BEST CRIME STORIES

OF THE YEAR

VOLUME 3

T0347748

BEST CRIME STORIES

OF THE YEAR

VOLUME 3

EDITED BY

AMOR TOWLES

SERIES EDITOR

OTTO PENZLER

HEAD
ZEUS

An Aries Book

First published in the US in 2023 as *The Mysterious Bookshop Presents the Best Mystery Stories of the Year 2023* by The Mysterious Press, an imprint of Penzler Publishers

First published in the UK in 2023 by Head of Zeus
This paperback edition first published in 2024 by Head of Zeus,
part of Bloomsbury Publishing Plc

Compilation copyright © 2023 by The Mysterious Press
Foreword copyright © 2023 by Otto Penzler
Introduction copyright © 2023 by Cetology, Inc

The moral right of Amor Towles to be identified as the editor
of this work has been asserted in accordance with the
Copyright, Designs and Patents Act of 1988.

The list of individual titles and respective copyrights to be found on pages
527–528 constitutes an extension of this copyright page.

All rights reserved. No part of this publication may be
reproduced, stored in a retrieval system, or transmitted in any form
or by any means, electronic, mechanical, photocopying, recording,
or otherwise, without the prior permission of both the copyright
owner and the above publisher of this book.

This is an anthology of fiction. All characters, organizations,
and events portrayed in this novel are either products of
the author's imagination or are used fictitiously.

9 7 5 3 1 2 4 6 8

A catalogue record for this book is available from the British Library.

ISBN (PB): 9781837932993
ISBN (E): 9781837932955

Interior design by Maria Fernandez

Printed and bound in Great Britain by
CPI Group (UK) Ltd, Croydon CR0 4YY

Head of Zeus
5–8 Hardwick Street
London EC1R 4RG

WWW.HEADOFZEUS.COM

BEST CRIME STORIES

STORIES

OF THE YEAR

VOLUME 3

CONTENTS

Bonus Story

The Best Crime Stories 2023 Honour Roll

About the Editors   529

FOREWORD

Welcome to the third annual volume of *The Mysterious Book-shop Presents the Best Mystery Stories of the Year*. Having previously been the series editor of twenty-four volumes of *The Best American Mystery Stories of the Year*, the notion of writing something original as a foreword to the book is daunting, somewhat relieved by the expectation that not everyone (does anyone?) reads and/or remembers what deathless prose I have contributed to previous editions.

I have written and spoken about mystery fiction frequently (some ungenerous soul might say ad nauseam) through the years and have maintained that one of its appeals is that it is a literary presentation of a fundamental life force: a battle between those who value Good in opposition to the spear carriers of Evil.

Ruminating on it recently, however, I think this may be less true at this time than it was when I first became interested in crime fiction. As character and psychological elements of a story have transcended plots and clues, as the reason *why* a murder was committed has transcended the question of *who* committed it or *how* it was done, it seems to be that the two omnipresent factors in contemporary crime fiction are Death and Sin.

Death appears to provide the minds of readers with a greater fund of innocent amusement than any other single subject except love but, of course, in crime fiction they are not mutually exclusive components of a novel or short story. Furthermore, when Death is accompanied by Sin in its most repugnant shapes, the fun increases exponentially. Some readers prefer the intellectual cheerfulness of a detective story while others have a taste that runs more to noir fiction, but in either case the story generally requires at least one dead body and at least one very wicked person for it to provide that frisson of pleasure that may be had while viewing horrible events from a safe distance.

Here, then, in the 2023 edition of this distinguished series, is a collection of stories nearly all of which are about Death and Sin, with plenty of dead bodies and an abundance of wicked people. They are designed, albeit unconsciously for the most part, to make you feel that it's good to be alive and, while alive, on the whole, to be good.

It should be noted, in a parenthetical aside, that mystery writers are, with (very) few exceptions, good. It is fundamental to their jobs to be aware of the fact that your sins will be discovered, no matter how clever you think you are. This is why, it should be further noted, mystery fiction is such a good influence in an increasingly degenerate world and why it is so popular with academics, lawyers, politicians, business leaders, and others who have reputations to protect; reading mysteries improves their morals and keeps them out of excessive mischief.

While it is redundant for me to write it again, since I have done it in each of the previous volumes of this and the earlier series, I feel compelled to issue fair warning by stating that many people regard a "mystery" only as a detective story. I regard the detective story as one subgenre of a much bigger genre, which I define as any work of fiction in which a crime, or the threat of a crime, is central to the theme or the plot.

While I love good puzzles and tales of pure ratiocination, few of these are written today, as the mystery genre has evolved (or devolved, depending upon your point of view) into a more character-driven form of literature, as noted previously. The line between mystery fiction and general fiction has become more and more blurred in recent years, producing fewer memorable detective stories but more significant literature.

It has been my goal in these anthologies to recognize that fact and to reflect it between these covers. The best writing makes it into the book. Fame, friendship, original venue, reputation, subject—none of it matters. It isn't only the qualification of being the best writer that will earn a place in the Table of Contents; it also must be the best story.

As frequent readers of this series are aware, each annual volume would, I am convinced, require three years to compile were it not for the uncanny ability of my colleague, Michele Slung, to read, absorb, and evaluate thousands of pages in what appears to be a nano-second. After culling the non-mysteries, as well as those crime stories perpetrated by writers who may want to consider careers in carpentry or knitting instead of wasting valuable trees for their efforts, I read stacks of them, finally settling on the best—or, at least, my favorites—many of which are then passed on to the guest editor, who this year is the remarkable Amor Towles.

Perhaps surprisingly, after graduating from Yale College and receiving an MA in English from Stanford University, Towles worked as an investment professional for over twenty years before becoming a full-time writer. His novels *Rules of Civility* (2011), *A Gentleman in Moscow* (2016), which was on the bestseller list of the *New York Times* for two years, and *The Lincoln Highway* (2021) have collectively sold more than six million copies and been translated into more than thirty languages.

Before the novels, and before his life in finance, he wrote short stories that have appeared in the *Paris Review*, *Granta*, *British Vogue*, and *Audible Originals*. Towles also wrote the introduction to Scribner's seventy-fifth anniversary edition of F. Scott Fitzgerald's *Tender Is the Night* and the Penguin Classics edition of Ernest Hemingway's *The Sun Also Rises*.

My sincere thanks go to this supernaturally gifted author, as well as to the previous guest editors who helped make this series both distinguished and successful, Lee Child and Sara Paretsky.

While Michele and I engage in a relentless quest to locate and read every mystery/crime/suspense story published, I live in fear that we will miss a worthy one, so if you are an author, editor, or publisher, or care about one, please feel free to send a book, magazine, or tear sheet to me c/o The Mysterious Bookshop, 58 Warren Street, New York, NY 10007. If it first appeared electronically, you must submit a hard copy. It is vital to include the author's contact information. No unpublished material will be considered for what should be obvious reasons. No material will be returned. If you distrust the postal service, enclose a self-addressed, stamped postcard and I'll confirm that it was received.

To be eligible for the 2024 edition, a story must have been written or translated into English and first issued in the calendar year 2023 with a 2023 publication date. The earlier in the year I receive the story, the more fondly I regard it. For reasons known only to the dunderheads who wait until Christmas week to submit a story published in the spring, holding eligible stories for months before submitting them occurs every year, causing severe irritability while I read a stack of stories while friends are trimming the Christmas tree or otherwise celebrating the holiday season. It had better be a damned good story if you do this.

Because of the very tight production schedule for this book, I am being neither whimsical nor arrogant when I state that the absolute deadline for me to receive a story is December 31. If the story arrives one day later, it will not be read. Sorry.

Otto Penzler

INTRODUCTION

Before you begin reading this anthology, I ask you to join me in honoring that unsung hero of murder mysteries: the cadaver.

Male or female, old or young, rich or poor, for over a hundred years the cadaver has been accommodating, gracious, and generally on time. There is no other figure in crime who has proven to be more reliable. Since the murder mystery first gained popularity, there have been two world wars, multiple economic crises, dance crazes and moonshots, the advents of radio, cinema, television, and the internet. Ideas of right and wrong have evolved, tastes have changed, the science of criminology has advanced by leaps and bounds. But through it all, the cadaver has shown up without complaint to do its job. A clock-puncher of the highest order, if you will.

Over this time frame, many of our most revered detectives have proven themselves to be rather difficult to work with. They have been variously arrogant, irascible, antisocial, or persnickety. Witnesses have often been skittish or defensive. Many of them have intentionally sowed confusion through lies of commission or omission that spring from their own sins and prejudices.

But, decade in and decade out, the cadaver has remembered his lines and hit his mark. This is despite the fact that it has borne the brunt of a thousand humiliations. Never mind that it has been subjected to the most definitive form of violence—homicide. It has then had to lie undiscovered, often in a cellar or back alley overnight. Once the police arrive, our cadaver is poked and prodded, its pockets searched. Having been shuttled to the morgue and laid out on a slab under the unforgiving florescent light, it is cut open, unceremoniously.

Almost from the moment the corpse is discovered, it becomes the subject of slander. Friends, family, and acquaintances who tended to be complimentary and discreet when our victim was alive, are suddenly enumerating personal failings and sharing rumors of infidelity or financial malfeasance. And all of this—the loss of life, the autopsies, the recriminations—the cadaver has suffered in silence for over a century, on our behalf.

THE GOLDEN AGE

The cadaver's unwavering professionalism is all the more admirable given the diminishment of its standing over the decades.

If we look back to the early part of the twentieth century—the so-called Golden Age of detective fiction, when the form was reaching its apotheosis in the works of Agatha Christie—the cadaver maintained an almost enviable position of status and influence. After all, it was the cadaver who set the wheels of a mystery in motion.

The stories of the era tended to begin in a relatively benign and inviting manner. A small assembly of family members, friends, and acquaintances, for instance, might gather for the weekend in a rambling country manor with a variety of servants in attendance. The setting and circumstances are not that different from what we might expect to find in a play by Anton Chekov or a novel by Henry James. At least, that is, until with the scream of a house-maid, the cadaver is discovered. Its sudden appearance sprawled on the study floor with its head caved in, or slumped over the kitchen table with a knife in its back is what transforms the book in our hand, taking us from the realm of domestic drama or social comedy into the realm of the whodunit.

But in the Golden Age, the cadaver didn't simply get things going. It maintained its position at the center of the story from the moment of its discovery until the denouement. For in the era, there was a general understanding among writers and readers that the solving of the entire puzzle required an understanding of the victim. Not simply what she was doing in the hours leading up to her demise, but what she had done in the past and what she intended to do in the future.

As Hercule Poirot often pointed out, it was the psychology of the victim that was paramount. In life, was the cadaver lascivious? Unscrupulous? Greedy? To understand who was most likely to monkey with the brakes of his car or poison his cup of tea, one first had to understand whom he had loved and whom he had spurned; whom he had enriched and whom he had cheated.

In the Golden Age, while the cadaver gave its life fairly early in the story, it could take comfort that it would remain of primary concern to the writer and reader until the mystery was resolved and the murderer brought to justice in the book's final pages. And surely this was no small cause for consolation. As Lord Henry observed in Oscar Wilde's *The Picture of Dorian Gray,* "There is only one thing in the world worse than being talked about, and that is not being talked about."

THE HARDBOILED ERA

But time moves on. In the years before and after the Second World War, a new form of mystery rose to prominence in the United States: the hardboiled detective story. Spearheaded by Dashiell Hammett, refined by Raymond Chandler, perfected by Ross Macdonald, the hardboiled style dominated the mystery genre for almost half a century in print and film, at home and abroad.

Unlike the detectives of the Golden Age, who were often aristocratic in bearing and schooled in etiquette, the hardboiled detectives were men who disdained artifice and favored plain speaking. They hung their hats in shabby offices, gathered information in bars and flophouses, and went home to sleep in one-bedroom apartments alone. If they ever set foot in a mansion it was because they'd been summoned by a client whom they neither envied nor admired. Leading rugged lives, earning meager livings, prepared to expect the worst of everyone, the hardboiled detectives were consummate professionals in the most world-weary of industries. All of which felt to readers both refreshing and truer to life.

But when Hammett, Chandler, and Macdonald opted to foreground the gritty, quotidian life of the detective-for-hire, one consequence was that the role of the cadaver shrank in importance. For these detectives were not hired to solve murders (a task that was the purview of the police). Instead, they were hired to solve messy domestic problems. In Hammett's *The Maltese Falcon,* Sam Spade is hired by Miss Wonderly to follow a man who has run off with her sister. In *The Big Sleep,* Philip Marlowe is hired by General Sternwood to help resolve a blackmailing attempt stemming from his daughter's gambling debts. In *The Drowning Pool,* Lew Archer is hired by Mrs. Slocum to investigate a libelous letter. Infidelities, coveted objects, missing people, these are the nettlesome problems that the hardboiled detective tackles for fifty dollars a day plus expenses.

Once the hardboiled detective accepted a case, what tended to follow were the drab necessities of investigation as he pounded the pavement, flipped through phone books, gathered information from government agencies, and interviewed low-rent professionals in low-rent offices. In other words, he completed the sort of menial tasks that might fill the days of cub reporters, insurance adjusters, and door-to-door salesmen. An unglamorous man in an unglamorous trade pursuing an unglamorous process step by step.

But somewhere along the way, as our detective follows the loose threads of the case in his plodding fashion, he happens upon a body. It is our old friend the cadaver, of course, but she has undergone a change. For she is no longer one of the principals of the story. She is now a minor character: a hotel clerk, shady attorney, or two-bit criminal whom the detective has already spoken to once. It is when the detective returns to ask a follow-up question that he discovers the body on the floor behind a desk, or in the bathroom drowned in the tub, or stuffed in the trunk of a car with a bullet hole in the head.

The body in the hardboiled stories is decidedly not at the center of the narrative action. We will not spend time investigating his or her past or personality. Nor are we likely to feel much moral outrage or shed sentimental tears over their demise. This is not to say that the victim's death is irrelevant. The cadaver in the hardboiled detective story fulfills two very important purposes. First, its appearance alerts both the detective and the reader that what had seemed a simple, domestic matter is, in fact, part of a larger, messier reality—one which will ultimately reveal an intricate web of desires, multiple sinners, and a raft of ugly truths.

The second purpose the cadaver fulfills is that of a timely confirmation. Up to this point in the story, the detective has followed multiple false leads and arrived at multiple dead ends, such that he has begun to wonder if he's wasting his time. The sudden appearance of the body signals that he is on the right track. Some visit he has paid, some question he has asked has unnerved someone. The someone in question has emerged from the shadows to silence this relatively insignificant player because he or she happened to know something incriminating that the detective was on the verge of discovering. Thus, when we and the detective come upon this corpse, we may paradoxically feel a sense of elation. For, however in the dark we remain, we can leave the scene of this crime confident that the game is afoot.

Does our friend the cadaver bemoan his diminished role in the hardboiled mystery? Does he object to his incidental relationship to events, and the near inconsequentiality of his passing? He does not. He fulfills his role with all the humility and discipline of the devoted actor who, once a leading man, is now relegated to the playing of minor parts.

The Modern Era

In the last decades of the twentieth century, the murder mystery witnessed the advent of a new era—one defined by crimes that were darker and more violent. These stories have manifested themselves in a variety of forms, but no subset of the genre has better expressed the new modality than the hunt for the serial killer. While this strain of the murder mystery genre may not be everyone's cup of tea, it has had undeniably broad appeal, being central to many of the most popular mystery series in print and on screen.

The success of the serial killer hunt as a narrative form is due to a variety of reasons, the most important of which is that it is particularly effective at raising our heart rate. By definition, a serial killer is going to commit multiple acts of homicide. As such, the detective (and the reader) are in a race against time. The longer it takes for the detective to discover the identity of the murderer, the more innocent people will be killed. In addition, serial killers tend to pursue their vocations through particularly gruesome means. Thus, the serial killer narrative can quicken our pulse in the manner of a horror story. But the serial killer narrative also raises our heartrate by hinting at our own vulnerability.

In the Golden Age or the hardboiled era, there was no reason for us to imagine ourselves as potential targets. The Golden Age victims tended to killed because of the lives they'd led and the hardboiled victim tended to be killed because they'd made a habit of swimming in murky waters. In each case, these were circumstances that we could eye safely from a distance. But in the serial killer hunt, the victims are generally chosen by the killer at random or as part of an obscure obsession. In reading these books, we cannot help but imagine that we, too, could be attacked one night—while getting into our car in an empty garage, while jogging through the park, or worst of all, while asleep in our own beds. It's a rather unpleasant but stimulating aspect of the genre.

A second reason the serial killer hunt has been successful with readers is that it amplifies the battle between detective and villain. By definition a serial killer has repeatedly gotten away with murder. Within the boundaries of the genre, this is generally because the killer is unusually intelligent, methodical, and ruthless.

Advances in technology and the science of criminology have given modern detectives all manner of new tools to trap their quarry. They have access to DNA analysis, sophisticated forensics, a ubiquity of security cameras, and facial recognition software. For a killer to succeed in the modern era, she has to gain as much mastery over modern criminology as the detective has, so that she can anticipate all the various means by which she might get caught.

This makes the serial killer narrative less an investigation than a game of cat and mouse that tests the proficiency, patience, and nerve of two antagonists. The elevated heart rate, the sense that we could be a victim, the unusual abilities of the killer all result in our being a little more gripped by events on the page and a little more satisfied once the killer is brought to justice.

Well, being a little more gripped and a little more satisfied is all well and good for the reader. But what of our friend the cadaver? What if we take a moment to look at these developments from its point of view? In so doing, most of what we discover is dispiriting.

For in the era of the serial killer narrative, the cadaver must experience whole new levels of tribulation. In these stories, the victim has often been tortured or sexually assaulted before being killed. Once dead, its corpse may get skinned, chopped up, even eaten. Some of the serial killer mysteries begin with a body part washed up on a beach or a skeleton unearthed in the woods, victims so beyond recognition that their identification poses a significant challenge, never mind how, where, or why they were killed.

The sad truth is that in the serial killer narrative, the identity of the victim barely matters. It is one clue among many in the ongoing hunt for the villain. Where once the understanding of the victim's background and psychology was paramount, now the physical attributes of the *various* victims are studied along with the settings of the crimes and the specifics of the brutality in search of a pattern that will give the detective insight into the background and psychology of the killer.

The cadaver, having played such a central part in the mysteries of the Golden Age, having been then relegated in the hardboiled era to an incidental role, must bear the ultimate indignity in the serial killer stories of becoming a prop. And yet, despite all that, our cadaver persists.

For over a hundred years we have taken great pleasure in reading the mystery story, discovering profound satisfactions in each of its incarnations. During that time, more than a few of the detectives have gained international fame along with the authors who invented them and the actors who portrayed them.

So, it seems only fair that before you read on, you take a moment to pour yourself an ounce or two of your favorite spirit, make yourself comfortable in your favorite chair, and then join me in raising a glass to that humble and reliable individual without whom the whole genre would not exist.

Amor Towles
New York City
The Ides of March, 2023

Doug Allyn *has twice won the Edgar Allan Poe Award and is the record holder in the Ellery Queen Mystery Magazine Reader's Award competition. Allyn is one of the best short-story writers of his generation—probably of all time. He is also a novelist with a number of critically acclaimed books in print.*

The author of twelve novels and more than a hundred forty short stories, Allyn has been published internationally in English, German, French, and Japanese. His most recent, Murder in Paradise *(with James Patterson), was on the NYT Best Sellers list for several weeks. More than two dozen of his tales have been optioned for development as feature films and television.*

Allyn studied creative writing and criminal psychology at the University of Michigan while moonlighting as a guitarist in the rock group Devil's Triangle and reviewing books for the Flint Journal. *His background includes Chinese language studies at Indiana University and extended duty with USAF Intelligence in southeast Asia during the Vietnam War.*

Career highlights? Sipping champagne with Mickey Spillane and waltzing with Mary Higgins Clark.

BLIND BASEBALL
Doug Allyn

The roadside bomb was a beauty. Neatly wired, compact. First-rate workmanship. Good. Every tech's nightmare is getting blown away by some kid's cobble job.

This unit was cached in a school-boy's backpack, hidden under a cardboard box by the roadside. Four bricks of Semtex wrapped with duct tape, with its trigger—no, two triggers—in plain view. The wiring was laid out in straight lines, the soldered joints sheathed in shrink tubes. Precise, professional work.

All good. And yet—

A snake of unease began uncoiling in my gut as the instincts honed by two long tours in Iraq kicked in. Something felt *off* about this setup. The triggers were obvious, a trip wire half-buried in the dust of the gravel road, and a mercury switch parked on top of the Semtex bricks, both in plain sight. I was *supposed* to find them, and assume that defusing the unit would be easy-peasy, but . . .

It couldn't be. Because the rest of the workmanship was too damn good.

So . . . There would be at *least* one more trigger, possibly two more. The backpack was almost certainly resting on a contact switch held open by its weight. Lift the bag, or even bump it?

Hello, Jesus.

Okay. Disarming a contact switch is tricky, but manageable. I've cleared dozens of them. But if this bomber was crafty enough to wire up three triggers . . . ? He rigged four. Or even five . . . ?

No. The fifth would be riskier for him than for me. Things can go south in a build, a static spark, a stray wire. Each trigger increases the chances of an accidental blast. So. Not five, but definitely four. Two I could see already, which left two more to find. The real question was . . . How good *is* this guy? Good enough to kill me?

Maybe.

He already had me sweating through my fatigues.

I leaned back to clear my head, shrugging my shoulders to loosen up. Not so easy to do. I was in a bulky blast suit, rigged out like a deep-sea diver, full body armor plus a Lexan face shield. The suit would absorb much of the blast from a four-brick bomb, but not all. With luck, I'd only lose my arms.

Personally, I'd rather lose my head.

I sucked in a deep breath, but it didn't help. An oil refinery a few kilometers up the road made the air as sour as a bus-station john.

Our platoon was halted on a turnoff just west of the Dover Road, thirty kilometers north of Baghdad, roughly eight clicks out from the UN base at Taji. The rutted gravel side road passes through a dozen sun-baked villages like this one. If I'd ever known its name, I couldn't recall it. A few dozen dirt-poor Sunni families live in cinder-block apartments on the west side while even poorer refugees squat on the far side, in cracker-box shacks patched together out of crates, pallets, whatever scraps they can scavenge. The clutter offers good cover for bombers, so we find IEDs here fairly often.

Hadn't seen one here for a while, though. A few weeks? And that one was a cobble job, not nearly as neat as—

The bomb before that.

Damn.

I *knew* I'd seen this guy's work before. *Four* triggers the last time, two visible plus a pressure switch underneath, and a cell phone wired up as a detonator. It was a tricky disarm, but I'd managed it with no trouble. So. If it *was* the same muji, I'd already beaten him once. And yet? Here we were again, in the same damn place, staring at basically the same damn setup.

Groundhog Day.

But it wouldn't be *exactly* the same. I'd disarmed his work before, and he *knew* that, so he'd add some twist to make this rig deadlier than the last one. He'd wire up a trigger I couldn't find. And so far, I hadn't.

I was sweating bullets now, my breathing had gone shallow, and my mouth was dry as the dirt road. *Settle down!*

This was my second tour in Iraq, our unit had disarmed seventy-one IEDs, and we were all still breathing. So now? Seventy-two. First-rate craftsmanship, and—familiar. I chewed on that for a moment. I'd definitely seen this muji's work before, but not *exactly* the same setup. The last rig had a cell-phone trigger. I didn't see one here. And the last time it was . . . C-4 stashed under a broken crate by the roadside maybe . . . twenty meters south—

"What's happening, Sarge?" Lieutenant Tarleton's voice was a whisper in my ear bud. The LT is new, with the unit five months. Has a lot to learn, but at least he knows it.

"Stay off the coms, LT," Marco Romero said. "You're keeping me awake."

Marco's our sniper and class clown. Grew up in Chicago's gangland and considers Iraq a vacation spot. If Tarleton took offense, Marco wouldn't care.

"Copy that," LT said. "Unit's buttoned up, Luke."

"Roger that."

The squad was deployed in a fifty-meter semicircle, hunkered down in positions of opportunity. Three were crouched in the lee of a burned-out basement, the LT and Willy were huddled behind a wrecked taxi. Marco was on a rooftop across the road, watching our back trail. Most of us were second- or third-tour vets, so they'd all gone to ground in good cover, safe as houses—so why the hell was I so jacked up?

For openers, I didn't like that trip wire. Wires are risky. Any damn thing can set 'em off, a stray dog, kids at play. We spotted this one from the Humvee. Maybe a lucky gust uncovered it, but the Dover's always windy, so—more likely the bomber *expected* us to spot it, wanted us to stop near his backpack. And we had. So the wire had served its purpose.

My meter showed no juice on the line and it was slack. I could disconnect it. But as I reached out with my nippers, I noticed my hands were shaking . . .

Snip! I took a breath. Still here.

The mercury switch was next, also in plain sight, and the contacts were . . . clearly open. I could remove it safely too.

Snip . . . snip!

I desperately wanted to knuckle a bead of sweat off my nose, but couldn't risk lowering my face shield.

Next? The last time, he'd set a contact switch underneath the pack, held open by the bomb's weight. I'd disarmed it, and he knew that. Leave that one for last. I swallowed, or tried to. My throat felt like I'd been gargling gravel.

So far, I was only seeing exactly what the muji *wanted* me to see, and every reflex I'd honed in two deployments was telling me I was missing something. Something important. *Damn it!*

I leaned in, practically shoving my nose into the damn bag, scanning it from inches away, mentally dividing it into sections.

Upper right, nothing showing. Lower right, nothing there either. Upper left—ah. *Thank you, Lord! There it was!* A wire so fine it looked like a loose thread. But it disappeared through a tiny slit in the lining. Using my needle-nosed pliers, I widened the slit just a tad . . .

And touched plastic. He'd sewn the cell phone into the lining this time! Which meant the pack could be triggered remotely! If that phone rang, it would be the last thing I'd hear in this world and the muji could be dialing it this second!

No time for finesse. Slitting the lining, I slid the phone out just far enough to access the battery slot. Popping open the cover, I—

Stopped. Stunned.

Empty! The freakin' battery slot was empty!

I almost laughed out loud. After all his fine work, the muji bomber had forgotten to arm the ordnance. This phone couldn't set off a sneeze.

But even as I grinned with relief at his rookie mistake, I kept seeing the rest of his handiwork; the redundant triggers, shrink tubes—

No. This muji did not *forget* a battery. He'd saved himself ten bucks because he knew the phone wouldn't be the trigger, because—

Because I'd found the phone the last time, so he *expected* me to find this one as well. And he didn't care.

Because the damned phone *wasn't* the trigger. It was a distraction, set to keep me occupied while—I missed something else completely!

My God!

Staggering to my feet in the blast suit, clumsy as a beached whale, I looked wildly around for—*hell!* I had no idea.

But the squad wasn't safely hunkered down anymore. Lieutenant Tarleton had moved away from cover. He was standing in the middle of the road now, scoping out an apartment building with his weapon.

The building was five floors, maybe sixty units, each with its own balcony. LT was aiming at the roof—no. Just below it. At a fourth-floor balcony. Then I saw it too, a movement. Someone was up there. A looky loo? No. The building was bomb damaged, with yellow warning tape strung all over it. Nobody in his right mind would be up there.

LT fired off a warning burst from his M4, splintering a doorjamb near the watcher, who ducked down out of sight.

But he didn't run. A local would have scampered off like a scalded dog. Our watcher just took cover, which made him a mujahideen, hoping for a shot at us. And the LT was giving him a target—

Suddenly the muji popped up with an AK-47 and cranked off a wild burst toward the lieutenant, the slugs kicking up the dirt near Tarleton's feet. The LT scrambled back behind the ruined taxi next to Willy.

The same place they'd holed up the last time we were here.

And that's when I got it.

Raising my fist in the air, I waved it in a circle. "Everybody out! Into the street! On my six! My six! *Move! Move! Move!*"

No hesitation! The team rose as one man—but the muji heard me too! He popped up to see what was happening—a fatal mistake. Willy cranked off a burst of full-auto, must have hit him five times. The muji's body was jerking from the impact even as he lunged forward, throwing himself over the railing into space—

No!

"LT!" I screamed into my collar mike. "Get into the street!"

The muji's body slammed down onto a pile of broken concrete—

And the taxi exploded into a massive fireball!

The ground bucked beneath my feet, hurling me into the sky! And then I was tumbling back down on top of the backpack bomb, desperately trying to turn my face away—

I woke up in a white room. White ceiling, white tiled floor, white sheets. A white machine winking silently by my bedside. I had no freaking idea where I was at first, couldn't remember what happened, but as I wrestled my way back to full awareness, I realized why the sharp reek of disinfectant and background noise seemed so familiar.

I'd been here before. Eight months ago, I'd sat by Ben Cooley's bedside for most of a week, waiting for him to die. Which he did. In a cubicle exactly like this one.

And now? I was in the cubicle. Maybe in the same damn bed. In Germany. In the USAF base hospital at Ramstein.

Dying?

I tried to sit up. *God!* My body was one giant, throbbing ache, yet somehow the pain felt—distant. Which meant the docs had me cruising on heavy meds, but I still couldn't think why—and then my memory began flickering back to life like a slide projector with a faulty switch, and—*whoa!*

In a total panic now, I swept the bedsheets aside to take a frantic inventory. My legs and lower body were patched over with a crazy quilt of bandages, mostly greased gauze, for burns. But there were no casts, so no bones broken, and no surgical drains jammed into my guts that would indicate internal injuries.

My right arm was bandaged, but I could move it freely. My left was in a plastic cast, strapped to my chest, so it was either broken or dislo—

Oh.

Damn it. I swallowed. Hard.

The cast was—short. *Way* too short. I clumsily laid my right arm across it to compare—but I already knew.

My left hand was gone. Completely. And maybe . . . seven or eight inches of my forearm along with it. Blown off or amputated, roughly halfway between my wrist and elbow.

Son of a *bitch!*

I was still trying to process this when the privacy curtain parted and an army nurse poked her head in. Square-faced, heavyset, salt-and-pepper hair cropped boot-camp short. She was wearing a white coat over a desert camouflage uniform. Thirtyish tops, but her eyes looked a lot older.

"We're awake," she said, with professional cheer. "Welcome back."

"My unit," I managed, "what happened to them?"

"Sorry, Sergeant, I don't have that information."

Like hell you don't. Damn it! I sagged back on the pillow, swallowing the bile surging in my throat.

"I can check with your unit—"

"Don't play me, lady, please. If anyone else came through, you'd say so. Or they'd be here."

"Someone *is* here. A tech sergeant from Intel has been waiting out in the hall to debrief you."

"Waiting? How long have I been here?"

"Four days." She scanned the dials on the contraption beside the bed, tapping one with a fingernail. "The sergeant checks in every few hours to see how you're doing."

"And how *am* I doing? For real?"

She hesitated.

"It's okay. I know I'm minus a mitt. Is anything else fubar?"

"Your blast suit protected your upper body from the shrapnel, but the explosion threw you about forty feet. You've sustained massive bruising on your torso, rib cage, thighs, practically everywhere. You look like a building fell on you, Sergeant. We closed a five-inch gash on your sternum, possibly from the same shard that severed your wrist. But that aside, on my mother's life, I swear nothing else is—*fudged* up beyond all recognition. You should make a full recovery, except for—well." She didn't bother with the obvious. "Can I get you anything?"

"Yes, ma'am. You can send that sergeant in. Let's get to it."

The tech looked like an NBA ballplayer, tall, Black, and slim as a whip, sporting a gold tooth in front. His fatigues were faded, but his jump boots had a high shine. A dogface, not a rear-echelon type. His nametag read Jeffers.

"Sergeant Duroy," he nodded, pulling a plastic chair up beside my bed. "I know you're hurting, so I'll be brief. We got most of what we need from your Humvee's video—"

"My outfit?" I grated. "Did anyone else—?"

Jeffers shook his head. Once. The darkness in his eyes told me the rest. I sagged back on my pillow, choking on the worst news I've ever heard.

"Why them and not me? Why the hell am I still alive?"

"The shock waves from the taxi blast blew you clear of the unit you were disarming. You're about the luckiest mofo on this planet, son."

"Funny, I don't feel all that lucky."

"Maybe it'll come later. The blast blew out the audio from the vehicle cams, but the video shows you yelling something at your squad just before the bang. What was that about?"

"Groundhog Day," I said bitterly.

"Say what?"

"The roadside bomb was just bait. He left the trip wire exposed so we'd spot it and stop to deactivate it, which we did. But halfway into the disarm, I remembered disabling an IED at the same spot a few months back. There wasn't much cover so the squad deployed to the same positions they'd taken before. The muji knew where we'd go to ground because he'd watched us last time. He mined every bit of cover with antipersonnel explosives."

"Groundhog Day," Jefferson echoed, nodding. "I'll put it in the manual. Your lieutenant, Tarleton? Was new to the unit. First tour. Was his inexperience an issue?"

"No. We'd been in the field five months. He was still learning, but he knew it. He was quick on the uptake, a good officer."

Jeffers nodded, accepting it. "Your squad was shorthanded?"

"Aren't they all? We were down two. Corporal Peschanski was home on emergency leave—"

"Did her absence affect what happened?"

"Only the body count. She was a spotter for our sniper, Romero. She would have been with him . . . on a rooftop, I think."

"Then it's lucky she wasn't," he nodded. "And Specialist Blumenthal?"

"The medics sent Blu stateside a few months ago. COPD. He couldn't breathe."

"He was also having serious problems with alcohol."

"Not to my knowledge."

"Nobody's trying to hang your buddy out—"

"You heard me the first time, dog. Blu couldn't breathe."

"It's a moot point." Jeffers shrugged. "He's separated from the service."

"Along with the rest of us," I said bitterly. "Anything else?"

"No, we're good. Thanks for your time." Jeffers rose to go, but paused at the curtain. "One last thing. Did your unit have some kind of special insurance policy?"

"What?"

"Insurance. More than the standard GI—"

"I got no idea what you're talking about. Why?"

"A couple of civilian types have been sniffing around, asking the staff about your chances of recovery. I ran 'em off, but vultures always circle back. I'm sorry as hell about your friends, Sergeant Duroy. Good luck to you."

I managed a nod, and Jeffers left. Luck? Even minus half my arm, I'd used up my luck allotment for this lifetime. I had no freakin' clue what the insurance business might be about, but I filed Jeffers's warning away. In my line of work, when somebody says *duck?* You don't ask why.

You duck.

I was up and moving the following day, wobbling down the hospital hallways like a wino. Groggy, off-balance. The walk to the end of the hall felt like a forty-mile hike in full battle rattle. But the second day was easier, and by the second week, I could feel my energy seeping back, a tad more each day. The medics were already taking laser measurements of my right hand, and showing me the 3D computer mock-ups on a laptop. My new lefty prosthesis would be state of the art, they said. Better than before.

They were wrong, but not by much. The hand itself was a fair facsimile that could almost pass for real if you ignored the rivets at the finger joints, but my forearm looked like a spare part from *The Terminator*, a set of titanium bones with pulleys, powered by nylon cables. Long sleeves covered it, but it still felt—alien.

After a few fittings, my myoelectric plastic paw was fully functional, with magnetic implants that responded to the nanovolts of my radial and ulnar nerves, much like the original. I couldn't deal cards or pick up a dime, but I could make a fist, wave hello, and scratch my butt. But the first time I picked up a china coffee mug, it slipped through my fingers. I caught it—

And crushed it to powder, shards flying around the room like shrapnel. There was a stunned silence. The medics eyed each other anxiously. I guessed that wasn't supposed to happen. Good to know, though.

The techs decided the power surge was due to an upgrade from alkaline to lithium-ion batteries. I had no idea what that meant, but if we dialed the power down to half strength, my flesh-toned titanium miracle could manage basic tasks.

Full power was more fun. I could shatter cups, bend forks, and probably break bones if I wasn't careful. The techs wanted a few more weeks to tweak the bugs out, but close enough would have to be good enough.

A career counselor suggested that my experience would be invaluable at Fort Riley. I asked for an honorable discharge instead.

I'd paid my dues in places most Americans can't find on a map. My friends were gone, and I needed to get back to my world, to Vale County on Michigan's north shore. I was desperate to heft axes and chainsaws again, to measure myself against the big pines in the snowy silence of the deep woods.

I'd been to war. I wasn't sure who won, but I knew who'd lost. It was time to go home.

The big Stihl 880 chainsaw was screaming, cranked wide open as I swung the blade back and forth like a scythe, clearing the brush away from the red pine's trunk. The tree was a giant, an eighty-footer with a forty-inch bole, a century old, tall and straight as a mast. Dropped, lopped, and trucked to the mill? A thousand-dollar tree.

Kicking the slashed brush aside, I set my stance in the snow, then cut a ten-inch notch into the trunk. Circling the pine, I double-checked my escape route, then cranked up the saw again, slanting the blade down toward my first kerf at a forty-degree angle—

"Hello?"

I was so focused on making my cut dead-nuts accurate the voice didn't register at first.

"Hello? Sergeant Duroy?"

A woman's voice. I ignored it. I hear voices sometimes. The VA docs say it's a common problem for injured vets. It will pass. I absently tried to identify it as I continued my downward cut. The ghost voices that call to me at night are usually from the platoon, but this one wasn't familiar—I paused, straightening up to look around—*whoa!*

A woman was marching toward me through the snow, directly in the path of the big pine—the massive tree shuddered beside me, uttering a final groan as it slowly tilted and began to topple.

"Lady, look out!" I shouted, waving my arms wildly. "Run left! *Left, left, left!*"

Startled, she froze, then saw the tree hurtling down on her like a freight train plunging out of the sky. On sheer instinct, she sprinted to her right, diving clear at the last instant, tumbling through the snow.

The tree slammed down hard, bounced four feet in the air, then crashed down again, roughly where she'd been standing.

She sat on her butt in the snow a moment, looking a bit dazed, then got to her feet, dusting herself off.

"What in the hell was that?" she snapped. "Aren't you supposed to yell timber or something?" She was a tall woman, maybe thirty, ash-blond hair cropped boyishly short, expensive cashmere coat, black slacks, high-fashion boots. City girl.

"Sorry," I said, "I thought I was alone. What are you doing out here?"

"Looking for you, if you're Sergeant Luke Duroy."

"I'm not a sergeant anymore. Who are you?"

"Lauren Tarleton," she said, circling the pine stump to offer her gloved hand. "You served in my brother's unit. Lieutenant Leonard Tarleton?"

LT's sister. Of course. Up close, the family resemblance was striking, in a good way. She was more handsome than pretty, I suppose. I'm six three, a buck eighty, muscle and bone and not much else. In heels, LT's sister could almost look me in the eye. Hers were blue-gray, bright as high beams.

"What can I do for you, ma'am?"

"It's what I can do for you, Serg—*Mister*—Duroy," she said, handing me a business card. Lauren Tarleton, attorney at law. An address in Cleveland. "Do you recall Corporal Nikki Peschanski?"

"Peach? Sure. We served together, until—well. Until we didn't. How's she doing?"

"She's here, actually, in Valhalla, at the Holiday Inn. She's looking forward to seeing you."

"I doubt I'd be good company. I'm not interested in reliving the good old days in Iraq, ma'am."

"This isn't an auld lang syne visit, Luke, it's business. A significant sum of money is involved—"

"She's welcome to my end."

"It's not that simple."

"It is to me. I'm not a soldier anymore, lady, I'm a logger, and we only get paid for timber delivered to the mill. So if there's nothing more . . . ?"

"There is, actually. My brother has left me a—*situation*, Sergeant. I hoped you could help. Len said you were the best of the best, the crazy bravest man he ever knew. How many bombs did you disarm?"

"I— Seventy-one."

"I can't even comprehend the kind of courage that would take. I was really looking forward to meeting that guy."

"You missed him," I said. "He got blown to hell in Iraq." I raised the chainsaw to restart it.

"Wait!" she said, grabbing my wrist, then pulling away, startled at the feel of ice-cold metal. "Do you know what a tontine is, Sergeant?"

"A what?"

"A tontine. It's complicated. I'll explain over dinner, Holiday Inn, six o'clock, I'm buying. No dress code, no excuses, and I promise you won't be bored. Don't be late, please. We have a lot to discuss." She didn't wait for my answer, just turned and stalked off through the snow, retracing her own footprints.

I watched her go, then cranked up my saw, lopped off a big bough, and watched it fall.

"Timber," I said.

I worked through the afternoon, dropping trees, limbing the logs, planning to give the dinner a pass. I have trouble enough blotting out memories of battle and bombs, but . . .

My problems weren't Peach's fault. She probably had questions, and I owed her the courtesy of a meet. And I had to admit, LT's sister had captured my interest, and not just about the tontine, whatever that was. I used to be the guy she came to meet. And I wondered how much of him was left.

So, at five, I loaded my tools into my Dodge Ram pickup, stopped by my rented cabin to swap my coveralls for clean jeans and a Detroit Lions sweatshirt, then drove into Valhalla.

The town's a resort now, dreaming on the northern shore of Lake Michigan, but in its heyday it was a boomtown. Lumber barons made fortunes off the sweat and blood of the loggers who harvested the lumber that built the nation, creating a hard-nosed, woodland culture that still survives.

The Holiday Inn sits in the middle of Olde Town, a six-block preserve of nineteenth-century buildings, cobblestone streets, and globular streetlamps. Quaint, cute, and mostly bogus. In the logging era, streets were a mire of mud and horse hockey, bordered by boardwalks. It's prettier now, but about as historic as a Hallmark Card.

I found my dinner dates in a quiet corner of the rustic dining room, Lauren Tarleton in slacks and a black turtleneck, Nikki "Peach" Peschanski in sweatpants, tennies, and a bulky holiday sweater that didn't come close to covering her baby bump.

Peach saw me coming and rose hesitantly, offering her hand, unsure of how I would react. Circling the table, I wrapped her in a bear hug that we both held for a very long time, then I eased her down in her chair, bussing the top of her curly hair before taking a seat.

"Well, I'm glad we cleared up that particular worry," Lauren said drily.

"Not quite," I said. "Whose is it, Peach?"

"LT's," she said, watching me. Nikki's half-Italian, but it's the half that shows dark eyes, dark curly hair, and, at the moment, a belly round as a bowling ball.

"Wow. That's the best news I've had since—awhile. How are you holding up?"

"I'm good. The baby's healthy, that's what matters now."

"You went home on leave a few months before things went sideways. You didn't write, didn't Skype. What happened?"

"I reported my pregnancy, listed the father as unknown, and resigned. I had to break contact with the unit to keep my medical benefits."

"Under the Uniform Code of Military Justice, an affair with a subordinate brings an automatic court-martial and dishonorable discharge," Lauren put in.

"Len planned to resign at the end of tour," Peach continued. "We'd get married, get on with our lives—" She broke off, looking away.

"Sorry, Peach," I said. "You two deserved better."

"You all did," Lauren said. "Which brings us to the business at hand. The tontine."

"Which is what, exactly?" I asked, swiveling to face her. A very pleasant view. Her pixie haircut gave her a boyish look, but the rest of her wasn't a bit boyish.

"In the nineteenth century, a tontine was a bet against death," she explained, waving me to a seat. "A group of investors would pool their money and share out the interest it earned. Over time, as members passed away, their shares remained, increasing the payout to the survivors, until the last man standing inherited the pool, which often made him rich overnight."

"Good for him," Peach said. "What's that got to do with us?"

"A few months after joining your unit, my brother won big in a poker game."

"And took a lot of static about it," I added. "FNGs are supposed to lose politely."

"FNG?" she echoed.

"Effing new guy," Peach said. "Gambling's technically against regs, but it was a war zone. There was always a game—hearts, euchre, something. Nobody blamed Len for getting lucky."

"Even so, winning the money troubled him," Lauren said, "so he wired it home and asked me to buy term insurance policies for each member of his platoon, making each of you the beneficiaries of the others. If the worst happened to someone, *something* good would come of it."

"Like a tontine," Peach nodded.

"Too much like one, actually. Tontines are banned under the UCMJ. Obviously, if one soldier's death could profit others in his unit—"

"He might 'accidentally' get capped in a battle," I said. "But if tontines are banned . . . ?"

"Only as originally written," Lauren continued. "We added a rider that stated the benefits are only to be released after completion of a task on behalf of the insured. In effect, the payout becomes a wage for a service rendered."

"What kind of a service?" Peach asked.

"I have no idea," Lauren said, leaning back in her chair, eyeing us both. "Leonard enclosed seven numbered envelopes, to be opened by the survivors. He assumed it would be the whole platoon seeing to the last wish of a fallen comrade, not—you two seeing to all the others." Her gesture took in our tiny trio, seated around the small table.

And I felt a chill, the lightest wisp of a feather brushing across the back of my neck.

Eyes. Someone was watching us.

It couldn't be real. I knew that. We were in a busy restaurant in my hometown, for Pete's sake. And yet— Damn. There it was again, soft as a whisper in the dark. Shifting casually in my seat, I glanced around the room, scanning faces, stances . . .

There was nothing. A tableful of hunters in blaze orange duds and Sorel boots, wolfing down steaks and beers, other tables of moms and pops, some with kids, some without, and— *There.*

Sitting at the bar, a silver-haired daddy in a pricey pinstripe suit, salt-and-pepper goatee, military brush cut. He was scanning his menu a bit too pointedly. Just my imagination? Maybe. But after two tours of disarming ordnance, I've learned to trust my hunches—

"Is something wrong?" Lauren asked. She'd noticed me eyeing Mr. Pinstripe across the room.

"Not a thing," I lied, turning back to her. "Go on, please."

"As the tasks in the envelopes are completed, the payout is divided between the final beneficiaries."

"By that, you mean—us? Luke and me?" Peach asked, waggling a finger between us.

"Actually, there's a third survivor. Specialist Kurt Blumenthal was still with your unit when Len drew up the pool, but he apparently took a settlement from the insurance cartel and opted out. I haven't been able to contact him."

"If Blu collected fifty bucks, he went off on a bender," Peach said. "He's a lush. Bottom line, what's this payout you're talking about?"

"Whatever it is, count me out, Peach," I said. "My mistake erased our whole crew."

"Get over yourself, Duroy!" she snapped. "It wasn't just you, it happened to all of us! Hell, I wasn't even *there!* We got it right seventy-one times, and what*ever* happened with seventy-two, LT's baby doesn't own any part of it. I'm eight months pregnant, I run out of gas walking around a block. I'm in no shape to handle—whatever's in those envelopes."

"It's not that simple," I began—

"Actually, it is," Lauren said flatly. "The policies require all tasks to be completed. If you opt out and Peach is unable to complete a task on her own, the pool reverts to the insurer, with no payout. Game over."

"Even so, I can't—"

"Tell you what, hotshot," Peach snapped, cutting me off as she rose clumsily to her feet. "Junior and I have to hit the john every twenty minutes. So while we're gone, why don't you think things through and decide if you're gonna do one last solid for the crew, or punk out on us." She rose and waddled off.

"I'll go with." Lauren said, hastily rising to follow Peach.

I watched the two women move through the crowded room, Peach, still cute as a bug, even with the baby weight, Lauren Tarleton slim as a gazelle. I sensed a stare again, quickly glanced at the suit at the bar. There were two of them now, and the bigger one was checking me out. Making no pretense of doing anything else.

Okay . . . game on.

I gave the women a few moments to vanish, then rose and headed for the men's. When the big guy rose to follow, I wasn't a bit surprised.

The men's john was a half-dozen metal stalls and as many sinks in a Masonite shelf, a choice of air dryers or paper towels. I rested a haunch against the counter and folded my arms. Waiting.

Not for long. The bruiser I'd spotted in the dining room pushed in, then stopped, surprised. Big guy, sports coat over a

Pistons T-shirt, a three-day stubble, and a bulge under his left arm. Shoulder holster.

"Lookin' for a date, buddy?" he growled.

"From the way you were checking me out in the dining room, I thought you might want to talk. And here we are. What's up?"

Before the bruiser could answer, the door behind him pushed open and Mr. Pinstripe joined us. Older than I'd thought, fiftyish, but in good shape. Razor-cut hair, tailored suit, repp tie, and clearly in charge. He nodded to his bull-shouldered buddy, who leaned against the door to insure our privacy.

"Sergeant Duroy," Silver Fox nodded, offering his hand, "my name is Morton Canfield. My oversized friend here is Cheech Marino. We'd like a moment of your time."

"Why?"

"For openers, so you can count your money," Canfield said. Snaking an envelope out of his jacket, he tossed it to me. "There's ten thousand US there. Check the count if you like, then put it in your pocket. It's yours. Free and clear. All we need is your signature, relinquishing any claim to the late Leonard Tarleton's estate."

"I don't have a claim."

"All the better." Canfield shrugged. "Our job is to settle small problems before the lawyers get involved. Take the money, sign the form, and let the party begin."

"Or what?"

"Or—? Sorry, I don't follow."

"Sure you do. You're offering me serious cash to do something. What happens if I don't take it?"

"It's free money," Cheech snorted. "Your buddy Blumenthal grabbed it in a heartbeat. You'd be a moron not to take it. Are you a moron?"

"No need for crudeness," Canfield said hastily. "Let me speak plainly, Mr. Duroy. The company's offering you ten K to—"

"Which company?"

"Our office represents a number of them, in this case a cartel of underwriters. Insurers often join forces to deal with nuisance claims."

"So I'm a nuisance worth ten K?"

"You're a sucker," Marino snapped, clearly annoyed. "The ten is cash in your hand. Try to squeeze us for more, you could land in real trouble—"

I couldn't help smiling.

"Did I say something funny, sport?"

"A few months ago, my unit was eight people. Today it's two. If you think you're more trouble than that, think again."

"You don't get the picture, pal," Cheech said. "If you don't sign, me and Mr. Canfield don't get paid. And we like gettin' paid. Take the bird in the hand, while you've still got a hand that works."

"I'll give it some thought," I said. "Move away from the door."

"Why don't you move me—oh, wait," he said, grinning. "Lemme put one hand behind my back—"

"Cheech!" Canfield's voice cracked like a whip. "Let the man pass. Mr. Duroy seems like a bright guy. Once he thinks it over, he'll do the smart thing."

"He don't look smart to me," Cheech said. "If he isn't, maybe we'll have better luck leanin' on his knocked-up girlfriend. Are you the daddy, Duroy? Or did your whole crew get a shot?"

It almost worked. I was casually dialing my prosthesis up to full juice, when I realized it was what they wanted. They wanted a scrum in a men's room. They'd rough me up, plant the money on me, their word against mine as to what happened. It might almost be worth it to find out how much damage full power on the prosthetic arm could do . . . but not quite.

So I didn't take the bait. And the big guy stepped aside, just enough to let me pass, clearly hoping I'd swing away.

And it was tempting. I thought about grabbing his wrist, giving it a full-power squeeze, then see if he still wanted to fight me one-handed. But both men were armed, and I couldn't come up with a scenario that didn't end up with somebody bleeding out. So I swallowed my rage, edged past Cheech, close enough to smell his aftershave, leaving the big ape grinning. Without a mark on him.

I stalked back to the table, steaming, and dropped into my seat. Peach glanced up, and her smile instantly vanished.

"What's wrong?" she demanded.

"Ask our friend, here," I said, jerking a thumb at Lauren. "I just got braced by two studs who work for the insurance companies that are on the hook for LT's game."

"What did they want?" Peach asked.

"To buy me off. Offered ten grand to walk away. Or else. The same deal Blumenthal took."

"Did you take it?" Lauren asked.

"Hell no. I don't like being pushed any more than I like being played, lady. Count me in. What's the game?"

"Just like that?" Lauren asked.

"Don't argue with the man," Peach countered. "Shut up and deal, Counselor. How does this thing work?"

Lauren drew a slip of paper out of her briefcase, along with a pair of black horn-rims that made her look even brighter.

"The tontine requires the survivors resolve the issues cited in the letters to the satisfaction of an officer of the court. I can serve, for the time being. In the end, a judge will review it to ensure the terms have been met."

"Why so complicated?" I asked.

"Substantial sums are involved, Mr. Duroy."

"How substantial?" Peach demanded. "How much are we talking about?"

Lauren hesitated, then shrugged. "The tontine pool is funded by seven term insurance policies at two and a half apiece. With four decedents, and one dropout, the remaining shares will come to you two. A total of roughly half a million, US. Each."

The background noise in the restaurant suddenly seemed very loud. "Holy crap," Peach said softly.

I didn't say anything. Couldn't.

"Okayyy," Peach nodded slowly, "that's a pot worth playing for. But how does it work, exactly? How do we win our shares?"

Lauren tapped a quick text into her smartphone, then placed it at the edge of the table, facing us.

"From this point forward, we'll record each step, to verify that the tasks were properly explained and completed." She quickly recited her name, the date, and our identities into the phone. Then she turned it again to face the table, opened her briefcase, took out a sheaf of black envelopes, and dealt them out on the table. Each bore a number but no other identification.

A sobering moment. In a way, the envelopes were as much a final monument as a tombstone. After checking a file, Lauren removed three of the envelopes from the stack.

"These three are yours and Specialist Blumenthal's. The remaining four describe tasks to be completed on behalf of a decedent. If resolved successfully, the benefits pay into the tontine pool and you go on to the next, until all four have been completed. If you fail, the game ends with no payoff. Do you have any questions?"

We didn't.

"Then let's proceed. Who wants to draw the first envelope?"

"Ladies first," I said. Peach reached for the fanned-out envelopes, then paused with her hand in midair.

"Holy crap," she said, grinning. "This isn't a tontine, guys, it's Blind Baseball."

I cocked my head, then nodded.

"Sorry," Lauren said, "you've lost me."

"Blind Baseball's a variation of stud poker," I explained. "All cards are dealt face down, so you bet blind, without knowing what's in your hand."

"It's always the last game of the night, when everybody's fried," Peach added. "Guys get nuts and go all in when they've got nothing."

"It's the game we were playing the night Len won big," I added.

"Okay, the name of this game is Blind Baseball, people," Peach said, grinning wildly. "Let's play."

Drawing an envelope from the stack, she tore it open, withdrew a short note, and scanned it quickly. "It's Artie's," she said, glancing up at me, her eyes swimming.

"What's it say?" I asked.

Peach shook her head, then passed it to Lauren, who raised an eyebrow for permission, then read it quietly aloud.

The note was written by Lt. Tarleton to outline the situation. LT identified himself, name, rank, serial number, and the date, roughly four months previous. And then the task.

"On the behalf of Specialist Arthur McVey—" I found myself hanging on every word, entranced. Lauren's voice was an eerie echo of her brother's. I've been hearing voices in my dreams. Now it was like LT was speaking to us from the next world, asking for one final favor. . . .

"That's it?" Peach asked when Lauren finished. "We track down Artie's dad, buy the old fart a drink, and hand him a check?"

"It appears so," Lauren acknowledged.

"That doesn't make sense," I said. "His dad ditched his family when Artie was just a kid. He hadn't seen him in years."

"The point of the game is unfinished business," Lauren said. "Perhaps my brother knew Artie wanted to make amends—"

"It doesn't matter *why* he wanted it done," Peach said impatiently. "Eyes on the prize, guys. We do the damn job, we get paid. Right?"

"Exactly," Lauren said. "I'll phone my office and have our investigators locate McVey Senior. If he's still above ground, it shouldn't take long."

It didn't. Lauren got a call back twenty minutes later. Arthur McVey Senior was alive and well, and living in Cincinnati.

Lauren booked a flight for the next morning and we agreed to meet at the airport. But as we were leaving, I scanned the room and spotted Canfield and Cheech at the bar. Cheech shot me with a fingertip, then blew away the imaginary smoke.

I didn't return fire. I should have.

The flight from Valhalla down to Cincinnati was a brief one. Barely an hour in the air. We hired a car at the airport, then Lauren used GPS to wend our way through the Bottoms, the seediest district of Cincy, looking for an address she'd gotten from her firm's investigator.

I don't know Cincinnati well, but I'd been here before. The first week after I joined the unit, Artie McVey became my rabbi. He took me under his wing, helped me to blend in with fourteen edgy strangers whose lives depended on my green skills. He taught me when to stand up for myself and, more importantly, when to shut up. Coaching me wasn't his *assignment*. We were intruders in an alien land, and he went out of his way to help me. Even took me home with him on leave once. Here. To Cincinnati. I met the gran who raised him and dated his girlfriend's sister.

So when Lauren parked in front of a seedy riverfront dive bar, Muldoon's Mill, I actually remembered the place. Artie and I spent a long afternoon in the joint, maybe . . . six years ago?

It could have been six minutes. Inside, nothing had changed. Sawdust on the floors, tinny country music from a battered neon jukebox. The regulars were rummies or dockworkers knocking back bracers before a shift, or washing out the aftertaste.

When I'd been here with Artie, we took a table in the corner, ordered a pitcher, then nursed it for an hour.

At the time, I thought he might be looking for a fight, it was that kind of joint. He wasn't, though. He just sipped his brew in stony silence and took no offense when a wino blundered against our table and cursed us out, weaving his way to the men's.

Later, when I asked him what was up with that place, Artie said he was just curious about it, but didn't say why. It was a clear signal to let it drop, so I did.

Until today. This time, I knew exactly why this place was important to Artie, and he must have told LT about it.

Arthur McVey Senior, Artie's wayward dad, was parked on a stool at the end of the bar, which was obviously his home away from home. In the same dive where Artie and I wasted a long afternoon, all those years ago. I hadn't made the connection then, but no Sherlocking was required this time. A quick glance at the mug shot supplied by Lauren's office was all it took.

The old-timer was sitting alone, nursing a double bourbon with a beer chaser. Seedy, dressed in faded denims and a flannel shirt that looked slept in, he seriously needed a shave. And probably delousing.

The three of us took a table in a quiet corner. Peach frowned at the mug shot.

"You sure that's him?" Peach said doubtfully. "He looks too old."

"I know how to find out," I said, rising. I made my way to the bar and took the stool next to the old-timer. Up close, there was no doubt. Years of boozing had taken their toll, but his resemblance to Arthur was unmistakable. A narrow hawk face, deep seams of surly disappointment around the eyes and mouth.

"Yo, you're Arthur McVey, right?"

He didn't even look up. "Whatever you're sellin', I ain't buyin'. Screw off."

"My name's Duroy, sir, I served in Iraq with your boy."

"Which one?" A response that surprised me.

"Do you have more than one son in the service?"

He mulled that a moment, "Nah, I got the two boys, Art and Jimmy, but just the one joined the service. Arthur. Jimmy's in the joint—got busted years ago, ran down a kid on a bike, drunk drivin'. Kinda lost touch with Arthur after that. Or maybe before. How's Arthur doing?"

I turned slowly to face him. "He—you must have been notified."

"Notified?"

"Mr. McVey, Arthur's dead. He was killed in Iraq a few months ago."

The old man didn't flinch at that, just frowned.

"Yeah," he nodded, "I guess I do remember somethin' about that. Got blowed up, right? Stupid bastard. Never shoulda mixed into that mess over there. Should've stayed home, found work, looked after his own."

"Like you did?" I asked evenly.

"My luck ain't been the best. My wife run off, you know."

"Hard to believe."

McVey knocked back his bourbon with a single gulp, chased it with beer, dribbling foam down his stubbled chin. "So? You bring a man bad news, least you can do is stand him a round."

"Actually, I can do better than that," I said, signaling the bartender, pointing a finger at his empty glass, stifling the urge to backhand the old sot out of his chair. "My friends have something for you. From Arthur."

"Yeah?" he asked, brightening a bit. "Them two broads you come in with? Works for me." He stumbled to his feet, then followed me back to our table, carrying his beer. But his pace faltered as he saw Peach, then he stopped.

"Nice try, but forget it, sonny," the old man said bitterly, turning to me. "This ain't my first rodeo."

"What are you talking about?"

"Your knocked-up girlfriend there. She ain't the first honey showed up carryin' somebody's woods colt, lookin' for a handout. This is where you tell me Arthur's the father, and I sign on to pay a bunch of child support. Is the other broad a lawyer?"

"The attorney part's right," Lauren said, rising to offer her hand, which he ignored. "Have a seat, Mr. McVey. I have a letter for you, sir, from your son. And a check."

"Check?" he echoed, brightening.

"Perhaps you'd care to read the letter first?"

"Ain't got my glasses," McVey said, pulling up a chair. "You read it. What's this about a check?"

"The letter will explain. Would you do the honors, Sergeant?"

I took the letter, opened it, and began. "Hey Pop, if you're reading this, I'm gone. Since we don't talk much, or at all, really, I wanted one last chance to say I'm sorry. I'm sorry you missed our high-school ball games. Me and Jimmy both lettered, but I was just a ham-and-egger. Jimmy was golden. Sorry you missed seeing him back then."

I paused. "Are you following this all right?"

McVey nodded, spinning a grimy fingertip to urge me on.

"I know you've had your troubles, Pop, I get that, especially now that I've got some of my own. Jimmy never got it, though. Every game, he'd look for you in the stands. It was freakin' comical. And now this last thing has happened, and I'm on to whatever's next. I want to leave you something, to make up for what you missed. The family we could've been. I'm leaving a check with my lieutenant, to forward to his lawyer. Something to remember your boys by."

Lauren passed him a check. McVey's eyes widened.

"*Jesus H. Christ!* A hundred thou? A hundred freakin' thousand. Is this legit?"

"Absolutely," Lauren said. "Your son had a term insurance policy worth far more," Lauren said, watching him. There was something in her eyes . . . I didn't get it. And then I did.

McVey grinned in drunken wonder at his magical pass to a new life—then he blinked.

"Wait—this ain't signed."

"Unfortunately, Arthur met his end before endorsing it," Lauren nodded, "an oversight that can't be corrected now—"

"—With Artie being dead and all," Peach put in. "But it must warm your heart to know your boy was thinking of you at the end of his life."

"I don't get it," the old man said.

"That pretty much sums it up," I said. "You don't get it."

"The check's like a keepsake, something to remember Artie by," Peach said. "Auld lang syne and all that."

"But—ain't there no insurance money?"

"There was," Lauren agreed. "Arthur's GI insurance went to your mother-in-law—"

"—the gran you dumped him on when he was eight years old," Peach said. "Remember her? The woman who actually raised your boys?"

"So . . . you clowns came all this way to tell me I don't get nothing?"

"What do you think you deserve?" Peach asked, exasperated. "A gold star for being a deadbeat dad?"

"Artie and I sat in this dive for most of an afternoon a few years back," I added. "You were sitting at the bar, twenty feet away, and didn't even know who he was."

"Ah, to hell with youse," he growled, tearing up the check, throwing the scraps at the two women.

Snatching up her drink, Peach threw it in his face! Both of them lunged up out of their chairs, facing off across the table.

"You snotty little bitch!"

"Go ahead, Pops!" Peach snapped back, jutting her jaw out to offer him a better target. "Clock a pregnant lady in an Irish bar! I can take a punch and it'll be worth it to see you get stomped!" She was begging to get decked and every eye in the room was locked on the drama, guys already coming up out of their seats—

"Time to go," Lauren said hastily, pulling Peach back. I seized the old man's shoulder, locking my prosthesis on his left bicep with a force that widened his eyes, sitting him down hard before he could swing. Lauren already had Peach in tow, heading for the door. I trailed them out, backing all the way, making sure no one followed us.

As we stumbled into the street, I wasn't sure if Peach was laughing, or crying, or both at the same time. For Arthur? Or for all of us?

But as we hurried across the street to our ride, I felt a feathery chill brush my neck. I glanced around quickly. There was no one near, but up the block, a black Range Rover was gunning out of its parking slot, burning rubber. I couldn't make out the driver through the smoked windshield, but didn't need to.

I damn well *knew* who it was, and they were headed straight at us!

Spreading my arms, I swept the two women out of the street, sending them sprawling over the curb as the Range Rover blew past, missing us by inches, shaking us with its windblast.

I tried to get a license plate, but a van crossed the intersection behind it. By the time it cleared, the Rover had mixed into traffic. Nothing to see but taillights.

"What the hell was that about?" Peach demanded as we straightened up, dusting ourselves off.

"That was trouble, lady. I think the insurance company thugs who braced me in Valhalla tracked us here, and this game just got serious. In a tontine, we'd just outlast the other players, but we're playing Blind Baseball against a cartel with serious money on the table. I don't know if that was a close call or a warning—"

"They're the ones that need a warning," Peach snapped. "We're not amateurs. They come at us again, we'll put somebody down."

"With what?" I said, holding the passenger's door for her, then slipping behind the wheel. "We're on the move and you can't get weapons through an airport."

"Hold it right there," Lauren said. "I'm an officer of the court. You can't consider violence—"

"Lady, where we've been, people kill for a cross word somebody said fifty years ago," Peach countered. "For this kind of money, we should expect the game to get rough. No weapons, no problem.

We'll improvise. There's always something handy. Salad fork, tire iron—"

Lauren was staring at her in disbelief—and Peach burst out laughing. "Jeez, Counselor, if you could see your face. I'm kidding, for Pete's sake. Just kidding."

But she damn well wasn't. I knew it, and from the look Lauren gave her, I was fairly sure she suspected it too. But we all let it pass. For now.

"How did they find us so quickly?" Lauren asked, as I eased the rental car into traffic.

"They're hired guns, working for a cartel with deep pockets," I said. "We'd better count on them showing up from here on."

"And if they do?" Peach grinned wickedly. "We'll . . . improvise."

"Maybe we can ditch them if we move fast enough," I said, weaving through traffic, picking up speed. "Where to next, Counselor?"

She popped her briefcase, and held up the envelopes. Peach chose one, and opened it, read it, then shook her head slowly. "Chicago," she said.

"Whoa," I said. "It's Marco's turn?"

She nodded, still reading.

"I'm sorry," Lauren said, "which one was Marco?"

"Marco Romero was our sniper," Peach explained. "My partner. Crack shot, could cap a bandit at a thousand yards. I was his spotter for two years, should have been beside him, but— well. Anyway, I already know what his task will be, it's all he ever talked about. LT would have heard about it."

"His brother," I said. "He'd want someone to get him out."

"Out of what?" Lauren asked.

"A street gang," I explained. "Marco was a Chicago gang-banger, grew up running with a crew in Pilsen. He enlisted to stay out of jail, but once he got clear and got his head screwed on straight, he was desperate to get his younger brother out too."

"And how do you do that, exactly?"

"The same way we'll handle the insurance goons," Peach said, her eyes glittering. "We improvise."

⚬━━⚬

We caught a shuttle flight out of Cincy's Lunken Airport, a forty-minute hop to Chicago. After renting another car, it was only a short cruise from O'Hare to Pilsen, in Chi-Town's violent Lower West Side.

Tough neighborhoods. Run-down older homes, most of them WWII vintage or before, sagging roofs and porches, in sad need of paint, with an obvious crack house every few blocks, multistory buildings, first-floor windows completely boarded up, replacement steel doors set in reinforced frames, painted up to look old. I was at the wheel, and slowed as we passed a crack house.

"Is that the address?" Lauren asked, frowning.

"No, it's the crew's headquarters and place of business," Peach said. "Marco showed us a picture of it once. His younger brother lives in the next block."

The house was as seedy and run-down as its neighbors, with one striking difference. A beautifully restored '63 Lincoln Continental, gleaming with fresh wax, was parked on the postage stamp of a front lawn. I pulled up beside it, pausing to admire it as we walked to the house. Looked, but didn't touch. It was that pretty. Midnight blue, big as a boat. They don't make 'em like that anymore.

A gaunt Hispanic woman answered the door, silver hair awry, faded flowered housedress, bunny slippers, ancient eyes.

"Qué?"

"Mrs. Gutierrez?" Lauren asked.

"No policía," Peach added quickly. *"Amigos de Marco."*

"It's okay, *abuela,*" a teenaged kid said, stepping out of a doorway behind her, pulling an Oakland Raiders muscle T-shirt on over his head. Taking his time, showing off his abs and gang tats. "I know the little one. You're Peach, right? Marco's buddy? Marco put you on once when we was talkin' on Skype. Come on through." He led us down a dim hallway to a seedy sitting room that looked out over the street. Sagging sofa patched with a flannel blanket. He didn't offer us seats, just turned to face us.

"So what's all this?" he demanded, swiping at an invisible drip on the end of his nose. "Is your kid my brother's or something?"

"Nope," Peach said, "but Marco would have wanted us to look in on you. He was worried about the life you're in."

"*My* life? He shoulda stewed more about his own. I ain't the one who got blown to hell. What do you want?"

"We're keeping a promise," Peach said. "We made a . . . deal, that if things went bad, we'd see to each other's families. We're here to help."

"Don't need no help. I'm cool. It's tough about Marco, but he bought into all that patriotic crap, and look what it got him. Slip me a few bucks if you want, you won't hurt my pride." He scratched idly at one of the gang tats on his arms. It was a faded tattoo, ridged with a fresh scab.

"It's a little heavier than that," Peach said. "Marco wanted you out of thug life, out of the Pilsen Projects crew."

"Then it's lucky he bought the farm," the kid said evenly. "Saved himself a big disappointment. I'm good where I am."

"Your brother wanted to get you into a better life."

"Better than what?" Chato asked, annoyed now. "See that Lincoln parked out front, lady? It's a resto-mod '63, cherry as brand new. Voodoo V-Eight, tricked out suspension, discs all around. It's Juice's ride, the shot caller with the Pilsen crew. I ain't some wannabe, I'm his damn driver."

"You mean you're his teenage fall guy," Lauren said bluntly. "If your boss gets stopped in that car with weapons or dope, he'll walk away, you'll claim the weight and take a deal for juvenile detention, then sit in a cell until your eighteenth birthday."

"I can do that time standing on my head," Chato scoffed. "Driver always takes the fall. Whatever happens to the car lands on me, that's the game. So what?"

"As an attorney, I've worked cases like yours many times." Lauren sighed. "Here's the part your homies leave out. The day you walk out of juvy, the sweet ride's over. You're just another street punk, bottom of the ladder. The cops will be all over you—"

"I won't give nothin' up—"

"Do you think your boss will take that chance? Some wannabe in your own crew will blow your head off and make his rep on your bones."

"You don't know what you're talking about!"

"But your brother did. He knew exactly how the thug life ends up. He got out, and he wanted you out."

"Fat lot of good it did him. He got himself killed for strangers!"

"We weren't strangers . . ." Peach began, but I waved her to silence. Out on the street, a black Range Rover had slowed to a crawl as it passed the parked Lincoln, clearly giving the driver time to read the street addresses. It kept on at the same speed, then eased around the next corner, made a U-turn, and stopped. And sat there. Idling. White exhaust snaking up into the dark.

"What's up?" Chato asked, joining me at the window, still scratching his arm.

"Do you know that car?"

"I know it ain't from around here," he snorted. "Sweet ride like that would get jacked at a corner, waitin' for a light to change."

"If that's the Rover that took a run at us in Cincy, they're getting pretty bold," Peach said.

"A little too bold," I said. "See that silver Ford, parked in the next block, across the street? It was idling, but it shut down as the Range Rover rolled up."

"The silver Ford's the law," Chato said. "Dumbasses stake out the clubhouse in unmarked cars like we won't notice. The crew shuts down business while they're on us, open up five minutes after they're gone."

Chato was getting edgier by the minute, a case of nerves that had nothing to do with the cops up the street. He was using meth, not an addict yet, but on the way. Which made up my mind.

The idling Rover and the two thugs were just sitting there, waiting to take another crack at us at their convenience. Confident. And careless.

Casually dialing my faux forearm to full power, I edged over beside Peach.

"The kid's getting antsier by the second. He wants us gone, but doesn't want to push it. If his boss trusts him with his car, he's probably holding a stash for him as well. It'll be somewhere in the house, probably close at hand, easy to get at. Find it."

Peach moved off casually, circling the room before heading toward the kitchen to talk to Chato's grandmother. Or so it seemed. Halfway down the corridor she paused, only for a second, gave a barely perceptible nod, as though to herself, then continued on.

She'd turned up his meth stash in less than a minute. Good time, but not exceptional for somebody who's been trained to sniff out IEDs. A bomb can be planted almost anywhere, in a basement, on a roof, and still do its job. A gangster with a meth habit needs his junk available. And so it was. For both of us.

I motioned for Lauren to join us at the window and pointed out at the idling Rover across the way.

"Things are about to get complicated," I said quietly. "Why don't you explain to young Mr. Romero what his options can be if he quits his crew."

"But—"

"*Keep him distracted*," I hissed, smiling when I said it, but already moving off down the hallway to the spot where Peach had paused. I had no problem spotting the stash. There was an overhead vent with no screws holding it in place. I slid it out and a glassine packet dropped into my palm. Eight ounces or so, just below the limit for hard time, on the edge between delivery weight and personal use—

"Hey!" Chato barked. The kid was sharper than I'd thought, but still a step slow. The keys to the Lincoln were on a nail by the door. I pocketed them along with the drugs as the kid grabbed my shoulder, spinning me around. "What the hell do you think you're doing?"

"Borrowing your boss's ride," I said. "He won't mind, right?"

I clamped onto Chato's wrist, harder than I'd meant to, actually, but I was angry and the unit tracks my nerve impulses, which crank up with my temper. It had the desired effect, though. Chato went white, gasped, and nearly fell. He staggered as I led him to a kitchen chair, thrust him down in it.

"Stay put," I growled, "or I swear I'll snap your wrist like a matchstick!" He was smarter than I'd thought. He believed me, probably because I meant it.

"What are you doing with my boss's stash?"

"Saving your life. Meth will kill you, and your boss's stash seems a little light to me. I'd guess you've been experimenting a little."

He went absolutely gray. "No, I ain't. Swear to God."

"Don't take this wrong, kid, but you're maybe the worst liar I've ever seen. You just don't have the knack for it."

"Which is kind of a compliment, if you think about it," Peach put in. "It means you don't lie enough to be good at it."

"But it also means that when your boss hears about what happened tonight, he'll read you like an email and put a bullet in your head."

"What do you mean 'when he hears'? Nothing's happened."

"Not yet." I nodded to Peach, who clamped onto the kid's wrist in a come-along hold. "But it's about to. You'd better plan on leaving with us, kid. Trying to explain this mess will only get you killed."

"What mess?" he yelled after me, in a total panic. "*Wait—!*" But I was already out the door, trotting across the lawn to his ride.

The big Lincoln wasn't even locked. Everyone in the neighborhood would know who owned it and wouldn't dare touch it. But I wasn't from the neighborhood.

Sliding in behind the wheel, I fired it up. The oversized V-8 rumbled instantly to life, growling with power. Sixty-threes didn't come with seat belts, but this car wasn't original. Its resto-mod body *looked* classic, but everything under the hood was totally up to date, including a seat-belt rig worthy of a NASCAR racer.

I strapped myself in as tightly as I could, then dropped the Lincoln into drive and floored it. Pedal to the metal!

The big cruiser lunged off the lawn like it had been launched from the Space Center, skidding broadside into the street as I whipped the wheel around, then fishtailing in the opposite direction as I countered the skid, aiming its whale-sized nose directly at the idling Range Rover. I caught a glimpse of Cheech's wide eyes in the Lincoln's high beams a split second before the Linc leapt over the curb and plowed into the Range Rover broadside!

I slammed hard against the safety belts, banging my mouth off the steering wheel. I'd expected an airbag to absorb part of the jolt, but the Lincoln apparently wasn't *that* modern. Still, basic physics applied. Five thousand pounds of Detroit iron smashing into a Brit SUV at forty miles an hour? The Range Rover went airborne, flipping over as though it had been tossed by a pro wrestler, crashing down hard on its shotgun side. The windshield and sunroof blew out, and it was lucky they did, because the driver's door was jammed shut.

Dazed by the impact, leaking blood from a gash on my chin, it took me a moment to clear my head and get myself unstrapped, but then I was out of the Lincoln and scrambling up onto the Range Rover. The driver's-side window was shatterproof but twisted out of its frame. Gripping it with my powered arm, I tore it out and tossed it aside.

Below me, Canfield and his bruiser buddy were in a tangled pile against the passenger door, struggling to free themselves.

The older man's eyes met mine for a mad moment.

"Help us!" Canfield pleaded. "For God's sake, man!"

No problem. Popping open Chato's baggie of crystal meth, I shook it out on them, dusting them like snowmen. Then I scrambled down off the Rover, backed away from it, and dropped to my knees.

The unmarked silver Ford came roaring up, skidding to a halt with its strobe lights ablaze. Two plainclothes cops bailed out while their car was still rocking. A salt-and-pepper team, one white and much older, the other a young bronze-toned woman, both in leather jackets and jeans, both armed with Glock automatics aimed straight at me.

"On your knees!" the woman shouted.

I was already on my knees, but I nodded to show I understood.

"Hands behind your head!"

"Sorry, ma'am, can't do that," I said.

"What?"

A picture's worth a thousand words. Grasping my prosthesis with my right hand, I gave it a quick twist, pulled it off, then lowered it to the pavement in front of me. "Will that do?"

The two cops were so startled I thought they might shoot me by accident.

"Guys, the crash was my fault. My artificial hand came loose, I lost control. But right now I smell gasoline. You'd best get those guys out of the Rover before it blows!"

Which they did. I stood aside, reattaching my arm, while the two officers wrestled Canfield and his thug buddy out through the shattered windshield to safety. But when they realized both men were liberally dusted with a controlled substance? And armed? The conversation went south in a hurry. Canfield tried to bluster his way out of it, but this was Chicago. The stakeout cops weren't buying. The two mercenary goons left in an EMT bus, handcuffed to their gurneys, with a uniformed officer standing guard over them.

My questioning went slightly better. A wounded warrior, back from Iraq to visit a dead buddy's family. I borrowed his boss's car to make a beer run, but my government-issue arm came loose (I waggled it for emphasis), and I lost control of the Lincoln. Sorry about that.

They didn't believe me for a second, but the gang boss's Lincoln plowing into a Rover dusted with meth gave them an excuse to search Juice's car and raid the drug house, which they proceeded to do after calling in a small army of street cops, plus a SWAT team.

And during the ensuing confusion, an older cop took me aside. He was a Gulf War vet, and he *strongly* suggested that if I had no urgent business in Cook County, I might want to answer any follow-up questions by email. From far away.

It was excellent advice. But I didn't take it. I *did* have pressing business in Cook County.

Morton Canfield woke slowly in a white room. White ceiling, white tiled floor, white sheets. A computer monitor winked silently by his bedside. Dazed and disoriented, he had no idea where he was at first, but I could see his panic rising as he surfaced out of the haze. His eyes widened even more when he realized his left hand was handcuffed to the bed frame, and that I was sitting in a plastic chair beside his bed.

"Hey," I said cheerfully. "Welcome back. Before you ask, you're in the detention wing of Rush Medical Center, one of the best hospitals in Chi-Town. Your partner's two doors down, strapped to a rack. He took a swing at the cop who was trying to pull him out of the wreck. You should hire smarter help."

"What—" He coughed. "What the hell happened?"

"You had an accident, Mr. Canfield. It was totally my fault. I had some trouble with my prosthesis, lost control, and banged into you."

"But—if you hit us, why am *I* restrained?" He jerked his left wrist against the handcuff.

"That would probably be about the methamphetamine the cops found scattered all over you guys and your vehicle."

"Meth?" he echoed, dazed. "But . . . we didn't—you planted it on us!"

"You can fly that story if you like. It'll be a tough sell, though. The cops think I'm a low-rent hero, a wounded warrior and all that. And since you and your buddy were parked across from a known drug house, dusted with crystal and packing guns—"

"They'll never make this stick," Canfield snapped. "The company has an army of lawyers on speed dial. I'll be out of here before these yokels finish their paperwork!" As he spoke, his eyes were darting about wildly.

"Looking for this?" I asked, holding up his cell phone. He snatched it out of my hand, but the instant he touched the dial—a blinding flash flared on his nightstand, sending a tiny puff of smoke toward the ceiling!

"What—?" Canfield stammered, dropping his phone. "What the hell was that?"

"A visual aid," I said, leaning in. "You seem like a bright guy, so let's settle our business here and now. That little flash was a pinch of magnesium dust, triggered by your phone. Totally harmless. But that same pinch of dust sitting on a brick of Semtex or C-four? It could bring down this building on top of you, or blow a car into the next county and you with it. In tech school, when you learn to disarm bombs, you also learn how to build them. I was top of my class."

I leaned in closer, our faces only inches apart. "Listen up, Mr. Canfield, because I'll only say this once. If you ever come near one of my friends again, or I even see you in the same neighborhood, that little pop you just heard will be the last thing you *ever* hear. Nod if you understand."

He hesitated, but only for a second. Then managed a jerk of his head. I settled for that.

"Good," I said, rising to go. "Normally I'd say 'see you around,' but you'd better pray I don't."

"You won't," he said, swallowing. "I'm done with this. I swear it."

"Do we believe him?" Lauren Tarleton asked. We were seated at a small table in an O'Hare International café, waiting for our flight to be called. Me, Peach, Lauren, and a tattooed teenage thug who was nervously eyeballing every pedestrian who passed. Not so easy to do in one of the nation's busiest airports.

"I think he probably meant it when he said it," I said, "but he's a mercenary. If they bump his paycheck, he may come at us again."

"Better if it's him," Chato said. "You know what he looks like. It's the ones you don't know you gotta worry about."

"The kid's got a point," Peach said.

"I ain't a kid, but I probably won't get much older. Thanks to y'all, I'm about to be dead as Tupac."

"Actually, we saved your crummy life," I countered. "You grew up gangster, and that movie always ends with you dead or in prison. Your brother Marco knew it, and down deep? So do you."

"What I *know* is, I was aces till you wrecked Juice's Lincoln and got the clubhouse raided. Now my own crew will be looking to bust a cap in my ass."

"The boy's right about one thing," Lauren said, glancing around at each of us. "This business is turning out to be a lot more dangerous than any of us expected. If Canfield quits, the insurance cartel will just hire someone else. You two might want to rethink this."

"Lady," Peach sighed, shaking her curly head. "Compared to where we've been, this 'danger' you're talking about is like spring break. We've survived contact with the enemy twice, and came out ahead. If we underestimated the risk, we don't anymore. We'll be okay."

"Even so—"

"Fine, let's put it to a vote," Peach said impatiently. "I'm still in, all the way. Luke?"

I nodded. "Lauren?"

"Absolutely," she said. "Leonard started this, I'll see it through, all the way."

"I vote . . ." Chato began.

"You don't get a vote," Peach said.

"Sure I do. Marco was my brother, so I get his vote. And I'm voting myself in. It's a one-time deal and y'all better take it. You need me more'n I need you."

"How do you figure?" Peach demanded.

"Lady, I drove Juice's Lincoln the better part of a year, outran the law four different times, never got caught, never got a ticket or put so much as a freakin' *scratch* on that ride. Duroy here borrows it five minutes, totals it out, puts two mopes in the hospital, and gets half my crew arrested. Y'all obviously are in serious need of a wheelman, and thanks to your pal jamming me up, I'm available."

"It's not that simple, sonny," Peach said. "Did you miss the part about our situation being risky?"

"Riskier than Juice draggin' me into an alley to ask how his ride got wrecked?"

No one had an answer for that. Which was an answer, of sorts.

"I knew it," Chato said, trying not to look smug. And failing. "Y'all are marshmallows. I'm hired, ain't I?"

"God," Peach groaned, "it's like having Marco back, in the worst way."

"Saving this kid was what Marco wanted," I said. "Anyway, he's right. We can't leave him here, and the way things are, having a hotshot getaway driver might come in handy."

"We don't even know where we're going next," Peach said.

"Then let's find out," Lauren said. Fishing the final two envelopes out of her briefcase, she handed them to Peach. And I found myself smiling, eyeing Peach across the table, knowing she was feeling it too. We all were. Feeling the *buzz*. The adrenaline rush you get before heading into action.

She offered me the choice but I nodded it away. "Let the kid draw."

"All right, ladies and germs," Peach said, shuffling the envelopes, "New blood at the table. The name of this game is Blind Baseball. Pick an envelope, sonny, and tell us where we're going."

The question comes up at every seminar and signing. Where do you get your ideas? Forget the usual suspects: nightly news, scholarly research, and even an occasional dream. This story, "Blind Baseball," has its roots in the seventeenth-century, with the birth of an odd insurance format called a tontine. A circle of investors (sometimes numbering in the thousands) each contribute a given amount of money, for life. Each participant receives a yearly interest payment from the pool, which grows as the years pass and so do the donors, as their donations remain in the fund. The last survivor wins everyone else's shares, and becomes wealthy overnight.

Gee, what could possibly go wrong?

The odd thing about the story idea? I first encountered tontines in a book of my mom's when I was a very little kid. Why would it pop up all these years later to drive a new tale? That's a question for a much longer essay.

God, I do love this game.

Derrick Belanger *is a best-selling author and educator most noted for his publications and lectures on Sherlock Holmes and Sir Arthur Conan Doyle. His company, Belanger Books, is one of the world's top publishers of new Sherlock Holmes books and is the only authorized publisher of the original August Derleth Solar Pons collections as well as new Solar Pons adventures. In January 2020, Belanger was awarded the Susan Z. Diamond Beacon Award in recognition of outstanding efforts to introduce young people to Sherlock Holmes. Find him at belangerbooks.com.*

THE ADVENTURE OF THE MISQUOTED MACBETH

Derrick Belanger

The Bible instructs us to love our brothers, but I confess I felt little of the sentiment in question as I stared at the letter from San Francisco. I had a strong sense of what kind of news the missive contained.

"This one's travelled a long way, Doctor," Mrs. Hudson said, holding out the letter.

I had just come home from a long day of work; fortunately, Holmes's day was even longer than mine and my detective friend had not yet returned from his investigations. I knew his current case concerned the murder of a mudlark. It was the type of case he took when the client, in this case a desperate street Arab who was the victim's kin, had nowhere else to turn. Holmes did not profit from these cases, but they kept his mind occupied and proved to me there was a heart inside his cold exterior.

"Em, do me a favour, Mrs. Hudson, and please don't mention this letter to Mr. Holmes. It, em, involves a surprise I'm planning for him," I blubbered, uncomfortable at telling my landlady a falsehood.

The creases around Mrs. Hudson's eyes flattened as she opened them wide. "A surprise? For Mr. Holmes?" she said, astonished. Then she let out a soft chuckle. "You don't need to worry. Your secret's safe with me." I was unsure that she believed me, but I was certain she would not breathe a word to Holmes.

I quickly ascended the steps to 221B and tore open the letter, reading with dread. As my worst fears were confirmed, nay, exceeded, I felt my face reddening and anger rising within me. My brother was penniless and very ill, residing in a hospital. He asked me to journey to see him one last time, for he feared his drinking had finally got the better of him. The signature was in a shaky hand.

I tore the letter into pieces and threw them in the wastepaper basket. Then I reached for paper, ink, and pen and wrote a frenzied response telling my brother how much I despised him, how he had squandered his life as a drunkard and run through our father's inheritance without ever doing an honest day's work. When I reached the final lines and saw the loathing and ill will inked upon the page, I had second thoughts. I crumpled my letter into a ball and tossed it away, realising that I needed a clearer head before deciding on a course of action.

It was but a few days later, on a chilly spring afternoon in the year of 1884, when a case was brought to Sherlock Holmes that serendipitously led me to a conclusion on the matter of my kin. I had returned to 221B Baker Street in a foul mood, lamenting to Holmes over the crowded London streets and the unseasonable cold. The frost really was not out of the ordinary, but since receiving my brother's letter I had found a long list of things about which to complain. Holmes must have noted the change in my mood, but he did not comment, nor did he say anything when I built a fire in the hearth. We could have easily worn wool and drunk tea to stay warm and not wasted the coal.

I was sitting in my armchair across from Holmes, grumbling about the new French Minister of Foreign Affairs, when the bell rang downstairs, and soon after Mrs. Hudson came to our door. She handed Holmes a card. My friend read it and gave a nod.

"Send the gentleman up."

"A new client?" I asked.

"That depends on whether I take his case." Holmes had been smoking his clay pipe and looking towards the flames, puzzling over some problem. A new case might prove beneficial since he had brought the mudlark investigation to a swift conclusion. The less he had to do, the more likely he was to become bored, and that was when he chose less savoury ways to occupy his time.

There was a knock and Holmes called out, "Enter!"

I turned, and started at the sight of the man who might become Holmes's next client. It was as though the giant Antaeus himself were stepping into our sitting room, a massive figure who had to stoop so as not to scrape his head against the doorway. His chest was Herculean, his arms were thick as tree trunks, and his looks brutish. An unevenly trimmed black beard hid some of his pock-marked face, and a lion's mane of hair fell over his forehead. His nose was stubby, his eyes dark and beady.

"Which one of you is Sherlock Holmes?" he asked in a baritone, guttural voice.

The appearance of this creature had me at a loss for words, but Holmes gave a few coughs and whisked away smoke from his face. "Excuse me," he said, calmly extinguishing his pipe. "I wanted to get in the last few puffs of this excellent Turkish blend. I am Mr. Sherlock Holmes, and this is my friend and associate, Dr. Watson. Please join us."

Holmes motioned for the goliath to sit in the cane-back wicker chair between himself and me. The giant sauntered over and lowered himself, the chair giving a long, pitiful creak.

"Watson, this is Mr. Phineas Armstrong. At least that is what his card indicates. I believe the name is an alias, isn't that right, Mr. Armstrong?"

The brute glowered at Holmes. "What are you getting at?" he snarled, leaning forward in threatening fashion.

My friend studied his fingernails. "I do believe it is time to file these down," he mused. "Have no fear of our guest, Watson. While he is a sizeable man and appears quite menacing, Mr. Armstrong is as gentle as a newborn babe."

I am not sure who had a more startled look upon his face, Armstrong or I. Holmes, unruffled, elaborated on his statement:

"Look to his hands, Watson. Note how they are smooth and free of calluses." Holmes made a fist to show off his own rough hands. "Unlike mine, the hands of a fighter.

"You will also observe the high quality of his suit. It is new, well pressed, and with rather expensive silver cuff links. An unusual fashion choice for a man who wears his hair as though it were brushed by a whirlwind and speaks as though he made his home in Limehouse.

"Lastly, the name Armstrong furthers his act. A brutish outer appearance coupled with the name Arm-strong suggests a man you would not want to cross." He turned to our visitor. "Now, Mr. Armstrong, I should appreciate it if you dropped your charade and told us your real name, and more importantly, why you are here."

I had been watching Armstrong's expression turn from one of shock to one of absolute pleasure, like that of a child beholding a magic trick.

"Well done, Mr. Holmes, well done," he said now in the Queen's English. "You're everything Lestrade said you'd be."

Holmes arched his brows. "Lestrade sent you?"

"In a manner of speaking. He's mentioned you. Said your detective skills could almost keep up with his own—" Armstrong stared blankly "—and your fees were reasonable too."

"Did he, now?" Holmes responded, his lips closing in a thin line.

"Oh, don't you worry, Mr. Holmes. You'll be well compensated for your work."

"I do not yet know what that work is," Holmes answered. "Nor do you know if I shall accept your case."

Mr. Armstrong raised his hands as if telling a robber not to shoot. "I understand. I probably shouldn't have mentioned that bit about Lestrade . . ." He shook his head. "Let me tell you the nature of the case and then you can make up your mind."

Holmes nodded his approval.

Armstrong leaned forward and began his tale, moving his hands expressively as he spoke. "I should begin by telling you that Hale, Chauncey Hale, is my birth name, though I did legally change it to Armstrong, and debt collection is my game. I didn't set out to be a debt collector, no, sir. Chemistry was my field of study, and I started out at King's, thinking that would be how I made my way in life. Fate took a bad turn, and a case of the pox left my face as cratered as the moon. Always looking for a way to flip my luck from bad to good, I saw how intimidated people were when they encountered me with my new face, and I thought there had to be some money in it for me.

"So, a few years back, I turned to debt collection, and not just any debt collection, but the collection of large sums. You see, I can charge twenty percent of the debt for my services. Fear makes the men pay up. Banks are much happier to get their money and pay a hefty fee than to send a client to debtors' prison where the person may never work off what is owed. Better to pay me and have eighty percent immediately."

"Your work must be quite lucrative," I said, thinking of all the people I knew who had gambled away their fortunes. Even I myself had been in debt several times from making bad bets at the races.

"It is, Doctor. I have a gentleman's salary. There's no end to those who owe money, regardless of whether the markets are up or down. And if I keep bringing in payments, I should be in business for the rest of my life. And that brings me to why I'm here."

Holmes leaned forward. His gaze became more focused, and I could see that he would concentrate on the colossus's every word.

"Continue."

"Yesterday, I had three payments to collect. All were for large sums of money from gentlemen who had fallen on hard times. The first two were easy enough to . . . let's say coax into finding the necessary resources. Alas, I'm sure that they ended up even deeper in debt by borrowing to cover what they owed." He shrugged. "Better than hanging from a noose tied with their own hands."

"Really, sir!" I was disgusted at how nonchalantly this brute discussed the misery of his fellow man.

"It is but the truth, Doctor," Armstrong answered casually. "I take no pleasure in this. No one ought to be blamed for a task society considers necessary."

I was about to reply with some choice words, but Holmes held up both his index fingers.

"Mr. Armstrong," he said in a tone of boredom. "Pray, keep the asides to a minimum."

Armstrong grumbled that he was only trying to defend himself. "It was late in the afternoon," he then continued, "when I came to my third and final collection of the day. Since the first two had taken longer than anticipated, I was torn about how to approach this one. You see, I keep a red setter at home. I pay the neighbour lad to take her out each day after he gets home from school; however, he had some oral examination yesterday, so I had to get home and give Lady a run of the park before she made a mess of the house.

"My last scheduled visit of the day was to the home of one Jacob Snerley, a former bank manager who owed five hundred pounds. The man had worked for Horace and Sons, but when the bank discovered how much debt he was in, he was sacked. They thought it looked poor for a company that was entrusted with people's fortunes to have a manager who was so bad at managing his own."

"Understandable," Holmes agreed. "And who owns Mr. Snerley's loans?"

"A lender by the name of Bentley mostly, but there are a few brokers as well."

"Thank you," Holmes said, and I could tell he was storing this information in his mind. "Carry on."

"I decided that I would go over to Snerley's house in Upper Grosvenor Street, threaten that I'd return to see him that evening and he'd better have the money or I'd haul him off to prison myself. That would give him plenty of time to gather the necessary funds and myself plenty of time to care for my dog."

"Weren't you concerned that he might flee in the interim?" I asked.

"That was a concern of mine, Doctor," the giant said with a grin. I could tell he was a man who enjoyed the sound of his own voice. He was having a grand time telling his tale. "However, when I got to the house I knew, or at least I thought I knew, that he wasn't going anywhere. The property was worth vastly more than what he owed, a two-storey house with a manicured lawn. If the man fled, then the loan agency could foreclose on his house. Before I rapped on the door, I already knew that I'd suggest Snerley take a small mortgage, easy to arrange for someone who's worked in the City—"

"One moment," Holmes interrupted the potential client. "Just because a man can lay hold of some money doesn't mean that he will act upon your request. There must have been more to your certainty that he would not run off without paying his debts."

"You are an observant fellow, Mr. Holmes. Yes, I noticed through the window when I approached the house that the furniture had beige cloths draped over it. I figured Snerley was having the house painted. Someone who improves his property isn't going to up and leave. The man appeared to have resources; he just wasn't directing them properly."

Holmes thought for a moment, nodded, and then said, "*Appeared* . . ." as though he were questioning the debt collector's word choice. "Very good, Mr. Armstrong. Pray continue your story."

"I was surprised, gentlemen, that when I knocked on the front door, it was answered by Snerley himself, and he was as tall and almost as ugly as I am, and also scarred. Before I had a chance to introduce myself, he handed me a thin envelope and said, 'I've been expecting you. Here.'

"I thanked him, but he sneered at me. 'Don't dawdle. Be off with you, now,' he said. I did not like his tone of voice, but this was a stroke of good fortune, so I simply tipped my hat and turned on my heels.

"I caught a hansom to my house in Marylebone, took Lady for a long stroll, and then spent the remainder of the evening catching up with the news. It was not until this morning when I was preparing to hand in the debts I had collected that I opened Snerley's envelope." Armstrong ground his teeth while taking an envelope from his inner pocket. "Here, Mr. Holmes, have a look. No cheque inside. Only a piece of paper with some gibberish on it."

Holmes opened the envelope and took out a sheet of paper, which he proceeded to unfold. I noted that his eyes widened for a fleeting moment. He scoffed and then handed the paper to me.

I was surprised to see scrawled there in pencil a number of the opening lines of Shakespeare's *Macbeth*:

FIRST WITCH: WHEN SHALL WE THREE MEET AGAIN? WHEN THE MOON NEITHER WAXES NOR WANES?

SECOND WITCH: WHEN THE HURLYBURLY'S DONE. WHEN THE BATTLE'S LOST AND WON.

THIRD WITCH: THAT WILL BE THE ARRIVAL OF THE SUN.

FIRST WITCH: WHERE THE PLACE?

SECOND WITCH: UPON THE SAINT.

THIRD WITCH: THERE TO MEET WITH MACBETH.

"Tell me," said Holmes in a rather uninterested voice. "What did you do next?"

"Well, after I cursed and complained to my poor dog, I took a cab over to Snerley's residence. When I arrived, I saw this little fellow slipping a letter through the letter box. I asked if he happened to know whether Mr. Snerley was home. He told me that he wasn't. We struck up a conversation, and it turns out the man was Snerley's landlord! So, not only did Snerley not own the house, but the place was furnished, so he didn't even own the furniture. I had nothing to use as collateral and the thief had slipped away. If only I'd opened that envelope when it was handed to me!"

He used some rather uncouth words to describe himself before continuing. "So, that's about it, Mr. Holmes. I have to find Snerley and collect the debt from him, if possible. I can probably get a few days of grace from my employers, but after that, they'll drop me, and I'll lose my payment. Twenty percent it is, Mr. Holmes, but more than that, I'll lose my reputation for always collecting my debts. In fact, if you can get Snerley and the money to me in forty-eight hours, I'll give you half . . . no . . . sixty percent of my fee as payment. What do you say, old man?"

Holmes's face still displayed an expression of ennui. He glanced over the paper that bore the *Macbeth* quote one more time, then reached out and let the paper glide into the fire. Armstrong's jaw dropped, just as my own did, on watching Holmes destroy what appeared to be a piece of evidence.

"What'd you do that for?"

"Because, Mr. Armstrong," Holmes said as he grabbed the poker and stirred the fire, "the message provided no value to your case, but it does provide a touch of warmth to the room." He returned the poker to its rack and leaned back in his seat. "Now, Mr. Armstrong, your fee is quite generous, and I do believe I can bring your case to a conclusion within the time you have in mind."

At Holmes's words, the Hercules let out a sigh of relief. "Thank you, Mr. Holmes. Lestrade was right to recommend you."

"Just a moment," my friend cautioned. "I do have a few questions before I give you my final agreement."

"Of course."

"First, you mentioned that Snerley was ugly and scarred."

"That's right. A truly repulsive fellow."

"How so?"

"Well, he has a twisted face, as if his eyes and ears don't quite line up. They are misaligned, with his left side higher than his right."

"And the scar?"

"Ghastly, Mr. Holmes. It stretches from here"— Armstrong tapped his left temple then moved his finger down his face, from just under his eye to the corner of his lips— "to here."

Holmes nodded. "Well, he should be easy enough to find." He then asked, "What additional information did you learn from Mr. Snerley's landlord?"

"Not much. He said Snerley was a fine tenant who always paid on time. In fact, he is paid up until the end of the week. I'll be honest, Mr. Holmes. I find it odd that Snerley pays his rent and fixes up the interior of his home, but doesn't make any payments towards his debt."

"A good point, Mr. Armstrong. One that I hope to clarify for you."

Once Armstrong had departed, Holmes practically threw my coat to me from the wardrobe. "Get ready, Watson. We must hurry to Snerley's house."

I buttoned up my outer garment. "Why the urgency?"

Holmes swung open the door, cape in hand, urging me to head downstairs. "I must inspect the house, though I fear it has already been cleared."

We exited into Baker Street, damp and rather glum this afternoon. Fortunately, we did not need to wait for long. A four-wheeler approached, and soon we were off to Snerley's residence.

"I take it there is more to the case than an escaped debtor," I remarked dryly.

"There is indeed, Watson. How much more I hope to elucidate when we arrive in Upper Grosvenor Street."

Holmes settled into a monk-like trance as he focused on the fragments of the case. I also reflected on what I knew, wondering if there was any significance to the letter Holmes had thrown into the fire. I decided against it, for why would my friend destroy a piece of evidence? Still, his methods sometimes appeared to make as much sense as the ramblings of a Bedlam resident.

Despite my best efforts to focus on the problem at hand or even to clear my mind and just listen to the clopping of the hooves upon the cobblestones, my thoughts returned to my brother and his situation. A bitterness grew in my heart. I remembered our good times together growing up, playing rugby in the field near our house, jumping off rope swings into the pond near our school. What a waste for a lad with so much promise to end up a hospitalised drunkard in a faraway land.

The Snerley residence, handsome and well-kept, was nestled between a Georgian cottage and a row of terraced houses. Upon our arrival, Holmes awoke from his trance and practically sprang out of the carriage, not even pausing to request that our driver wait while we inspected the house.

My friend rushed up the garden path to the entrance. He tried the door, found it locked, and removed a pick from his trouser pocket.

"Stand behind me," he commanded, so that I blocked anyone from seeing us breaking in.

While Holmes worked, I turned my head and looked through the front bay window, where I could see a fine but worn green couch. Something about it puzzled me, but I could not place my finger on why that particular piece of furniture should draw my attention. The lock clicked open, and Holmes entered the house. I followed, shutting the door behind me.

The front parlour was sparsely furnished. There was the green couch I had spied through the window, with a matching set of cushioned chairs. A small mahogany card table stood in the centre of the seating arrangement. The table was quite worn and looked as if it might serve more frequently as a footrest than as a device for playing bridge.

Holmes stared at the floor. "Bah!" he let out, clenching his right hand. He stepped over to the dining room behind the parlour and let out another "Bah!"

"It is as I feared, Watson. Just look at the floor."

"Could do with a touch of the mop."

"Exactly." Holmes bent down and swiped his index finger across the wooden boards, then showed me the dust upon its tip. "It will be like that throughout the house. In every room, except in the front parlour."

"Why would Snerley only clean the parlour?"

"Because that is where he and his unsavoury guests met." Holmes returned to the parlour, crouched down by the furniture, and began moving the chairs around and peering underneath. "This ensures that they can't be identified. I should almost say that the precautions they took suffice to identify them, but without conclusive evidence I—aha!"

Holmes had moved the couch back, and now in one corner picked up what appeared to be a long strand of white hair. He held it up to the window, a look of triumph taking shape upon his face. "Ah, Watson, as I suspected. I will verify with my microscope at

home, but I am certain this strand of hair is from our adversary."
Holmes gave one of his odd silent laughs. He was certainly in
high spirits.

"I don't recall Armstrong saying that Snerley had white hair."

"He didn't. In fact, my friend, Armstrong never met
Mr. Snerley."

"Really, Holmes, you are making little sense."

"Come, Watson. Our cab is waiting and I have what I need.
We shall return to Baker Street, and there I can explain everything to you."

We rode back to Baker Street in silence. I wanted Holmes to give
me a hint at least as to what he had discovered, but I knew better
than to press my friend. Back in our rooms, Holmes went straight
to his desk and placed the hair he had found under his microscope.
He looked through the lens for just a second, then turned to me,
a wry smile upon his face.

"As I suspected."

"What is so suspicious about a strand of white hair?"

"It is the type of white hair. It is a strand not from an elderly
man but from one who lacks pigment."

"Albinism?" I asked, surprised that Armstrong had left out this
important detail. "You believe that Snerley is an albino."

"Not Snerley, no. But one of his two associates is. The other is
the man whom Armstrong met."

Holmes saw my befuddlement. He invited me to join him in
our seats by the hearth so as to explain himself, though not before
calling down to Mrs. Hudson to request warm brandy. Once our
landlady had served us our drinks, my friend leaned back and
revealed all to me.

"As you surmised, Watson, when Mr. Armstrong first brought
me the case, I didn't think it was worth my time. It was only when
he showed me that note he had received that my interest was
piqued. When he described Mr. Snerley, I knew we were dealing
with true villainy."

"But you destroyed the note," I countered. "Why would you
destroy a piece of evidence?"

Holmes took a swig of his brandy before answering. "For two reasons. First, I had gleaned all the information I needed from the note. Second, I wanted Mr. Armstrong to see me destroy it in case our antagonists were to go after him. If he told them he had spoken to a detective who destroyed the note because it was worthless, there was a better chance they would do him no serious harm."

"I see," I said curtly, wishing that Holmes had told me the logic behind his actions earlier. "So, the note was never intended for Armstrong?"

"No, I am certain that our client was mistaken for a courier."

"Armstrong? If he showed up at my door, I'm not sure I'd hand a letter over to such a character."

Holmes gave me a look of disparagement. "Remember, the man who greeted Armstrong told him not to dawdle. The letter needed to be delivered promptly. I am sure that the true messenger showed up after Armstrong had left. That's when the coverings were removed from the furniture, and the parlour was cleaned."

At Holmes's words, I recalled Armstrong telling us that the furniture was covered in cloths as though the room were being prepared to be painted. At this point my mind started working. I understood why I had thought there was something odd about the green couch I had spied through the window. There was no covering. I remembered Holmes's remarks on the parlour having been cleaned.

"That is where the villains met. They covered the furniture and later, when they cleaned everything thoroughly—though not thoroughly enough—they removed the coverings. They did not want any evidence, such as a strand of hair from an albino, to be discovered. If they had not abandoned the house in such a hurry, I am sure that they would have left no trail for me to follow."

"And you couldn't share any of this information with me?"

"Do not be offended, Watson. Until we inspected Snerley's house, all was mere speculation. I had to see the evidence, and then determine how seriously to take the plan laid out in the note."

"Plan? It was just a quote from *Macbeth*."

"Ah, that is where you are mistaken, my dear Watson. While the words are taken in part from *Macbeth*, they are misquoted. The original quotation reads: 'First witch: When shall we three meet again, in thunder, lightning, or in rain? Second witch: When the hurley-burley's done, when the battle's lost and won, that will be ere the set of sun. Third witch: Where's the place? Second witch: Upon the heath. Third witch: There we go to meet Macbeth.' If you recall, Watson, the note Armstrong received quoted several of those lines incorrectly. The first witch said that the three witches would meet again *when the moon neither waxes nor wanes*, not in thunder, lightning, or in rain."

"I do seem to remember that, Holmes, but I'll have to take your word for it since you destroyed the note."

My friend nodded. He knew that I lacked the faculty of etching something into my mind by way of a mere glance.

"The note also said that the time they will meet is on the arrival of the sun instead of at the setting of the sun," Holmes explained. "And the last change was that they would meet Macbeth not upon the heath, but upon the Saint."

"Most interesting, Holmes, but what does it all mean?"

"It means, my friend, that our three ne'er-do-wells are planning to meet at Saint Katharine Docks at dawn on Thursday."

"Thursday? In two days? But . . ." I blubbered. "How could you read all that from the note?"

Holmes fixed me with a steely-eyed gaze. "The pieces are all there, my friend. I simply had to look for what had been altered from the original. First, the time of the meeting: when the moon neither waxes nor wanes. That would mean a new or full moon. There is a full moon tomorrow evening. This is followed by the line that the time is at the arrival of the sun, so that would mean dawn, the dawn after the full moon, ergo, Thursday morning. The quote concludes by saying the three will meet upon the Saint to find Macbeth. While there are many churches and cathedrals in London named after saints, the wording that they shall meet *upon the saint* would indicate a location such as a field or a dock. The most likely answer, then, is that the three men will meet at Saint Katharine Docks."

"Remarkable, Holmes!" I said, once again astonished at my friend's skills.

"Merely logic, Watson."

"But who are the three men of whom you speak? There's Snerley, but what of the other two?"

"Have you read in *The Times* of a notorious thief known as MacAlister?"

"Yes . . ." I whistled. "The less respectable papers call him the Albino Butcher. Works alongside a nasty brute named Fibbs, a man with a ghastly face and . . ." I paused. "Holmes, that means . . ."

"Yes, Watson, it means that Snerley is working with two of London's most notorious criminals. I now must learn why."

"Isn't it obvious? The man is in debt. He's reached for the bottom to dig himself out of the hole he's created for himself."

Holmes tapped the fingers of his right hand on the arm of his chair while his left hand held his chin. "Perhaps, Watson, but a man, a professional man, doesn't usually delve down so quickly. You could be right; however, I wonder if there is more to it in this case. Tomorrow, I shall make enquiries as to the character of Mr. Snerley. I believe I can answer many of my questions, and those that I can't shall be answered by Snerley after we apprehend him."

"You are certain that you can catch him."

"I am. We now know the time and location. The question still remains as to why they are meeting at Saint Katharine's. It is either to perform a robbery of some sort or to flee the city. A robbery appears more likely. All will be revealed in just over a day's time."

I had a light schedule the following day, and while I supplied routine medications to my patients, my mind kept turning to Holmes and the case of Mr. Snerley. I could not help but wonder how a banker could drift into a life of crime. Then I thought of my own problem with gambling and how I, at times, had to watch myself to make sure I did not lose all my savings. I also thought of my ill brother and for the first time felt a pang of sympathy for the man. He had fallen on hard times and was in hospital. He could have become a thief, or worse.

Before going home for the day, I made sure to clear my diary. I knew that I might be up all night and not find rest until early or even late in the morning. I would be in no condition to treat patients.

When I returned to Baker Street, I opened the door and found a well-groomed, bespectacled, elderly man sitting by the fire.

"Ah," he said in a high-pitched, scratchy voice, "you must be Dr. Watson. Mr. Holmes told me about you, said you were a fine fellow."

"That's very kind of you to mention. Is Mr. Holmes here?"

The lined face of the elderly man softened, and I noted the steel-grey eyes of my friend. "Why, Watson, he is right here. I have just arrived, haven't had a chance to change out of my disguise."

I complimented Holmes on his extraordinary outfit and asked what the occasion was.

"Why, to gather information on Snerley, of course. A stern yet well-dressed older gentleman can take on many roles. Today, I used this disguise to impersonate a bank inspector, an officer of the law, and a visiting professor of medicine."

My friend invited me to sit with him. He lit a pipe and I cut myself a Cuban cigar. As smoke began to drift to the ceiling, Holmes began his tale.

"I first went to Threadneedle Street to visit the bank which formerly employed Snerley, an institution by the name of Horace and Sons. At first, the owners were tight-lipped about any information on a former employee. Some stern gazes and veiled threats helped loosen their tongues and they then answered all my questions. Mr. Snerley was a model employee and well regarded. The man is relatively young, in his thirties, and had built up a reputation for kindness and competence. But, as Mr. Armstrong said, when a debt collector came to the bank enquiring about Mr. Snerley, the owners felt compelled to show him the door.

"They did not know the reason for Snerley's debt. They asked him, but he refused to answer, merely agreeing with some sadness to leave their employ.

"I also enquired about any special new assets set to arrive at the bank. Michael Horace, the elder brother, was surprised I asked, because they had been advised that a rare jewel would be delivered to the bank late this evening."

"Don't you mean tomorrow at dawn?" I asked.

"Actually, I must humbly admit that I was wrong on that count. The jewel that is being delivered is a large rare yellow diamond of an intense and vivid hue. It is called the Australian Sun—the sun referred to in the misquoted *Macbeth*—and is set to arrive on a special freighter this evening at ten o'clock."

"Snerley and his associates plan to steal it at the docks, eh?"

"Yes, but I've already notified Gregson, and he assures me the force will be out in full to protect the diamond and arrest the trio. We shall join them at the dock shortly after dinner."

After leaving the bank, Holmes continued, he had gone to Snerley's residence in the guise of a police inspector. He claimed that he was investigating the disappearance of Mr. Snerley. From the banker's former neighbours, Holmes learned that Snerley was the type of person who helped carry in baskets for elderly people returning from the market.

One neighbour who had been close to Snerley revealed that the man had a sister who, like my brother, was the black sheep of the family. She was a drunk who squandered money and had ended up in debtors' prison. When his sister became ill, Snerley borrowed heavily to pay off his sister's debt. She died soon after being released. That was all the man knew.

"You said that you took on the guise of a bank inspector and an officer of the law, but you also mentioned you were a professor of medicine."

"Ah, very good, Watson." My friend nodded. "I ended my day at the hospital where Snerley's sister had been treated. I claimed I was doing research on the effects of excessive alcohol on the female body. It is there that I verified that the death of Miss Snerley was indeed from liver failure.

"Now, Watson, do you have your trusted Webley?"

"Give me a minute, and it will be at my side," I responded, patting my hip.

"Excellent. You might need it at the dock later on."

The fog for which our fair city is so noted was absent that evening, and the dock was well lit by the light of the full moon. As Holmes and I watched, together with Inspector Gregson and his men, the steamer carrying the Australian Sun docked. None of us saw any signs of the criminal trio we were hoping to apprehend.

The guards from the bank arrived with an armoured carriage to transport the rare jewel to the vault of Horace and Sons. Gregson spoke with the head of the guards and Holmes walked around the carriage, ensuring that it was secure. I began to wonder if the villains might be scared off by the presence of so many officers.

"Looks like you were wrong about this one, Mr. Holmes," Gregson told my friend in a flat voice. Unlike Lestrade, Gregson did not take every opportunity to gloat. He had in fact hoped to apprehend two of London's most dangerous criminals that night.

"Perhaps," Holmes responded, deep in thought. After a brief pause, I could see a gleam come into his eyes. "Inspector, I have an idea that will ensure that the diamond arrives safely at its destination."

"Go on."

"Let us have the bank carriage leave the dock, but instead of carrying the true diamond, it will carry a decoy along with us and an additional two of your men."

"And what of the actual diamond?"

"We shall leave it here, under guard by your best men. Surely nothing will happen to the gem with so many officers around."

Gregson agreed. Per Holmes's orders, the inspector called on one of his men to fetch a small box from the ship containing a much less valuable jewel than the Australian Sun. In the cargo were a number of gems worth only a few hundred pounds. While the jewel was being retrieved, Gregson beckoned over two of his best constables, Lockley and Stark, and Holmes related the plan to them.

A few minutes later, a sergeant handed the replacement jewel to Lockley, and the two constables entered the armoured carriage. Holmes and I followed, and soon we were travelling along the streets of London.

If the villains were watching, as Holmes surmised, then they would now believe that we were escorting the Australian Sun to the vault of Horace and Sons. We were in the back for half an hour. The mood was tense as the officers and I clutched at our guns, waiting for the fiends to strike. Holmes remained calm, biding his time.

Constable Stark grumbled that he wished he had a touch of snuff, and Lockley used his sleeve over and over to wipe the sweat from his brow. Like mine, their minds must have wandered to the possibility of Holmes's plan going wrong. What if the villains overtook the carriage and forced us into a gang hideaway where their sheer numbers could overwhelm us? I shuddered at the thought of fighting a wave of ruffians, armed with sharp blades, furious at finding they had been tricked. But then the carriage stopped and we heard noises outside; no sound of violence, only regular chatter. A man in a thick Scottish accent said:

"We just need to make sure nothing's gone amiss."

A key turned in the lock and Holmes nodded towards us to be at the ready.

"Here you are, officer," said the guard as the back of the carriage swung open and moonlight streamed in.

"Now!" Holmes shouted, and we jumped out, surrounding two police officers and one of the guards. The guard, of course, was innocent. The two police officers, on the other hand, were none other than MacAlister, the Albino Butcher, and his grotesque henchman Fibbs, both in disguise.

"What is this?!" shouted Fibbs as the darbies closed around his wrists.

MacAlister made no attempt to conceal his true self. He threw a satchel at one of the officers, trying to break through their ranks. He might have succeeded, had I not been standing directly in his path, the barrel of my Webley aimed straight at his face.

The albino growled, but gave up the fight. "It was that fool Snerley who tipped you off, wasn't it?" MacAlister spat at Holmes. "I should have killed the traitor when I had the chance!"

Holmes did not respond. The two villains kept yelling threats as they were locked away in the back of the armoured vehicle.

We would have driven off right then and there, had not a loud moan come from an abandoned building next to the scene. A search of the premises revealed the two constables whom MacAlister and Fibbs had stripped of their uniforms, as well as Mr. Snerley himself. All three were bound and gagged. When freed, the constables explained that Snerley had stopped Fibbs from killing them. The banker had threatened to shout for help if the officers were harmed. He thus compelled the villains merely to tie up their victims. Then, however, MacAlister hit Snerley over the head from behind, knocking him unconscious. Fibbs tied him up as well and said that he planned to kill all three of them once they had obtained the diamond.

"I never wanted any of this," Snerley lamented to Holmes. "I only wanted to save my sister."

Snerley was the opposite of the henchmen, a rather handsome fellow with striking blue eyes, a soft face, a square jaw, and broad shoulders. I could tell that he was the kind of man whose character was solid, but who had taken a wrong turn. He explained that after losing his job, he had been unable to lay hold of the funds to pay off his debts. Desperate, he began looking towards the underworld. MacAlister had got wind of the banker's plight and approached him with an offer. If he helped in stealing the Australian Sun, he would receive one third of the money from the sale.

"I had knowledge of when the jewel was arriving, which I provided to MacAlister and Fibbs. I knew how dangerous those two were, but I told myself that they were sincere when they assured me that no one needed to get hurt."

The plan was to stop the armoured carriage as constables in disguise and claim that a police informant had relayed a rumour that the diamond might be stolen. MacAlister had a fake diamond in his satchel. His intention was to swap it for the real one. It would most likely have been days or even longer before the forgery was detected.

"I've ruined my life, I have," Snerley choked, trying his best to contain his tears. "But I'd do it all over again, to provide my sister with the opportunity to die in the comfort of her home. I had to give her that. After all, she was my sister."

The plight of Mr. Snerley moved not only me but also Sherlock Holmes. My friend used the power of the press to have Snerley's story told as though he were working as a police informant, a man who had risked his life and career to stop two of London's most notorious villains. The constables who were captured with Snerley spoke of his valour and how he had saved their lives. Within a few weeks, the banker became a hero of London. He served as a witness against MacAlister and Fibbs, and for his help the charges against him were dropped.

"After all, Watson," Holmes explained to me. "The man's motives were pure even if his means were illicit. In the end, little harm was done. He saved the lives of two constables and ensured that MacAlister and Fibbs will spend their lives behind bars."

I concurred with my friend. Due to all the coverage in the papers, Horace and Sons rehired Mr. Snerley. A hero brings in exceptional business, and they paid all his debts to free his mind of this burden.

Holmes, for his part, earned his payment from Mr. Armstrong and then had his time occupied by a case involving a high-level Member of Parliament.

As for me, the tale of Mr. Snerley led me to realise the importance of family. After much contemplation, I informed Holmes that I would be away on a lengthy sojourn to San Francisco. Holmes never enquired as to the reason for my leave. Perhaps he knew and was kind enough to remain silent.

I was fortunate to arrive in time and to spend the few weeks my brother had left in his company. It was during those precious weeks that I learned much about myself and what it behoves one to hold dear to one's heart. It was also the time during which I met the first true love of my life, though that is a tale for another day.

In October 2020, Martin Rosenstock enquired if I'd be interested in writing a story for the then upcoming book, Sherlock Holmes: A Detective's Life, *and if so, would I set the story between 1882–1886. I jumped at the opportunity to write a Sherlock Holmes story for the book. I decided to set my story in 1884 to connect the story with the timeline proposed by William Baring-Gould that Watson traveled to San Francisco in the latter part of 1884 to tend to his ailing brother. I would use Watson's strained relationship with his brother as a bookend for the story. The next step was coming up with the story itself.*

The idea for "The Adventure of the Misquoted Macbeth" came from a Shakespeare unit I was co-teaching at Horizon High School. I am a high school Special Education teacher and as part of the unit of study, I, along with my teaching partners Steve Lash and Jim Madole, did a reading of the three witches opening from Macbeth. *My mind often randomly latches on to ideas, and while reading this particular section, I thought of the problem for the story. Since the witches are asking where to meet again, I thought it would be a great puzzle for Sherlock Holmes to solve if someone took the witches' lines, changed them slightly, and made it so that they would be alluding to the location of a theft. Once I had the problem and an idea for the story's conclusion, it started to write itself. It was developed through further discussions of* Macbeth *with fellow teacher Max Anderson as well as my two developmental readers, Chuck Davis and my brother, Brian. With their help, I was able to connect the dots of the plot and have a fine Sherlock Holmes adventure. Truly, though, the majority of credit for what made this a polished story deserves to go to my editor, Martin Rosenstock. I've worked with Martin on two books now and his edits and revision suggestions always make my stories significantly better. I look forward to working with him again on future endeavors.*

T. C. Boyle *is the author of thirty-one books of fiction, including, most recently,* Blue Skies *and* I Walk Between the Raindrops.

PRINCESS

T. Coraghessan Boyle

S he tried the door. The door was unlocked. She went in.

The moment was layered and complex, almost like a fairy tale, but where were the three bears? Upstairs, barking. Did bears bark? No, but dogs did, and that was what was going on here, dogs barking and scrabbling with their black shiny toenails—pawnails?—at the shutfast door at the top of the stairway, the stairway that was carpeted and strewn with soft welcoming shadows cast by various objects in the dimmered glow of the lamp behind the couch that was only ten feet from where she was standing. There were pillows on the couch, a whole flotilla of them, and there were two armchairs flanking it, a coffee table, bookshelves, the black nullity of a flat-screen TV affixed to the wall across from her. When she moved, and she moved only a foot or two into the room—edging, that was what she was doing, edging in—the screen gave back her reflection in a way that was too obscure to matter.

There might have been a voice calling from the room at the top of the stairs—"Cameron, is that you? Hello? Is anybody there?"—but it was lost in the uproar of the barking and it wouldn't have applied to her in any case because her name wasn't Cameron and she wasn't there anyway, was she? She was still back at the party, the barbecue she'd lucked into on this fine, cheery holiday afternoon that had somehow become night when she wasn't devoting her full attention to the *details*. In her right hand was a plastic sack containing spareribs lathered in a gooey red sauce, two ears of corn still wrapped in the blackened tinfoil in which they'd been roasted over the grill, a container of what looked to be potato salad, and dessert, lots of dessert—two napoleons, a wedge of cherry pie, and a fistful of chocolate-dipped strawberries she'd picked out herself, after the hostess, whose name might have been Renée—she reminded her of her mother on one of her mother's good days—had insisted that she take some food with her, because *I don't know what we're going to do with it all.*

She remembered that there had been a band at the party—bass, guitar, drums, a singer—the joyous reverberative thump of which had led her to push open the back gate off the alley and give all those wondering faces a friendly little nod and let herself in, which was okay, fine, no problem, everybody a friend of somebody's. And she remembered the champagne, good champagne from France and colder than winter in Poughkeepsie, which helped moderate the buzz she'd been riding for three sleepless days and nights now—and the singer from the band, who'd come up to her at the buffet table as if he wanted something from her and made some sort of lame joke about the way she was going at the dessert display and then flapped away like a six-foot crow once she opened up her smile and he got a good look at her teeth and the sore at the corner of her mouth she couldn't stop picking at, and so fuck him, fuck everybody. But that was her right hand, weighed down with all that food she didn't really feel like eating, not at this point, when the only thing she wanted was to crash, as if that would have been understandable to any of them standing around locked into their tunnel vision that featured nobody but themselves, and what about her left hand? What was this? She saw that she had a plastic sack dangling from the bunched fingers of that hand too, and for a minute, what with the newness of the surroundings and the barking of the dogs and the voice that had gone unanswered and had stopped expecting anything now, she momentarily blanked on what was in there. Until the dogs seemed to run out of breath and she remembered: makeup. Blush, foundation, and eyeliner she'd borrowed from the Rite-Aid somewhere down the street and around the corner out on the boulevard that was like a stage set, same streetlamps, same tired palms, same traffic lights going green and going red and going green.

Okay, all right, fine. But she didn't need makeup now—that would be for tomorrow. The food too. What she needed now, because her legs felt as limp and soft-boned as the barbecued ribs in their squishy plastic bag, was sleep. A bed. Sheets. A blanket. What were all these doors? Doors didn't exist for nothing. There had to be a bed behind one of them, didn't there?

Dawn's son had got home at eleven thirty, same as the last two nights, because they'd given him an extra shift so baggers with seniority could take the holiday off. There was the sound of his car in the drive and then the front door slamming, right on cue. If her eyes drifted to the clock radio on the nightstand it was only a reflex, and because she was already in bed, reading and half watching some outer-space slasher movie (with the sound muted so she didn't have to hear the screams), she didn't bother to go downstairs. Cameron ate at the store, anyway, and if he was hungry, there were cold cuts and a fruit salad in the refrigerator. She thought of texting him about the fruit salad, which she'd just made that night, but if he opened the refrigerator door he couldn't miss it, so why bother? At some point she drifted off with the book still propped up in her hands, as she did every night, both dogs and three of the cats stretched out in various configurations beside her and at the foot of the bed. Usually she slept through the night, but not this night, because at 2:36 A.M. both dogs rose up on their haunches and started barking for all they were worth.

The first door she tried was locked so she went to the next one, which gave onto a bathroom—or half bath, actually, as she saw when she flicked the light on. It was like any bathroom in anybody's house—toilet, sink, mirror, towel rack, framed cartoon on the wall—and if it could have been cleaner she wasn't complaining. The cartoon was a Gary Larson, the one with the two dogs in a courtroom full of cats—cat judge, cat lawyers, cat jury. It was funny, but she'd seen it before, and whoever used this bathroom must have seen it a thousand times now, and how funny was that?

She could have looked at herself in the mirror but she didn't because looking at herself right then was outside the realm of

66   T. CORAGHESSAN BOYLE

possibility, but the idea of the bathroom, the fact of it and the
fact she was in it, reminded her that she had to pee and this
was as good a time as any. When she was done, she flushed and
put down the lid, washed her hands, and went back out into
the main room, where she plopped herself down on the couch
for a minute, just to stop things from spinning. That was when
she noticed that there were two more doors to try, one giving
onto what looked to be a study with a desk and laptop and the
other—bingo!—revealing the bedroom she'd been looking for,
and if the dogs had started up again, it was nothing to her. She
belonged here. This was her room. Or it ought to have been,
because whether she'd grown up in this house or not it was the
room she would have chosen, though the clothes hanging in the
closet were the wrong size and the colors and patterns weren't
even close to her style. And the shoes! They made her feel sorry
for whoever had actually taken the time to go to the store and
pick them out and put down cash for them—or a credit card, as
the case may be. She reflected briefly on the fact that she once
had a credit card herself and how nice that was—hand it across
the counter and you got whatever you wanted.

Except drugs. Drugs were cash only.

The food she left in the bathroom, but she kept the makeup
with her, and maybe she even sat down at the vanity and tried the
blush and the lipstick, not that it mattered at this point. In the
morning, she told herself. In the morning everything would be
different. But—and here's where the cold hard world interceded to
cut her down the way it always did—she'd barely closed her eyes
before she woke to the overhead light and the three faces lined up
in a row, staring down at her.

"Why didn't you let the dogs out?"

"I would have, if I'd known, but I was afraid to, because it
could have been anybody down there. With a knife or a gun or
who knows what?"

She was sitting on the couch in the living room, the couch
where the girl had apparently stretched herself out and left a long
red smear of something on one of the pillows, which turned out

to be barbecue sauce, thankfully, and not blood. Dawn herself had taken a washcloth to it first thing in the morning—after photographing it, that is. For evidence. Not that the police needed it, since they already had the girl in custody.

She'd been on the phone pretty much the whole morning, talking her way through last night's events, as if she could somehow neutralize them, make them make sense. At the moment, she was talking to Chrissie Wagner, who lived directly across the street and, like her, was a single mother, which was part of their bond, which went beyond just being neighbors. The other part was that they were both junior-high teachers, though in different school districts.

"I hear you, I mean, it's terrifying, but Buster's so huge he'd scare off anybody, right? Even if he is a big pussycat. And Ernie's a pipsqueak, but I've seen him get riled up—like the time that woman came around canvassing for the mayor's race, remember that?"

"Ankle biter," she said, and laughed at the memory. "But you know what I'm saying. First thing I did was lock the bedroom door, and Cameron was downstairs in his room and he always locks his because he doesn't want anybody going in there—me, that is—so I texted him not to make a sound and dialed 911. Why risk the dogs getting hurt?"

"What about Tammy?"

"Talk about small mercies—she was spending the night at Beau's house, because she'd had a couple of beers at his family's Memorial Day party and didn't want to drive. Or so she said over the phone." Her daughter—seventeen, combative, pampered, and privileged, and way too obsessed with crime shows and doom-scrolling—would have been seriously traumatized, or worse, because her door was never locked. And that was something Dawn didn't want to even begin to imagine, this girl pushing her way in while Tammy was lying there asleep in her own bed with her movie posters on the wall and the Minnie Mouse night-light she'd had since she was three years old pushing back the shadows.

She gazed out the window at the sunstruck palms that lined the street out front, the safe and tranquil street in a decidedly safe middle-class neighborhood, where the only crimes were committed in her daughter's imagination. Or had been till now. *Home invasion.* Frightening words, chilling words, words out of the morning paper, which was always suffused with somebody else's misery but never hers, never theirs. Was she even going to tell Tammy? And, if so, how was she going to put it? Especially since the girl had gone into Tammy's room and had maybe even sat at the vanity, trying on makeup she'd probably stolen from Rite-Aid, though she hadn't attempted to take anything from the house, not Tammy's laptop or iPad or anything else as far as she could see. Which was strange. And then the whole thing with the bed . . .

The 911 operator had instructed her to stay in her room with the door locked and definitely not try to confront whoever it was who'd broken into the house and flushed the toilet and flicked the lights on and off. Just sit tight. They were on their way.

The police arrived within ten minutes, give them credit there. They didn't use their siren or the flashing lights, and they parked two doors down and came up on foot for the element of surprise. They wound up going in through the front door, which Cameron must have forgotten to lock when he got back from work (though, of course, he never forgot to lock his bedroom door—that was automatic for him, even if he was just jumping up from his console to get a soda out of the refrigerator). They found the girl in Tammy's bed, fast asleep, the comforter and sheets stripped back and thrown on the floor as if they were of no use to her. She herself didn't really get a good look at her from the window, three A.M., the nearest streetlamp a dull blur at the far end of the block, but she seemed slim and maybe even pretty, and she was wearing a rumpled yellow tunic dress that left her legs bare and her shoes were high-top sneakers. By then the police had brought the squad car into the driveway, and one of them put a hand on the girl's head to keep her from banging it on the doorframe as they put her in the back seat, just like in the movies.

She tried to tell them she lived there—look at the evidence right before their eyes, because here she was, in her own room, in her own bed—but one of the three faces staring down at her, the one that wasn't mushrooming out of the collar of a neat blue uniform, belonged to a kid of sixteen or seventeen, acne, arms like two strings of dangling sausages and hair that might have been cool if somebody would only get their shit together and cut it right, and he was saying, "She's lying, I've never seen her before. She broke in, she's the one—*she broke in!*"

She was only the tiniest bit drunk at this point and the crank buzz that had kept her going for all these glorious, blazing mile-a-minute days had totally deserted her, to the point where her whole body felt as if it were encased in cement and all she wanted from this world and this existence was sleep, but she looked at the kid's big dumb dump truck of a face, and couldn't help herself, so she said, "You're the one that broke in. Oh, my God, Officer, Officer, who is he? What's he doing here?"

"She's lying!" the kid repeated, and now the cops were giving him the look and so she kept it up, repeating "My God, my God," till it was like a little song she was singing to put herself to sleep.

That set him off. His face clenched, and he started barking like the dogs upstairs, "Yeah, right, prove it. What's the address, huh? The phone number? The name on the mailbox? My mom. What's my mom's name?"

The thing was, there was nothing they could charge her with besides trespassing, since she hadn't broken in and hadn't stolen anything, but when they asked Dawn if she wanted to press charges she said yes. As much as she'd have liked to be sympathetic, she just couldn't get past the sense of violation, which made her feel dirty and insecure in her own home, and that was inexcusable, absolutely and categorically, and so yes, she was going to press charges. As it turned out, the girl was twenty-two, her name was Tanya Swifbein, and she had no fixed address. She'd been arrested only once before, for disturbing the peace; no details on that beyond what you could glean from the charge itself, but she'd disturbed the peace in this household, that was for sure. Tammy had wound up spending the entire weekend at Beau's, without calling or even texting, which was beyond irritating, and when she came in late Monday night with bloodshot eyes and liquor on her breath, she just said, "Mom, don't, because I'm not going to talk about it, okay?," and slammed the door to her room so hard the pictures on the wall rattled in their frames. Two minutes later, she was back out in the hallway, demanding to know who'd been in her room.

So the story came out, and before Dawn could even catch her breath her daughter had apportioned the blame—it was her fault, all her fault. And her stupid brother's. "What, am I going to get head lice now from my own pillow? Or AIDS or whatever? Some street person sleeping in my bed? Is that fair? Is that right? Is that what you want?"

What was fair and what wasn't didn't enter the equation. She said, "I put everything in the wash—with bleach—and vacuumed the rug twice, and I know, I know, honey, because I feel violated too."

Tammy just glared at her, then stalked back into her room and angrily stripped the bed, bundling everything up—sheets, pillows, blankets, the bedspread her dead grandmother had crocheted for her—and tramped through the house and out the back door, where she stuffed it all in the trash can, the sentry lights snapping on to catch the hard white flash of her elbows and the suffering icon of her face.

So they booked her and let her go, back out into a night that was starting to brighten around the edges. She was cold, wrapping her arms around herself and making sleeves of both hands, but her actual sleeves were attached to her denim jacket with the butterfly patch flapping across the shoulders and her shades in the pocket, which was back at Luther's, she thought, or at least she hoped it was, but where was Luther's from here? She had no idea and she hadn't gone a block before she had to go down on her hands and knees on somebody's front lawn and vomit up the dregs of the champagne. She would have stretched out right there on the grass and slept until the sun came up and fried her like an egg, but here was the gardener slamming out of his truck with all his rakes and hoses and gardening paraphernalia strapped to the top of it, and so she pushed herself up and started off down the street, going nowhere. Of course, she didn't have a phone. Her phone had disappeared somewhere along the line there, so she couldn't call Luther and wouldn't have known the phone number, in any case—or even, for that matter, what his last name was. The street was Marigold, wasn't it? If she could find Marigold, she'd recognize the house for sure, but where was Marigold? She didn't have a clue. Meanwhile, her feet were like boxcars, giant boxcars strapped to her ankles, and she dragged them along with her down the block till she saw what looked to be a park up ahead, and that seemed like just the place because there'd be a bench there, and maybe a restroom, a water fountain, and she could sleep, just sleep, and worry about the rest later.

Well, there was a bench there, as it turned out, standard issue, painted a graffiti-hatched forest green, but only one bench, a solitary bench, and a bum was curled up on it, his face turned away from her like a promise he wasn't about to keep. The restroom was locked, but she found a water fountain and drank till she could feel it coming up, then slapped water on her face and ran it through her hair and saw that there was a dirt path behind the restroom that led up into some sort of dense undergrowth, where at least she could crash for a while and just let things settle. She didn't want to get high—she was no addict, not really, not like some of them—but the thought of it, of the way the first hit made her feel invincible, like a superhero supercharged with energy, made her calculate: sleep first, then figure out how to find Luther, then see what the day would bring.

Birds spoke to her, saying what they were going to say in their own language, and then the sun jumped over the ridge to explode in her face like a supernova, bushes to the right of her, bushes to the left, nature just an endless repetition of the obvious—but here, what was this? Somebody had dug out a little nest under one of the bushes and lined it with flattened strips of cardboard that weren't even that dirty—a bed, a bed made just for her. But then, as she brushed back the fringe of dried-out vegetation that hung over the cardboard like a canopy, she saw the rest, and it was so sudden and inadmissible it was like being attacked by all the snarling bears and wolves in the deepest, darkest forests of the earth: there was another human being there, a girl, a little girl, but she wasn't breathing and she wasn't moving and if her eyes were open she wasn't seeing anything.

To get this straight, to get it precisely right: she'd never seen a corpse before, because that wasn't who she was. Even her grandfather, when he died, did it elsewhere and came back to them in a glazed ceramic jar the color of olive oil and if there were pictures on TV of the dead bodies lying sprawled in the streets of Ukraine, she wasn't there, was she? But she was here now, and here was this little girl stuffed half in and half out of a black plastic trash bag somebody had stashed under a bush in a public park in the Golden State of California.

Of course, and Dawn could have predicted it, the girl—Tanya— never showed up for her court date and there was nothing anybody could do about that, not until the next time she got arrested, anyway. The Memorial Day weekend gave way to a non-holiday weekend and then another one after that, and the whole incident began to fade. The school year was winding down, which meant tests and grades and the usual madhouse rush. She and Tammy went shopping for a dress for commencement, Cameron picked up an extra day a week at the market, the weather turned hot. Both dogs got tapeworm—which was disgusting—and had to stay out in the yard till the pills went to work. Her car didn't seem to want to start in the mornings, and, when it did, it spewed a black cloud of exhaust as she wheeled out onto the street, which meant that she was going to have to take it to the garage, whatever that was going to cost. The lawn needed cutting. There were more weeds in the flower bed than flowers.

It was her daughter who told her about the little girl in the trash bag, who'd been found in the park not ten blocks from here, and how nobody knew who she was or what had happened to her, more evidence of the corruption of the world. As if she needed it. As if any of them needed it.

The girl was estimated to be between eight and ten years old. She was thin, skinny, as if she hadn't had enough to eat, as if she'd been abused, and the police were asking for the public's help in identifying her. She was wearing pink Crocs, pajamas in a blue-and-white polar-bear print, and a yellow visor bearing the logo "Princess" in a bold black looping cursive. She didn't have any ID on her—what eight-year-old did?—and no distinguishing marks, as far as the police could see.

When Dawn did an online search, the picture that came up—a police sketch of the girl's face and torso—jumped out at her. She'd seen her someplace, she was sure of it, but where? It couldn't have been at school—the girl was too young, a child, just a child. Her face was narrow and serious, but the eyes were all wrong and the mouth too, slack and lifeless and like no mouth she'd ever seen. But then she had to remind herself that this was only a sketch, not a photo—a photo would have been more than anybody could bear.

She should have flagged somebody down, but once she was back out on the street the words just couldn't seem to get past the barrier of her brain: *There's this dead girl, this dead body? Like back there in the bushes?* She was trembling, that was what she was doing, lifting her big boxcar feet one step at a time and trembling all over, even though it wasn't cold, or not especially, the sun tracking her everywhere she went. There were people sitting on a bench at the bus stop, and she almost leaned in over their bowed heads and slumped shoulders and told them, but then they would have called the police and the police would automatically assume she was the guilty party. She'd already been photographed and fingerprinted and all the rest of it, and wasn't that enough for one night? So she just kept walking, like a zombie, and everything was sorrowful now, everything.

Luther said he'd been looking for her and that was why he'd happened to be driving by and also just happened to have a box of Dunkin' Donuts on the front seat, including two of the Bavarian Kremes that were her favorite, and so she was rescued by her knight in shining leather and all that started up again.

She didn't tell him about the girl, didn't tell anybody, but she was tempted to borrow his phone to call her mother back in New York and just sob over the line because her mother didn't want to hear from her anymore and was not now or ever again going to send her money only to have it go up a glass tube. *Was that clear? Yes, mom, clear as Smirnoff* (which was what her mother drank, in a tall glass, all day long). She stayed away from partying for a couple days, just to get her strength back, and once she was oriented she went to her storage locker and picked up a few things to wear and two twenties from the stash she kept there in the inside pocket of the black puffer jacket she was going to wear on the airplane back to New York when her mother finally relented and sent her a ticket. She slept for most of two days straight and made sure to brush her teeth when she was conscious, though the damage was already done and if she ever got to a dentist it was going to cost more than she'd ever make in this lifetime, and then it was Friday and she and Luther scored and she became the single most powerful woman alive on the planet and everything was under control.

She could see what Tammy was doing, pushing the limits and using the break-in as an excuse, but when she stayed out all night on a school night, Dawn took away her car keys and grounded her. Which led to the usual fights and tantrums and threats, with the added anxiety of graduation hanging over it all.

"I'm not even going to go, okay? Is that what you want?"

"Suit yourself," she said, sounding just like her own mother.

But of course that was all nonsense and as the day approached Tammy relented, as they both knew she would, and they wound up holding a reception at the house for her and Beau and a few of her friends, catered by Hana Sushi and floated on a raft of carnations and white roses and baby's breath. There was dancing and a computer collage of the kids at all ages and fruit punch and sodas but no alcohol, not till they were of age—she was sorry, but that was the way it was going to have to be—and if a couple of the kids who kept slipping in and out were glassy-eyed by the end of the night, she understood there were times when you just had to let the boundaries drift. As long as nobody got hurt. That was the worry, always the worry, but beyond a certain point there was nothing you could do about it.

As for the little girl, the child stuffed into a trash bag and abandoned like a dead animal, she realized she'd been right—she had seen her before. A week after the discovery of the body, the newspaper identified the girl as a former local resident, Evena Clarkson, and they ran a photo of her with a plea for anyone who might have seen anything unusual to come forward. In the photo, the girl was smiling into the lens, her eyes as wide as the world, her shoulders arched and her head cocked as if she'd been dancing for the camera, and that's when it clicked.

Back in February, she'd gone along with Chrissie to talent night at the elementary school because Chrissie's son, Robert, who was something of a piano prodigy, was to be one of the performers. It was the usual sort of thing, kids singing along to pre-recorded tracks or even, for the minimally talented, lip-synching, but then this girl had stepped out of the wings alone, leaned into the microphone, and delivered an a-capella ballad that hushed the whole auditorium. Dawn recognized the song—it was from an animated feature Tammy had been obsessed with at that age—and maybe that had something to do with it, with the rush of her feelings from back then, when everything was so much simpler, but she'd found herself on the verge of tears. The girl had presence. She had talent. And when her voice rose up you forgot the echoey sound system and the imperfect lighting that made all the performers look as if they were carved of stone, because you were soaring right along with her.

This time the party was all in her head. It had been days now and she was getting delusional, which always happened to her at the end, because her body was trying to tell her something. (And she wasn't listening.) After the fight with Luther—and with Bob, his friend Bob, a king shit if there ever was one—she'd gone outside for a breath of air, not depleted, not fully, not yet, and found herself going off down the street in whatever direction her feet seemed to want to take her. It was a neighborhood, and it was beginning to look familiar to her, palm trees with fronds like heaps of dirty clothes, cars parked bumper to bumper, hardly any lights on anywhere and everybody in bed because it was two A.M. or three A.M. or something like that. She might as well have been following a trail of bread crumbs because she went straight to the house, which she couldn't have found on any rational basis, even if you'd given her a map.

The dogs didn't bark. They were out back in the fenced-in yard, having committed some sort of crime, and that made them unsure of themselves. Timid, they were timid, and when she held out her hand the big one came up to the fence and licked it, his tongue working at her fingers like a warm washcloth. This time the front door was locked. But she climbed over the fence and got in the yard with the dogs and they were just fine with that and so was she. Was the kitchen window open? Or maybe just cracked an inch to let in a seep of the cool night air flowing off the ocean that was however many blocks away? It was. And she didn't really think beyond appreciating that it had to be lifted as silently as possible. Of course, the dogs were right there, just watching her, cheering her on in a silent steadfast way and thinking, no doubt, that she was going to let them in. Which she wasn't.

She stood in the kitchen a moment, just feeling things, listening, taking in the strange mélange of odors—of cooking, of dog, of dust and mold and the ancient grease worked into the burners of the stove—till they felt familiar. Then she went on through the living room with its dimmered lights and heaped-up pillows, eased open the bedroom door and got into bed, and so what if there was some-body already in it? This was her tale, and nobody else's.

---

* Over the past Memorial Day weekend, my sister-in-law experienced a break-in at her house that gave me the impetus for this story. The details—right down to the two plastic bags, one of barbecued ribs, the other of makeup—came to me ready-made. My curiosity was aroused. Who was this girl? What was she thinking? How competent, mentally, was she? Was she in an altered state? What did she want? The first lines came to me, and suddenly I was plunged into the narrative, deep in a world of fairy-tale tropes and human wanting. We all need to belong, we all need a bed, we all need a home.

Joslyn Chase *is the prize-winning author of mysteries and thrillers, including* Nocturne in Ashes, *the explosive novel surrounding events set off by Mt. Rainier's fictional eruption. Chase's short stories have appeared in* Alfred Hitchcock's Mystery Magazine, Fiction River Magazine, *and* Mystery Magazine, *among others. Known for her fast-paced suspense fiction, Chase's books are full of surprising twists and delectable turns. Her love for travel has led her to ride camels through the Nubian desert, fend off monkeys on the Rock of Gibraltar, and hike the Bavarian Alps. But she still believes that sometimes the best adventure comes in getting the words on the page and in the thrill of reading a great story. Visit her online at joslynchase.com.*

COLD HANDS, WARM HEART

Joslyn Chase

H al loved early morning on the Hood Canal. The air fell sweet and cold on his skin, reminding him of those icebox plums William Carlos Williams apologized for in the poem. Behind him, to the east, the pale autumn sun crested the darkened ridge, tinting the clouds pink and sending fingers of misted light across the sky.

He eased the boat out and nosed it toward the hatchery. Mooch, his net man, sprawled in the bow, catching a few more winks, his snoring lost amid the purr of the motor. The faint stench of fish, which he could never fully scrub from the boat's interior, set his stomach growling and Hal peeled back the soggy paper towel from his microwaved breakfast sandwich and took a large bite.

He chewed slowly. The English muffin felt rubbery between his teeth and the lump of egg and sausage retained only the faintest hint of warmth. Still, he wouldn't dream of trading these crystal mornings on the canal for a hot breakfast. They sustained him far better than food.

Hal idled the engine, letting the boat drift beneath a patch of clouds. The conditions were perfect for salmon, and he hoped to catch his limit. For the both of them.

"Wake up, Mooch! Make yourself useful."

Hal watched the young man roll off the chair like liquid, suddenly alert and eager. He remembered having that kind of loose, well-toned muscle and indefatigable vitality. Decades gone, but on a day like this, the distant echo rose to a roar.

Grinning, he prepared a lure and cast a line. Immediately, he felt the boost like a tonic in his blood. Less than five minutes passed before he got a bite and reeled in a silvery pink salmon, thrashing in the new light of morning.

Mooch netted the fish and they both cast another line. The quick and easy first catch of the day had set a tone, but the next hour passed without a bite as the clouds dissipated under the rising sun, turning the water's surface to burnished copper.

Hal resorted to trolling, moving gently along the canal, and was rewarded with a tug on the line. With a surge of anticipation, he worked to pull in the catch but knew within seconds that he hadn't hooked a live fish.

Mooch leaned over, knife in hand to cut him loose, but Hal felt the line jerk and release.

"Hold up," he said. "Let's see what we caught."

He spun the reel. It turned easily in his hands but with enough heft to let him know he'd hooked *something*. Most likely a clump of aquatic weeds or the proverbial old shoe. He had a whole collection of baseball caps he'd reeled in off the bottom of the canal. Some of them were pretty nice.

And—Hal felt a little leap of hope—he'd be lying if he didn't admit to a bit of foolish dreaming about finding treasure or at least a piece of jewelry worth hawking. It could happen.

A gust of wind roughened the gleaming water and the boat slapped up and down on the surface. Hal braced himself and peered down into the layered green depths, watching them shift and waver like a watery kaleidoscope.

He held his breath, waiting to discover what would emerge. As the thing on the end of the line rose and bobbed to the surface,

Hal leaned farther over the side and promptly parted ways with his breakfast sandwich.

Chief Deputy Randall Steadman tucked his uniform shirt into his pants and zipped up with a little more effort than usual. After a two-week vacation and all the indulgences that came with it, the uniform fit more snugly than he liked. He made a mental note to do something about that.

The bedclothes rustled as Vivi rolled over, one bare leg thrusting out from beneath the sheets. She gave a long, growling murmur and opened her eyes, squinting at him through a tangle of pale blonde hair.

"You've had . . ." She fumbled for her phone on the bedside table and rubbed at the corners of her eyes with a pink-nailed finger. "You've had four and a half hours of sleep, Rand. Can't you ease your way back to work? Maybe take it in stages? The shock could kill you."

He laughed and leaned down to kiss his wife. "We did have a wonderful time, didn't we?"

Gripping him by the front of his shirt, she pulled him close and he breathed in the smell of her. Baby powder, with faint citrus overtones. "Marvelous," she said.

"Go back to sleep, Vivi. I'll see you tonight."

Steadman drank a mugful of steaming coffee—unsweetened and black—on his way to the station, finishing it as he pulled into the parking lot. He left the mug, with its bitter dregs, to give his car that new coffee smell and hurried up the steps. He'd enjoyed every minute of his vacation, but now that he was back, he was eager to get to work.

"Nice tan, Chief."

His partner, Deputy Cory Frost, waited for him in the corridor. They'd worked together for two years, and Steadman was well able to read the slant in Frost's eyebrows, the twitch at the corner of his mouth, and know what they meant.

They had a case.

And not just any case, Steadman deduced, but what his mother would have called a dilly. He figured Frost could hardly wait to tell him about it.

They entered the office pen together and Steadman was met with a flurry of questions.

"How was Hawaii, Chief?"

"What'd you bring me?"

"Frost filled you in yet?"

Steadman waved, encompassing everyone in the gesture, and deposited an enormous box of macadamia turtles on Lily's desk. She squealed.

"All for me?"

"All for you, darlin'. But I trust you'll share."

Everyone laughed and Lieutenant Lily Jamieson tore the cellophane wrapping off the box and opened it, passing it around. Silence fell over the detective division as people munched and everyone waited for Frost to break the ice.

"Do you remember hearing anything about a mysterious dismembered hand, Chief?"

"Sure. Garth told me about it from his days on the force. Back around 2007, wasn't it? Someone found a lone human hand off Highway 101, near Hoodsport."

"It was 2005, actually," Frost said, "and it was chewed to the bone by coyotes. Never identified. The case went cold."

"Right. Well . . . ?"

Frost cleared his throat. "Day before yesterday, a couple fishermen snagged a human hand out of the Hood Canal. We're thinking it could be a matched pair. Neal's working on it now."

"Did you send down divers?"

"Yes, we hauled a 1993 Audi S4 off the bottom of the canal. It was resting on a submerged sandbar or no one ever would have known it was there. You know how deep the canal is."

"I do," Steadman said. "Deep enough to swallow a scad of secrets and never make them known. I'm guessing there was more in the car than a vintage cassette deck."

"You got that right, Chief. We found the skeleton of a young female in the back seat, largely intact except for the hands. One was reeled in by the fishermen and there's no sign of the other."

Lily plunked the box of chocolates down on her desk. "I'm combing through dental records of missing young women," she said. "I expect to have something soon."

Steadman looked around at his team. Good people. People willing to serve, to work late into the night, to dig as deep and as long as necessary to see justice done. He loved his wife, his family—they were the most important thing in the world to him. But by everything good in this world, he was glad to be back at work. Doing what he was meant to be doing.

"All right, everybody. I want an ID on the remains and the name of the car's owner ASAP." He caught Frost's eye and nodded toward the hall. "Let's go see Neal."

Dr. Carolyn Neal's lab was in the basement, underground, as seemed befitting for one who spends her days with the dead. He and Frost forsook the elevator and took the stairs, part of his plan for reducing the bulge at his waistline.

As they descended, Steadman felt the walls darken and close in. He knew it was only illusion, merely generated inside his head and possibly spurred by the chemical odors and the deeper, indelible smell of rot beneath.

If anything, the lighting here was brighter, harsher, than above ground. As if in defiance of the dark. Steadman pushed open the door to the lab, steeling himself for what might lie ahead. He'd seen some pretty stark sights on the tables in Dr. Neal's lab.

Today, he was greeted by the skeletal remains of a young woman, and by the older woman leaning over them in mask and gown.

"Careful, Chief," she said. "You're going green, losing that lovely tan you picked up in Hawaii. How was it?"

"Paradise, doctor."

"A far cry from what you came home to. I understand, and I'll do my best with this one."

"As you always do."

Carolyn Neal's bloodshot eyes met his over the edge of her surgical mask. She nodded.

"Cause of death?" Steadman asked.

Neal lifted the skull from the metal table and turned it, showing Steadman the cracked depression along the left side.

Frost stepped closer and she angled it so he could see as well. "Any ideas about the weapon?" he asked.

"Something heavy and cylindrical," Neal replied. "A baseball bat. A marble rolling pin."

"A lead pipe," Frost suggested.

Neal gave him a look. "This isn't a game of Clue, but yes—a lead pipe could have done it."

She picked up the victim's wrist bones and pointed out the differences between the right and the left. "The right hand was severed, probably with a hacksaw or similar instrument. I surmise the left hand came away by more natural means."

"Such as?" Steadman said.

"I'm running tests on the hands now, but let's assume for the moment that they both came from this girl. And let's assume she lost them postmortem, and that the Audi went into the canal around the same time the first hand was found. In 2005."

"Okay."

"That means the car was submerged for seventeen years. The mechanism holding the windows in place would have rusted out at some point, causing the windows to fall down and allowing access to underwater predators. The bones were picked pretty clean and a few of the toes are missing. The connective tissues have deteriorated and that's how the hand came away when hooked by the fisherman."

A steady beep filled the room and Dr. Neal crossed to open a machine resembling a microwave oven. She extracted two bony, severed appendages and carried them on a metal tray to where Steadman waited.

"It's official," she proclaimed. "They're a match. Reunited after all these years."

He watched in silence as Neal placed the hands in their respective places, doing what she could for the dead girl's dignity. He and Frost left without another word.

Back at his desk, Steadman asked, "What else did you find inside the car?"

Frost pulled the lid off a cardboard box and placed three sealed evidence bags on Steadman's blotter. They contained a rusty key on an indeterminate fob, a blue-stone class ring on a chain, and a fancy beaded hair ornament marked as a barrette.

Steadman studied the beaded bauble. "Are you certain that's a barrette, Frost?"

His partner raised an eyebrow. "Sure. What else?"

Steadman fingered it through the plastic. "Could be a roach clip. Who was the car's registered owner?"

Across the aisle, Lily hung up her phone and said, "I should have that information for you soon, boss. But first, you'll be happy to hear we have a possible name to go with those bones."

She snatched a file folder from her desk and raced toward the door. Steadman and Frost followed her back down the stairs to Dr. Neal's lab. The three of them watched Neal slide an X-ray film onto the light box and compare it to the film she'd taken from the corpse.

"It's affirmative, Chief. This is your girl."

Steadman read the name on the file. "Amber Dawson. Missing since 2005. Her file's been on ice for seventeen years." He turned to Lily. "Find out if she still has family in the area."

"I did, boss. And she does. Amber's mom and stepdad live out Lake Cushman way. I'll text you the address."

"Lily, you're one in a million. Let's go, Frost."

Frost's voice echoed in the stairwell amid the sound of his pounding feet.

"I'm already gone."

The house smelled of paint. Not fresh enough to be wet, but not long out of the can. Beneath his feet, the carpet felt springy and Steadman guessed the café au lait berber was new as well. The Pratt family stronghold—where Amber Dawson had fit in as stepdaughter—had received a recent face-lift, but the 1970's split-level bone structure remained.

In the living room, he and Frost perched on faux leather and looked across at Greg Pratt. The man was seated in a worn recliner cranked into the upright position. From the way it creaked and wobbled, Steadman suspected that might be the only position the chair could still achieve. No doubt, furniture replacement was next on the list of home improvements.

Pratt's hair was a muted brown, still thick but with hints of gray at the temples. His skin was only a shade or two lighter, giving him an odd homogenous appearance as if he, like his house, had been doused in paint. Which explained the bold-print T-shirt he wore in contrast.

Barbara Pratt, Amber's mother, sat on a hardback chair next to her husband. Her spine was ramrod straight, her face thin and white as skim milk as Steadman delivered the news. He feared she might pitch forward onto the new carpet.

"Are you certain about this?" Greg Pratt asked, shifting his weight so the chair groaned beneath him. "Have you really found Amber?"

"We have," Steadman said. "Dental records confirm it. I'm sorry," he added, looking at Mrs. Pratt.

She looked dazed. Her lip trembled and he saw her tighten her jaw, getting a grip. "No, no—it's good to know after all this time." She pulled in a deep breath and let it out in a shaky sigh. "It opens an old wound, brings back the . . . the pain. But it's also a relief. Can you understand that, Sheriff?"

"I'm just a deputy, ma'am, but yes—I think I understand a little about what you mean."

Silence stretched for several seconds, then Frost cleared his throat and leaned forward. "We're sorry to bother you with this now," he said, "but we need to ask you some questions. We can come back later, but—"

"No!" Amber's mother snapped out the word. Her dark brown eyes were now hard and shiny, reminding Steadman of an angry sparrow. "I don't want to let another minute go by," she said. "We'll do everything we can to help you catch the man who did this to Amber." She jutted her chin toward her husband and he leaned forward.

"Absolutely," he said. "What do you need to know?"

Steadman addressed himself to Barbara Pratt. "How long have the two of you been married?"

"We'll celebrate our twenty-year anniversary next month," she told him.

"So, you were married and living together with Amber in this house when she disappeared."

"Yes, and Kyle too, of course."

"Kyle?"

"He's my son," Barbara said. "He was five at the time."

"Amber's brother, then, and your stepson," Steadman said to Greg.

"Yes, and he adored her," Barbara told him, her face wistful, a tiny sad smile on her lips. "She loved him too . . . so much. With the big age difference, she was almost like a second mother to him."

Steadman turned to Greg. "What did you do for a living, Mr. Pratt?"

"I was—and still am—a math teacher at the high school. I retire next year." He shifted again on the squeaky chair. "In fact, Amber was in my class. I could barely keep ahead of her. She was brilliant, by far the brightest math student at the school."

"She had a scholarship, you know," Barbara said. "Full-ride. MIT, Stanford, or Princeton. She could take her pick and was still deciding."

"Wow," Steadman said. "Impressive."

"Damn straight," Greg said, his face flushed, forehead furrowed. "That girl could have made a real difference in the world. She would have, she *should* have . . ." He broke off, breathing hard, eyes fierce beneath wild brows.

Barbara Pratt began weeping, soft and silent but for her shuddering indrawn breaths. Steadman gathered his weight beneath him and started to rise, but she threw out her hand in a chopping motion.

"Don't go," she commanded, wiping her eyes with short, irritated jabs. "Ask whatever you need to."

Steadman settled back in his seat, recognizing her impulse to act, in spite of the emotional onslaught. He glanced at Frost and caught a slight movement from the shadows beyond the split-level staircase. Focusing, he saw a young man standing in the hallway and beckoned him into the room.

"Oh, Kyle," Barbara said as he sank onto an ottoman, "I didn't realize you were home."

"Got off work early. I was taking a nap." Kyle's coffee-dark hair was flat on one side and fluffed on the other, like some kind of avant-garde style. His eyes were slightly unfocused as he swept his gaze across Steadman and Frost, taking in their uniforms and solemn manner.

"They found Amber," he said in a dull, flat voice.

"Yes," his mother said, her voice catching as she bit her lip.

The boy sat on the low footstool, staring at the wall, his face emotionless. One arm hung slack, fingers almost touching the new carpet. Steadman noticed the other hand clenched tight in his lap, the knuckles turned white.

Frost had been taking notes. He held up his pencil and asked, "Have you ever owned a gold-colored Audi or remember seeing one in the neighborhood around the time Amber went missing?"

Barbara shook her head. "I don't notice makes or models of cars. Greg?"

Greg's forehead wrinkled but he said, "I can't help either. Why? What's the connection?"

Steadman explained about the car in the canal and watched Barbara Pratt struggle again to keep control. The pain washed over her face in waves, twisting her pretty features. He looked away but didn't get up.

"Who would do such a thing?" she managed at last. "Amber was a sweetheart, and so special. So—" She buried her face in her hands and Kyle rose to stand behind her, rubbing her shoulders. A minute passed before Frost spoke again.

"What can you tell us about the day Amber disappeared?"

Greg answered. "It was a Saturday. I cut the grass and fiddled with the car. Barbara worked around the house and then put in a shift at the hospital. Amber spent the day with her boyfriend, Marshall Miller."

"The last time we saw her was at the breakfast table. She asked me to braid her hair, but I was busy flipping pancakes. She told me never mind, gave me a kiss, and . . ." Her voice trailed off as her mind traveled a long, bitter road she'd been down many times.

Steadman let a moment pass, then he said, "Do you think Marshall Miller had anything to do with Amber's disappearance?"

"Of course we do," Greg said, "but the police grilled him at the time and got nowhere. Days and weeks passed, the case turned cold, and in time, they gave up. There was nothing to go on."

"Can you think of any reason he might have harmed her?"

Steadman felt the room go still. Greg looked at Kyle, who stopped rubbing his mother's shoulders and returned to the footstool.

"A week or two after Amber left," Greg explained, "Kyle found her diary hidden in her room."

"I tried to read it," Kyle said. "I thought it could help us find her. But I couldn't make out some of her handwriting, and a lot of what I could read didn't make a whole lot of sense to me. At the time."

Kyle paused and ran a hand through the flattened side of his hair, fluffing it. "The last page of her diary said something strange. I thought Amber was being funny. It said, 'Today is the day I tell Marsh I'm cooking his bun.' It seemed like a weird thing to say, and I had no idea what it meant."

"He brought it to us," Greg said, leveling a hard look at Steadman. "We knew what it meant."

In the car, there was only the low rumble of the motor as Steadman turned out of the neighborhood and started down toward the coastal highway. The pain in the Pratt house had been palpable and he sensed the same subdued feeling in Frost that he was dealing with himself.

He buzzed down the windows, letting a brisk breeze flush out the mental cobwebs. Tall pines lined the road on both sides, rising from a carpet of feathery ferns, and the air smelled damp and earthy. The dashboard radio squawked once, spitting out a few blips of static, then went silent.

"Chief, I—" Frost abandoned whatever he'd been about to say as his phone emitted Lily's ringtone. "Hello," he answered. "Give me what you got."

He listened, thanked Lily, and ended the call. "Find a place to turn around, Chief. We're going back."

"Something we forgot to ask the Pratts?"

"Not exactly. Lily figured out who owned the Audi. A woman named Faye Turner. She lives across the street from the Pratts, used to run a nursery there and has a house on the premises."

"Interesting," Steadman said as he backed into a rutted logging road and made the turn.

He rolled to a stop in front of Faye Turner's house and let his eye wander over the broken, moss-scummed glass panels of a decrepit greenhouse. A weed-choked path led to a sagging shed where several bags of mulch lay like a handful of tossed pebbles, some of them split open, growing weeds of their own.

Steadman had noticed these things before, packed them away in his cranial filing system, but now they took on significance and he was eager to learn more about this new piece of the puzzle.

"I always hated that good-for-nothing car," Faye Turner told them.

They were seated on the front porch, he and Frost on a splintered wooden bench swing of questionable stability and the old lady in a creaky rocking chair. She had white, fly-away hair spread thinly over a blue-veined scalp and wide, blinking eyes. To Steadman, she looked like a startled ostrich just lifting its head from the sand.

"I always had to make sure I parked on a hill," she said, "nose out. More often'n not I'd have to pop the clutch to get it going." She held out a wavering hand for Frost's inspection. "See the scar? That's from the permanent blister I had, cranking on the key to get the thing started."

Frost gave due respect to the scar, then asked, "What happened to the Audi?"

Faye got contemplative, gazing at the spider-festooned ceiling while the chair rocked and creaked beneath her. Finally, she said, "It disappeared from my driveway sometime during September 2005."

"That was a long time ago," Steadman said. "What makes you so certain?"

"Rudy's birthday is in September. He just turned seventeen."

Steadman waited, but she didn't seem inclined to elaborate. "That's wonderful, Ms. Turner. But . . . ?" He made a rolling motion with one hand.

"In September 2005, I was visiting my son in Cincinnati and meeting my brand new grandson, Rudy. When I got back, the car was gone."

"Why didn't you report it stolen?" Frost asked.

Faye gave him a scornful look. "Not very perceptive for a detective, are you, son? Good riddance, I thought. The neighbor girl—her name was Amber Dawson—disappeared around the same time, so I figured she took it and run. More power to her. I was young once."

"How would she get the key?" Steadman asked.

Faye snorted and leaned back so far in the chair Steadman feared it might tip. "Any number of ways. I kept a spare on a nail I pounded into the wall behind the counter at the nursery. All she had to do was help herself."

"Is this the key?" Frost asked, holding out the sealed plastic bag.

Faye took the bag, dropping it into her lap. She peered at the key and the blob-shaped fob, moving them, running her finger along their ridges. "Yes, this is the spare key. I bought this fob at a roadside trading post when I first came to Washington. It's a cameo of George's head, if you couldn't tell."

"I couldn't," Steadman said, smiling. "Who else had access to the key, Ms. Turner?"

She rocked and creaked. Steadman counted six times back and forth before she answered. "My granddaughter Tiffany used to work for me now and again, helping out around the nursery. And there was young Wes, came in to heft the heavy stuff—bags of potting soil, mulch, terra cotta pots and such."

Frost held out the ring and the bag marked as a barrette. "Do you recognize either of these items?" he asked.

The bags joined the key in her lap and she rocked, holding each up to inspect it by the midday light streaming onto the porch. "I'm not sure about the ring," she said. "Lots of kids used to wear those things. But the barrette looks like the kind of fluff Tiffany liked to wear in her hair."

Steadman met Frost's gaze, saw the barely lifted eyebrow.

"Did Tiffany spend time in the car?"

"Sure, she borrowed it now and again. Always asked permission, far as I know." The chair stopped creaking as Faye leaned forward. "I guess all these questions mean you found the car after umpteen years."

Steadman bent to meet her eye, keeping his face deliberately solemn. "Yes, we found the car. It's a bit rusty, missing a few parts, but you can have it back when we're done with it."

Faye pushed back in the chair, sending it into a rocking frenzy. She cackled long and hard.

"Oh, Sheriff," she said, "you are a wag."

The sun hung low in the western sky as Steadman climbed from the car and stretched his legs. He and Frost had timed their arrival to come at the end of the work day, beating the rush hour traffic through Tacoma before stopping for a late lunch at a Jack in the Box in Federal Way. So much for his plans to get skinny.

They hoped to catch Marshall Miller just as he was arriving home from work, assuming he had a desk job. As he followed Frost up the flagstone walk, Steadman noted the neatly trimmed lawn, the sprawl of rollerblades and baseball gloves on the front porch, the tole-painted welcome sign hanging beside the front door. A pleasant and homey place. He cringed a little, knowing their visit might well put a dent in that harmonious atmosphere.

Frost rang the bell, a classic two-tone that made Steadman think of Avon calling. He heard a clatter of footsteps and the door was wrenched open by a freckle-faced girl about seven years old, wearing tap shoes with big black bows. She looked disappointed to see them and stepped back, to be replaced by a small, grubby boy who stared, wide-eyed and wordless, at their uniforms.

"Mom!" the girl called out, leaving the door standing open while she went in search of her mother. A petite, pretty woman in jeans and a purple sweater came forward from the nether regions of the house, wiping her hands on a dish towel. Her face went from inquiring to wary in a fraction of a second.

"Hello," Frost greeted her. "Mrs. Miller?"

The woman nodded, throwing the dish towel over one shoulder and placing a protective hand on her son's downy head.

"We're sorry to disturb you, but we were hoping to catch your husband, Marshall, at home. Is he here?"

"Not yet. I don't expect him for another half hour."

"All right, then. We'll wait in the car."

She hesitated, glancing down the road as if wishing her husband would suddenly appear, then said, "Why don't you come in."

She showed them into a small living room with a bay window overlooking the front yard. The brown leather couch and love seat were scattered with colorful throw pillows and framed family photos lined the walls. The small boy followed them in, continuing to stare as he plunked random keys on the upright piano with a grimy finger. The girl clacked up the stairs, the sound of the taps diminishing as she moved down the hall.

Steadman pushed aside a few pillows and sank onto the couch, next to Frost. Mrs. Miller sat on the love seat, twisting the dish towel in her hands.

"It's ironic," she said. "We bought a house on this side of the water because the company Marshall works for was based here in Lakeland and we wanted to avoid a long commute. A year later, the company moved across the Sound to Silverdale and now Marshall makes that long commute every day."

Steadman gave her a sympathetic look. "Best laid plans, blown apart. Sorry."

She tipped her head in acknowledgment, then said, "I'm curious to know what this is about."

Steadman leaned forward, resting his elbows on his knees and clasping his hands. "Mrs. Miller, does the name Amber Dawson mean anything to you?"

He watched the color wash out of her face, leaving two coral spots of brush-applied rouge high and dry on her cheekbones. She swallowed hard. "If you've ever heard someone talk about 'the one that got away,' for Marshall, that was Amber."

She paused, biting her lip. "This was years before Marshall and I met. In fact, if she hadn't disappeared like that, my life would have been a whole lot different. He'd have married her."

She stopped, pressing two fingers against her forehead as if pushing away a burgeoning headache. "She was pregnant, you know."

"So we heard," Steadman said.

"Marshall was thrilled. He told me Amber was the most amazing person he's ever known and he was over the moon about the baby. And then she just . . . disappeared. It broke him."

She looked up and Steadman watched her face change as she looked out the window. "He's home," she said. "Please . . ."

Steadman waited for her to finish, but she only gave him a look and went to the door. After a brief, whispered conference with her husband, she kissed him and took the little boy by the hand into the kitchen.

Frost made the introductions and explained the reason for their visit. Marshall Miller was a large man, good-looking and clean-shaven, with a ready smile. He still looked much like the football player he'd been in high school, though getting a little thick through the waist and jowls. He sat on the love seat where his wife had been, ankles crossed, hands in his lap.

Frost cleared his throat. "Will you describe what happened the last time you saw Amber?"

Marshall closed his eyes and furrows rose on his forehead. "I tried so hard to remember every little detail for the police. I told about this day so many times. I wanted her back. I just wanted Amber back."

He paused, pulling in a deep breath and letting it out slow. "And then, when I knew she wasn't coming back, I tried so hard to forget it all. It's been years, a lifetime."

"I know," Steadman said. "Take your time, do the best you can."

Marshall uncrossed his ankles and leaned his head back against the upholstery, thinking, remembering. "We were such kids," he said with a bitter laugh. "We didn't have a clue about real life, but I can still remember the way I felt. Like top of the world."

He was silent for a moment, eyes distant, turned inward. Then he spoke.

"We bought fried chicken, that last day, and went on a picnic by the lake. It was a Saturday, one of those hot, end-of-summer days. People were fishing, there were a couple of kayaks out on the water and kids splashing around on the shore. We laid on a blanket and stared up into the tree branches, talking about all sorts of things and then, right out of the blue, she tells me she's pregnant."

Steadman watched the Adam's apple in Marshall's throat convulse as he struggled to swallow his emotions. "I was ecstatic. It wasn't the way we'd planned it, but it seemed like a wonderful sign. We were meant to be together. We were going to be a family, and I was going to marry the most beautiful, the most brilliant girl in the world."

Marshall lifted his head and straightened himself on the love seat. "I wanted to do it right then, I couldn't wait. But Amber just laughed and tweaked my nose. She liked to do that. She said, 'we have time to do this right.' Then, her mood darkened. She said she might have to give up her scholarship and her mom and stepdad would be mad. That kind of put a damper on things and it was getting dark. Amber said she had to get home, so I dropped her off at her house. That's the last time I ever saw her."

To Steadman, a trained lawman, Marshall Miller seemed open and sincere. Until Frost asked his next question: "Did you ever drive or ride in a gold-colored Audi sedan?"

A layer of dark pink slid across Marshall's face and he dropped his gaze before answering, "No, I don't think so. I really can't remember."

"What about these?" Frost asked, producing the bagged items from the car. "Do you recognize any of these?"

Marshall poked at the bags, looking them over. "No, I'm sorry," he said.

Steadman grabbed the bag with the class ring in it and joined Marshall on the love seat. "See this?" he said, smoothing the plastic so they could both see the *MM* engraved inside the ring. "Isn't this yours?" he asked. "MM for Marshall Miller?"

A pained look settled over Marshall's face and he gritted his teeth. "Okay, yes. That's my ring. I gave it to Amber and she wore it on a chain around her neck."

"So why not tell us about it?" Frost said.

"I . . . I panicked when I saw it. You're looking for someone to blame for Amber's disappearance. I have a different life now. A wife, a family. Maybe you think I killed Amber, but I swear to you I didn't!"

"Sure Marshall, but what else are you going to say?" Frost asked. "We didn't really come here expecting you to confess."

"It's the truth," Marshall said. "I could never have hurt Amber. I missed her terribly. I mourned her for years, but now . . ."

"Now, things are different," Steadman said. "You've moved on, we get that. But Amber—by all accounts a bright star and lovely person—wasn't able to move on. She was snuffed out."

He stood and straightened his uniform. "We're going to determine the person responsible for that and find justice for Amber. Good day, Mr. Miller."

Their meeting with the Millers hadn't taken enough time to get them past the rush hour. Steadman fought his way through endless streams of traffic, irritated by the constant necessary adjustments to speed and lane of travel. When the rain came, pelting down in a noisy sheet that almost obliterated his view through the windshield, it only seemed like a logical addition to his day.

Neither of them spoke until they'd passed the Point of Tacoma, where the congestion thinned and the rain receded to a misty drizzle. Steadman felt his grip on the steering wheel loosen a bit in response and he took a deep breath, feeling his chest expand, the air filling his lungs.

"I like him for this," Frost said. "He's certainly hiding something. He loved Amber, that's clear enough, but . . ."

"But love can do strange things to a person," Steadman agreed. "He's got a lot to lose now. He'll fight to keep it."

"He admits the ring is his, but that doesn't necessarily prove he was in the car. We need to place him in that car."

Steadman signaled and changed lanes, steering onto the Tacoma Narrows bridge. "Let's have Forensics run another check on the items from the car, see if they can pick up any DNA."

"Good idea."

Lily's ringtone chimed through the car and Frost picked up the call, putting it on speaker.

"I'm still digging, boss," she told Steadman, "and I came across something interesting. Faye Turner's car received a photo radar ticket—during the time she claimed to be in Cincinnati."

"How was the ticket resolved?" Steadman asked.

"It was paid by check. Signed by Faye Turner."

"Good work, Lily. We're going to swing by and drop off some evidence for further analysis. Have a clear print copy of that ticket ready for us."

"Will do, boss."

Less than ninety minutes later, they were back at Faye's. It was dark and chilly, and Steadman hoped they wouldn't be returning to the splintery porch swing for this conversation. Instead, Faye beckoned them into a tiny, musty-smelling sitting room where the three of them perched in such proximity that they were nearly touching, kneecap to kneecap.

Faye didn't offer them anything to drink and that was just as well. Steadman wanted to get right to it. He'd had a chance to examine the ticket and he sensed some meat on that bone.

"Ms. Turner," he said, "your Audi S4 received a photo radar citation during the time you were in Cincinnati visiting your son. Why would you pay a speeding ticket when you weren't the one driving the car?"

"Did I?" Faye said. "I don't remember."

Frost held out the printed ticket. "Do you recognize the young woman in the photo, Faye?"

Faye took the sheet of paper, squinting at it for several seconds before handing it back with a resigned sigh.

"That's my granddaughter, Tiffany."

"Can you give us Tiffany's address?" Frost asked.

As Faye wrote the address in Frost's proffered notebook, Steadman studied the photo once again. The girl behind the wheel was wearing something in her hair. Something that looked remarkably like the beaded clip he'd just dropped off at Forensics.

Steadman caught glimpses of morning sunlight sparkling off Dyes Inlet as he drove up Highway 3 in Silverdale. The day was fine, warm for November and edged with the kind of autumn crispness he loved. In the seat beside him, Frost crinkled the wrapper on his egg and croissant sandwich and the smell of it made Steadman's stomach growl. He'd opted for a bowl of Special K with skim milk.

Last night, after speaking with Faye's granddaughter Tiffany, they'd signed off for the day, but Steadman had hardly been able to sleep. He was eager to continue the investigation, and Tiffany had given them a lot to go on.

Steadman took the exit near the mall and navigated a gauntlet of traffic lights, finally turning into the parking lot of the tech company where Marshall Miller worked. Steadman slammed his car door and took a moment to stretch his legs, smoothing out the wrinkles in his uniform. Frost was doing the same on his side of the car.

Marshall's face, when he saw them enter his office, was a curious mix of dread and relief. Steadman guessed he was resigned to telling them everything and relieved to be doing it here and not in the family citadel.

"We spoke with Tiffany Curtis last night, Marshall," Steadman told him. "Do you remember her?"

The tinge of pink Steadman had seen before returned in Marshall Miller's face, but he kept his head up, eyes open, waiting for the ax to fall. Almost begging for it.

"Care to change your story about the car?" Frost asked.

"Yes, okay," Marshall said, "I was in the car, but only one time." The pink deepened. "And only in the back seat."

"Tell us about it," Steadman invited.

"Tiffany was . . . well, you know the type of girl—always flirting, suggestive. She was constantly after me, offering herself up. I avoided her, tried to ignore her, but she *was* really pretty. And really persistent."

He let his head fall, chin to chest, and several seconds passed before he continued. "She caught me in a weak moment. It only happened once, and I was so ashamed afterward I wouldn't speak to her. I didn't even want to look at her."

"How did she react to that?" Steadman asked.

"Made her mad. She threatened to tell Amber."

"Did she?"

"No."

"Then what?"

"Then nothing. Absolutely nothing. I just pretended it never happened and I never told anyone about it. Including my wife. Can we keep it that way?"

"Depends," Steadman said.

"Depends on what?"

"Did you kill Amber Dawson?"

Marshall's face twisted. "Deputy Steadman, I think you know I didn't. I want you to catch the guy who did and send him straight to hell."

Once more behind the wheel, Steadman reflected that if he spent as much time on the treadmill and asleep in bed as he did on the road, he'd be a much healthier man. Still, driving gave him time for contemplation. And discussion with his partner.

"So, what have we got, Frost? Lay out the suspects, as you see them."

Frost pulled the notepad from his breast pocket and paged through it.

"I still say Marshall Miller is our best bet," he said. "He was very convincing back there, but some people can lie like a champ."

"What would be his motive?"

"I can think of several. He says he loved Amber and was thrilled about the prospect of marrying her and having the baby. But what if that's not true, just a cover? What if he had some kind of fantasy about a big football career—he was their star player, after all—and he saw Amber's pregnancy standing in his way?"

"Sounds plausible. Other possibilities?"

"Maybe Tiffany did tell Amber about her and Marshall in the back seat of grandma's car. Maybe they argued, and things got out of hand."

Steadman shrugged. "Worth looking into. He does seem to have the best opportunity for the crime. Who else?"

"Well, there's the parents. I guess either one of them might conceivably have done it after Marshall took Amber home."

"Motive?"

"We should look into the insurance angle. Or maybe there's a sexual component, something hinky with the stepdad. That could give either one of them motive."

"Did you get that feeling?" Steadman asked.

Frost was making notes on the pad. He stopped and tilted his head, thinking. "No, I didn't get that feeling," he admitted, "but that doesn't mean it couldn't have happened like that."

"True. Anyone else?"

"Tiffany Curtis might have been jealous enough to take Amber out." He flipped a page on his notepad. "But I can't picture it. The woman is tiny. If she did it, she had help."

"What about Faye Turner?" Steadman asked.

"She was in Cincinnati."

"Was she?"

"Right, Chief. I'll check on that too."

"Of course, there's one more we haven't even considered yet," Steadman said, veering right at Gorst to stay on Highway 3.

"Oh yeah, I was going to mention that. According to Tiffany, Miller wasn't the only guy she spent time with in that car. Is that where we're headed now, Chief?"

"Certainly is. Wes Hamilton, Faye Turner's handyman."

Wes Hamilton lived in Belfair, at the end of a shady lane lined with shacks and rusted-out trailer houses. Steadman stifled a groan as he made the turn onto the street. He'd spent too many hours in this part of town during his patrol years, breaking up meth labs and hauling in guys on domestic violence charges.

It depressed him—the squalor, the wasted lives, the hopeless faces. This boneyard of broken dreams and broken people. He told himself every one of them would get out if they could. Surely, every one of them had tried, multiple times, losing a little more hope with every attempt as they fell back into the bucket of crabs. Waving claws, pulling them down.

No one would *want* to live like this.

The Hamilton house was a dingy yellow square on a cinderblock foundation, about the size of Steadman's living room. There was no front porch, only a rise of three cracked concrete steps up to the front door. A window to the left of the door was boarded shut with rusty nails and a mangy black cat missing an eye slunk along the cinderblock base, probably a pretty good hunting ground for mice.

Wes answered their knock wearing plaid boxers and a faded blue terry-cloth robe. He held a can of Budweiser in one hand and a lit cigarette in the other. He didn't invite them in.

Frost laid the groundwork for their conversation, covering the basics, then Steadman threw his first question.

"Tiffany Curtis admits she often borrowed her grandmother's car so you and she could drive someplace private and smoke marijuana. Does that match your memory, Wes?"

He pulled a drag off the cigarette and nodded through the exhale. "Sure, Tiff and I did that some. No law against it."

"Now," Frost said. "Back then, it was different."

"Is that why you're here, deputy? To nail me for smoking pot?"

"No, that is not why we're here," Steadman said, making his voice extra stern. "Let's keep our focus here. Tell me about your work at Faye Turner's nursery. Is that how you met Tiffany?"

"Yeah, the old lady called me in sometimes to shift stuff around. Heavy stuff she couldn't handle."

"What about Amber Dawson?"

Wes took a final puff on the cigarette and flipped the butt, sending it into the dirt. "Nah," he said, "Amber had two legs. She could walk on her own. I never had to shift her anywhere."

Steadman moved half a step closer, near enough to smell the beer and Hamilton's bad breath. "Very amusing, Wes. Now, talk to me about how well you knew Amber."

"Well enough to say hi, is all. She had no interest in me, so I returned the favor. She was all about her math equations and football boyfriend."

"Really?" said Frost. "Because Tiffany told us you 'had the hots' for Amber."

"Tcha!" He huffed indignantly. "She was gorgeous, okay? I was a red-blooded American boy and she got my blood pumping all right. Doesn't mean anything ever happened between us."

"You sure about that, Wes?" Steadman asked. "We can place you in the car where her body was found."

"I already told you," he said, gesturing with his beer can so that some slopped out over the side. "I was in the car a number of times. But never with Amber. I don't know anything about what happened to Amber. Are we done here?"

Frost's phone rang. Lily's jingle. He held up a finger and stepped away to take the call. Steadman stayed where he was, legs apart, spine straight, his gaze fastened to Wes Hamilton's face, watching the man sweat in the November sun.

Frost finished the call and returned to the step. "No, we're not done here, Wes. Our lieutenant just got a call from Tiffany. Something she forgot to tell us and wanted to get off her chest. She says the last time the two of you were out in grandma's car was the day Amber went missing. She says you offered to return the car to the nursery and you dropped her off at home."

Steadman tensed. They'd treed this fox and a cornered fox can be antsy and unpredictable.

"Looks like you were the last one to drive the murder car, Wes," he said. "Right into the Hood Canal."

Wes Hamilton didn't run. He didn't slam the door or pull a knife out of the pocket of his robe. He put down the can of beer and moved out onto the step, hands open, palm up and held out at his sides.

"No, I returned the car, like I said. The nursery was locked up, so I couldn't put the keys away. I stashed them above the visor so Tiff could return them later."

"So you claim," Steadman said.

"It's the truth. You can ask Amber's little brother. He was standing on the porch across the street, watching me."

Frost scoffed. "He was five years old."

"Ask him," Wes said. "He'll remember. He was crying and hiding on the porch because Amber and Greg Pratt were tearing it up inside. He was scared. I talked to him, told him everything was going to be okay."

He hawked a wad of spittle into the weeds and dirt. "Shows how wrong I can be."

Logging in another hour behind the wheel, Steadman drove west, into the setting sun. He was grateful when they reached the turnoff to Lake Cushman and the tall pines closed in, giving him some relief from the glare. He pulled into the Pratt's driveway and climbed from the car. Someone nearby was burning leaves, the odor hung pungent in the air. The smell of autumn.

Seated again in the newly painted living room—he and Frost on faux leather and the Pratts on their customary chairs across the carpet—Steadman got right to the point.

"Tell me about the fight you had with Amber on the night she disappeared," he said to Greg.

Greg stared, twisting his mouth into a downward curve, shrugging his shoulders in a show of ignorance. "There was no fight. Like I told you, she never came home from her day out with Marshall Miller."

"We can ask Kyle about it. He was there."

Greg shook his head. "Kyle was five years old. He doesn't remember anything about that night. Not reliably."

"Why don't we ask him," Steadman said.

Kyle, like before, had materialized from the shadows and entered the room. He stood behind Greg's recliner, grim-faced and pale.

"What do you remember about that night, Kyle?" Steadman asked.

The young man stood silent for so long that Steadman was beginning to think he wouldn't answer, that maybe Greg Pratt was right and the child had no memory of the events. At last, he spoke, his voice tight, controlled.

"I loved Amber," he said. "She was more than a sister to me. She was my champion."

No one said anything and a moment passed before he went on.

"Amber was smart. Not just math smart, but smart about life. She was kind and she cared about people." His voice broke. "She cared about me."

Steadman made a small move with his hand, motioning Kyle to the ottoman where he'd sat the last time, but the young man ignored him.

"That night, I was asleep," he said. "The shouting woke me up. I was scared, so I went into my mom's room, but she wasn't there. Greg and Amber were yelling at each other. It was loud and they were angry. So angry. I went out on the porch to wait for mom to come home."

"What were they fighting about?" Frost asked.

Another bout of silence, then Kyle said, "I don't know. I don't know!"

He pulled in a breath that had a sob in it, but he choked it back. "I saw the handyman from the flower place across the street. He drove the old lady's car and left it, then he saw me and came over. He heard the shouting and he told me to stay on the porch and wait for my mom. He said everything would be all right."

The room went quiet again. Only Kyle's shuddering breaths punctuated the silence. "Then he left, and everything wasn't all right. I tried to wait on the porch, but I got cold. I went back to bed and the shouting stopped. I fell asleep. When I woke up, Amber was gone and I never saw her again."

Kyle took a step back and brought his arm from behind the recliner. He was holding a gun. He pointed it at Greg Pratt's head.

Barbara Pratt gasped. "No, Kyle!"

"You killed her!" Kyle shrilled. "I kept hoping she'd come home, kept pushing my memories from that night away, pushing them down. Deep. I wanted to believe she was coming home."

"Kyle," Steadman said, "put the gun down. You did good remembering, but we can take it from here."

"Kyle, please," his mother pleaded.

"No." He shook his head violently. "I can't push it down anymore. I have to face the truth now. She's gone. She's spent the last seventeen years underwater. Because of you!"

His gun hand wavered and Steadman feared he might set off the trigger, whether he meant to or not.

"I have to let the memory of that night surface, *Dad.*" He spoke the word with bitterness. "I have to face the fact that you killed my sister!"

"No," Greg said. "I didn't."

"I know you did, and you're going to confess. Or I'm going to shoot you."

"Kyle," Steadman said, keeping his voice calm and even. "This is not the way. You don't want to carry that burden. Put the weapon down."

"Admit it," Kyle shouted. His breathing was heavy now, an anguished panting, and Steadman knew the overload of emotion could easily lead to a tragedy even greater than the family had already borne.

"Let's do this right, Kyle," he said. "I promise you I will bring the full weight of the law to bear here. Let me help you."

The young man's voice rose to a shriek. "I want Amber back!" His eyes, wide and wild, drilled into Greg's. Steadman's focus shifted slightly to take in the man in the chair. His face had gone gray, aged by twenty years, as if the bedrock beneath had risen to the surface, revealing the visage of torment and regret.

"You're right, Kyle," he said, his voice toneless, hollow. "I killed Amber. I hacked off her hand and dumped her in the canal."

"Greg?" Barbara's voice sounded small and lost.

Kyle grew very still, a statue with dead solid aim.

"I let her rot there," Greg said, his features twisting with what Steadman took to be self-loathing. "Food for fishes. I did it. So, shoot me, Kyle. Pull the trigger and put me out of my misery."

"*Your* misery! What about my misery? What about mom's misery?"

Steadman couldn't spare a glance for mom. She was too far in his peripheral vision, and he had to stay focused on the two in front of him. He knew Frost would be looking after her. He had a soft spot for mothers.

"Is shooting you going to make my misery go away?" Kyle screamed. "No, damn you. It won't!"

He dropped the gun to the brand-new carpet where it fell with a muffled *thunk*.

"Live with the misery, Greg. I hope it eats you alive."

Steadman sat across the scarred table from Greg. He felt tired, smothered under a heaviness, like body armor that can stop a bullet but does nothing to protect the tender soul. He ached.

The interrogation room, stark and painted in two-tone shades of grubby blue, was cold and bare, adorned only by the one-way mirror to his left. Frost, Lily, and one of his sergeants were on the other side of the glass, waiting for him to begin.

He adjusted his chair. It scraped over the industrial tile like nails on a chalkboard, and Steadman winced. "Talk to me, Greg. I want to know what happened that night."

Greg Pratt slumped in his chair. Weighed down as he felt, Steadman knew the man across from him carried a far heavier burden. He could almost smell the despair.

"I never meant to hurt Amber," he said, his voice low but rising as he spoke. "I was so proud of her, so excited to see where life would take her. I knew she'd go farther than I ever could. Her mind was like . . . like a finely crafted instrument that would only grow more capable, more inventive, with time and maturity. She was brilliant."

Steadman said nothing, simply waited.

"I was champing with eagerness to see her step into that scholarship—whichever one she chose—and watch her take off."

Steadman realized Greg had been thinking of Amber as an extension of himself. Sometimes parents do that. Even stepparents.

"She came home that night and I went into the kitchen to talk to her. She had a glass of water and she was swallowing a pill. I

asked about her outing with Marshall. We talked about some of
the equations and theories she was working on."

Greg stared down at his hands, spreading them open, exam-
ining them like he'd never seen them before. "I picked up the
pill bottle—really just for something to do with my hands—and
I eventually noticed I was holding prenatal vitamins. I froze.
Paralyzed."

Steadman pictured the scene, imagined the punch in the gut as
Greg realized the significance of the bottle in his hand.

"I knew, in that moment. I saw everything change. I saw my
shooting star burning out before she ever left the ground."

Greg's voice thickened, clogging in his throat. "I confronted
her. She admitted she was pregnant, and she was glowing. She
didn't see. She didn't understand, like I did, how this would
damage everything she'd been working for."

Steadman waited while Greg struggled to rein in his emotions.
He heard the man swallow, hard and slow, before he went on.

"I suggested we should get in touch with a doctor and she
agreed. We discussed which clinic she should go to and it took
several minutes for us to realize we were each talking about a different kind of doctor. When I made it clear I thought she should
abort the pregnancy, she flipped."

He let out a shaky breath. "That's when the shouting began."

A moment passed, and Steadman let it go without speaking.
Greg wouldn't hold anything back now, but it might take some
time for the whole sordid story to come out.

"We argued. She outright refused to consider an abortion. She
said she was going to give up her scholarship and marry Marshall.
She wouldn't see reason. Finally, she just turned and walked away.
I saw everything good ending. I snapped. I picked up the rolling
pin and . . . I stopped her." A bitter smile touched his lips. "I
stopped her from ruining her future."

Once that admission was out of the way, the rest of the story
seeped out of him like pus from a wound.

"I had to get rid of her before Barbara came home from her
night shift. I knew she'd be found eventually, and I thought if
I . . ." Another long, hard swallow. "I thought if I cut off her

hands and head and disposed of them separately, no one would ever be able to identify her and no one would ever know what happened.

"I went to the garage for a hacksaw and on the way back to the kitchen, I looked out the window and noticed Faye Turner's old Audi parked across the street. I knew she was out of town, and I thought it would be easy to steal the car and use it to take the body away.

"I ran across to the car. It was unlocked and I found the keys in the visor. It felt like a sign. I got in and pulled the car up close to the house, loaded the body into the back seat, along with a shovel and the hacksaw. I cleaned up in the kitchen and then I started driving."

A long pause while Steadman watched Greg's distant-focused eyes taking him back to that night seventeen years ago.

"I didn't know where to go, but I somehow ended up driving alongside the canal and I knew it was deep water, deep enough for submarines. I hatched the idea to drive the car over the edge and sink it. I picked a spot close enough I could walk home before daylight, and I found a secluded area where I planned to take off the head and hands and bury them in scattered locations."

Steadman noticed that once Greg reached the point in his account where he admitted to killing Amber, he ceased to refer to her by name. She had become "the body." That had been the only way he could deal with her disposal.

"I dragged the body into the bushes and got the hacksaw . . . but I couldn't do it. I managed one hand, but I just couldn't stomach any more. I dragged the body back to the car and returned for the hand."

He shook his head. "It was gone."

Greg covered his face with his hands, rubbing his fingers along his eye sockets. "Well, that spooked me, and I was done. Done. I put the car in neutral and pushed it over the edge. Then I walked home and tried to sleep."

He let out a low, humorless laugh. "It was a week before I could sleep again. I sweated it out when the hand turned up and became a curiosity in the news, but no one ever made the connection. Coyotes chewed it up good."

Furrows creased his forehead, and he spent a long moment staring down at the table.

"I thought it was over," he said. "But it was never over, and it never will be. Not for me."

Steadman drove home. It was late as he pulled into the driveway, but he knew Vivi would have a plate warming in the oven for him. She always did.

The lawn shone silver in the moonlight, sheened with frost, and a sharp nip in the air left no doubt that winter was in the wings. Steadman stopped on the front walk and stood with his head tipped back, stretching his neck. He looked into the sky with its expanse of darkness and light, coexistent and eternal.

He rolled his head side to side, loosening the tight muscles in his shoulders and at the base of his neck. Time to go inside.

He hung his coat on its peg and went straight to the bedroom. He wanted to change, get out of his wrinkled uniform, stained with the stink of the day, before he kissed his wife hello.

He came to her in the living room and sank onto the couch beside her. She was bathed in mellow light from the table lamp, her fine ash-blond hair polished to gold, looking every bit the angel she was.

"Oh, Rand," she said, gently pushing him into a supine position and taking his feet in her lap. "It was a difficult one, wasn't it?"

"It was," he admitted, letting out a long, murmuring sigh. "But it's over now. All wrapped up after seventeen years. Maybe now the healing can start."

"You need another vacation," Vivi said, rubbing the ache from his toes, massaging his heels and ankles.

"No," Steadman said, falling to the edge of sleep. "All I need is you."

Chief Deputy Randall Steadman is the hero of my thriller novel, Steadman's Blind, *and a favorite character of mine. So, when I was invited to submit a story for* Mystery, Crime, and Mayhem's Cold Cases *edition, I started casting around in my mind for the makings of another Steadman story. I wanted to set this mystery in his jurisdiction, near the beautiful Hood Canal of Washington state, where I lived for several years before moving to Germany. And I wanted it to be intriguing. What I reeled in was a single human hand, severed and unidentified. A case gone cold. I wondered what might happen seventeen years later when the other hand turned up. "Cold Hands, Warm Heart," is the result of Steadman's journey down that road.*

Andrew Grant *was born in Birmingham, England. He graduated from the University of Sheffield, ran an independent theater company, then worked in the telecommunications industry for fifteen years before establishing himself as a critically acclaimed author. He published nine novels under his own name then—writing as Andrew Child—began a collaboration with his brother Lee to continue the internationally bestselling Jack Reacher series. He is married to novelist Tasha Alexander and lives in Wyoming. Find him online at andrewgrantbooks.com and jackreacher.com.*

NEW KID IN TOWN

Andrew Child

Reacher expected a truck, but he wound up in a car. He expected to be kept waiting in the hot Texas sun, but he got a ride almost at once. He expected trouble when he saw a skinny guy in a suit stick his nose into someone else's business, and on that score at least, he wasn't wrong.

The rest area parking lot was maybe half-full, but, human behavior being what it is, the vehicles weren't evenly distributed. There were clumps of cars and trucks all bunched up together in some places, and other sections with three or four empty spaces in a row. The skinny guy had been about to climb into a silver sedan on the right-hand side of one of these gaps, thirty yards from where Reacher was standing. Another guy was heading for a dull blue pickup on the left-hand side. He would be in his late twenties, Reacher guessed. Early thirties at the most. He wasn't especially tall, only around five ten, but he was broad. His sleeveless T-shirt was stretched tight across his chest. His arms were thick. They were covered with a bright, swirling mass of tattoos. So were his calves, which bulged out below his knee-length shorts. He wore black boots, unlaced and gaping open. His head was shaved. And he was hurrying after a girl.

She looked around ten years old, with blond hair in braids and a yellow sundress and sandals. She stretched for the door handle, then pulled her arm back and darted toward the rear of the truck.

The tattooed guy grabbed her by the hair and pulled her back. "Dad!" The girl's voice was shrill. "Let go."

The skinny guy paused, one foot inside his car. He shifted his weight. Set his foot back on the asphalt. Turned to face the other man and the child. "Hey," he said. "Stop that, you asshole. Let her go."

Reacher clamped the lid back down on his carry-out coffee cup and started to move. If it had been any other kind of dispute—a squabble over dinged paintwork, a contest for the most convenient parking spot—he might have left them to it. But this involved a kid. And as things stood, the way he saw them, there was no prospect of a happy ending.

There were twenty-five yards between Reacher and the three people.

The tattooed guy kept hold of the girl's hair for another couple seconds. He was acting on his own timetable. He wanted that to be clear. Then he put his hand flat on her chest, slammed her against the side of the truck, and held her there for a few moments as if the pressure would fix her in place.

Fifteen yards between them.

The skinny guy took a step, stiff and tentative. The tattooed guy took a bigger step, confident and aggressive. They locked eyes. Neither of them spoke.

Five yards.

The skinny guy edged back. The tattooed guy moved forward. He raised his fist. Cocked his arm. They were seconds away from *game over*. Moments away. Then Reacher stepped between them.

"In the car," Reacher said to the skinny guy.

The guy didn't react for a moment. He was too shocked. The giant, messy figure in front of him seemed to have appeared out of nowhere. Six foot five. Two hundred and fifty pounds. Chest like a refrigerator. Arms like most people's legs. He could have been a villain in a horror movie. Or the thing you run from in a nightmare. Then the guy's senses kicked in and he scrambled backward and did what he'd been told.

Reacher turned to the girl. "In the truck."

She climbed up onto the step, pulled open the door, jumped inside, and disappeared from sight.

"Your kid?" Reacher said to the tattooed guy.

The guy didn't answer. He glared back. But he did lower his fist.

Which was smart, under the circumstances.

"Want to keep her?"

The guy strode forward. "You're not taking—"

Reacher shoved him back, one handed. "Do you want to keep her?"

The guy raised his arm again and took a wild swing. He was aiming for the side of Reacher's head. Reacher leaned back and watched the guy's fist sail harmlessly past.

"Behave yourself." Reacher checked the lid on his coffee cup. "Don't make me kick your ass in front of the kid. So. You want to keep her?"

"Damn right."

"Because if you don't, no problem. We can call Child Protective Services right now. They'll take her off your hands, no questions asked."

"No one's taking my kid. Not you. Not the government."

"Maybe. Maybe not. Depends if you hurt her again."

The guy didn't respond.

Reacher said, "Well?"

"I didn't hurt her. You don't understand. Kids, they act out. You have to—"

"Show me your wallet."

"What?"

"Your wallet."

"You want money, you're SOL." The guy took a billfold from his back pocket and held it up. It was made of imitation snakeskin, frayed and stained and sorry looking.

Reacher took it and flipped it open, then turned it around to show he'd seen the guy's driver's license. "Here's something you didn't know. I used to be a military cop. One of the guys from my unit is a Texas Ranger now. I'm going to give him a call. Have him put a flag on your address. Any domestic disturbances, any visits to the emergency room, he'll hear about them. Your kid stubs her toe too often and—"

"What? He'll arrest me? Bullshit."

"No." Reacher shook his head. "He'll call me. Then you'll wish he'd arrested you."

Mason Greenwood sat in his house, in front of his computer, one hundred and fifty miles away, safely out of the heat and the dust. He was working. Although, he was almost embarrassed to call it that when he thought of the way business used to be done. He was earning a living, then. Providing a service. Meeting a demand. There was no arguing with that. And no one could call him lazy. He put in more hours than he had to. Way more. But then he'd always been a hands-on kind of guy. He could buy his stock from elsewhere, but he preferred to produce it himself. He enjoyed it. And he could automate the transactions as well as the security. There are bots that can handle pretty much everything these days. Maybe he'd use them, at some future point. Not yet, though. Not while he was still expanding. Looking for new markets. Like the client he was getting ready to pitch. From Japan. They were sticklers for etiquette, those guys. He'd read all about them. Done his research. They needed to be handled carefully. And he didn't want to risk a lucrative revenue stream for the sake of a few more hours at the keyboard.

Greenwood figured he'd get the deal squared away then head into town, such as it was, and celebrate. He liked the place. In many ways, the two years he'd been there had been the best of his life. Certainly the safest. But it wasn't exactly a heaving metropolis. There wasn't much in the way of fresh blood. Usually. When someone new arrived, it was an event to be savored. Especially if she was young. Pretty. And happy to stick around for a while. As had happened two weeks ago. Greenwood had enjoyed the chase. But now he figured it was time to close another kind of deal.

The old V8 spluttered into life. The truck shivered as the tattooed guy dropped it into Drive. Its rear tires squealed as he hit the gas. Reacher watched until it disappeared onto the highway, then started toward the section where the trucks were parked.

"Hey." The skinny guy rolled down his window. "I want to thank you."

"No need." Reacher kept on walking.

The guy fired up his engine and reversed out after him. "Let me at least drive you to your car. Is it far?"

"I don't have a car."

"Your truck, then."

"Don't have a truck."

"Then where are you going?"

Reacher shrugged. "Wherever the first driver who offers me a ride is going."

"You're looking to hitch a ride?"

"That's what I said."

"And you really don't mind where?"

"Somewhere west of here, preferably."

"Why west?"

"Because I just came from the east."

"Oh. Okay. Well, I'm heading west. South first, then west. Want to ride with me for a while?"

Reacher stopped and looked at the guy's car. He figured it was German. Not new. Ten years old, at least, based on the style and the degree of fade shown by the three expired parking permits stuck on the inside of the windshield. Maybe fifteen years. But a good brand. And it seemed in good shape. Clean. Well maintained. Which meant there was a good chance it would be reliable. A critical factor in that part of Texas. There could be hundreds of miles between one town and the next. Not the kind of place you want to break down. Not unless you want to be dinner for the vultures. "How much gas have you got?"

"Full tank."

"Range?"

The guy pressed a button at the end of one of the stalks that stuck out from the steering column. "Three hundred and fifty-eight miles. If you trust the computer."

Reacher nodded, walked around the front of the car, and climbed into the passenger seat.

The guy shifted into Drive but kept his foot on the brake. "Where's your stuff?"

"What stuff?"

"I don't know. Clothes. Luggage. Suitcases, or whatever."

"I'm wearing my clothes. My stuffs in my pocket. I don't need any luggage."

"The clothes you're wearing—they're all you have?"

"How many clothes can a person wear at one time?"

"What happens when they get dirty? What do you wear when they're in the wash?"

"I don't wash them. I buy new ones."

"Isn't that a bit wasteful?"

"No."

"Oh. Okay. Each to their own, I guess." The guy stretched across and held out his hand. "Charles. Charles Bell. People call me Chuck."

"Reacher."

Bell shifted his foot to the gas pedal and set off slowly toward the exit.

"So," Reacher said, once they were on the highway, "where are we headed?"

"Small town. Near the border. La Tortuga."

"Why there?"

"Long story."

Reacher didn't reply.

"Some . . . thing I'm looking for might be there."

"What kind of thing?"

Bell turned away and looked out of his side window for a long moment. "A place. An opportunity. My background's in power generation. Renewables, most recently. Solar's my specialty. I work for a nonprofit now. Small outfit. Just me, actually. I'm looking to put a coalition together. You know all the talk about a border wall? I want to build one. But out of solar panels. Half the power for the United States, half for Mexico. Something to unite us. Not divide us. And help the planet at the same time."

Reacher said nothing.

Bell said, "You think I'm crazy."

"I was thinking about your idea. This town, it's the place you want to build your wall?"

"I don't know. I've been searching for the right place for a while. A long time. This might be it. Or it might not." Bell loosened his tie. "We'll soon see."

"I wish you luck."

"Thanks." Bell wiped perspiration from his forehead, despite the air being cranked down low. "How about you, Reacher? What do you do for a living?"

"Nothing. I'm retired."

"From what?"

"The army."

"Oh." Bell was quiet for a moment. "I hear that a lot of ex-military guys go into law enforcement. Or join private contracting firms. Things like that."

"Some do. Not me."

"So if you don't work, what do you do?"

Reacher shrugged. "I keep busy."

Mason Greenwood hit the key to end the virtual chat, then double-checked that the secure connection had really been terminated. Some might have called that kind of behavior paranoid. He called it prudent. And he wasn't in jail, or worse, which to his way of thinking was proof he was right to act that way.

He stood up, stretched the knots out of his shoulders, and made his way to the kitchen. It was also at the back of the house. All the rooms he used were. The front part of the building was just for show. Anyone driving by would think nothing had changed since he bought the place, if they thought anything about it at all. It still looked ramshackle. Almost derelict. Or *rustic*, as the sleazy real estate guy he'd dealt with out of Fort Stockton had called it. Keeping it that way had been his biggest challenge. He needed to avoid drawing attention. Not altogether, of course. The kind of attention he attracted personally was fine. The kind in the town. In the bar. The kind that came from being the first person in a decade to land there with money. And no federal warrants. The kind from the local losers, who were looking for ways to get paid. And from the ladies, who were looking for . . . other things. He thought.

It was just his home Greenwood needed to keep discreet. In particular, the part where he worked. His studio. His computers. His pair of satellite dishes to guarantee uninterrupted internet access. And his backup generator to keep everything working when the local supply struggled to keep up. The answer had been to tent the place. Then to hire two construction crews. One made up of old lazy guys who hung around out front, sitting in the sun, drinking beer, wheeling the odd barrow around and occasionally sawing random pieces of wood. And another of top-line professionals brought in from over the border and paid extra to keep out of sight. Their job was to build essentially a whole new house—compact, efficient, and tailored to his exact needs—hidden inside the existing structure.

Greenwood opened the fridge and pulled out a bottle of champagne. Dom Pérignon, 2008. He couldn't honestly tell the difference between vintages. He couldn't tell the difference between champagne and sparkling wine from the grocery store, but he did have a degree of brand awareness. He knew which labels were supposed to be the best, and that's what he felt he deserved. Particularly at that moment. The call had been a success. A triumph, in fact. His preparation had paid off. His due diligence. The guy he'd uncovered was a human gold mine. He represented a group of other like-minded individuals. People with very particular tastes. The kind of tastes he was uniquely positioned to cater for. And on top of their tastes was their appetite. They sounded insatiable. They were going to set him up for life. He popped the cork, grabbed a glass, and headed back to his office. He needed to trawl through his archives. His filing system didn't quite mesh with the way his new best customer defined his group's requirements and he didn't want to miss anything. Not with the kind of volume they were talking about. He reckoned he should have enough material stored away for two months. Ten weeks, if he was lucky. He needed to make sure. Then, start work on a new production schedule. Procuring the raw material might be a challenge. The specification was very narrow. He checked his watch. There was plenty of time before he needed to leave for the bar. And if he was a little late, so what? It wasn't like he had any competition.

Bell stayed on I-10 for twenty miles, then coasted around a cloverleaf onto a state highway for seventy miles, then switched to a county road. Each one was narrower than the one before. Each one was quieter. Clearly there was no border crossing at the town they were heading for, Reacher thought, official or unofficial. The roads were too small, and the traffic was too light. He turned to ask Bell for more details but paused. It might have been the angle of the sun, or the tint of the windows, but he thought Bell appeared different. His skin seemed a couple shades paler than when they'd left the rest area. It looked clammy, and his eyes seemed to be bulging a little.

"Chuck?" Reacher said. "You okay?"

"Of course." Bell took his left hand off the wheel and shook it like he'd just washed it and couldn't find a towel. "Why?"

"How much farther are we going?"

Bell checked the odometer. "Fifty miles. Sixty, maybe."

"What kind of place is it?"

Bell shook his left arm again. "Not entirely sure. Never been before. Just seen it on Google Earth."

"Is there a doctor's office there? Or an emergency room?"

"Why? Are you sick?"

"No. But I think you are."

Bell slumped a little in his seat. "I'm fine. Just tired."

"Want to stop? Take a break?"

"No." Bell wiped his forehead. "Got to keep going."

"Why? What's the rush? Is there some kind of race to build this solar wall?"

Bell managed a weak smile. "No. It's just . . . when I set my mind on something . . ."

"I understand. I feel the same way. But a little tactical flexibility can be a good thing."

"I guess." Bell took a couple deep breaths. "Maybe a rest would be nice. But I don't want to stop. Not for long. So how about we pull over. I get in the back. Stretch out, maybe take a nap. You drive the rest of the way."

It was possible, Reacher thought. He did know how to drive. Although he didn't like it much. It wasn't a technical issue. Operating a vehicle was straightforward enough. He'd been trained in the army. He'd done it many times since then and never had any collisions. Not accidental ones, anyway. It was more a question of temperament. He was better suited for explosive bursts of action or long spells of inactivity. Not the kind of measured concentration needed to successfully navigate traffic and pedestrians. But just then, there wasn't any traffic. There weren't any pedestrians. And there did seem to be a real risk of Bell collapsing at the wheel.

Mason Greenwood was three-quarters of the way through his bottle of bubbly. With each glass, he'd cranked his music up a little louder, which wasn't a problem. No one would be able to hear it. His house was the second-farthest building from the center of town. He'd have preferred the farthest, all things being equal. He'd almost bought the farthest. But there were two things wrong with it. First, the layout. It was basically a big wooden shed. It had been built for storage back in the days when the town straddled a trade route that came up from Mexico and then split, east and west. So there were no living quarters. Greenwood would have had to build two new structures. A fake section, to fool any passersby, and a concealed section, for him to live and work in. Which wouldn't have been the end of the world. He would have considered it, if it weren't for the second issue. The real deal-breaker. A complete lack of water.

With each glass he'd also come closer to the conclusion that he had far fewer of the kind of files he would need for his new Japanese customer. At the rate he was finding them, maybe only enough for a month. Six weeks at the outside. Which might be a problem. It left him far less time to ramp up production. He would have to jump on the procurement issue right away. He hadn't dealt with that specific subset for some time. He'd have to develop new contacts. He couldn't suddenly get back in touch with his old ones. That would be too suspicious. It was more than ten years since he'd done that kind of business, he realized. Where had the time gone? He had no idea. But the length of the interval did explain why he was having less luck with the computer search than he'd expected. Some of his inventory from those days would be on paper. Which could offer a reprieve. If he could find the right pages, he could scan them. Make digital copies. It would be time-consuming but possible. And he could start at once. Get a few batches done. See what the quality was like. Confirm whether he'd found a lifeline, or not. He checked his watch. He was definitely going to be late to the bar. But so what? It wasn't like he had any competition.

Bell passed out on the back seat before the car got moving again. Reacher switched on the radio, tuned it to a blues channel to cover Bell's raspy snoring, and settled in for the balance of the journey. There were fifty-four miles remaining. Reacher covered them in forty-nine minutes. He had no problem with traffic. He only saw three other cars the whole time, all heading in the opposite direction, plus one Coca-Cola delivery truck.

The town of La Tortuga was spread out over a low, shallow hill. First, they passed a scattering of small, low houses, mostly painted peach or yellow, with wide verandas and flat terra-cotta roofs. Then they came to the commercial section, higher up, spread along both sides of a single street. There were a few shops. A tiny post office. A diner. And in the center on the north side, a hotel. The only building with a second floor. Reacher parked by the entrance and turned to rouse Bell.

Inside, they found a stern-looking woman sitting behind a reception counter. The top was made of richly polished mahogany. There was a bud vase holding a single yellow rose and a copper bowl containing three folded copies of a local map. The walls and ceiling were white, the floor was tiled, and above their heads a fan moved lethargically, barely stirring the air. Bell asked for two rooms and handed the woman a credit card. She produced a cell phone, connected a small square device, and pulled the card through a slot on its edge. In his pocket, Bell's phone made a quiet *ting*. The woman returned Bell's card and followed it with a pair of keys on oversized brass fobs, numbered *one* and *two*.

"Rooms are at the top of the stairs," she said. "Dinner's in the bar, five until eight. Bar closes at ten. Breakfast's six until eight. Questions?"

Reacher and Bell shook their heads and made their way to the foot of the stairs. Bell was breathing heavily by the time he'd hauled his suitcase and backpack to the top, and the sheen of sweat had returned to his forehead. He handed a key to Reacher, checked the number on the one he'd kept, and used it to open the door to his left.

"I'm still feeling tired," Bell said. "Think I'll lie down for a while. In fact, I'm going to call it a day. See you in the morning?"

Reacher said, "Sure."

After checking his room, which he found satisfactory—a bed, a chair, a closet, and to his surprise, a little bathroom enclosed in an oval-shaped plastic unit wedged in the corner—Reacher headed back downstairs. He stepped outside, thinking some fresh air would be welcome after the time he'd spent in Bell's car. To the west, he could see the jagged outline of the peaks of the Great Bend National Park. They looked close enough to touch, but Reacher figured they must be at least fifty miles away. The town's single street continued to the east, seeming to lead nowhere in particular. To the south was Mexico, separated by a metal fence. It looked like a line of twenty-foot knife blades, glinting maliciously in the fading sunlight. If Bell wanted his solar project to literally span the border, he was going to have to look elsewhere. Reacher felt suddenly sorry for the guy. His enthusiasm for being outside waned. Plus, it was still oppressively hot. He decided to scratch his walk, go back inside, and see what kind of food the place had to offer.

The bar took up the full depth of the hotel. It had a window facing to the front. Another to the back. And it was about a quarter of the building's width. Which made it bigger than Reacher was expecting. And there were more people than he was expecting. Fourteen, including the guy who was serving the drinks. There was a group of four men, maybe in their forties, thin and wiry and tanned, who probably worked outside, all drinking beer from tall, frosted glasses. There were four couples, ranging in age from late twenties to early seventies, Reacher guessed. And a young woman, sitting on her own. A very young woman. She had shoulder-length blond hair. Bright blue eyes. No makeup. She was wearing a white sundress with a pink-and-red flower pattern embroidered into it. She didn't look a day over sixteen. And she was halfway through a margarita, with another empty glass at her side.

Reacher took a seat at a small round table with his back against the wall where he could see both windows and the door. An old habit. One that had served him well. The bartender approached, and he ordered two cheeseburgers and a coffee. He watched the other guests while he waited for his food, and the whole time he could feel the woman watching him. She kept it up while he ate his burgers, and when he finished and pushed his plate aside, she took a last sip of her drink and came over to his table.

"Mind if I join you?"

Reacher didn't answer right away.

"I know what you're thinking," the woman said. "This is a setup. Where are the cameras? Where are the cops? But you can relax. I might not look it, but I'm thirty-two years old. It's a family thing. You should see my mother. She's sixty, and she still gets carded. So. Can I sit?"

"I guess," Reacher said.

"I haven't seen you here before." The woman turned and gestured for the bartender to bring her another drink. "What's your story?"

"What makes you think I have a story?"

"Everyone has a story."

"They do? Then what's yours?"

The woman smiled. "Touché. But mine's boring. I'm running away from a bad situation. This is as far as I've got. Kind of run out of steam, I suppose."

"How long have you been here?"

The woman shrugged. "A couple of weeks."

"How long are you staying?"

She shrugged again. "A couple more? Who knows? How about you?"

"I just arrived. I'll be gone in the morning."

"Really? Huh."

The bartender dropped off a fresh margarita for the woman and topped up Reacher's coffee.

"I'm Heidi, by the way."

"Reacher."

"Well, Mr. Here Today, Gone Tomorrow, Reacher. What are you running from?"

"Nothing."

"Then what are you running to?"

"Nothing."

"Really? Neither? You sure?"

"Absolutely."

"How so?"

"Running's not a thing I like to do."

"Interesting." Heidi picked up her drink. She took a long sip and kept her eyes on Reacher's the whole time. "So what kind of things do you like to do?"

Reacher smiled. "Lots of things."

"Example?"

"Some things are easier to show than tell."

"That's very true. Maybe—"

A guy had just come through the door. He was about five foot eight, stocky, with buzz-cut hair and a pinched, pockmarked face. Possibly early forties. Wearing a white dress shirt untucked over loose gray jeans. He was gesturing urgently for Heidi to join him.

"Excuse me." A frown crossed her face. "One minute. Let me get rid of this jackass."

Heidi crossed to face the guy. There was lots of gesturing. Lots of scowling. Eventually, the guy grabbed Heidi's arm. She pulled free and hurried back to the table. She sat down. He followed. He stood about six feet away from her and crossed his arms. Reacher waited a moment to give him a chance to find some manners. The guy stayed where he was. Reacher stood up. The guy backed off, all the way to the far wall, but he didn't leave the room. And he didn't stop glaring at Heidi.

"Ignore him," Heidi said. She took another long swig of her drink. "Now, where were we?"

"He's a little hard to ignore," Reacher said. "Who is he?"

"Some idiot. He hangs around with this other guy. An asshole named Greenwood. He's older. Kind of sleazy. Hits on me every time he sees me. Gets mad if I talk to anyone else. I thought Greenwood might be here tonight. I was glad when he didn't show up. But this one? He's harmless."

"He's annoying. He should leave. For his own safety."

"No." Heidi sucked down the rest of her drink then got to her feet. "We should leave. Carry on our conversation somewhere else. Somewhere more private."

Heidi was gone when Reacher woke the next morning. There was just a tiny depression in the pillow next to his and a slight hint of her perfume lingering on the sheets. Reacher stayed in bed for another five minutes, then got up and showered. He got dressed, folded his toothbrush, put it in his pocket, and went to knock on Bell's door.

Bell cracked the door, then opened it all the way when he saw it was Reacher.

"Feeling better?" Reacher stepped inside.

"I think so." Bell straightened his crumpled blue pajamas and ran his fingers through his hair.

"Then it's time to say goodbye." Reacher held out his hand. "Good luck with your wall."

"You're leaving? No. You can't. I need your help."

"With what? I'm not a solar coalition type of guy."

Bell shuffled back and sat on the edge of the bed. "Neither am I, to tell you the truth. I used to be. I did work in the power industry. I did specialize in solar. But then . . . stuff happened. I lost that job. I'm a private investigator, now. I'm here looking for someone. A missing girl. I'm not feeling well and the kind of people—"

"You're not a PI, Chuck," Reacher said.

"How do you know?"

"Your car. It's too upmarket. It's German. It has Connecticut plates. And it has parking permits inside the windshield and half of a dealer's decal on the edge of the trunk lid. A PI would have a domestic car. Or a Honda or Toyota. He'd have local plates, even if they were fake. He'd have nothing that would make it easy for someone to identify the car if they saw it twice. And he'd certainly have nothing that suggested where he lives. Or lived."

Bell slumped forward and buried his head in his hands. "So you won't help."

"I didn't say that. But if you want my help, you better start with the truth."

Bell looked up. "Only the PI part wasn't true. I am here because of a missing girl. I am looking for someone. I swear."

"What girl?"

"My daughter."

"When did you last see her?"

Bell blinked twice. "Fifteen years ago."

"That's a long time, Chuck." Reacher tried to soften his voice. "Are you sure . . ."

"She's still alive? Fair question. But, yes. I'm sure. Here's what happened. My wife left me. Fifteen years ago. She ran away, actually. With our daughter. I never stopped looking for her. It's why I lost my job, in the end. I only caught up with her six months ago. And by then my daughter had gone her own way. My wife—my ex—was alone."

"What's your daughter's name?"

"Holly."

"Holly's age? Description?"

Bell grabbed his wallet from the nightstand and pulled out some papers. One must have been a picture of Holly when she was little. Bell shuffled another piece to the front, unfolded it, and held it out for Reacher to see. It showed someone who looked like a late teenager. With blond, shoulder-length hair. And bright blue eyes.

Well now, Reacher thought. *This could get interesting.* The picture looked kind of like Heidi. The woman from last night. Although, there was something strange about the image. It had an odd quality to it. Almost synthetic.

"It's a computer simulation," Bell said. "I didn't have any recent pictures of her. Her mom didn't have any up-to-date ones either, so we had to use this special software. You feed in the pictures you do have, tell it how much time has passed, add any details about accidents or tattoos or piercings or whatever that you know about, and it calculates the person's probable appearance now."

Reacher looked at Bell. Wondered how old he was. Whether he could have a daughter who was thirty-two. Probably not, Reacher thought. But if it was true that Heidi's family looked freakily young . . .

"Eighteen," Bell said. "You asked Holly's age."

Reacher suppressed a smile of relief. "Okay. Good. So, how do you know she's around here?"

"She communicates with her mom via a computer chat room. I found out her screen name. Then I paid someone I know to hack into the system and trace the IP address of the computer she was using. Most recently, it was here. And before you ask, yes, that was very expensive. And yes, that was very illegal. But we're talking about finding my daughter. I don't care about what's legal."

"No judgment." Reacher held up his hand. "But I do have one question. Something that could be a problem."

Bell looked suddenly worried. "Oh. What?"

"Suppose we find her. What do you want me to do? If she doesn't want to come with you, I'm not going to help you kidnap her."

"Kidnap her? God, no. I'd never do a thing like that. I'm going into this with my eyes open. I know how long it's been. How much water's under the bridge. I'm going to take it slow. Step one, make sure she's okay. Step two, make sure she knows I want to be back in her life. And make sure she knows how to contact me, if she wants that too. And I'm going to be patient. I'm not going to force anything."

"Okay. That sounds good. But not too challenging. Physically, anyway. Which brings us back to where we started. Why do you need my help?"

"Two things. First, finding her. And second . . ." Bell paused for a moment. "Second, honestly, for moral support. I need a friend by my side. I didn't think I would, but I do. You saw me yesterday.

The state I was in. The closer we got, the worse I felt. I thought my heart was going to give out."

"I'll stand by you. But finding her? You know where she is. You said your guy hacked her address."

"What? No. Not her address. The IP address of her computer. The chat room service she uses has all kinds of encryption built-in. To disguise the location of the users. The best my guy could do was narrow it down to this town. Not to an individual house."

"So we're close. This town's pretty small. We should start by showing her picture around. Someone's bound to have seen her."

"Yes. Let me change. Actually, I better hop in the shower real quick. I was sweating like a pig last night."

"All right. I'll go grab some coffee. See you downstairs in ten."

Mason Greenwood forced himself to breathe. *It's all right*, he told himself. *Everything's going to be okay. You just have to run. To disappear. You always knew this day would come. It's what you prepared for. The catalyst is different, that's all. No biggie. No need to panic. Just follow the plan . . .*

But which plan? He had two levels. *One*, for if he had a little time. If he picked up a software warning, for example, tripped by the FBI's bots trying to break into his system. Or if he got a coded message from one of the agents whose kids' college funds he was boosting. He'd be able to take more stuff. Personal items that he had in everyday use, or his old paper archives. Things he could load into the RV before tripping the degausser—the device which blasts out a magnetic pulse strong enough to irrevocably wipe all the hard drives in the house—and setting the timer on the incendiaries. *One* was preferable, for sure. But there was also *Two*. The real emergency level. If his perimeter alarm was triggered, say. Or he spotted the feds sneaking through his yard on his motion-sensing, infrared CCTV system. Then he'd have to drop everything and run to the RV. Which was a thing of beauty, he always thought. He'd designed its special features himself. The lead-shielded backup hard drives, so the bulk of his work would never be lost. The high-volume freshwater tank—automatically flushed and refilled every morning—and the additional solar panels for the AC, so he could stay off-grid for longer, even in Texas in the height of summer. The auxiliary gas tanks, which were always completely topped off. The remote switches for the degausser and the incendiaries. The self-detaching umbilicals for keeping the batteries charged. And then the feature he was most proud of, which wasn't actually part of the RV at all. The thing that made the RV unstoppable. The special panel in the garage wall. It looked normal. Felt normal. But it was actually just a thin skin. The RV could burst through with no danger of damage at all. And no need to wait for a door to crawl open. RVs are tall. His was fourteen feet, counting the equipment on the roof. A door would take several seconds to get clear. The difference between escape and capture. He knew because a guy had gotten close once before. Some kind of deranged relative, when he lived in Maine. That time, the door had jammed and he had to bust through a section of frame and drywall. Which did his car no favors at all. He had to ditch it two streets away.

So, level one, or two? Not two, he decided. The situation was serious, but it wasn't desperately urgent. The police were going to find out. There was no way to avoid that. But not until someone alerted them. That could take a while. Then they'd have to make their way out to La Tortuga. There was no police station within fifty miles. That was one of the things that had originally attracted him to the place. He probably had the rest of the day, minimum. Which pointed to level one. Greenwood took another minute to work on his breathing. Then he went to his office. His paper archives were still spread out all over the floor from the night before when he'd been searching for the files he wanted for the Japanese. He'd definitely need them. He started to gather them together, then paused. A new thought had entered his brain. A different way of looking at his situation. The plans he'd made were designed to protect him from threats arising from his professional life. But his current problem had nothing to do with his work. It was entirely personal. There was no connection to his business persona. No trail going back for decades, intrinsically bound up with troves of incriminating evidence. It was a one-off. A blip. Something completely out of character. Something anyone could have done. He wasn't the new kid anymore. The unknown quantity. The person at the forefront of everyone's minds. The one everyone wondered about. But someone else was. Someone who'd been seen in the hotel bar last night. The person who had, actually, started the chain of events that led to the tragedy. The person who should be held responsible. Who would be held responsible.

If Greenwood approached things in the right way.

Reacher was halfway through his second cup of coffee when a guy approached his table in the bar.

"Excuse me, Mr. Reacher?"

The guy was about six feet even, with a big round head, broad shoulders, burly arms, but a narrow waist and incredibly skinny legs. His hair was slicked back and tied up in a ponytail. His shirt was covered in palm trees and parrots like the kind Reacher had seen people wearing in Hawaii. His pants were some kind of pale-colored chinos, and on his feet he had dusty little beige espadrilles.

Reacher took another sip of coffee. "Yes. That's me."

"Come quickly. Please. It's your friend. Mr. Shell."

"Mr. Bell?"

"Yes. Sorry. Bell. He needs your help."

"Why? What's he done?"

"He's not well. He's collapsed. He's asking for you."

"Where is he?"

"Out back. Behind the hotel."

"He wasn't loading the truck on his own, was he?" Reacher drained his cup. "I told him not to. He promised he wouldn't."

"He was, sir, yes. He begged me not to tell you. He knew you'd be mad at him. But please. Come quick. It's bad. I think he needs to go to the hospital."

Reacher stood up. "Which way?"

"Down the corridor. Left before the stairs."

Reacher's standard operating procedure was to never allow anyone suspicious to get behind him, but that day he made an exception. For two reasons. He figured the guy wouldn't make a move until they were outside, where he'd likely have reinforcements. And he wanted to be first to the exit door. He moved fast, to look like he'd bought into the urgency of the situation and to make sure the top-heavy guy had to hurry to keep up. To build momentum. So that when Reacher opened the door and politely stood aside, the guy was past him and outside before he realized the mistake he'd made. Then all Reacher had to do was let go of the door. Let it close. Stand to the side away from the hinge. And wait.

Reacher pictured the scene. The top-heavy guy would slow down. Stop. Look around. Realize he'd come out alone. Glance at his buddies for confirmation, if anyone was backing his play. Conclude that Reacher would be running the opposite way, back along the corridor inside the hotel. He'd rush back to correct the error. Barge open the door. And race through. At which point his participation in the day's events would be brought to an end.

It took twenty seconds for the door to swing open. Reacher was ready. He was watching for it. He knew the exact height of his target. The exact trajectory it would follow. Which led to a perfectly executed blow. Reacher's fist connected with the guy's temple with maximum force. It was lights-out, instantly. And, as an added bonus, the other side of the guy's head cracked against the outside face of the door on his way to the ground. Reacher scooped up the inert body and held it in front of him as he stepped outside, just in case anyone had ideas about gunplay. No one did. There was only one other person there. The guy from the bar the previous night. The one who'd harassed Heidi. He was standing next to an ancient pickup. A Chevy, with orange and white paint dulled by years of sun and sand.

"Heidi told me you were an idiot," Reacher said. "Is that true?"

The guy didn't respond.

"See what happened to your friend?" Reacher dumped the body on the ground. "That's what's going to happen to you. It has to. It's a rule. It happens to anyone who tries to attack me."

The guy shuffled back a little, but he didn't speak.

"There's only one way to avoid it," Reacher said. "Answer a couple of questions. Are you smart enough to do that?"

The guy's hand started to creep toward the back of his waistband. "Stop," Reacher said. "Keep your hand still. Tell me who sent you. And where you were supposed to take me. Tell the truth, and I'll let you walk away."

The guy didn't answer. His hand continued to move.

"Last chance."

The guy's hand sped up. Reacher raised his knee and drove the ball of his foot into the guy's abdomen. He flew back and folded at the waist. His face hit the ground. His body slammed down after it. Reacher stepped closer and kicked him again. In the head this time. Just to be sure.

There was a pistol tucked into the back of the guy's jeans. A Beretta M9. Reacher took it, along with a spare magazine. He checked the guy's pockets. He found a wallet. It held $100 in notes. Reacher took the cash too. Spoils of war. You lose, you give up your treasure. An ancient tradition. The only other item was a phone. A modern one with a big screen and no buttons. Reacher added it to his haul. He figured he'd investigate it at his leisure when the bodies were secure and he was in a less exposed position.

The top-heavy guy's pockets yielded a similar crop. A gun. A spare mag. Cash. And two phones, this time. One modern. One old-fashioned. The kind that flips open, with a real keyboard and a much smaller display. A second phone was an anomaly. It made Reacher suspicious. He pressed one of the keys. The screen lit up. It said, *Enter PIN* in black letters against a pale blue background. Reacher tried 1111. The phone vibrated. The screen momentarily went blank, then *Enter PIN* reappeared. Reacher tried 1234. A digital clock appeared, along with a symbol. An envelope. Indicating that a text message was waiting. Reacher used the menu to open it and the screen filled with characters:

> Thanks for last nite! Magic! Breakfast at old
> warehouse? I have something for you!
> Heidi xxx

Reacher read it twice. This was why Heidi had left so early? She'd snuck off to hook up with this guy? Seriously? Then a whole different explanation sprang into his mind. One he liked even less.

The map Reacher took from the hotel's reception showed a place called the Old Warehouse. It was the last site marked on the eastern side of town. When Reacher stopped the captured pickup a hundred yards short, he figured it was more like a dilapidated shed. It looked dirty. Rickety. On the verge of collapse. But his aesthetic and structural complaints were the least of his worries. He'd been drawn into a tactical nightmare. There was only a single road, in and out. He should have scouted an alternative escape route. He should have been approaching from the opposite side. He should have been there hours earlier. In a less distinctive vehicle. And without two hostages hastily secured in the load bed. He should have walked away. He wanted to walk away. But—Heidi. Someone had sent that text. If it was Heidi herself, and it was intended for the top-heavy guy, then no harm, no foul. Under the circumstances, Reacher would be delighted if that was the explanation. Because if someone else had sent it, that meant Heidi was being held captive. Or worse.

Reacher jammed the spare magazines between the squab of the passenger seat and its backrest. He tucked one Beretta under his right thigh. Wound down his window. Took the other Beretta in his left hand. Shifted back into Drive. Shook his head. And continued toward the warehouse. He made it all the way to the structure unopposed. He drove in through a gap in the wooden siding. No one shot at him, so he kept going until he was as deep in the shadows as he could get.

Reacher stepped back out through the gap in the wall and cursed another weakness in his situation. His complete lack of intel. He had no idea how the plan was supposed to unfold. All he could do was put himself in the shoes of whoever he imagined was behind it. Try to anticipate what they wanted to achieve and how they would go about it. And act accordingly. He sat down and leaned gingerly against the wooden planks in the spot where he'd be most visible from the road. Put his hands behind his back. Brought his chin down onto his chest. And waited.

Ten minutes ticked by. The temperature rose another three or four degrees. Reacher felt the sweat prickling his scalp and soaking his shirt. Then he heard a vehicle. It drew closer. Slowed down. Its wheels swapped pavement for gravel. It kept coming. And coming. Straight toward him. For a crazy moment, Reacher thought he was going to get run over. Then it crunched to a stop. The motor died. A door opened. Reacher held his breath. Feet hit the ground. They took a step. Another. Another. And stopped. About level with knees, Reacher thought. He still didn't breathe. He couldn't. Not without his chest moving. He held on for another thirty seconds. Then snapped his head up and whipped both arms around to the front, a Beretta firmly in each hand.

The guy who'd approached leaped back, panicked at first, but he quickly regained control and kept moving, smoothly, until he was thirty yards away. A reasonable position, since he had a hunting rifle in his hands and was pointing it straight at Reacher's chest.

"Drop the guns," the guy said. "It's over. You'd never hit me from there."

"Want to bet?" Reacher got to his feet and darted behind the guy's car. It was a Toyota Prius. Dark blue, with a pale dusting of sand. There was a body in the passenger seat. It was Heidi's. She had no visible injuries, but Reacher knew she was dead. She had the unnatural stillness that only comes when every electrical impulse has shut down and the last vestige of life has passed. Reacher ducked down and shifted to place the car's engine block, such as it was, between him and the guy with the rifle. He cocked the hammer on one of his guns, slid the other into his waistband, then relaxed his arms and rested his hands on his knees.

"What's your name?" Reacher said.

"What the hell?" the guy said. "You're not going to live to tell anyone. It's Greenwood. Mason Greenwood."

"Why did you kill the woman?"

"I didn't." Greenwood smirked. "You did. I was out hunting and I heard a commotion over here, so I came to investigate. Saw you strangling the girl. Then you threw her down. So I shot you, hoping to save her. But I was too late. She must have banged her head on a rock. Shame, really."

"Meaning you strangled her. You threw her down. She hit her head on something else. Somewhere else. And you're trying to pin it on me."

"I didn't throw her down. I let her go. Then she slipped. Hit her head. It was an accident, really. And I'm not *trying* to pin the whole thing on you. I'm succeeding."

"It won't work, Greenwood. Trust me. I used to investigate homicides. Your plan is full of holes. The police will know the body was moved. Your hands are way smaller than mine, so the bruises on her neck won't add up. And you won't be able to find a rock that matches the crack in her skull."

"You know what, Reacher? If we were in a city, some of that might matter. It might matter in a town. Even a small one. But out here? After the sun and the critters have worked on her body for a day or two? Forget it. And there's something else. Whoever drags his ass all the way out here will be at the top of his boss's shit list when I call it in. They're not going to be looking for clues. They'll be looking for a closed case. One that means the next crappy job gets dumped on someone else. And who are you? The new kid in town. The perfect one to take the blame. No one knows you. No one will vouch for you. No one will miss you."

"You have a very depressing worldview, Greenwood. But maybe you're right. Maybe the safest way forward is for me to call it in. And to identify you as the perpetrator at the same time."

"For you to call it in? You think you can call with a rifle bullet in your brain?"

"How's that bullet going to get into my brain, Greenwood? How good a shot do you think you are? Because if you miss high, I've got a clear shot with two guns while you reload. And if you miss low, you hit your car. Most likely immobilizing it. Which is going to complicate your story, some. You heard a disturbance. Shot up your own car. Then shot me? I don't think that'll fly."

"I won't miss. And if I do, I can reload as many times as I want. You'll never hit me from there. Not if you had ten handguns."

"You sure? Let's find out. Take a shot. See what happens."

Greenwood raised the rifle. Took a breath. Started to squeeze the trigger. Then, a box fixed to his belt started to bleep and buzz.

The rifle discharged. The bullet hit the side of the warehouse, twenty feet above the ground.

Reacher stood up straight. Feet apart. Shoulders square. Arms out in front. He aimed. Pulled the trigger. And watched Greenwood buckle and fall. He approached the body. Kicked the rifle away. Raised the pistol again, ready for the customary two insurance shots to the head. Old habits die hard. But he didn't pull the trigger. He was thinking about Greenwood's theory. About lazy cops looking for easily closed cases. There might be something in that. In which case he could give them two. And maybe give Heidi's death a little meaning too. It would take a little staging, but maybe he could make it look like she'd defended herself. Escaped from Greenwood's chokehold. Ran a little. Turned. Shot him so he couldn't come after her again. Then slipped and hit her head. It might work. And if it didn't, no one would be any worse off.

Reacher emptied Greenwood's pockets, then went to work on positioning the bodies. It was unpleasant work. Hot. Smelly. Awkward. He didn't enjoy it. But he was pleased with the result. When he was done, he moved into the shade at the side of the warehouse and checked Greenwood's things. There were only two. His phone and the box from his belt that had bleeped and distracted him. Reacher started with that one. It looked a bit like an old-fashioned radio pager, only it was thinner and it had a bigger screen. Part of the screen had a printed, permanent display. It was a list. *Zone One* to *Zone Six*. And the boxes next to zones five and six were checked. It was for a security alarm, Reacher figured. He couldn't think of another kind of system that used zones in that way. Presumably for Greenwood's house. Someone must have broken into it at the exact same time Greenwood was trying to frame Reacher. Which could have been a coincidence, of course. A lucky break for some local hoodlum, chancing their arm. But Reacher wasn't a big believer in coincidences.

The best Reacher could figure it, Greenwood had lured Heidi someplace and killed her there. Presumably out of jealousy. Maybe her death was premeditated. Maybe things got out of control and she slipped, as Greenwood claimed. But either way, he would have kept her body on ice until his stooges delivered Reacher to the warehouse for the frame-up. With the extra cell phone in his pocket, complete with its incriminating message.

Maybe that place was Greenwood's house. A logical place for a rendezvous. Familiar. Not suspicious. And which had just been broken into. Which could have been a coincidence.

Neither stooge had called or texted Greenwood to say they'd arrived, since they were both unconscious. Yet Greenwood arrived at the old warehouse within ten minutes. Which meant his house, if that was where he'd killed Heidi, was likely within visual range. Reacher moved away from the building and looked back toward the town. One structure jumped out at him. The next one in line. Another old place, a quarter of a mile away.

Reacher parked the orange-and-white pickup at the front of the building. It was wide and low, with a deep porch with anchors for a swing chair, made of gnarled old wood, topped with shingles that were warped and bleached by the sun. He stepped onto the porch and peered through the dusty windows. The place looked deserted. He made his way around the side. The wall was plain and featureless. He turned the next corner and almost walked into a car. A silver sedan. German. Connecticut plates. Ten or fifteen years old. Belonging to Chuck Bell. But no longer in good shape. Because it had been driven into the rear wall of the garage. Through the rear wall, in fact. It had smashed into an RV that was parked inside, then it had been pulled back out. The driver's door was standing open, but there was no sign of a driver.

Reacher ducked down and went through the hole in the wall. He skirted around the RV and used a door that led to a kitchen. A super modern space, nothing like the outside of the place at all. It was all stainless steel and granite, and there were all kinds of appliances Reacher didn't even recognize. The only thing he was familiar with was an empty champagne bottle sitting on one of the countertops. He ignored it and moved on to the next room. An office. There were three wide desks, covered with computer monitors. A row of file cabinets along the opposite wall. Heaps of folders on the floor. Along with a person: Bell. He was slumped against the pedestal of the center desk. His face was contorted. His skin was gray. His hair was damp and plastered to his scalp. He was breathing, but fast and shallow. He saw Reacher and managed to lift one hand just enough to beckon him over. He seemed like he wanted to talk, so Reacher leaned in close.

"Sorry." Bell's voice was a rasping whisper. "Lied. Again."

"It's okay," Reacher said. "Don't try to talk."

"Didn't hack chat room. Hacked this guy. He . . ."

"Take it easy." Reacher put his hand on Bell's shoulder. "I'll get you to the hospital."

"No." Bell paused, gasping for air. "Too late. Promise. Burn it. Burn it." Then his head slumped to the side and the last of the light left his eyes. Reacher sat on the floor next to Bell and felt for a pulse in his neck, just to be sure. There wasn't one. Reacher stayed for another minute. He felt like rushing away would be disrespectful, somehow. Then he noticed Bell's other hand was crushing a piece of paper to his chest. Reacher pried it free, and immediately wished he hadn't. The paper was letter-sized. It was printed on the other side. A color photograph of two people. A man and a little girl. Both were naked. Both Reacher recognized. The man was Greenwood. Maybe fifteen years younger. Reacher needed to be sure about the girl. He slid his hand inside Bell's jacket and pulled out his wallet. He opened it and took out a photograph. The one he'd glimpsed at the hotel. Bell's daughter, when she was three.

Bell's ex-wife hadn't taken her. Greenwood had.

Reacher stood. He wished with all his being that he hadn't already killed Greenwood. Because he wanted to do it again. And again. And again. He wondered if that was why Bell had come. For vengeance? And then something Greenwood had said at the warehouse came back to him. *You're the new kid. No one knows you.* He'd meant Reacher, but he was wrong. Reacher and Bell had arrived together. Only Reacher was driving at the time. Bell was in the back seat. Technically he'd entered the town a moment later. So Bell was the new kid. *The perfect one to take the blame.*

Blame? Reacher thought. Or credit?

Reacher hoisted Bell's body up and over his shoulder. He had some arson to attend to. A couple trussed-up stooges to deal with. But first, there was a shooting he had to restage.

A vital ingredient of any good story—regardless of length—is a strand that somehow connects its characters to ourselves in a way that feels familiar and plausible. This is especially true in mysteries where choices and consequences can quickly spiral away from the realm of our real, everyday lives.

When I began the process of writing "New Kid in Town," I was thinking about the way we often make decisions based on the predicted outcome of our actions. These can be trivial—if I watch this movie, will I enjoy it? Important—if I switch jobs, will I prosper, or will I wind up getting fired? Or particularly for the characters in a mystery, life and death—how can I evade arrest for a heinous crime, or escape from a psychotic killer?

The more experience we have gained, and the more data we have accumulated, the more accurate our prediction of the future is likely to be. Throw in a wild card, however, like a newcomer whose reaction to stress is unknown, and you have the potential for serious drama. Make that newcomer Jack Reacher, and the ride is likely to get very wild indeed. . . .

Aaron Philip Clark *is a native of Los Angeles, CA. He is a novelist, screen-writer, and former Los Angeles Police Department recruit. He's the author of the International Thriller Award-nominated Detective Trevor Finnegan series and the winner of the 2021 Book Pipeline Adaptation Award.*

Clark's forthcoming novel, All the Smoke, *is a psychological thriller set in the hip hop music industry and draws inspiration from* The Talented Mr. Ripley *and other works by Patricia Highsmith.*

In addition to writing, Clark teaches creative writing at UCLA Extension. To learn more about Aaron Philip Clark, visit AaronPhilipClark.com and follow him on social media @_WriteMeAWorld.

DEATH AT THE SUNDIAL MOTEL

Aaron Philip Clark

The Sundial Motel was a relic on a dirt road. An old behe-moth, it had forty rooms across six floors. It was the last stateside motel before reaching the Mexican border. When the property was converted into studio apartments rented by the week, it became affordable housing for those struggling to survive, many undocumented like Alma Henri and her son, Criston.

Ernesto spoke softly when he told Alma that Criston was dead. At first, the words struck her ears oddly, sounding like gibberish spoken through a funnel. It was as if she were listening to a song on a forty-five record, slowed, warped, the needle slipping out of the groove. But she knew this song—borne of her greatest fear, something that dwelled inside her, shone brighter each time Criston would venture out into the world. And it had been this way since he was seventeen when they came to the States. Now, he was dead at twenty, and Alma knew nothing except his body was lying in the street a few blocks from where she stood.

"I can take you to him," Ernesto said as they stood in Apart-ment 3. Though she was not tall, she towered over the boy, stout and bowlegged. The cheap floor lamp washed his face in gilded radiance while casting a grand shadow on the wall. "The police are there, so we'll need to be careful," he said. Alma knew what he meant. Like her, he was without papers, undocumented. The motel had become a haven for her and others who had escaped violence and famine in places stricken by death.

"All right," she said.

Ernesto looked to his mother as if to request permission to leave. Though Alma had seen the boy wander the Sundial's grounds and adjacent streets unsupervised at all hours, she thought it was a respectful gesture. Ernesto's mother was a frail woman sitting in a worn recliner. She was dressed in a hand-stitched frock of patchwork fabric and a knit cap because she had lost much of her hair in a fire. His mother nodded, and Ernesto got up from the bed's edge, drew air into his chest, and turned to Alma. "Follow me," he said.

Alma walked with Ernesto into the chilly San Ysidro night that carried dust on the wind. She was without her jacket but didn't feel cold. The boy led her down the sidewalk toward a cluster of red and blue lights in the distance. Her dreadlocks were wrapped in a scarf, and her once-white canvas sneakers were stained and threadbare. As they got closer to the commotion, each step felt like weights were anchored to her feet. When they were close enough to see the cordoned-off scene, the two stood under a bus stop's awning across the street. "There," Ernesto said, pointing to the skinny figure on the ground. An orphaned shoe was on the curb, and an arm stuck out underneath a sheet. A crushed gold watch still on the bloody wrist shimmered like a beacon in the dark. It felt like the arm had been reaching for something, for someone.

"Did you see what happened?" Alma asked, unable to cry. She had learned to stomach her pain, never showing it in front of Criston. Even in frightful moments, times she was certain they'd be sent back to Haiti, her face was stone. Fear had become a constant in her life, and it ruled her even now. Fear of deportation. Fear of not being able to protect her child. It was a feeling she had come to accept, just as she would now have to accept his loss.

"No, Miss Alma. I'm sorry."

"All right," she said. "Thank you." And with that, the boy left.

The night's air was all over her as she watched men and women with badges in uniforms and suits walk past her son's body as if it were no more significant than the hydrant feet from where he lay. An ambulance was parked, but its lights were off—there wasn't any need. The emergency had passed. The paramedics conversed with deputies, paper cups of hot liquid steaming in their hands. Their attention was on a howling man, who stood dressed in a tan jacket, jeans, and boots. The man's legs seemed weak, his torso a boulder affixed on two twigs. His laughter caused tremors that threatened his footing. He steadied himself with the aid of an officer's shoulder.

Alma grew up with drunks—piggish men—she recognized them by how they moved and spoke. The alcohol fouled their breath, got into their muscles and bones—seized their thoughts. Their bodies would confess what their mouths worked to hide. "I'm fine . . . I only had one," they'd say.

Alma shuddered at the thought of Criston dying in the street, taking his last breath without her there to comfort him. It was inexplicable. Mothers weren't supposed to bury their sons. She wondered how long Criston had been dead and what would happen to him next. Alma wanted to go to him, hug his thin body, tell him how much he was loved. It would surely mean her deportation, but what good was staying in the States now that her *pitit gason* was gone?

More deputies arrived in cruisers and SUVs, red and blue lights flashing. Alma had lived to avoid people in uniforms, especially the police, and now there were many standing near the pickup truck, shining flashlights against its front end. She didn't know the truck's model, but it looked American, with a long, wide body, and she could see the damage: a dented hood, cracked headlight, a broken side-view mirror.

Alma tasted a bitter taint in her throat. She coughed hard, nearly lost her balance. Then vomited onto her shoes. The earth spun, and Criston's voice in her head was all she could hear. Not as a man, but as a tender boy, timid, holding on to her apron strings. The Lord told her he had a good heart and would grow to be a good man, and he was . . .

Unable to watch anymore, Alma left and returned to the Sundial. Her neighbors, many who knew Criston, stood with candles and prayed the rosary outside her apartment. Alma didn't speak to them as she opened the door, but she nodded appreciatively. She noticed the vomit had dried on her shoes as her feet crossed the threshold. Once inside, she collapsed to the floor and wept.

Alma had attended worship services at St. Francis Church each week, but today everything felt different—foreign. She had never been in the priest's chambers. The room was paneled in mahogany, the carpet blood-red, and a dust-coated window offered the only measure of light. It rattled as the Santa Ana winds blew, whipping up the earth. Alma could see the brown billows sweeping across the empty desert and thought of her son. Criston loved the desert, though she didn't understand why. "It's so filthy," she'd tell him as he admired its scope. "It is what it is," he'd say without further explanation.

"Yes, that's my son," Alma said. She was sitting across from the priest, looking at an image of Criston's nude body on a metal table. The fact that it was on the priest's cell phone only made the process of identifying her son's remains all the more disheartening, which Alma didn't think was possible.

"The coroner will make arrangements with you. He will not ask about your status. Though I suggest you have the body brought here," the priest said. He had olive skin and was cloaked in a black cassock, fitted with a red sash around his waist. "You have my deepest condolences. May God bless you."

"How did they tell you he died, Father?"

"I was told a motorist struck him."

"And the driver?"

"I'm not certain."

"He's a man . . . I think he could be the police or a government official," she said.

The priest looked away as if he had heard something in the distance, but there was only silence. He turned to her slowly until their eyes met. "How do you know that?" he asked.

"I saw Criston in the street," she said. "And the truck that hit him and the man, I believe, was driving it. I didn't get close. I was afraid of what I'd do if I got close."

"That was wise," he said. "No reason to put yourself in jeopardy."

"Where can I bury my son?"

"We can have the funeral here at the church. All that's required is a simple donation."

"A fee?" Alma felt invisible, like the priest was looking through her. She wanted to scream.

"It will need to be a quick burial as we don't handle preserving the body."

"Where will he be kept?"

"The basement," he said. "It doesn't get very warm down there this time of year."

"The basement," Alma repeated. There was anger in her voice but also shame. The priest looked anxious, and she pressed on. "What about an investigation? Something should be done."

"Investigation into what, pray tell?"

"He was hit. That isn't something that just happens."

"I understand it was an accident. A dark road, no sidewalk. Perhaps he wandered into the traffic."

"My son never wandered," she said. "Especially not into someone's vehicle. The man who hit him was drunk, I know it."

"Miss Alma, I can't speak to any of that, but I would caution you not to make any allegations that could put you and those at the Sundial in danger. Your choices don't only impact you. Leave the matter to the police. If alcohol was involved, I'm sure the evidence will come to light." Alma nodded, though she felt sickened by each word he spoke. "It's best we mourn Criston and know that it was just his time. He's in the heavens now, with the Creator. It's where he was needed."

"But my son should be here with me!"

The priest reached for Alma's hand. She wanted to pull away but surrendered to his touch. No one had touched her since Criston hugged her the morning of his death. It was all the comfort she was awarded, even if it was out of pity. "You're familiar with the Book of Revelations?" he asked.

"I know the prophecies."

"Good," he said. "Then you know that everything must end. But what some won't tell you is that the prophecies in the book may have already come to pass."

"I don't understand."

"What if we exist after the destruction told in the text? A people born out of time. Living in limbo, waiting for God to turn off the lights."

"That carries no importance to me."

"What I'm trying to say is death isn't the end. It's a beginning. In the heavens is where we truly belong." He reached his arms above his head and shook them violently as if it were a ritual calling of haints. "He's up there, Miss Alma, and he's looking down on you, and he wants you to go on living."

"Stop," Alma said, slamming her fist on the priest's desk. "Your words are meaningless." She rubbed her temples and stood up from the chair with a sigh.

"Excuse me?"

"Save it for your sermons," she said. "My son was killed, and you want me to forget?"

"Please, Miss Alma . . ."

"Why can't you speak to the police for me?" she asked. "See if they checked the driver's blood . . ."

"It wouldn't do any good."

"Why?"

"Leave it, Miss Alma." The priest spoke sternly as if she were a child. "There are things about living in this country you still don't understand."

Alma didn't need to understand and knew when a man was hiding something. She snatched a letter opener from a small jar on the priest's desk and held it tightly in her palm, studying its tip, appreciating its heft.

"I know why God took my Criston," she said. "It was to punish me." Alma moved closer to the priest, and she laid her hand on his shoulder. "When I first came to this church, all I felt was guilt. Do you remember what I confessed to you?"

"I do," the priest said.

"You told me that I'd be forgiven," she said. "I know that's what you're supposed to say, but I didn't believe you. God's seen what I've done, looked into my heart, and he knows what I am."

"And what are you, Miss Alma?"

"Nothing good," she said. "In my village, they called me *destriktè . . .*"

"What is that?"

"Destroyer," she said, bringing the letter opener to the priest's throat and pressing its tip into the flaccid flesh, to the right of his Adam's apple. "Why don't the police come for us? Arrest us? Deport us?"

"If you want to continue living at the Sundial, be careful what you do next—"

She pricked him, producing a dollop of blood. It ran down the priest's neck until it reached his collar, spreading into the white fibers. "You are not the first man I've made bleed," she said.

"Please, think about what you're doing!"

"Tell me what arrangement you have with the police." She pressed the opener's point farther into his neck. It was like jabbing a pen into an inflated balloon. She knew his neck would burst like an opened valve with a little more pressure.

"There is no arrangement!"

"Stop lying," she said, needling his neck more, twisting the blade's point until more blood trickled. Killing him would be easy as slaughtering a chicken and she imagined how undetectable his blood would look seeping into the red carpet.

The priest's eyes were locked on hers. Alma wondered what he saw in her brown pools with green halos. Perhaps the emptiness she felt? Hollowed and heartbroken now that Criston was gone. Could he see it? Somewhere behind her severe glare, that she didn't fear prison or death or purgatory? Damnation had already come to her.

"Okay, okay," he said, exasperated. "Apartment twenty-two. You'll find answers there." Blood slipped down the opener's edge to Alma's finger. It was warm and oily.

"What about it?" Alma asked, releasing the priest.

He coiled back into the chair. "Go, see for yourself. But once you do, you can never set foot in this church again. What I've told you could ruin everything."

"If what you've told me is anything but the truth, then God help you."

"Oh, Miss Alma," he said, removing his bloodstained collar. "The only thing left now is God."

When Alma returned to the Sundial, she didn't encounter anyone, though she could sense eyes on her peering from behind curtains. Most residents at the Sundial had mastered the art of minding their business. They rarely asked one another about who they had been in their home countries. Everyone had given up something—status, career, a family. They were transients hoping to one day become citizens of a country they knew little about but had placed all their hopes in. There was a common yearning to remember where they came from and hold on to tradition, beliefs, and pride for who they were, even if their worlds had changed.

Alma hadn't worked at the janitorial company that morning and was certain she had sacrificed her job, which had been her only personal source of income for a year. Alma was paid five dollars an hour to clean office buildings throughout San Diego County, and the company's owner, a man she knew only as Mr. Rattler, paid her cash each week. She didn't bother explaining to him she'd lost her son. Rattler rarely remembered her name and reminded the workers that they were replaceable.

A note was tacked on Alma's door from the motel's manager—a reminder that her rent would be due in three days. She would have to go into her and Criston's savings to pay it. No longer would she have what he made at the gas station to help with expenses. She ripped the note from the door, went inside, and sat on her bed.

If Criston were to have a tombstone, she considered what it would say—*Beloved Son, Shining Light*? Old photos and texts had become precious now; she read them and sobbed. When she came to the last message Criston had sent her, she read it aloud:

"On my way home. Picked up pain haïtien."

Alma loved bread and coffee at breakfast, and she could see him like a shimmer in the dark, coming home after his shift as a gas station attendant, bread tucked under his arm, delighted to serve it to her in the morning.

Alma didn't trust the priest and couldn't fathom what she'd find in Apartment 22. She removed a long wooden box under her bed, opened it, and pulled a blade from its sheath. Alma's reflection showed clearly in its metal. It was a *manchèt*, often called a machete in the States.

In Haiti, it had been Alma's weapon of choice. She preferred it over a gun or knife, though she had used both in her line of work. The *manchèt* was decades older than her, passed down through generations. It was a humble weapon with a handle wrapped in crocodile skin, long, curved, and sharp. It had been used in revolutions, helped secure schools for children, kept bandits at bay, protected the wealthy, and later cleared an escape path through the dense jungle when men came to take Criston's life.

She slipped the blade back into its leather sheath, tied its braided strap around her waist, put on a long coat that best hid the weapon, and left the apartment.

Apartment 22 was located at the rear of the motel and faced a parking lot. When night fell, the lot became the site of fights, drug use, sex in cars. She and Criston only ventured to the rear of the motel in daylight, usually to throw garbage into the roach-infested dumpster or pour frying oil into the dirt.

It was five minutes to 2 P.M. She stood at the foot of the stairs leading to Apartment 22. Many of the Sundial's residents would begin making lunch soon, and she anticipated the smells of plantains, chicken adobo, stewed corn, and beef braised in mole. It always astonished her that the most delectable smelling dishes were made on two-burner stoves and ovens that couldn't fit most roast pans. Alma climbed the stairs to the unit, and when she reached the door, she stood in front, unsure of what to do next. The window's curtain was drawn, and she couldn't hear anyone inside, despite the thin doors and single-pane glass that made for cold, drafty nights. Alma felt uneasy and thought it best to watch and wait. She walked downstairs into the parking lot and waited near the dumpster. She debated returning to her apartment, believing 22 to be empty and the priest to have lied. Then she saw Ernesto carrying a grocery bag, walking from the front of the building. He went upstairs to Apartment 22 and knocked. The door opened, and he entered.

Alma continued to wait near the dumpster. When the boy appeared, he headed downstairs. She moved quickly, meeting the boy as he came down the last few steps. When Ernesto saw Alma, he stopped. She crouched down until their eyes met and said, "Hello again."

"Hello," Ernesto said, standing meekly in a windbreaker a size too small.

"Can I ask what you were doing in that apartment?"

"I make deliveries," he said.

"Is that your job?"

"People pay me to bring them things."

"What people?"

"I should go," he said, moving away from Alma. "I have more deliveries."

"Wait, please? Can you tell me who you gave the food to?"

Ernesto was hesitant and looked up toward Apartment 22. "I shouldn't."

"I promise, you won't get in trouble," Alma said. "But if someone in there needs help, we should help them, right? Just like you helped me when you took me to see my son."

Ernesto nodded. "I bring food to the sick girl."

"A sick girl lives there?"

"Yes."

"Do you think I can see her?"

"Why?" he asked.

"If she's sick, I'd like to help."

"Were you a doctor?" he asked. "I mean before you came here?"

"No, but I've helped many girls before. Many of them were sick."

"You have medicine? Can you make her better?"

"I can try," she said.

"All right," he said, overcoming his hesitation. "I believe you, Miss Alma." She followed Ernesto upstairs to Apartment 22. The boy knocked twice. Alma stood out of view. When the door opened, a man's voice said, "What is it, boy? You forget something?"

Ernesto lowered his head, didn't speak. Alma nudged the boy aside and pushed her way into the apartment.

A withered man with wrinkled brown skin stood disheveled, holding his pants to his waist with one hand and an unlit cigarette in the other. He was missing most of his teeth, save for two that poked up from his bottom gum. It reminded Alma of the fence pickets orphaned in the sand after flooding demolished her childhood home in Haiti.

"Who are you?" he asked. A baggy sweatshirt swallowed up his frail limbs. "You need to leave." He glared as if trying to see through smoke, and Alma thought his vision might be poor. She noticed a girl asleep on the single bed. Heavy makeup was on her face: red lipstick layered to a thick sheen. The apartment smelled of jasmine; a large yellow candle burned on the stove.

She looked back at the doorway, and Ernesto was gone. The frail man looked as if he wanted to retaliate but did nothing. "Don't move," she said, walking to the corner of the room where a video camera was mounted to a tripod. It looked older than one Criston had bought at the Sunday Swap Meet last year. Instead of a slot for a memory card, there was a chamber where a tape would go.

"What's wrong with the girl?" she asked.

"She's ill, has a condition."

"Why do you need a camera?"

"Please, leave. You're going to make it bad for all of us. No one comes into Apartment Twenty-Two without permission. That's the rule."

"Whose rule?" she asked, but the man didn't answer. "Where's her family?"

"Who the hell are you to be asking about her family? I told you to leave."

"Careful, old man," she said, raising her fist. "Tell me, where are her people?"

He began to sulk, then answered, "Deported."

"To where?"

"I don't know," he said. "Honduras, I think. I just watch her, that's it—"

"And who told you to watch her?"

"I can't tell you that. Please, I beg you, leave before you make things worse."

"No," she said, looking at the sleeping girl.

"There's nothing you can do, leave her," he said. "You'll only ruin your life."

"Be more concerned with yourself," she said, pulling her coat back to reveal the *manchèt* on her hip.

"You don't have to hurt me. I'm nobody—"

"Tell me why she's here."

"He makes me do this," he cried.

"Who makes you?"

"Please," he begged, his hands steepled as if he were praying. "I don't know his name, but he'll send me back to Cebu. I can't go back."

"Why isn't she waking up?"

"It's the medicine," he said. "All I do is give her the medicine, but I never touch her."

"Show me."

"Here." The man took a prescription bottle from the kitchen counter and handed it to Alma. At least twenty capsules were filled with white powder. The label was removed. She presumed the drug was powerful enough to keep the girl heavily sedated for what could have been hours.

"When will this *man* be back?"

"After sundown," he said. Fear had strangled his vocal cords, and he sounded hoarse. "The boy brings dinner. Then he comes, and I can go home."

"She never goes out?" she asked, setting the bottle on the counter.

"Never," he said. "Your accent . . ." He searched Alma's face, leaning forward, glaring. "You're Haitian."

"What?"

"Yes, it's you. I heard about your boy."

"What do you know about it?"

"My wife died six months ago," he said, growing misty-eyed. "I'm very sorry."

"And did she approve of you watching this girl?"

"The job came after," he said. "My body is broken, can't work in the factory anymore. Needed money to live."

"So you became this man's watchdog?"

"He said I only had to sit with the girl during the day."

"How old is she?"

"I don't know . . . I don't ask questions," he said. "I rarely talk to her and only do what he tells me." He put the cigarette to his lips and dug inside his pocket.

Alma's hand moved to the *manchèt*. "Easy," she said, watching the man closely. His hand shook terribly as he pulled out a lighter, worked his thumb over the spool until it produced a small flame.

"Please, believe me, I tried to help her," he said, lighting the cigarette and taking a drag. "I swear I did, but she wouldn't listen. Told me it was better than living on the streets . . . better than dying in the desert."

"She's going to leave this place," Alma said. "You're going to help me."

"But you don't understand—"

"I'm not giving you a choice." She pulled the *manchèt* from the sheath and held it high. The man backed away. "Do you see her? She's not yet a woman, just made to look like one."

The man gazed at the sleeping girl. The cigarette was a dangling branch of ash. "What was I supposed to do?"

"That's between you and God. Now tell me about the man."

"He comes and goes. Doesn't talk too much," he said. "Pays me, and I leave."

"Don't lie to me," she said. "There must be something." Her patience was wearing thin; she brought the *manchèt* to his neck, and he trembled.

"Wait. Wait," he said, pumping his hands. "I have something."

"What?"

"In the recorder."

Alma pressed a button on the camera, and the chamber opened. Inside was a small tape; she feared what was on it.

"You record for him?"

"He makes me sometimes . . ." The man took a step forward and reached for the camera. "Do you want to see? Should I play it?"

She gripped his hand tightly, then yanked it away. He seemed surprised by her strength or perhaps the ease with which she moved. Grabbing the man came easy for her, as did many things that involved force.

"I'll do it," she said, pressing the play button. Time-code appeared over black on the small three-inch screen. Then she saw the sleeping girl step into the frame. She was naked and small and climbed onto the bed. A man approached, only a white towel wrapped around his waist. His chest was specked gray and black, and his skin was blotchy and red. He was big, wide-shouldered, with a lapping belly. Alma recognized him instantly as the one who had killed her boy. He wrapped his arms around the girl, and she disappeared in his embrace.

"He has other tapes," he said in a husky whisper. "Many . . ."

"You should have given it to the police."

"The police? I would have been deported."

"Better than dying here."

"Dying?" he asked. "But I had no choice. I'm not a bad man—not like him."

Alma couldn't watch anymore. She stopped playing the tape, ejected it, and put it in her pocket. "You always have a choice," she said. Her heart was beating with ferocity. She knocked over the recorder and tripod. Pieces of plastic broke off onto the floor. The screen cracked, and the focus ring became dislodged from the housing. It was loud and violent, but the sleeping girl didn't wake.

"The man will come soon," he said. "He'll see the camera and want to know what happened."

"And then what?" she asked. "You think I should fear him?"

The man was silent.

"Those pills . . ." Alma snatched the pill bottle from the counter and rattled it. "You know what they are?"

"No," he said. "Makes the girl tired. She sleeps for hours."

Alma took off the cap and sniffed the capsules. They smelled metallic. "Leave before you join your wife."

He ashed his cigarette into the kitchen sink and moved toward the door. Alma followed close behind him. He opened it. She took hold of his arm in the doorway and spun him to face her. Alma stared at him as she had stared at many men before. Under different circumstances, she would have pushed the man from the landing and watched him fall to the concrete, but that would bring unnecessary attention.

"Please," he said, more afraid than before. "I'll do whatever you want."

"Go back to your apartment. Not a word to anyone."

"Yes," he said. "But what are you going to do?"

Alma didn't respond and looked to the sun. It was resplendent and flooded the desert with golden light. It glowed against her skin, and she was reminded of Criston's smile and how it made her feel safe, loved.

"What about the tape?" the man asked. "What will you do with it?"

"I don't know."

"Give it to me," he said. "Please, let me make it right."

"How?"

"I'll find a way."

Alma looked skeptical. "Now you're fearless?"

"The others . . . I never believed they could help her, but you—"

"Others?"

"Some her family, some strangers," he said. "Everyone was sent back to their countries beaten—even crippled."

"Take it," Alma said, handing the man the tape. "Now, go." He put it into his pocket, hobbled down the stairs, and didn't look back.

Alma waited by the dumpster. All she could think about was the girl in the apartment. Enslaved. Victimized. It could have been Alma's fate in Haiti had it not been for her mother, who taught her how to wield a blade and where to put it if a man ever came for her. She had lost count of the men her *manchèt* had blessed, but she remembered how it felt when she dug its tip into their thighs, penciled their groins, tattooed her initials deep so they'd never forget.

It was sundown; Alma had waited hours. She was tired and hungry. When Ernesto returned, he was carrying containers of food and bottled water. She watched him go upstairs and knock on the door to Apartment 22. "Is that food for the girl?" Alma called to him from the bottom of the stairs.

"Yes," the boy said, arms working hard to manage the containers. "Tacos."

"You can put it down," she said, walking up the stairs. "Don't take it in just yet."

"Did you help her?" Ernesto asked with worry as he placed the container on the step. "Is she better?"

"I'm trying." Alma crouched next to the food and opened both containers, which held refried beans, rice, and what looked like beef and chicken tacos. "The door is unlocked," she said. "Take this food to her." She handed him one of the containers. "I will tend to the other." Ernesto went into the apartment with the container while Alma opened the meal she set aside for the man. She removed capsules from the pill bottle and began opening them, pouring the powder into the food.

Ernesto returned minutes later. "Is she awake?" Alma asked as she poured the last of the white powder from the capsules into the beans.

"Yes," he said. "She's eating now. Where's the old man?"

"Gone."

He studied Alma for a moment. "I know what you're going to do," he said. He reminded her of Criston, precocious and astute. "Will it kill him?"

Alma had poured at least ten capsules into the container, folding the powder into the rice and beans with a plastic knife. "I hope so," she said. The boy looked on as she continued to stir the drug into the food.

"Can I watch?" he asked.

Alma's heart was heavy. "Him die?"

"Yes."

"Have you ever seen someone die?"

"No," Ernesto said.

"It stays with you . . . something you can't forget."

"Even if they deserve it?"

"Stays longer when they deserve it." She was disturbed by the boy's request but more so by her calm delivery. Her hands were steady as she prepared the man's last meal. "You're just a boy," she said. "Best to keep being that."

Ernesto's foot was fidgety, like he was kicking imaginary dust. "I lied before, Miss Alma . . . I saw when Criston was hit."

She reached out her hand, and Ernesto took it. "I know," she said. "It's all right."

He pulled away, putting his hands into his pockets, and looked on with curiosity. Alma closed the food container. "You should go home," she said.

Before leaving, Ernesto asked, "Who are you, Miss Alma?" Alma knew what the boy meant, but it was complicated. "I'm a mother."

"That makes you brave?"

"Maybe," she said.

"I don't like being afraid . . . I wish I could have helped her."

"You're helping her now," Alma said. The boy looked as if he were going to smile, then left.

Alma stepped into the apartment and set the man's food on the counter. She could see the girl better now. Her face told of the horror she was living. The drug had taken its toll: eyes drained of life, pain-filled.

"What are you doing in here?" the girl asked. "What do you want?"

"To help."

"Is that his food? Why do you have it?"

"I need him to eat it all," Alma said. "It's the only way you'll get out of here."

"What did you do to it?"

"The drug he's been giving you, I mixed it in."

"That will kill him, won't it?"

"Yes, I believe it will."

"Then what?" she asked, looking at the broken camera on the floor. "Where will I go?"

"You can come with me," she said. "I'm leaving this place."

"But I'm sick . . . he made me sick," the girl said. "I'm not good without the pills."

"I can get you to a doctor." Alma stood over the bed as the girl continued to eat. "And I can get us money."

"You'd do that?"

"Yes."

The girl looked at the alarm clock on the nightstand. "He comes soon, and he'll be drunk."

"All right."

"I have to get cleaned up. He gets angry if I don't smell good." The girl pushed the food aside and slowly scooted to the edge of the bed. She slipped her feet into beach sandals and stretched her arms above her head. The oversized shirt looked more like a nightgown and poorly hid the bruises on her arms and thighs.

"What's your name?" Alma asked.

"Carina."

"You?"

"Call me Alma. He'll need to eat everything, Carina—every bit of it."

"He will. Always does." Carina went into the bathroom and began brushing her teeth.

"I'll be outside," Alma said. "It may take some time before . . ."

Carina spat the white foam into the sink. "It's just one more night," she said somberly. "Did the boy tell you about me? Is that why you came?"

"No," Alma said. "I didn't know. If I did . . ."

"You would have been sent away like my family . . . he deported everyone who tried to help me."

"He has that power?"

"Homeland Security," she said. "I've seen his badge." Carina cupped water into her hands and drank. She swished it around in her mouth. "He's here," she said before spitting out the water.

"That's his truck's engine." A backfire followed a faint clamor. "You have to go."

Alma quickly walked to the door, then stopped short of opening it. "I'll be back in an hour," she said.

"Okay," Carina said, spritzing her skin with cheap-smelling perfume. "An hour."

As Alma walked downstairs, she saw the truck that had hit Criston parked and the Homeland Security officer getting out. She was sure to keep out of sight, moving to the other end of the landing, away from Apartment 22. She peeped around the corner as he stumbled. As Carina had predicted, he was drunk and dressed in jeans and a flannel shirt. He fiddled with his keys while slurring, muttering to himself. Alma watched him climb to the top of the stairs, taking bold, reckless steps, and thought—a just God would see that he tripped to the bottom, neck snapped. Then, she wouldn't have to take matters into her own hands. But as long as she could remember, justice came without divinity; rather, it took a woman's dedicated hand.

The hour passed quickly, and Alma found herself standing outside the door of Apartment 22. A woman and man were arguing in the parking lot near a rusted van. The air smelled of marijuana. The two were cursing, throwing beer bottles. She couldn't hear a sound from inside the apartment.

Alma knocked gently and waited with her hand on her *manchèt*'s handle. She knocked again, slightly harder, and the door opened. Carina stood draped in a blanket. The color was gone from her face. Alma stepped into the apartment and saw the man sitting shirtless in a chair. He was a mass of pink flesh, bloated and greasy. Next to him was the empty container of food.

"She told me everything," he said, barely able to speak. "You're both dead." His breathing was wispy. Sweat poured from his brow, and his legs shook uncontrollably. He tried to stand but fell back into the chair.

"I wanted him to know," Carina said, holding the man's cell phone in one hand, "so he knew what was happening to him."

Alma picked up the man's pants at the foot of the bed. She dug into the pockets, removed his wallet, flipped it open to his driver's license. "Thadius Wayne Jackson," she said.

"I'm a cop . . ." Jackson coughed. "You did this to a cop."

"You were police . . . a murderer . . . and a rapist."

He coughed again, nearly fell from the chair. "Carina," he said. "Please, baby? I love you. Don't do this to me."

"Love?" Alma shook her head, remembering all the men in her village who had claimed love for women they brutalized.

Jackson's breathing worsened, along with the shaking. His face contorted into something horrid and *baby* became *bitch*. "You goddamn bitch!" he said, foaming at the mouth. Alma had seen men make these types of faces, working desperately to drown out fear with rage. She was certain those men like Jackson became seething beasts in the afterlife.

After Jackson had what Alma presumed was a seizure, he slipped from the chair onto the floor. There were more convulsions. Then his body was still, and Alma knew he was dead.

She found a bottle of bleach, filled the kitchen sink, and submerged Jackson's cell phone. Then, she and Carina left the apartment and walked to Alma's unit as if nothing had happened. Carina showered and changed into Criston's clothes: sweatpants and a T-shirt. As Carina slept in Criston's bed, Alma listened for sirens, wondering if anyone would find Jackson and care enough to call the police. But the night was quiet, and Alma soon fell asleep.

In the morning's light and without makeup, Carina looked slightly younger than Criston. Alma served her bread and milk and watched as she devoured four loaves, stopping at the fifth when she began to feel ill. Alma knew it wasn't because she was full of bread, but her body was craving the drugs and her withdrawal would need to be managed. She served her a hearty black tea and Carina seemed to improve.

After breakfast, they packed the car with as much as it would fit, and she drove to St. Francis. She marched into the priest's chambers. "I want to see my son," she said. "Take me to his body."

"You can't barge in here," the priest said from behind his desk. "I told you never to come back."

"I went to Apartment Twenty-Two." Alma looked to Carina as she stood wearing Criston's hoodie and pants; she had cuffed the legs so they fit better. "He kept her there drugged, but you knew that, didn't you?"

He stammered. "Of course not," he said. "This is terrible. We should call the police!"

"You know we can't do that . . . but that's why you sent me there, isn't it? You wanted to be rid of me. Maybe you hoped I'd be deported or worse?" In his eyes, Alma saw no shame or remorse. "How long have you owned the Sundial?" she asked.

"Oh, Miss Alma," he snickered. "I've misjudged you."

"I've known too many men like you," she said. "Unholy men that breathe to exploit and corrupt everything they touch."

Carina locked the door.

"Are you too blind to see that I'm the only reason you had a roof over your heads . . . the only reason *you* people can live safely in this country?"

"Safely? You preyed on us. Took our pennies to live in that slum, corrupted the gospel while letting a cop do whatever he wanted to a defenseless girl."

"What do you want?" he asked in a cold sweat.

"You're going to give us money," Alma said. "Enough for us to get out of town, and tomorrow morning, my son will be buried in the church's cemetery, as promised."

"And if I don't?"

She pulled the *manchèt* from its sheath. "I pick up where I left off."

The priest touched his neck, feeling the scar left behind by Alma's last visit. He opened his desk drawer, removed a metal box. "I see now . . . you are the monster you confessed to being." He unlocked the box with a brass key. Inside, he took out a stack of bills. He handed them to Alma, and she put the money into her coat pocket. "This is all I can offer you. As for Criston's remains, they are in the basement. He'll be buried tomorrow as you wish, then I want the both of you gone from the Sundial and this town."

Alma and Carina followed the priest downstairs to the basement, where a makeshift coffin was surrounded by clutter: boxed paper goods and crates of wine.

"Leave when you're done," the priest said. "And God help you."

Alma ignored him and opened the coffin. She nearly collapsed at the sight of Criston. Carina came to her aid, took her hand, gripped it tight, and together they cried until Alma felt strong again. "That was his favorite sweatshirt," Alma said, running her hands down the arm of Carina's hoodie. It was stained with her tears.

"I'd like to know more about him," Carina said. "I feel like he saved my life . . ."

"Yes," Alma said, smiling. "I suppose in a way he did." She touched her son's hand. His skin felt like a thin sheet of wax, slightly moist.

"Can I ask you something?"

"All right."

"Why did you leave Haiti?"

Alma swallowed hard. "My son fell in love," she said, "with a boy who was very dear to him. But those in our village saw their love as unconsecrated."

"What happened?"

"The church condemned them, and Criston's lover was murdered. He was probably no older than you are now."

"I'm so sorry."

"That night we fled for America," she said, still looking at her son's body, wistfully. "Seems like all I've ever known is death."

Carina touched Alma's cheek and she flinched. "Maybe it doesn't have to be that way anymore?"

"I pray for something better," she said, resting her cheek in the girl's warm palm.

Outside the church, they stood shielding their eyes from the desert wind. A storm was forming in the distance. Dark clouds were closing in; the sun had disappeared. Alma remembered what the priest said about Revelations. For a moment, she wondered if he was right—had God come to turn off the lights? Then she thought of her son, how his love made her worst days bearable—how he gave her hope and perhaps sent Carina to her so she could be a mother again, and she prayed for more time . . .

They got into the car and started down the road, driving away from St. Francis. Ahead of them, dust kicked up in the distance as police cars approached. Red and blue lights, blaring sirens. Carina took Alma's hand and looked at her, but Alma said nothing. When their eyes finally met, Carina said, "Thank you."

They continued to drive, Alma picking up speed, hand in hand into the storm . . .

The editors, Gary Phillips and Gar Anthony Haywood, wanted to put together a story collection that honored the courage of teenager Darnella Frazier, who filmed the homicide of George Floyd. The collection aimed to spotlight characters who witness injustice and take a stand. When considering the plot and setting, I called upon my time working with immigrant populations, specifically refugees and asylees in San Diego. I wanted to pen a story that looked at the complexities that undocumented people face, especially when victimized. As an extremely vulnerable population, justice often eludes them. They are routinely preyed upon and exploited. For Alma, the protagonist in the story, the killing of her son by a drunk driver who avoids prosecution leads her to a young girl in peril. Unable to turn a blind eye, Alma is determined to get justice for the girl and her son by any means necessary.

A former journalist, folk singer, and attorney, **Jeffery Deaver** *is an international number-one bestselling author. His novels have appeared on bestseller lists around the world, including* The New York Times, The Times of London, *Italy's* Corriere della Sera, The Sydney Morning Herald, *and the* Los Angeles Times. *His books are sold in one hundred fifty countries and translated into twenty-five languages.*

He has served two terms as the president of the Mystery Writers of America, which also recently named him a Grand Master.

The author of forty-five novels, multiple collections of short stories, and a nonfiction law book, and a lyricist of a country-western album, he's received or been short-listed for dozens of awards. His The Bodies Left Behind *was named Novel of the Year by the International Thriller Writers association, and his Lincoln Rhyme thriller* The Broken Window *and a stand-alone,* Edge, *were also nominated for that prize, as was a short story published recently. He has been awarded the Steel Dagger and the Short Story Dagger from the British Crime Writers' Association and the Nero Award, and he is a three-time recipient of the Ellery Queen Readers Award for Best Short Story of the Year and a winner of the British Thumping Good Read Award.* Solitude Creek *and* The Cold Moon *were both given the number one ranking by* Kono Misurteri Ga Sugoi *in Japan. The Cold Moon was also named the Book of the Year by the Mystery Writers Association of Japan. In addition, the Japanese Adventure Fiction Association awarded* The Cold Moon *and* Carte Blanche *their annual Grand Prix award. His book* The Kill Room *was awarded the Political Thriller of the Year by Killer Nashville. And his collection of short stories* Trouble in Mind *was nominated for best anthology by that organization as well. His most recent novel,* The Never Game, *was named one of the top ten crime books of the year by* The New York Times.

Deaver has been honored with the Lifetime Achievement Award by the Bouchercon World Mystery Convention and by the Raymond Chandler Lifetime Achievement Award in Italy. The Strand Magazine also has presented him with a Lifetime Achievement Award. Deaver has been nominated for eight Edgar Awards from the Mystery Writers of America, an Anthony, a Shamus, and a Gumshoe. He was shortlisted for the ITV3 Crime Thriller Award for Best International Author. Roadside Crosses *was on the shortlist for the Prix Polar International 2013. He's also been shortlisted for a Shamus.*

His book A Maiden's Grave *was made into an HBO movie starring James Garner and Marlee Matlin, and his novel* The Bone Collector *was a feature release from Universal Pictures, starring Denzel Washington and Angelina Jolie. Lifetime aired an adaptation of his* The Devil's Teardrop. *NBC aired a TV series based on the Lincoln Rhyme books, called* Lincoln Rhyme: Hunt for the Bone Collector. *His Colter Shaw thriller* The Never Game *will be a CBS prime time show later this year.*

Readers can visit his website at jefferydeaver.com.

DODGE

Jeffery Deaver

*T*he phone chimes like a knife-tapped glass.
Not loud but enough to waken.
A text.
The message is simple:

Back off—Last warning.

Below is the black triangle of an attached sound recording.
A pause and then it downloads and plays.
First the scream, then the woman's voice. "No, please . . . No . . . Kill me! Please. Just—"
A final scream and the recording ends.

WEDNESDAY, APRIL 5

Today would be out of the ordinary.

He was looking forward to it.

Cautiously.

The twenty-nine-year-old deputy pulled his somber-gray squad car into the strip mall parking lot, slowed to a stop and looked around him, past the parents shopping now that the children were in classrooms, past DIYers loading paint and Sheetrock into their pickups, past the skinny truant teens clustered together, aimless, faces sporadically obscured by dense masses of vaping steam.

A few glances his way.

Always, with the car. Always, with a man in a Sheriff's Office uniform, crew cut, unsmiling, brown eyes that "meant business," he'd been told, though by a drunk he was arresting for public urination so the observation was a bit suspect.

What's he up to? the people here would be wondering.

Shoplifters? A fight? An arrest was always good to video and upload to TikTok, even if it didn't result in nearly as many views or likes as one would want. Supply and demand.

Deputy Anthony Lombardi noticed the man waving, eight rows away.

He steered in that direction, then pulled into a space facing Dollar General.

Lombardi killed the engine and climbed out.

The two men met on the sidewalk in front of the store. "Marshal Greene?"

They shook hands and Greene displayed an ID and a badge; it was a silver star, like what old-time sheriffs wore, in the movies at least. No need for Lombardi to flash anything; his Sheriff's Office uniform, along with a name tag, said it all. There was the squad car too.

Edward Greene was of medium build—if he'd done a college sport it would've been baseball. He was dressed in a dark suit, white shirt, dark blue tie. Neatly trimmed dark hair. Carefully shaven, as, Lombardi supposed, all marshals had to be. A serious face and still, brown eyes—which most definitely meant business.

"Welcome to Upper Falls. Or you can call it what we do: just the Falls."

"Looks like a lovely place." Greene had a lilt to his voice situating him somewhere in the South, though a few years ago.

Lombardi chuckled. "Parts are. Yessir." He had been a Harbinger County Sheriff's Office deputy since the army. Unlike some of his coworkers, even at this age, he was in basic-training shape. One hundred seventy-three pounds on his six-foot frame.

He had a full head of brown hair and a face that looked like that of an actor on a prime-time police or hospital show. Not the lead but serving a role to advance important plot developments every third episode or so.

"Now, Deputy—"

"Let's make it Tony, how about?"

He said this automatically, then wondered if it was it okay to go first name.

Apparently so.

A nod. "And I'm Ed. I need a pit stop and refill. Where's good for coffee?"

Lombardi stabbed a slim finger at Maggie's.

He could use some caffeine too. He hadn't fallen asleep until the wee hours because he kept thinking about the Sheriff's phone call at nine P.M.—the special assignment.

Out of the ordinary . . .

They walked into the bright place, just past bustling hour, and were assaulted by a tidal wave of smells. Fry fat predominated.

Greene hit the restroom while Lombardi took a booth. When the marshal returned they ordered coffee. He asked, "Anything else? Uncle Sam's buying."

Lombardi was hesitating, as if eating would seem unprofessional in the eyes of a law enforcer who would be, the deputy felt, superior to him in all respects.

Then the marshal rapped the laminated menu. "How about burgers all around? You're in a diner you eat diner food. Though I'll bet the mac 'n' cheese isn't bad."

"Burgers're better. The mac can be gluey."

Spry Kate, in her seventies, poured the coffee and took the order, then headed to the kitchen.

Sipping, Greene nodded. "Yessir. That *is* fine. Now, Tony, let me explain what I'm here for. And we'll see where you stand."

Odd phrasing. "All right." And he stepped on the "sir," before it peeked out.

Lombardi lifted the mug. Greene too, like they were toasting. Ceramic did not meet ceramic.

"Did your sheriff brief you?" Greene asked.

"Some. There's a manhunt. You're covering this part of the state and could use somebody local."

A nod. "Pretty much. Now, the Marshal's Office, it's sort of a grab bag. We guard federal judges and transport prisoners. Then there's the Witness Security Program. What I do. You know, whistleblowers, people who testify against the mob and cartels."

Lombardi and Jess liked their true crime shows. He didn't think there'd been a show about the US Marshals. It could be a good one.

Greene continued, "I got this one family set up, new identities, new home, after the husband testified in Chicago—he was a bookkeeper and got the FBI some spreadsheets that brought down a big drug ring."

Lombardi's face grew still. It was clear where this was going.

The marshal's hands encircled the mug. "An assistant in our department? She was kidnapped and tortured and gave up the location." Greene hesitated. "Everybody breaks. Just a matter of time. Joanne worked for us six years. Married, children." He stopped speaking before his voice cracked, which it was just about to do.

"Sorry to hear that."

"Yeah." Nearly a whisper.

The burgers landed and, without ketchup or other doctoring, Greene started eating, small bites. The tough story about his assistant had dampened his appetite, it was clear. Still, he nodded his approval. "Place must be an institution."

"From miles around." Lombardi turned his patty yellow and red, then cut the sandwich in half, which he always did, and then ate too, more slowly. He and Jess had talked about when the kids arrived: they'd make sure mealtimes lasted a while. They'd talk about their days—their jobs and school, the news, anything. Like on *Blue Bloods*, at the end of each show.

Then: Stay on this, he told himself. Focus.

Wiping his lips with a napkin, Greene continued, "So, there it is. I lost a coworker, and my witness and his wife. I'd become friends with them. A lot of the people we protect, they're just assholes. Mob, petty criminals. But these were good, solid folk."

Lombardi started on the second portion of his burger. The fries were vanishing too. He ate them with a knife and fork to make them last. Maggie's was known for its fries.

"So I dropped everything. Told my bosses, this's all I'm working on, finding their killer. Didn't have any luck for weeks but then I get a lead from a CI . . ." He hesitated.

"Confidential informant."

"That the perp's here in Upper Falls. And he tells me something else. The killer's found out I'm full-time on the case now and's going to do whatever it takes to stop me. See, I have kind of a reputation: I never stop till the perp's collared."

"So he's gunning for you at the same time you're gunning for him."

"That's it, Deputy. Except for one thing: The killer's not a 'he.'"

"You seen this man?"

She flashed her phone at the bartender. He looked up with a vaguely out of alignment expression. He was a tall blond of an age somewhere between thirty and fifty. He clearly partook of the wares he sold.

He looked first at her gray eyes and then at the phone, his face ill at ease.

Constant Marlowe was still as a cat eying an unfortunate sparrow.

Studying the picture. "No."

"Look again."

He did. "No."

She lowered the phone. "I saw him walk out the front door here ten minutes ago." Her voice was low and more raspy than usual.

He wasn't happy that she'd snagged him in a lie, with her trap. He decided to ignore her and returned to dunking glasses in a glass-dunking soapy water thing.

Marlowe said, "Let's try it again. The truth. I'm going to show you another picture, another man." She leaned forward a bit more. "And I don't have time for bullshit."

She was on a tight timetable.

Was he wondering if he was in physical danger? Probably not. The gaunt woman was five six and one hundred twenty pounds and not toting a kitchen knife or axe, and the bartender would surely have some defenses against the creepy meth crowd wandering through Upper Falls like bit players in a zombie movie. At least there'd be a fish-knocking club under the bar, and likely a firearm.

Still, somebody'd once said she was a walking high-tension wire, and you never knew when crazy might rear. She'd be telegraphing some of this now.

"Look, Miss . . ."

She displayed the shot. The dark-haired man in the image was in his forties, wearing a suit jacket and tie-less white shirt. A good-looking, if nondescript businessman. He was gazing off to the side and didn't appear to know he was being photographed. The Chicago lakefront was in the background.

He studied this one hard. Maybe she'd go away. "No. I don't think so. I can tell you he's not a regular."

"No. He wouldn't be. He's not local. I'm just asking if you saw him here, or maybe around town."

He sighed. "No, lady. Haven't seen anybody like that. You know, it's policy you don't order anything you gotta leave." Clearly he was hoping she'd be forced out on this technicality. He took to studying the hot water once more.

Pale afternoon light bled through the smeared and fly-dotted windows of what called itself a tap room, in which were twenty tables and six patrons.

"When does the next bartender come on?"

"Okay. I really gotta ask you to go."

"A Coke, Pepsi." She put a fifty down.

Another sigh. "I can't change that."

"Not asking you to. Take a look at the picture again."

He glanced behind her. "Keep your money. It's on the house. Drink up and leave. Please. There's a restaurant up the street, out the door. You turn right, you can't miss it. Odie's Café. Maybe you'll have some luck there. And the pies can't be beat."

He looked back to the suds when her expression made clear she didn't give shit about pie.

Two stools down was a heavy man, who looked sixty but was probably younger. She walked up to him, showed him the phone and was about to speak.

"No, no, no." A voice from behind.

She cut her eyes to the mirror, past the bottles of low- to mid-brand booze. It was as neglected as the windows. She saw the big man who'd spoken. A bouncer.

Marlowe turned, leaving the patron at the bar to gloom over his whiskey, and the bartender to soap and swizzle and rack glassware. There was nothing else to clean. It may have been near lunchtime but none of the patrons was eating lunch.

She looked over who'd approached and thought: lumberjack. He was big, six one or so, and two hundred ten or twenty. He was in black jeans, flecked with dots of yellow—pollen time in the region. His black boots were scuffed. And the lumberjack impression was inevitable, as he was wearing an honest-to-God red-and-black plaid flannel shirt. He had a broad, creased face and his teeth were smoker stained.

Marlowe looked behind him at the table where he'd been sitting, along with two slighter men, one in dress slacks and a shirt, the other in jeans and a hoodie. They were, like everyone else here, white. And any coloration to the skin came from bottles, not the sun. She'd noted the beverages of choice. For a tap room, Hogan's apparently sold a lot more hard liquor than draft beer.

Before he could speak again, she asked, "Who are you?" Belligerent. A quality she could toss but usually had no desire to.

"A manager."

He stood close, just inside that circle of comfort we can't define in terms of inches but all recognize. She didn't step back but just looked up into his face. Bourbon overcame his cloying aftershave, but just barely.

His brown eyes did the Scan: her dark red and brunette ponytailed hair, her pale forehead, on which was a three-inch scar, her black leather jacket, which was unzipped, her white tee, dotted with a few faint stains, blue jeans and black ankle boots that might have come from the same Chinese cobbling factory as his.

His eyes returned, a brief hiccup, to her chest. Given her build, men's gazes often lingered. Constant Marlowe had spent thirty-two years on this busy earth. There were many, many other things worth getting riled about.

And here, beneath the Hanes T, was the most unappealing of Nike sports bras. Who could figure?

"I'm looking for this man." She displayed the picture. He glanced but gave no reaction.

"Better you leave."

"I paid for a drink. Or tried to."

"Nup, better you leave, little lady."

No worries about this either. She called men "dicks" and "pricks" and "assholes" about as often as someone lobbed a corresponding phrase her way.

She clicked an exasperated tongue and walked to the other occupied table—two paunchy, gray-complected men—and held out the phone for them in one hand. The fifty, which she'd picked up from the bar, was in the other. "Can you tell me if you've seen—"

"No." Lumberjack had followed and now gripped her arm.

He didn't say the b-word or the c-word, insults that were as meaningless to her as the sentence, "Have a nice day."

But he touched.

That made a difference.

Like a striking snake, she ripped her arm away, slammed her elbow into his forearm, and knocked it back. He winced and blinked in surprise. The audience stirred.

"Rudy," the bartender said. "Just, no. Don't—"

Lumberjack Rudy's palm shot out. "Yo, dog. Quiet." He stepped back and stared down at her. A cold smile blossomed.

"That's not going to do, little lady. Out you go." His powerful fist encircled her biceps once more and this time he turned and shifted his weight to deflect or stop elbows cold. He started to guide her out the door.

This stopped fast when her Smith & Wesson Bodyguard .380 appeared, jammed under his chin. She carried it in a battered leather holster, held taut between the Walmart jeans and the silver Victoria's Secret briefs.

"Oh, shit."

Gasps from the patrons.

"No," she said calmly.

He released her arm and stepped back, lifting his palms. "Just go your way. All good."

She stepped back and looked around the room. The table men had stood. She said, "Sit," and they sat.

The bartender looked at the phone.

Marlowe said, "You really want the cops in here?"

It was Rudy who shook his head, and the bartender returned to suds.

Cops were the last thing she wanted here too.

She looked Lumberjack over. He was no longer shocked or intimidated. The sneery smile had returned.

"You have a piece?"

"Sure don't."

"Tug it up, turn around."

He hesitated, then decided her eyes meant she was wild enough to pull the trigger.

High-tension . . .

He grimaced and did as told. She pulled from his unpleasantly sweaty waistband the small semiauto, an Italian .25. Her Smittie was small too but in her hand it didn't look silly—the way this weapon would in his.

She said to the bartender, "You have anything underneath?"

"Baseball bat is all." His voice trembled. "Look, I don't want any trouble."

Keeping the gun on Rudy, she walked to the table he'd been sitting at and said to his two companions, "Stand up. Up with *your* shirts. They did. Neither was armed. She nodded at the chairs and they settled.

She glanced at the other three patrons. And knew they were clean. You get a feel.

Looking Rudy up and down. Broad shoulders, meaty hands. Strong, yes. But a fair measure of his bulk was the sort that arises when you start drinking whiskey around noon.

She went to her backpack, which she'd set on the floor when she'd entered. From inside she extracted a gray bag that looked like a pocketbook a woman in the 1950s might carry, a clutch. It was made of carbon fiber, nearly impossible to cut open. Marlowe worked the combination lock at one end and unzipped it. Into this went his gun.

And then hers.

She sealed up the bag and clicked the lock.

Constant Marlowe, now in a mood, had just taken weapons off the table.

Rudy's face tightened, perplexed.

She then removed her jacket and set it on the barstool. On one arm was a tattoo of a hawk's head. On the other, the letters DK.

"You touched me twice without consent. Now, I'm consenting." She balled up her fists, dropped into the stance.

"You're kidding." With a smile, Rudy glanced back at the table to where his friends sat. "She's kidding."

They were not smiling. He was a bully and she was unhinged. This could go bad in several ways.

"Seriously? I'm not going to hit a girl."

Too damn much talk in this world.

Marlowe moved in fast and launched a stunning uppercut with her left. His head snapped back and he tottered, while she danced away, out of range.

Rudy blinked. Astonishment held off the fury, though only for a few seconds.

His friends rose.

Both Rudy and Marlowe barked, "No!" They sat.

Now came the c-word, snarled out.

She stepped back to let him rip off his lumberjack shirt. He, too, had a tee on underneath and, for that matter, his chest was noteworthy, though not as muscular as it had once been.

He plunged forward, swinging wildly.

She zipped away, back and sideways. She'd memorized the position of the tables.

Footwork, always footwork . . .

A high feint and, when his arms went up, she sent a forceful jab into the left portion of his gut. He grunted.

Rudy was clearly an enforcer but one who enforced with threats and guns and pipes. Never his fists, it was obvious. He hadn't been in a fight for a while, maybe he'd never been in a real one. Probably it was all push and shove and sneer and insult, like on the schoolyard. And watch all the boxing and mixed martial arts videos you want, you'll never learn a single thing from the tube.

His meaty paw caught her on the shoulder. It had inertia and she staggered back. The blow ached; it didn't sting. In boxing the difference was significant.

He reminded her of a prison guard once who thought her bulk and muscle were all she needed to put Marlowe down. They went at it for a while, the blows furious, until Marlowe got bored and finished it with a series of lightning jabs. She wasn't the least winded—and those were the days when she smoked.

Enjoying his shoulder success, he tried it again. Could he possibly be surprised when, expecting it, she dodged and delivered a left hook to his jaw? Spit flew. Arms sagged.

When defenses are down, never, ever wait.

A combination uppercut and jabs to the abdomen.

It wasn't enough to incapacitate a big man, so she escaped out of reach quickly.

"Jesus." In fury, he pounced, trying some kind of weird Chuck Norris move. She easily stepped aside and Rudy backed up fast when she crouched again and swayed left and right, ready to strike.

He had strength, but no strategy, in a sport where strategy was vital.

Her blows concentrated on the face and solar plexus—the only two targets that would do any good. Hitting him elsewhere was like slugging a side of meat, wasting energy.

The one thing she had to be careful of—where he could do some damage—was grabbing her shirt, controlling her movement, and swinging at her face or getting her in a chokehold. He tried this several times. There was no rule that prohibited grabbing and choking. No rules at all, other than hers: they couldn't shoot each other.

But she managed to avoid the groping claws.

His unfocused bounding and flailing were taking their toll. Rudy was now breathing hard and the lunges were slower. His behavior fit the pattern she was oh-so-familiar with: a man, twice her size, getting beaten by a "girl." He was embarrassed and furious, two emotions that have no business in a fight. They gave birth to an even worse liability: desperation.

Then, thinking once more of the urgency of her mission here in Upper Falls, she decided it was time.

Marlowe eased in, quarter turned to the right and when he tried to grab her—now a laughably predictable maneuver—she swiveled and came back with a roundhouse right to his nose.

Two back-to-back left and right jabs into the gut. Without the slick surface of gloves hitting skin, bare-knuckle fights were largely silent. This particular assault was punctuated with his noisy grunts.

Rudy went down to his knees and Marlowe bounded back once more, though this time it was solely to avoid getting puked on. All things considered, the blows had been tame—she didn't want to rupture anything—but when they joined the whiskey the result was inevitable.

The utter silence that followed his retching was broken by words behind her.

"Well, that didn't last long."

The man stood in the back of the room. He'd emerged from a doorway. He was wearing a nice suit, a rich navy-blue one, and a light pink dress shirt, open at the collar. Oxford shoes, brown. He was about fifty, squat and fat. Hair red, face round and freckled. He didn't get outside much either.

She went to the bar, pulled her jacket back on. "Water."

"Ice?"

Marlowe didn't answer but gave him a look. He slid the glass toward her, ice-free, worried he'd gotten it wrong.

She drank half down. Then opened the clutch bag, got her gun out and tucked it away. Rudy's went into her pocket.

The round man said to the men at Rudy's table, "Get him home."

They rose quickly.

Marlowe said, "Tell him his gun'll be in one of the trash cans outside. He can figure out which one."

"Yes, ma'am." Hoodie frowned, wondering if this word fell into the same bad-call category as "little lady."

They walked to Rudy and helped him up. The lumberjack was muttering something. Maybe explaining that she'd cheated, took advantage of the fact she was a woman.

The redheaded man in the back, nodding at the mess on the floor, said to the bartender, "Clean that up."

"Yessir."

To Marlowe, the man asked, "So who are you?"

The bartender said, "She was—"

"I wasn't talking to you, Des."

"No, sir."

The big man sat at the just-vacated table. She joined him.

"I was watching." He nodded to the ceiling. A camera.

"You need better security guards."

A sigh. "Man is a trial. He's my half-brother. From my mother's third marriage."

Marlowe had no interest in dissecting weird genealogy. "You're—?"

"Wexler. Tomas Wexler." He added that he was the owner. "What did he do to you? Rudy?"

"He touched me."

"But you *were* bothering my clientele."

She scoffed. The only thing these barflies would be bothered by was a short pour.

He seemed to get it and gave a faint smile of concession.

Out came her phone. "I'm looking for this man."

Wexler glanced at the screen, shook his head.

She sighed, slipped the mobile away. She looked over the room slowly, left to right, up and down. "You own a place like this, I'm guessing you're . . . Connected." Emphasis on the word.

"Some."

"And I assume you and the police or deputies or whatever passes for law here aren't best of friends."

"That would be a correct assumption."

"You help me find him, it'll be worth five K."

A reddish eyebrow involuntarily rose. Surprise vanished, replaced by business.

"Half up front. Nonrefundable. Give me his particulars and I'll see what I can do."

She reached into her backpack and dug around the cluttered interior until she found an envelope of cash. She counted out the bills and slid them over.

Wexler asked, "So, this man, what do you want him for?"

Rather than explain that she'd come to Upper Falls, Wisconsin, to murder him, Marlowe said only, "That's my business. Yours is to take the money and not ask questions."

"You don't hear much about a woman doing that."

"No, you don't," US Marshal Ed Greene offered absently. He'd lost his taste for food. The remaining half of the burger and most of the fries sat intact.

Tony Lombardi wanted the rest of his own lunch but thought it would look bad, him scarfing down the food. "Women, breaking the law, you think of them abusing their kids or shooting a cheating husband. Not torturing people."

Greene displayed an iPad.

On it was a security camera image of a woman in her early thirties. She had thick hair, red and brown, pulled into a tight ponytail. She was in jeans, a sweatshirt, and a well-worn black leather jacket. Boots. Crouching at the door of a small warehouse, she held a pistol.

"Rival crew's stash. She was hired to torch it. Which she did. Then shot one of the minders in the knee. Didn't have to. She just did."

"What's her name?"

"Constant Marlowe. Not 'Constance.' 'Constant.'"

"Never heard of that," Lombardi said. "That a scar on her forehead?"

"That's right."

She was pretty despite that. Maybe it made her prettier.

"What's her story?"

"From what I hear, the wiring's off. She's just, well, *bad*. A sociopath. In juvie a half-dozen times before she was eighteen. She was a boxer for a while. Good but she got banned—ignored the ref too much. At the gyms she made some contacts, Mob and some of the bigger indie crews. She started doing odd jobs. It worked out: nobody suspects a woman's going to kill. That's how she got close to my assistant.

"So, the boxing? She can kick ass. And she's a good shot. She parked three a few inches from my head at fifty feet when I was following up on a tip. Only it was a setup to take me out."

"Fifty feet? A handgun?"

"Yep."

Pistols were nowhere near as accurate as movies made them out to be.

Greene lifted an eyebrow. "I by rights should not be here now."

Lombardi had never been shot at and he'd never fired his own weapon in his seven years with the HCSO. Drawn but not fired.

"Are you sure she's after you?"

Greene was silent for a moment. "About a week ago I got a message late at night. A text. She told me to back off. It was her last warning." He hesitated. Then: "And she attached a recording she'd made of Joanne while she was torturing her."

"Oh, my Lord." Now Lombardi's gut twisted again, and he wondered if he'd be sick.

No. *Control it, Deputy.* He did.

"Back off," Greene whispered, shaking his head. Then he focused again. "Okay, Tony. This brings us to the crux of the matter. She's decided to have our—what would you call it?—"

The deputy suggested, "Showdown? Like in the streets of Dodge, some old Western."

Greene smiled, pleasing Lombardi. "I like that. Gunfighters . . . Okay, we know she's here in the county somewhere. The plan's like any other manhunt. You and me, with a little luck, we find her. Call in backup from your outfit, tactical. Or WSP. We collar her and that's that. But—"

"The wrinkle is she's hunting for you too."

A nod. "Right. Now, why I called your sheriff: I don't know this area and I need somebody local. I want it to be you. I like the cut of your jib."

Something about sailing, he believed, but didn't want to ask. Obviously a compliment.

"But you have to know there's a risk. I understand if you want to pass."

So this was the We'll-see-where-you-stand part.

Lombardi thought about his past week: Three DUIs, one domestic, two shopliftings, a naked crazy man, processing a meth OD, and a missing six-year-old found in eighteen minutes. Oh, and volunteering for the Benevolent Association's pancake breakfast, where he was pretty talented at the griddle.

"I'm in." he said. And surprised himself—and apparently the marshal too—by sticking out his hand to shake, as if they'd just come to mutually acceptable terms on a used car.

Some days he liked the uniform, other days he didn't.

This was a didn't day.

Marshal Ed Greene looked every inch the investigator. Which is what Anthony Lombardi wanted to be someday, of course. The man's suit was dark and rich, the starched shirt white as a cumulonimbus. The blue of the tie was like the sash worn by the European general in a movie he and Jess had seen recently.

As they walked into the parking lot, he wondered if he, too, should dress plain-clothed. But wasn't sure he should ask about it.

Jessica, last night: "You look nervous."

"Do I?" he'd replied. Feeling nervous.

"Don't be cowed. He should be thanking *you* for helping."

True, he guessed. He just wanted to make sure this out-of-the-ordinary day went smooth as planed oak.

He asked Greene, "I too obvious?"

"What's that?"

"The uniform."

Lombardi's suits were almost like new, since he wore them only for church and the occasional wedding or funeral.

Greene was considering the question.

"Probably better to leave it. My shield doesn't mean much here. You, in uniform, kind of . . ." He sought a word. "Validates us."

"Make sense."

The marshal said he'd drive. Lombardi in a uniform was one thing but rolling up somewhere in a marked cruiser could give Marlowe advanced warning.

Good thinking.

The men climbed into Greene's vehicle. It was a Chevy Malibu. Apart from the cruiser Lombardi was never in a sedan. He and Jess owned SUVs. Hers was the bigger because she did the gardening and—when the kids came—she'd be the taxi.

As they pulled out from the parking lot Greene asked where tweakers might hang out in the Falls. He wanted to talk to some. He still wasn't sure why Marlowe was in Harbinger County but some of the crews she worked with were into meth distribution.

"There's a trailer park a lot of 'em live in. And kind of a camp in a forest preserve. We roust them, they leave, they come back." Lombardi thought they were, on the whole, sad people.

He gave the marshal directions to the park.

They were halfway there when the man's phone hummed.

He glanced at the text, lifted a surprised eyebrow. "Well. Got a lead. Our data surveillance people just had a credit card hit. The name on the card was an alias she's used before. At a motel in Harvey. Nearby?"

"Town next door. Twenty minutes on the highway. Turn right, next light."

"It's the Western Valley Lodge."

"Dive of a place—right by the railroad, which they don't mention on the billboards. And it's a meth quick mart. Girls too."

Lombardi's heart began to thud fast. Audible to him. Was it to the marshal?

Of course not.

"Left, next intersection."

"Might be a waste of time but . . ." Greene shrugged. "I'm the eternal optimist. When I first heard that, I was a kid. I thought it was *internal* optimist. You have children?"

"Not yet. It's part of the grand plan."

"Your wife work?"

"Teacher. She says maybe she'll just buy one in her class. Easier and they're house-trained."

Greene didn't smile. Should he have said Jess "joked"? Greene wouldn't really think she was serious about buying a kid, would he?

Then he told himself to relax.

Confidence . . . .

"You have a family, Ed?"

"I do. My wife's an administrator, Chicago PD. Two boys. High school and middle. Into soccer. Well, and girls. But that goes without saying."

"Your next right. How do you like working the city?"

"Well, never dull. But there're issues. Everything we do, we've got to keep the press in mind."

"We've got one paper, the *County Gazette*. They dropped the Police Blotter page when they had to cut back. Now it's ag event stories, local politics, and classifieds."

Greene looked his way. The handsome face smiled. "I detecting a little dissatisfaction? You thinking of moving to the big city?"

A shrug. "You never know. Have more chances to move up. And the pay's better than here, gotta be."

"It's a balance. Parts of the city're war zones. You go into apartments you never know if they're waiting for you. There're plenty of Marlowes out there. Don't give a shit if they kill a cop. Fact is, sometimes they go out hunting for us. Gives them street cred. Plenty of weapons too. Hey, want some advice?

"Okay."

"You ever serve paper?"

Lombardi said, "Warrants? Sure."

"Best way to do it is kneeling in front of the door when you knock."

"Kneel?"

"Yep. If there's a shooter inside they aim for your chest through the door. And you can't stand to the side either, since they've conned to that and fire there too. Keep low."

"Hm." Lombardi was scheduled to serve divorce papers on Harvey Engels and the man was never sober, and he sure did like to shoot his Browning twelve-gauge at the moon. Lombardi'd remember the trick.

He told the marshal, "Give you an idea of policing around here, last year I collared a perp for kidnapping a cow."

"You mean, like rustling?" Greene smiled. "Speaking of Westerns."

"No, Jon Perry drove onto Elbert Sands's place at midnight with a transport and made off with a Hereford. Sands was four months behind on a debt."

"And he didn't put up livestock for collateral. So it had to be snatched."

"Exactly right. Jon could've got a judgment and had the sheriff levy on it. But took the matter into his own hands."

Greene frowned. "Any Stockholm syndrome?"

When hostages form an emotional bond—sometimes even a romantic one—with their kidnapper.

Lombardi laughed. "That is a situation I do not want to even imagine."

The detective looked around again, squinting at the woods. He'd been doing this frequently.

"You think she has a long gun?"

"Don't know. I heard she did some shooting in the army. She was in for a year before she got kicked out. Dishonorable. Suspected of stealing small arms for the black market."

"She could be targeting us?" Lombardi, too, looked around, spine shivering.

"She won't know this car. But it's a habit. Ever since that text she sent."

"Must get tiring."

"Beats the alternative."

Constant Marlowe was reflecting that motels like the Western Valley Lodge, old, cheap, built on funky land, always smelled the same.

Cleanser and something gamy, an almost human-body smell.

And not perfumed necks or wrists. From the nether regions.

Marlowe was presently rearranging furniture.

Her Honda was elsewhere, a half mile away, in an abandoned carwash bay. A lot was abandoned in the scuffed town of Harvey, adjoining slightly less-scuffed Upper Falls. Plenty of spots to hide a sedan, even one as orange as hers.

She'd been here for thirty minutes after making some stops on her way from Hogan's Tap Room. Her jacket off, Marlowe muscled the low, wide dresser to a spot about twelve feet in front of the door. She then began filling the drawers with gallon jugs of distilled water. Eighteen of them. It was a trick she'd learned from a mob triggerman. While the barrier wasn't wholly bulletproof it could be counted on to deflect and absorb enough incoming slugs to give you some cover, confuse your attacker, and buy you time to return fire.

Some might consider this excessive, even paranoid. But up against this particular opponent there was no such thing as too much preparation.

She examined what lay on the bed—the contents of her backpack, along with some recent purchases. Her eyes strayed to one small plastic bag, yellow. She debated. She wanted to indulge. Constant Marlowe had trouble with impulse control.

Like the time she parked a slug in the knee of that human trafficker because . . . well, because she *wanted* to park a slug in him. Sometimes you just couldn't help herself.

The bag?

Later. Now, she had to remain vigilant. No distractions.

Every so often she would look out the window at a pile of junk across the parking lot. What she studied while doing this was the mirrored medicine cabinet door that she'd unscrewed from its hinges. Outside she'd propped it against a trash bag and aimed it in the direction of the front of the parking lot. She could glance through the slit between the two curtains, look at the mirror, and get an early warning of cars coming this way.

Even five seconds made a difference.

On the floor behind the dresser she set out the magazines for her pistol—not the hidden Bodyguard but her big 9 mm. A total of forty-five rounds was at her disposal, plus one in the chamber.

She set the bedside lamp between the dresser and the door. She clicked it on and removed the shade. This would blind an attacker and illuminate the target for her.

She looked at the yellow plastic bag again.

No.

Settling herself behind the waterlogged piece of laminated furniture, she gripped the SIG Sauer and flicked off the safety, waiting for her prey, thinking of how best to place the kill shot.

The motel was a worn-out place that wouldn't've been stylish even in the late fifties when it was fresh-paint new. Functional then, functional now.

The rectangular structure, concrete with sea-blue trim, nestled in a valley, surrounded by pine forest.

"She drives an orange Accord," Marshal Ed Greene told Lombardi as he made a circuit of the parking lot. The place was not busy today. There were only a half-dozen vehicles in the lot and no orange Hondas. An unfortunate tweaker, midtwenties, who'd have the teeth of a seventy-year-old, to the extent he had teeth at all, sat on a curb nearby. Waiting for a delivery, probably. Nearby was an emaciated, scabby prostitute, smoking.

On this very out-of-the-ordinary day, these crimes were not Tony Lombardi's affair.

The marshal parked under the overhang in front of the motel office and got out, hand near his hip, looking around. He bent down to the open door. "Keep an eye out. I'll just be a minute."

When the marshal went inside, Lombardi studied the area. No residential buildings. The road was home to commercial operations as tired as the motel. Warehouses, self-storage, a gravel and stone company, a car-painting shop, a truck-repair place specializing in big rigs. These businesses, too, seemed to belong to a different era. Pre-digital, pre-cable.

From nowhere, a thought hit him. Hard. Constant Marlowe was a killer and, it sounded like, a sadist maybe. Definitely a sociopath. But she *was* a woman. His imagination unspooled. What if she wounded the marshal, or killed him, and it was up to Lombardi to shoot her?

Could he do it?

Oh, man . . .

The thought sat heavy and dark in his heart.

But only for a moment.

Of course he could. And he'd do it without hesitating. Because if she took him out too, think what that would do to Jess? And to Joseph and Anabelle Rose, future dreams though they were. He—

Greene opened the door and dropped into the driver's seat. "Bingo. Got her."

Heart rate up again. "Yeah?"

"The clerk ID'd her picture. Her room's around back. I've got the key."

"They gave it to you, no warrant?"

A shrug. "Sometimes good citizens step up and do their duty."

Greene put the car in gear and drove forward.

"What if she comes back while we're in there?"

"Then the clerk calls us. I gave him my mobile."

"He did that too?"

Greene chuckled. "Well, that part cost me forty. Civic duty only gets you so far."

"You have a budget for stuff like that?"

"Of course. Don't you?"

"No."

"Tell your sheriff. You'd be amazed at what a little cash buys you."

"I'll do that."

Tony Lombardi was getting a whole continuing ed course today, all to himself.

Another glance toward the early warning mirror.

Yes, Marlowe saw a car approaching.

It was a dark Chevy Malibu, moving slowly toward the back of the motel, where her room was located. It turned into a parking space about three or four rooms away.

Breathing slowly now. Calm. Prepared.

Ready to kill.

No car doors slammed. He'd left it open for the silence. An old trick. There was the faint sound of a footstep, gritty. Marlowe had decided not to stuff plugs into her ears; she needed to hear his approach and would just have to endure the stunning blast of the gunshots.

Come on . . .

She flipped the SIG off safety.

And here he was.

A shadow appeared beneath the door.

He didn't move for a long moment. On the one hand, he would be thinking—as she hoped—that she was gone. He would break in and wait for her. On the other, he'd wonder if this was a trap and she was waiting for him.

Marlowe believed she and her adversary were equally intelligent, equally skilled at strategy and tactics.

Then something curious happened.

He was whispering. And someone whispered back.

Two people?

What was this about?

So, her enemy had backup.

The door lock clicked as a key card was pressed next to it. He'd sweet-talked the desk clerk into giving him a copy.

Her right index finger, tipped in black polish, slipped from outside the trigger guard to inside. This gun had a very light pull.

Five seconds passed.

Ten.

Her teeth were clamped tight, impatience growing to irritation.

Come on in, both of you. Plenty of ammunition to go around.

Let's get this over with.

Another whisper? Hard to tell. Might have been the wind. The shadows beneath the door vanished. A moment later two car doors slammed, an engine started, and the tire squeal announced an urgent departure, robbing her of the chance to run outside and empty her weapon into the back of his head.

Goddamn . . .

Marlowe exhaled long, closing her eyes, lowering her head in anger. She safety'd the gun, put it into her waistband and began to dig through her backpack.

"What was it?" Tony Lombardi asked.

The marshal didn't answer; he was concentrating on piloting his rental car quickly along the road the motel was located on. Squinting and glancing from asphalt to hillside and back again.

He skidded the Chevy onto a badly maintained road that ascended steeply. At the top, he made another left, and after a short drive, stopped on the crest of the hill overlooking the Western Valley Lodge.

Greene climbed out and nodded for Lombardi to do the same. The men peered down at the motel.

"I want to see if her lights go on or a curtain moves."

"You think she's there? But her car?"

"She could've parked it someplace else and hiked over here."

Lombardi had never thought of that.

They stared for three or four minutes. Room 188 remained asleep.

"You asked me what it was, Tony. A feel. That it was a trap."

"She was going to shoot us, just like that?"

"Wasn't going to give us a coupon for the buffet breakfast." The marshal looked him over. "You all right?"

He wasn't going to fake it. "Sort of."

"Never get over it—being in a firefight or *almost* being in a firefight."

"So, what was it? That feeling. Where did it come from?"

The marshal said nothing for a moment. "I wish I could tell you. Experience, I guess. I've got a few years on you."

"Sixth sense?"

"Call it that." Greene shook his head. "Every time I think I have one up on her, she does something like this." He stiffened suddenly and leaned forward. "Wait . . . What's that? No . . ."

Lombardi squinted and saw a figure in dark clothing, backpack over the shoulder, hopping a fence on the far side of the motel.

Likely a woman, given the ponytail. She vanished into tall weeds and brush.

"Goddamn it." Greene's eyes squeezed shut briefly in anger.

"How'd that happen?"

"Probably broke through the adjoining door to the unit behind hers." The marshal was squinting into the distance. "And hell, we can't follow her, not in the car. We'd have to go all the way around the forest preserve. And she'll be long gone by the time we get there."

The men got into the Malibu once more. Greene sighed in frustration and piloted the car down the hillside. At the intersection he turned toward the mall where they'd first met.

After a few minutes of silence the marshal mused, "She's got to stay somewhere."

It was Lombardi's turn to be the expert. "Not a lot of options in the Falls. Motels mostly. Bed and breakfasts. A few Airbnbs. Hm, you know, Ed, we got a dozen or so abandoned farmhouses in the south county. I don't know if she'd know about them. But, this weather, all she'd need is a sleeping bag. I can radio in, get some addresses."

"That's good thinking."

The deputy kept from smiling.

"I'll check motels," the marshal said. "And call my credit card people again. She won't use this alias but she's got others."

The marshal gripped the wheel firmly. His anger was thick. He was probably thinking about Joanne, the assistant Constant Marlowe had tortured and killed.

Fifteen minutes later they were back at the strip mall and parked near Lombardi's squad car in front of the Dollar Store.

The men decided they would work in their respective mobile "offices" and meet up at Maggie's in a half hour to compare notes. Maybe some cake would be in order.

Lombardi climbed from the car. He turned and bent down. "Hey, Marshal? Ed?"

The man looked up.

"Appreciate you letting me work with you."

"Appreciate you helping. You make a good partner."

Lombardi tried not to let the pride blossom in his face. He wasn't sure he was successful at this.

He got into his cruiser and started the engine. He lifted the mic and called in to Sandra, one of the office's administrators, asking her to pull together a list of foreclosed farms.

Lombardi sat back, thinking about what he'd learned today.

Kneeling in front of the door when serving warrants, not closing car doors when you didn't want to announce your presence, using credit cards to track suspects, setting up a fund to pay for information, remembering that a suspect might park their car in a place that police couldn't easily get to in their vehicles . . .

At this last thought, something began to nag.

What was it?

Think . . .

Oh, okay. What to make of this? The marshal had said Marlowe would hike through the forest preserve to get to her car.

Well, it *was* a county preserve but how did he know that? And that it wasn't just a forest?

He'd said he didn't know the area.

And something else: Greene hadn't asked directions back here to the mall or used GPS. It was a complicated route from the Western Valley Lodge. Lombardi himself would have used the nav system.

Then, something even stranger arose, more troubling.

The two of them had found Marlowe. Why not call in a tactical team to stake out the room or, if she was in it, do a dynamic entry to take her? Which Greene had said they'd do.

For some reason the marshal had wanted to be at the motel alone with Lombardi and Marlowe.

He debated only seconds. Gut churning, Lombardi logged on to the computer mounted in front of the cruiser's dashboard. He googled "US Marshal's Office, Chicago." The site came up quickly and he clicked on "Personnel." When the page came up he began scrolling through names.

Lombardi was then aware of a shadow outside. He turned to his left and saw, no more than three feet away, Ed Greene, or whoever he was, looking at the deputy's computer screen.

The man's lips were pressed together in disappointment . . .

Neither of the men moved for a moment.

As Tony Lombardi's hand lurched forward, the man lifted his Glock and shot him in the face.

Constant Marlowe pulled her old orange car to the curb in a part of the village of Upper Falls that was much better than the neighborhood surrounding the Western Valley Motel, where her trap had failed so spectacularly.

A touch to her back waistband to orient herself to the location of the Smith & Wesson—it sometimes shifted as she drove—and then she stepped through a thicket of untrimmed brush. She stopped at the edge of the parking lot. Quite the scene unfolded before her, a full-on carnival, illuminated in the approaching dusk by the whipsaw lights of the emergency vehicles.

Dozens of people stood in clusters on the exterior side of the yellow police tape. They were staring toward the Dollar General store, from which the hind end of a Sheriff's Office cruiser protruded, surrounded by an ice field of glass shards. A multitude of cell phones were at work, taking pictures and videos. Dozens of law enforcers were present. She focused on two: both gray-uniformed men, one older, one younger. They stood beside an HCSO cruiser. On the side were the stenciled messages: *Call 911 in EMERGENCY* and *We serve and protect.*

The elder of the pair was decked out with significant gingerbread on shoulder and chest—bars and pins and insignia.

He was the one Marlowe walked up to. "Sheriff?"

The man looked down at her from his six-four stature. His face was outdoorsman wrinkled and was of a physique that featured thin legs and a belly that swelled a few inches over his belt. His hair and drooping mustache were gray, a shade between that of his outfit and the paint job of the cruiser.

His expression was both weary and cautious. "Press?"

"What?"

"Are you a reporter?'

"No."

"You know something about the incident here?"

She held up a wallet containing on one side her employer picture ID and on the other a gold badge. "Special Agent Constant Marlowe, Illinois Department of Criminal Investigations. And in answer to your question, yes, I do."

"The man who shot your deputy is Paul Offenbach," she said to Sheriff Louie Braddock.

She and the sheriff were sitting in the front seat of the cruiser. His large hands were atop the steering wheel, thumbs hooked beneath and eight fingers rising and falling as if he were playing ragtime.

It had taken a few minutes to verify Marlowe's identity. Braddock had contacted the DCI headquarters in Springfield to get confirmation. The agent in charge confirmed that there was a Constant Anne Marlowe on the force. But he didn't know anything about her going to Wisconsin. She was presently on a leave of absence.

He texted a picture, which matched, but Braddock, not quite satisfied, had run her prints. Finally claimed identity aligned with corporeal form.

"Said he was a US Marshal. Name of Greene."

"Offenbach does that. Assumes identities. How far did his credentials hold up?"

"Good enough. There's even an Edward Greene in the US Marshall's office in Chicago. My deputy got suspicious and was on their website when he got shot."

"How is he?"

"Hit in the face. There's an answer."

"He'll live?"

"They say. Though I would cast some doubt on his returning to his chosen profession. Which he loved."

"How'd that happen?" A nod toward the cruiser, atop the bits of shiny glass.

Braddock explained that he'd interviewed the deputy as best he could. The officer had said—well, written down—that just as he saw the gun, he went not for his own pistol, but the gear shift and hit the gas.

"Man fired a few more shots, missed, and then, with all the people around, took off." He swiveled his long, stern face her way. "Now, time to hear *your* story, Agent Marlowe."

"Offenbach's a career criminal out of Chicago. Independent but he works with crews there and along the lakeshore to Minnesota. I've been after him for a couple of weeks. He and two men stole a truck with a million worth of opioids and fent. Vandalia County."

"Right over the border. We work with their Sheriff's Department. High-speed pursuits this way, high-speed pursuits that way."

"Did you know a Cynthia Hooper? Deputy there."

"No." His cowboy face was still. "And I caught that verb."

"The robbery hadn't been reported yet. She sees a van off the road and goes to check it out. Probably just thought it was an accident. The three perps're still there. Offenbach tortured her and killed her." With some effort Constant Marlowe controlled the rage.

"My Lord. Why?"

"Because he's a goddamn sadist. He enjoys it. Cyn and I worked together, drug task-forced, her outfit and mine. She was a friend."

Marlowe heard Cynthia's lilting voice. She often did.

So there's something I want to bring up . . .

"Well, I am sorry."

"Last night I get a call from one of my CIs. Offenbach's here in Harbinger. I drive up."

The sheriff was thoughtful now. "Leave of absence, hmm? Didn't feel your comrades in the Land of Lincoln were doing enough to track him down."

Hardly a need to confirm.

"This morning I start walking around town, flashing his picture, to see if anybody's seen him."

The sheriff gave a coy smile. "But maybe it was more than looking for leads. You were playing bait, hoping he'd come after you."

Again, no need to corroborate.

"He's into the narco trade, so I was talking to some of your tweakers, dropping twenties. Thinking he might be where they hang. Never saw him. But the name Wexler came up."

A troubled look momentarily flickered in the sheriff's eyes.

"I went into his place. Hogan's. Had a slugfest with one of his boys." She shrugged. "Had to make them believe I wasn't law."

"What happened with Wexler?"

"Paid him twenty-five hundred down to give me Offenbach."

"My, you got yourself some budget."

"From my savings. Personal."

"Oh."

"Either Wexler'd do what I asked and give me Offenbach. Or he'd dime me out to Offenbach and pocket two fees. Turned out to be the second. I spotted one of his men following me from the bar to the Western Valley Lodge. He got word to Offenbach where I was staying."

"Western Valley? Had a complaint about damaged rooms and a missing guest not an hour ago. Seems you've had a busy day in the Falls, Agent Marlowe."

She gave no reaction but continued, "So Offenbach—playing the marshal—shows up. Somehow he got the key—"

"That'd be Wexler. Nearly every business in town, he speaks, they jump."

Constant Marlowe cast anger the way other people throw off shadows on a bright day. She controlled herself once more. "He was about to walk in. But changed his mind. Got spooked, I guess. Took off before I could do anything."

"'Do anything.'?" With this the sheriff looked at her the way he would probably regard a DUI who claimed he'd had only two beers before driving into a street sign.

She clarified, "Arrest him."

And Sheriff Braddock became the second person in the space of a few hours she lied to about her intention to murder Paul Offenbach.

A loud roar of a diesel engine. The tow truck was lifting the cruiser's rear. Tiny cubes of glass fell like glittery hail.

"Your deputy . . ."

"Tony Lombardi."

"How'd he end up in this?"

"Offenbach's story was he was hunting for you because you murdered his assistant and went on to kill a couple in the Witness Protection Program. And Tony said, that is, *wrote*, before he went into surgery, that you sent him a text and a tape of somebody screaming to scare you off."

Jesus . . . Marlowe steadied her center. This wasn't easy. "No, *he* sent *me* the text."

"And the recording was your friend?" Braddock added in a whisper, "Being murdered."

She nodded. If she'd answered, the words might have become a scream.

"Almighty."

With a clattering grind, the tow truck dragged the cruiser free.

"This's not the sort of thing we see 'round here, crime-wise. Don't think you see it *anywhere*."

"Offenbach's unique. Pure sociopath. But add to that he's brilliant. He's a chess player, paid half his college tuition that way. He plays four or five games at a time. Sometimes blindfolded."

"You can do that?"

Marlowe: "He could hire a triggerman to shoot me in the back from a hundred yards. Plans like this are what he enjoys."

"You know a lot about him."

A nod.

Braddock asked, "Why didn't you contact us?"

"I work best alone." Which was true but left out more than it told. "Your deputy, he have a family?"

"A wife. And they're peas in a pod. Do everything together. Fish, hunt, cycle . . . that's the *proper* kind of cycling. Harleys. Jessica's with him now and woe to any nurse that tries to pry her away." One hand left the wheel briefly to smooth the mustache. "What was the point of it? Faking he was a marshal?"

"I had to guess, he wanted a cop as a human shield."

"What?"

"Offenbach'd find me. He and the deputy'd move in and then he'd get behind Tony, knowing I'd hesitate. That's all you need for advantage. A few seconds. He'd take me out, and then him."

"Dealt with some pretty downward individuals in my day but never anybody like him." Braddock glanced—for the third time—at her scar. It had happened when she was at a match in Trenton. Boxing gloves don't cut flesh like that. The scar occurred after the fight was over, outside.

The sheriff's fingers flipped up and down atop the wheel. She wondered if he actually did play a keyboard.

"I'll need you to stay around. If we find Offenbach you'll be a material witness."

"You won't find him. He's gone now."

"You know that for a fact?"

"He tried for me and he blew it, and now you and WSP'll be all over the county. He'll fall back—go underground. Chicago, or one of his places in Florida or offshore. He'll set up another trap for me someplace else."

"We'll take that under advisement. I assume the Western Valley Lodge isn't your real accommodations. Where're you staying, Agent Marlowe?"

"We've got each other's phone numbers."

"Ah. Probably best to keep information like that close to your vest." A shake of his head. "Jugs of water in the dresser. What was that all about?"

She gave him a nod. "Night, Sheriff."

As she walked to her own car, she kept an eye on the nearby woods, which would be a good place for a shooter to set up shop.

Because she knew as well as she knew it was a cool spring evening scented with jasmine, that Paul Offenbach had gone nowhere.

He was still in or around Upper Falls, Wisconsin, and here he would remain until one of two things happened. He killed her, or she killed him.

He sat on the porch of a rambling house, a century old, in the low hills in unincorporated Harbinger County.

A twenty-five-year-old Macallan scotch beside him, Paul Offenbach was looking over the view, rolling and gentle, well on its way to April budding. In his sure hands, a pen knife made the circuit of the inside of his pipe. While the smoking implement certainly had to be cleaned with some frequency, scraping wasn't necessary.

He simply enjoyed the sound. It was like blade on bone.

Offenbach had come to the house frequently when young and the four-thousand-square-foot structure held fond memories for him. Also, nice, it was largely untraceable. So, with no living relatives in the Midwest any longer, Offenbach had used it as a safehouse and for storage and as a staging area for jobs in northern Illinois and Southern Wisconsin. Here he had several million untraceable dollars and two dozen weapons. No drugs. After the Old Bennett Road robbery in Vandalia County, Illinois, he'd sold the entire stash immediately. Narcotics were far too easy to—literally—sniff out.

The scraping put him in mind of the deputy, Cynthia Hooper, he'd learned her name was, who'd stumbled on the scene—to her misfortune, and his delight.

Scraping, the sound of the razor knife on bone . . .

Offenbach used to wonder—with concern—why he got such pleasure from pain—eating chocolate pleasure, drinking single-malt pleasure, orgasmic pleasure. While someone else might enjoy hearing the moans and whispers of their lover during the throws of coupling, he slipped into an ecstatic reverie at the sound of screams, the smell of blood, the gasping begs to stop . . .

This was not a fault, not a crime. How could it be? He was simply being true to his nature. A shark wasn't bad when it dined on a dangling limb. According to these rules of the world, irrefutable, Offenbach was in the right when he created pain.

He eased back in the comfortable chair and lifted his phone again. He listened to the recording he'd made of Cynthia Hooper.

No, please, don't . . . Why? It hurts . . . Just kill me . . .

He'd made several copies, in case one was accidentally erased.

He scanned the rooms he could see from where he sat. He would miss this place. Now that he'd been identified as the mastermind of Old Bennett Road drug van heist and as the shooter of earnest and insecure Deputy Tony Lombardi, it was time to leave the country.

Though not before finishing up what he'd come here for.

Completing the mission now delayed.

His plan—mapped out like a game of his beloved chess—had nearly worked.

He wanted to hunt down Constant Marlowe outside Illinois—in a place where she'd have few allies. Wisconsin was good. Harbinger County made sense with his connections.

A contact would get her the message that he was here, and Marlowe would believe it was legit because it would come from one of her trusted confidential informants.

There was no risk she'd talk to the county deputies up here. In fact, she'd avoid them at all costs; her goal was to murder, not arrest, him.

Offenbach decided he'd front that he was a law enforcer—US marshal seemed good; he had quite enjoyed *The Fugitive.* He'd bought the badge and ID card for two thousand. Expensive but they were the real thing and, if scanned, which he doubted the Sheriff's Office would even know how to do, the bar code was genuine.

He had borrowed the name of a real marshal in the Chicago office, Edward Greene, who, his contact told him, was out of the office on assignment in Indiana.

As for the bio—married, with two children, well, *that* was a joke. Paul Offenbach had relationships with women but they invariably involved some dealmaking—with hefty bonuses paid when the evening went rougher than planned. He occasionally lost control when it came to that sort of playtime.

The man in Chicago who had turned Marlowe's confidential informant—and who was extremely well compensated by Offenbach—also provided a picture of Marlowe breaking into a warehouse. It was not, however, a rival gangs' facility. She was the lead tactical agent in a raid of a human trafficker's hideout. (Several things he'd told hapless Deputy Lombardi were true: Marlowe did shoot the man in the knee. And, no, she didn't need to.)

Then it was on to Upper Falls to meet the deputy, have an excellent hamburger, and seduce the unfortunate kid. He'd used charm, informal mentoring, and a southern accent, which he'd found tended to make people trust and believe you.

The text he'd received as they were driving to the meth site was not from any computer credit card outfit—if such a thing existed. It was from Tomas Wexler, who was being paid 10K to help him find and eliminate Marlowe. One of Wexler's men had tracked her to the Western Valley Lodge, where a clerk would hand over a key to her room.

He and the kid were all set to go. He had pictured the scene so clearly he could taste it. Open the door. If she were there, he'd shove Tony in first and when she hesitated to shoot a uniformed law enforcer he'd kill her and then put two into the deputy's head.

If she weren't inside, they would wait and play out the same scenario when she returned.

Such a perfect plan . . .

But it hadn't worked out that way.

Just before they'd gone inside, he'd noticed on a pile of trash a perfectly good drug cabinet mirror. It was partially covered with trash but, judging the angles, he realized it would give her a view of any cars approaching.

She was inside. And anyone entering would be seen only in silhouette. She wouldn't see that one of the two was a cop, but assume he was one of Offenbach's associates.

They retreated, to make new plans.

But no new plans were possible.

Because of his big mistake.

Supposedly a stranger to town, how did he know the route from the motel back to the strip mall.

And Lombardi probably wondered too why the marshal hadn't called the sheriff or the state police and requested a tac team at the motel.

So, it was goodbye to the poor Tony Lombardi.

Though die he did not.

But in a way Offenbach enjoyed this outcome more.

A shattered face . . . Think of the pain.

He checked the news from Northern Illinois. He'd been following a trial in Vandalia County, Illinois. The authorities there believed they'd caught one of the two men present with Offenbach at the site of the robbery and murder of Cynthia Hooper three weeks ago. The evidence was weak but the myopic pit bull of a prosecutor, a man named Evan Quill, had pushed forward with the trial anyway.

Interesting to see how *that* circus would play out, Offenbach reflected.

According to the feed, the matter was now in the jury's hands.

Inhaling the whisky, thinking of the house once more. Young Paul had come here as often as he could to escape from his junior mobster father. Paul hadn't minded the man's criminal career—he himself had paid for much of his college education running numbers in the Windy City. It was the man's personality: he was a narcissistic bully, who never once touched Paul, his brother, or their mother, but abused them relentless with his sarcasm and insults. The words landed like whiplashes.

Still, he had his father to thank for starting young Offenbach's own criminal empire; he'd blackmailed the philandering man for his nest egg—a story he had never told to another soul on earth.

Other memories about the house: the bedroom on the third floor where he and his cousin Sarah had played, among other things. The expansive dining room where the family guests had boisterous meals. The musty basement smelling of heating oil, where—when older and he had the place to himself—he'd tied a drifter to a set of box springs and started experimenting, finding that this aroused him far more than Sarah, or any female, ever could.

In one way, he was regretting that Constant Marlowe would die. There was an appeal about her. In some respects she reminded him of himself. No interest in rules. No interest in following orders. Blunt, physical. He'd edited her bio for Tony Lombardi but much of what he'd told the deputy was close to the truth. She was a former award-winning prizefighter, with hundreds of titles under her belt. Nearly undefeated. She hadn't been banned at all—in fact, she'd been much in demand by promoters through her retirement. She still kept up with the sport, boxing in recreational leagues, like the Illinois Public Safety Boxing Club, where she'd take on other women cops and firefighters. She especially liked fighting female prison guards.

The job attracted large, tough women; Marlowe, the word was, didn't like things easy.

Yes, she'd been in the army, and there'd been trouble, though it had nothing to do with peddling stolen arms, and her discharge was honorable. The reprimands were always for the same thing: if she learned of any soldier—enlisted or officer—guilty of harassment, and if the victim had been bullied to silence, Constant Marlowe delivered her own justice. Curiously, afterward, when asked about the bruise or the broken wrist, the men invariably reported that the injuries came from being mugged or a rock-climbing accident.

Ah, Constant . . .

A shame to say goodbye.

But speaking of being true to your nature . . . Offenbach concluded he'd never met anyone more self-destructive than she was.

Suicidal probably.

Tomorrow he would simply help her fulfill that destiny.

How exactly he'd accomplish that he wasn't sure. But this was one thing he'd found about himself. When confronted with a problem, he would sit back, smoke his pipe and let the ideas emerge. They would. Time. That was the key. Just the right amount. He'd made good money playing fast chess, but the games were always in the Rapid category, ten to sixty minutes per match, never Blitz or Bullet, in which the entire contest had to take place under ten minutes and under three, respectively. He knew perfection required planning, but that too much planning could ruin it.

Winning the game after losing your queen, money laundering, meth, bribery, shipping girls from Colombia to Indianapolis . . . murdering your nemesis. As difficult as those challenges were, Paul Offenbach would always find a solution.

He turned the chair so the last slice of sun was visible over the hills, filled the bowl of the half-bent taper pipe with Astley's No. 2 and flicked a blue flame from his hissing butane lighter—the same one he'd used on Cynthia Hooper, he now recalled.

Constant Marlowe walked along a path that wound from the parking lot to the entrance of St. Francis Hospital in the northern part of Upper Falls.

The institution was situated on about four acres of land, well-tended though lacking in colorful petals; commonplace grass predominated. All pleasant, neat, easy on the eyes. But the corker was the narrow river running fast along the eastern edge, fed by one of the waterfalls that gave the town its name.

This cascade was modest, about twenty feet high, discoloring to rich brown rock—white in its natural state—it poured along. The more impressive chutes were downstream.

Inside the immaculate hospital, Marlowe was directed to the ICU, on the ground floor. Once there she located Room 5, in front of which sat a blonde in her late twenties, solidly built, talking on a cell phone. She wore a navy-blue, form-fitting dress and flesh-colored stockings. Marlowe could not remember the last time she'd donned that particular accessory; she'd received a pair as a gift six months or so ago. They sat unopened. Somewhere.

The woman wore an ID badge on a lanyard around her neck, showing her picture and bearing the words: *Langston Hughes Middle School.*

A county Sheriff's Office deputy sat across from her, guard duty.

Marlowe showed her ID and he nodded.

The caller put her phone away and turned her pretty face toward her with a questioning look.

Marlowe introduced herself to Jessica Lombardi.

They shook hands.

"How is he?"

"It'll be a long haul. But we'll get him better." Her eyes were determined and her jaw set and Marlowe remembered what Sheriff Braddock had said.

Woe to any nurse that tries to pry her away . . .

"How's the coffee here?" Marlowe asked.

"Only half as dreadful as you think."

"Let's take a chance."

They walked up the corridor filled with the unsettling scents of houses of healing. In the cafeteria Marlowe bought two large cups.

"To eat?" she called to Jessica, who'd taken a table by a window, overlooking one of the streams. She shook her head.

Marlowe joined her and sat. The sugar packets and pods of half-and-half were wasted.

The women sipped.

Jessica's sharp, hazel eyes looked at the walls. "Did you know that orange paint like that makes you eat faster?"

"I didn't."

"Our lunchroom at school? Wasted the paint job. Kidums have twenty minutes. So they better scarf it all down before the bell." Her voice caught. A moment later she said, "Tony was lucky." Jessica explained that the bullet had hit his cheek and gone clean through. Missed everything vital, though it had come close and if he had not accelerated as fast as he had, he would have died when Offenbach fired the other shots, which missed him entirely.

"God was looking out for him." Her eyes were on Marlowe's. Not the scar. "You like being police as much as Tony does?"

"Suits me."

"Him too. You're a detective."

"Pretty much."

"That's what he wanted to be. *Wants* to be. He'd be good." A glance at Marlowe's naked left ring finger. "Some men have skill by the bucket. They just need to think a little more highly of themselves."

A nod in response. Then Marlowe said, "You know that somebody was helping Offenbach."

"I heard. Wexler." She grimaced.

The coffee was, in truth, not as bad as she'd expected. Hunger pinged. But later. "When Sheriff Braddock mentioned him, he gave a reaction, just like that. But didn't say anything more. What do you know about him?"

Jessica's lips tightened and the gaze aimed at the brash walls grew cold. Marlowe could just imagine her confronting an out-of-order middle schooler who was armed with a joint or graffiti spray can. "He's awful. Tony was telling me what he does. Those people in the woods, on meth? We know he sells to them. And there's been talk about trafficking in Milwaukee. Women and girls. Disgusting," she spat out. "And he's got a half brother, Rudy, who's a mean bully."

Though a very bad boxer.

"The Falls used to be a nice town. But Tony said that people like Wexler've moved out of the cities. They're in the small towns now. Less police to hassle them." Concern blossomed in her round, pretty face. "Tony can't talk, but he writes things. He said there was a woman Offenbach was here to kill. Is that you?"

"That's right."

"It didn't work out. So *both* of them, Wexler *and* Offenbach, aren't very happy with you. You'll be careful?"

Watching your back for threats from two people isn't a lot harder than from one.

Marlowe asked, "Why is Wexler still free?"

She scoffed, disgust in her face. "The word is that he's really smart and keeps himself insulated from the dirty work. Tony says that. But I don't know I agree with him. Sheriff Braddock's been around. He knows his business. No, it's that Wexler owns half the real estate in the county, and a dozen businesses. He hires people for good jobs, people who could only get work that involves asking what kind of side dish do you want? Gets people jobs in the county government—whether they're any good or not."

Marlowe recalled that when Wexler told the motel clerk to hand over the key to Offenbach he jumped to.

"Tony was on patrol one time and found some meth on a man who works for Wexler. The guy was hanging around the high school and that just burned up Tony. But the Sheriff let him go. Could've been a felony. Tony called him on it. Braddock said, Look, we got water moccasins here. A more dangerous snake you will not find. But we let 'em be. They eat rats and cottonmouths. And to kill one you gotta go into a river or pond, their territory, and that is one job we are not prepared for." She sighed.

Marlowe decided Braddock wasn't a corrupt man but, despite the grizzled gunslinger look, he was weak and didn't want to risk a plum job in a pleasant enough town by taking on a danger like Wexler. Oh, there'd be justice of sorts for Braddock: The sheriff would have to process crime scenes where high schoolers died with a needle in their arm, and he'd head home to dinner, with his only company on the drive his hot shame.

But for Constant Marlowe, no. Justice of sorts wasn't enough.

She was not, however, the sheriff of Harbinger County.

The woman started to sip coffee but put the Styrofoam cup down. She crossed her arms and gazed out the window. "And you know the worst of it? About Tony?"

"What's that?"

"He shouldn't even be here." Her face revealed more disgust than anger, as she nodded up the hall. "He wasn't supposed to be the deputy going to meet the marshal. Braddock was going to give it to somebody else. Pete Jacobson. But he said he couldn't do it. He had to take the day off. His mother was sick, he said. But he lied. He skipped work so he could go gambling, a poker tournament. The sheriff called Tony for the job."

She sighed and her face went still as stone. "Tony wasn't sure. Wasn't sure he could do it—work with some big fancy US marshal. I talked him into it. I told him he could."

Marlowe wondered if she'd cry. But no, she controlled herself, merely shook her head. "I guess you want to see him but he's probably still sleeping, I'm afraid."

Marlowe said, "Let's wake him up, why don't we? I don't think he'll mind."

She hid her orange Accord behind a dumpster in the parking lot of a metal fabricating company on the west side of Upper Falls.

Constant Marlowe then walked fifty yards to her motel, carting her backpack, green quilted rifle case, and a plastic bag containing purchases from a deli.

Cozy Staye—the weird final "e" maybe an attempt to Old Englishize—was her real residence here, her base of operation. She'd checked in last night—after a fast drive from Vandalia County.

She reached for her key and found she still had Rudy's gun, that little .25, in her pocket. She'd forgotten to leave it in a downtown trash can, as promised. Had he gotten coated with the dregs from discarded coffee cups and soda cans as he dug?

Hope so.

The motel, horseshoe shaped, was in need of several new layers of bile yellow paint. The parking lot was five years late for hot asphalt. The neighborhood was populated with some folk not of the finest moral stature, it seemed. You checked in at a window of thick Plexiglas in need of Windex, and it was there that you received towels and your TV remote control. The vending machine had one of the most impressive clasps and locks Marlowe had ever seen.

Inside her room, she set what she carried on the bed, chained the door, and angled the desk chair under the knob; without any such measures, it could be kicked in by a sturdy twelve-year-old.

Marlowe opened her backpack and removed the yellow plastic bag whose contents had so tempted her as she waited for Offenbach at the Western Valley Lodge.

No distractions . . .

Now, she was free to indulge.

From the bag she lifted out the package of Oreo cookies. She preferred the ones with double cream filling, though the deli had only the regular ones. They would certainly do.

Marlowe enjoyed three with a small bottle of whole milk before her phone hummed.

A caller ID number popped up on the screen.

Hell . . .

Don't answer.

Then decided: But better to know where you stand.

"Yes?"

"Constant."

Assistant Special Agent in Charge of the Department of Criminal Investigation's Chicago office, Richard Avery, had a distinctive voice. Light and melodic. She'd always wondered if he sang in a choir.

"I just heard from Downstate. You're in Wisconsin?"

She'd known that news of Braddock's phone call to check her credentials would eventually make its way to Avery, who was her ultimate supervisor.

"That's right."

She'd hoped to stay in the brush until Offenbach was dead. But that plan had derailed after Deputy Tony Lombardi was shot.

"Explain."

She tried to keep impatience out of her rough voice: "I got a tip Offenbach was here. From one of my CIs. Marcus Washington. South Chicago. You know him. He's given us good stuff before."

Avery, who was about fifty, looked the part of a special agent. Broad shoulders atop a torso that narrowed to thin hips and legs, with a powerful chest and a taut gut in between. A law degree and some prosecuting experience figured on his résumé. Though he wore nice suits and stylish cuff links, he wasn't above strapping on a body plate and kicking in a door to collar a suspect. She believed that, like her, Avery far preferred raids to paperwork.

But administrator he had become. And now was a time for administering.

"You're on leave of absence. You can't be investigating."

She didn't ask, *And why not?* Her silence, however, did.

Avery's voice softened. "I know how you're feeling, after . . . what happened. But we've got interstate protocols. They work. Up there, in Wisconsin, you're out of jurisdiction. And a county deputy's been shot? Are we in any way . . . ?"

Right up front, Marlowe had asked herself if she could have anticipated that Offenbach would enlist a young law enforcer to be his shield. She'd answered no, and that was the end of it. It angered her now that he was concerned about ass-covering.

"No, we're not," she said sharply. Marlowe had earned more than a few complaints in her years at the DCI, and most of those were for a simple reason: she had zero patience for politics, incompetence, misguided ambition . . . well, the list of infractions was long.

Avery would now be deciding: why bother to wag fingers, especially with Constant Marlowe. He said and asked what he needed to. Time to move on.

"Anything pan out? Offenbach?"

"All the leads've dried up."

"You think he's there?"

Once you lie, better to stay the course.

"Doubt it. Too hot for him here. You shoot a uniform, you know how it is."

"You're coming back to Chicago?"

"Hopewell first, to see how the trial's going."

One of the suspects in the Old Bennett Road heist was on trial for felony murder in Cynthia Hooper's death. She'd heard the trial would be winding up tomorrow. There was no doubt about Offenbach's guilt; they had a video of him at the scene. But as for the man presently on trial neither his innocence nor guilt was clear-cut.

"Where you're staying? Is it safe?"

"I'm in cover. It's good."

As melodic as ever, his voice managed to turn gruff. "If you're on leave of absence, act like you're on leave of absence. Watch TV, jog, go do whatever one does in wherever you are. Don't go traipsing off after him."

"'Night, Richard."

She disconnected and looked at the bag that contained the deli sandwiches she'd bought. They went into the fridgette. She'd eat them tomorrow or she'd throw them out. Probably it'd be the trash. She had two more Oreos and finished the milk.

Removing the rifle from the case, she pulled the bolt out and sighted down the bore—from the stock end, of course. Clear. No reason for it not to be but you always made sure. The weapon smelled of oil and Goodes cleaner and, wafting sweetly from the rich wooden stock, Pledge furniture polish.

She had an affection for long guns. In the army she'd been a sniper and had taken those skills with her when she joined the Illinois Department of Criminal Investigation's tactical team. The gun was a Winchester Model 70. On the market since the 1930s it was a workhorse for hunters. It was called the "rifleman's rifle" and could be used for any game, since you could buy it chambered for calibers from flat and fast .223 up to the punishing .338. Hers took one of the bigger rounds, the .308.

This particular 70 had been the gun her father taught her to hunt with, and she'd inherited it—along with a slew of debt and a sizeable store of methamphetamine—when he met an unfortunate but inevitable end. He was fifty, she twenty-five.

Marlowe had little time for sentiment, and if, for instance, she had to bail out of a bad situation and leave the gun behind, so be it. What she liked about this weapon was not its history but that it was as familiar in her hands as a lover's neck and shoulders.

It was also accurate as sin.

And one other attribute: It had been bought by her father years ago with no documentation. It was untraceable.

Because the bullets were large, the magazine, which was not detachable, could hold only three. But Constant Marlowe had never needed excessive ammunition. If she had to kill with a long gun, one round would do the trick.

The bolt went back in, and, finger on the trigger, she pushed it forward and then down, so there'd be no tension on the firing pin spring. She returned the weapon to the case.

Marlowe stripped, showered. She dressed in boxers and a tee, then spent some lengthy time drying her abundant hair.

Placing her SIG, safety'd, on the bedside table, she slid under the covers, but remained sitting upright. She placed a call.

"Hey." The voice was as baritone as Avery's was tenor.

"You're not sleeping."

"In bed with a pizza," said Evan Quill.

The man had OCD and for him to dine in bed meant he was beyond exhausted. This happened with every trial he'd ever run, as long as she'd known him.

Quill was prosecuting the case she'd just alluded to: the man accused of being a conspirator in Cynthia's death.

Maybe innocent, maybe not . . .

"I got a call. Richard Avery."

"And?"

"Heard I was up here, on vacation. Wasn't happy, but he won't dare do anything about it."

"I heard about the deputy who was shot. How is he?"

"Point blank, face. He'll live. But still . . . Oh, Quinn, I almost had him. He sensed my trap. How does he do that?"

There was a pause.

"I'll start drafting extradition papers to get him back to Illinois if he's collared up there."

This probably wasn't his chiding her for wanting to circumvent the judicial process and deliver a writ of execution personally. He was the sort who would be thinking logically and methodically of tasks that lay ahead in the lengthy process of the law. Unlike her, Evan Quill didn't improvise and he didn't break rules.

She asked, "And the trial?"

A hesitation. "Gone to the jury. I'm confident. He's got no defense, some bizarre alibi that he was plotting to murder a pervert."

"What?"

"Yep. And a mysterious stranger on Route Twenty-Eight who really did it."

"The man on the grassy knoll."

Quill said, "There's one in every case. Somebody else done it. You sure he's still in Harbinger?"

"I'm sure."

He didn't respond for a moment. She asked, "Any thoughts, how long the panel'll be out?"

"You want to flip a quarter?"

"Be careful, Quill."

Did he laugh at this? Couldn't be sure. He said, "I'll be in court. Armed guards."

"You won't be in court forever. . . . And you never know how Offenbach'll come at you. Need some sleep. I'll call tomorrow."

After another pause, he said, "Wait. Ask you a serious question?"

"Hm?"

When she heard it, she laughed and gave him an answer.

Then they disconnected.

She plugged her phone in to charge and snapped the lights out. She lay down in bed and stared at the bumpy ceiling, hoping for sleep, though guessing it would be some time coming.

"I'm aching."

Marlowe points out: "You just ran ten miles this morning."

The women are in Stanley's Restaurant off Route 44, one in a beige uniform, one in jeans and a white tee. They are the same age, though Marlowe seems older. Maybe that's because of the rugged outfit. Maybe because of the gray eyes, which are burdened. This is true even when her lips arc into a smile. This is rare.

Vandalia County Deputy Cynthia Hooper waves for two more beers. Stanley's chills the mugs Antarctic, so that the first several sips require a napkin around the icy handle. They arrive and the women wrap and clink for a second time tonight.

Drinking is fine; they're off duty.

Marlowe is impressed with her friend's prowess at long-distance running. She herself now allows: "I run. But only when I'm being chased. Or chasing."

Hooper offers: "But now I know if it's chased or chasing, I can make it a full ten miles."

Marlowe nods in concession to the logic.

Hooper then says, "So there's something I want to bring up."

Sounding serious.

Marlowe sips and waits. She's not good with solemn conversations. Avoids them like hornets.

"I'd really like it if you'd be my daughter's or son's godmother."

"Well, you know I will." Marlowe tilts her head. "Is there some news you want to share?"

"Oh, my Lord no. Not yet."

"And what about the middle step?"

"A man? I'm working on it. That position is still help-wanted. But you know? Last week I lit up Bernie Fromm. Speeding. He's got a nice smile. And that guy is built, I'll tell you. He told me a joke while I wrote him up."

"What was it?"

"The joke? Okay." Hopper sips and sets her palms flat on the table, as if the gag might escape if she doesn't hold on. "You have to ask me two questions. The first is 'What do you do for a living?' The second is 'What's the hardest part about it?' Go ahead."

Marlowe frowns. "I'm supposed to ask you?"

"Right, go ahead."

"What do you do for a living?"

Hooper replies, "I'm a comedian."

"And what's the hardest—"

"Timing."

Marlowe, surprising herself, laughs hard. "Anybody telling a joke getting cited, he goes straight to the top of the datable list." She then asks, "You sure you want your kid to have a godmother that's a cop?"

"Oh, cops're a dime a dozen. I want her to have a godmother who's a badass."

Which requires another mug clink.

Hooper says, "Let's order. I can't stay late. Early watch tomorrow."

"Anything good?"

The deputy scoffs. "Not hardly. There've been complaints of kids four-wheeling behind a development."

"Where?"

"Old Bennett Road. You ever hear of it?"

"No, never have," Marlowe says and opens the menu.

THURSDAY, APRIL 6

Detective work is about unraveling puzzles, often in the most unlikely ways.

This was one of the things Constant Marlowe liked about it.

As she walked into the ancient red brick building on Hammett Street in downtown Upper Falls, she wondered if the solution to the hunt for Paul Offenbach would be inside.

Today, in a nearly identical outfit to yesterday's but with a black tee, she climbed the stairs and at the metal detector perplexed the guard when she announced she was armed and displayed her IDCI badge.

She didn't wait for any protocols or procedures. She simply said, "Official business," and steamed past him, leaving the near-retirement-age fellow to decide if making trouble was *worth* the trouble.

In the Recorder of Deeds office, she used the same two words with the clerk, an enthusiastic woman in her midtwenties who warmed immediately to the intrigue and said, "Whatever I can do. You bet." Marlowe wondered if she'd salute.

"Here's what I need: any record of property in the county owned by Paul or any other Offenbach."

Her visit last night to St. Francis Hospital had been partly to have some words with Jessica Lombardi and offer sympathy to Tony, which she'd done when they had wakened him.

She'd also wanted to question him.

Let's wake him up, why don't we? I don't think he'll mind. . . .

He'd been more than willing to help, writing down in loopy, morphine-slacked handwriting that the deputy had learned Offenbach was phony because he claimed he knew nothing of the county when in fact he seemed quite familiar with the geography.

Maybe he'd owned property here at some point, Marlowe speculated. Maybe he still did.

And if so, maybe that's where he was hiding out.

Because of the age of the county building Marlowe had the idea that the records woman would lug out huge, dusty tomes of maps on crisp, yellowing paper.

But computers had come to Harbinger County the same time they had everywhere else. The blonde—she was born to define "pert"—sat on a stool before her terminal and typed in the request with lightning strokes, despite long turquoise nails.

In minutes, the results were in, and it was clear that the puzzle wasn't going to be solved here.

No record showed an Offenbach, Paul or otherwise, owning property in Harbinger County or anywhere else in the state.

"Can you tell me what this is about?" the woman asked, and Marlowe knew from the shine in her eyes that she was a fan of true-crime shows.

"An investigation."

Which wasn't quite the level of detail the woman wanted.

Then she added, "Between you and me, it's classified. But big."

The clerk's eyes lit up.

Marlowe asked, "Is there a Vital Statistic Department here?"

"Yes, Officer . . . Detective?"

"It's agent."

Even better. "Second floor."

Upstairs, Marlowe met the woman who presided over this operation. She was pleasant enough but unconcerned about criminal conspiracies and wanted to get back to a stack of birth certificates. Maybe nine months before, a period of bad storms took out the power for a few days and kept Harbinger couples inside with not much else to do.

This official let Marlowe do her own searching and after a brief lesson on how the computer system worked, she was turned loose to dig.

With far less impressive fingertip velocity than the *Forensic Files* clerk's downstairs, she typed in her request.

The only hit she had was that in 1939, Emma Offenbach, a resident of Harbinger County, married Nigel Cotter, also a resident, and became Emma Cotter.

Was this gold, or not?

It was back down to Deeds to find out. Now the target of the day was property owned by Nigel Cotter. "From the late thirties to date."

"I'm on it, Agent."

The cerulean nails tap-danced once more and soon there was an answer.

Cotter had sold a house in 1940 and bought another the same year. It was located at One Trail Ridge Road. When Cotter passed in 1964, the house went to another Cotter, who kept title in his name . . . until it was transferred to an Illinois limited liability corporation ten years ago.

"Will there be a big arrest, like they show on *Small Town Murders?* They're reenactments but they're still pretty okay. You watch it?"

"It's a good one."

Constant Marlowe did not own a television set.

She stepped into a dim corridor, tugged out her phone, and called a contact in the Illinois Secretary of State's Office. Two minutes later her friend said that Marlowe had been right in her assumption: managers of the LLC owning the house at One Trail Ridge Road were in Nassau, the Bahamas.

In the same building where Paul Offenbach had an office.

The puzzle was almost complete. One piece remained to be found.

The most delicate one of all.

"Travis."

Offenbach nodded to the solidly built man, midthirties, in jeans and a gray tee. The garment was tight, showing off muscles and a potbelly. His hair was dark and thick, and his face round. Offenbach had known him for several months and in all that time he'd never known him to be clean-shaven. Not sporting an intentional beard, as Offenbach did from time to time, just stubble.

Maybe lazy.

Maybe a look.

The two men were outside a dilapidated shack on narrow, winding Trail Ridge, which was surrounded by pine and oak forests and dense tangles of a thousand species of plants. The men were two miles from the terminus of the road, where the Offenbach-Cotter family house was located.

Travis had just driven up from Illinois, in a commercial van, the logo on the side reading *Henrietta's Florist*, surrounded by colorful bouquets. This was at Offenbach's request. He wanted a vehicle that would blend in, not a Tony Soprano black Escalade, his wheels of choice in Chicago.

"What's the plan?"

Offenbach pointed the way the man had come. "Go back to 22, turn right toward Upper Falls. About four miles, there's an outlet mall. Park there, facing out. You need a good view of the highway. Watch for an orange Honda Accord, coming this way."

"That'll be her?"

He didn't answer. Who else would it be?

"Call me, so I'll be ready."

"And if somebody else's with her?"

His first reaction was to snap sarcastically, *And what on earth difference would that make?*

But he just said, "We go forward anyway." Offenbach was a smart man and connections and deductions came instantly to him. He had to remind himself that the rest of the world was not like that. He offended people from time to time. And offended people could be dangerous. He'd had to kill several of them.

"All right." Travis grunted. He climbed back in his florist van and returned to the highway.

Offenbach walked inside the shack. Closed the door. The groaning of rusty metal was loud.

He looked around, inhaling hot air aromatic of dust and mold. The interior was about eight hundred square feet, and largely empty, though a card table sat in one corner beside an old office chair, the upholstery ripped as if shredded by a bear's claws. The other decorations: hypodermic needles, broken meth and crack pipes, and rocks thrown through the windowpanes, all of which were shattered. What was there about human nature that could not allow a single piece of glass in an abandoned building to remain intact?

The shack was at a bend in Trail Ridge and the front window offered a perfect view of his shooting range—exactly where Constant Marlowe would be driving on her way to the Cotter house.

Last night, after the whisky and pipe, he'd gone to bed without a solution to the problem.

Now he had one.

A half hour ago Tomas Wexler had called.

"Offenbach. Listen, Marlowe made your house."

"How?"

It was supposed to be hidden legally.

"Digging in Public Records. I've got somebody works there. My niece. She's a ditz but she does what she's told. Always lets me know if somebody from out of town's nosing around." A pause. "For this, Offenbach, I get points off my next delivery?"

He had agreed.

Now, he'd go with the simple solution. Marlowe would have looked over a map and seen that there was only one way to his family's house—straight up Trail Ridge. Her plan would be to drive close, then pull off the road and hike up, undetected, through the brush.

But she wouldn't get that far.

As she slowed for the curve, he would open fire with his Bushmaster assault rifle, modified to be fully automatic.

Your destiny, Constant . . .

Suicidal probably . . .

He'd be doing her a favor.

As he slipped a magazine in, and chambered a round, he happened to think of the comic books his father had owned. These were not about superheroes but soldiers in World War II. Big American GIs fighting Germans and Japanese inked into embarrassing ethnic stereotypes. The lieutenant or dogface heroes were forever letting loose with their Tommy guns. The artists had written the sound in angled, boldface, all-cap type.

BUDDA BUDDA BUDDA . . .

So, kill his nemesis. Take the millions waiting for him in the house and then get to a private airport where a pilot who was making a great deal of money would spirit him off to a dirt field in Ontario . . . and onward from there to a new life.

He checked the stubby black gun. He had an extra magazine in his pocket. Unnecessary—the field of fire was a mere thirty feet away—but its presence reassured him.

He moved the grizzly-ripped chair to the window overlooking the road, which was partially covered by a tattered drape that was gray but had probably started the decade white.

Aiming out the window, he reminded himself to grip tightly. With the gun in full auto mode, the muzzle rose like basketball player about to dunk.

He set his phone on the sill. It was on silent and he didn't want to miss Travis's call. Just then, two things happened at once: the left panel of the curtain flew violently inward and there was a loud snapping bang from the floor.

This was followed by a third occurrence: a rolling boom of a long gun in the distance.

Offenbach dropped the assault rifle and flattened himself on the filthy and fragrant oak panels beneath him.

A wave of disgust. Marlowe had figured the whole damn thing out. She'd probably looked at Google Maps and found both his house and the shack. She understood that this was a perfect ambush spot.

Another crack as a slug dug wood out of the floor closer to him. Another boom of thunder.

He grabbed his phone to call Travis and tell him to get to the top of the hill where Marlowe would be shooting from. He would also ask angrily, by the way, why had he let a goddamn bright orange car get past him?

And then: He closed his eyes briefly, hearing a creak from the ancient floorboards.

He turned and saw her.

Constant Marlowe was aiming her gun, a small semiauto, at his head. Her phone was in her other hand. She said into the device, "I'm good. Thanks. You can go." She put the mobile away.

Who was the sniper?

Hardly mattered.

Endgame. He had tortured and killed her friend and now she was going to do what she'd come to Harbinger County for: to murder him.

She'd won.

Offenbach sighed.

Okay. Pull the trigger. Get it over with. His thoughts were not on his mother, certainly not on his father, nor one of the many women he'd had over his years. Cousin Sarah made a fleeting appearance. Then he pictured chess grandmaster Garry Kasparov.

He braced, wondering how long he would be conscious after the slug hit.

But she didn't shoot.

Her gravelly voice: "Toss your sidearm to me. And you know how to do it."

He pulled the Glock from his belt with thumb and index finger only. And pitched it to her feet.

She placed the semiauto on the chair and tucked her own pistol away in her front waistband, where she could draw it easily if need be. She collected the assault rifle and dropped the magazine, then ejected the chambered round. She used the tip of this bullet to push out the two pins holding the upper to the main receiver of the weapon. The gun separated into two pieces. She threw the pins out the window into the brush and the gun parts to the floor.

The assault rifle was now just a conversation piece.

"Stand up and pull up your shirt. And turn in a circle."

He did as she'd asked.

"Now your pant cuffs."

He complied; he never wore ankle holsters.

He reflected, so there *is* another way to get to Trail Ridge Road, other than from Route 22. It probably involved Marlowe hiking several miles through forest and underbrush. The foliage was dense here. It would have been a tough trek.

And what was *this*?

He squinted, watching Marlowe take something from her jacket pocket.

Offenbach was confused, thinking, *Why would she be carrying around a small gray purse?*

Constant Marlowe had never seen Paul Offenbach up close. Doing so now, she thought he was smaller than she'd expected.

But this was not uncommon in her line of work. Often the mental picture of your prey swells in size during the pursuit.

Which doesn't mean they are any less dangerous when you finally go nose to nose.

The guns were tucked away in the locked fiber pouch. Her jacket was off, as was his. The two stood six feet apart in the middle of the shack, which was lit by sunlight streaming through the windows and cracks in the walls. Dust motes and pollen spores floated slowly around them.

She occasionally wondered why she was drawn to hand-to-hand combat, why she carried the gray pouch everywhere. One person said it might be because she was testing herself. Another had suggested that, being a woman, she had the advantage of surprise.

She'd been amused that it was *men* giving these opinions.

In fact, the answer was that it simply was more satisfying than guns, knives . . . and, if she were being honest, handcuffs and Miranda warnings.

In this particular instance it was because she intended to beat Cynthia Hooper's killer to death. In the motel she would have been content to shoot him. Now she had the chance to make him feel what her friend had.

Her fists balled, her center of gravity low, she swayed back and forth, ready to meet an attack.

Offenbach was calm—eerily calm. He slipped into a martial arts stance. A real one, not like Rudy's bizarre mock-up. Marlowe had never had the patience to learn any. The training took forever and sparring was, for her, more like dancing. To be a boxer, you did jump rope and calisthenics and punching bags, you ran. Then you got in the ring and you hit and hit and hit.

Coming in fast, keeping his fists centered and head down, he drove her back with a series of carefully aimed blows. She blocked most, though took a stinging connect in the chest. Breastbone at least, not solar plexus. But he didn't withdraw fast enough and she landed an uppercut on his chin.

His head snapped back and he barked a faint cry and his eyes instantly teared. A hand went to his mouth.

Maybe martial arts senseis don't teach one of the first rules in street fighting: keep your tongue from between your teeth.

Offenbach's face returned to calm and he spat blood.

Her serene eyes matched his. Hatred abounded in both quarters but there was not a breath of distracting anger between them.

They collided once, twice, three times, forearms deflecting forearms, some blows landing. He was strong and had speed behind his lunges.

Unlike Lumberjack Rudy, he didn't try to grab her shirt. His choice probably was not a playing-fair issue. She guessed he believed that trying the maneuver would tie up one of his hands for the grip, which meant losing a defense barrier, exposing his face to a chain of vicious lightning blows.

His aim was good—and he nailed her chin once—but she knew how to roll to trick the energy, and the blow did little damage.

Boxing was about learning, and she was seeing that he had a limited number of punches in his repertoire. Marlowe soon memorized them all and lined up several defensive responses.

Again and again she danced in, deflected or took a sloppy blow, and delivered her signature triplet left-right-left, which had earned her hundreds of points and a number of knockouts. Some of these were technical, some were wholesale unconsciousness—no more satisfying moment exists in the world of prizefighting.

More blood eased from his mouth. More moisture from eyes and nose. His breath came in gasps as he grew winded. She had stepped back often, making him charge her, which used far more effort. For the first time in the battle his eyes were uncertain.

He eased back, gathered himself, and spit more blood on the floor. He held up a hand.

Ignoring it, she charged in fast and landed a solid right on his chin once more.

He glared angrily.

Did he really think she'd give him a moment's rest?

This was hardly a refereed match.

No rules, except for the guns.

He began, flailing, to force her back. Fine with Marlowe. She avoided his fists and watched his energy evaporate.

"You know I'm a very rich man." The words were spaced out by hard inhaling and exhaling. "How'd you like to be a rich woman?"

Constant Marlowe rarely said a single word during a fight. And never listened to any, except those like "Enough" and "You win."

As he paused, waiting perhaps for a response, she struck like a hungry rattlesnake: leaping in low and when he lifted his left to block the blow, he realized too late it was a feint; she drove her left fist into his jaw hard. Spit and blood flew.

It would have been a bad bruise—had he survived the fight. Which Marlowe was determined he would not.

A flash of fury in his eyes. Then, snap, calm was back.

They pummeled some.

They backed away, they circled.

They attacked.

The money gambit hadn't worked. The great chess player, the great planner needed a new tactic.

"You want to know what I used on her?" Gasps. "Hurting people can be complicated. I think simple is better. Don't you want to know?"

She came in fast but he blocked both blows, though she could feel his arms had grown weaker. Flailing does that. Compact movement is the only way to fight.

"A razor knife. And the lighter I use for my pipe. It's like a little blow torch."

Marlowe noted that he was favoring his left shoulder.

"After you slip something metal under the skin, you can heat it up with the torch. Or you can just raise blisters with the flame itself. Depends on your mood."

Marlowe observed, too, that his right ankle was weaker than the other.

"My, that woman could scream . . ."

Left shoulder, right ankle . . .

The body is a funny thing. Even before you feel the pain of a damaged foot, your wiring tells you exactly how much it's going to hurt if you move a certain way and does what it can, all by itself, to take over your movement and keep you free from pain.

Marlowe now ducked and moved in to Offenbach's right. To spare his damaged ankle, his body shifted weight to his left foot and instructed the left arm to rise, steadying himself.

When she drove her blow not into his body but his left fist itself, she was prepared for her knuckles to meet bone. He was not.

Two of Offenbach's fingers snapped—left ring and pinkie.

He barked a guttural cry, and she leaped away. Unfair, somebody might say, to target a hand. But one could also put into that category distracting your opponent with details of torturing her friend.

His left arm useless, Offenbach now came in fast and low, then just before jabbing with his right, stopped and kicked hard. He aimed for her groin, as if momentarily forgetting the different physical structures of the two sexes. Marlowe let the blow land. It hurt but didn't paralyze.

Ache, not sting.

She grabbed his foot and twisted.

Offenbach went down on his face.

He lay stunned.

She could easily have dropped a knee into a kidney, paralyzing him. Then rolled him over and done the same to his throat, concluding her mission in Wisconsin.

Marlowe did not do this, however. It wasn't her boxing instinct that said you sportingly let your opponents rise and collect themselves before reengaging. No, it was that the fight had lasted only five or six minutes and her intention was to make him suffer for the same amount of time Cynthia had: at least a full ten.

He lifted his head and when he realized she wasn't attacking him from behind, took a moment to rest.

Or that's what she thought.

In fact, Offenbach had been scanning the floor of the cabin. He crawled forward fast and scooped up a handful of hypodermics and broken drug pipes, not caring about his wounds to his own palm and fingers. He flung the handful hard. She dodged most but a shard from a shattered glass bong struck her on the cheek. She ignored the diversion and when he rolled to his feet and charged, she deflected his roundhouse.

In the ring, Marlowe was known for her unrelenting attacks.

And this was how she now advanced on Paul Offenbach.

Jab, jab, uppercut, driving him back.

His defense was in shambles. Her vicious left hook connected squarely with his chin, snapping his head back. Her right drove into his midsection—not always a good strategy in the ring with a pro, who'd do daily sit-ups to tighten the muscles into boards. But that was not Paul Offenbach. The blow was aimed perfectly. It shot the air from his lungs.

He dropped onto his back, gasping, paralyzed.

"Uh, uh, uh . . ." His arms were spread out like he'd been making snow angels. Fingers curled, chest rising and falling.

She straddled him.

No banter, of course. No final words.

Marlowe gripped his hair and tugged back to fully expose his throat. He tried to lift his arms; they weren't responding.

Their eyes met and she lifted her right fist, which some reporter had described—ironically now—as her "killer weapon."

Her arm had not yet descended when a voice from behind her barked, "No!"

Two gray-uniformed men lunged forward, gripped her arms with fierce pressure, and pulled her off.

"Truck driver called in about gunfire somewhere around Trail Ridge."

Sheriff Louie Braddock was standing with his arms crossed, dead center in the dusty pull-off in front of the dilapidated shack. Constant Marlowe wondered what the structure had been used for. If a residence, it would have been less than appealing even when fresh.

"He said he thought it was a rifle. You know, boom, not a snap. Isn't season now, so we had to check it out. You know anything about a long gun around here?"

"Do not, Sheriff."

He looked toward Paul Offenbach, cuffed and being looked after by some medics.

"So he didn't leave town."

"Appears I was wrong."

The sheriff scoffed.

Marlowe glanced toward Route 22. Deputies had stopped traffic temporarily. At the intersection sat a florist's van, black and dusty. Henrietta's Florist. The dark-haired driver stared at the excitement. Flashing lights were a perennial draw.

"You'll want him extradited down to Illinois, and I'd have to talk to our DA, but I think she'll agree to you folks having him first. We have him on attempted murder here and the weapons charge. You've got the full monty."

She nodded her thanks. She hadn't expected this, considering she'd just tried to murder somebody in his jurisdiction.

"Thanks. I'm a friend of the DA in Vandalia. We'll make sure he comes back here for the Lombardi trial."

Braddock said, "If I know your state law, Agent Marlowe, he'll get life in Illinois, and attempt here're buy him sixty years. That man is not seeing the outside of a cell ever."

The Motorola on the sheriff's hip clattered with a staticky transmission. Loud.

"Sheriff, you there?"

"Kelly, I'm still on Trail Ridge. Offenbach'll be in for processing. Give it thirty, forty—"

"Sheriff. There's a situation."

The dispatcher's voice sounded unsteady. Usually they were calmer than this. It takes a certain type of person to do 911 work.

"Go ahead."

"It's Tomas Wexler. He's dead."

The sheriff said nothing for a few seconds. "Okay. Why don't you keep going here?"

"Shot. He was on Clement Road at a light. Looks like somebody pulled up and shot through his side window."

"Just like Tony got shot," Braddock said, half to himself.

"Six rounds. Small caliber. Looks like a twenty-five."

"Where on Clement?

"That stretch along the preserve. Near Osceola Trail."

"So, no cameras."

"Not a one."

"Anybody see anything?"

"Not so far."

Braddock asked, "When d'it happen?"

"Pete thinks an hour ago, two maybe."

"I'll be there when I'm finished up."

"All right."

He turned to Marlowe, looked down at her eyes, ten inches below his. "You heard?"

Hard not to, with that volume.

She nodded.

"I'll be blunt with you, Agent Marlowe. Where were you the last two hours?"

"Don't recall, other than trying to find him." A nod toward Offenbach, who happened to be staring at her with a look that radiated not a shred of emotion. Dead eyes, she thought. Dead eyes.

Hands on hips, Braddock surveyed the shack and the tangle of brush and vines behind it. The growth reminded Marlowe of the land bordering her own property, which was halfway between Chicago and the Wisconsin state line. The house was a bungalow, many years old. As for the yard itself, front and back, she'd had the grass removed and replaced with gravel, atop plastic sheets to stifle weeds.

"If I was to check firearms records, would I find that you've ever bought a twenty-five-caliber handgun?"

"Never have. No stopping power. Only three-eighty, nine, and forty-five ACP."

"Ah . . ." Braddock's eyes took in a hawk making leisurely circles overhead. "Shooter was smart. Probably stayed inside the vehicle. All the ejected brass ended up there, so he didn't have to worry about wasting time picking them up off the ground."

"Makes sense," she said. Many a killer had been caught because of fingerprints left on the cartridges ejected from semiauto weapons. They wipe the gun but don't think to clean the brass.

Braddock said in a low voice, "I'm going to take your statement about what happened here, Agent Marlowe. And then I think I'd like you to get out of Harbinger County."

She shrugged. "No reason for me to stay."

"You're a good shot," Constant Marlowe said to Jessica Lombardi as the woman handed over the green rifle case containing the Winchester 70. "You placed them right where they needed to be."

The woman said, "We take deer for food. Tony has a ragout recipe that—I was going to say it's to die for. Bad choice of words."

The two women were standing in the parking lot outside the hospital, near the cascade that was truly lovely, even if it was a lesser one.

The water, clear as polished window glass, fell and fell, shattered and regrouped and changed into rainbows whenever the sun was freed by gaps in the staunch clouds.

Marlowe put the rifle and ammo box into her trunk and closed the lid.

After she'd learned from Tony about Offenbach's prior connection to Harbinger County, and about the Cotter house, she'd come up with her plan.

She knew from Jessica that Wexler had people inside county offices. They'd know to call him if anybody came in inquiring about Offenbach and any property he or his family might have owned. Or at the least if an out-of-towner started asking odd questions.

Marlowe supposed it was the pert True Crime Girl, which was a disappointment. But she'd learned long ago what you see isn't always what truly is.

Wexler would have called Offenbach to report Marlowe had made the Cotter house.

Offenbach would set a trap for her on Trail Ridge, knowing that she'd sneak up to the house to kill him.

A trap that she'd use against them.

Marlowe had then gone to Jessica—the last piece of the puzzle. She recalled that Braddock had said both Tony and Jessica were hunters. So she'd asked, "Will you help me get the man who shot Tony?"

"Offenbach?" Her daunting eyes had glowed. "You bet I will."

There had been a pause. Marlowe had added, "When I say *get*, I don't mean arrest. Do you understand what I'm saying?" She had noted that Jessica wore a cross and some of the flower arrangements in her husband's room bore the symbol, as well.

Jessica didn't hesitate. "Tony and I're religious. We go every Sunday. I teach Bible school. The Thou Shalt Not Kill—it's the Sixth Commandment in our church—it means you can't kill the *innocent*. No rule against murdering the evil. What do you want me to do?"

Now, eyes on the tumbling water, the woman said, "It didn't turn out the way we wanted."

"No. At least he'll spend the rest of his life in a small concrete box. That's something."

Justice of sorts . . .

Marlowe sloughed off her disappointment.

"I've got something for you."

She walked to the passenger-side door and opened it. She lifted a thick manila envelope off the seat and handed it to Jessica.

"What's this?"

"Don't open it here." They weren't alone. Staff, discharged patients, and family members were walking between the parking lot and the hospital.

A frown of curiosity appeared in the round, freckled face.

Marlowe said, "It's two hundred and fifty thousand dollars."

"*What?*"

"I got to Offenbach's house on Trail Ridge before the deputies. He had a go bag. You know what that is?"

"We watched *Breaking Bad.*" Jessica offered it back "But we can't take it."

"It's laundered. Offenbach would never have traceable cash."

"I don't mean that. It's just it's not ours."

Marlowe had anticipated the reaction. She had a plan for this too. "There's something called the crime victims reparation fund. Every state's got one. Consider it's from there. Tony's rehab's going to be expensive."

Jessica stared down at the envelope.

"If you don't want to spend it, use it to start the fire in the barbecue when you're cooking your venison burgers."

The envelope disappeared into her purse.

You staying around here?"

"No, I'm going back to Hopewell. Vandalia County." She explained about the trial of the man who might be one of Offenbach's associates at Cynthia's murder.

She added, "The facts aren't clear. I don't want an innocent man to go to jail. I don't want a guilty one to go free."

Marlowe walked around to the driver's side of the car, the orange shade glowing like lava in the sunlight.

Jessica said, "That trial? It'll be over soon?"

"It's gone to the jury. They could come back today. Could be next week."

"Tony and me? We'll pray that God sees that justice is done."

Constant Marlowe nodded her thanks and sat down behind the wheel, thinking, *And maybe, just maybe, She would.*

Brendan DuBois *is the award-winning* New York Times *bestselling author of twenty-six novels, including the Lewis Cole series. He has also written* The First Lady *and* The Cornwalls Are Gone *(2019), co-authored with James Patterson,* The Summer House *(2020), and* Blowback *(2022). The year 2023 saw DuBois release two additional novels with Patterson:* Countdown *and* Cross Down. *He has also published nearly two hundred short stories.*

His stories have won three Shamus Awards from the Private Eye Writers of America, two Barry Awards, two Derringer Awards, and the Ellery Queen Readers Award. He has also been nominated for three Edgar Allan Poe awards from the Mystery Writers of America.

In 2021 he received the Edward D. Hoch Memorial Golden Derringer for Lifetime Achievement from the Short Mystery Fiction Society.

This is his seventh appearance in this annual collection.

He is also a Jeopardy! *game show champion.*

THE LANDSCAPER'S WIFE

Brendan DuBois

It was a late spring day when my landscaper—Hiram Grant—took a midmorning break and came up on my porch, where I was sitting in one of the two wooden rocking chairs with my cane held between my legs. Hiram was solid, built wide, wearing soiled khaki pants tucked into muddy Wellington boots and wearing a gray hoodie on top.

The sleeves of the hoodie were pushed back, revealing long beefy forearms and dark tattoos. He had a thick, full beard and the top of his head was razored tight, leaving just a faint stubble. One of his upper canine teeth was missing, leaving a dark gap.

Out in front, along the shoreline of my small man-made pond, Hiram's assistant Cray Lister was raking out dead leaves from the pond's bottom. Cray has worked for Hiram since getting out on parole from the state prison in Concord two years earlier.

We rocked silently in the chairs for a couple minutes, the low azalea bushes and holly in front of us, getting high enough to block the view of the pond. Even after having moved here more than five years ago, I still found it hard to adjust to how quiet everything was. The Granite State was known for lots of things—from cheap state booze to its presidential primary—and closed-mouth neighbors was one of them. My closest neighbor, Sally Turner; her husband Bob had been dead and buried for a year before I found out, only because mail going to him had ended up in my mailbox.

At the time Sally had shrugged and said, "Didn't want to bother you none, that's all."

Hiram coughed, which was usually a sign that he was going to say something.

"Well," he said.

"Yes?"

"Maura still taking good care of you?"

I said, "Yes, of course."

Maura was Hiram's wife and my housekeeper, who came in every week to vacuum, dust, wash the floors and countertops, and move things around so I couldn't find them later.

"Good."

A few more minutes passed. I wondered if that bit was going to be this morning's message of the day.

I was wrong.

He said, "You see how much gas prices have gone up?"

"That I have."

"I mean, I know you don't drive around much, but I sometimes drive up to an hour to take care of my old-time customers. Not new ones, Christ, I'm only taking on new customers who live within ten minutes of me, but it used to cost me forty bucks to fill up the tank for one of my trucks, and now it's close to a hundred. But it's not just gas, it's anything with oil, like fertilizer and plastic parts. My idiot helper Cray two weeks ago ran over one of my rakes. Last year it cost me fifteen bucks and now it's twenty-eight. Everything's going up."

I nodded. I saw where this was going. Hiram and I had a deal that he got paid a hundred dollars a week, week after week, without him sending me an invoice and me getting lawn mowing, tree trimming, gutter cleaning, and snowplowing in return without having to ask.

But his costs were going up.

I was going to be reasonable.

"Go ahead, Hiram," I said.

He heaved himself out of the chair.

"I need to start charging you more, sorry."

"I understand."

Hiram looked out at Cray, still raking my pond.

"Glad to hear that, John," he said. "Starting next Friday, it's going to be a thousand dollars."

My mouth went dry.

"A week?"

He clomped down the front porch steps. "Hell, no, I'm not that unreasonable. A thousand a month. In cash. Prefer hundreds, if that's okay."

I didn't say anything.

His empty chair kept rocking back and forth for a while.

That night I was alone out on my porch, most of the lights off so that the night insects wouldn't be attracted to come over and bother me. In my right hand I held a tumbler of Jameson and ice cubes. I really craved a nice craft beer from California—like a Lost Abbey Cable Car or an Anchorage Wendigo—but I've not had a single Californian beer since moving to New Hampshire five years ago. I still occasionally liked a store-bought beer like Sam Adams or Michelob, but those were watery imitations of what I really craved.

The Jameson and ice was unsatisfactory replacement since in my prior life in California, not once I had ever sipped on a whiskey.

I took a swallow, shivered some as the icy burning feeling traveled down my throat.

What was Hiram up to?

Why the sudden and drastic price increase?

I stayed outside, watched the fireflies dance and swirl out there, and decided I didn't have enough information to make a guess as to what was going on with my landscape.

Another sip.

Out in the woods to the side of my yard—separating me from my other neighbors, the McAdams—there was a harsh shriek from some animal that repeated itself twice before it getting quiet again.

Quiet it was.

Other night birds and animals had immediately shut up, not wanting to draw attention to themselves to what bloody business was going on.

Like being in the yard at San Quentin, seeing somebody getting shanked, and instantly turning around to look at the position of the sun in the sky, or bending over to tie your shoes.

That's what it was like.

I finished my whiskey, grabbed my cane, and leaned into it as I got back into the house.

I left the cane at the side of the door, tossed the ice cubes from my tumbler into the sink, and washed, rinsed, and dried the glass.

Next was a careful stroll through the house, making sure the windows and the three doors—the front door, the kitchen door at the rear, and the one leading into the garage—were all locked.

They were.

There was one more door, leading into the cellar.

No need to check that.

It was always locked.

Two days later I was outside again on my porch, washing four skinny paint brushes in two small plastic buckets—one with tepid soapy water and the other with tepid rinse water—and slowly took my time, washing, rinsing, and repeating when necessary. When I was satisfied that they were clean, I would next pat them dry with a paper towel and then let them lie out on the porch to dry.

I looked up when a black Ford Ranger pickup truck came up my driveway and stopped. The door opened up and Maura Grant stepped out, Hiram's wife and my housecleaner. She had on black stretch yoga shorts, a Red Sox T-shirt, and sandals. Her thick hair was black and trimmed to shoulder length, and she reached into the truck bed, picked up a vacuum cleaner and a bulging bag carrying her cleaning supplies. The first time she came here, a year after I had moved in, I went to help her and she had smirked and said, "You're the one with the cane. Go away or I'll kick it out from under you."

She came up the flagstone path to the porch and said, "What room should I skip today?"

"The studio" I said.

Maura paused. "That's the third time in a row I haven't done that messy shithole."

"That's because I know where everything is and don't want it moved."

Maura showed a familiar smile. "Okay. This time. No studio. But one of these days your paint tubes and those rags are gonna light off from spontaneous combustion, and you'll remember this conversation, and you'll think, 'damn, should have listened to Maura.'"

I twirled my cane again in my hands. "I think that every day."

"Doubt it," she said, walking past me. Her toenails were painted bright red.

I got back to work.

Two and a half hours later I was reading Doris Kearns Goodwin's latest work of history, when Maura came out to join me on the porch. It had gotten warmer and she had taken off her Red Sox T-shirt and her sandals. Her face was flushed with sweat, her perfect hair was matted some, and she was wearing a black sports bra to go with her tight yoga shorts.

She said, "Everything's done, except your studio. And your sacred cellar. Why is that door always locked?"

"That's where I bury the bodies," I said.

"Not funny the first time, not funny the tenth," she said. She stroked a piece of wet hair across her forehead. The black sports bra looked very nice on her tanned body.

"Off to take a shower."

"Sounds good."

Two minutes later I got up to the bathroom, heard the water running in the shower. I leaned the cane up against the near vanity, stripped, and gently slid open the shower curtain. Maura was in the middle of washing her hair and turned and smiled at me.

"Do your back?" I asked, stepping in. "Do your front?"

A nice inviting grin came my way. She ducked her head under the shower head, the streams of water and soap running down her curves, and she slipped into my hug and kissed me.

"But some jokes last forever," she said, one hand reaching down to squeeze my butt.

Later we were in my bed, cuddling. She idly played with my chest hairs. "You know what I like about your cane and injured hip?"

"It stirs up your maternal instincts and makes you want to take care of me?"

"As if," she said. "Having two of Hiram's sons have knocked out any maternal instinct I may have possessed. No, the reason I like your banged-up hip is that I like being on top, riding along like a cowgirl. Hiram would never allow that. It'd hurt his feelings or whatever, so he needs to be on top, grunting and grinding along like a bear in heat. Score another one for the patriarchy."

"That's a picture I'd like to forget," I said.

She laughed, tugged at a few chest hairs. "Good luck with that. Hey, can you see the time?"

"It's two o'clock."

"'Kay, time for me to go," she said, getting up, me looking in appreciation at her body. "Need to dry my hair, get dressed, be on time for my next appointment."

"Don't you get tired of Hiram keeping track of all your moves?"

She padded her way nude to the bathroom. "I do, but I might have some slack time coming up in the next few weeks. I think my husband has something new coming up to keep him occupied."

"What's that?"

Maura turned. "For some reason, he's coming after you, John. Hard."

Maura's words rattled around me during the afternoon, while I tried to get some painting done in my little studio. At one time

I think it had been designed for a nursery—Disney-style wallpaper and light pink trim along the baseboards—but something tragic had obviously happened before I moved in because everything else in the room was spotless, like the expected crib, drawers, and bassinet had never appeared.

The place was now a mess, and Maura always did her best, but I earlier told her that a good vacuum and dusting would suit me just fine. There were paint-splattered drop cloths on the floor, three easels—only one in use—and a stack of framed and stretched white canvases. Two work tables were covered with Mason jars holding a variety of paintbrushes, along with tubes of oil paint, color charts, a crowded bookshelf with books about painting, especially ones for enthusiastic amateurs.

Like me.

I spent an hour working on what I could see out the well-washed windows, which was my pond. Two weeks ago I had snapped a photo of a Great Blue Heron standing and fishing in a corner of my pond, along with a bunch of cattails, and that's what I spent my time with, listening to NPR from Concord and trying to focus.

I nearly succeeded.

With everything put away and capped—lots of expensive tubes of oil paint were tossed out earlier in my career when I forgot to put the caps back on—and after scrubbing my hands clean and drying them, I went downstairs and stopped in front of my cellar door. I punched in the five-key code and the lock snapped open, and with my cane, I went down the stairs, switching on the light to illuminate what I've been hiding all these years.

As I reached the bottom, I remembered the joking times Maura had guessed what was down here:

"A wine cellar?"

"A man cave with the largest TV screen possible?"

"John's last stand, complete with weapons and enough freeze-dried food to last five years?"

And the last one—which came closer than she realized—"the embalmed bodies of your enemies?"

Not quite.

I switched on another set of lights, and the cellar came into focus.

A treadmill.

A speed bag.

A punching bag.

A number of weight systems.

Shelves holding a number of weights.

A framed high-definition poster of Muhammed Ali yelling at a fallen Sonny Liston to get up off the mat and continue their controversial fight in the small town of Lewiston, Maine.

Not a gun in sight.

I hate guns.

I went to the treadmill and soon I was jogging away, looking to do five miles before getting to the speed bag.

Three days later Hiram and his man Cray returned to my property and quickly got to work, with Hiram standing on a pile of brown mulch from the rear of his pickup truck and shoveling it off in big wide sprays, with Cray trying to catch up by scooping it into on big pile.

I sat in my usual chair, cane held between my legs, and watched the work proceed.

When Hiram was done and so was Cray, he told Cray, "Ten minute break, okay?"

"Sure," Cray said, wiping the sweat away with his soiled hand, the stain from the bark mulch smearing brown on his craggy face. He went to the cab of the truck, took out a cooler, removed a bottle of water, and plopped himself down in shade from the truck.

From the truck Hiram took a battered metal cup, dipped it into my pond, spat it out, and then repeated, swallowing the second swig. He came over and clomped up to join me on the porch, and sat down.

As always, we kept quiet as we both rocked in our chairs, presumably admiring the view.

I broke the silence and said, "I was thinking of adding something to the property."

A few seconds passed. "Like what?"

"Like a stone bench, right in front of the near flower bed, so I can get a better view of the pond."

"What kind of bench?"

"A good one," I said. "Polished granite. Set deep and hard into the ground, so that frost heaves won't move it, and a century after I'm gone, kids and others can sit on the bench and still use it."

Hiram said, "A bit tricky, but I think I can do it. My sons Bruce and Roy get out of school shortly, they could give me an extra hand if I need it. Purmort Stoneworks'll probably have what you need. I'll bring in my John Deere with the rear excavator to give you a nice deep hole."

"Sounds good."

"You want to come with me to the Stoneworks, pick something out?"

"No," I said. "Traveling too long hurts my hip."

"Yeah, I remember."

More than ten minutes had passed and either Hiram was being nice to his boy Cray—doubtful—or he was waiting for me to speak up more.

I said, "Isn't Bruce the one planning to go to the university in the fall?"

"Planning and doing are two separate things," Hiram said.

"Meaning?"

"Meaning it's a father's responsibility to get his kids ready for the future. You tell me, what kind of future is coming? One where computers get more complicated, or one where the whole system collapses, and those who know how to do things with their hands thrive?"

"Maybe it's the kid's choice."

"You a dad?"

"No."

"That's it, then," he said.

Cray snuck a look over to us, amazed that his break time was still stretching out. I said, "We need to talk about the price increase."

"Go ahead."

"I understand the cost of everything going up, that you have more expenses to pay," I said. "But Hiram, be reasonable. To go from a hundred dollars a week to a thousand dollars a month . . . that's just not right."

"Sure it is," he said. "Old law says so."

"What law is that?"

"Law of supply and demand," he said. "I got the demand, and you got the supply."

"I don't think that's how it really works—"

"Well, that's how I see it," he interrupted. "I got the demand, and you got the supply. You think you can fool everyone in town by living simple-like and walking around like a cripple and selling your paintings at craft fairs, but you're rich, John Delaney. Rich. And I want my part of it."

That led to a few more seconds of silence, and Hiram got off the chair.

Back into my locked cellar once again for another workout, and I felt like running more, so I spent a good ten minutes longer on my treadmill, running to nowhere.

I tried not to dwell on that expression.

When the treadmill bleeped itself off and slowed down, I rubbed my face, arms, and legs with a white towel, and just paced around the cellar for a few minutes to cool off.

I stopped in front of my Muhammed Ali and Sonny Liston poster.

Slid three fingers on the side, and gently pulled it free.

It swung out on hidden and well-lubricated hinges, revealing a metal safe built into the concrete. I twirled the combination dial from memory; below the dial was a thumb sensor. I pushed in with my thumb—a very expensive security system that would only unlock the safe after the right combination has been dialed in and the system detected normal temperature, blood pressure, and heart rate from the thumb, derailing any "Mission: Impossible" moves using a severed thumb—and I unlocked the safe and pull the heavy door free.

Two hidden lights silently came on.

There were stacks of fifty-dollar bills and one hundred dollar bills, along with polished mahogany boxes containing five hundred gold Krugerrands from South Africa.

Yes indeed, as Hiram said, I was rich.

But how did he know?

And why the demand?

I had theories but I'd have to think them through.

I closed the safe door, locked it, spun the dial, and put Muhammad and Sonny back in place.

I should go for another five-mile run, but instead, I wanted a Sam Adams beer and to sit on my porch.

I went upstairs, switching off the lights, retrieving my cane, and with beer in hand, I limped out to the porch, just in time to meet Molly, our local UPS driver.

She handed over an Amazon box. She was short, stocky, and had dragons tattooed on both shins.

"Hell of a nice day, John, isn't it," she said.

"The very best," I said.

Molly looked at my cane. "How's that hip of yours?"

"Still the same."

She shook her head. "You take care."

"I will," I said, and that was the truth.

Two days later Hiram came by unexpectedly, and by himself.

I didn't like it.

I sat up straighter in my rocking chair, made sure my cane was firm in my hands.

He walked up, carrying something in one hand.

An iPad, its gray carrying case smeared with dirt and oil.

Hiram nodded, sat down, and opened up the iPad, started going through the screens.

"Here," he said, holding it out to me. "Went to Purmort Stone-works, took a few photos of what they got for granite benches. See anything you like?"

I took the iPad from his thick callused hands, started swiping the screens, thinking how odd it was, having this normal conversation, with that damn large elephant taking up most of the room.

There were tall ones, thin ones, solid blocks, and some that were decorative.

Then a couple clear-cut and polished granite slabs called to me.

"This one," I said. "I like this one."

He leaned over. I could smell stale tobacco and fresh sweat.

"Yeah," he said. "Simple design, solid base, nice sloping back you can lean against. I'd probably have to excavate a good six or eight foot deep trench, put some crushed stone in it, make sure it stays in one place, summer or winter. You want I should order it?"

"Please," I said.

"'Kay," he said, taking the iPad back, closing the screen.

I said, "What makes you think I'm rich, Hiram?"

He grinned. "Easy to tell, once you know where and how to look."

"You want to tell me?"

Hiram said, "You want me to give up my trade secrets?"

"I don't give a shit about your planting, watering, and fertilizer routines," I said. "Those secrets are safe. But you've got to tell me why you think I'm rich, before this goes any further."

The satisfied and happy grin got wider, like, *I know something you don't know.*

"This place had a hefty tax lien on it before you bought it," Hiram said. "Using a bank money order, you cleared it. Same thing for the house. No loans, no mortgages. Cash. And that's what you use, all the time. Cash at Hannaford's, cash at the local eateries, cash at the hardware store."

I said, "I like cash."

He said, "And where do you keep your money tree? I know all the plants on your property."

"I live light," I said. "I make a living."

"Right, right," Hiram said. "Your painting career. C'mon, you only sell them at local art shows and a few storefronts downtown."

"There are other markets," I said, feeling disquiet at how far Hiram had gone into his research.

I had thought years back that moving to a small town meant anonymous living and fading into the background, but now it was becoming the very opposite: Being a stranger from a strange land meant I was different, something to examine, something to question.

Hiram said, "What, private collectors? Museums? Are you really that good, John?"

I was trying hard to keep my bluff going, while my hands were tight on my cane.

"That's right," I said.

Hiram shook his head. "My son Bruce, the one who wants to college in the fall, he knows computers in and out, and the damn internet. He knows all that shit. I asked him to do research on an artist named John Delaney. You. I've seen your paintings at the Fine Arts and Collectibles downtown. You sign them 'J. Delaney.' Right? You don't have a . . . what you call it, a pseudo . . . pseudo . . ."

"Pseudonym, no I don't use a pseudonym."

"Well, John, you know what he found out? There's no artists named John Delaney in New Hampshire, New England, or the entire United States. What does that mean?"

Stuck in a corner, I had nothing to say.

But Hiram did.

"I'll tell you what," he said. "Somehow you ended up here, in Purmort, with a lot of cash. Probably on the run. Stolen from someone or somebody that has a long memory, a long reach. The money's enough to live comfortably on for the rest of your life, and then some, without you standing out apart. You bought this house, tried to blend in, set up a fake career so you could claim a yearly income. But if you look closely, it all falls apart. Like a support sill chewed out by termites."

"Nice analogy," I said.

He shrugged, got up. "Whatever. That's why I'm charging you what I'm charging you, and if that money doesn't come to me by day after tomorrow, you can figure out what happens next. So I'll see you then."

He started down the porch steps with his iPad in hand, and turned and said, "Oh, and by the way, thanks for confirming what I mostly guessed, that you're rich."

My mouth was dry and felt pasty. "How did that happen?"

Another unfriendly smile. "You chose that granite bench without even asking me the cost."

He took two steps. "Goddamn fool."

That night sleep didn't come easy, as I tossed and turned on my bed on the second floor. The opening line from the famed novel *Rebecca* kept echoing and echoing in my mind.

Last night I dreamt I went to Manderley again.

Yeah.

Except for me.

Last night I dreamt I fled Los Angeles again.

Ah, Los Angeles.

More than a hundred feet up in the air, in your air-conditioned cabin, with switches and levers at your smooth fingertips, gently moving tons of shipping containers, the lord of the sky and the port as far as the eyes could see. Making an obscene amount of money, you and your union buds controlling the nation, because you were the chokepoint where offshore shipping and goods came in. Which meant a lot of squeezed money being passed around large tables, handed over to you in white envelopes, and just living the good life.

Until I learned it was time to go, and go fast, and go hard.

The past five years had been a change, but also bliss, as I got used to the solitude and the quiet. In some ways it was the happiest I had ever been, not having the pressure of being high up over the Port of Los Angeles, not wondering if somebody in the union might get pissed over me at some slight—imagined or real—and ambushing me one night in the parking lot with the two traditional shots to the back of the head.

But now my bliss was being disturbed, bullied by a nearly illiterate peasant, my comfortable and anonymous retirement threatened.

That kind of threat would have lasted about ten minutes back in LA, with five minutes being spent on how many fingers of Hiram I wanted to break to teach him a lesson.

But here? Now?

Last night I dreamt I fled Los Angeles again.

Three days later I was back on my porch, nearly finishing my latest Doris Kearns Goodwin book, when Maura Grant came by for her usual housecleaning visit.

The black Ford Ranger pickup truck came up my dirt driveway, stopped.

I waited.

Something was off, something seemed wrong.

It took longer than usual for Maura to come out

I leaned forward in my rocking chair.

The door opened and she got out, but she moved slow.

It took two tries for her to get her cleaning supplies out of the truck bed.

I almost grabbed my cane and stood up to help her, but I remembered the first and last time I had tried that, so I sat still.

Maura labored as she came up to my porch, and she had sunglasses on.

A cold and hard sensation settled in my chest.

"Hey," I said.

"Hey," she said.

I said, "You know, the place is in pretty good shape. Why don't you drop your stuff and relax on the porch with me, have some lemonade, and we can talk about things. Shoes and ships. Sealing wax. Cabbages and kings. You'll still get paid."

Maura shook her head. "No, I don't take charity. What room again?"

"The studio," I said.

"All right," I said.

She nodded. "Do me a favor?"

"Without a doubt."

"Don't ask me to take off my sunglasses."

Maura went into my house and I sat there, thinking, reminiscing, maybe even plotting some.

I know what happened. I just knew.

But what would I do if she said something stupid like falling down the stairs, or bumping into a bookshelf, or having a planter fall on her head?

I kept on waiting.

Maura came out, voice strong but trembling. "I'm done, but there's enough time for the studio if you want."

I got up and leaned into my cane, walked over to her.

She stood still.

Like she was waiting.

I slowly brushed her hair, and then took off her sunglasses.

One eye was heavily bruised, nearly swollen shut.

The other was bruised as well, just not as severe as the first one.

"I told you not to ask me to take off my sunglasses."

I gently slipped them back onto her face.

"I know," I said. "I didn't."

Her Red Sox T-shirt was sweaty and I should have asked permission, but I didn't, and I lifted the shirt to reveal yellow and blue bruises around her ribcage. I dropped the shirt and said, "You're actually ahead of schedule."

"John, really, I'm not in the mood for a shower, or anything else."

I took her hand.

"Let me just start, and I'll stop the moment you ask me."

On my bed I draped a spare sheet and helped Maura get undressed, my temples throbbing, my heart moving slowly and hard. There was one more dark bruise, on front of her left thigh. I helped her into bed, best as I could, holding my cane, and then I limped into the bathroom and came back with a Tupperware bowl with warm, soapy water.

"A sponge bath?" she said, giving me the first smile I'd seen that day.

"That's right, just lay back and let me do all the work."

"Washing a nude woman in your bedroom, you consider that work?" she said.

A faint hint of a smile that encouraged me some.

I moved quietly and smoothly, washing her from feet to forehead, turning her on the side a few times, and she gasped in pain once when she was on her left thigh.

By the time I was slowly toweling her off she was weeping, chin trembling, and I wanted to say something supportive, but my throat was thick and I couldn't think of anything to say.

Much to my surprise, she came back after the dinner hour, and again walked slowly up to my porch. I put my book down and she sat next to me, took off her sunglasses. Maura had on black capri pants and a long-sleeved blue-checked blouse.

But no sunglasses.

Her eyes still looked awful.

Maura said, "Before you ask, Hiram's cousin is the chief of police, and the two officers that's the department are related to Hiram either through blood or marriage. The only women's counseling center in this part of the county closed last year because of budget cuts. That leaves me with few skills, not much cash, responsible for my sons."

I said, "Glad I didn't ask."

"All right then."

I reached over, gently took her hand. Squeezed it. Got a slight squeeze back. I said, "Anything in particular set him off this time?"

"Besides being drunk and mean down to the marrow of his bones?" she asked. "No, it wasn't a new topic, but his reaction was new."

"What was the topic?"

"Bruce."

"Your son?"

"You know of any other Bruces I hang with?"

"Sorry," I said. "Stupid comment. Go on."

"We were talking about Bruce's future," Maura said. "We both had been drinking, which meant it sort of spiraled. No excuse, Christ, I'm not one of those who excuses a man who beats a woman, but I kept on saying Bruce should go to college, and Hiram said, no, he and his brother Roy were both going to work for him after graduating high school, and that was it. No way was he going to waste money on a computer education when Bruce could get a better education working with his dad."

I kept quiet. Times like these, you can't interrupt. You can only listen.

Maura said, "And I told him, no way was my smart and oldest son going to root around in dirt and plants for the rest of his life, like his dumb dad . . . and that set him off."

I still kept my mouth shut.

"It was a hell of a fight, and I got him good, kneeing him twice in the balls, but then he got a kitchen knife and threatened to slice off my hair, and then cut my throat. I had to give up then. I didn't want to. But I did give up . . . though I'm glad his balls were aching, 'cause that meant I didn't have to put up with any more of his attention."

A few more seconds passed and I said, "What now?"

"Now? We'll both give each other the cold shoulder drill, and things will be frosty in the house, and then we'll start talking in a while to make the boys feel okay, and life goes on."

"Sorry."

"Unless you got other plans, that's the way of my world."

"Well," I said, "to be bold, I do have other plans. If you're interested. About going upstairs."

Her little smile looked odd and twisted near her bruised eyes.

"The spirit is willing," she said, "but my flesh is aching and weak."

"You wouldn't have to do anything," I said. "Just lay back and let me do all the work."

She seemed to consider that and nodded and got up. "Second time in a row you mentioned me, my naked body, and work. What, did you go to a Catholic school or something?"

I stood up as well. "Jesuit."

"Close enough," she said.

The next time Hiram came back he and Cray mowed my lawn, while a sullen-looking Bruce Grant trimmed my shrubbery, using an old-fashioned pair of garden shears. His younger brother Roy picked up the clippings and tossed them in the back of his dad's truck. I sat on the porch, cane in one hand, white business-sized envelope in the other.

When Hiram barked out that it was break time, I left my porch, limped over to him. He was wearing heavy Timberland boots, white socks, cut-off dungaree shorts, and a soiled white tank top T-shirt.

As I got closer, I thought that Hiram probably didn't understand irony, for in some circles—not mine—his shirt was called a wife-beater.

He took a crumpled handkerchief, wiped his sweaty face, and said, "Hey."

I nodded.

"Here you go," I said, handing over the white envelope.

A big grin came over his sweaty face. "Well, well, well."

He took the envelope and roughly tore it open, like a worried dad looking for a ransom note. He pawed through it and the grin evaporated.

"This is freakin' light."

"Yes."

"Five hundred dollars light."

"Good job," I said. "You can count without moving your lips."

He crumpled up the envelope and the five hundred-dollar bills in his fist.

"What the hell? Where's the rest? Don't tell me you don't have it."

I leaned on my cane. "Oh, I have it. And then some. But there's a new deal. You promise me, right now, that you won't raise a hand against Maura, then you get the rest of the five hundred dollars, and the rest of the monthly payments without any argument on my part."

The money and envelope remained crushed in his fist. His face reddened more and his eyes narrowed.

"You are way the fuck out of line."

"I beg to disagree."

He stepped forward, held up his fist to my face. "You see that truck? That belongs to me. See the lawnmowers? They belong to me. Those boys are mine. And Maura belongs to me, and whatever I do with my property is my business, not yours."

"Ever hear of Lincoln?" I asked. "The guy that's on your penny? He and Congress freed the slaves nearly two centuries ago. Maura's not property. You don't own her."

"She does what I tell her to do," he said. "Not you. Back off."

"I doubt I can," I said.

Then he laughed. "What, you going to hit me with your cane? Kick me with your good leg? Hell, Maura told me you don't have a single gun in your house. You know how weird that is around here?"

I tightened my hand on my cane. "I'm not afraid of you, Hiram."

He nodded, shoved the envelope into a pocket. "You should be. You really should be, John. You know why? Because I have access to your house, thanks to Maura. And I've got friends in the Purmort police and the county sheriff's office. Bet if I had them run your fingerprints, I could find out pretty quick who you are. Right? Because even though Maura does a lousy job cleaning up my house, I know she does good work for her customers. But even Maura can't clean up all your fingerprints, can she?"

I kept quiet.

Hiram said, "With that info in my hand, what, it might take a week or so for it to get to the right people. Or wrong people, in your case. I got a lot of friends who are out on parole, or served their terms, both here and in Massachusetts. A few words to the right people and one night, John Delaney—or whatever the hell your name is—you're gonna wake up one night with someone sawing off your head."

I still kept quiet.

"Made myself clear?"

"Unfortunately, yes."

A satisfied nod. "I'm in a good mood, John. Putting Maura in her place always cheers me up. So I'll let your underpayment slide this time. But a month from now, I expect full payment. Any questions?"

"Not at the moment."

"Good," he said. "Now me and my crew gotta get back to work." Another smile. "Don't want you to think I'm cheating you."

On the porch alone again, at dusk. Bats swooping and diving over my front lawn, hunting and thinning out the herd of mosquitoes out there. There were hunters and then there were hunters. Hiram was definitely a hunter, roaming his own lands, not worried about a damn thing.

I had earlier come to him, thinking I was the hunter, trying to put him in a place where he would say yes to me, and it had been an utter failure.

Like my final months at the Port of LA.

When I thought I was top of the world, both figuratively and literally, having a great union job, bringing in some serious bucks, and being part of an illegal and secret organization that was skimming millions.

I thought I was the hunter, until I overhead some of my colleagues, drinking and smoking heavily one night, who explained that at a certain point, I would be a sacrificial goat. The plan was to take the blame and lifetime jail sentence to protect the others because of indictments soon coming this way.

That's when I left LA, taking along a new identity and a good piece of the stolen funds.

Hunters.

Out there on the pond, I heard a skittering noise from above, and then there was a flur of feathers and a *splash!* of water, as a kingfisher grabbed a frog or a small fish from my pond.

Had to either keep hiding or keep hunting.

It grew darker as I finished off my whiskey, wishing again for a nice cold California craft beer.

The next time Maura visited the bruising about her eyes had eased, but her lower lip was puffy and reddened, and she said, "No questions, all right? Don't feel like answering anything today, John."

I was in the kitchen, cane against the counter, washing my few breakfast dishes.

"All right," I said.

With her cleaning supplies at her feet, Maura said, "Which room should I skip today?"

"The downstairs bathroom."

"Really? Not the studio?"

I said, "You were right. I don't want spontaneous combustion or anything similar to light off the place. But you can give it a quick sweep and tidying up. Don't worry about taking too much time."

"I'll take any time I want," she said.

"Makes sense."

She gathered up her supplies, headed to the stairs leading upstairs. "Spontaneous combustion. Love the sound of that. Hiram's got lots of gasoline and fertilizer stored in the side barn. Would be nice to have that go up spontaneously."

Maura reached the bottom of the stairs. "With Hiram in it."

We took a shower together but there was tension in the air, like walking past an electrical substation, and she sat in a chair outside the bathroom while I took a big fluffy blue towel and rubbed her dry. I started at her feet, worked up her long, strong, and tanned legs—being gentle around the faded bruise on her thigh—and had her stand so I could dry off her lower torso. No fondling, no rubbing, no teasing, just a good fluffy dry.

Up her belly and sweet breasts, and her back, and neck, and shoulders.

She sighed a bit as I worked the towel hard into her shoulders, and then I turned gentle when I did her thick hair.

I took a hairbrush and worked her hair for a while, and she said, "Hiram never touches me, you know that?"

"I did not know that," I said.

"Oh, he'll give me a slap on my ass when he squeezes by me in the kitchen, and when he's in the mood, he'll give me a good rutting. And you've seen the other ways he treats me. Do I need to draw a picture?"

"No."

She sighed, pulled the hairbrush away. "It's tiring, you know. My grandparents lived to their nineties, which means a long life is in my genetic makeup. Divorce means starting over with little or no money, and no place to go. I've been to Manchester maybe six or seven times, and Boston, just once. And Florida when I was a kid. Where would I go, since Hiram would follow me and make my life hell?"

I stepped back as she got up, towel wrapped around her waist, and I went with her into the bedroom.

Strange kink, I know, but I enjoy seeing a woman get dressed almost as much as seeing her get undressed.

Once she got her clothes back on, slipped her feet into her comfortable sneakers, Maura looked straight at me and said, "I wish he was gone."

"I'm sure."

Her gaze was as cold as I had ever seen it. "Don't patronize me, John. I don't mean gone like moving to Montana. I mean gone. Permanently. Do I have to spell it out for you?"

I handed Maura her small black purse. "No. I get it."

"Glad you do."

Two days later Rudy O'Halloran of Purmort Stoneworks came by in his red Chevrolet pickup truck with its logo on the side, to check out where my new granite bench was going to be installed. He measured, probed, and put stakes out with orange tape, out-lining the work area.

Rudy was about a half foot shorter than me, tanned, wide, wearing dusty jeans and a black T-shirt, and when I shook his hand, I noticed how hard and callused it was. His fleshy face and jowls bore gray-white stubble.

He had a ready grin but there seemed to be a shadow about him as he worked.

"Sorry you got Hiram Grant to do your job," he said.

"He's my landscaper," I said. "It seemed logical."

Rudy shook his head. "Logic's got nothing to do with. Logic means you should have hired me, straight off."

"I thought going through Hiram made sense."

"You thought wrong," he said. "Thing is, the son-of-a-bitch is tighter than a tick. He'll contract out to me for the granite bench and supports, but that's it. He'll do the excavation work, put in the crushed stone for support, and install the damn thing himself."

I didn't like where this was going. "You mean he'll do a lousy job?"

His face seemed to pale out. "No, I'd never say that, and I hope you don't say that to him. All I'm saying is that Hiram will do a good job for you, but I'd do a great job."

I heard the *squawk-squawk-squawk* of a kingfisher scoping out my pond.

"No offense, Rudy, but when we started talking about Hiram, you looked like a con man being ushered into a priest's rectory," I said. "What's up?"

Rudy said, "I like you, John, honestly I do. So do me a favor and don't get Hiram riled up by anything I said. Hiram ain't much for sharing, that's why he'd only get the granite bench and supports from me, not let me in on the installation."

"Sure," I said. "That'll be my new goal in life. Not to rile up Hiram Grant."

He said, "I can see you're not taking me seriously. Again, I'll deny I ever said this, but I like you, and you're from away, so remember this. Over next in Hancock, this young fella filled with enthusiasm and a nice bankroll, and a couple of college degrees, started up his own landscaping business a few years back. Name was Frankie Boyd. Hiram didn't pay him attention because what did a young guy know about landscaping?"

Rudy rubbed at his chin. "Thing was, the young guy knew what some people wanted. He made it a point of being green, Earth-friendly, and working with the environment with natural stuff. Hiram started losing customers. Hiram tried to be friendly, in his own way, and told the fella the county wasn't big enough for both of them, so why didn't he set up shop somewhere else. That didn't work. Tires getting slashed, fertilizer bags slit open and soaked with gasoline, and then an outbuilding burning down didn't work."

"What did work?" I asked.

A shrug. "Something. Poor Frankie Boyd one day up and disappeared. Was never seen again."

My feet and hands were feeling cool. "What, did he move to Wyoming or something?"

"You not listening," Rudy said. "He disappeared. Everyone around here knew what really happened, and that Hiram did it.

Lots of quarries and deep woods around here to hide a body. The young man's family raised a fuss but after a few weeks, the local cops and the state police made it, a what-you-call-it, a cold case."

He checked his watch. "Jesus, look at the time. Need to get back to work and make sure your granite bench gets prepped in time. But John?"

Earlier I had welcomed Rudy's visit but now I wanted him to leave.

"Yes?"

"Be smart," he said. "Don't turn into a cold case."

I woke up that night, remembering some about my past life. Top of the world on a ship-to-shore crane, the essential part of any port in removing containers from a container ship. It was a constant knife-edge of work, checking the wind, the weather, softly manipulating the controls to lower the grappling equipment to the containers piled up on the ships.

Ships.

They had so many containers loaded aboard that they looked like big office buildings tilted on their sides.

On one particular day one of the union reps cornered me in the break room and said, "Like the way you do your job. Efficient, not too fast, you keep your mouth shut, the union and the company have no complaints about you."

"Thanks."

A hard slap to my shoulder. "Thing is, we gotta know how deep your loyalty runs to your brothers. There's gonna be a test today."

"Written or oral?" I asked.

He grinned. His teeth were way too bright.

"At ten A.M. this morning there's gonna be an accident on the C Dock. You're gonna be a witness, and you're going to witness an accident."

An "or else" was implied in that sentence, but I didn't press the matter.

I brushed past him and, in thirty minutes, was high up in my cab. I did my day's assignments and kept it focused, until ten A.M. came.

Now what?

Way down below on the C Dock, two men in suits were arguing. I was way too high to know what was going on, and didn't particularly care.

One of the men abruptly turned around, started walking away, heading to the near buildings. The one who remained on the dock, shook his head, took out a pack of cigarettes, lit one up.

It happened quickly.

From one of the overhead support systems, a heavy cable with a block at the end of it swung down, moving quicker and quicker, until it hit the man square in the back of his head.

It was like he'd been struck by some cosmic baseball bat.

He flew off the deck, arms and legs spread out, right into LA harbor.

Later, when I was being interviewed by various labor and police inspectors, I kept on saying the same thing, over and over again:

"It looked like an accident."

Three days later Maura came by to do my house, and she limped, and didn't have much to say. When she was done, Maura came out on the porch, still dressed and carrying her cleaning gear, and said, "Everything's clean. I worked on schedule today. Didn't skip anything. Except for your mysterious cellar."

"All right," I said. "What's going on at home?"

"Why do you care?"

"I do," I said. "I saw you limping."

Maura shrugged. "Maybe I fell and slipped on something. Or a door closed on me. Or I took a tumble down the stairs. Why do you care?"

"I do," I said. "Tell me what we really happened."

Another shrug. "We had another fight about our boy's future. This one was worse, 'cause we weren't drinking. Made it more real, nastier. I said Bruce deserved to make his own future, to set a life for himself, and he said Bruce's future was going to stay right here in Montcalm, along with his brother Roy. And that was that. When I pressed him is when he threw me down, and kicked me, and kicked me, and kicked me."

"Sorry again, Maura."

She picked up her cleaning gear, started limping down the stairs.

"Prove it," she said.

The day after Maura's visit, Hiram backed his truck into my yard, right up to where Rudy had marked off the spot for my granite bench. He and his worker Cray got out and climbed in back of the truck, started shoveling crushed stone into a pile on the grass.

The worked with silent and glum efficiency, not once saying a word. When they had gotten most of the stone out of the truck's bed, Cray stayed behind while Hiram leaped to my lawn.

He slammed open the tailgate, grabbed one end of a blue tarp that was protecting the truck bed, and he and Cray pulled the tarp and swept the remaining stones out, holding the tarp carefully so nothing fell out.

The two went to the pile, dumped the rest of the stone onto it. Cray started folding up the tarp and Hiram came over to me, walked onto the porch, and sat down. His lower legs and his hands were dusted gray with stone dust.

We sat quiet for a couple minutes. I said, "Want a drink?"

"No," Hiram said. "I want that five hundred bucks you owed me from your first payment."

I said, "I thought you were going to let that pass."

"I lied."

"Or did you change your mind?"

He rocked the chair back and forth. "Maybe I did."

"What caused it?"

He got up from the chair. "Drove by and stopped and saw you talking to Maura on the porch."

"I didn't see you on the state road."

"Didn't have to," Hiram said. "Used an old pair of binoculars. Saw you both quite good. Lots of talking. Can't read lips but I can tell you weren't talking about the best way to dust your furniture."

Well, there you go.

Hiram said, "I won't stand you talking lots to my wife. She's mine. Not yours. Got it?"

I said, "I'll pay you the next time you come by."

"Count on it," he said, clomping down my steps, his worker Cray carefully putting the folded swatch of tarp back in the truck, like he had been yelled at earlier for doing it wrong.

Back in my basement gym, running and running, realizing not for the last time that I was running in place.

Pretty good metaphor for what my life had become.

Staying in place.

Satisfactory most times, but not when someone was threatening me.

Time to start moving for real.

In Montcalm there was one small convenience store—Montcalm Country Store—where you could gas up your car and get essentials, like toilet paper or cans of Dinty Moore Beef Stew. For real shopping, you had to drive almost an hour to the Exit 14 Shopping Plaza, just off I-89, which had a CVS Pharmacy, a shoe store, a Verizon store, and a Walmart.

I own an old Volkswagen Golf that served me well, and which bore a handicapped parking placard. I went in, did my shopping, and poked around, and when I returned home, there was a surprise for me.

A granite bench, waiting to be installed.

After I parked my car and brought my groceries into the house, I went over and examined the bench. It was wrapped in plastic and padding, but I forced one hand in and rubbed the stone.

It felt smooth and well-worked.

I looked to my pond.

Imagined how it would be, sitting here, looking at my pond.

Looking at it in peace.

Hiram came by the next day, accompanied by his worker Cray and his son Bruce. On a trailer hitched to his pickup truck was a flatbed trailer, and on it was a compact John Deere excavator, with a folded-up backhoe and small plow on the other end. Cray and Bruce emerged from a Honda sedan, its fenders dented and rusted.

I went over, leaning into my cane, watched as the two young men undid wide yellow tie-down straps from around the excavator's tires, and lowered two trailer ramps to my driveway. Hiram climbed up on the trailer and then the John Deere, started up the engine, and backed it down. He maneuvered it over to the stone pile and my flower bed, switched off the engine.

He talked some to Cray and Bruce, and they nodded and went back to the Honda, started it up, and drove off.

Good.

Hiram came up to me.

"You got the five hundred bucks?"

"I do," I said. "Are you going to install the bench all by yourself?"

He grinned. "What, you think I'm going to pay those two boys good money to spend most of their time standing around, looking at me work?"

I said, "Still a big job."

He looked back at the John Deere, which also had a small plow on the other end.

"Me and this green devil will get the job done," he said. "I'll get the hole dug, plow in some crushed stone, lower the bench, put more stone around the supports, more dirt, and then she'll be done."

I spent a few moments looking at the controls.

Hiram laughed. "You look like some ignorant savage staring at his first motor. Bet you've never learned how to use one of these."

"You're right," I said, my voice quiet.

"You want to learn?"

"Not if you're teaching," I said.

He laughed again. "Idiot. So useless, so soft. One of these days the lights are going to go out, and the internet is going to be silenced, and it's going to be guys like me who survive. Who can hunt and dress a deer, run machinery, and be a mechanic or electrician or anything else."

Hiram went to the John Deere and said, "Go away, soft man. I've got work to do, and when I'm done, I'll want my five hundred dollars."

I sat on my porch for the next hour, watching and grudgingly admiring Hiram's work as he excavated the deep hole, rotating the excavator to dump the dirt nearby, making a pile next to the pile of crushed stone.

I had his five hundred dollars in my pocket, and held my cane between my legs, idly unscrewing and screwing the hard brass top.

Then he paused, took a shovel, and jumped into the hole. It was about chest-high to him, and he worked with the shovel to square off the edges of the rectangular-sized hole.

I had to give him credit. Even as a wife-beater, blackmailer, and probable murderer, he did have pride in his work.

Thing was, so did I.

He tossed the shovel out when he was finished, and grunted and heaved himself out of the hole. Hiram stood up, brushed his hands together to get the excess dirt off, and I limped my way over to him, holding out the five hundred-dollar bills.

His eyes lit right up.

He held his hand out and I brushed his hand away, and punched him hard in the chest.

His eyes widened and he let out a muffled "oof" and took two steps back and fell into the freshly dug hole.

I stepped to the edge and he got to his feet, eyes narrow and raging, and he said, "What the fuck was that all about? I'm gonna get out of here and beat the ever-living shit out of you."

"I doubt it," I said.

I took a step back and he placed both beefy hands on the edge of the hole, to lift himself up.

I twisted the top of my cane, loosening it, and slid out a narrow and razor-sharp edged sword. I slapped him twice across his hands and he yelped, and fell back, holding up his bleeding hands in disbelief, like the proverbial ninety-eight-pound weakling had turned around and suddenly nailed him.

"What . . . what . . ."

I said, "Us soft guys sometimes can be a surprise."

Two more motions of the sword cane.

He fell back and sit down, still looking surprised. I went forward, knelt down on the grass.

Blood was oozing through his fingers against his chest, where I had stabbed him, and his other hand was against his throat, where I had slit him. Blood was trickling through his fingers there as well.

"Hiram, you had a good thing going here," I said. "Constant payment, never caused you a problem, never gave you a complaint. But you got greedy, got stupid, and threatened me."

His face was starting to pale out. Hiram couldn't talk.

I said, "You're bleeding out. It's going to be painful, as you suffocate. And all because you were greedy."

I got up, brushed some dirt and grass off my knees. "Just so you know, I've been fucking Maura for the past year. And Bruce will be going to college this fall."

I walked over to the John Deere, gave a cool and professional look at the controls, and got to work, first sliding on a pair of latex gloves from my back pocket.

First thing first, plowing crushed stone over Hiram's body.

I didn't know how much time I had, but I kept up a steady pace, unwrapping the concrete bench, using straps and the excavator to lower it onto the crushed stone. I borrowed Hiram's level to make sure it was balanced, and then plowed in the rest of the crushed stone, and then the dirt. I used a shovel to smooth everything out.

Even with the raw dirt, the bench looked pretty good.

I was pleased with the results, but there was more work to be done.

The next day Maura came by, and she parked her Ford Ranger and walked over to my shiny new granite bench. It was barely a day old and I was already enjoying the view. Getting off the porch gave me a nice eye-level view of my pond.

I had my cane in my hand, and Maua came up, nodded, and took the other side of the bench.

Maura said, "Hiram's missing."

"Really?"

"Yes," she said. "Have the police come by yet?"

"No," I said. "Why should they?"

Maura said, "According to his customer schedule, he was due here yesterday to install the bench." She rubbed the stone with her left hand. "I see he did it. Then he was due to go to the Newmans', to trim their shrubbery. He never showed up."

"Well," I said. "Did he call you, or leave a message?"

"Hiram? No, that would never happen. But about a half hour ago the police found his truck and trailer, up on Monroe Hill, on an old logging road."

"Was he in it?"

"No," she said. "But there was blood on the steering wheel and the upholstery. The State Police are analyzing it, trying to see if it has his DNA or not. Might take a few days."

I touched the stone as well. It did feel nice. "How are you doing?'

She got up. "Better than I expected."

As Maura walked back to her truck, she said, "Thanks, John," and I pretended not to hear her.

Later I made two phone calls and then returned back to my peaceful bench.

A week after Maura's visit an unmarked police cruiser came up my driveway, and two plainclothes detectives stepped out. Even before they ID'd themselves, the black Impala and the way the woman and man were dressed and carried themselves said *cop cop cop*.

I stood up and limped over to them, offered them my hand.

"John Delaney."

The man said, "Bob Woods."

The woman said, "Caitlan Bailey."

Bob added, "We're both detectives with the New Hampshire State Police. Can we have a few minutes of your time?"

I limped back to my house. "You can have as much time as you'd like."

They joined me on the porch and I took one chair, and Detective Bailey sat in the other. Detective Woods leaned against the wooden railing and I said, "You're here about Hiram Grant, aren't you?"

The woman detective said, "What makes you say that?"

I held my cane with one hand. "Stands to reason. Word is all over town that he's missing, and since I was his last customer, and probably the last one to see him alive, I'm sure you have questions. Go ahead, ask away."

Both of them pulled out little notebooks and the questions started, one right after another, soon their voices sounding like they were twins.

"Are you sure you didn't see Hiram Grant later that day?"

"Positive," I said. I jostled my cane. "As you can see, I don't get around much."

"Did Hiram seem to be not his self that day? Like he was upset or worried about something?"

I said, "Not to speak ill of the dead, Hiram always seemed like he was upset about something."

A sharp question. "What makes you think he's dead?"

"Stands to reason, doesn't it? His truck and equipment abandoned on a logging road. Blood found in the truck's cab. Even though it's not been released to the press, I'd bet the blood you found there was his."

"Did anything unusual happen while he was here?"

I pointed to my new granite bench. "He installed my new bench. I've had that on order for a few weeks. It gives me a better view of my pond."

"Who helped him install the bench?"

I said, "He did it himself."

"Really? That seems to be one complicated job."

"It certainly was," I said. "But Hiram wanted to do it himself. He was always tight with money, you know, and if he could get away with putting it in without any help, well, that's the way he rolled."

"Was there anyone that might have a grudge against him?"

I didn't say anything.

The male detective said, "Mister Delaney, do you know anyone who might have a grudge against him?"

I spoke slowly. "Well, I know that he would beat his wife. Maura comes around every now and then to give my house a cleaning. A couple of times I saw bruises on her face."

The male detective said, "We know about Mrs. Grant. It's being looked into. But was there anybody else?"

I kept quiet again, and said, "Look, I don't want to make trouble, or get myself into trouble."

The female detective said, "You won't. We promise."

"It probably doesn't mean anything."

"Please," she said. "You don't know what any piece of information might help."

I waited for a moment longer, and I said, "I guess this is common knowledge around town, so you'll probably hear it from others, if you start digging. The thing is, a few years back, another landscaper came around, starting up a business and competing with Hiram Grant. I think his name was Frankie something. Started with a B. Boyle, Baker? I can't remember. But I do remember that Hiram didn't like Frankie on his turf, taking away his customers. There was some vandalism done at Frankie's place, and then . . ."

The detectives didn't say anything.

"Then Frankie disappeared," I said. "Left everything behind. I thought it was weird that nothing ever came of it, but later I found out that nearly everyone on the police department here is related to Hiram."

"I see."

I tapped my cane on the porch planks. "Oh, something else just came to mind."

"Sir?"

"He was over at my house, a couple of weeks ago, trimming the hedges, and he had one of his sons working for him. I said to Hiram that he was a good-looking boy, and wasn't family great. He sort of snorted and said, 'Families suck, especially ones that keep on poking around where they shouldn't.' He seemed angry at that so I didn't press him."

Both detectives looked at each other, trying to play cool but I saw it in their eyes. A few more questions and then they said they were done for now, and each handed over a business card.

The male detective said, "If you think of anything, anything at all, no matter how minor, give us a call."

I pocketed both cards and slowly stood up. "Absolutely, detectives. Absolutely."

We all shook hands and the woman detective said, "Mr. Delaney, I hope I'm not being rude or intrusive, but what happened to your hip?"

"Fate," I said.

It was another week before Maura Grant came back to my house, and I was sitting on my new granite bench, reading a history book by Alex Kershaw. She had on a yellow sundress speckled with little blue flowers, and leather sandals. Her toenails were freshly painted bright red.

She filled out the dress nicely but she just gave me a nod as she sat down next to me on the bench.

I tried not to see the irony in the situation.

Maura sat down heavily next to me, her legs stretched out.

"Things suck so bad," she said.

"No news about Hiram?"

She gave me an odd look. "No, there's no news about Hiram. He's been missing two weeks." She paused. "Do you know anything?"

"I had two state police detectives interview me last week."

"Guy and gal duo?"

"That's right," I said.

"What did you tell them?"

"The truth," I said. "I also mentioned Hiram's feud with that young landscaper who was here a couple of years ago."

"Frankie Boyd," she said.

"That's right," I said. "I had heard . . . rumors about Hiram doing something."

"Funny you should mention that," she said. "I got word from a gal who works in county dispatch. Seems both the county sheriff and the state police got anonymous phone tips that the Boyd family was involved in Hiram's case, because of that very same something."

"Were they able to trace the calls?"

She shook her head. "Nope. I guess a burner phone was used, the one you pick up at a Walmart or a drugstore. I hope something comes up about it, 'cause they've been after me ever since he disappeared. Asking about my bruises, my busted lip, my black eyes. Kept on pressing me. They even checked my bank accounts, to see if I paid off somebody to kill the son of a bitch. Asked me if I had a lover who might have done it."

The air seemed heavy.

"And you said . . ."

Maura said, "Relax. I kept your name out of it."

"Why should I relax?"

"You know why."

"I do?"

Maura said, "You walk with a cane, you got a bum leg or hip, but I see how you look at things. And I think you could have taken care of my asshole husband without being found out."

"Maura, honestly, I have no idea what you're talking about. The last time I saw Hiram, he was driving out after installing my granite bench. That's it."

"You don't trust me to keep my mouth shut?"

"Maura, please."

She abruptly stood up. "You think I'm wearing a wire? Is that it? Here."

Maura grasped the hem of her sundress, pulled it up over her body and over her head, now just wearing a white bra and white cotton panties. With quick motions of her hands, those two articles of clothing were gone, and she took her time, moving around in a circle.

Despite the tension in the air, I was still struck by the curvy eroticism of her body.

"See?" she said. "No wire. What do you have to say now, John?"

I said, "I'm hoping I can take you upstairs for a more thorough examination."

Her face was set, like a piece of stone. I kept quiet. Her expression didn't change.

She laughed. "All right, that sounds great."

About an hour later it was nearing dusk, and we were both back on the new granite bench, sipping Jameson and water. We were both wearing light blue cotton robes.

Maura said, "This is bracing and all, but right now, I could use a cold beer."

"I'll make it a point to start stocking some."

She eyed me over her drink. "That's one heck of an assumption, John."

Oops.

"You're absolutely right," I said. "My apologies."

She smiled. "Got you."

I smiled back. "Glad to be gotten."

We both took more sips of our drinks. Maura said, "Earlier, when I said things suck, I wasn't joking."

"Go on."

She said, "We all know Hiram's dead. His truck and trailer were found abandoned, his blood was on the steering wheel and upholstery. He's not coming back. Again, thank you."

"Maura," I said, my voice strained. "Please don't say thank you again. I don't know what you're talking about."

"Says you," she said. "Anyway, with him gone, I'm getting lots of phone calls from suppliers and vendors. First up they're all concerned and shit, and then they want to know when they're going to get paid. Idiots don't realize that his life insurance policy won't go into effect until he's pronounced dead, and in New Hampshire, that'll take four years."

"A lawyer told you?"

"Are you nuts? No, I looked it up on a computer at a library over in Wentworth. You and I both know that in a case involving a missing or dead spouse, the survivor is always the number-one suspect. And I'm not going to do anything to make the state police think that, by them seeing my computer browser history."

"Pretty smart," I said.

"Yeah, but I need some more smarts, on how to live on my cleaning business and not much else," she said. "Hiram was an asshole, but at least he was an asshole who was bringing in money every week. Now that income stream is gone. I could probably sell his landscaping equipment, but shit, in this economy? How much would I get? See what I mean when I say things suck? I'm running out of money, John. I need help."

When you toss a rock in a pond, like mine, the ripples go far and away.

She said, "I know you got money, John. Hiram told me so. Told me how he upped your fee from a hundred bucks a month to a thousand bucks a month, and you were a pussy about it. Barely put up a fuss. You'll help me, won't you?"

"I'll see what I can do," I said, speaking carefully.

The tone of her voice changed. "You will, will you. Aren't you the generous one. Well, before my curvy bottom leaves this nice granite bench, we're going to come to some sort of agreement."

I said, "There's usually an 'or else' attached with that."

A sly smile emerged. "Or I go to the state police, filled with guilt. Saying you and I have been having an affair for a long time. That Hiram beat me. That one night I got mad and told Hiram I was stepping out with you, and he gave me a really bad beat-down, I'll also say how you and I plotted to get rid of him. Of course, I was just under a lot of pressure at the time, and never thought you'd actually do it. How would you like it then, that you got under suspicion instead of Boyd's family? Your background, your finances, everything in your house searched."

The sly smile stayed as she continued looking at me.

I cleared my throat. "You make a good case."

"You know it," she said. "I've been thinking about it for a long time. And there's something else. I want to leave Montcalm. Leave it with you."

The ripples were growing wider.

"Go on."

"I hate it here. I want to go far, far away."

"How far?"

"California," she said. "Los Angeles."

Of all the towns in all the world, she picks one I can't possibly return to.

"Can't be done," I said. "I was there once. Hated it. Traffic and smog. How about Florida?"

"Bleh," she said. "Too flat, too hot. All of the plants and trees look alien. I've always dreamed of LA, seeing the Hollywood sign, and so much else. Besides, I know you were there more than once. You lived there, for a long time, didn't you?"

I didn't want to say any more.

"You can never trust your cleaning lady," she said. "Way, way deep in back of your closet, I found some autographed Lakers' basketball T-shirts. From the players' names, it looked like you collected them for at least six years. Am I right?"

I stared at my pond. "And your sons?"

"Bruce turns eighteen in a couple of months, his brother Roy is sixteen and can live with him, or Hiram's mother, I really don't give a shit."

She sipped her drink again, stretched out her shapely legs.

I said, "Just to make sure I understand where you're coming from, you want me to help support you, get your bills paid, and sometime soon, we leave Montcalm and head out to live in LA. Am I right? Did I get that straight?"

Maura smiled, slipped her tongue out, and played it along the rim of her glass.

"Exactly so, John," she said. "What do you think?"

I glanced over at my pond and my quiet and secluded property. I sighed.

"I think I'm going to need another granite bench."

Last summer my wife and I had our thirty-plus-year-old (and overgrown) landscaping torn up and replaced with new pieces of shrubbery. As the land-scapers were skillfully doing their work, it struck me that there must be some sort of crime story that could take place with such a routine event.

After some pondering, it came to me: a new arrival in a small New Hampshire town hires a landscaper to do work in and around his home. But the landscaper is suspicious of this newcomer with apparent wealth and no means of support.

The landscaper decides to blackmail his customer.

As my story eventually proves, he chose poorly.

Kerry Hammond *decided to give up the practice of law to commit crimes—on the page. Her work has appeared in* Malice Domestic: Mystery Most Geographical *and* Malice Domestic: Mystery Most Diabolical. *Her love of travel means that her stories often to take place in foreign locales she has (or wants to) visit, or while her characters are en route to their next adventure. She's a huge fan of the subtle surprise ending and is happiest when her readers didn't see the ending coming.*

STRANGERS AT A TABLE

Kerry Hammond

"You mean like the Miss Marple book?"

Michelle sipped her wine and looked at the other three passengers at her table in the dining car of the California Zephyr. Her blond bangs were a bit too long, and she had a habit of swiping her hand across her forehead to move them to the side, out of her eyes. She was a petite woman in her early fifties, with a thin face and straight, white teeth. She was shy and frequently avoided looking people in the eye when talking to them. She was at the end of a cross-country train journey, a gift to herself when her divorce was finalized.

"It was a short story actually, not a book. But yes, like Miss Marple." Janie smiled at the others, clearly proud of herself. An aspiring theater actress in her late twenties, Janie was traveling to Denver to audition for The Denver Theatre Company. One of the actresses had quit without notice, and Janie's best friend, Helen, had gotten her an audition. Helen told the company that Janie had already relocated to the Colorado capital and would be able to start immediately. Afraid to fly, Janie's mother had convinced her that train travel might be fun.

"The story was called 'The Tuesday Night Club,' and it was one of my favorites. Everyone always underestimated Miss Marple, and she always showed them in the end." Janie was beginning to think that her mother might be right. This trip might be fun after all.

"Full disclosure," she said, "not only have I read every Miss Marple mystery ever written, I'm also named after Jane Marple. My mother was a huge Agatha Christie fan but thought the name Agatha would be way too old-fashioned."

She registered confusion from the two men and continued. "Here's what we should do: let's each take turns and tell a story. Some little mystery that we have personal knowledge of because it happened to us or to someone we know. It doesn't have to be a story about murder, of course. That kind of stuff is for the movies and mystery books. I don't care if it's the case of the stolen newspaper." She said this last part in the voice of a news reporter, her expression serious.

"Just something to get us all thinking, you know? Just for fun. Look, none of us have met before, so we won't know the people involved in the stories. It's not like we're breaking anyone's confidence. And with no knowledge of the players in the story, we also won't have an unfair advantage when we try and solve the puzzle."

The others were silent as they considered Janie's suggestion. "So we each tell our little puzzler, and the others try and guess the solution. But we have to know the solution so we can confirm if anyone gets it right?" said Daniel, a forty-five-year-old attorney from Denver. He had missed his flight out of Chicago because of a snowstorm and decided to catch the train instead. The next flight with an empty seat was two days away and the thought of sitting in a hotel room in Chicago, snowed in, was worse than an eighteen-hour Amtrak train ride. "I guess it could be fun," he said, spinning his wedding ring around his finger. It was clear from the tone in his voice that he thought it would be anything *but* fun.

"If you don't know the solution, that's okay too," said Janie. "Maybe as a group we can figure it out."

The dining car was nearly empty, the dinner service was over, and just a few passengers remained, finishing their drinks. The serving staff had cleared the tables and were chatting with each other as they restocked supplies behind the bar. They appeared in no hurry to close down the room. Outside the window, the snow swirled, but the landscape was nearly invisible, swallowed by the winter night.

"What about you, Hank? Are you in?" Hank was a government employee who had recently retired after forty years with the National Park Service. He was headed back home to Denver after visiting his daughter and her husband in Chicago. He was a widower and preferred train travel to air travel because, as he put it, "I'm not in a hurry to get anywhere anytime soon."

"I may have to go last. I'm just not sure I have a story to contribute," said Hank, racking his brain for something, anything interesting that he could tell. He had lived a quiet life. Married at nineteen, two children by twenty-two, and only one job his whole life. Nothing exciting had ever really happened to him. Except there was that one time that . . . no, he couldn't tell that story to total strangers.

"Great, then it's settled," said Janie. "We each tell a story, and then the others have a chance to ask questions before we reveal the solution, if we know it. The storyteller has to answer the questions honestly, though. No lying or evading the truth. Got it?"

"Got it," they all said in unison.

"Are you going to go first then, Janie?" said Daniel. He sipped his martini as he loosened his necktie.

"I am," she said. "Get ready, because this is a good one." The other three passengers found themselves leaning forward in anticipation, vibrating slightly in their seats with the movement of the train.

"It happened when I was seven years old. I was small for my age, and I was born with a flair for the dramatic, so I liked to hide from my parents to see what they would do. I would slip away in department stores and hide in the middle of those circular clothes racks. It took them ages to find me and my mother always threatened to put me on a leash if I didn't stop wandering. But she never did, of course. I even secretly suspected that she liked the few minutes of peace and quiet when I was gone. But sorry, that's not relevant to the story.

"One day, my mother took me with her to the mall. I was mad at her for some reason, and to this day, I can't remember why. Anyway, I was up to my usual tricks, and I found a rack full of men's pants and I hid in the middle. I sat down on the leg of the rack, pleased with myself, hoping to make her suffer. I heard someone coming near the rack and expected my mother to part the pants and grab me, but instead, I heard two people talking. It was a man and a woman, and they were arguing.

"He was telling her that she needed to stop calling him at home because his wife was starting to get suspicious. I was only seven, but my parents had a friend who left his wife for his dental hygienist, so I knew what was going on. This guy was cheating on his wife, and this woman was trying to break up his marriage. The thing was, I knew the man's voice.

"I held my breath and peeked out between two pairs of cor- duroy pants, and sure enough, I did know him. He was the guy who always waited on my mother at the post office. Mr. Riley, or Rawlings, or something like that. He actually lived a couple of streets away from us. I'd seen his wife before, walking her dog around the neighborhood."

"Did he see you when you poked your head out?" asked Michelle, speaking to Janie but looking down at her wineglass.

"No, they were too intent on each other. He was so mad, his face was bright red. He had a grip on her arm, and she was trying to yank it free. She was like, 'If you don't let me go, I'm going to call your wife right now and tell her about us.'

"That seemed to startle him, and he let go of her arm. That's when I stuck my head back in. I was scared of being seen. But here's the kicker." Janie paused for effect. She knew she had them in the palm of her hand. She would nail that audition; she was sure of it.

"A couple of weeks later, I heard my mom tell my dad that Mr. what's-his-name, Riley or Rawlings, at the post office was getting a divorce. His wife caught him cheating and left him. Took him for everything he had.

"The mystery you have to solve is, how did she find out?" Janie finished her story with a flourish, waving her hand in the air and tipping her head in a kind of bow.

"Well, that's easy," said Hank. "The mistress told her."

"Nope," said Janie. "Try again."

"How do you even know how she found out?" said Michelle.

"That isn't relevant to the mystery," said Janie. "You just have to trust that I know and give me your best guess. Any more questions?"

"No questions, but I know the answer," said Daniel with a smirk. "It's elementary, my dear Watson."

"Wrong detective, but okay, smart guy, tell us. How did his wife find out?" said Janie.

"It's easy, *you* told her."

"And what makes you think that?" said Janie, with a smirk that told him he was headed in the right direction but wasn't quite there.

"Because you knew his wife and where she lived. It would be easy for you to approach her when she was out walking her dog." He paused, and a look from Janie made him change course. "Or, you wrote her a note and slipped it under her door."

"Is he right?" said Michelle.

"He is," said Janie. "Or mostly. I actually slipped the note in her mailbox. Even at seven, I had an understanding of irony. What better way to call out her postman husband's infidelity than to leave a note in her mailbox? I found a note my mom wrote to my dad and tried to mimic how an adult would write in cursive. I don't know if I pulled it off or if she guessed that a child had written the note. What I do know is that she must have believed me and confronted him because she divorced the jerk soon after. Well done, Daniel. Since you guessed correctly, you get to go next."

"All right then," said Daniel. "I've got a story, but I don't know the solution. It's either unsolved or not the mystery it appeared to be at the time."

"Cool," said Janie. "Maybe three fresh sets of eyes can solve the cold case."

"Well," began Daniel, "it was about three years ago. I had an elderly client who came to me for a will. I'll call this client Mr. Smith." His brow furrowed, and he paused for a moment. "Let me back up a bit. I think I told you that I was an estate planning attorney. I recently retired from practice but have retained my license to practice law. When I did have my practice, I prepared documents like wills, trusts, and powers of attorney for my clients. In the course of business, clients tended to confide in me about extremely personal matters, sometimes with information that wasn't even related to the legal work I was handling for them.

"On this occasion, my client told me that he had two daughters. One was a bright and beautiful woman who had gone to culinary school and had successfully started her own catering company. She was the apple of his eye, as the saying goes, and he wanted to leave his vast fortune to her. She was his little princess, the good daughter.

"The problem was, he had another daughter. She was the black sheep of the family. She'd dropped out of high school and gotten caught up with the wrong crowd. She got involved in drugs at a young age and had been in and out of rehab several times. He had tried to help that daughter, but all of his attempts had failed, and he wanted to leave her out of the will completely. He was afraid she would spend any money she inherited on drugs and alcohol.

"Disinheriting a child is sticky, but not uncommon. I created a will that left everything to the good daughter and nothing to the black sheep."

"So, what's the mystery?" asked Janie impatiently.

"I'm getting to that, Miss Marple. Keep your pants on," said Daniel teasingly. "My client was in his seventies but in good health and very active. He could theoretically have lived for another twenty years. However, three months after I delivered the paperwork to him and he signed all of the documents, he was dead.

"The good daughter showed up one Sunday for their weekly brunch and found him at the bottom of the stairs, his neck broken.

"The police investigated and were pretty convinced there was foul play involved but couldn't find any solid evidence. The good daughter was catering a big event when he fell and had about three hundred people who could give her an alibi, so she was in the clear.

"The police then contacted me and asked me about Mr. Smith's will. I explained that the good daughter inherited everything and that my client had disinherited the black sheep but admitted that I didn't know if he had told either of the girls about the changes to his will. You see, the previous will left his fortune to the two daughters equally.

"They came to the same conclusion as I did. If he hadn't told his daughters about the new will, the black sheep would have thought she would benefit from his death, giving her a motive to get rid of him. She would think that she stood to inherit half of his fortune, which is what would have happened if the first will were still valid.

"So, the police investigated the black sheep, and after quite a bit of pushback, she told them she had been at an AA meeting when the old guy fell down the stairs. Apparently, there were several people that backed up her story."

"So, who does that leave?" said Michelle. "Did anyone else inherit, even a smaller amount?"

"No one else inherited. The good daughter inherited about twenty million dollars and was his sole heir. The black sheep got nothing, but to her credit, she didn't even try to contest the will."

"Was the good daughter married?" asked Janie. "A greedy husband who couldn't wait for his father-in-law to live another twenty years before his wife inherited the money would have a strong motive. He could have bumped off the old guy."

"Good guess, but no, she wasn't married. And she wasn't even dating at the time," said Daniel.

No one spoke. Michelle swirled the wine in her glass, Janie stared out the window at the snow, and Hank sat with his eyes closed in contemplation, or maybe he was sleeping, it wasn't clear.

"Have I stumped Jane Marple's namesake?" said Daniel. "Not to worry, the police were stumped too. They found no unexpected fingerprints in the house. Even though he was a wealthy man, he had no security cameras on the premises, so there was no video footage of his last hours. His property was quite secluded, so his neighbors were miles away. The closest one worked as a flight attendant and was gone for days at a time. When Mr. Smith fell, she was on a plane headed for London."

"Well, I'm stumped," said Michelle.

"You've got me too," said Hank.

"I'm not giving up yet," said Janie. "I may need to sleep on it."

"By all means," said Daniel. "Like I said, I don't know the answer. It's unlikely that the police will ever know what happened. Eventually, it was ruled an accidental death. The case isn't even cold at this point, it's closed."

One of the waiters approached the table. "I'm sorry, but we do need to close the dining car now."

Janie furrowed her brow. "Oh no, we won't be able to get to more mysteries." She pushed back her chair and gave a reluctant half smile. "Oh well, you solved my mystery, and Daniel gave us one we can sleep on. Maybe I'll see you all in the morning before we reach Denver."

They said their goodbyes and prepared to leave the dining car. Daniel and Michelle went to their sleeper compartments, and Hank and Janie went back to their coach seats.

Janie had trouble sleeping that night, but not because of the movement of the train. She couldn't stop thinking about Daniel's client. What were the police missing? Daniel said they suspected foul play, so there had to be something there.

The next morning Janie ate a breakfast bar from her backpack and enjoyed the scenery rolling by from her seat by the window. She had blown her food budget on dinner last night, so she didn't make any reservations for breakfast in the dining car. She'd get a bite with Helen when she arrived in Denver.

As the train got close to Denver's Union Station, the passengers started to gather their belongings. Janie zipped her backpack and walked down the aisle toward the door. When the train stopped, she stepped down on the platform and looked around for Helen. She found her standing a few cars down, waving like a madwoman.

When she reached her, Janie gave Helen a big hug. As she was about to let go, she spotted Daniel over Helen's shoulder, kissing a young brunette. "Hang on a second, Helen. I want to say goodbye to someone I met on the train."

As Janie started to jog over to where Daniel and the woman stood, they turned away from her, walking toward the parking lot. The woman put her hand on Daniel's shoulder, and the large wedding ring on her finger sparkled in the sunlight. Just as Janie was about to call out his name, Daniel stopped and opened the passenger door of an SUV that was parked at the curb. On the side of the vehicle was a sign that read *Princess Catering*.

Janie stopped and stared at the vehicle.

The puzzle pieces started to slowly fall into place, and she stood on the sidewalk, her mouth frozen into the shape of an *O*. Ahead of her, Daniel kissed the woman and closed her car door. As he started to walk around to the driver's side, he spotted Janie standing on the curb. He looked taken aback but quickly recovered his composure. He put his hand up to shade his eyes, looked straight at her, and winked.

---

*I find that I meet the most interesting people when I travel. I strike up conversations about the most diverse subjects, so why not murder? Traveling by train is by far the best way to go and when I recently had to cancel a cross-country train trip, I decided that if I couldn't experience riding the rails, I would write a story about it. "Strangers at a Table" helped fill the gap that my canceled trip left, and allowed me to give a nod to Patricia Highsmith and Agatha Christie, two of my favorite authors.

Working as a typographer, **Victor Kreuiter** *witnessed the death of the linotype machine and the proof press. Few tears were shed. He learned some years later of the birth of the Macintosh computer, paid it little attention, and wasn't sure it would survive. It did, and more than half his career was spent working on a Mac. He went from a trade shop, working fifty hours a week, to the graphics department of one of the country's top public relations firms, where he worked fifty-plus hours a week as a vice president. Retiring after more than forty years in the printing industry, he returned to writing fiction, and has since been published in* Ellery Queen Mystery Magazine, Tough, Mystery, Halfway Down the Stairs, Literally Stories, *and other online and print publications. He rarely uses pen and paper, writing mostly on a MacBook.*

MILLER AND BELL

Victor Kreuiter

Dutch Miller listened for as long as he could stomach it. There were three of them sitting in Deena Hoke's cramped living room, listening to her drone on and on. Miller had been lured with the story of fast work and a big take. Deena'd been hyping the thing for over an hour and the longer she went on the less likely it sounded. Miller didn't know the other two guys, was unfamiliar with the city where it would happen, and was unsure about the target. As she prattled on about how easy and rewarding it would be he made up his mind: it was a wild goose chase.

He stood up and stretched, his move to show he was going to leave. She looked at him, scowled, and pointed a finger.

"Sit down, Dutch. Now."

He didn't sit down. He frowned, stared at her, walked to Deena, hung his head—wanting to appear contrite—and said, "Sorry Deena. I'm out." He didn't want to make a scene, didn't want any drama, but was no longer interested. Decision final.

He hadn't seen Deena Hoke in years and hadn't ever really known her well. He looked into her eyes, shrugged out an apology, and was turning toward the door when she grabbed his arm.

"You're not leaving," she said. She leaned closer until they were face to face. "Nobody's quitting. Not now, not after you've heard the plan." Was it a threat? It took him a second to realize she'd threatened him. He wondered how Deena Hoke had convinced herself she had the stones to do that.

And she'd touched him. Dutch Miller did not like being touched.

He punched her. One time, a knockout punch.

He stepped back, glanced at the other two in the room, then looked down at her, crumpled on the floor. "I'm out," he said. "When she wakes up tell her I'm not interested. Tell her I'm not a snitch, I won't pay any attention if she goes through with this thing, but tell her if she comes after me it won't end well." He stood silent for a moment, expecting a comment or a question, anything. Nothing was said and he left.

Miller had retired at fifty-eight. Why hadn't he stayed retired? That's what he thought about as he drove home, a twelve-hour drive.

The invitation arrived like this: a guy who knew a guy who knew a guy knocked on his door one afternoon and said Deena Hoke wanted him for a job she had lined up. Miller should have played stupid or claimed he was somebody else or just slammed the door. But he hadn't. He'd been living in a small town on the Missouri-Iowa border for just over two years, in a small, forgotten farmhouse on a forgotten corner of an immense corporate farm where he paid rent once a year—cash—to a guy who collected rent once a year. That guy never offered a receipt and Miller never asked for one.

He didn't ask the guy who knew a guy who knew a guy how he'd found him. He should have.

Dutch Miller associated with no one, nobody bothered him, he kept his nose clean and paid cash for what few bills he had. He watched a lot of TV, did a little fishing, a little reading, took walks, and worked on keeping the past in the past.

After the knock on his door—a rare thing—he'd listened to the guy who knew a guy who knew a guy, all the time knowing he knew better than to listen. Who was this guy? He never found out. He knew the name Deena Hoke, but that name came with baggage, most of it negative. He'd been bored living on the Missouri-Iowa border, and a little lonely, so he made a mistake. He thought about those things on the drive back home.

Dutch knew Deena's husband was dead. He'd heard the rumors that Deena had killed him and a friend of his. Those rumors were a couple years old.

When Deena's eyes fluttered open the room was empty. Her eye was swollen and her head throbbed. She knew the job was queered . . . word would get out and there was no way she could get anyone interested again. To soothe her rage she went on a bender. Meth and coke were available, so she got some. Weed? Why not? Alcohol? Lots. Going on a week later she was sitting in a dive bar, late afternoon, drinking, talking too loud, and she mentioned Dutch Miller's name to the bartender, like he wanted to listen to her any more than he already had. There was a guy in the back, sitting alone, reading a newspaper, half listening. Hearing Miller's name he folded his paper, chewed on his lip, got up, and walked to the bar and offered to buy Deena Hoke a drink. It wasn't a tough sell.

She had one on him and mentioned she'd like another and that was okay with him. He motioned to the bartender for two more. When that one was gone he said, "You know Dutch Miller?" Deena got all quiet when he asked that, like she'd been offended. He watched her rummy brain try to do something with that question, but figured after another drink or two she'd forget all about it, and he was right.

Before the night was over he'd seen her without any clothes on, told her that he was falling for her and they might make it as a couple, and she'd told him that she knew Dutch Miller and Miller had ruined her perfectly good plan.

"Where'd you find Dutch Miller?" he asked her. She'd already explained her plan, which he listened to patiently. He told her it sounded "solid," but it wasn't. He waited for her to shut up, which she rarely did, but he was patient. After he showed her how much he was falling for her, she answered all his questions.

His name was Dwight Thomlinson and he knew a guy who had been looking for Dutch Miller for a long, long time. The next morning he called the guy and asked if he was still looking for Dutch Miller and when the guy said "yes," Dwight told him he had good news.

It took Dwight a day and a half to find Deena's guy, the guy who knew a guy who knew a guy. When he found the guy—a fat old man who insisted on being called "Big Tim"—Dwight gave the guy two thousand dollars to tell him where he'd found Dutch Miller. Then he told the guy they should never see each other again. Ever. Then he ditched Deena. What did he need her for?

Dutch Miller's reputation was made when he killed two lunkheads in a wildlife preserve in Arkansas and drove off with their money and the drugs they'd stolen. The guy who owned those drugs was middle management—worked out of Cincinnati—but he had influence both up and down the ladder, and he was impressed when Miller looked him up and returned his money and the drugs. Dutch had been paid handsomely to end the two lives; he figured the smart thing to do was return the money and the drugs to their rightful owner, which he did. He liked things squared up. The middle manager offered Dutch Miller a job, Dutch declined, which disappointed the guy, but the middle manager was relieved to have his drugs back so he gave Dutch some money out of his own pocket and told him if he was ever in the neighborhood . . .

That guy never told anyone, but he was afraid of Dutch Miller the first time he laid eyes on him.

Miller drifted around, a freelancer. He wasn't popular, he wasn't friendly, he associated with no one and anyone claiming they'd had a genuine conversation with him was lying. But he was eminently reliable. Nobody who worked with him was ever disappointed. He moved often, and before each move he'd find himself some kind of preacher, some kind of evangelist, and would unburden himself.

"Why am I like this?" he'd ask them. "Why do I live like this, doing these wrong things? What's the matter with me? Why don't I feel anything?" He'd dive right in, telling them everything, and when he talked like that, his confessor would usually get all serious, head down, ask him to pray and tell him God can forgive anything, but only if. The "only if" was always the deal killer. Miller would leave behind some significant cash with each person who'd listened to his story, then explain how revealing anything about him would be a terrible mistake for the confessor, his family, and his parish. Then Dutch would disappear.

Older, all that bouncing around began to bother him. It bothered him there was nothing in his past he wanted to remember, and it bothered him that his future looked like his past.

In his time at the Missouri-Iowa border he grew fascinated—captivated, actually—with two things: gangster movies and meditation.

He watched a lot of TV, and stumbled onto foreign gangster movies: Japanese, Korean, Chinese, Filipino . . . Indian. He was mesmerized. These movies preached a kind of honor that appealed to him. The gangsters had a code. They were sworn to some version of family. They had rituals and ceremonies and adhered to them. He lacked those things in his life.

Meditation?

Out for a drive the spring after he arrived, with no particular destination, he drove into Fairfield, Iowa, home of The Maharishi University and the epicenter of Transcendental Meditation in the US. He got hooked. It was something real to aspire to; it was soothing. It made him feel noble. It required—and this fit perfectly into Miller's lifestyle—it required no one other than himself. Him. Alone. He bought books on meditation, attended lectures every time he returned, which was once or twice a year, and breathed deeper and grew calmer with his new awareness. His mind linked the gangsters in the movies and their rituals and their code of conduct with this meditation. It made perfect sense to him. He meditated . . . or at least he'd learned to sit silently for an hour a day. Sometimes more.

Dwight Thomlinson called the guy he notified, told him he needed his help to get to Dutch Miller, and that guy was on the road an hour later.

Deena Hoke pieced it together slowly. After the second day Dwight didn't show up she got mad as hell. She laid off the drugs a bit and realized she'd been foolish. She thought real hard about the questions Dwight had asked her and tried to remember how she'd answered. The guy who knew a guy who knew a guy? She went to him, they drank a bit, she cried on his shoulder and when he finally fessed up that he'd told Dwight where he'd found Dutch Miller, Deena sobered up real fast, held a gun to his head and told him she understood that two thousand dollars is two thousand dollars, but she was disappointed in him. She told him that going forward he had to actually shut his trap. He promised he would.

Deena knew a guy—a big guy with no brains and nothing to do—and told him about some big money near the Missouri-Iowa border and how they could get it. She invited him to her place and took off all her clothes and asked him if he liked what he saw and he said he sure did. Then she told him about the guy who knew a guy who knew a guy and that he'd have to be taken care of eventually—he was okay with that—and then she said they had to get to the Missouri-Iowa border and get that money. She talked it up quite a bit. It was gonna be easy and rewarding.

Dutch Miller was sitting in a diner, eating breakfast, when a guy walked in, and Dutch knew immediately that the guy was trouble. How did he know?

"I know trouble before trouble starts," he told a preacher in Indiana once. The preacher was very, very successful, a regular on another preacher's TV show, and had a great big church that filled up twice on Sundays. This preacher also had a taste for drink and drugs.

"I could use you," the preacher had told Dutch. "You got a gift," the preacher said. "Your perceptions, that's a gift from God." This preacher, himself, needed someone confess to, and he'd confessed a bunch of stuff to Dutch, which made Dutch uncomfortable. The preacher offered Dutch a security position with his ministry. Dutch turned him down. He offered it several more times. Dutch said he'd think about it, then relocated.

The guy who walked into the diner was Dwight Thomlinson and he took a seat in a booth and twenty minutes later a truck pulled into the parking lot and a guy got out of that truck and walked into the diner, stopped at the cashier, and asked for a cup of coffee, then walked over and sat opposite Dwight Thomlinson.

When he was seventeen, Randall Bell walked away from a juvenile facility in Florida where he was being detained until his eighteenth birthday. He'd been arrested twice, both times for home invasion. He kicked around for a couple months, made his way up to Virginia, and that's where he met Dutch Miller, a cocky drug dealer in his late twenties, who would do about anything for money.

Randall Bell was an anomaly. He appeared to be a hick, which in fact he was, but his IQ was off the charts; he excelled in all academics and made it look easy. It's not a nice thing to say, but his people were pure trash. As a small child, as a boy, he was an introvert; then he was an introverted adolescent. The summer between his sophomore and junior years he transformed into a troubled, introverted teenager. The incident that put him away was a spur-of-the-moment thing; he beat up an elderly couple pretty bad and the next morning was caught in their car. His family didn't show up in the courtroom, didn't visit him at the detention center, never called and never wrote. When he walked away from the juvenile facility, as far as he was concerned he had no family.

In Virginia he tried to steal junk food from a rural convenience store where Dutch Miller's team were selling drugs from behind the cash register. He was, of course, caught, and turned over to Dutch Miller, who slapped him around a little and then—seeing something in the boy—put him to work. Randall Bell doubled Miller's business in a year and they became something like father and son.

Two years later, Bell, who by then knew damn near everything about Dutch Miller's businesses, shot Miller in the back of the head and drove off in Miller's car with around $350,000 in cash. He left the car at a shopping mall in Youngstown, Ohio, keys in the ignition.

Two days later he stepped off a bus in Kansas City, Missouri, and from that point on he introduced himself as Dutch Miller.

Why he chose that name is left to those with extensive psychological training.

The Dutch Miller name carried a bit of mystique. First there was the real Dutch Miller, the drug dealer who'd been shot and robbed. That story was common and for that reason didn't last long. But the second Dutch Miller? Randall Bell's Dutch Miller?

Among those clinging to the bottom rung of criminality's ladder, *that* Dutch Miller was the cowboy who could, would, and did.

That Dutch Miller was low-key, quiet, smart, and dependable. He was around when good money was to be made and when the good money was made he disappeared with his share, sometimes with more. Word was he could speak Spanish and disappeared into Mexico. Word was he could blend in with anybody anywhere anytime. Word was he did not show fear and did not panic. Word was you couldn't spot him in a crowd totaling three. Word was he was polite, gracious, and deferential, never spent a dime he didn't have to, lived like a hermit, and had a bundle of money.

Word was word was word was. His name didn't come up often, but when it did, folks listened.

Dwight Thomlinson had heard about the money. He'd been told about the money and even met folks who claimed ownership of some of that money. Those folks held some sway in Thomlinson's world and he knew they would appreciate—reward—the person who found it. That was Dwight's angle.

Deena Hoke? Deena was not right in the head. She had trouble controlling her temper. Paranoid? Probably. None too bright. The intoxicants she used too frequently didn't help. But she'd decided she wanted something out of Dutch Miller and would decide what it was after she had his scalp in her hands.

On the way to that small town on the Missouri-Iowa border, she talked nonstop about how, once there, she'd observe Miller for a day or two while she fine-tuned the plan. "We'll just kick back, have some drinks and roll around in bed," she told her new partner. He loved hearing that. She did all the driving. He had a couple too many DUIs and was due to show up in court a couple months ago. He drank, she drove.

Dwight located Dutch Miller in two days. Miller, aware that trouble had arrived, helped him by spending both days shopping along the tiny main street, something he almost never did. He stopped at the two strip malls and had lunch and dinner out. These things were unusual for him, and had he been asked why, he would have said "instinct," because that's what it was. He knew those guys were looking for him and thought it better they find him sooner rather than let the whole thing drag on. He watched them follow him home one evening, trailing behind a quarter mile or so, then drive right past his lane. He felt good about that.

On her first day on the Missouri-Iowa border, Deena Hoke saw Dwight Thomlinson walking down the main drag and knew right away she had to act fast. She and the muscle had checked into a motel; she'd left him with a bottle and cable TV and told him she was going to look at the lay of the land. She parked her car and caught Thomlinson in front of a hardware store. He smiled and she didn't.

"What?" he said. "You think I cut you out?"

Deena Hoke wasn't drunk, but she'd been on maintenance amphetamines for a couple days. "I ought to shoot you where you stand," she said.

He frowned. "Come on, Deena," he said, then smiled and said, "turn around."

Deena turned around and saw the guy Dwight Thomlinson was partnering with. He looked smarter than her guy. She turned back to Thomlinson and said, "I want a share."

Thomlinson nodded. "Okay, that's not unreasonable, so let's talk."

Miller's farmhouse was about three miles outside of town, down a private lane. It had electricity paid for, unknowingly, by the corporation that owned the farm. Same with water, which was low pressure but good enough. The septic tank worked. In the winter

Miller's truck was parked in a dilapidated barn the corporation thought had been torn down years earlier.

For two days he drove back and forth—home to town . . . town to home—until he was confident he'd revealed his whereabouts to Dwight Thomlinson. He put a case of beer in the bed of his pickup while Thomlinson watched from across the street, then went back into the store and bought another case. It was all show; Dutch Miller did not drink alcohol. Ever. He'd never been an idea man, but he'd seen movies where guys with real brains could sort through their difficulties. This had convinced him that he could do it, too, or at least learn to.

In American movies, tough guys drank all the time, smoked all the time, yakked away all the time. In the movies he'd been watching nobody did that. He figured that was smarter.

His Deena sighting was strictly luck. He was at one of the town's four stoplights when she walked right in front of his truck, never glancing left or right. She looked wired. Miller took that as a positive.

The first night after he'd seen both Thomlinson and Deena, Miller stayed up late, light on in the living room, watching a movie about a gangster hunted by rivals and receiving no help from his family. It looked like his family had sold him out. Then it turned out they were being threatened by the same rivals and were scared. Then they threw in with the rivals. Then they tried to help him, but he was afraid they were setting him up. Eventually the gangster who was being hunted just killed them all, family and foes. That's what Dutch would do.

The next day he stayed home, listening to cars pass on the road down the lane. He meditated in the morning and in the afternoon paged through a book on budo and serenity.

They came at night.

The banging on his door happened about ten. There was shouting. "Mister! Hey! Mister!" He waited, and the banging on the door increased. "There's an accident out on the two-lane. We need help! We need your help now!"

When he opened the door, Dwight Thomlinson was pointing a gun at him; Miller didn't even look surprised and Dwight could see that. That was unnerving. Miller backed into the room and Thomlinson stepped in and the guy who had met Thomlinson at the diner stayed by the door.

Miller sat down on his couch and nobody said a word. Eventually Miller pointed at a closet right next to the door, right where Dwight Thomlinson was standing, and Thomlinson opened that door and smiled. There were two large duffel bags in there, one stacked on the other.

"That's my money," Miller said.

Why did that make Thomlinson feel so funny?

"There's close to four hundred thousand in each of them bags," Miller said. "That's what you're here for, isn't it?"

Thomlinson looked all around the room, slowly, wondering where Miller's gun was. He kept his gun on Miller, kept his eyes on Miller, and talked over his shoulder to his partner.

"Look in them bags, will you, Errol?" he said.

Errol started to move, but hadn't put one foot into Miller's living room when two shots hit him, both from his right. He fell hard, into the living room. Thomlinson backed up a step, then two, then watched as Deena Hoke stepped into the room. She looked at Miller, looked at Dwight and nodded, then shot Errol two more times. For Deena, good-and-dead beat dead any day.

"Get the bags," Thomlinson said.

Deena glanced at the bags, walked right past them, and dropped the barrel of her gun on Dutch Miller's forehead.

"Deena, that ain't part of this plan," Thomlinson said. "Stop," he said. "Deena, back up."

"I'm gonna kill Dutch Miller," she said.

Miller grabbed her wrist and swung her around, using her body as a shield, then grabbed the gun out of her hand, pointed and pulled the trigger, managing to shoot a startled Dwight Thomlinson two times in the chest. Miller turned her around again and punched Deena Hoke in the face, twice. Her eyes rolled back and she went limp.

He walked over to Thomlinson. He was shot good enough.

Miller tied up Deena's wrists real tight, then tied her ankles, left her on the floor, and went outside. Two cars. He figured it was Dwight's in the yard. Deena's was most likely down the lane a bit.

He went back in, sat on her chest, and slapped her until her eyes flickered.

"You alone?" he asked.

She gasped, struggled just a bit, looked up at him. "I'm alone," she said. "It's just me and Dwight."

He wrapped both hands around her neck, leaned down on her, and squeezed until he thought he ought to stop.

"You really come alone?" he asked.

She answered every question he asked, then she followed orders, calling her guy, telling him to be ready, she'd be there in twenty minutes.

Twenty minutes later they pulled up at the hotel. Her muscle jumped in the car and when she was back out on the highway the muscle felt a barrel press against the back of his head.

"Do not turn around," Miller said. "Put your hands on top of your head and leave them there. If they come down for any reason I have to shoot you."

Back at Miller's house they strolled into the farmhouse. When the guy saw the body in Miller's living room, he jumped, pushed at Deena's back, tried to go around, and Dutch Miller shot him three times, twice in motion, once as he lay on the floor. Then Miller handed the gun to Deena. She looked at it, pointed it at Miller's head and pulled the trigger once, twice, then once more. Nothing. When she looked at Dutch Miller he was frowning. "Christ, Deena, did you think I'd give you a loaded gun?"

Then he hit her once more, and down she went.

When Deena came to, Dutch Miller was standing in the doorway. Her wrists were bound. Her ankles were bound. She was on the floor and looked up at Dutch and started crying.

"I'm conflicted," Miller said to her. He waited for a reply but none came, she was crying too hard. He'd been thinking about how he'd killed her husband and the other guy years earlier. It had been a contract job. He figured she'd never known. He thought it was funny that he was probably going to have to kill her now. It was like in the movies, the family thing and how you can think it's over but it's not. There's always somebody else coming at you, because everyone has a role to play and they have to stay in that role because that's where their honor is. The honor is in accepting your role and being proud of the way you handle the responsibility of what you have to do.

He didn't think it was honorable for Deena Hoke to be crying. "I'm going to have to kill you," he said, and she wailed.

Minutes later he walked out to her car, drove it up to the house so the front bumper kissed the front of the house, shut it off, and got out. Then he went and got Dwight's car, drove it up on the pad that sat outside the front door and got the bumper to kiss the door frame. He got out, walked around and went in the back door, came out with a gas can and poured gasoline over both cars. He went back in, sat on the couch perfectly still, silent, eyes closed, breathing slowly, counting each inhale, each exhale. He counted close to five hundred, then grabbed the duffel bags and carried them out to his truck. Back into the house one more time, scattered all his clothes around the house, doused the place, and then got in his truck and drove a hundred feet or so down the lane and waited there, foot on the brake, until he could see flames climbing the curtains in the front window. Then he drove off.

He'd lived there two years. There'd never been a photo on a wall, a calendar on a door, or a piece of mail delivered.

Miller drove to Cleveland, three or four miles an hour over the speed limit all the way. He got breakfast from a fast-food window in Springfield, Illinois, and dinner near Dayton, the same way. When he arrived in Cleveland, he became Randall Bell again. The idea for the switch came to him during the drive and to him—him coming up with that idea—that showed he was getting smarter. He credited it to watching those gangster movies and meditating. All that had made him more receptive to his own personal skills, his own personal truth. It was the circle of life, or something like that. He'd seen it in the gangster movies. He read about it in the books he bought in Fairfield, Iowa. At one of the lectures he'd attended in Fairfield he'd been told to become truly yourself, "you have to do the work."

He'd done the work, he was sure of it. That's why he became Randall Bell again.

In Cleveland Randall Bell paid cash for a laundromat—he bought it cheap and fixed it up. The guy he bought it from handed him off to an accountant who could make Randall Bell look like an upstanding businessman.

Within a year Randall Bell met a nice woman. He met her renting gangster movies in the shop she ran; it offered all kinds of Korean stuff: food, cosmetics, magazines, cheap dishes and cheap glasses and coffee cups; she was Korean. Her English wasn't too good, but that didn't bother him. She described her life to him in her pidgin English and he listened, trying to understand, realizing her life had been tough, like his own. She'd had to scramble to survive; she'd had to start over multiple times. When he told her about his life—leaving out the killing—she listened closely, nodding.

They married. The ceremony was small, held in a community center that catered to immigrants. It was him, her, her mother, an aunt who barely spoke, and an officiant, the whole thing in Korean. He liked it. It was a simple ceremony and some sort of noodle soup that was required at Korean weddings was served. He liked that too.

After the wedding her mother lived with them, which was fine with Bell. Finally, family again.

His wife and mother-in-law told him they had some family in Minnesota and they went there every year to hold some traditional ceremonies, or rituals, or something like that. His wife insisted they go. "Got to do," she said. She said that multiple times: "Got to do." Sounded like more ceremonies to him, and it sounded like it was centered on family. He figured some honor was involved too. It sounded good.

They went in the late fall, leaving on a Friday at noon, driving continually for twelve-plus hours until, on Minnesota State

Route 1, an hour or two east of Fergus Falls, they got lost. The wife was driving.

Mother and daughter got talking in their other language, arguing maybe, then they started laughing with each other. Bell laughed too. Everybody was smiling and excited and they drove on until Bell's wife said she had to pee. The mother-in-law started laughing and his wife was trying not to laugh because she had to pee so bad. Bell said he could take a pee, too, so they pulled off on a small lane, a logging road, and his wife got out, ran to the side of the car, pulled down her jeans and squatted, laughing hard. He cracked his door and was starting to get out when he felt the hairs on his neck stand up.

He ducked. A gun went off, a bullet whizzing past his head and blasting through the windshield. He swatted with his right arm and his right hand, got a hand on the gun then dove over the seat and put his other hand to his mother-in-law's neck and squeezed. That stopped her screaming. He looked to his wife, standing up, scrambling, then he shot his mother-in-law in the head and jumped out of the car.

His wife was running down the rutted lane. It would have been much smarter, he thought, to run through the brush. Why didn't she think to run through the brush?

He got back to Brainerd, Minnesota, without incident, worrying about that windshield the whole time. A cop seeing that windshield would be trouble. In Brainerd he stole a car and drove to Chicago. He dumped the car and from there it was Amtrak to Cleveland.

The remains of his wife and mother-in-law would be found in the spring. By then he was living in Tampa, where he'd bought a car wash. He would sell that car wash for cash a year later, below asking price, and drift toward Pensacola. In Pensacola he called himself Brad. Sometimes Brad Miller, sometimes Brad Bell. That turned out to be a problem when he was T-boned at the corner of Main and Palafox by a drunk.

When he woke up in the hospital there was a man sitting on a chair, doing what looked like a crossword puzzle in the newspaper.

"Say there," the man said when he saw Bell awake. He pulled his chair closer, smiled, and introduced himself as Detective Ray Yustiz. "You," he said, "have a couple names—at least that's what we've been able to dig up so far—and we'd like to know why that is."

Brad Bell, that's what Miller thought. *Brad Bell. Go with Brad Bell.*

He felt tight in the chest, weak all over. One leg was elevated. His neck was wrapped up real tight. He struggled to crane his neck and see his body; when he did he saw his right arm was in a cast, wrist to shoulder. He tried to pull his left hand into sight; he heard jingling and his hand jerked to a stop about mattress level. He was cuffed to the bed.

He looked at Yustiz.

"You don't have a driver's license," Yustiz said. "And where in heaven's name did you get those license plates?" The detective's smiled faded. "You're not insured," he said, "and the title isn't in the truck or in your wallet and we haven't gone into that little bungalow you're living in to see if it's there because we're not going in without a legal search warrant." The smile was gone. "You could agree to allow us to go in, you know, and tell us where we could find that title."

The cop stood up and looked down at Brad Bell, shoved his hands into his pockets, and shook his head slowly and took a deep breath.

Bell went into defense mode. No expression. Didn't say a word. Closed his eyes slowly and kept them closed.

"You know how long you been in here?" Bell didn't answer. Didn't open his eyes.

"Two days," the cop said. "And there is so little we know about you, and so much we have to find out."

Bell fell asleep again. It didn't take much effort.

When he woke up again it was a day later. At least it felt like that to Brad Bell. He opened his eyes slowly, thinking he had to be careful. He heard some murmuring, shuffling feet, then somebody walked into the room.

Detective Ray Yustiz appeared over his bed, staring down at him, hands shoved into his pockets, lips tight. "Morning," he said.

No reply.

"You're an interesting guy," Yustiz said. He turned around, said something in Spanish to somebody near the door, then turned back, looked down, and said, "The name Dutch Miller mean anything to you?"

I've lived my entire life in the Midwest and am a proponent of the Midwestern lifestyle. (Don't ask. There are no specifics.) In the Midwest the defining cities are four, five, six, seven, even eight hours apart. Detroit, Cleveland, Cincinnati. Indianapolis. Minneapolis, Milwaukee, Chicago. St. Louis and Kansas City. What's beyond and in between? Smaller cities, bigger towns, smaller towns, and small places stitched into the landscape with a factory of some sort, an array of grain silos, a rail yard, or proximity to an interstate. Randall Bell, aka Dutch Miller, is comfortable—reassured, even—knowing the Midwest holds 750,000 square miles of territory where he can enshroud himself, live quietly, frugally, and in relative peace. If the Midwest is Flyover Country, or the Heartland, or the Rust Belt, he never noticed and wouldn't have cared. He's a character with a changing, unsettled identity and, if he is uncertain about who he is, who he might be, and how he might be, he is preternaturally true to himself, whoever he is. He's not a good person. Good and bad are foreign concepts to a man like him.

I have other characters in other stories I've written with similar, indeterminate identities. I don't think I'm sharp enough to know what that says about me, but I am curious.

David Krugler *writes spy thrillers set during World War II.* The Dead Don't Bleed *and* Rip the Angels from Heaven *feature a young intelligence officer who stumbles upon Soviet espionage inside the top-secret atomic bomb project. His short stories have been published in* Mystery Magazine *and* Ellery Queen Mystery Magazine. *Writing fiction with a historical bent comes naturally to Krugler—for his day job, he works as a professor of history. He is steadily working his way across the globe by visiting a foreign capital every chance he gets. Learn more about Krugler and his writing at davidkrugler.com.*

TWO SHARKS WALK INTO A BAR

David Krugler

Carol's Pub had the sorriest, most raggedy-assed pool table Meredith had ever seen. The felt was scuffed, nicked, and stained; the cushions, battered and uneven. A folded piece of cardboard—torn from the lid of a beer bottle case—leveled one leg on the warped linoleum flooring. The pocket points were misaligned and two had hairline cracks. Cigarette burns marred the edging, dark welts curling like sneers from the composite plastic.

The location befit the table's condition. Way back of the tavern, wedged into a nook haphazardly created by a windowless brick wall, walk-in cooler, and broom and mop rack. A narrow plywood mantel for bottles and ashtrays jutted from the brick wall. A faded Bicentennial banner sagged from two nails. Someone had penned a mustache on George Washington, a beard on Thomas Jefferson, and goggles on Benjamin Franklin. Four stools with ripped cushions, a Pabst light with fringed shade, and two long-haired punks in Levis, T-shirts, and neck chains completed the decor.

Punk One was taking a shot. A hard left cut on the seven ball into a side pocket. Meredith didn't watch the balls. She took in his stance, grip, elbow angle, and bridge, keeping her eyes on the cue's glide as he shot. Smooth, not too hard, but with a wobble. Unconsciously, he slipped his bridge as he finished, probably because he was thinking too hard about keeping his right elbow aligned with the cue. He still dropped the seven ball, left himself good for a corner pocket kiss on the one ball.

"Is the girls' room back here?" Meredith asked before he could shoot. She put the slightest lilt into her voice, just a hint of Laverne and Shirley, while looking around quizzically.

The shooter looked up from the table. Punk Two perched on a stool with his boots hooked on its rail, cue in hand. They scoped her out, squinting through the bangs drifting over their eyebrows. Punk Two took a theatrical drag on his king-size.

"Nah, babe, s'round the bar, back that'a way," he drawled, gesturing vaguely. The Southern accent gave him away as a recent arrival in Chicago. Carol's, a honky-tonk joint, was in Uptown, a beatdown neighborhood recently taking in lots of poor whites from Appalachia.

"Thanks!" She twirled around and returned to the bar where Darren was waiting. For this job, Meredith wore shorts, a fitted tee, and flats. July, and the city was as humid as a jungle. Just about every other woman in the bar wore a similar outfit. Darren wanted her to wear stiletto heels with straps. *Meri, you flex your right foot when you're shooting, let him see that shoe dangle just so, for sure he won't be thinking about his next shot!* Took her five minutes to explain why stiletto heels with straps didn't go with shorts and a tee. Maybe they would find a mark with a foot fetish. Or maybe the mark would wonder why the hell she was sporting those shoes and tumble to the ploy.

Meredith slid onto the stool Darren had been guarding for her.

"Table?" he asked.

"About fell off a dump truck."

"Rough, huh."

"Worse than Canton."

"Jeez. Natives?"

"Two hillbillies."

He smirked. "Your people. Maybe they're your second cousins."

"Wouldn't that be something?" Meredith decided to say. She had worked hard to lose her accent, but Darren still teased her about being from Kentucky.

"Sandbag 'em?" he asked.

"Too obvious."

"Rope-a-Dope?"

"Thought about it, but no."

"Explain."

"Pro: They're young and think they're hot shit. One I saw shoot, s'got a wobble. We could work that. Con: They know better than to bang those beat-up rails."

"Try a Bicker?"

"They'll just bail."

"For Chrissake, then what?"

That edge to his voice, already—they weren't ten minutes in yet. Darren's nerves were fraying a lot lately.

"I'm thinking we could—"

"What can I getcha, hon?" the barmaid interjected. Like the two pool players, she had a Southern accent.

"Rum and coke, lotsa ice," Meredith answered.

"Sure thing."

Turning back to Darren, Meredith said, "Dazzle, we should go with that."

"For real?"

"Yep."

He didn't respond. Took a long drink of his Miller High Life, drew on his Kent, blew smoke. Then:

"I need to see for myself."

"No."

"No?" The edge had sharpened.

Meredith put on a smile, squeezed his bicep. "I already asked if the bathrooms were back there. You take a look now and then we ask to play, they'll know we've been checking them out. You gotta trust me on this, Dare-bear."

"Dare-bear, ain't that sweet," the barmaid said with a big grin, setting down Meredith's drink. She looked to be on the right side of forty, hair piled high and tied with a checked handkerchief, sleeves rolled on plump arms.

Meredith flinched, worried Darren would lose his temper because his pet name had been overheard, but he smiled and held out his palms. "Yep, I'm just a big ole sack of sugar, ma'am," he said.

"You're a big ole sumpin-sumpin, that's for sure," the barmaid said, admiring Darren's broad shoulders and powerful chest. No doubt about it, Darren was handsome, strong jaw and planed cheeks, just enough rough touches—bump on the bridge of his nose, crooked eyebrows—to keep him from being a pretty boy.

The barmaid took a dollar from their bills on the bar and headed to the cash register.

"So, no Sandbag, no Rope-a-Dope, no Bicker," Darren said. "Dazzle. I don't know . . ."

The Sandbag was a tried-and-true hustle. Grab a warped house cue, let the mark see that. Make a shot now and then, near-miss others, selling it (a groan, a curse, a look of self-disgust) so the mark doesn't notice he's getting left with not-so-easy shots. Throw the first two games, win the third with a "lucky" shot. Scratch on the eight ball to finish the fourth, beg for a rematch. No scratch this time.

Rope-a-Dope was Darren's creation, named after Ali and Foreman's famous bout. Darren came out shooting hard, muscling the cue and deliberately slamming the pocket points off-center so the balls careened right out. Without realizing it, the marks also started hitting hard, some kind of macho reflex, as if they couldn't let big ole Darren look stronger than them. On the fifth game, Darren "suddenly" found his aim, nailing the balls dead center.

In Bicker, she and Darren played doubles and sniped at one another about misses, giving each other dirty looks as the insults got more barbed before they "made up" and took game five. Acting-wise, the Bicker was easy—Darren's folks had split when he was ten, Meredith's when she was twelve.

Dazzle was Meredith's baby. Took a certain type of mark. Young, loaded, arrogant. A guy who hated to lose. Especially to a woman. Meredith would prime the mark by whispering to Darren, who would shake his head.

"What?" the mark would ask.

"She wants to play you solo."

"So?"

Then Darren would tell him how much money Meredith wanted to bet. That put the mark on the spot but good. Back down from playing a girl, look chicken? Darren had to be smart, name a figure at the outer limit of what he guessed the mark was carrying. Every time they had run Dazzle, he'd always hooked the mark, who put up all his cash. And Meredith had won every time. No holding back, as in Sandbag or Bicker—she went straight for the kill, working to run the table from her first shot. Darren had dubbed it Dazzle for Meredith's ability to plot out her seven shots from the get-go, the way she'd skip the obvious makes to do a reverse bank or a tricky combo, all to set herself up for the run. Despite his admiration, Darren always resisted going with Dazzle. Not only did it sideline him, he didn't like the idea of all their cash riding on Meredith's cue.

"How you gonna run Dazzle on two marks?" he now said truculently. "What if you can't cut the weaker one from his partner?"

Don't push it, Meredith told herself. "Okay, no Dazzle," she said. "Maybe we could Bicker them, if we ease into it, keep it light."

He nodded briskly, stubbed his cigarette. "Let's do that."

She sipped her drink, didn't respond, keeping her gaze on the mirrored backbar. Darren caught her look in the reflection.

"What?"

"Nothing."

He sighed impatiently. "What aren't you saying, Meri?"

"It's just . . . well, okay, I keep thinking about the transmission."

"Dammit, you know better'n that." Darren grabbed his cigarettes, tapped out another Kent, snapped open his Zippo.

"I know, I know, I shouldn't have brought it up. Forget I said anything."

An ironclad rule: never, ever hustle because you're desperate. Even the best player could psych himself out that way. *Need fifty bucks to make the rent . . . fridge is bare-ass empty . . .* Or, as Meredith and Darren had found out that morning, they needed 282 dollars to replace the transmission on Darren's 1967 Nova. Meredith had noticed the clanking when they left Canton, every time she shifted. *You hear that?* she had asked Darren. *Hear what?* He was cranky, trying to crib a nap while she drove. *That clanking*, she'd said. *I don't hear shit*, he'd answered. She'd persisted, slowed the car, told him to downshift into fourth while she kept the clutch in. He'd done it, clumsily, because he was using his left hand. *Gear box feels tight, doesn't it?* she'd asked. *I guess so*, he'd said. Darren liked fast cars, but he didn't know anything about them. Meredith's dad, a mechanic, had taken her to his shop when he had visitation; she knew engines. She'd gotten the repair quote from the first shop they saw once they hit Chicago. The car was drivable, short-term, but they couldn't leave town without the repair. Pushing Dazzle just to get that 282 dollars—that was bad luck, as she'd just admitted to Darren. He was in no mood for an apology though.

"Can I count on you or what? You gonna play your part?" About to lose his temper.

"Yeah, you can count on me," she shot back. "How 'bout you? Maybe you oughta lay off that beer, your hand looks a little shaky."

In an instant, that look. Eyes flashing, jaw clenching, shoulder and bicep muscles going taut. As he released a gritted hiss, Meredith flashed a smile.

"See, babe? Just practicing the Bicker."

Darren relaxed, allowed himself a grin. "Oh, that was a good one, Meri, you really had me there for a second."

"It's one of our best acts, isn't it? The Bicker."

"Never let us down yet."

"I never failed on Dazzle yet, either."

"Meri, c'mon . . ."

She put her hand on his thigh, leaned to whisper. "We'll do whatever you want, Dare-Bear. All I'm saying is, see what you think after you get a look at these two. I think they're here warming up on this rat-trap of a table so they can hustle someplace else. Which means they're carrying a lotta bread."

"All right, I'll think about it. Follow my lead."

"Always, always."

The punk Meredith had seen shooting said his name was Lester. His boots put him a tick over six feet. Lean torso, ropy muscles, faint freckling on his cheeks. His hands were chafed, grime under his nails. His buddy Virgil was a few inches shorter, with a squat build, short arms, and thick wrists. He sported a bristly mustache under a pug nose. Meredith hoped Darren saw what she saw: both men had telltale wads of cash in the front pockets of their jeans. Maybe, just maybe, he'd go for the Dazzle if the Bicker worked out.

"Yeah, sure," Lester answered Darren's suggestion they play doubles. He didn't say anything about money and neither did Darren.

"Find the little girls' room, little lady?" Virgil asked, laughing at his joke.

"Oh, sure, thanks for the directions!" Meredith smiled, playing along.

Darren racked for eight ball. She reached for a cue.

"Let me do that," Darren commanded. "You don't know anything about pool sticks." The opening ruse: boss her around. He held a cue out and peered down its shaft, looking for a warp. Lester and Virgil had brought custom cues, the cases stacked on the wall shelf. They exchanged looks as Darren proclaimed, "This'll do."

Virgil broke hard, careened the three ball straight into the right corner pocket at the foot of the table. The spread left him an easy shot on the six ball in the left corner, but then he missed cutting the one into the left side pocket. "Awwh, hell," he groaned. "I shoulda made that."

Meredith noticed Virgil left the cue ball tight against the rail, without a clear shot for them. A classic Sandbag—the hillbillies were trying to hustle them. But the Bicker played well against a Sandbag. Nothing like a couple arguing to create a distraction.

"So we're the stripey balls, right, hon?" Meredith asked as Darren stood to take his turn.

"Obviously," he answered sarcastically. He made a show of studying the leave: squatting down to scrutinize the rail, staring at various stripes. He came down hard on the cue ball from an awkward angle. The tip glanced off and struck the felt—a scratch.

"Oops," Meredith giggled.

He glared. "You think you coulda done better?"

So much for easing into it, keeping the squabble light.

"We'll see, won't we?"

Lester shot next. Sunk the one ball his partner had missed, then tried a reverse bank on the four that came up short, intentionally. He left Meredith two clean shots, one easier than the other. Which one she took would tell him and Virgil a lot. If she took the hard shot, a cut on the twelve, she'd set herself up for a good run, at least three more balls, and they'd know she could shoot. The sure shot, on the fourteen, would leave her behind the eight ball. *Recon*, she and Darren called this ploy, furtively setting up your opponent so you could appraise them. Time to mess with their heads, she thought.

She studied the lay, then looked expectantly at Darren. "I'm thinking I should try for this purple one"—she pointed at the twelve—"cuz then I can—"

"No, no, no!" Darren jumped up from his stool, immediately sensing what she was up to. "You can't make that shot. Take the fourteen." He grabbed the cue from her hands and pantomimed the shot for her.

"Are you sure?"

"Yes—do it already!"

Meredith shot, sank the fourteen. Predictably, the cue ball settled an inch behind the eight. Now the hustle was primed. Virgil and Lester could see she knew how to read the table but that her boyfriend was too dense to give her a chance. Hopefully, that would embolden them to casually propose playing for money, especially once she and Darren really started to bicker.

And bicker they did, for the rest of that game and straight through the next, Darren laying it on strong, telling her she shot like a girl and coming over to arrange her stance and shot, moving her arms around as if she was a rag doll. For her part, Meredith started pushing back, changing her compliance to petulance, then irritation. "Well, you're not making your shots either" . . .

"I didn't have anything to shoot at!" They lost the first game, and the second. Darren pounded the cue on the floor. "Well, this is a waste of time. C'mon, let's go," he snapped at Meredith.

Lester piped up. "No, man, this is fun. Maybe we oughta make the next game a little interesting, whattya say?"

"You mean like for money?" Darren laughed derisively, jerked his head toward Meredith. "You think I'm gonna play for money with her as my partner?" He ostentatiously took out his wallet, extended it. "Why don't you just help yourself and get it over with?"

Darren's acting was good. Too good, Meredith thought. But she stayed in character, lowering her head at his abuse.

"Well, we could handicap," Lester said. "How's that?"

"After the break, we'll take two of your balls off the table straightaway."

Darren pretended to think about the offer. "Three. You saw how lousy she is."

Lester looked at Virgil, who nodded and said, "Fifty bucks a game."

"Sure."

"Rack 'em," Lester told Darren.

They threw that game, but Darren eased up toward the end, stopped dictating her shots, stopped belittling her. When she sunk a ball, he offered grudging praise. Darren put another fifty up; they lost it.

"Double-or-nothing?" Lester asked casually.

"You mean a hundred?"

Lester ticked his chin.

"We're still handicapping, right?"

"Yep."

"Well, man, I—oh hell, why not?" Darren bent to retrieve the rack.

Showtime for Meredith. They needed to win, but if Darren upped his game, the hillbillies would catch on and refuse a rematch. If Lester and Virgil quit after losing this game, she and Darren only broke even. Another double-or-nothing—200 dollars—almost fetched them what they needed for the car. Don't think that, she rebuked herself. She needed to stay deep in the hustle, concentrate on looking like an amateur on a lucky streak . . .

"I made it, I made it!" She squealed with delight as she just—*just*—dropped the eight ball in the side pocket on her third turn, after clearing their last ball off the table. Darren had played masterfully, sinking only one or two each turn, always leaving Virgil with a tough shot. Meredith brought the cue ball perilously close to the pocket, counting on the rough felt to stop it from following the eight ball in.

"You almost scratched," Darren glowered.

Meredith's face fell. Was he still in character, pushing the hillbillies to believe that she would start missing after being rebuked, or did he mean it? Too often, the Bicker started to feel real.

"Good game," Virgil said flatly.

"Guess that makes us even," Lester said, handing over a hundred dollars. As Darren slipped the bills into his front pocket, Lester asked, "Want to go again?"

"How much?"

"Thought we agreed on double-or-nothing the last round."

"So two hundred?"

"That's double a hundred, ain't it?"

Darren ignored the crack. "All right—rack 'em."

"No handicap this time," Virgil piped up from his stool.

"You're the ones suggested it," Darren protested.

"Sure. But the little lady's on a roll now. Cain't expect us to play for two-hundred bucks with y'all three balls ahead."

Darren appeared to think, then leveled his gaze at Meredith. "You better play good."

"I will," she shot back.

And did she ever, Darren too. They were all-in now. Meredith lived for this moment, when she could stop missing, could shrug off the ditz act; and she could shoot to kill. The Bicker was off—she and Darren were a team again. They had to put these hillbillies down, just like they'd put the two ironworkers down in Canton on the eleventh game of nine ball, clearing 160 dollars; just like they'd taken the sixth game in Cincinnati the week before in a fierce round of Rope-a-Dope. When all the money was on the line, they both came alive, prowling the table, chalk squeaking as they readied their cues, single-minded and relentless, pouncing on every ball like panthers on prey. Darren was one of the finest short game players she'd ever seen, since she took to hanging out in her Uncle Filbert's pool hall after her folks split up. Sure-footed, a power-hitter with admirable control.

For her part, Meredith had a glide as straight as a rifle shot. She could take a ball clear across the green, drop it without fail, never needing a friendly roll off the pocket point. And her leaves! As Darren said, the night they met and she took him for 300 bucks, she could read the table like a book. More like a board, she liked to think, chess being the other game her Uncle Filbert had taught her. Always thinking several shots ahead, surveying the spread, seeing her balls as pieces to move around the table, which is why she could pull off the Dazzle. She was good on her own, but a solo hustle as a woman was difficult and dangerous. Constantly being hit on and pawed, never knowing when a mark might get violent. She had already had two close scrapes when she hooked up with Darren. For a while, they'd been good together, and not just on the pool table. Then Darren started losing his temper over the littlest things. His beer wasn't cold enough, she'd left a towel on the hotel bathroom floor. Whatever was eating him, he wouldn't say, but he was getting moodier and more unpredictable. As the bruise on her right forearm kept reminding her.

"Awwh, Goddammit all," Virgil groaned as Darren dropped the eight ball into a corner pocket. He handed over 200 dollars and sullenly watched Darren pocket the cash.

"I'm done," Lester said, unscrewing his custom cue.

"You cain't quit on me now, partner," Virgil protested.

"You wanna play, keep playin', I ain't gonna stop you."

The perfect setup! Meredith jumped up from her stool, ran over to Darren, and whispered into his ear. "Let's go big, baby, let's do the Dazzle."

He scowled and shook his head. "No, I don't think so."

Was he playing along or really saying no? Meredith couldn't tell. "What?" Virgil asked.

"She wants, well, she wants to play more doubles."

So he *was* nixing the Dazzle. Couldn't he see how easily she could beat Virgil?

Virgil said, "Well, man, I cain't play doubles without a partner," giving Lester a dismissive nod. "But how about you and me play one-on-one, big man? Maybe a little nine ball?"

It was like he wanted to hand his cash over to them! All Darren had to say was, "Sure, but why don't you play her instead?" Meredith could stroke a nine-ball rack like a yo-yo: up, down, and all the way around.

But Darren didn't say that. What he said was, "If I'm gonna play you solo, it's gotta be worth my while." His gaze flickered over the thick pad of bills still evident in Virgil's front pocket.

Meredith didn't let her face show what she was thinking. Nine ball was not Darren's best game.

Virgil smiled. "You wanna bet big, you mean."

Darren nodded.

Virgil didn't say anything for a moment. The bar had become louder—a country band was playing up front. Cigarette smoke hung heavy in the air, the Pabst light over the pool table made jerky rotations, hueing the scuffed felt in a pale red circle. Taking a long drag on his cigarette, Virgil said, "Awright man, you wanna up the stakes, you got it. Why don't we play for something you cain't afford to lose?"

"Yeah? What's that?"

Another drag, exhale. When the smoke cleared from his face, Virgil pointed at Meredith:

"Her."

Meredith let out a shocked yelp.

Darren laughed. "Funny."

"I ain't joshin' ya."

"That is not cool, you understand?" Darren squared his shoulders and took a step toward Virgil.

Who didn't back down. "Don't you wanna know what I'm gonna put up?"

Darren shook his head but Virgil spoke anyway.

"My ride, that's what I'll put up." He reached into his pocket and took out a key ring, jangled it. "Oughta come take a look, man, it's a sweet machine."

Darren looked over at Meredith, who had lowered her head, hands clenched in her lap. She could break character, she knew. Just stand up and say, "No way, we're done." Or should she stay quiet, see how Darren played it? He might convince Virgil to stick with cash—double-or-nothing would put four hundred dollars on the table. So long as he didn't think about how the Nova needed a new transmission, and he didn't agree to see the car.

"I'm not saying yes, understand? But I'll look at your car."

Meredith jumped up, ran over, and grabbed his forearm. "Baby, no, you can't—"

He shrugged her off. "We're just taking a look, okay, nobody's bet nothing."

"I don't care, you can't do this!"

But Darren was already following Virgil and Lester out the bar's side door. Meredith hurried after them. The street was narrow and lined with parked cars. The canopies of ash and elm trees arched over the pavement. Brick apartment buildings and cut stone single-family homes loomed behind high iron fences. *No Trespassing* signs abounded, as did alarm company shields with silhouetted pistols or German shepherds. Virgil led them down the block and greeted a teen with unruly curls falling past his shoulders. He was perched on a milk crate upturned on the government strip.

"Any trouble, Duane?"

"Naw."

"My sister's kid," Virgil explained. "Cain't leave a car like mine unattended 'round these parts."

Darren wasn't listening. He was all-eyes on a 1975 Pontiac Firebird, cherry red with a black stenciled phoenix spreading its wings just below the hood header. Rally II rims, whitewall Goodrich radials, black leather bucket seats, six-speed transmission, power windows. The setting sun, slanting through the shade trees, brightened the waxed finish. Darren ran his finger along the edge of the driver's side door, peering into the interior.

"You got papers?" he asked.

Meredith's stomach heaved. He was going to take the bet! She rushed over. "Dare-Bear, we should—"

"Right here." Virgil tugged a worn, folded sheet from his wallet. Darren studied the title and handed it back.

"Darren!"

"Gimme a moment, yeah?" he said to Virgil, who nodded. Darren guided Meredith behind the nearest tree.

"We should do it," he whispered. "I won't lose, I promise." Stroking her hand, like a nervous beau about to propose.

"Are you outta your mind? You can't treat me like a hunk of meat!"

"I won't lose, baby."

"What if you do?"

He squeezed her hand. "Then we'll cut and run."

She jerked free. "You don't think they'll be ready for that? Lester'll be on me like white on rice."

"I won't lose, baby," he said again.

"No. I don't wanna do it."

He gently lifted her chin with his fingers, looked into her eyes. "Trust me. I got this. One game'a nine-ball and that car's ours."

She met his gaze. They weren't supposed to think about the prizes before they played, were they?

"Promise you won't leave me, no matter what."

"I promise. But I'm not going to lose. Believe you me, I got this hillbilly's number."

Darren's table, his break. He barely kissed the one bill, nudging the rack, leaving no leaves. But Virgil understood that opener, kissed the one ball right back. Darren brought it out and dropped it with a masterful massé. He was just able to nick the two ball, but the hillbilly wedged the two ball right back in the rack and back-spun the cue ball into the kitchen. Darren couldn't hit the two ball, so Virgil had ball-in-hand—he could put the cue ball wherever he wanted. He lined himself up for another kiss of the two and again back-spun the cue ball into the kitchen.

Meredith saw what was happening—Virgil was running his own Rope-a-Dope, in reverse! Toying with Darren, pushing him toward a hard shot just to break up the rack. If he did that, the way Virgil had composed the lay, the seven ball would push the nine toward the corner pocket and leave the two on a straight line toward the nine. In this game, you didn't have to sink the balls in numerical order to win, not if you slopped, bumped, or banged the nine ball in any way you could.

Meredith licked dry lips. "Hey, baby, before—"

Crack! Darren muscled his shot, breaking up the clustered balls. They veered this way and that, in seemingly random directions, but just as she feared, the two ball left a clear shot on the nine.

Darren stared at the table, too stunned even to swear. He wiped his brow.

"Well, would you look at that?" Virgil said, chalking his cue. But he wasn't looking at the table—he was staring at Meredith. Lester had sidled into the passageway to the bar, blocking the only exit.

"Listen, man, you gotta gimme another chance, another game—"

"Hold your horses now, I gotta make the shot," Virgil said. He bent over the table, shot carefully and slowly. The nine ball dropped with a thud.

"No, no, no," Meredith whimpered.

"Another game, we have to play again," Darren insisted. "I let you play after you lost."

"How we gonna go double-or-nothing now? I ain't got but one car, and less your pretty little lady's got a twin, you only got one'a her."

Meredith ran to Darren and jumped on him, wrapping her arms and legs around him. "Get me outta here, you promised!" she hissed into his ear.

"Okay, okay, I won't let them take you," he whispered. He nudged her off, getting her feet on the floor. Her hands dropped to his waist, letting go slowly. Virgil and Lester stood side-by-side in the doorway, arms crossed.

"Now look," Darren began nervously. "This bet, you know we were just joking around, right? She's not my slave, I can't just turn her over to you."

"Was you joking when you asked to see the title to my Firebird?" Virgil asked coldly.

"That didn't mean anything."

"Where we come from, a bet's a bet. We can do this the honest way and you don't get hurt, or we can do it the hard way."

Darren's face tightened. He clenched his fists. "Bring it on, hillbilly."

Virgil smirked. Lester put two fingers in his mouth and let out an ear-splitting whistle. From the bar, two men stood and started to come their way. They were older, both big and round-shouldered, thick arms.

Meredith figured they had a few seconds, no more, to reach the side door before the reinforcements arrived. Darren could lower his shoulder, knock Virgil into Lester and clear a path. If they moved now!

"Darren, let's go!" She grabbed his wrist, ready to hang on for dear life.

"I'm sorry, Meri," he said, yanking his arm free. Head down, he rammed Lester with lowered shoulder, slamming him to the floor. Virgil tried to grab Darren's arm but he shook him off, plowed straight through a clot of women, knocking one to the ground. The two men from the bar charged toward Darren.

"You BAAA-STARD!" Meredith's bellow halted all conversations mid-sentence. Even the band stopped playing. Everyone turned their heads to gape at Meredith, who stood in the passageway, arms in the air, a slim pretty young woman in a fitted tee and shorts, sun-streaked brown hair pulled back into a ponytail. Then their heads swiveled to watch a broad-shouldered man sprint through the side door.

"Well, I sure hope that wasn't directed at *me*," the band singer quipped. Laughter rippled through the bar. A few patrons gave Meredith lingering, curious looks; most resumed talking, drinking, smoking, flirting. The band went back to their cover of "Please Stay Tuned."

One of Virgil's friends ticked his head toward the door. *Go after him?* Virgil shook his head. They nodded and returned to the bar.

Meredith strode over to Lester, who was now on his knees, grimacing as he started to stand. She extended a hand.

"Sorry about that. You hurt?"

"Ahh, I'll be fine. Your old man's a bull, though, I'll give him that."

"*Ex*-old man, thanks to you." Meredith was all smiles as she hugged Lester and then Virgil, kissing them both on the cheek.

"Happy to help," Virgil said. "Gotta say, we had to have Filbert tell us twice what you wanted to do."

"I know, sorry. I tried to keep this hustle simple."

"Once we understood it through and through, we knew we could do it."

Through and through. Good phrase, Meredith thought. As in, she was through with Darren. For a short time, she had hoped he would get over whatever was eating him, get back to being the fun-loving, pool-sharking man she'd fallen in with. But when he got physical—uh-uh, no way she was giving him another chance. While he slept off his beer and whiskey one night in Canton, she snuck out to the hotel lobby and called her Uncle Filbert at his pool hall in Lexington, where she had met Lester and Virgil. Before she left town for good, the three of them had played something like a thousand games of cutthroat together. She had heard they'd ended up in Chicago. *Know how to get ahold of them?* Meredith had asked Filbert. *'Spect I can do that*, he had answered. Feeding dime after dime into the pay phone for the long-distance call, she had outlined her plan, Filbert repeating each step back to her to make sure he understood. *All set*, he told her the following night when she snuck out for another call. *Saturday night, Carol's Pub in Uptown—they'll be there.*

"Boy, you sure can act, Meredith," Lester now said, rubbing his chest where Darren had butted him. "S'like you'd never seen us before."

"You boys did pretty good yourselves."

"How'd you know he'd go for my car?" Virgil asked.

"On our way here, I told him the transmission on his Nova felt off. I'd called ahead to a garage, told the mechanic I'd give him twenty bucks to pop the hood and tell us we needed two-hundred-eighty-two bucks to fix it."

Virgil chortled. "So there's nothing wrong with his car?"

"Nope, not a lick."

"Too bad he got away with it."

"Did he?" Meredith grinned as she pulled Darren's key ring from her shorts pocket.

Both men gaped. "How'd you do that?" Lester asked.

"Remember when I jumped on him after Virgil won, how I wrapped myself around him? When he let me down, I picked his pockets."

Virgil nodded admiringly but Lester looked worried.

"Should we be worried about him coming back?"

Meredith firmly shook her head. "After ditching me like that? He'll slink off, find some place to hustle a stake to get out of town. And I'll never have to see him again."

"What'd he do to you?" Lester said.

She let her stoic expression serve as reply; Lester didn't press.

"Gotta say, I was frettin' a bit over playing nine ball," Virgil said. "But he took the bait just like you said he would, breaking the rack wide open."

"That's his weakness," Meredith said. "No patience. Hey, here's your bread back." She counted off two-hundred dollars and pressed them into Virgil's hand.

"You don't gotta do that," he protested awkwardly.

"Take it. I pulled it outta his pocket when I snagged the keys."

He dipped his chin and accepted the cash. "So what's next, Meredith? You wanna stick around a few days, get to know Chicago?"

Why not? She'd been so focused on running the hustle to rid herself of Darren, she hadn't thought about what came next.

"I'd like that, sure," she answered.

"You can stay with my sister."

"That sounds great."

"Maybe you can teach us a thing or too," Lester said.

"You bet." Meredith looked at the beat-up, raggedy, sorry-ass table that had aided her liberation. "S'long as it's not here."

---

*This piece started with two off-the-cuff decisions: I wanted to write about a couple and I wanted to set the story in the 1970s (in my humble opinion, a much *cooler decade than conventional wisdom allows). But what were Meredith and Darren going to do besides drive around in their Chevy Nova? I got an answer—and a first line—when I wandered into a dive bar in Chicago and shot a few games of eight ball on the sorriest, most raggedy-assed pool table I've ever seen. The story started clicking then. (It sure helped that the bar's decor dated to the Carter administration.) Whatever was going to happen, I just knew, had to happen because of that pool table. Right after our two sharks, Meredith and Darren, walk into a bar . . .*

Tom Larsen *was born and raised in New Jersey and was awarded a degree in Civil Engineering from Rutgers University. He is the author of six novels in the crime genre.*

Larsen's short fiction has been published in Alfred Hitchcock Mystery Magazine, Mystery Tribune, Sherlock Holmes Mystery Magazine, *and* Black Cat Mystery Magazine. *His nonfiction work has appeared in four volumes of the anthology series "Best New True Crime Stories."*

Larsen's short story "El Cuerpo en el Barril" ("The Body in the Barrel") was the recipient of the 2020 Black Orchid Novella Award and appears in the anthology Best Mystery Stories of the Year 2022 *from the Mysterious Press.*

POBRE MARIA: A CAPITÁN GUILLÉN MYSTERY OF ECUADOR

Tom Larsen

"Somebody better be dead," Guillén barked. The *Policía Nacional* dispatch officers had become used to his trademark way of answering the phone at late hours, but whoever was calling had not. A silence greeted him from the other end of the line.

"*¡Mande! ¿Quién es?*" Capitán Ernesto Guillén had little patience at the best of times, and this was not the best of times. "Answer me!" he demanded.

"It's Sergeant Ortiz," a timid voice responded.

"Ortiz?" Guillén was on his feet by now, padding barefoot across the cold tile floor toward the bathroom. "Why are you calling me?"

"It's your desk phone," Ortiz explained. "It kept ringing. We ignored it for a while, but it wouldn't stop. Finally, Lieutenant Rodriguez said that *I* should answer it."

"Rodriguez! What a coward!" Guillén cleared his throat. "Well, come on, man. Out with it! What is this about?"

"A woman died last night," Ortiz said. "At the public hospital."

"A woman died in a hospital? What are the odds?"

"He said it was a suspicious death."

"Who said this? The person that called my direct line at two o'clock in the morning?"

"Yes!" Words started tumbling from the sergeant's mouth like water over river rocks. "He said it was a *suspicious death*. Those were his exact words. And he won't deal with anyone but you."

"What's his name? This fellow who called."

"I don't know. He wouldn't say."

"You're a detective, Ortiz. Detect!"

"Yes, sir."

Guillén sighed. It was no fun berating this new generation of policemen. If a superior officer had talked to him like that when he was a sergeant, he would have, at a minimum, called him an *hijodeputa*—a sonofabitch.

"Okay," he said, when it appeared that no more information was forthcoming from the terrified sergeant. "Pick me up in one hour."

"An hour? But—"

"Yes, an hour! Why? Is the woman going to be any less dead?"

"No, sir. It's just . . . There's one more thing."

"Oh?"

"Yes, sir. This woman? She is apparently the daughter of a very influential man."

"*¡Madre de Dios!* Why didn't you say that in the first place?"

"Sorry, sir."

"Sorry, sir," Guillén mimicked. "All right, then. Twenty minutes." He ended the call and tossed the phone onto his bed. In Guillén's world, "a very influential man" was code for "money to be made."

In his midfifties, Guillén at five foot nine was tall for an *ecuatoriano*, but at a hundred-eighty pounds he was also quite overweight. As a result, he never left home without being immaculately dressed. He had his suits especially tailored for their slimming effects and wore long ties, like the current American president, because he had been told that they, too, would help distract from his bulk.

Tightening his belt, he found that he had lost a few pounds and, momentarily, he missed his wife. They had been separated for two years but would never divorce. They were Catholic, after all. Alicia had a tongue that could cut you like a new razor, but she cooked like an angel.

He glared at his reflection in the mirror. Twenty minutes. No time for a shower, which meant an extra heavy dose of cologne.

It couldn't be helped. Ernesto Guillén feared no man, but he had learned that it was never advisable to keep a powerful man waiting.

And, what about that? Guillén wondered as he knotted his tie. *How was it that the daughter of a man this powerful ended up in the public hospital, where medical care was free, and you got what you paid for?*

The answer was obvious when he thought about it for a few minutes. This woman was estranged from her powerful father. That added a layer of complexity to the case. He would have to solve the crime while keeping the details from the newspapers. *And that is why they called me directly,* he thought with some pride as he went out to the street to await the arrival of Sergeant Ortiz.

"Ernesto. Thank you for coming so quickly."

"Of course, Mauricio."

Mauricio Segreda was the personal attorney, confidante, and fixer of problems for José Neira, one of the richest men in Cuenca. After five years in the Air Force, Neira had purchased an old twin-engine Cessna 310 and began delivering supplies to oil exploration teams in the jungle. After thirty years, in which time his fleet had grown to eighteen planes, he sold the business and began a second career as a politician. He had served two terms as mayor of Cuenca and one as the governor of Azuay province. A devastating defeat in the 2008 presidential election soured him on politics and he returned to making money with a vengeance. He now owned houses, condominiums, and commercial buildings from Cuenca to Quito.

Segreda was similar in size to Guillén, but rather than trying to disguise his obesity, he seemed to celebrate it. His suit was more expensive than the captain's, but the jacket hugged him tightly at the shoulders and the sleeves were too short. The trousers struggled to contain his bulk at the waist. His jacket hung open and his tie was stained and rumpled.

Even at three in the morning, Guillén wouldn't be caught dead dressed like that.

"How can I help?" he said, his hands folded in front of him, his facial expression the epitome of concern. Segreda was already on the move, toward the freight elevator.

The elevator began its slow ascent to the fourth floor. "What is going on?" Guillén said, with a sharper tone than was perhaps advisable. Segreda may not have looked like much, but he was the right arm of one of richest and most powerful men in the region.

"What is happening," Segreda said, "is that Don José's daughter has passed away under suspicious circumstances.

"Suspicious circumstances?" Guillén said. "She died in this hospital, no?"

"Yes. And before you say anything, I know . . . and Don José knows as well. People die in the hospital all the time."

Especially this one, Guillén thought but didn't say.

Segreda stopped in front of a door to what appeared to be a storage closet. Noticing Guillén's puzzled look as he took a key from his pocket, he smiled briefly.

"The administrator was kind enough to provide me a key so that we can enter and leave without bothering the staff."

Guillén smiled as well. The Neira family trust had contributed millions of dollars to some of the finest hospitals in town. Here, where the corridors smelled faintly of urine and the rooms resembled prison cells, the donations were undoubtedly smaller and of a more personal nature. As in directly into the pocket of the administrator.

"So the administrator called you when Don José's daughter was admitted?"

"Yes. He has been very good about that." The two men shared another brief smile. *Money talks!*

"This is not the young lady's first time here?"

They were in the room now, and Segreda searched for and found the light switch before answering.

"Maria has a history of illicit drug use. So yes, she has made a number of visits to this hospital." He shook his head slightly side to side. "It was only a matter of time, I suppose, but Don José is devastated nonetheless."

Guillén knew that José Neira had two daughters—one a doctor and one an attorney—and a son who held a high-level position in his business. He didn't need to be told that Maria was Neira's illegitimate daughter. He kept tabs on her, contributed to her support, but kept her several arm's lengths from his *real* family. Guillén knew that he could pressure Segreda and get some details, but that would just be gossip. He had work to do.

The two fluorescent ceiling lights flickered on and off a few times before settling into a pale yellow glow. The room was indeed a storage closet, although slightly larger than Guillén had expected—perhaps three meters square. The walls had been painted a light green at one time but were now cracked and filthy. The ceiling was stained from water leaks. The entire room smelled of dampness. Brooms, mops, buckets, and what appeared to be spare parts from various pieces of medical equipment littered the floor.

"It's cold enough to hang meat in here," Guillén said, and shivered. The window was wide open, and a large floor fan pulled the night air into the room, directing it at an old hospital bed. One of the bed's wheels had been removed, and that corner was supported by a block of wood. As he approached the bed, Guillén saw what appeared at first to be a pile of dirty sheets.

"Sonofabitch!" Guillén stopped moving. "That's her?"

"Yes, that is Maria." Segreda spoke from near the door, as far as possible from the woman's body without leaving the room.

Guillén stood motionless for a moment. *I will find who did this to you*, he promised, under his breath. Not a man known for his compassion, he always felt an overwhelming sense of sadness when encountering someone whose life had been cut short.

His wife used to say, "You care more for the dead than you do the living." Maybe she was right. He shook his head and took in a big gulp of cool air to clear his head.

"*Listo*," he said, all business now. "She died of drugs? An overdose?"

"She was murdered!" Segreda exclaimed.

"So you say." Guillén dropped any deference to the fat man. This was a crime scene, and he was in charge. He pulled back the sheet at the head of the bed and was startled to see the woman's bare feet.

"*Hijodeputas*," Guillén muttered. "Couldn't take five seconds to lay her out properly." Moving to the other end of the bed, he pulled the sheet back once again, revealing a grotesque mask of death. Maria's neck was arched back as if she had recoiled in fright from something. Her mouth was open, revealing a hellscape of broken teeth and blackened gums, the sure signs of an addict. The attendants had not even taken the time to close the poor woman's eyes. They stared up at him as if begging him for relief. He stood looking into them for a few seconds and then used his thumb to close them gently, one at a time.

When he lifted and released her right arm, it fell back onto the bed. Rigor wouldn't set in for about twelve hours, probably longer in the coolness of the room. Still, her body was cold to the touch, and when he turned her on her side, her back showed evidence of lividity. Five, maybe six hours she had been dead.

"When did they call you?"

Segreda jumped as if surprised to hear another human voice. "Just before midnight," he managed to say, his voice like the sound of dry leaves being raked across concrete.

Guillén looked at his wristwatch. "So, she lay there dead for three hours before anybody noticed," he said, his voice barely audible.

"You may want to look away," he warned, but Segreda had already done so, placing a forearm against the door and resting his head on it. Guillén pulled back the sheet. The woman, who appeared to be about thirty, had small breasts, and he could see the outline of her ribs through her skin. Her stomach was concave and showed the markings of physical abuse. Some had scarred over, but a few were fresh, probably inflicted within the twenty-four hours before her death. What appeared to be a couple cigarette burns had become infected. Strings of yellowish pus had oozed from them and now lay dry and crusty against her brown skin.

Guillén scanned the rest of her body before covering her with the sheet once again. Her legs were atrophied, signifying a life of inactivity. The soles of her feet were black, indicating that she had walked barefoot a lot. Her arms were similarly cadaverous and bore no signs of needle marks. Whatever her drug of choice had been, she took it orally, not via the spike.

Guillén had succeeded in extricating the stricken attorney from the room by the time Sergeant Ortiz returned with Styrofoam containers of coffee and a greasy paper sack of empanadas.

"You didn't get yourself anything?" Guillén dug a meaty paw into the sack and came out with a fistful of crispy dough-wrapped chicken, still steaming from the fryer.

"I didn't know if I was supposed to," Ortiz responded, handing Guillén his change, mostly one-dollar coins.

Guillén shrugged. It wasn't up to him to train the young sergeant in the intricacies of his job. "Mauricio?" He extended the bag toward the attorney, who sat on a metal bench against the wall with his head in his hands.

"No," said Segreda without looking up. "I can't eat now. Not after what I saw in there."

Guillén shrugged one more time and retrieved another steaming empanada from the bag. "Some coffee, perhaps?"

"Yes, thank you, Ernesto. You are very kind." Segreda sat up straighter and took the Styrofoam container. He was light-skinned for an ecuatoriano and now so much blood had drained from his face that he appeared nearly white.

"You!" Guillén turned to face Ortiz and took a small notebook from the inside of his jacket. He scribbled something and tore a page from the book. "Go to this address and bring me the man who lives there."

"Will I need backup?" Ortiz asked, his wide expressive face exposing his nervousness.

"This man is seventy-two years of age," Guillén scoffed. "I think you can handle him."

"Yes, sir." The crestfallen sergeant turned to go. *What would it take to earn the respect of his boss?*

Ortiz was ten meters down the hall when Guillén called to him. "Be sure that Señor Torres brings his kit with him."

"His kit?" Ortiz called over his shoulder.

"Yes. His kit."

Guillén appeared not inclined to clarify, so Ortiz hurried off.

"It is certainly possible that she was poisoned," Guillén said. He sat on the bench next to the stricken attorney. "There is no evidence of external physical trauma, but she died in extreme pain. You can tell by the way her expression is frozen in anguish. A few poisons—not many—will cause such pain. But Torres will tell us for sure."

"Who is this man? Señor Torres?"

Guillén read suspicion on Segreda's face.

"Doctor Alberto Torres was the best toxicological chemist that ever worked for the Policía Nacional. He's retired now, but he has expensive tastes, and a government pension is not enough to satisfy such tastes."

"Ahhh," Segreda murmured. The captain had carefully crafted his answer so as to relax the man and it appeared to have done so. The fact that Torres was retired told the anxious attorney that there would be no direct police involvement. The fact that the man had expensive tastes told Segreda that his discretion would cost his employer a good deal of money, but he had plenty. Segreda—and his employer—always felt comfortable dealing with the monetary aspect of any transaction. It was the human factor that often baffled them.

Dr. Torres was dressed as if he were headed out to a high-society dinner, not a hush-hush autopsy at four in the morning. He was short and thin, and his dark black hair, neatly groomed beard, and designer eyeglasses made him appear much younger than seventy-two. He wore a tailored gray suit, a light blue shirt, and a red and black regimentally striped tie. Trailing in his wake, Sergeant Ortiz struggled to carry a leather satchel four or five times the size of a normal doctor's bag. The faux leather case showed every bit of *its* age. The outer casing was cracked and faded, the brass latches were dull and tarnished, and Ortiz had to carry the case in his arms because one of the carrying straps had worn completely through. He set the case down next to the bed and stood up, stretching his back and rubbing feeling back into his hands and forearms.

"Ernesto. *¿Cómo le va?*"

"*Muy bien,* Señor Doctor." Guillén barely touched the man's extended hand, as if he were afraid that years of rooting around in people's diseased organs might have somehow infected it. "This is—"

"Zapata!" Segreda interrupted. "Juan Zapata."

"Yes, Juan Zapata," Guillén agreed, unable to completely hide his amusement at the man's ham-handed attempt to disguise himself. Segreda didn't know that the fact that Guillén had summoned him was enough to guarantee the good doctor's silence. No one dared to cross the big man.

The formalities dispensed with, the four of them crowded into the small room. Dr. Torres approached the bed and pulled the sheet back with one quick movement. The other three flinched at this sudden exposing of Maria's naked body, but Torres paid them no mind. To the doctor a human body, naked or clothed, dead or alive, was nothing more than a lab specimen to be probed and prodded, sliced apart, and examined until it revealed its secrets to him.

Torres took a small penlight from his jacket pocket. Forcing the woman's eyelids open, he peered into them, then examined the nasal cavities and finally her mouth. He leaned in so close that it appeared to Guillén that the diminutive doctor might crawl in through the gaping aperture in order to examine her from the inside.

"Come. Look at this." Torres moved to one side, but even so there was only room for one more person next to him. It was Guillén who strode across the room and leaned over the body, trying to see what the doctor's extended finger was indicating.

"See there?" Torres shown the penlight into the open mouth. "See how the entrance to her esophagus is red and inflamed?"

"Yes, I see it now." Guillén stood. "But what does it mean?"

"Well, I could draw some blood to be absolutely sure, but I think it's safe to say that someone stuffed a rag down her throat.

A rag soaked in something extremely toxic. As I said, I'll take a blood sample, but I suspect strychnine or something similar." He pushed down on the woman's chin, but even using two hands he couldn't straighten her neck. "See there," he exclaimed, as if addressing a group of first year med students. "The drug would decrease very quickly the amount of adenosine triphosphate in the neck muscles, which would account for the localized rigidity. Yes, I'm quite sure that strychnine is the culprit here."

"Well, Mauricio," Guillén said, turning away from the bed, "Dr. Torres is never wrong. We can now be sure that it was murder. Now, you must decide what—" He stopped in mid-sentence. His black eyes scanned the small room. "Where is he?" he demanded, sending a murderous glare in Ortiz's direction. "Segreda! Where is he?"

"He left. Right after the doctor . . ." Words failed the stricken sergeant at that point, leaving him with an open-mouthed stare as he pointed to the door.

"Who is Segreda?" Dr. Torres wondered, but no one answered.

"*¡Maldición!*" An angry Captain Guillén is a sight to behold. He seemed to swell in size, as if compressed air had been pumped into his body. His swarthy face turned two shades darker and his eyes bulged.

"Come on!" Guillén headed for the door with Ortiz a step behind.

"I will call you," Guillén told Torres over his shoulder.

"I am counting on it."

Hearing but choosing to ignore the implied threat, Guillén nearly tore the door from its hinges as he bulled his way out of the room. Ortiz followed as if being pulled along by an invisible string.

Sergeant Ortiz tried to keep up with the enraged captain as he stomped down the corridor. The elevator ride from the fourth floor passed in silence, except for the captain's labored breathing, which threatened to suck all the oxygen from the small, closed-in space.

"Drive!" Guillén demanded.

"Where to, sir?" Ortiz was almost afraid to ask. Did Guillén expect him to know where they were headed?

"Just drive!" Guillén waved a hand in the general direction of downtown as he pulled his cell phone out and punched in a number.

"Rodriguez!" he said when his call was answered. "Get off your ass and get someone out to the public hospital. There's a room on the fourth floor. A storage closet. I want a man on the door at once!" There was a short pause. "Because it's a crime scene!"

Guillén broke the connection without further explanation. "¡Pendejo!" he muttered, and then fell silent.

Guillén was angry, anyone could tell by looking at him. His dark eyes bulged, his nostrils flared like a bull's, and his hands were balled into fists. He was angry at Segreda and his boss José Neira, but if the truth were to be known, he was most angry at himself. They had played him for a fool. Neira knew, or strongly suspected, who had killed his daughter. But given her history of drug abuse he needed definitive confirmation that she *had* been murdered. Of course he didn't want a full police investigation, which would drag on forever and probably prove inconclusive anyway. He wanted personally to punish the culprit. What then, does a man of Neira's power and influence do?

He has his attorney call his personal hired cop! Guillén pounded the door in frustration, causing Ortiz to jerk the wheel and nearly sideswipe a parked car.

The predawn streets were deserted. Ortiz, hands at ten and two, was making good time, yet he was a nervous wreck. *Was he driving too fast? Not fast enough? And where the hell were they going anyway?* He didn't dare to ask. That wasn't the way things worked when you served under the Great Captain. You did as you were told, no more and no less.

"Where are we?" Guillén bellowed without warning.

"Avenida González Suárez. We're coming up on the *Cementerio Municipal.*"

"Turn! To the right, just before the cemetery! Right there, goddammit! At the light."

Ortiz put all his one hundred thirty-five pounds into mashing the brake pedal. He held it for a count of two, and then hit the accelerator while cranking the wheel hard to the right.

"I always wanted to do that," he said with a nervous laugh when the car had righted itself. Guillén smiled, but it was so brief that Ortiz missed it.

"Floor it!" he said, and Ortiz did.

"Where are we headed?"

"The airport. Neira keeps a small hangar there for his personal plane."

"Do you think that's where they have him? The man who killed his daughter?" It was hard to read Guillén's expression, but Ortiz would forever after think that the big man was regarding him with a newfound respect. "I'm a cop too," Ortiz said, and this time he saw the grin on the captain's face.

"You could get in trouble for your part in this, you know," Guillén said as the airport control tower came into view.

"Not as long as I'm with you." Emboldened now, the young sergeant blew through a red light. He would always remember *that* moment as the time that he made the sour old captain laugh.

Cuenca's Aeropuerto Mariscal Lamar is small, just one runway for both incoming and outgoing flights, with a sweeping turnaround at each end. Pilots hate to fly into Cuenca because of its short runway and the heavily populated area surrounding it.

Most flights in and out of Cuenca occur in the early morning hours, so the small parking area in front of the terminal building was abuzz with activity. Taxis dropped off and picked up fares, and porters in blue jumpsuits jostled for position.

"Over there." Guillén pointed to an opening in the tall chain-link fence. Ortiz squealed to a stop at the small guard shack. The guard, a sleepy-eyed old fart in a black uniform, looked ready to scold Ortiz for his unsafe driving until Guillén leaned across the seat, thrusting his shield in the man's face.

"Neira's hangar," he said. "Where is it?"

The guard lost his ability to speak, finally pointing a trembling finger over his shoulder to the south.

"Raise the arm!" Guillén demanded. "Anybody else been in here this morning?"

The arm raised as if by magic, and the guard opened his mouth and then clamped it shut. That alone told Guillén everything he needed to know. Neira had tossed the minimum-wage flunky a few dollars to keep his presence at the airport hidden. But the guard hadn't reckoned on being faced with this glaring madman.

Neira and likely one or more of his henchmen were in the hangar, doing who knows what to some poor bastard. As Guillén knew all too well, Ecuadorian males consider revenge to be among the most honorable acts a man can perform. Neira may not have acknowledged his love child, may not have protected her as a father should, but he would sure as hell avenge her death.

"I'll deal with you later," Guillén promised the guard, and Ortiz piloted the sedan onto the frontage road that ran parallel to the runway. Had either of them looked in the rearview mirror, they would have seen the guard leave his shack, run out to the street, and jump on the first city bus that came by.

"Down there. I think it's the second one from the south end." The springs of the sergeant's car protested as Guillén rocked forward and then back in his excitement and frustration. They approached Neira's hangar, a steel-clad building painted yellow, blue, and red, the colors of the Ecuadorian flag. A wind sock mounted on the peak of the roof hung nearly vertical in the pre-dawn stillness. The front door, encompassing nearly the entire face of the building, had been raised, and huge sodium arc lights illuminated the interior.

"*¡Mierda!*" Guillén grasped the dashboard with both hands. "Look what they're doing!"

A blue and white single engine plane was emerging from the building, pulled slowly forward by the plane's spinning propeller. The high whine of the engine reached their ears, and Ortiz reacted instinctively, mashing the accelerator to the floor. The little sedan hesitated, its own engine whined dangerously, and then it lurched forward and stalled.

Why couldn't we have taken the captain's SUV? Ortiz asked himself.

"Come on, man," Guillén urged. "Go!"

By the time Ortiz had managed to restart the engine, Neira's plane had reached the runway and was taxiing away from them, gaining speed as it went. Ortiz engaged the clutch, hit the gas with less force this time, and maneuvered the little sedan onto the tarmac.

The plane accelerated away from them and then slowed as it reached the end of the short runway. They heard the whine of the plane's engine decrease in pitch. Emboldened, Sergeant Ortiz gave the little car more gas and they began to close the gap.

Three things happened in rapid succession. Neira turned the little two-seater in a tight circle and came back on the runway headed directly at them, a pair of blue and white police cars tore down the runway from the terminal area, lights flashing and sirens blaring, and a Copa Airlines Airbus A-320 emerged from the low lying bank of clouds on its final approach to the one and only runway available.

"What do I do?" Ortiz screamed.

"Whatever you do, don't stop. Don't slow down!"

No one would ever say that Captain Guillén was a man given to contemplation—self or otherwise. But with Neira's Cessna bearing down on them, everything seemed to slow down for him. He watched in the rearview mirror as the police cars gained on them. He wondered who was behind the wheels of the two vehicles. Were they on Neira's payroll? The idea made him grin. What irony it would be if the corrupt Captain Guillén died from a gunshot fired by another, probably younger, corrupt cop. An upstart, a pretender. His grin melted and was replaced by a scowl.

He glanced at Ortiz, whose hands were no longer at ten and two. One had a death grip on the steering wheel and the other was clutching with equal ferocity the golden Jesus on the cross that he wore on a chain around his neck.

"Why are we doing this?" Ortiz's scream cut through the fog bank that had formed in the captain's brain.

"Because we're cops, goddammit!"

They were close enough to the small oncoming plane that Guillén could see clearly the pilot was, as he suspected, José Neira. Even at seventy-five, the man cut an impressive figure, displaying all the attributes of health, wealth, and success. The man who occupied the jump seat displayed none of these. He'd been drugged, of course, and his head lolled against the side window.

Without warning, the onrushing Cessna started to take off. The engine shuddered and the entire plane shook. They hadn't taxied far enough to execute a clean takeoff, even Guillén knew that. But the old flying ace would not be denied. His face contorted and he pulled back on the stick with such force that Guillén thought he might pitch over backward. The plane rose and cleared the oncoming sedan by only a foot or two.

A darkness came over them, accompanied by a thundering roar. The pilot of the A-320, the absolute biggest plane that was allowed to land at the Cuenca airport, had managed to abort the landing and passed over them, so close that Guillén and Ortiz could have counted the rivets in the bottom of the fuselage if they had so desired.

"Slow down!" Guillén yelled as he stuck his head out of the car window. He saw the small plane pass within what seemed like inches of the big plane. Neira powered it into a steep climb. Guillén couldn't hear the sound of the little plane's engine above the deafening roar of the jet engines, but he knew something was wrong.

Sure enough, the entire plane shook once again, and a puff of black smoke emerged from the engine compartment. The engine stalled at about fifteen hundred feet, but Neira managed to bring the plane's nose down so that it was nearly horizontal. Then the door against which Neira's captive was leaning flew open and the captive pitched headfirst out of the cabin. Guillén figured that Neira had planned to take his daughter's killer high up in the Andes Mountains and push him out in some remote area where the animals and the elements would render the body unrecognizable long before it was discovered.

Guillén looked away before the body hit the ground. In doing so he realized that the car was not slowing down. Sergeant Ortiz was making the sign of the cross over and over, while his left hand still gripped the wheel and tears streamed down his face. Guillén kicked out, making enough contact with the sergeant's leg that his foot came off the accelerator. Ortiz came out of his trancelike state, grasped the wheel with both hands, and stood on the brakes.

In the lightening sky above, they saw that Neira had somehow wrestled the sputtering airplane into a controlled dive. They got out of the car and stood with their mouths agape as the Cessna plummeted toward earth. There was no doubt in Guillén's mind that the old fighter pilot would manage to put the plane exactly where he wanted it—right on top of the lifeless body of his daughter's murderer.

It had been a busy week, and Captain Guillén was tired as he slid onto a stool in the elegant wood-paneled bar of the Hotel Colonial in Cuenca's Old Town. A fiery plane crash involving one of the richest and most well-respected men in the province drew government agencies from throughout the country as well as newspaper and TV reporters from far and wide.

"How are you holding up, Ernesto?"

"As well as can be expected, Mauricio. And you?"

José Neira's personal attorney made a vague hand motion that was meant to indicate that he was okay as well, but one look at him told a different story. The rumpled suit he wore could have been the same one he had on when Guillén and Ortiz met him at the hospital. His white shirt was stained and wrinkled. Guillén had managed to slip home and put on a fresh suit and had a shave, haircut, and manicure as a gift to himself on the successful conclusion to a case that could have ended his career.

Segreda had helped, with his access to powerful men and women and, apparently, unlimited access to Neira's fortune, or at least enough of it to grease the wheels of the lumbering freight train that was Ecuador's justice system.

DINASED, the forensic arm of the Policía Nacional, did their part by performing their usual bumbling, incoherent investigation. In the end they could identify neither of the bodies, or what was left of them after the fifteen hundred degree fire, ignited by the Cessna's exploding fuel tank.

The story put out by Mauricio Segreda and backed by Guillén and Ortiz was that an unknown male, possibly a Colombian, had kidnapped Señor Neira and demanded, in addition to a substantial amount of money, that Neira fly him out of the country. Despite heroic efforts by Captain Guillén and Sergeant Ortiz, the light plane lifted off from the airport at 6:10 that morning, narrowly missing an inbound flight from Quito. Witnesses on the plane and on the ground testified to the skill and bravery of the Cessna's pilot.

The small plane developed engine trouble, and taking advantage of his captor's panic, Neira had overpowered him and pushed him out the door. Then, realizing that there was no way to avoid a crash, Neira had heroically maneuvered the plane away from the densely populated area surrounding the airport and sacrificed himself by slamming the plane onto the deserted tarmac. Against all odds he crashed right on top of the mangled body of his kidnapper.

The two men sat in silence for a while. Guillén sipped his bourbon while Segreda slammed his and ordered another.

"Here you go, Ernesto." Segreda reached inside his jacket and came out with a thick envelope. "Even from the grave, Don José pays his debts."

Guillén took the envelope and slid it into his inside jacket pocket.

"There's enough there for everyone. You, the old doctor. And your man, the sergeant. I'll leave it up to you how you want to divide it." Segreda gave him an alcohol-fueled smirk and a lazy wink. They were two of a kind, after all. Men who knew how to get things done and profited from that knowledge.

Guillén fixed the man with an icy stare until he looked away.

"What is your problem?" Segreda mumbled.

What was the captain's problem, indeed? A rich and powerful man was being hailed as a hero, even though he had taken another man's life. That would never have bothered him before. The still-unidentified man was, after all, a murderer himself. And what of young Maria? Her body had been cremated on the sly. An ignominious end for sure, but not unexpected. The cardboard box containing her ashes had ended up in his closet. Now that things had quieted down, he would undertake the search for someone who truly cared for Maria—if such a person existed—and return her ashes.

And Sergeant Ortiz. What about him? He had acquitted himself well that night, and he deserved a share of the money.

That was no problem. The problem lay with this newly conflicted version of Ernesto Guillén. Was it right for him to corrupt this young cop, send him down the tortuous path that he himself had embarked upon without a second thought twenty-five years ago?

And what had it all gotten him? It had all started out so innocently, at least in his mind. A few extra bucks to help feed his growing family. Everybody did that. Didn't they? But in typical Guillén fashion, he had taken it to the extreme, covering up, or even engaging in, ever more serious crimes, for ever larger paydays. In the process he had grown fat and arrogant, to the point where his adult children rarely spoke to him. And Alicia, the only woman he had ever truly loved. She had told him that she had only endured their marriage so the kids would have a father, and now that they were grown, she had no reason to stay. Guillén had laughed in her face then, but he wasn't laughing now.

Guillén had fooled himself into thinking that by doing the bidding of rich and powerful men, he was somehow one of them. José Neira had shown him what a chump he had been. Neira had used him, allowing him to risk his career just so that he could avenge his daughter's death.

What the hell was going on? Why, now, was he having these thoughts? He glanced over at the fat lawyer, who was mumbling something under his breath as he stared into his whiskey glass. Guillén needed someone to talk to, but not this bloated bag of pus.

He got up from his stool, walked to the far end of the bar, and spoke quietly on his cell phone.

"I have to go, Mauricio." Guillén drained the remainder of his drink and extended his hand.

"So soon?" Glassy-eyed from drink and slurring his words, Segreda managed a leering grin. "Have you got a date?"

"As a matter of fact, I do."

"Yeah? What's her name?"

"Alicia." Guillén clapped the man on his back so hard that some of his drink spilled, and walked out into the afternoon sunshine.

My wife and I spent six years in Cuenca, Ecuador, high in the Andes Mountains. It was the most rewarding period of my life in terms of my literary career. Ecuador is a country that values its artists and backs that up with funding for programs that support music, art, literature, and culture—from the biggest city to the smallest village.

I was able to meet several fantastic Ecuadorian writers. I personally think it is a crime that these authors, every bit as talented as any in South America, have not received recognition commensurate with their talents.

As a mystery writer I was fascinated to learn everything I could about the workings of the policía nacional, *Ecuador's national police force. There are a lot of corrupt cops, sure, but there are also many talented and dedicated officers. I like to think that my protagonist, Ernesto Guillén, is a combination of the two.*

Avram Lavinsky *wrote his first mystery short story at the age of eleven but channeled most of the creative energy of his formative years into songwriting and music composition, eventually earning a gold record for his work with the band* Blues Traveler.

In 2021, he attended the New England Crime Bake writing workshop and, captivated by the welcoming and supportive mystery-writing community, began to devote more effort to authoring within the genre. "Playing God" was originally written based on a writing prompt from that workshop.

In 2022, he was short-listed for the Brooklyn Non-Fiction Prize and the Al Blanchard Award for New England's best crime short story. His work has appeared in Boston Literary Magazine, *the* San Antonio Review, Mystery Tribune, Savage Planets, Shotgun Honey, *and* Deadly Nightshade: Best New England Crime Stories 2022. *He has also earned starred reviews from the industry's toughest critics, his three teenage sons, although not often.*

PLAYING GOD

Avram Lavinsky

PRESENT DAY

S tan Kaplan didn't need to open the letter to know the two words printed on the folded page within. Or to know that it was the last. He placed it under his arm with the sales circulars and the insurance offers. He swung shut the coppery door to mailbox 3B, removed his key, and started back up the stairs.

Alone in his apartment, he inserted a pinky under the top flap and tore open the hand-addressed envelope. He withdrew the letter, folded it, and placed it in his hip pocket. He tossed the envelope and all the other mail into the recycling bin under the kitchen sink.

In the living room, at the side table his wife had picked out when they first moved in, he reached for his favorite picture of them together, the one from the boardwalk at Coney Island. He had one arm over her shoulder and the other extended beyond the edge of the image to hold his phone. They both wore dark sunglasses. Behind them stretched a three-tiered railing of metal pipe and beyond that, endless water, and beyond that, endless sky. He ran a forefinger over the top of the silvery frame, feeling the tight grain of the combed metal and displacing a layer of dust that swirled up into the light from the nearby window like a tiny solar flare. He lifted the photo and pressed his wife's image to his lips.

He left the apartment, pulled the door closed behind him, and checked the knob to make sure he'd locked it, half laughing at the absurdity of this particular habit in his current situation. He took the empty elevator to the fifteenth floor.

The steel stairs to the roof clanged under his Nikes. He leaned into the push bar, and with a clack, the fire door unlatched. Somewhere below, the honk of a horn echoed between the buildings. He squinted against the sunshine and made his way across the asphalt surface to the hip-high brick parapet capped with rounded masonry. He stepped up onto it. Teetering, he closed his eyes.

EIGHT YEARS AGO

Aviva Kirchner hugged the round plastic hamper to her body and made her way to one of four washing machines lining the back wall of the basement laundry room. She flipped up the lid of the washer and hoisted the rim of the hamper toward the opening.

Paul, her husband of less than a year, clomped down the stairs barefoot behind her with the other hamper, the wooden runners groaning beneath his weight.

Aviva's body stiffened. She coaxed out the last remaining item from the hamper, a yellow pillowcase, flinging it into the washer with a flick of her slender wrist. She set the hamper down and, with the back of her forearm, swept a few stray strands of wavy black hair back from her brow.

Paul crouched to keep from banging his head on one of the naked bulbs at the center of the ceiling, its stark light revealing curtains of churning motes thick with lint. He dropped the second hamper and gave it a shove. It skidded briefly on the concrete floor behind Aviva.

She flinched at the sound but didn't turn to look. She poured a cap of detergent and a smaller cap of fabric softener into the machine. She wound the dial and pulled the knob outward. It clicked, and the sound of running water drowned out the bull-like breathing of her husband at her back.

A sudden movement in the shadow along the wall in front of her caused Aviva to freeze where she stood. She could make out the outline of Paul's raised arm angled toward her head.

The bullet tore through the gray matter of her brain, destroying the centers for processing sound before the soundwaves from the report ever reached her ears. Her arm shot out awkwardly as her chest and shoulders crashed onto the edge of the washing machine. Her knees struck the floor, and she folded backward over her legs.

It struck Paul that she looked like a magician's assistant, one of those female contortionists somehow crammed into one half of an ornate box, ready for the giant buzz-saw blade to pass down the center line and cut her in two.

He thought about cutting her up. It seemed to him that she had something more coming to her. Even now, she seemed to defy him, to bait him. He searched her open eyes for remorse at what she'd caused but found only the white gleam of the light bulb overhead.

The expanding pool of blood beneath her head ebbed toward his bare feet. He turned and clomped back up the stairs to finish the job, emitting faint wheezes of self-pity each time he exhaled.

Eight Years Ago

Rabbi Eron Danovitch had worked as a chaplain with the New York City Police Department for just under two years when he got the call. A detective named Fitzgerald with the Thirteenth Precinct requested that Danovitch join her to comfort the Roth family as she notified them of the loss of their only daughter,

Aviva Roth Kirchner, in what appeared to be a murder-suicide perpetrated by her husband.

Danovitch had just traveled back from working the burial of a retired sergeant in Yonkers as part of his duties with the Ceremonial Unit. Detective Fitzgerald picked him up at One Police Plaza, and they made good time heading uptown on First Avenue. They entered Stuyvesant Town at Eighteenth Street and parked in a loading zone.

Luckily, Detective Fitzgerald knew her way around the looping access roads and the dozens of identical brick buildings. They followed a curving path past a row of basketball courts on one side and climbed a few cement stairs to enter a vestibule.

Detective Fitzgerald found the intercom button with the name Roth beside it in faded ink and held it down. "NYPD. We need a word with the Roth family."

After a few awkward seconds, a buzzer sounded, and the door unlatched.

The two stepped into the lobby. The elevator's outer door, a weighty metal slab painted candy-apple red, had a small rectangular window crisscrossed with wire in a diamond pattern like the fire doors in schools. They pulled it open and stepped in. The detective pressed the eighth-floor button, and the slowest elevator in New York jerked to life, inching its way upward.

When they finally reached apartment 8E, Fitzgerald rapped on the door three times. She unclipped the badge from her belt as footsteps crescendoed inside and then stopped. She raised the badge to chin level. The peephole darkened. The door opened a few inches, and the chain snapped taut.

Even with only one quarter of the woman's face visible, Fitzgerald and Danovitch could see the terror in her expression.

"Mrs. Roth. I'm Detective Fitzgerald. This is Rabbi Danovitch. He's a police chaplain. Could we come in please?"

Not for the first time, Danovitch contemplated his own presence as a portent to the family of the victim. As if a solemn-faced New York City detective in a suit at your door didn't confirm your worst nightmare, here stood an NYPD chaplain to erase any remaining hope.

The door swung inward, and a woman regarded them from the narrow entrance hall. Petite and slender to the point of frailty, she had an oaky complexion and a lined face that still bore traces of beauty beneath the cumulative effect of troubled years.

Her expression the rabbi understood well. She knew. But she couldn't let herself believe. Not yet.

"We'd like to come in and sit down, please," said the detective.

The three walked the walk of the condemned down the narrow entrance hall into the living room. From a photo atop the lid of a baby grand piano, a much younger and supremely radiant Mrs. Roth beamed at them, a swaddled baby resting a tiny head on her shoulder. In the next frame, a daughter in mid-stride, her black cap and gown accentuating skin fairer than her mother's, though she shared the same radiant smile, accepted a handshake and a high school diploma from a waiting school principal in a more ornate gown of regal violet. In the next, the same young woman held a bridal bouquet, still looking girlish in a simple white veil and wedding gown, her petite frame dwarfed by the bear of a man in the tuxedo next to her, the edge of a paisley-pattern vest showing across his massive chest.

Mrs. Roth motioned with an unsteady hand toward a couch and drifted to the far end of it. Detective Fitzgerald waited to see her sit prior to seating herself. Danovitch sat on a wooden chair with a spindled back facing them both.

An ancient woman in a gossamer robe drifted into the room from another narrow hall on the other side.

"Mama," said Mrs. Roth, a forced calm in her voice, "they're from the police."

"What has happened?" The older woman had an Eastern European accent Danovitch couldn't quite place.

Danovitch welcomed her presence. They needed the bereaved mother to have company. Per protocol, they wouldn't have left her alone without at least seeing to some arrangements with a family member or a neighbor.

A stifling sense of helplessness gnawed at him, a sense of a greater pain soon to follow, the way a tickle in the back of the throat portends the entire illness to come. Perhaps it was the nature of a murder-suicide. The perpetrator had put himself well beyond the reach of law enforcement. No justice. Not in this world, and Danovitch's religion did not place great faith in any other.

Fitzgerald leveled a mournful smile at the grandmother. "Why don't you sit and join us as well, please."

The grandmother slowly wilted into an armchair.

"I'm sorry," said Fitzgerald, "but Aviva Roth Kirchner and her husband, Paul, were both killed this morning."

PRESENT DAY

As the only Unitarian Minister in the unit, Deacon Eugene Bradley responded to more calls than any of New York's other twelve police chaplains. He couldn't avoid it. His was the faith that welcomed all faiths, and so he remained dispatch's second choice to comfort citizens of any denomination.

Emotionally drained from four different bereaved families that day, he felt ill-prepared for the conflict on the twelfth floor of the building on the Upper East Side.

Along with the two detectives from the Nineteenth Precinct, he had been prepared to notify and comfort the jumper's niece, who lived nine floors above her deceased uncle in an apartment with impressive views of the East River and Roosevelt Island.

But it turned out she not only knew about her uncle's death, she had strong opinions about it.

"I'm not buying it!" Her eyes flashed a challenge behind the glassy layer of tears. "He wouldn't."

"He wasn't depressed?" The senior detective, a guy named Van Tyne, had a basso voice that any clergyman would die for.

"It's winter in New York. Everybody's depressed. I just don't believe he'd do that to himself."

"We did find a note in his pocket," said the detective. "A bit mysterious."

"Of course you did. Let me guess. It said, 'Zero days.'"

Van Tyne shared a wide-eyed glance with the chubby-cheeked junior detective, Pearson, or maybe Paulson. Bradley hadn't quite gotten his name.

"We only called you people about those letters around a hundred times. I knew something like this would happen."

"Are you saying your uncle received threatening letters, and you notified the police?"

"Probably a couple thousand of them."

"A couple thousand threatening letters?" Van Tyne's gray eyebrows rose until the creases in his forehead turned to taut bands.

"Not like you're picturing. My uncle got one letter every day from the same sender."

"Every day. One threatening letter?"

"Judge for yourself." The niece marched off and returned a moment later with a shoebox. "We have nine or ten boxes full."

Van Tyne placed the box on a side table next to a photo of the victim. He pulled a pair of blue latex gloves from the inside pocket of his jacket, and stretched them over his hands.

Removing the lid, he took one letter from the pile within and inspected it while Deacon Bradley and the junior detective looked on. No return address. The American Flag Forever stamp had a postmark that read "NEW YORK NY 10001" in letters along the perimeter of an inky circle around the date.

He removed a folded piece of printer paper from the envelope. In block letters at the center was the message, "31 Days." Nothing more. The half circle of the capital *D* in "Days" had a wide horseshoe shape. The lowercase *a* had a distinctive hook at the lower right.

He placed the letter back in its envelope and took up another. Same forever stamp. Same zip code on the postmark. He opened it. It read "24 Days." The *D* and the *a* had the same telltale features.

"So it was some kind of countdown?"

"He told me that at first, they counted up. I can't imagine why." She pressed her lips together in thought for a moment. "Sometimes I felt like he knew more than he was telling me. Then last year they started counting down. That's when he got nervous. But the cops kept telling us to bug off."

"It's not their fault." Shaking his head, the junior detective cut in for the first time. "The letters aren't really threats. There's no crime there."

"That's what *they* told us. We sent one to a lab. It took two months and six hundred bucks. Nothing."

"No prints? No DNA?" asked Van Tyne.

"Nope. And now somebody pushed him off that roof. I just know it."

"Tell me why you're so sure," said Van Tyne.

"Like you said. It was a countdown. And today's day zero."

Eight Years Ago

It had been the grandmother's request. Once she had learned that Aviva's body couldn't possibly be released for burial within twenty-four hours in keeping with Jewish custom, she had begged Danovitch to say a mourner's *kaddish* at her granddaughter's side, so the rabbi found himself back in the passenger seat of Detective Fitzgerald's unmarked Dodge sedan, heading to the forensic lab.

"Probably would have been easier to walk." The detective waved the back of her hand at a yellow taxi that cut her off with only inches to spare.

The Office of the Chief Medical Examiner of New York was tucked behind Bellevue Hospital on East Twenty-Sixth Street. Miraculously, they found a legal parking spot on Twenty-Fifth. They strode past students with an assortment of facial piercings outside a Hunter College dormitory. At the office's main entrance, Danovitch followed Detective Fitzgerald to the stainless-steel awning and into the rhythmic vacuum of a revolving door.

For all the graveside prayers Danovitch had offered, he'd never encountered any place like the autopsy room of the Forensic Biology Lab. It struck him as part hospital, part butcher shop, with the row of rolling stainless-steel tables and the clocklike hanging scales.

Fitzgerald, seemingly unfazed, passed Danovitch a mask and a folded plastic apron. He gladly donned both.

The horrid smell of rotting flesh mingled with acrid detergents. The first body he encountered soured his stomach. He had never known a human corpse could bloat to that degree: the eyes swollen shut, the tongue seeming to occupy all of the open mouth.

It dawned on Danovitch that he knew nothing of death. Perhaps his entire life's journey in search of spiritual understanding had been no more than a desperate flight from the indignity and insignificance that lay so starkly before him on that table.

He recognized the naked woman on the fourth table: Aviva Roth Kirchner, no longer childlike but still beautiful, her skin porcelain-white except for a faint bluish band along her side that darkened toward the metallic surface of the table.

Just beyond her, the naked corpse of Paul Kirchner appeared monstrously large by comparison. With a week's grizzle on his cheeks, he had a predatory look even in death. Beneath his thick body hair, dark blue lines marbled his skin. His privates seemed absurdly thick, and Danovitch wondered if some strange post-mortem physiology caused changes of that nature. Each of his thighs looked heavier than both of Aviva's combined.

In that moment, Danovitch hated his own maleness, the hormones coursing through him with all the impulses they could bring. He hated his own feeble attempts to provide hope and comfort while the Paul Kirchners of the world leveraged despair and pain every day to hoard away the only currency they knew. Power. All for Power. Most of all, he hated the criminal justice system so unable to do anything about it.

As Detective Fitzgerald launched into a technical discussion with a medical examiner, Danovitch walked to Aviva's side and angled himself so that he did not have to view her murderer.

He rocked back and forth gently at the waist as he prayed, moving within the familiar rhythm of the mourner's *kaddish* he had uttered a thousand times, pronouncing the words in Hebrew but considering the English meaning as he did. He rattled off the litany of adjectives describing his God, *glorified and celebrated, lauded and praised, acclaimed and honored, extolled and exalted*. In all his life, he had never felt such futility in those words.

Seven Years Ago

A young patrol officer pulled the yellow police tape taut and tied the end to an alternate-side-parking sign. Catching sight of Rabbi Danovitch in uniform, he put the roll of tape under his arm and saluted him.

Farther down the block, next to a double-parked box truck, a detective near retirement age took notes as a man in a navy-blue freight service uniform spoke. The detective gave Danovitch an abbreviated salute, the pen still in his hand.

Danovitch saluted and approached the patrol officer.

"Afternoon, Rabbi," said the officer. "That's the husband over there wearing out the pavement."

He gestured toward a fair-skinned man pacing between the stoops of two brownstones, a bag of some kind clutched in one shaking hand. "His name's Kaplan, Stan Kaplan. Said he tried to grab her by the shoulder but ended up with a handful of her scarf."

Beyond a crouching investigator, a woman lay sprawled in the middle of the side street. Long waves of hair vanished in a pool of blood nearly as dark as the asphalt. The unnatural angles of her limbs brought to mind a tangled marionette.

"The trucker already admitted he was on his phone." The officer eyed the man in the freight service uniform. "He never even saw her until he climbed out." He shook his head. "She was only twenty-four. Two years younger than *my* wife."

As Danovitch approached the husband with measured steps, he realized that what he had mistaken for a bag was actually the wife's scarf as the officer had said, silky, with a gold and black pattern. He couldn't blame the husband for clinging to it.

"Mr. Kaplan. I'm Rabbi Danovitch. I'm an NYPD chaplain."

Kaplan stopped short and stared at the six-pointed star at the top of Danovitch's badge. "You're a rabbi?"

"Yes."

"Why are you here?"

"The officers noticed you and your wife are Jewish and asked me to help in any way I can."

"I don't think anybody can help. I don't know . . . I'm just so . . . angry."

"It's okay to be angry."

Kaplan rubbed the scarf across his cheek with a shaking hand.

After a few seconds of silence, Danovitch went on. "It's normal. Anyone would be." Danovitch gestured at the trucker.

"I'm not angry with *him*," said Kaplan.

Danovitch waited for Kaplan to continue. When he didn't, he asked, "Who are you angry with?"

Kaplan seemed about to speak but then compressed his lips tightly.

"It's all right. You can tell me. Whatever it is."

"I'm angry with *me*," Kaplan said in a squelched tremor.

"You tried," said Danovitch. "You're only human."

Kaplan said nothing.

"You weren't behind that wheel."

Kaplan raised his eyes to Danovitch's. "You don't understand." He drew back the corner of his mouth into a snarl. "I pushed her."

The words sent a jolt through Danovitch's midsection.

"We argued. She had her finger in my face. I batted it away." Kaplan's eyes, bloodshot at the edges, searched the rabbi's. "Then we had our hands on each other. And I did. I pushed her. Right into the street." Kaplan's face seemed to develop strange contours around the brow ridge and cheekbones. It seemed to undulate, defying three-dimensional logic like an Escher lithograph.

Danovitch cleared his throat, his voice sputtering. "You . . . didn't tell the responding officer or the detective that."

Kaplan shook his head. "I couldn't do it."

His voice seemed to crackle, as if funneling through a bullhorn at Danovitch's ear. In fact, all the sounds on the cordoned-off side street seemed to ring in Danovitch's brain at once, the cooing of the pigeons absurdly loud, the groan of a truck downshifting on the avenue nearly deafening.

"I'm not even sure why I told you," said Kaplan. "You said I could tell you anything. I just . . . believed you, I guess."

Danovitch chose his next words carefully. "Are you going to tell *them*?" He glanced at the patrol officer and the detective, feeling their eyes drift momentarily toward him.

"I don't want to spend the rest of my life in jail." The sibilant consonants of Kaplan's words continued to hiss and distort in Danovitch's ears. "Guess you'll be telling them anyway."

Danovitch exhaled to steady himself. "I can't. Not if you don't want me to. What you tell me is privileged."

Harsh metallic clicks, painfully loud, pierced Danovitch's consciousness. The truck driver had turned his back to the detective, who was slapping the cuffs onto the man's wrists.

"Mr. Kaplan," said Danovitch, his voice drawn thin, "I can't tell you what you should and should not say. I can only ask that you think of *that man* as you make your decision."

PRESENT DAY

Deacon Bradley's living room still smelled of polyurethane. With the help of a rented sander, he and his wife, Elaine, had restored the parquet floor to gleaming glory in November. With the room finally reassembled, Bradley was admiring the holiday cards spread out on the hearth.

In the photos, all the children of their friends seemed to have turned into young adults overnight. It made him feel old. He noticed how many of his police friends sent pictures with kids but no spouse. Some years, divorce seemed to rampage through the police force like a plague.

He picked up one nondenominational card. No picture, but the words "Joy and Light" stretched out across the front, embossed in a metallic rose-red. He checked the back. "Happy Holidays" was printed in a shiny pine-green, and below that the hand-printed name, Eron Danovitch.

Bradley went to set the card down, but something made him stop. A closer look at the name gave him a prickly sensation in his spine. The half circle of the capital *D* in Danovitch went past the vertical line in a wide horseshoe shape. The lowercase *a* had a distinctive hook at the lower right.

PRESENT DAY

The two men met in a coffee shop, but with the weather so unseasonably warm, they got their coffees to go and crossed the street to stroll Prospect Park. Danovitch inquired politely about Bradley's wife, Elaine, and they both lamented the injury-plagued Brooklyn Nets.

They found a bench overlooking the lake, and after a long silence, Bradley said, "That one case. It just seems like you haven't been the same since. You know the one."

"The Kirchner case." Danovitch's mouth took on a sour twist. "I think if it hadn't been that one, it would have been the next or the one after that. I don't know if another case will ever shock me like that one did, but they all haunt you, you know?"

Bradley struggled to choose his next words. "Eron, I know you did something . . . from the handwriting on your holiday card . . . and I need you to explain it to me."

A swelling breeze caused branches along the water's edge to sway, their inky reflections strobing across the rippling surface.

"I've always known I'd have to explain it to someone eventually," said Danovitch, his face betraying nothing. "I certainly never thought it would be you, but I'm glad it is." He sipped his coffee. His eyes narrowed against the sunlight as they scanned the silvery shimmer along the expanse of the lake.

"I know," said Bradley, "you would never push anyone off a roof," his tone a little less certain than he had intended.

"Nah," said Danovitch, exhaling, a brittleness creeping into his voice. "Not with my hands anyway."

Bradley said nothing.

"I'm not going to sugarcoat it for you," said Danovitch. "I did what I had to do. You can do what you have to do as well. I don't care who you tell about it."

"What you *had* to do?" said Bradley. "I found the file on the Kaplan woman's death. All you *had* to do was comfort Stan, the bereaved husband. Anonymous letters? Why would you play mind games with him for seven years?"

"I think it started before I even met him. Like you said, maybe that Kirchner case changed me. Did you hear much about it?"

"Not the particulars, no."

"The husband shot his wife in the back of the head in their basement. Then he walked upstairs and shot himself. She wanted out. One of those 'if I can't have her, nobody can deals.'" Danovitch winced stiffly.

"The family asked me to go say a *kaddish* by the bodies. I go to the autopsy room, and they're both laid out naked on tables, side by side, not six feet apart. She looked like a kid. Whole life ahead of her. He looked like a rhino. Probably three times her weight. Ball sack like a breadbasket.

"So I'm saying the *kaddish*, line after line about the greatness of God, and I knew, for the first time, why my people have been repeating those words for all these centuries. It's not because God is great. It's because we are so freaking small. We are so ungodly."

On a tree branch at the side of the lake, a hawk shifted with a brief beating of wings. White feathers with gray bands flashed and then disappeared behind the pine needles.

"Kaplan told me he killed his wife," said Danovitch. "He told me he pushed her in front of that box truck. He wouldn't tell anyone else though. So I couldn't either. He let the trucker take the fall for it. They cuffed him and took him away right in front of us. Poor bastard didn't even know enough to keep his mouth shut about texting on the road."

"So you thought you'd creep Kaplan out with threatening letters?"

"I don't know. I just wanted to remind him. At first anyway. Every day he walked free was another day in a cell for that poor trucker. The guy ended up getting the max. Seven years. I sent the first letter the first day he spent in prison."

"So that explains why you counted up at first. But then you started counting down."

"Once the trucker had a release date, I thought maybe I could at least get Kaplan thinking by counting down to it."

"You think he even got that? That he even understood what the letters meant?"

"I didn't care what he understood. Or maybe I did. It's not like the trucker would ever come after him. He's a gentle soul. I visited him at Rikers. He wasn't cut out for the place. But if Kaplan happened to think the guy knew what he'd done and meant to settle the score, that would have suited me fine."

"But why bother keeping the secret of his confession if you're going to disregard your oath and torture the man?"

For the first time, Bradley saw anger smoldering in Danovitch's face. "I didn't torture anybody. The only person torturing someone was Kaplan torturing that trucker. He got beat down multiple times in that prison yard and God knows what else indoors. He had a wife that left him and a daughter whose first communion he just missed. Kaplan took everything from him."

"We all feel it," said Bradley. "We all get angry at the injustice. If it started getting the better of you, you could have come to someone on the unit. You could have come to me. We could have talked about it."

"I know."

"Only Kaplan, right? No others?"

"One daily letter campaign is about all I can handle."

"You wouldn't ever do anything like this again, would you?"

"I don't know. When I heard Kaplan killed himself, my outrage kind of drained. Maybe not my disgust. Now I just feel disgusted with myself too."

Bradley pointed a finger into the air as if trying to prove some theorem on an invisible whiteboard. "If you knew he would kill himself, if you pulled his strings to make him do it, then that's way over the line. Like the homicide detectives say, nobody gets to play God."

"Then I guess you'll have to report me."

"Not this conversation. I'm on the job. This is privileged."

"But you recognized my handwriting from my holiday card. Nothing stopping you from sharing that info. You have to. Can't impede the investigation. No choice."

"I just . . ." Bradley's shoulders caved, his face suddenly weary. "I just love the Chaplains Unit. I love the PD. I can't do it. I can't spread all that shame."

Danovitch sipped his lukewarm coffee and scanned the trees for the hawk but saw only the gently swaying clusters of pine needles. "I guess we all play God once in a while, some just a little more mercifully than others."

Writing prompts don't often motivate me. I don't like that sense that a bunch of other authors are trolling the same waters as me for inspiration. The prompt that inspired "Playing God" felt different though.

Saturday, November 13, 2021, at the New England Crime Bake writer's conference, during the last panel discussion of the day entitled "Meet the Experts," someone asked about law enforcement resources for bereaved families of homicide victims.

Bestselling author Bruce Robert Coffin fielded the question. He explained that in Portland, Maine, during his years as a detective sergeant, they had a police chaplain to help with that. Then he said something like, "Someone should really write a story about a police chaplain. It'd be a fresh topic. I've never read one."

I looked around at all the people who had welcomed me so warmly to their community, and all I could think was, "Which one of you thinks you're stealing my prompt?"

I started researching the story as soon as I got home, just online at first. Later, I connected with Tom Zahradnik, chaplain for the Port Jervis, New Jersey, Police Department, who was very generous with his guidance.

To catalyze the spiritual crisis that tortures Chaplain Eron Danovitch in the story, I drew on another experience from New England Crime Bake. On the last day of the workshop, Death Inspector Michelle Clark discussed her role in law enforcement and presented slides. All her cases were fascinating. Many were disturbing. But one truly haunted me, a murder-suicide perpetrated by a husband against his young wife. I knew I needed to convey only a fraction of the horror and senselessness in those images to give the story emotional impact.

Jessi Lewis *grew up on a blueberry farm in rural Virginia. She was* Oxford American's *Debut Fiction Prize winner in 2018. In addition, her work has been published in* Alaska Quarterly Review, The Massachusetts Review, The Hopkins Review, The Pinch, Yemassee, *and* Appalachian Heritage, *among others. Lewis's novel manuscript,* She Spoke Wire, *was a finalist for the PEN/Bellwether Prize for Socially Engaged Fiction. She received an honorable mention in* Best American Short Stories 2020.

EARS

Jessi Lewis

When they bought Ears on the side of Route 50, Ruby's mother haggled expertly, noting that the lady-dog's nipples were stretched low after weaning puppies. The seller was a man in his sixties with thick glasses and overalls covered in motor oil. He had little use for a lady-dog like that.

Ruby watched the sale from the truck. Her mother's lit cigarette stuck out the side of her mouth at a sharp angle during the conversation. Her hair was blown out big the way it always was when they went into town. As the price dropped down from sixty dollars, the cigarette moved up and down, dropping ash. That day was Ruby's eighth birthday, when all she wanted was a puppy—maybe a dachshund or a greyhound. But her mother paid ten dollars for the dirt-doused Ears, including collar and name tag. Her mother looked at Ruby's reddening face and rolled her eyes. They made room on the bench seat for the dog.

"Be grateful. You'll never find a more loving girl."

Ears's claws scraped roughly on the truck seat. Her panting was wet on Ruby's cheek.

"What kind of a name is Ears?" Ruby said, convincing herself to pat the dog's side. Ears wasn't beautiful as she sat on the seat panting—she was stretched from pregnancy and scarred from a slash of barbed wire across her chest. Ears turned to the window and whined gently. Ruby's mother sighed and waved with two fingers to Ears's prior owner turning his truck onto the highway westward.

Then her mother said, "There is nothing more unappreci- ated than a bitch dog—a mother dog—that's up for sale. Ten dollars—" she paused to hold a hand up to the tan skin of her forehead, "Can you believe that? Someday you'll see it and wish you weren't born a girl. And her name is 'Ears,'" she added, touching a finger to make Ears's right ear swing, "because look at them. Look at them."

With every mention of her name, the dog looked up expecting a command. Ruby's mother looked tough as she smiled at Ears and bit too hard into the cigarette filter.

The rough-coated dog, Ears, a Heinz 57 with oversized Labrador ears, pit bull chest, and German shepherd tail, obsessively followed her girl. Even that summer, in the yard, when the warm came in and lay over their roof and groundhogs scrambled in between field and tree, Ears didn't let herself become distracted. That summer, the sky and the ease of time would alter for Ruby, but the warm body of Ears leaning against her would not.

Ruby sat cross-legged in the dirt, ripping up the grass at her ankles methodically. They waited for Ruby's mother to get ready to go to town. Ears drifted in and out of sleep, only to snap at a passing bee every once in a while. When there was little switch- grass left, Ruby smacked the ground, stood, and strode to the base of the poplar tree in the corner of the yard. Ears followed.

Here, Ruby kept items hidden that only Ears knew about. The stash included a *MAD* magazine that didn't make a whole lot of sense to Ruby and four cigarettes she'd stolen for a day she couldn't predict. Ruby included Ears's greatest finds there too—an old raccoon sternum bone, a half-eaten, grayed ball, and a deer antler. Ruby pulled this collection out from the base of the poplar, wrapped in a green hand towel that her mother hadn't noticed was missing. Ruby held each item up to the summer sun and squinted. Ears ambled close, her legs stiff. She chewed on the bones a bit, snuffled around the ball, then leaned again on Ruby despite the heat.

Ruby practiced holding a cigarette in her hand. Her mother had a way of holding a cigarette in different situations, and Ruby was careful to practice each form.

In the yard, in the yellow light, with gnat clouds moving over the grass, Ruby took a cigarette and stuck it out the side of her mouth. She looked to Ears, and the lady-dog looked at her, a deer tick crawling up the smooth of her snout. Ruby reached to remove it and pressed its hard body under her shoe.

"No, you don't know, Ears. You just don't know," she practiced.

Ruby brushed her hair back, cigarette akimbo, and listened carefully to see if she could tell what was taking her mother so long. Their house was so small it was easy to hear from the front yard what was happening inside. Sometimes, she could even hear her mother turn newspaper pages and the wet note of a coffee mug coming to rest on the table. Ruby listened and Ears lowered her head to rest it on Ruby's knee. There was a light sound of clinking, then the opening of the bathroom window.

"She's done showering, now she's putting crap on her face," Ruby said.

The house was a tiny structure framed by cornfield, then apple trees, none of which belonged to her mother. Originally, the orchard owners used the rental to lodge seasonal workers instead.

The driveway was a three-mile dirt road that looked like every dirt road. But Ruby knew it better than anyone—each bump, each pocket of dust. Now, she heard the low rumble of a little car with too much work done on the engine. She knew who this was. Ears barked and sat up. Ruby hid the cigarette with the others in the pocket of her jeans. It was Dennis, her mother's boyfriend, in his little Chevy with the nodding Hawaiian lady on the dash. Dennis let the engine murmur and waved Ruby over. Ears followed her, then growled low at the open window.

"Ears," Dennis said, "it's just me. What a guard you got there," he said. Dennis had a deep respect for Ears.

Ears sat in response to Ruby's finger pointing at the ground. Ruby leaned toward the car's open window. They both eyed Dennis. He had grown a thin mustache that Ruby did not like. It would never get thicker.

"Listen," Dennis said, "is your mother at home?"

Dennis was a bank teller, tie still on.

"Yes, sir. We are getting ready to go into town."

"Yeah? How soon?" he said, and his voice quivered.

She shrugged. His eyes looked from her to the front door of the house. He wiped his palms on his jeans. "Has she been out a lot this week? Maybe going to the bar in town?"

"Don' know," Ruby said.

A lie. Her mother never kept anything quiet, and had asked once or twice if it was okay for her to stay out all night and not come back until morning. Ruby always said it was okay, that she and Ears were fine at night if they had the television for company and Ruby's ongoing paint-by-numbers project. Her mother never actually stayed out all night though. She'd always come in around two or three in the morning and make Ruby put on the Michael Jackson record—something to end her night right. They'd dance oddly on the green carpet, Ruby wiggling on her heels, her mother shimmying, Ears wagging.

Right now, though, it felt important to lie. Dennis was going to start crying—the tide rose over his pupils. Looking through his driver's door, Ruby eyed his hands. They had formed fists on his thighs.

"You don't know," Dennis said. He sighed and let his eyes stay on the house's front door. His lips twitched. "God damn it, Ruby," he said, spitting a little. "You're certain you don't know? Certain-certain?"

Ruby nodded as she took a step back. Dennis's voice wasn't right and he had never cursed at her before.

"Okay. Fine, girl. That's fine." He pressed his forehead to the steering wheel. "Tell her," he said to the steering wheel, "tell her I'll be back in a bit. Don't go to town until I get back."

"You okay?" she asked and he glared. "Yes, sir."

He nodded and waved in the direction of the house.

Dennis reversed the car in the dust and drove back toward the highway. Ruby and Ears watched his dust cloud disappear, and then Ruby made a decision and stomped up the steps. She stepped one foot onto the green linoleum of the mudroom and called out, "Mama! Ma? Dennis was here."

There was no response. Her mother couldn't hear her over the hair dryer.

"C'mon, Ears," she said, "we'll just wait." The last time she had interrupted her mother she had been pulled into the bathroom. Ruby's mother spoke as she used lipstick for blush and Ruby was required to sit on the toilet and listen. In the end, her mother fished a tampon out of the drawer and showed Ruby how to push the soft body through the plastic tube.

Her mother had said, "We better talk about these things before time gets past us. My mother never bothered and that's why—you know, Ruby." Ruby had kept her eyes on the tub drain the whole time. Ears cried in the hallway to be let in on the conversation.

Rather than go through that again, it was easier for Ruby to wait until her mother walked out on the porch as she always did, all made up, her eyes fresh and strong in the light, her long white leather purse with the tassels swinging. Then Ruby would tell her about Dennis.

Ruby could guess that there was something wrong with Dennis that her mother wouldn't want to discuss anyway. For the last three weeks, her mother had been careful to wear nicer things when they went into town because she kept coming across Rex, an old friend from high school. He had moved back home to help his father's carpentry business that served the rich little houses all the way to the edge of the district. Ruby liked the way he looked because he was blond, and she hadn't been around too many blond men with goatees. He was sizable too—towering on the sidewalk outside the hardware store whenever they'd run into him.

Running into Rex had taught Ruby to listen carefully. She didn't mind being overlooked so much, but she tried to spend that time studying her mother, the way she spoke her *o*s like her Jersey parents, the way she leaned on one hip.

Whenever her mother met a man on the street or in a restaurant, she held a cigarette daintily in her hand as though holding a pencil. When she'd bring it to her mouth, it was like she was kissing it.

Ruby practiced this once she'd landed back in the green of the yard. Ears's head was back in her lap.

Ruby's mother used to smoke this way around Dennis. Ruby could admit that she liked Dennis better than Rex. While he didn't have Rex's big shoulders and he spoke with a voice that was low, yet squeaky, he still really seemed to give a damn. He helped her mother pay the bills when her mother cried over them late at night. He called every once in a while and talked to Ruby—only if her mother was in the shower or made a face and waved away the telephone. Rex, on the other hand, didn't talk to Ruby at all. He looked to her mother when they came across him on the street, and he never let his eyes drift down to Ruby's height.

Either way, Ruby could imagine that kissing Dennis was far better. Rex seemed like he would have clunky lips, like he'd suck too hard or slobber too much. She had seen Dennis kiss her mother expertly. Her mother's back was always against the passenger side door of his car when he'd drop her off. He'd have one hand on her mother's waist squeezing tightly at her hip, the other touching the skin of her collar bone. Sometimes her mother would make a soft sound that made Ruby's neck hair stand. Sometimes her mother would unwrap his hands and end the kiss early as though his grip had been too tight.

Now Ruby thought about Dennis's shaking shoulders against the seat of his little car. She took the cigarette out of her one hand and rolled it back and forth between both.

"Ears? Huh? What do you think? Need a light?"

Ears stood up and walked over to their special collection in the grass. The dog looked down at the antler, picked it up in her jowls, and dropped it again. Ruby followed, then rolled everything back up into the dirty hand towel. Her mother would be out any minute with a smack if the secret cigarettes were found. Ruby went to the base of the tree and pushed the little bundle back into the hole, perfectly tight for its contents. The tree bark scraped at her knuckles.

Ruby saw the copperhead before it made its move, but she never heard it. Its brown bow tie coloring dragged tight to the trunk of the tree and Ruby's wrist almost touched its slick head. She fell back from her sitting kneel and the snake reared, coiling. It moved its head to a silent beat. Ruby cried out as Ears scratched over her legs. The dog rose to stand between them and barked her harsh single warning sound.

Ears dodged and darted as the snake took bites of air in her direction. Ears moved her front paws like a boxer's fists, drew her lips back and snapped over and over. Her white teeth clacked.

"Ears, no, get back, back away," Ruby yelled.

The copperhead snapped again, this time catching a bit of fur from Ears's front leg. Ears danced backward, surprised at the bite, then forward again, rearing back on her hind legs for a second. When their jaws met, Ears caught the copperhead in her mouth. The dog shook hard. The snake went limp.

"Ear-y?" Ruby said.

The dog turned, the snake sagging in her mouth, but its ugly head had clamped tight to Ears's snout and dug its fangs deep. Ears dropped the snake. It hung on her snout from its fangs until she shook her head. The snake flew through the air and lay limp on the line between yard and the young cornfield. Ears took to rubbing her snout with both paws and crying gently.

Ruby landed on her knees in front of Ears.

"Ears—Ears, let me see."

She turned the dog's head to see the bite marks. Already the skin was swelling at the puncture points. Ears pulled away and cried as though burned. Ruby struggled to think of what to do. She stood and circled her dog twice, looking from the destroyed snake's body to the house and back. She tied her hair into a ponytail twice.

It made sense to call for her mother, to drag her away from the mirror, to beg her to take Ears to the veterinary hospital. But Ruby knew that that place was expensive and Ears had only cost ten dollars in the first place.

"Or maybe we go to the Mulroneys' place," Ruby said as she dropped back to her knees next to Ears. Ruby considered the wideness of the dog's eyes and immediately shook her own head at this thought too.

The Mulroney couple lived in a trailer on the other side of the cornfield—five acres away. Melinda Mulroney taught home economics at the high school and Greg Mulroney worked on a turkey farm. He had fat, leathery hands. But Mr. Mulroney tended to put dogs out of their misery more often than he took them to the vet. That's what happened to Trudy, their beagle, who had met a raccoon late at night and had her eyes scratched. Ruby shook her head again. The Mulroneys were nice, but they weren't an option either.

"Ears, don't worry," she said, rubbing the velvet of her flop ears gently. "You aren't going to get put down. I promise this—," she looked around the yard again for an answer. "I should make you something—like from a medicine woman? Dr. Quinn?"

Ears was panting now and tried to lick her own snout with her tongue. She looked up to Ruby and whined gently. One ear stood straight, the other flopped.

Ruby could see the swell even more clearly now under the dog's skin. It was spreading. She reached to touch the two fang marks. When her fingers met the fur, Ears growled. It made Ruby's tennis shoes scratch over the grass. She clasped her hands together.

"Ears, what do I do now? You tell me if you're going to get all pissy."

The dog stood slowly and looked to Ruby, as though considering what she should do with her child. Ears's tongue still hung out of her mouth, her pupils small and nervous. She plodded over to the porch and drank a little water, crying at the pain of it. Ruby watched as Ears lapped, then as the dog walked to the side of the porch and crawled under, her back legs dragging under the skirting boards.

"Ears, no. Come back. We can take care of you." Her back paw disappeared, dragging in the rocks.

"Ear-y, c'mon out now. C'mon," Ruby called louder this time. She patted her thigh.

Ears did not reconsider.

Ruby knelt for a second eyeing the darkness and the form of Ears's left ear—all she could see. She wondered if there'd be more snakes under the porch, or black widows or something else with venom and a bite, legs, and eyes. She huffed once, got low, and scraped under the bottom board where there was just enough room for her hips to get through.

Ears moaned when Ruby crawled next to her. The lady-dog was on her side, panting hard. Two summer lizards scuttled out to the sunlight. Ruby drew herself in between Ears's four paws and leaned against the warmth of her fur. Through Ears's belly and rib cage, she could feel the movement of the dog's blood and organs, and the light fever that was rising to the surface. The bare dirt pressed against Ruby's cheek.

"Ears, you should be all right. No snake can win against you."

Ruby wasn't confident. She held her breath and tried to think about what to do next. The wind passed through the cornfield and the sound of the adolescent stalks dancing with each other gave some comfort. Ruby stayed. All she could see was the light in between the porch boards in perfect lines above her.

That's when Dennis's car drove up the road again—the same rough engine, the same avoidance of the potholes he had come to know so well over the last six months. Instead of idling on the road this time, he parked, but now Ruby could hear him gasp even when he hadn't opened his car door yet. When he got out, he was crying. Ruby listened and Ears tensed as she did too. Dennis called out over the yard, "Ruby! Ruby-girl?"

Ruby sat up on an elbow. Dennis could be the answer. He knew about snakes and voles and owls and things from Boy Scouts. Ears could have a better chance with Dennis on their side. She thought about calling out to him.

But then, Dennis let go of a sound from his throat like a hurt animal himself. It was deep and full of spittle. Ruby held her breath. Ears put one paw on top of Ruby's side.

"Ruby!" The word fell out of his mouth between sobs. Only a mockingbird replied. Dennis took the porch steps up to the front door. From Ruby's position, she could see his nice pointed boots through the cracks, the ridges of his legs and belt, and then something silvery in his hand. He snugged the silver into the waistband of his jeans and untucked his shirt to cover it.

"That woman, that girl," he said, "that fuckin' woman." When he banged on the front door, he placed his forehead against it and sobbed once, then twice. Ruby heard her mother's light footsteps from the bathroom. She opened the door and all Ruby could see of her was a dark skirt, bare feet, and a hand on Dennis's shoulders.

"What's wrong, Denny?" she asked. "Is Ruby out there? I've been making her wait forever."

"Tell me you didn't fuck a man in the back of his truck for all of the goddamn town to see, Emily."

"Who've you been talking to?" her mother asked in her deepening voice. Ruby considered this to be her mother's power voice. Whenever her mother spoke low she was getting ready to be tough, to hold back any smile below the high cheekbones that Ruby did not inherit. Her mother had complained once about how harsh her own voice could be—how manly—and Ruby hadn't understood the slight. She knew her mother's deep tones as muscle, as the power of a tight spine, a gripped fist.

Now, her mother led Dennis inside. The door closed.

"Ears," Ruby said, "I should go."

Ears chewed the corner of Ruby's shirt in a disoriented way, eyes unfocused.

"Please, Ears," Ruby said, trying to wiggle away. Her shirt ripped, and Ruby cursed under her breath. She moved to leave, but then there was yelling inside the house. Ruby hunkered back. Her mother and Dennis moved deeper into the living room.

Her mother called something about being stifled. Dennis roared louder: "—for you and your kid? What kind of woman are you? What kind of mother, Emily?"

There was a lower pitch, then even lower tones, then her mother saying, "You've got no goddamn right."

There was a crash—the heavy sound of somebody hitting the floor.

As far as Ruby could tell, one of them had hit the other, hard.

She hoped her mother was the one standing up strong, fist to her chest, knuckles aching. But Ruby could only hear a fraction, as though the argument was being screamed into somebody's deep purse. There was scraping on the floor, someone standing roughly to their feet.

Finally, there was a word, long and low and significant, but Ruby could not hear it clearly. It was followed by a loud sound, a deep bang, as though someone had dropped a cast iron pan on a stone. The whole world inside Ruby's head fractured. The bang made the darkness of the porch's crawl space wobble and Ruby felt sick. There was the sound of breaking. Then quiet.

Ruby waited and Ears breathed thick and heavy.

Her swollen snout threatened to block her eye. Wet rolled out of the nostril below the snake bite. When Ears breathed, the sound was raspy with drool.

"Ears, should I be sucking out the poison, or what?" Ruby said, ignoring the other questions she had, and the fear that rippled. It felt as though she had someone inside her chest, another voice telling her to stop speaking. *Please, stop being so loud.*

There was crying again, deep in the house, then closer through the opening of doors. Ruby held her breath. It was Dennis. He gasped as he closed the front door. The bottom of his shoes passed over the boards. Even from below the porch, Ruby could see dark staining his soles. He stood over the yard for a while, shoes looking down through the cracks.

Dennis yelled one last time, "Ruby!"

Ruby and Ears held still. Dennis took the steps two at a time, got into his car, turned the engine, and idled. He was out of sight, but Ruby waited, wondering how long he'd stay.

Eventually, Dennis reversed his car, and then rolled away and up the road. The sounds of the yard replaced him slowly. Cicadas gnawed at the air. The deep bang in the house beat around inside Ruby's head, but even that seemed to quiet when the cardinals started calling to each other in the poplar. Ruby breathed deep and matched the movement of her lungs to her lady-dog's. They lay under the porch together as though someone else might arrive, as though Dennis might come back, as though her mother might stride out on to the porch boards looking for her. But there was nothing, only soft sounds of wind and the warmth of the sun as it deepened toward afternoon.

"Ears," Ruby said, "what was it?"

Ruby tried not to let her mind wander to the inside of the house. She could taste the dirt of the sun-thirsty porch boards, and breathe in the ash that her mother took from the woodstove to throw over the ice in the winter. Ruby did know what the deep sound had been. She had heard Mr. Mulroney target practice with his handgun on the other side of the cornfield. He had offered her a chance to try once, the gun grim in its holster on his chest, and she had turned it down. Under the porch boards, for a moment, there was a pang in Ruby's stomach, somewhere full of nerves. She could feel the wave of it up her body—the knowing.

"Ears, please keep breathing. Oh my Gawd, I love you lady-dog." The dog complied, and Ruby listened to the sound of her animal struggle. Ruby turned to press her flat chest against Ears, so tight she could feel the dog's ribs, rough fur, and nipples through her T-shirt. She lifted her head to the dog's ear and listened to the wet breath, the strong pulse. Later she'd go inside to her mother, but here in the dark, lines of sunlight graphed out the girl's body and the dog's body, a pause before everything would catch up.

"Ears" is essentially a love story for a dog and it took me years to write it in a way that felt both sensitive and realistic. I've had so many people tell me that to hurt a canine in a story is to lose your audience, but I also believe that this piece should celebrate that vulnerable parental relationship between dog and kid. Now that I look back on this piece, I wonder how much of this was about my role as a mother, too, and whether I could stand up to the demands of it the way Ears could. But, it's also probably good to not think about this too much and to just keep writing.

Ashley Lister *holds a PhD in creative writing for his thesis on the relationship between plot and genre in short fiction. He is the author of more than sixty successful full-length titles and more than a hundred short stories. Aside from lecturing in creative writing, he is also the author of* How to Write Short Stories and Get Them Published.

THE SMOKING GUNNERS

Ashley Lister

B eatrix stood over the corpse, a smoking gun in her hand and a smile of almost comic regret playing on her lips. If not for the enormity of what she had done, Jim would have sworn she looked like a woman who wanted to say, "Oops!" or "fiddlesticks!" and then giggle as though the matter was of no consequence.

Instead, she glanced at Jim and murmured, "This looks bad doesn't it?" Not waiting for his response, flexing a diplomatic smile, she said, "But I promise you now: as bad as this looks, worse things have happened." Her features turned momentarily solemn as she added, "And we both know, too often, Wilkins has been the cause of those worse things."

Jim wanted to scream.

It was rare for anything about Beatrix to look bad but this scenario was an exception. She was a strikingly attractive brunette with her hair sculpted into a fashionable shaggy bob. Her scarlet heels accentuated her long coltish legs. The vibrant color of her shoes complemented Beatrix's scarlet nail polish and lipstick. The black stockings, thong, suspender belt, and balconette bra made her look as though she was posing for some tawdry photo shoot in a men's magazine. But, because she held a smoking gun as she stood over a still-warm corpse, he couldn't think of her as appearing desirable, sexy, or arousing. He could only concede that the scene looked bad.

"It looks bad," he groaned softly. Operating to the procedure he knew he had to follow, Jim pressed a finger against his earpiece and spoke for the microphone at his throat. "Ambulance to floor eight," he snapped. "Urgent. Also, I want a secure guard on all exits. Beatrix Geraghty must not leave the building." He glared at her and this time, looking as though he was saying it for her benefit, said, "Repeat: Beatrix Geraghty must not leave the building."

Jim glanced over his shoulder as though he expected to see subordinates rushing up to ask what was going on while demanding to know how he was going to explain this to his superiors. "You shot Wilkins?" Jim whispered. "Why? What happened?"

It crossed his mind that the questions were now redundant. He was standing in the open doorway of a hotel bedroom, looking in. Wilkins, face down on the floor and bleeding out from a GSW (gun shot wound) to the head, had his trousers around his ankles and his bare arse sticking high in the air. On the hotel bed the pristine sheets were hidden beneath an open briefcase filled with used fives, tens, and twenties. And the prostitute Jim had brought in for Wilkins, a prostitute that shouldn't really have been allowed anywhere near a man who had been arrested for sex-trafficking charges, a prostitute Jim had thought he could trust, was standing over Wilkins's corpse holding a smoking gun and wearing an expression of contrition that looked as sincere as a politician's promise.

"What happened?" Jim repeated dully. He was deliberately keeping his voice low for fear of starting to scream at her. "What the hell happened?"

"It's kind of a long story," Beatrix admitted.

She flashed a disarming grin that, on any other occasion, would have made him swoon. Her teeth were white and even and her smile made him think of sultry bedroom promises. Even in the panic of this moment he could feel the heat rising in his loins and he tried to quell his arousal by thinking of his now-doomed career.

"It's probably best if I tell you what occurred whilst we're somewhere else." She gave a light shrug and pointed her gun idly at Wilkins's corpse before adding, "This place is going to be very busy soon, and neither of us will be able to say a thing that won't be used against us as evidence." Without waiting She began to unroll the silencer from the barrel of the gun, before turning around and placing it on the bed next to the open case.

Jim didn't watch what she did with the silencer and was only vaguely aware that she was wiping down the gun, meticulously removing fingerprints. Beatrix had bent over, and Jim's gaze was riveted on the sight of her backside. Her buttocks, the lightly tanned color of a latte macchiato, were taut and muscular. The black fabric of her thong slipped between the peachlike orbs and molded itself to the plump shape of her labia. The shape of the lips looked swollen and he thought he could detect a glimmer of dewy wetness on the center of the crotch, as though this situation had brought her some arousal. The sight was sufficiently enticing to keep Jim enchanted until she stood up and turned to quizzically stare at him.

"It looks like you're drooling a little," Beatrix told him, pointing at the corner of her mouth to illustrate where she meant. "That's never a good look on a Detective Inspector. People will think you aren't able to control the situation."

Jim wiped his face with the back of his cuff and stepped into the room. "Wilkins is dead, and you shot him," he hissed in a stage whisper. "What's going on?"

Beatrix frowned. "You've said it yourself. Wilkins is dead and I shot him." Shaking her head as though dismissing the discussion, and clearly demonstrating disdain for the folly of Jim asking something to which he already knew the answer, she said, "Could you grab that briefcase for me whilst I get my coat? I'm trying not to touch anything. I don't want to leave fingerprints, do I?"

Too stunned to think of an appropriate response, Jim did as she asked. He wanted to know whose money he was holding, and how she thought she was going to walk out of a busy hotel, bustling with his fellow police officers, with guards on the door now looking out for her.

He snapped the clasps on the briefcase shut and turned to see that Beatrix had donned a man's camel-colored trench coat, cinched tightly at the waist, and accentuating her slender figure. The idea that she was wearing only the skimpiest lingerie beneath the coat made his cheeks flush and guided his thoughts away from more pressing issues such as the death of Wilkins, the money in the briefcase, and the consequences that were now going to fall on him.

"Let's get a drink," she said, donning a pair of sunglasses and stepping past him into the hotel corridor.

Jim cast a glance at Wilkins, decided the man wasn't going anywhere, and fell into step behind Beatrix's long-legged stride. They were on the eighth floor of the hotel and, on Jim's instruction, every room on the eighth was unoccupied to help ensure the security of their key witness. There were officers securing the fire escapes and stairwells, as well as a pair in front of the lift doors.

Approaching the pair in front of the lift doors Jim recognized both men. They were broad and clearly capable, with faces as impassive and unreadable as the hotel's wall art. One of them acknowledged Jim with a terse nod. Neither of them seemed to notice Beatrix, as though their job description specifically forbade them from seeing prostitutes. Jim knew, if Beatrix had been alone, they would have stepped in to stop her from making a getaway, following his command to prevent Beatrix Geraghty from leaving the building. But, because she was accompanied by their boss, the eighth-floor guards did not intervene.

Jim considered telling them they were no longer needed, that the man they were guarding was no longer going to make a statement in court, unless he was being interrogated by a barrister with a Ouija board.

Pragmatically, he decided that bombshell would wait.

He had to hear Beatrix's story before he set events in motion for her arrest on a charge of first-degree murder. Once he had her story, he would have a better idea of how his own miserable downfall was going to be intertwined with hers.

And yet, as much as he wanted to know what had happened, he remained silent as they stepped into the lift. He said nothing as they swiftly descended and continued to say nothing when the doors opened on the mezzanine floor where the hotel's bar was located.

"Bourbon," she told him, taking the briefcase from his hand and stepping toward a seat at an empty table that overlooked the lobby below them.

The bar was busy, many of the customers wearing the red and white shirts of the Arsenal home kit: *Emirates Fly Better* emblazoned across each breast. Seeing so many of them, Jim realized he had been lucky to secure the eighth floor for Wilkins when the hotel was clearly trying to cater for crowds attending an important weekend match. It looked as though the place was filled with Gooners, most of them having a congratulatory beer or two prior to going on elsewhere for a prolonged session of celebration and debauchery. Given the excited clamor of conversation, and the general geniality among them, Jim figured Arsenal must have won.

"Bourbon," Beatrix repeated, as though she knew his mind had wandered. "Make it a large one."

He was going to argue and say that he wanted to hold on to the briefcase, and thought they should remain together, until he had heard everything she had to say. She'd just killed an important witness. The only reason he was allowing her the courtesy of a final drink in the lobby was because he needed to know everything so he could work out how badly his career was going to suffer once she was arrested.

However, when Beatrix slipped onto the chair the split of her trench coat opened, revealing a tantalizing glimpse of stocking-clad leg and a milky-white band of flesh at the top of her thigh. Trying to resist the surge of desire that thrilled inside him, Jim nodded abrupt acceptance of her order and elbowed his way to the front of the bar.

He figured it was relatively safe leaving Beatrix alone for a moment. It looked like she was the only woman in the mezzanine bar, which made her easy to spot. Even if she made a break for it and started to run, there were CCTV cameras all over the place that would let him know where she was. On top of that, his officers at the front and back doors of the hotel were familiar with her appearance and had instructions to hold her if she tried to leave the building.

"So," Jim said, handing Beatrix her bourbon and slipping into the seat facing her. "What happened?"

At first she said nothing. She simply lifted the glass, placed it against her perfectly painted lips, and sipped at the golden liquid.

After allowing herself a moment to savor the taste her throat muscles briefly tightened. Jim could imagine the liquid sliding down her esophagus as she released a small sigh of satisfaction. When she stared at him her eyes were bright with excitement. "I promise you now," she told him, "as bad as this looks, worse things have happened. And we both know, too often, Wilkins has been the cause of those worse things."

"You said that before," he reminded her. "But you've not given me anything to support the idea."

"The media hype was big for Wilkins's arrest," she reminded him. "But it's going to be like nothing compared to what will happen now."

"What happened?" Jim asked, aware that he had posed the question several times now and was still waiting for an answer.

"Wilkins was first arrested a month ago," Beatrix told him, placing her glass on a coaster emblazoned with the hotel's name. "But you lot have known about him for years."

Jim had the good grace to blush. "There have been suspicions," he admitted. "But it's misleading to say we've known about him."

Beatrix lowered the glasses to the tip of her nose and peered over them as she studied his face. Her features wore the expression of a disappointed school mistress. "Wilkins's name was mentioned a decade ago in a report about sex-trafficking."

"A lot of people were mentioned in that report," Jim reminded her. "Many of them have been proven innocent over the years. There didn't seem to be any point in destroying careers unnecessarily."

She pushed the glasses back up the bridge of her nose and shook her head disdainfully. "Have you read the report?" she asked, taking another sip from her large bourbon. "Did you notice that senior police officers made sure that Wilkins's name was redacted from every published transcript?"

"Redaction isn't unusual," Jim assured her.

"Did you know the transcripts were redacted by a mason from Wilkins's lodge?"

Jim closed his eyes and shook his head.

"Have you ever wondered how he's managed to secure so many super-injunctions?" Beatrix asked. "Don't the words 'cover up' ever cross that pedestrian little policeman mind of yours?"

Jim opened his mouth to argue each of her points but Beatrix continued to speak before he could respond.

"Despite all the super-injunctions, one of the tabloids did an exposé on him and his links to the sex and drug trades the year after the sex-trafficking report." While he couldn't see her eyes, the tilt of her head made him think that she was staring at him with venomous intensity. "Did you ever read that?"

"I read it," Jim admitted. "And I also read the retraction they printed after a court case where Wilkins received record damages." He paused to take a sip from his own bottle of beer and said, "You do know, when they print those retractions, it's usually a sign that the story was made up and should never have been published in the first place?"

Beatrix shrugged. "That's one of the reasons why retractions are printed," she admitted. "One of the other reasons retractions occur happens when someone with power and authority, and a vested interest in concealing the truth, puts pressure on the publisher." She held up a finger, stopping him from interrupting, and added, "I recall that the information supporting that retraction came from one of Wilkins's lodge colleagues who happened to work at Scotland Yard." Her smile was cold as she asked, "Do you remember that detail?"

"Is that where you're going with this?" Jim wondered. "Masonic conspiracy theories?" He laughed drily and asked, "Was Wilkins Jack the Ripper as well?"

"Call it a conspiracy theory, if you want," she allowed. "Whatever you call it, it doesn't change the fact that Wilkins belongs to the same masonic lodge as the man who produced evidence to support Wilkins's claims of innocence."

"Masonic conspiracy theories," Jim sighed. "That's why you killed him?" He took a long swig from his bottle of beer and then shook his head. The shit was going to hit the fan in a spectacular way. He felt as though the beer was helping him celebrate the end of what had, for a while, been a rewarding career.

A Gunners supporter asked if he could take the third chair from their table and Jim nodded consent. Beatrix sipped her bourbon in silence. The chatter around them echoed hollowly because of the mezzanine's funky acoustics. Some of the sounds from the lobby reached them more loudly than conversation from adjacent tables in the bar. It made for a heady experience that didn't help Jim to feel calm or ready to accept his fate. He watched a trio of paramedics run into the hotel lobby below and then disappear inside one of the lifts.

Jim figured he knew where they were going.

A crackle in his earpiece made him start with surprise. One of the officers on the main door was asking for him. Jim tore the device from his ear and throat and pushed it into his pocket. He would communicate with his team when he was ready, not before.

When Jim next turned to face Beatrix she opened her lips, as though she had been waiting for him to glance at her. "Five years ago the FBI tried to have Wilkins extradited to the States."

"And he wasn't extradited because the case against him had no substance."

"He wasn't extradited," Beatrix contradicted, "because a lodge colleague in the home office refused to authorize the extradition."

Jim shook his head. "More masonic conspiracy theories?"

"No," she said quickly. "It's the same masonic conspiracy theory as I mentioned each time before. Wilkins has a masonic brother, or a family of masonic brothers, looking out for him."

Jim studied her without saying a word. He had a friend who said that arguing with conspiracy theorists was like playing chess with a pigeon, in that it knocks the pieces over, shits all over the board, and still struts around as though it was victorious. He groaned at the idea of his career going down the pan because of a conspiracy theory.

Beatrix fixed Jim with a challenging stare and said, "And now he's been arrested because of the Walsh sisters."

Jim couldn't argue with that. The story of the three Walsh sisters was a national tragedy. Two of them were dead. All of them had been the victims of sexual assault. And the one who hadn't died was on life support in a vegetative state.

The buzz on social media suggested that one of the Walsh sisters was a former victim of Wilkins's, and she was building an airtight case against him. But no one appeared to know which of the sisters this was. And, curiously, none of the usual newspapers had picked up on this as a story.

There was CCTV footage of Wilkins visiting the media offices where the Walsh sisters were working. There were mobile phone recordings, images, and sound, of Wilkins beating the eldest Walsh sister to death while one of the others tried to pull him away. There was the testimony of an emergency services operator who had overheard one of the Walsh women begging Wilkins to leave her sister alone. Forensic evidence, including fingerprints, blood, and semen samples, was sufficient to ensure Wilkins's conviction.

Yet it seemed, because of his connections, Wilkins wasn't going to be convicted. In return for his testimony, which would help to identify several of those who had escaped the original sex-trafficking charges, and for the information he could give incriminating the main profiteers from a drug cartel that he'd been involved with, Wilkins looked set to escape prosecution.

Jim could understand Beatrix's righteous anger but, as a police officer, he couldn't condone such a vigilante approach to justice. "Are you telling me you've just decided to take the law into your own hands and kill Wilkins because of this latest atrocity?" he asked eventually.

"Not at all," Beatrix laughed. "I decided to kill him when a group of people offered me a substantial amount of money in return for putting a bullet in Wilkins's head."

Jim studied her sullenly. "How the hell do you think you're going to get away with it?"

Instead of answering his question, Beatrix finished the last of her bourbon and then chased her tongue along her lips as she treated him to a smile. When she leaned forward he could see the enticing shape of her cleavage, forced up through her balconette bra. The flesh of her breasts looked milky, plump, and irresistible.

"You're going to get into trouble for what I've done, aren't you?"

Jim thought she was understating the severity of his problems. He would be a laughingstock. Not only would he be out of a job but the tabloids would string him up by the balls and beat him like a piñata.

She moved closer and placed a hand on his knee. Pushing her mouth close to his ear, speaking in a sultry whisper that was barely audible over the clamor of conversation from the football supporters around them, she said, "I need to make this up to you."

She wore a perfume of honeysuckle and violets, a smell that was light and innocent in contrast to the piquant tang of the bourbon on her breath. Even more exciting was the lingering scent of her beneath those aromas: the taste of her perspiration, nervousness, and sexual excitement.

Her fingers lingered on his knee for a moment before slipping softly upward. He could feel the weight of her caress on his thigh as her hand moved slowly higher and closer to his crotch.

"What are you doing, Beatrix?"

"I'm thanking you," she mumbled. Her fingers traced the shape of his thickening hardness through his pants. The glasses had slipped down her nose again and, this time, her eyes met his with a shine of eager need. "Do you want me to thank you?" she asked.

He hesitated for the longest moment.

What he wanted was a time machine that would take him back to earlier in the day, before he had been asked to organize the procurement of a prostitute for a protected witness who was supposed to be involved with sex-trafficking, drugs, and sexual assault charges. If he'd been able to take such a trip, he would have maintained his resolve, told his boss that, despite the promise of potential promotion, he still did not think it was acceptable to expect a Detective Inspector to act as a pimp. Such a refusal would have meant that Beatrix never got invited to the hotel and that would have meant his career was not being flushed down the pan.

But Beatrix wasn't offering him a time machine. She was only offering her gratitude and Jim figured that was the best offer he was going to get this evening.

He drained the last of his beer and said, "You want to thank me?"

"Would you like that?"

He nodded. "I'd like that very much," he told her.

Laughing, Beatrix snatched his hand and dragged him out of his chair. She pulled a path easily for the pair of them through the scarlet and white shirts of the bar's customers, urging Jim to follow her to the toilets.

He wanted to refuse. He wanted to tell her that, while it would be nice to see her gratitude, he had never had any desire to experience sex in public toilets. Before he could form that thought into words, she had pulled him into the dimly lit room, slammed the door behind them, and then pushed him into a cubicle.

Jim had never wanted to have sex in public toilets, but Beatrix certainly showed him that his lack of imagination had been keeping him from some surprisingly pleasant experiences.

Afterward, he was sufficiently distracted that Beatrix had time to pull herself away from him and move out of the cubicle. Shaking the threat of weariness from his thoughts, he quickly stood up, fearful she would be trying to make an escape while he was still on the lavatory seat.

But Beatrix had made no attempt to run. He saw that she was standing on the sink that faced their cubicle and reaching above her head into a panel of the suspended ceiling. The trench coat was still on the floor of the cubicle they had used. She was wearing only her heels, stockings, thong, and bra. Jim watched as she shifted the suspended ceiling panel aside, pulled out a rucksack, and dropped it on the floor.

"What are you doing?" he asked.

She didn't reply. She made sure the ceiling tile was back in its proper place and then dropped nimbly to the floor. Opening the rucksack she pulled out a pair of jeans, a sweatshirt, trainers, a cap and a large jacket. As Jim watched, Beatrix stripped off her stockings and heels, dropping them both into a wastebin, and pushed her way back into the cubicle they had used for sex. She closed the door behind herself.

"What are you doing?" he demanded.

"I'm saving your job," Beatrix explained. Her voice carried easily through the closed door. "The media would have a field day if they found out you were the one who hired a prostitute to visit Wilkins while he was in a hotel room waiting to give evidence."

Jim blushed. That worry had crossed his mind. It would likely be one of the main crosses on which he was crucified. "I'm not looking forward to that coming out," he admitted.

"That's not going to come out," she called cheerfully. "The agency that I work for will tie the original call back to a local masonic lodge. If anyone starts to investigate who ordered a hooker for Wilkins, the enquiry will throw so much shade on the Masons that Wilkins and myself will become inconsequential characters in the whole media circus."

Jim thought about this for a moment. He figured it was likely that her agency could make such a claim, and he knew that there were technologies that could change telephone information on official reports. Given the way she had been spouting masonic conspiracy theories earlier, it seemed plausible that she would happily throw lodge members under the bus. "Okay," he said eventually. "That would leave me in the clear. But what about you?"

She laughed, a sound that was sufficiently innocent and charming to make him feel ready to grow hard again. "Oh! Sweetheart," she breathed. "I didn't know you cared."

Quashing his need for her, and unhappy to think she was mocking him, Jim said, "My officers know your name."

"No," she corrected. "They know the name I use with the agency."

"The agency will have to give up your address."

She laughed again. "The agency don't know my address."

"There's footage of you from all the CCTV in this building," he said eventually. "You're not even going to be able to make it out of the hotel."

"I think I might," she said, opening the cubicle door.

The transformation had been surprisingly efficient. She was wearing a dark red Gunners football shirt that matched those worn by most of the men in the bar. Her irresistible legs were hidden beneath a pair of shapeless jeans and her scarlet heels had been replaced by a pair of androgynous trainers. When she donned a zip-up hoodie and baseball cap she looked sufficiently androgynous to pass for the twin of any of the Gooners he had seen in the bar this evening.

"You came in here with a glamorous-looking hooker," Beatrix explained. "And you're going to leave alone. The glamorous hooker has disappeared forever."

"And how are you getting out?"

"Over the next half hour a handful of those football supporters will visit and I'll simply step out with them. The CCTV footage will show two or three Gooners coming in and three or four leaving. I doubt anyone will notice the anomaly."

"And you've done all of that for this paltry sum of money?" he asked, holding up the briefcase.

"Of course not," she laughed. "That money is for you, to compensate you for the inconvenience of having to cover up for me and maybe miss out on the next promotion available." Her grin broadened as she added, "My payment is far more substantial and sitting in an off-shore tax haven, waiting for me to turn up there and start to spend it."

"This isn't right," Jim said eventually. "You should have simply left justice to take its course."

"Yeah," she agreed, pulling the brim of the baseball cap over her face. "The way justice has taken its course with all of Wilkins's other crimes." She grinned and added, "This looks bad. But I promise you now: as bad as this looks, worse things have happened." She was interrupted by four football supporters walking into the toilets and squeezing between her and Jim. He didn't see when she disappeared, or how she made it out of the room without him seeing. But he heard the words she hadn't spoken: "Too often, Wilkins has been the cause of those worse things." That unspoken sentiment made him think, on this occasion, things had probably worked out for the best.

---

* *The idea for this story came from wanting to subvert expectations. I was struck by a very clear image in my mind of the story's main character standing over a corpse, holding a smoking gun, and looking unashamedly guilty. I then wanted the narrative to justify the character's motives for committing a heinous act of cold-blooded murder so the reader could hopefully empathize with the choices that had led her to that point.*

I also wanted to do something with an irresistible femme fatale: *a woman who's so blatantly manipulating her male counterpart in the story that the reader's first reaction is to judge him an idiot for being so easily controlled.*

The story is set around a climate of biased media, corrupt police forces, and those murky figures in society who seem to avoid the repercussions of their abhorrent actions. However, those parts are completely made up and bear no relationship to what happens in the real world.

Sean McCluskey's *early fascination with mystery stories led him into law enforcement, where he's worked for his entire adult life. It also led to the Center for Fiction's writing classes at the Crime Fiction Academy in New York City, where he did his best to learn the secrets of the mysterious trade from high-ranking members of the outfit like Jonathan Santlofer and Alison Gaylin. His short stories have appeared or are forthcoming in* Ellery Queen Mystery Magazine, Crimespree Magazine, *and* Spinetingler Magazine.

MONDAY, TUESDAY, THURSDAY, WEDNESDAY

Sean McCluskey

MONDAY

The men introduced themselves as detectives Harris and Amenguale, but refused to sign the visitor's log. That would have irritated the doorman, even if they hadn't shown up just before midnight.

"It's awful late, fellas," said the doorman.

"I know," said Detective Amenguale. He tapped the badge on his lapel. "They taught us to tell time at the police academy."

"It's important we speak to Mr. Schulman upstairs," said Detective Harris, with an irritated glance at his partner. "Urgent, actually."

"Legal matters are handled by his attorneys," said the doorman. "I'm sure Mr. Schulman will want you to contact them. I have his law firm's card here." He reached for a drawer in the podium he stood behind.

"If Mr. Schulman tells us that, we'll leave," said Harris. "But it's vital we speak to him."

"Otherwise, you're obstructing justice," said Amenguale. "Then you'll need a lawyer's card for yourself, pops."

The doorman scowled. He was midsixties, not fat. His thick white hair and squared-off nose made him look like he should be engraved on Roman coinage. Amenguale was forty years younger, six inches taller, and muscular under a cheap suit. Harris was shorter and older than his partner. But he had flat eyes, dull like driveway gravel, that his tight smile never reached.

The doorman said, "I'll call him for you, officer." He lifted the podium's phone and tapped *Penthouse West*.

Amenguale glanced at Harris. Pursed his lips and nodded—*That's how you do it.* Harris shook his head and turned away, looking at the lobby's polished marble and dark glass.

"Mr. Schulman," the doorman said into his phone. "It's Silvio, downstairs. I'm sorry to call so late, sir. There're two police officers here, who say they need to speak to you." He listened. "I told them that, but they said it's urgent." He listened, woolly brow furrowed, then covered the mouthpiece. "May I tell Mr. Schulman what it's in reference to?"

Harris turned back. "His daughter."

"Sir, they say it's about Miss Apollonia." Silvio listened, nodded, and hung up. Jabbed buttons on his desk. "Please go right up." He pointed to gilded elevator doors, already opening.

"Thanks," Harris said. He strode toward them, Amenguale following. "Top floor, right?"

"I'll send it up," Silvio said. "Detective? Is she okay? Are you allowed to say? I've known her since she was little. She's a wonderful girl."

Harris shook his head. "I'm not allowed to say." The doors shut. The elevator rose smoothly as a champagne bubble.

"Don't talk to these people like that," said Harris. "It's not productive."

Amenguale snorted. "Guy's dressed like Captain Crunch, says I can't go upstairs? Fuck him."

"Just let me talk to Schulman."

The elevator doors opened. Not into a hallway, but an entry foyer almost as big as the lobby. Alon Schulman was there, in a terry-cloth robe over bare feet. His hair, gray and bald on top, was pulled into a ponytail. "Police?" he said. "Let me see your identification."

Amenguale tapped his badge again, but Schulman shook his head. "The cards. With the pictures." So they hauled out the wallets and flipped them open. Showed him laminated cards with photos and signatures. Miguel Amenguale and Ronald Harris. Detectives, 12th Precinct, New York City Police Department.

"NYPD?" said Schulman. "What are you doing in Connecticut?"

"We'll explain, Mr. Schulman." Harris motioned toward the apartment door. "May we come in?"

"No, we're fine here. What's the matter with my daughter?"

Amenguale pursed his lips again. Harris reached into his overcoat pocket and pulled out a flat slab, inside a plastic bag. Held it up. "Do you recognize this?"

Schulman squinted. The bag, EVIDENCE stamped across it, was hard to see through. "It looks like my daughter's computer tablet."

Harris turned the bag over. The tablet's screen was underneath. He tapped through the bag. The screen lit up.

An image appeared. A woman, young, with thick dark hair and light coffee skin. She was seated under harsh light. Silver tape bound her wrists to the chair. Her mouth was open, and her eyes were wide.

"That's my daughter," said Schulman.

Harris jabbed the tablet's screen. The picture sprang to life.

"Daddy!" the woman shrieked. "Please! Give them what they say! What they want!"

A gloved hand appeared in the picture, holding a small rectangular box with little metal spikes on top. A blue spark sizzled and popped between the spikes. The hand dove out of frame. The girl thrashed in the chair. "*Daddy!*" she wailed over the electric crackle. "*Tell them! Tell them about the—aah! Stop!*" She slumped forward, motionless in sudden silence. The hand reappeared, empty. It lifted her head. She breathed in shallow gasps, eyes shut. The video ran for several more seconds, then froze.

Schulman snatched the tablet. "Who did this? Who took her? Do you know?"

"We do," said Harris.

"Who? What do they want?"

Harris took the tablet back. "Mr. Schulman, it's important you do everything we say." He leaned in. "Because if you don't, we're going to kill her."

TUESDAY

"They said don't call the police," said Alon Schulman. "So I called my lawyers, and they called you."

Crenshaw, seated across the desk, nodded. "I've worked for Banks and Stokes in the past. Reputable firm."

"They spoke highly of you. Said you're an excellent investigator who's extremely discreet."

"I am."

Excellent remained to be seen, Schulman thought. But Crenshaw definitely looked *discreet*. Somewhere between thirty-five and fifty-five. Medium height, slender build, brown hair and eyes. Nondescript. He looked . . . vague. Like a hasty police sketch.

"I hope you're also fast," Schulman said.

Crenshaw nodded. "You mentioned a deadline."

"Thursday. They told me that's all the time Apollonia has."

"Let's not waste any. Tell me what happened."

Schulman described the previous night, detectives Amenguale and Harris, and the video of his daughter. Crenshaw didn't take notes—his clients didn't like written records.

"There is no NYPD 12th Precinct," Schulman said. "I googled it."

"It's from *Barney Miller*," said Crenshaw. "So are the names they used."

"The TV show? Why?"

"When I find them, I'll ask."

"Find them? I was under the impression you'd be negotiating the ransom and release."

"That's an option the firm is considering. But I'll have to find them to negotiate."

"They said they'd call."

"They also said they were cops."

"*Can* you find them?"

"Of course," said Crenshaw. "The trick is to do it without your daughter getting killed."

Schulman shook his head. Muttered something in Yiddish.

"What happened next?" Crenshaw asked.

"I brought them here, to my office. Harris asked about a courier service I use. He wanted details of a particular shipment."

"Tell me what you told them."

"There's a kid flying in Thursday night, from Dublin, to Stewart Airport, over in Orange County, New York. Those cheap flights Norwegian Air runs. He swallowed merchandise in Ireland. When he arrives, our people pick him up and bring him where he can . . . you know."

"Relieve himself," said Crenshaw. "Of the merchandise."

"Exactly."

"Drugs?"

"No. What do you take me for? Diamonds. From Antwerp."

"Then what?"

"They told me, you know, don't call the cops. Don't cancel the courier. If you do, she's dead. They left me the tablet. Dumped it on the desk. Said watch it all you want; see we're serious. The big one laughed. They said keep it close. We'll email you on it, to arrange giving her back."

Crenshaw looked at the desk, bare except for a Banks & Stokes business card. "Is the tablet still in here?"

Schulman looked around, red-eyed. Seven A.M., Tuesday, and he'd been up since just before midnight. "I think I left it upstairs. I was walking around, upset. I think I left it in her old room. I kept watching." He stood. "What are you thinking? Fingerprints? I don't think they touched it."

"No," said Crenshaw. "I'm thinking they left you a surveillance device."

"What?"

"Tablets have cameras and microphones, for video chat. Was it in the room when you called Banks and Stokes?"

Schulman screwed up his face and thought. "No."

"You're sure?"

"I couldn't find the number." Schulman tapped the business card. "I had to have the doorman bring it up. And I never call the firm from my cell phone. Always the desk."

"I need to see that video," said Crenshaw. "Without them seeing me." He walked around the desk, where shelves flanked a broad window. Sunrise glittered off the Long Island Sound, Manhattan hazy in the distance. Crenshaw took out his phone and tapped its camera to life. He propped it against a cut geode on a low shelf, aimed at the desk. Checked the angle onscreen. "Take the card away, please."

Schulman put the business card into his robe's pocket. "What are you doing?"

"I'm going to go out. After I do, get the tablet. Hold it on the blotter, lower left, and play the video. Then go put it someplace else. I'll watch the video from my phone."

"You're going to record in here?"

"After I watch, I'll delete the recording in front of you. In fact, I'll leave the phone here. You can smash it with this rock, if you want. Banks and Stokes will replace it."

"I don't like records of my business floating around. I'm sure you understand."

I do." Crenshaw walked out of the office, through a living room big enough to play volleyball in. Schulman followed.

"When you watch the video, try to seem upset," Crenshaw said.

"I *am* upset."

"Perfect. Tell me about your daughter."

"She's twenty-three. Lives in Boston, where she went to school—she dropped out. 'Finding her truth,' or some damn thing. I don't like the boyfriend she's living with."

Crenshaw opened the penthouse door. "Tell me about him."

"I only met him once. Scrawny, dresses funny. With a beard. His name's Aiden something. He's in a folk band. Their logo sticker's on Apollonia's tablet. That's how I recognized it." Schulman frowned. "Could he have something to do with this?"

"If he turns up, I'll ask. When you sit down, hold the tablet so I can see that sticker."

"All right."

"Is Apollonia's mother still around?"

"No, we divorced when she was little. Banks and Stokes took care of it."

Screwed her on the settlement, too, according to the file Crenshaw had read. "Are she and Apollonia close?"

"I'm not sure. I haven't spoken to my ex-wife in years, and Apollonia . . ." He sighed. Rubbed his eyes. "We've had arguments. Drifted apart."

"About her mother? The boyfriend?"

"Yes. And my business. Why is this relevant?"

"Right now, everything's relevant." Crenshaw pressed the elevator button. "Is Apollonia's mother part-Greek?"

"No, she's black. Why would she be Greek?"

"I was curious about your daughter's name."

"Her mother named her after a woman in a movie she liked."

Crenshaw thought for a second. "*The Godfather*?"

"*Purple Rain*."

The elevator arrived. Crenshaw stepped aboard.

"Where are you going?" Schulman asked.

Crenshaw said, "What's your doorman's name?"

"They were real assholes," said Silvio. "Pardon my French, sir, but they were extremely unprofessional. The big one, especially."

Crenshaw nodded. "They were the same with Mr. Schulman. Tried to push him around."

"No way," said Silvio. "Not Mr. Schulman. He's tough."

"I know. I'm with his law firm. We're going to file a complaint against those detectives." He nodded at the lobby cameras, up by the onyx molding. "I'll need to see any recordings."

"No problem, sir. I got the big one's badge number too. They wouldn't sign the guest book, but I wrote down their names."

"Good work." Crenshaw leaned over the counter as Silvio pushed buttons on the surveillance screens. "Is that a USB port? I'd like to download the footage onto a thumb drive."

"I don't know about computers, sir," said Silvio. "They just taught me to push buttons."

"You got their names. Didn't need a computer for that."

The older man beamed at the praise. "I got their license plate too. From the outside camera. They tore ass outta here. Nearly hit some people in the crosswalk. That's on video too. For the complaint."

"Mr. Schulman's going to be very happy with you, Silvio."

"Sir, it's none'a my business, but can you tell me if Miss Apollonia's all right? She's a sweetheart. I can't believe she's in trouble."

"She's not. They think her boyfriend's selling drugs, and the police want Apollonia to testify. But she said no, so they're pressuring her father. It's a common tactic."

"That's bullshit. 'Scuse me for saying, but they shouldn't be allowed to do that." He jabbed a button, and one of the screens froze. It showed a dark SUV darting from the curb. Moving fast, but the cameras were high-end. The license plate was clear.

"I hope you can do something about those guys, sir," said Silvio.

"I definitely will," said Crenshaw.

Crenshaw's office was in Manhattan, forty miles west of Stamford. The interstate was packed with commuter traffic at eight on a weekday morning, but Crenshaw didn't care—he was on company time.

While driving, he used his laptop to watch the surveillance footage. Amenguale and Harris wore dark suits and overcoats. Harris had accessorized his with a trilby that helped hide his face. Amenguale had long hair, with sideburns. Harris had a mustache; Amenguale, a goatee.

Then Crenshaw watched the recording of the tablet video, which he'd surreptitiously emailed to himself before leaving his phone with Schulman. Despite the angle and distance, the quality was good. Banks & Stokes issued pricey phones, with high-resolution cameras.

On-screen, Apollonia shrieked. Crenshaw watched as she struggled, then slumped. He frowned. Rewound the video and ran it again. *"Tell them!"* she screamed. *"Tell them about the—aah! Stop!"*

Crenshaw opened the car's center console. Inside was a cell phone, identical to the one he'd sacrificed to Schulman. While it powered up and downloaded his contacts from the cloud, he watched the video again. *"Daddy! Please!"*

His new phone buzzed—ready. He touched the icon for *B&S*.

"Good morning, Mr. Crenshaw." Nicole, his assistant, sounded impossibly peppy for eight A.M.

"Hello, Nicole. As a millennial computer genius, can you run a tag for me?"

"Let me have it."

Crenshaw recited the SUV's license plate and heard a keyboard rattle. Back when he was a cop, he'd have called it in to a bored or irritable dispatcher and waited for them to get around to it. But Nicole would have his information in seconds.

"It's registered to Car Horizons Incorporated, a vehicle rental company," Nicole said. "Not a chain. Business filings only show one location."

"Makes sense. They'd be looking for someplace that takes cash and isn't diligent about record keeping. Where is it?"

"Up in Newburgh. I'll text you the address."

"Thanks, Nicole. You rock, as young people say."

"Aw, so sweet. You want me to try and bust into Car Horizons' records? It's easier with the big companies, but sometimes we get lucky."

"No, I'll go and talk to somebody face-to-face. A *conversation*. That's what we old people call it."

"I may be quicker."

"That's okay. We've got until Thursday."

THURSDAY

"'Bout fuckin' time," said Amenguale.

"They're on schedule," Harris said. He glanced at the dashboard clock: 10:57. "Hell, they're early. Norwegian Airlines must've caught a tailwind."

They were in their rented SUV, outside the terminal at Stewart International Airport. A herd of people shuffled out the doors. Mostly young, casually dressed, pale and fair. Two stood out.

One was a short guy with a patchy beard. He wore shiny slacks and a wrinkled shirt, a yarmulke pinned to unkempt black hair. He carried a cardboard sign with *Mr. Stone* on it.

Which meant the kid with him was the courier. Tall, athletic, about nineteen, wearing a tracksuit and lugging two backpacks. Stumbling like a zombie, after his seven-hour flight. He dragged a rolling suitcase. His escort made no move to help.

"Why's he carrying luggage?" Amenguale asked. "He *is* luggage."

Harris didn't answer. His partner had two modes: asshole and silence. Amenguale—Harris still thought of him as "Amenguale," because he didn't know his real name—hadn't impressed him in the five days they'd worked together. The people who'd set up the job had paired them off. They didn't impress Harris much either. What impressed him was his promised share of a million two in diamonds.

The escort led the courier to the parking lot. They got in a faux wood-panel minivan, two rows from the SUV. Amenguale shifted it into gear.

"Don't follow too close," said Harris.

The minivan pulled out of the lot. Amenguale followed, cutting off a car leaving a spot. He swung onto the airport service road, a hundred yards behind the minivan.

Harris pulled on a baseball cap, a cheap blue novelty with POLICE printed across the front. With his windbreaker and cargo pants, it approximated a uniform. Amenguale was dressed the same, plus tactical gloves with solid knuckle guards.

The minivan turned onto International Boulevard, a two-mile stretch of road with the airport on one side and a state forest on the other. Nice and empty at eleven on a weekday.

Harris lifted a flat plastic box from the floor mat and stuck it on the windshield with suction cups. There was a smaller box, hand-sized, in the cup holder. Harris picked it up. A wire trailed from it, out a back window, onto the SUV's roof.

The minivan kept right, going slow. The SUV followed. A stream of traffic from the just-arrived flight flowed past on their left. It thinned to a trickle. Then nothing.

"Let's do it," said Harris.

Amenguale accelerated. Harris flicked a switch on the windshield box, and the red strobe lights on it started flashing. He tapped a button on the hand box. The siren they'd clamped to the SUV's luggage rack whooped.

The minivan jerked. Harris saw the driver looking back in the mirror. Amenguale stomped on the gas, closing the gap. "Pull over, you prick," he muttered. Harris held down the siren button, a sustained blast. The minivan wallowed into the breakdown lane and crunched to a grudging halt. Amenguale pulled close behind.

Harris got out and strode to the minivan's passenger side. The window was down, the courier getting some breeze after seven hours of recycled plane air.

"What's this about?" the driver demanded of Amenguale, who had arrived by his window. "You have to tell me what this about."

"Gimme your license," said Amenguale.

"Why? I wasn't speeding."

The courier was watching them. "Hey," Harris said. The kid turned. Bleary eyes and milky skin. "You speak English?" Harris asked.

"Yeah," said the courier. "I do." His Irish accent was almost cartoonish.

"Why are you talking to him?" the driver asked, turning from Amenguale. "You don't need to speak to him."

Harris opened the door. "Get out," he told the courier.

"He doesn't need to get out," the driver said. "You can't make him. I need to call somebody. You have to let me make a call." There was a phone in his hand, but Harris knew there was no cell service there. All electronic signal was drowned out by the shriek of the airport's radar. That was one of the reasons they'd chosen the spot.

Amenguale clamped a massive hand on the back of the driver's head. He shoved the small man forward, toward the steering wheel. Amenguale's other fist crashed into the base of his skull, enhanced by the reinforced glove. The driver slumped. Amenguale leaned in to hit him again.

"Holy shit!" the courier cried, his accent turning it into *hooly shyte*. Harris hauled him out by the warmup jacket. Shoved him against the minivan's flank, face-first.

"Put your hands behind your back," Harris said. The courier did, hands shaking as though palsied. Harris looped a zip tie over his wrists and pulled it tight. He led the courier by the arm back toward the SUV.

"I didn't do anything," the courier gasped, stumbling along.

"Relax," Harris said. "It'll be over soon." He bundled the kid into the back seat and belted him in. With another zip tie he secured his ankle to a seat stanchion.

At the minivan, Amenguale shoved the driver over into the passenger seat and bulled in after him. The taillights flashed, and it pulled away. Harris hustled around to the SUV's driver's seat and got in. Dropped the shifter into gear and followed.

They drove along International Boulevard until it ended. An airplane roared low overhead. Then onto a busy main road, cruising north. Harris tossed his cap onto the seat next to him. Yanked the box off the windshield and dropped it on the cap.

"Sir, am I in some kind'a trouble?" the courier asked.

"Just do what we tell you. It'll be all right."

"I don't really know that other guy. He was just givin' me a ride."

"It'll be all right," Harris repeated.

"Sir, could I use the toilet someplace?"

"Soon as we get where we're going. It won't be long."

"Could we please stop before that? A petrol station, maybe?" The kid squirmed. "I really gotta go."

"You will," Harris said. "Soon."

They turned east. Harris lowered his visor against the late-morning glare. Ahead, the minivan swerved in its lane and recovered. Harris shook his head. He wasn't impressed with Amenguale's driving, either.

After ten minutes, the minivan turned into the parking lot for the Lakeside Lodge motel, a squat concrete blockhouse, painted faded yellow. There was one other car in the lot, a battered pickup that had been in the same spot since Harris arrived on Sunday to rent their room.

Amenguale parked in front of room 17. Harris pulled in next to him, killed the engine, and got out. He went around and opened the passenger door.

"This isn't a police station," said the courier.

"You need the bathroom, right? The management lets us use them here, as a courtesy." Harris took trauma shears from his pocket and cut the zip tie on the kid's ankle. "Come on."

He led the kid to room 17. Amenguale was already there, fumbling in his pocket for the key. With his other arm, he held up the driver. The small man's eyes were ringed with bruises, nose and mouth bloody.

"Oh, my God," the courier moaned.

"What the hell'd you do?" Harris asked.

"He got mouthy," said Amenguale. He tossed the key to Harris. "Get the door, will ya?"

Harris opened the door. The room's signature stink of cigarettes and crack cocaine rolled out. He shoved the courier inside. Amenguale dumped the driver into a chair by the window. Harris shut the door and locked it.

The driver groaned. Blood and saliva bubbled from his mouth. Behind split lips, it looked like he had a couple teeth missing.

"You've got to be kidding me," Harris said.

Amenguale laughed. "Serves them right for killing Jesus." At Harris's look, he raised his hands and sighed. "What difference does it make?"

Harris pointed at the courier. "Take him into the bathroom and get him started." He looked at the blood on the carpet. "This job was supposed to be clean."

Amenguale dragged the courier toward the bathroom door. "Clean? We're about to be elbow-deep in this dude's shit. What, they're gonna keep our security deposit?" He opened the bathroom door. "Relax. It'll be—who the fuck?"

In the bathroom, Crenshaw raised his rifle. It was short, small-caliber, molded polymer and aluminum. It had an adapter on the muzzle to attach an automotive oil filter, as an untraceable suppressor. He aimed at Amenguale's face and fired.

The range was short, but Amenguale was big, and the small bullets were slowed by the filter. So Crenshaw pulled the trigger five times. The suppressed gunshots were no louder than enthusiastic hand claps. A brisk round of applause, and Amenguale went down.

Crenshaw stepped out, shouldering the courier aside. He turned and swung the rifle.

Then a number of things happened, very fast.

First, the courier tried to run. But he tripped over Amenguale and stumbled into Crenshaw, knocking him off-balance. Just a bit, but enough.

Harris dropped to his knees behind the chair. As he moved, he swept aside his jacket and pulled a gun from the holster on his belt.

Crenshaw aimed, struggling to steady the rifle. It had an electronic sight that superimposed a red crosshair where the bullets would hit. He centered it on what he could see of Harris's head and squeezed the trigger three times.

The first bullet went wide, because Crenshaw was off-balance. It hit the driver in the eye.

The second shot was better aimed, but by that time Harris had his gun raised, sighting in. The bullet meant for his head struck his hand. Blood sprayed, and the pistol tumbled away.

The third shot was off, because of the recoil from the second. It hit Harris in the head, but just barely. It skimmed his temple and clipped the tip off his ear.

Harris crashed to the floor. The driver slumped in the chair, blood pouring from his eye like a punctured wine cask. Crenshaw stood still, rifle aimed. He had two rounds left in the gun, and another magazine in his pocket. He wasn't worried about anybody outside hearing the suppressed shots—the place was built like a bomb shelter, and the closest occupied room was eight doors down.

Harris's pistol lay where he'd dropped it. He was on the floor behind the chair, grunting and moaning, legs kicking at nothing.

Crenshaw glanced at Amenguale. His nose was a cratered ruin. His eyes bulged, forced from their sockets by the hemorrhages behind them. It made him look both astonished and drowsy. No doubt he was dead.

The courier was on his knees. He tried to stand, awkward with his hands tied behind his back. Crenshaw hit him in the head with the rifle butt, knocking him on his ass. "Don't move," Crenshaw said, voice muffled by the neoprene mask he wore. The kid nodded frantically.

Crenshaw moved toward Harris, rifle aimed. He edged around the chair. Harris was on his back, head against the wall. Blood streamed down his face. He clutched his wounded hand, staring up at Crenshaw. At the gun.

"Wait," Harris said. "Just wait. That kid has a million bucks worth of diamonds in him."

"I know."

"It's all yours. I give up. I won't say anything to anyone."

"I need to ask you something," Crenshaw said.

"Yeah, I'll tell you. She's in—"

"Why *Barney Miller*?"

Harris gaped at him. "What?"

"When you talked to Schulman. The precinct, the names. I told him I'd ask."

"I . . . I watched it as a kid. With my mother. My name actually *is* Harris. But it's my first name, not my last. I made the ID cards, so they let me pick the names." He shrugged, awkward with the angle. "It was a joke. We all thought it was funny."

Crenshaw thought about it. "I guess you had to be there." He aimed at Harris's face and squeezed the trigger twice. *Clap-clap*.

Crenshaw pulled the window curtain open a bit. No nosy maid or curious tourist walking by. The parking lot was empty in the noonday sun. He reloaded his rifle as he walked back to the courier.

The kid looked up. A bruise was forming where Crenshaw had hit him, harder than he'd intended. He'd been angry about having his shot spoiled. Sloppy. Unprofessional.

"You speak English?" Crenshaw asked.

"Yeah."

"Stand up." The kid braced against the wall and struggled to his feet.

"Turn around," Crenshaw said. The courier started to, then hesitated.

"If I wanted to shoot you, I'd shoot you in the face," Crenshaw said. "Like everybody else in this room. Now turn around." He did, and Crenshaw took a knife from his pocket. Flicked out the blade and cut the zip tie. "Go in the bathroom." The courier went, rubbing his wrists. Crenshaw followed.

"Look in the tub," Crenshaw said. The kid pulled the grimy curtain aside. Saw the contractor garbage bags and the rolls of silver tape in there.

"That's where you two were going," said Crenshaw. "Afterward."

The kid mumbled something that sounded like *Hooly shyte*.

"Those men worked for a big organization," Crenshaw said. "They're everywhere. So if you're thinking about going to the police—"

"No way," said the kid. "I won't tell anybody. Swear to God."

"Don't interrupt me."

"I . . . I'm sorry?"

"It's rude."

"I'm really sorry."

"All right." Crenshaw pointed at the toilet. There was a plastic kitchen strainer in the bowl. Then to the sink, where a plain white box labeled *Bisacodyl* sat.

"What's that?" the courier asked.

"Laxatives."

The courier picked up the box. "How many do I eat?"

"They're suppositories."

"Oh."

"They work faster."

"I've never done it that way before."

"Then this must be a big day for you."

"Last time, they had one I could drink," said the courier. "Grape flavored. It was pretty good."

"You can't live in the past," said Crenshaw.

WEDNESDAY

The cabin was supposed to look like it was made of logs, but the vinyl siding was too even, too regular. It reminded Crenshaw of the icing on a cheap snack cake he'd liked as a child. He couldn't recall the name.

He lay in gloomy woods and looked at the cabin with binoculars. Its windows shone in the dusk, making halos in the fog. There was a car beside it, a Subaru with Massachusetts plates. Nicole had worked her magic and told him it was registered to an Aiden Gillespie, with a Boston address. A long way from home, here in western Pennsylvania.

The car had a bumper sticker, a skull and crossed fiddles, same as on the back of Apollonia's tablet. The band was called Silas Morning. The music on their website was like Woody Guthrie, with more bass and less talent.

Nicole had found tax records that said the cabin was owned by a Joseph Robson, who also lived in Boston. He and Gillespie had old addresses in common.

The SUV that Amenguale and Harris had driven wasn't there. That was okay—Crenshaw knew where it was.

The porch light snapped on. The front door opened and a scrawny man stepped out, wearing a sheepskin jacket against the early fall chill. His gaunt face and bushy beard made Crenshaw think of Civil War photos. The man shouted something over his shoulder as he slammed the door shut.

Crenshaw had a collapsible rifle in his backpack, but he hadn't assembled it. He was two hundred yards from the house, beyond the lightweight gun's effective range. So he watched the man stomp to the Subaru. He had a phone in one hand and a cigarette in the other. At the car he flicked the cigarette away, raised the phone to his ear, and yanked the door open. He sat behind the wheel for a minute, talking on the phone. Then he drove off, spraying gravel and pine needles.

Crenshaw waited until the engine noise faded. When the crickets returned, he crept toward the cabin. He drew his pistol from under his coat. It was a tiny semiauto,

.22 caliber, like the rifle, with a threaded barrel and a home-made suppressor.

As he reached the steps, the porch light went out.

Crenshaw stopped. There was a flicker of movement in the front window, a silhouette. Then nothing. He counted to twenty. Saw nothing.

He moved to the front door, pistol aimed, and tried the latch. He hadn't seen the man lock the door behind him, but it was locked now.

He peeked in the window. Saw a rustic living room, tweedy, rough-hewn furniture around a stone fireplace. An open pizza box on a coffee table, with one gummy-looking slice inside. Empty beer bottles on the table and floor.

Crenshaw circled the house. Found a side door, also locked. Looked in a window and saw a dim empty bedroom. The next window was an empty bathroom. Past that was a bigger window, lights on.

Crenshaw looked in, and saw Apollonia.

She was sitting on a bed, a laptop computer on her thighs and headphones on her ears. She was wearing a BU sweatshirt and flannel pajama shorts. Bobbing her head to whatever she was listening to. A cell phone lay beside her.

Crenshaw circled back to the front door. He opened his backpack and took out a chrome tube with a thin, narrow blade protruding from it. An electric lockpick. Imported German engineering. Pricey, but only the best from Banks & Stokes. He slid the blade into the keyhole, eased a tension wrench in beside it, and tapped the pick's button. The motor buzzed, and the blade vibrated against the lock pins, hammering them into position. Crenshaw turned the wrench. The lock clicked open.

He walked through to the back bedroom, checking doors on the way to make sure he hadn't overlooked anybody. He hadn't. The bedroom's door was partially closed. He pushed it open.

Apollonia jolted when she saw him. The gun and the mask tended to do that. He pulled the mask off and kept the pistol by his side.

Apollonia took the headphones off.

Crenshaw said. "Your father sent me."

"Thank God," she said, in a loud whisper. "We have to get out of here. The men who kidnapped me are in the other room. They've been drinking, but they might wake up." She moved to get up. Her hand, the one farther from him, darted under a pillow.

Crenshaw aimed his gun at her. "Stop."

She froze.

"Bring your hand out. Slow. And empty."

She did.

"There's nobody else here," Crenshaw said. "And no kidnappers I've heard of leave their victims with a phone."

She sighed. "Who told you? Aiden? Or those two assholes?"

"Nobody needed to tell me." He motioned to her sweatshirt with the pistol. "What did you study at Boston University?"

"Business. I'm my father's daughter, after all."

"I figured it wasn't drama. Your acting in that video was the first clue."

"What?" She sounded stung.

"The screaming at first—'Daddy, daddy, tell them'—wasn't too convincing. But then it changed. Much more realistic. I guess the guy with the stun gun's hand slipped?"

She shook her head, blew thick, glossy hair from her eyes. "Aiden. He wasn't supposed to actually hit me. Those things *hurt*."

"I know. They also don't work like the phasers on *Star Trek*. Nobody passes out from them. Just the opposite, actually."

"Well, they do on TV."

"And it was sloppy of your two detectives, not putting new plates on that SUV they rented."

"But those just lead to the rental place, right? And they paid cash, with a fake name and address."

"That wasn't too bad," said Crenshaw. "But one of the problems with those smaller places is that they can't just eat the loss the way a big national chain can, if somebody doesn't bring the car back. So they put GPS tracking in all their vehicles."

"Shit," said Apollonia. "Is that even legal?"

"Buried in the fine print. Legal enough."

"Seriously?"

"Trust me—I work for a law firm."

"So what did you do? Hack their computers?"

"I gave the kid behind the counter five hundred dollars for the login password to their tracker. That's the other problem with the small places. They don't pay their employees very well. The tracker stores the car's movement history. So I watched the SUV go from the rental lot to some fleabag motel near the airport on Sunday. Then out here, then over to your father's building Monday night, then back here for two days. And this afternoon it went back to the motel, where they're presumably staying until Norwegian Air 1842 lands at ten thirty tomorrow morning."

"Is there anything you don't know, Sherlock Holmes?"

"You could fill books with the things I don't know. For starters, who are your two phony cops?"

"The big Spanish-looking one was a bouncer at a club I liked. I used to fool around with him. The other guy was a bodyguard for one of my friends at boarding school."

"You fool around with him too?"

"God, no. He's, like, forty."

"None taken," said Crenshaw. "And who's Joe Robson? The guy who owns this place?"

"Aiden's stepfather. They used to come out here every summer. Their vacation paradise."

"Where'd Aiden go? To supervise the robbery?"

She scoffed. "I wouldn't put Aiden in charge of watering a cactus. We had a fight, so he flounced out. There's some skank bartender in town. He thinks I don't know they're screwing. Probably have been since they fell in love at thirteen, or something."

Crenshaw nodded. "Now I know everything."

"Bullshit. You don't know why I did it."

"You're angry about the way your father treated your mother. So you decided to break his heart, steal his money, and maybe get him killed by the people he does business with. Is that close?"

"Would they really kill him?"

"It's a distinct possibility."

"Hmm." She didn't look particularly horrified at the thought.

"If the diamonds actually got stolen, of course."

She sighed again. "It was still a pretty good plan. Yeah, a couple of missteps, but it would've worked just fine."

"Still is a pretty good plan," said Crenshaw. "Still can work, just fine."

She narrowed her eyes. "What are you saying?"

"Like I said, I'm with a law firm. We hate to see a good crime go to waste."

"I thought you worked for my father."

"I wasn't hired to guard his diamonds. I was hired to save you from kidnappers. But there aren't any. So I guess I'm here to save you from yourself." He walked around the bed, keeping the gun trained on her, and lifted the pillow. Saw a shiny little .38 revolver, which he picked up. "For example, I wouldn't want you to have a sudden attack of conscience and do something drastic."

"So what happens now?"

"It was a long drive out here," said Crenshaw. "I'm going to go in that other bedroom and take a nap. Around six A.M., you'll brief me on the plan you all came up with, and I'll drive over to New York to supervise the robbery. Then I'll bring the merchandise back. I assume you've arranged some way to sell it? Smart business major that you are?"

"Yeah. I have."

"Then it's all set." He dropped the revolver in his coat pocket. "When Aiden gets back, explain the new arrangement to him. If he has trouble understanding, come get me."

"I'll take care of Aiden," she said. Something in her voice. Her father's daughter.

When he got to the door, she said, "But maybe I'll just kill you while you sleep."

Crenshaw turned back. "Maybe. Or maybe those kidnappers murdered you before I ever got here. Then they stole those diamonds and found their own buyer for them. Either way, it'll be interesting."

"Or maybe I'll run away with Aiden while you're in New York," she said. "We'll start a new life together someplace."

"Without the diamonds?"

"We could live on love."

"Don't make me chase you," said Crenshaw. "Even doves have pride." He shut the door. He walked through the cabin to the smaller bedroom, which smelled of a pine air freshener that reminded him of Christmas. He locked the door behind him. Then he unlocked the window, eased it open, and slipped out. The ground behind the cabin sloped up, making it an easy step down to the dirt. He lowered the window behind him. Apollonia's room was around the corner; he wouldn't be seen.

Brisk steps brought him to the tree line. He crunched through the scrub and crouched behind taller growth, at an angle that let him see the spare bedroom's window and the spot where Aiden's car had been. After he got comfortable against a tree, he dug his rifle from his pack and twisted it together. Settled in to wait.

The best way to find out if you can trust somebody, Ernest Hemingway had said, *is to trust them*. All due respect to Papa, but Crenshaw disagreed. In his experience, the best way to find out if you could trust somebody was to let them *think* you trusted them. Then sit back and see what they did with it.

Maybe Apollonia really wanted to see this thing through, badly enough to let Crenshaw crash the party. Badly enough to *take care* of Aiden too. Or maybe she was calling Aiden at that very moment, telling him there was a new problem to take care of, so hurry back with your gun, baby, and we'll kill him in his sleep.

Either way, it would be interesting. *A life without risk isn't worth living*, as Charles Lindbergh had said. And if you couldn't trust an adulterous Nazi sympathizer, what had the world become? Crenshaw inserted a magazine into the rifle, pushed until it clicked, and chambered a round.

Probably, though, the interesting part wouldn't happen that night. It probably wouldn't happen until after the diamonds had been sold and the money got split. That's when people usually got silly. So no sense trying to surf a wave before it arrived.

He'd worry about it on Friday.

---

*I've always loved Richard Stark's Parker books and Lawrence Block's Keller stories, and what fascinated me about them was the clear-eyed focus on a *protagonist who makes no effort to be sympathetic, just interesting. These were stories where the lead character wasn't trying to solve anything or save anyone, and no heart of gold was going to make an unexpected appearance. Their only redeeming quality was that, bad as they were, their opponents were often worse. I thrilled at the chance to watch skilled, ruthless men skulk down dark streets where the only rules are made by the vicious or the clever. When Michael Bracken solicited submissions for* Mickey Finn: 21st Century Noir, *I had a chance to try and create a character who could skulk along behind them. Parker, Keller, and their ilk possess pragmatism, stoicism, and attention to detail—admirable traits, even if their actions aren't. Like Neal McCoy sang, "If you can't be good, be good at it."*

Michael Mallory *is the author of twenty-five books, both fiction and non-fiction, and some one hundred sixty short stories. He is the creator of "Amelia Watson" (the second wife of Dr. Watson) and hapless PI Dave Beauchamp, who stars in a series of comedic Hollywood mysteries. A former actor and theme park show writer, by day Mallory is an LA-based entertainment journalist and a film historian who has worked as a researcher and interviewer for the Academy of Motion Picture Arts and Sciences' Visual History Program. He can also tell you where to find the City of Angels' best British pubs and Mexican restaurants.*

WHAT THE CAT DRAGGED IN

Michael Mallory

"You can't do this to me!" Stacia Treen yelled at Jake Odenkirk, the editor of the *Rosaville Courier*, who was leaning back in his chair in the tiny office, twiddling a pencil.

"It's done," he replied. "You either cover the Rosaville Cat Show or tender your resignation."

"I'm the most experienced reporter you've got!"

It was true; Stacia Treen had spent the last seven years at the *Los Angeles Times* until falling victim to budget cuts.

"You're also the last hire," Odenkirk reminded her.

"Oh, please! I'm doing you a favor by working here and you . . . wait a minute. I get it now. This is about the Clementine DeWine piece, isn't it?"

Clementine DeWine was the town's most prominent realtor and the president of the Rosaville Chamber of Commerce. According to the owner of a local art gallery, she also had a history of favoring chamber applicants who shared her political leanings and opposing those who did not. Acting on the lead, Stacia tried to get a comment about it from DeWine herself but was rebuffed in no uncertain terms.

"DeWine demanded you rein me in, didn't she?" Stacia charged.

"She wanted you fired, Stace. I managed to placate her enough to keep you working here at my discretion, but the upshot is you are not to go near her again, which means you're through covering our happy little local government."

"I thought this was a free press!"

"It's a free newspaper," Odenkirk said. "There's a difference. We're a giveaway that survives on advertising and Clementine places a lot of ads with us. We're not the *LA Times*."

"Don't even think about saying, 'And if you don't like it here, go back.'"

"Have I ever said that?"

The truth was that Stacia Treen did not want to go back to LA. She'd grown tired of the City of Angels—its traffic, its high-cost lifestyle, its lack of angels—even before the double sucker punch of losing her job and a bad breakup with Rey, a deputy DA, who'd had more of a relationship with his job than with her. Wanting a fresh start, she remembered spending a weekend with Rey in Rosaville, just up California's central coast from San Luis Obispo, and thought it might be her perfect escape from the nuttiness of LA. And it was . . . for two months. Then she began to get restless (not to mention frustrated by her failed attempts to get that novel going) and applied for a job at the tiny *Rosaville Courier*. Jake Odenkirk had warned her that there was not a lot in the village for an investigative reporter to investigate. Stacia's nose for news, however, did not easily stuff up.

"Look, Stace, this is your decision," Odenkirk said. "The cat show beckons."

"You're the worst, you know that?" she replied. "Fine, give me the info for the damned cat show." After Odenkirk handed her the paper with all the pertinent background information, she added, "If the fuzzy little fur-turds get hungry, I know where they can dine on a great big rat."

Stacia spun around and marched out of the newspaper office, which was located on the second level of a building in the village's business district, and Odenkirk managed to suppress his chuckling until she was gone.

The annual town cat show took place that Saturday afternoon in the gym of Rosaville District High School, and it only took five minutes before Stacia Treen became allergic. The gym was packed with folding tables, each containing two or three filled cat cages. The guests of honor came in all sizes, colors, and patterns. The star of the show, though, was the size of a juvenile mountain lion—a gray Maine Coon Cat in a pen that made the surrounding cat carriers look like toiletry bags.

In the process of circling the room and talking to the cats' owners, Stacia quickly learned not to use that word. "We don't *own* anything," one woman indignantly told her. "We are 'parents.'"

Suddenly Stacia had the lead for her article.

Once she'd had her fill of felines (and pet parents), she retreated outdoors to continue sneezing. She noticed a man following her out. He was somewhere between forty and sixty, thin both of body and hair, and wore a bow tie.

"Can I help you?" she asked.

"I heard you tell someone you were a reporter," the man said, his voice surprisingly deep.

"That's right, for the *Rosaville Courier*. Why?"

"Well . . . I might have a story for you."

Oh, lord, she thought. "Is it about cats?"

"It's about *my* cat. He's semi-feral. I found him huddled under a tree, trying to survive on his own. He's a wonderful cat, but so independent. I don't really own him."

"Right, you're his parent."

"I'm more like Leo's roommate. He comes and goes when he pleases through a flap I put in the door. In fact, he pretty much has the run of my neighborhood. Everybody knows him. Sometimes my neighbors tell me he sits outside their windows and watches while they eat dinner."

Stacia glanced at her watch. "This is fascinating Mr. . . ."

"Lewis. Romero Lewis. I know you're busy, but it's regarding Leo's independence, see? I was curious as to where he went at night, so I got a little camera and fixed it to his collar. Last night he came back late, so I didn't look at the footage until this morning."

Great, a peeping tom cat, Stacia thought.

"What I saw alarmed me. I've never seen a murder before."

Stacia stared back at the man. "I'm sorry? You said *murder*?"

Romero Lewis nodded. "Leo looked in someone's window and the camera captured a woman being shot to death."

It took going to Romero Lewis's cabin-like house in a wooded, hilly area of the village, and actually seeing the video for herself, before Stacia believed.

The video, which Lewis had loaded onto his laptop, was shot from just above ground level and showed the inside of a house through a glass door. An ornate fireplace was built into the far wall in what was clearly a living room. A woman walked into view, talking to someone off camera. Even though there was no sound, Stacia could tell through her body language that she was agitated. Suddenly she attempted to run out of the room, but abruptly stopped and stiffened, a sliver of her back and one leg still visible. Then she fell down backward into the shot. From the right side of the picture an object appeared. As it moved in, Stacia could see it was a handgun with a long bulbous barrel, a silencer. The gloved hand holding the weapon became visible, as did an arm, then part of a torso, then . . .

The camera suddenly panned away and began to bounce its way through a bushy area, the feline cinematographer apparently having grown bored with the drama inside the house.

There was no way to tell who the killer was, even whether it was a man or a woman.

"My God," Stacia uttered. "You have no idea who that woman is?"

"Not a clue," Romero Lewis said. "I don't know the house, either, but it can't be too far away."

This was Rosaville, Stacia thought; *nothing* was too far away. "Have you contacted the police?"

Lewis looked at the floor. "No, because . . . well, I called them once before when I thought a bear was going through my trash. It turned out just to be a homeless guy. Another time I reported a wolf behind the house, which turned out to be somebody's service dog. Prior to that—"

"I get the picture," she said. "You've cried wolf—literally—so they no longer listen to you."

"But you saw the video for yourself. I'm not imagining this!"

Unless the murder on video was an elaborate practical joke involving the cat, Stacia had to agree the little man was not imagining it.

Then she had an idea.

"I think I might know how to identify the house," Stacia said. "I'll need a copy of that video."

"Give me your email and I'll send you the file," Lewis said.

By the time she left Romero Lewis's place, Stacia Treen was forming her plan. It would not be pleasant, but if it proved fruitful, it would enable her to solve the murder and bring Jake Odenkirk the biggest story his toy paper had ever seen.

"How *dare* you call me?" Clementine DeWine roared at the other end of the phone. "I thought I made it explicit to your supervisor that I *never* wanted to see you or hear from you again!"

"You did indeed make your desires clear to Mr. Odenkirk," Stacia replied, "and he indeed passed them along. But I have come across a problem that only you can solve."

After a pause, the realtor asked, "You want to buy a house?"

"I need to *identify* a house. Since you are the most knowledge-able realtor in town, I figured you'd know it immediately."

"Why do you want this property identified?"

Stacia breathed deeply and then said, "May we discuss this further over lunch? My treat."

Clementine DeWine agreed, but then chose the Seacastle Inn, which overlooked the ocean at Beachstone Bay. It served only the finest catch of the day at the most unreasonable prices on the coast ... imposing a two-dollar charge simply for looking at a menu. Even though the cost of this lunch would leave a major dent on Stacia's MasterCard, she viewed it as a wager against her future.

Clementine DeWine was not hard to spot in the foyer of the restaurant, since her picture could be found all over Rosaville, either in fliers, on signs, or in newspaper ads, though it was clear to Stacia that the ubiquitous photo was a minimum of fifteen years old. In person, Clementine had the kind of brick-colored hair that is not found in nature, a too-pink makeup base, and slightly droopy eyelids. Stacia introduced herself and the older woman looked her up and down before saying, "Let's get this over with" and signaling the maître d' that she was ready for a table.

Stacia ordered the salmon salad while Clementine started with chowder and moved on to the daily scallops special.

"Now then," DeWine said once the waiter had gone, "what is this about?"

Steeling herself for an adverse reaction, Stacia related how she'd met Romero Lewis and what she'd seen on the tape. When she had finished, Clementine said, "Is this a perverse attempt at humor?"

"I cannot honestly say that it isn't," Stacia replied, "but if so, it's a bad joke directed against Lewis. I've seen the video. This is not any kind of a gag on my part."

"Now I'm sorry I didn't order wine."

"Let's order some then."

Within a few minutes the waiter brought a bottle of Pinot Grigio to the table, and the two women decided it was best to eat before looking at the video. Stacia's salmon salad was excellent, but the aroma of Clementine's scallop fettuccini made her wish she'd ordered that instead. The wine was gone by the end of lunch, but Clementine declined to order another bottle. "One of us has to get back to work," she sniffed.

After the plates were cleared, Stacia pulled her tablet from her bag and set it up on the table, then clicked on the file Romero Lewis had sent.

Clementine watched in silence, though Stacia could see the alarm in her eyes. When it was finished, the realtor asked, "May I see that again?" Stacia replayed the video and afterward Clementine uttered, "Dear God."

"Do you recognize the house?" Stacia asked.

"No, but that does not matter since I recognize the woman. It's Marguerite Dornan."

"Then we must go to the police."

"That would be . . . difficult."

"Why? It's right there on the video."

"When was this grisly piece of *cinéma vérité* filmed?"

"A couple days ago, according to Mr. Lewis."

"Which is why the police would find this highly problematic. You see, Marguerite Dornan died a year ago."

"A year . . . are you sure?"

"Miss Treen, I attended her funeral."

The confirmation of Marguerite Dornan's funeral was in the newspaper files back at the *Courier* office. She was killed when her motorcycle plunged over the side of Highway 1 in Big Sur. After being listed missing for more than a month, her body was finally recovered on the rocky shore. She had no known relatives.

Having promised to keep Romero in the loop, Stacia was about to call him when an incoming call from Clementine DeWine prevented her.

"I believe I've pinpointed the house, based on that video of yours," she told Stacia. "Did you notice the fireplace behind Marguerite when she fell?"

"I saw there was one," Stacia said.

"You'll never be a realtor. It was quite distinctive, dramatic even, built of stone instead of brick or metal. There is a house on Monmouth Street that bears a matching chimney. It is not uncommon for the chimney and the hearth to be made of the same materials."

"Do you know the owner?"

"Not yet. Meet me there at four o'clock."

When Stacia arrived, Clementine was already there, her Jaguar parked in front of the house. Stacia pulled her Mini Cooper behind it.

"So, what are we going to do?" Stacia asked. "Just knock on the door and demand to go in?"

"I suggest you knock on the door and tell the person who lives there that you're writing a story for our local rag about people who retired to Rosaville after a career in the big city, and then we go in."

"How do you know whoever lives here retired from a career in the big city?"

"I don't. I don't have any idea who it is or what they've done. But if they did not come to our village from a metropolis, they'll say so immediately and tell us their background without asking."

"You know, Clementine, you're almost devious enough to be a reporter."

"Perish the thought!" the older woman said, marching up to the porch of the house.

"What if this isn't the right house?" Stacia asked, her hand poised to knock.

"Then we smile and say 'good day,' and leave. Now get to it."

It took two loud raps before a man answered. He was short, gray-haired, and over the cusp of fifty, Stacia guessed. He also had a crescent-shaped scar on his left cheek.

"Hi," she began, "my name is Stacia Treen and I'm a reporter for the *Rosaville Courier.* I'm working on a story about people who have come from a major city and relocated here in town, and I wonder if I might talk to you."

The man looked at her quizzically. "What are you talking about?"

"You are Clancy Jones, aren't you?" Stacia asked, making up the name on the spot.

"No, I'm not Clancy Jones. My name is Norm Sanders. You have the wrong person."

Before Stacia could say anything else, Clementine cried, "Oh, look at that lovely fireplace! I'm a realtor so houses fascinate me. I wonder if I might take a closer look at it." She pushed her way inside.

"Hey!" the man called. "You can't just barge in here."

"We won't be long," Stacia said, smiling, and following Clementine in.

"Oh, this is lovely!" Clementine enthused, pulling out a pair of glasses to examine it more closely. "Such artistic stonework. Are you thinking of selling this place?"

"The only thing I'm thinking is that you two need to leave. Now."

"Very well, we'll go," Clementine said, tossing a business card onto the hearth and moving back toward the door. "But if you do decide to sell, please come to me first. Thank you for your time, Mr. Sanders." Then she fumbled and dropped her glasses. "Oh, dear." Clementine quickly bent down and picked them up again. "Come along, Ms. Treen."

Once they were back on the sidewalk, Stacia said, "I'm not sure what we learned from that."

"The carpet has recently been shampooed, is what we've learned. When I pretended to drop my glasses, I felt it. It's still slightly damp. One can always tell when a carpet has been cleaned. The odd thing is that it was not the entire carpet, only that one spot."

"Blood, you think?"

"I doubt it was pine sap. The problem is we cannot prove anything."

"Are you sure we're not getting ahead of ourselves?" Stacia asked. "Maybe the man simply needed to clean his rug."

"Part of my job is sizing up people on sight," Clementine said. "I can tell immediately if someone is really interested in a property or simply wasting my time. Something about Norm Sanders is not right. I could sense it."

"So what do we do now?"

"I have to show a house this afternoon. As for you—"

Before she could finish, Stacia's phone rang.

"It's Lewis."

"That's that, then. Go see your friend and find out if the cat has solved the case yet."

Despite her allergies, Stacia Treen was learning to like Leo the Cat, who at this moment was sitting beside her on Romero Lewis's sofa, not encroaching on her space, but allowing her to scritch his ruff, no strings attached. For whatever reason, he was not making her sneeze.

"Can't you get a warrant and search the place?" Lewis was asking in response to the information she'd given him.

"In a word, no," Stacia said. "I'm not the police, nor is Clementine DeWine. Besides, that shampooed spot on the carpet proves that if Sanders is our killer, he's already cleaned up all traces of her."

"What do you mean *if* he's our killer? If it's not him, who is it? I mean, it's his house, isn't it?"

"We don't even know that conclusively. All I know for certain is that I saw him there."

"If we could only figure out why Marguerite Dornan was in the house."

"Romero, the bigger question is why she was *anywhere*. She's supposed to have died last year."

"Maybe we should get the police to dig up the grounds. They'll find her body."

"Which brings us back to that warrant problem."

Romero Lewis sighed and then turned to Leo. "I wish you could tell us more about what you saw that night. Then again, if you did, I might have to send you away for your own safety, given, a mad killer is on the loose."

"Even if he could talk, I don't think a court would put him on the stand. It's that camera of yours that's admissible." Suddenly Stacia Treen sat up at attention. "Holy . . . why didn't I think of this sooner? Where is that camera?"

Lewis went and got the tiny digital camera and handed it to her.

"Since this is a night-vision camera, maybe I should take it and visit the house again. If there's a patch on the property that looks like it's been recently dug up, I can record it and take that to the police."

"That sounds dangerous," Lewis said. "What if the guy's there?"

"I'll be careful. I don't suppose you'd like to come with me, would you?"

"No!" the man cried.

Good, Stacia thought.

Within twenty minutes she was at the house on Monmouth Street, which looked dark and empty. That was good; if no one was there, no one would catch her snooping around. A man was walking a dog on the street, so Stacia waited in her car until they had passed.

The pine-scented night was cool but not as cold as it sometimes got in Rosaville, with the winds blowing off the ocean. Turning on the camera and using its infrared lens to help guide her through the darkness, Stacia went up to the house and then around it on the side, looking carefully for any disturbance in the soil. The backyard was mostly brick, which would have made burial more difficult, but it was also quite obviously the vantage point from which Leo the Cat had peered in and watched the murder . . . or at least recorded it. With the curtains pulled back from the window, Stacia could barely make out the fireplace in the darkened house.

Then, with no warning, a face appeared on the other side of the glass, obscuring her view.

Stacia instinctively leapt backward but lost her balance and fell hard onto the brick surface, which caused her to cry out. Then she heard a door opening and, a second later, the beam of a flashlight was in her face, nearly blinding her.

"Oh, good God!" a voice said. "What are you doing here?"

"*Clementine*?" Stacia cried, recognizing the voice.

"Are you hurt?"

"My butt is cursing me out, but I think I can still walk."

"Then get up and come inside before somebody sees you!"

Once inside, they kept the lights off, their only illumination coming from the flashlight. Stacia asked, "Where's Norm Sanders?"

"I have no idea."

"How did you get in?"

"My dear, do you know how many houses I have had to break into over the years when the owners forgot to leave a key for me for a showing? It is really not that difficult."

"What if Sanders comes back?"

"I doubt he will," Clementine replied. "Follow me."

The realtor led the way into the kitchen and opened the refrigerator.

It, and the freezer, were completely empty, not even plugged in.

"Nobody actually lives here," Clementine said.

"What about all this furniture?"

"It's called staging. We all do it. You put prop furniture into a home before you show it to prospective buyers. It gives the place that lived-in feeling that buyers find so attractive."

"If nobody lives here, who is Sanders?"

"That is only one of the questions facing us," Clementine said. "The first is why Marguerite Dornan was murdered. The second is why she was still alive a year after her funeral. Only when we resolve those can we worry about what Sanders has to do with any of this."

"I can think of a fourth," Stacia said. "Why this house?"

"Aahh, very good. In fact, that might be the key question. If we can answer that, maybe the others will fall into place. Come along."

"Come along where?"

"My office—unless you've got something more important to do."

Stacia followed Clementine's car to the headquarters of DeWine & Associates, which was located in the West Village. (The fact that a place as small as Rosaville had to be divided into "East" and "West" was something she found both funny and puzzling.) Once there, the realtor powered up her computer. But after several minutes of typing and clicking, she said, "I do not understand this at all."

"What's wrong now?"

"There is no sales history for that house, not even a tax record. It's as if it did not exist."

"What does that mean?"

"For the life of me, I cannot imagine."

"You know, Clementine, maybe we were wrong about thinking that house is the key to all this. Maybe the real question we should be asking is who, exactly, was Marguerite Dornan?"

"Stace, I need that piece on the elephant seals," Jake Odenkirk reminded her.

"Hmmm? Oh, right. I just need to do a final proof on it."

Elephant seals, Stacia thought; like they were doing something different this year than they did any other year. Why not do a story on the phases of the moon?

She opened the file on the elephant seal story and gave it one last once-over, then forwarded it to Jake and got back to researching Marguerite Dornan.

Or trying to. It was like the woman didn't exist before coming to Rosaville. Suddenly something Romero Lewis had said flashed through her mind, and she cried, "Oh, no . . . *really*?"

"What's that?" Odenkirk called.

"Oh, nothing, Jake. Just thinking out loud."

"All right. Your story's good, by the way."

"Great, thanks," Stacia said, adding mentally: *You've no idea how satisfying it is to write about ugly, fish-reeking behemoths.* But if he was happy with the story, he'd be more of a mind to give her the rest of the afternoon off. She had to talk to Clementine about her realization.

Getting the time off proved no problem, and within fifteen minutes she was back at DeWine & Associates. Clementine was speaking on the phone with a client when Stacia walked in, and upon seeing her, said, "Darling, something's just come up. I'll have to get back to you. *Ciao.*" To Stacia she said, "You look like someone with information."

"If you wanted to stash a person where they'd never be found, where would you go?" the reporter asked.

"The William Morris Agency."

"What?"

"It's an old show business joke. If you want to disappear completely, sign with William Morris. You'll never be heard from again. My ex-husband was an actor."

"Clementine, I'm serious."

"All right, if I wanted to hide someone forever, I'd send them . . . oh, dear God, I'd send them *here.*"

"Exactly!" Stacia cried. "A town like this is the perfect place to put someone you don't ever want found again. A comment Romero Lewis made to me about having to send away his cat for its own safety finally sank in. I think he meant it as a joke, but it might be that elusive key we've been looking for."

Clementine sighed. "I thought reporters were supposed to be clear and precise."

"Witness relocation, Clementine. I think Marguerite Dornan was relocated here by the feds, and that house on Monmouth Street is a safe house owned by the government for just that purpose. That's why there are no local records."

"So you think Marguerite lived there?"

"Up until she had to disappear again. That's the only thing that logically explains how she can die and then come back and be murdered a year later . . . her first death was a fake! Let's say the person from whom she was being protected somehow found out where she was anyway, meaning that her life was in danger all over again. So the feds stage her death and move her to another location out of Rosaville."

"But how do you fake a body?" Clementine asked.

"The newspaper report said she'd been missing for a month before they found the body. My guess is they either used a substitute body, someone who died from another cause, or there never was any body."

"The casket at the funeral was closed," Clementine said. "But can you prove any of this?"

"No, but it's the one scenario that explains away all the peculiar facts," Stacia replied. "It's like Sherlock Holmes said, once you eliminate the impossible, whatever is left, no matter how improbable, is the answer."

"I'll take dream homes over Sherlock Holmes any day," the older woman sniffed. "But let's assume your hunch is correct. Why would Marguerite have returned here only to be murdered?"

"Well, I doubt she had being murdered on her itinerary. But why she came back at all is a question I can't answer. We'd have to ask an official of the witness protection program to find out, and from what little I understand about the system, they're not very forthcoming, for obvious reasons."

"Wouldn't the police know?" Clementine asked.

"I really don't think so. Things like this would be handled far above a city or county police force. It's the province of federal marshals or, depending on the venue, the . . ."

"The what? Don't leave me in suspense!"

"The district attorney's office."

"Let's ask them, then. Do you happen to know any?"

"I do," Stacia whispered, suddenly feeling chilled. "God help me."

Stacia Treen's first sight of Rosaville, California, had been in the company of Los Angeles Deputy DA Rey Morales, who had been dispatched to the village for some reason he never fully explained. That was last April . . . right around the time Marguerite Dornan "died."

Stacia didn't believe in coincidences.

And when you eliminate the impossible . . .

Stacia's hand hovered over her cell phone for a good half hour before she punched in the number.

He answered immediately.

"Hi, Rey, it's me," she said.

After a long, cold pause, he said, "Why?"

"Why what?"

"Why are you calling?"

"Well, funny thing, Rey. I'm living in Rosaville."

"You're . . . *what*?"

"I'm working up here for the local paper, but that's not why I called. I need to know if you've ever heard of someone named Marguerite Dornan."

The silence that followed went on so long that Stacia feared he might have disconnected the call. Finally Rey said, "I don't know what you're talking about" in a voice so cold it could have frozen the floor of Staples Center for a Kings game.

"Marguerite Dornan."

"I don't know any—"

"That interminable silence when you heard her name argues otherwise."

"I'm hanging up."

"She was murdered, Rey, this time for real. I know she was in the program and the fact that you and I came here last year right when she had her fatal 'accident' strongly implies that she came through the DA's office in LA. I want you to tell me about her."

"Drop it. Drop this whole thing."

"I can't, Rey. I want to solve her murder."

"You really think I'm going to jeopardize my job and the program itself so you can get a byline?"

"It's not just me. There's a realtor up here named DeWine who is also involved, as is a guy with a cat who—"

"A guy with a cat?"

"Look, never mind. Just tell me who Norm Sanders is and we'll call it even."

After another long pause, Morales said: "Whatever game you think you're playing, you'd be best to stop."

"The woman's dead, Rey, so there's no longer any need to protect her. I'd say your precious program failed her. Maybe that's what I should write about."

After a string of muttered four-letter words (at least he hasn't changed, Stacia thought) Rey said, "You don't know what kind of fire you're playing with, but I know you well enough to realize you're not just going to drop it. Don't leave town. Someone will be up to see you in a day or so to explain the facts of life." Then the line went dead.

As she clicked off her phone, Stacia realized she was dripping with sweat.

The next evening, Stacia returned home after interviewing a ninety-nine-year-old former actor who had retired to Rosaville and claimed to have the largest collection of locally reaped beach moonstones in the village (which, she rationalized, was at least better than a cat show). After taking a shower, she found a message on her cell from Clementine DeWine.

"You'll never guess what?" the woman began. "I've received a call from our friend Norm Sanders, and you were right . . . he *is* a federal agent working with the relocation program. I'm meeting him for dinner. I'll tell you all about it." And the message ended.

This was a story Stacia would have preferred getting firsthand, but it was hard to fight Clementine's competitive nature. Still, hadn't Rey said someone would be coming to see *her*?

Stacia had just finished her frozen chicken breast and corn dinner when her doorbell rang. Answering it, she saw a tall African American man in a dark blazer over khaki slacks, but no necktie.

"Ms. Treen?" he said.

"Who are you?"

"My name is Norman Sanders, I'm a federal marshal. May I come in?"

Stacia slammed the door in his face.

The bell rang again.

"Go away before I call the police!" she cried. "You're not Norm Sanders."

She stepped away from the door, and then noticed something sliding underneath it. It was an identification badge. Picking it up, she saw the federal insignia and a photo of the man on the other side of the door, looking about five years younger.

"Who sent you?" she called out.

"Rey Morales," the man replied. "Los Angeles County Deputy District Attorney."

"Oh, my God!" she cried, opening the door.

"It's good that you're careful," the man said evenly. "May I come in now?"

"No!" Stacia said. "You have to come with me instead. A woman's life is in danger."

Whoever it was that had answered the door of that house and identified himself as Norm Sanders was not Norm Sanders—and Clementine was meeting him for dinner!

"What is this?" Sanders asked.

"There's a fake Norman Sanders out there and he's with a friend of mine. If he lied about *who* he was, how can I trust that he's not the murderer?"

"Where did you see him?"

"In the safe house. The one on Monmouth Street."

"What did he look like?"

"Short, gray-haired—"

"Scar on his face?" Sanders asked, tracing it with his finger on his own cheek.

"Yes!"

"Damn! If he's with your friend, then you're right to worry. We have to get to them as soon as possible. Do you know where they went?"

"If I know Clementine, there's only one place."

Stacia got them to the Sandcastle Inn in her Mini Cooper in no time.

The maître d' had no reservation listed under the names of DeWine or Sanders, which was moot anyway, since everyone in the town knew Clementine by sight. "She has not been in here tonight," the man said. "If she happens to arrive, shall I give her a message?"

"Yes," Stacia said, backing toward the restaurant's front door, "tell her to run!"

Back in Stacia's Mini Cooper, which Norman Sanders had to squeeze into, she said, "I was sure this is where Clementine would insist upon dining tonight. I suppose I could try Chez Millau back in town." She was headed there, sliding through the village's few stop signs with abandon, before suddenly slamming on the brakes and screeching the car to a jarring halt.

"Hey, warn me the next time, okay?" Sanders said.

"Sorry, but I've just realized where they are," Stacia said. "The house."

As she careened through the narrow streets of the village, Stacia asked, "So who is it we're dealing with?"

"His name's Robert Plano," Sanders answered. "He's the guy we were trying to protect Jessica Walsham from. That's Marguerite Dornan to you."

"Mob?"

"Worse. He has his own global operation. Drugs, guns, children. He's as bad as you can get, but just like Capone, the only thing that stuck was income tax evasion. Jessica was a CPA who uncovered his money laundering. She testified against him, but Plano had a great legal team. He got off. We had to get Jessica out. She came here, but then we got word Plano had tracked her down, so she had to move again. Why she would come back here after relocating to Arizona is completely beyond comprehension."

They were in front of the house now, which appeared dark.

"No one home," Stacia said.

"I doubt that," Sanders answered. "You stay in the car. That's an order."

Before Federal Marshal Norman Sanders could completely unwedge himself from the Cooper, however, Stacia's door was yanked open. Glancing over in surprise, she first saw the barrel of a gun silencer an inch from her face. Behind it was the man with the scar.

"Out of the car and inside the house," Plano ordered, keeping the gun on her. "Sanders, put your weapon on the top of the car, slowly."

The marshal did so.

"You blink, Normie, and she gets it, then you get it."

"What did you do with Clementine?" Stacia asked.

"Inside."

The three of them approached the house, where the door was already open.

Clementine DeWine was inside the living room, lying on the prop couch, her hands and feet zip-tied.

"Let the women go, Robert," Sanders said.

"Oh, yeah, right."

"Do you know who this is?" Clementine asked, still indignant despite her condition.

"I know," Sanders said. "What I don't know is how he managed to glean information about this house and Jessica Walsham."

"It pays to have someone on the inside," Plano responded. "See, I found out you'd re-stashed Walsham and I was given her new contact number. I called her and told her I was you, and that she had to come back to this little hole in the ground, that it was a matter of life or death."

"And she did, just like that?" Stacia asked.

"Well, I told her that Bob Plano had discovered the location of her brand-new hiding place too, so she was only safe if she came back here, because no one would look in the same place twice." The criminal smiled, deepening his scar.

"What are you going to do with us?" Stacia asked.

"Same thing I did with Jessica. I've been working on the hole, making it bigger, so that it fits four as easily as one."

He still doesn't know about Lewis, Stacia thought thankfully.

"Four? How did you know I was going to come up here?" Sanders asked.

"Oh I knew you would be here," Plano said. "Like I said, it pays to have someone on the inside. Our mutual friend DDA Morales told me exactly when you'd be arriving so I could get rid of all the loose ends at the same time."

"*Rey*?" Stacia screamed, so loudly that it actually startled the man with the gun.

"Don't do that again," Plano barked, approaching her and putting the tip of the weapon to her forehead.

"Rey's involved in this?"

"Up to his career path."

Then Clementine DeWine began to laugh. "You think you're so smart, don't you, you sawed-off miscreant?" Clementine said.

"Watch it, lady," Plano warned.

"No, *you* watch it." She looked past him to the glass door. "It appears the cavalry has arrived."

"What?" Plano said, turning his head to look behind him.

With Plano's attention deflected, Norman Sanders clamped a hand on his wrist, forcing the gun down, and with his other hand grabbed him by the throat. Within seconds, the criminal's legs gave way and he sank to the floor, unconscious. Then the marshal removed the gun and went to help Clementine DeWine with her binds.

"That Mr. Spock thing really works?" Stacia said in amazement.

"If you know how to do it," Sanders said. "But it doesn't last forever. Before he comes to, why don't you turn on the lights and look around for more of those ties, or some rope, or anything to secure him with. By the way, what was that business about the cavalry?"

"Their commanding officer is still out there," Clementine said, and all three turned to the glass door where Leo the Cat was standing outside and washing his paw.

"Oh, no!" Stacia Treen yelled. "Oh, NO! You can't do this!"

"It's not my call, Stace," Jake Odenkirk said. "I've been on the phone with every government agent on the planet, and not a word of this is to be breathed to anyone, anywhere, at any time. Nothing, nada, zip, zilch, ix-nay, uh uh."

"This is the story of the year!"

"And you got it. You just can't share it, is all."

"This is *not* fair!"

"Sorry. My hands are tied."

"I doubt Clementine would think that's funny."

"Clementine has been briefed by the feds as well. And guess what? They're going to sell that not-so-safe house to her in return for her silence. The body of Marguerite Dornan has been removed from the hill behind the house, and DeWine plans to have the place blessed by a priest, just in case."

"I can't even write about my rotten ex going to prison?" Stacia whined.

"All hush-hush."

"You're enjoying this, aren't you?"

"Enjoying? No. I don't like the thought of losing my Lois Lane."

"Well, I'm glad you at least . . . *losing*? What do you mean *losing*? On top of everything else, I'm being fired?"

"No, but I figure you're going to resign," Odenkirk said.

"Why would I do that?"

"Because Clementine plans to ask you to join her in a newly formed private investigation firm."

"She . . . *what*?"

"She sees this as a whole new opportunity for her, and she feels the two of you worked so well together on the Marguerite Dornan case that you could keep going."

"She feels we worked *well* together?"

"That's what she told me. Clementine wants to base the new agency in Paso Robles and cover the entire county since there's not enough crime in Rosaville to keep you busy. She'll be by shortly to take you to lunch and pitch the idea."

"How come you know this before I do?" Stacia asked.

"Clementine called me for advice on how to deal with you."

"How to deal with *me*?

"I told her, of course, and wished her well on her new venture."

"You . . . you . . ." Stacia sputtered, and then slammed her mouth shut with a *clop*. After a few moments she said, "All right, fine. Maybe I'll do it. Maybe I'll become a PI. Maybe I'll work with a small-town tsarina who wanted to stifle my voice, if not get me fired! But no matter what I decide, I'm going to make Clementine take me to lunch at the cheapest, dirtiest, smelliest fish shack that can be found between here and San Luis Obispo!"

"Captain Rudy's in Morro Bay," Odenkirk said. "The food's fine, but they clean their own fish so the smell of the place would offend a seal. While you're there, tell Rudy if he takes out four ads with us, the fifth is free."

I believe that the genesis of most if not all stories comes from wondering, "What if . . . ?" Having once owned (or been owned by) a cat who came and went as he pleased and habitually peered at our neighbors through the windows of their homes, I began to wonder . . . what if the cat were to witness a terrible crime in the course of a nighttime jaunt and managed to bring home just enough evidence of it to raise alarm, but not enough to explain what actually happened? "What the Cat Dragged In" is the result. The story's setting, "Rosaville, California," is based on a real coastal village about two hundred thirty miles north of LA that is a favorite getaway spot for me and my family. Its name has been changed to protect me from the Chamber of Commerce.

Lou Manfredo *is the author of three highly acclaimed NYPD Detective Joe Rizzo novels:* Rizzo's War, Rizzo's Fire, *and* Rizzo's Daughter. *Kirkus declared Rizzo, "The most authentic cop in contemporary crime fiction," and the novels have been compared favorably to the late Ed McBain's legendary 87th Precinct novels.*

Manfredo's short fiction has appeared in various publications including Brooklyn Noir, New Jersey Noir, *and* Ellery Queen Mystery Magazine *as well as editions of* The Best American Mystery Stories; Best of BAMS, The First Ten Years; EQMM's The Crooked Road, Volume Two; *and Israel's* The Short Story Project.

A Brooklyn native and twenty-five-year veteran of its criminal justice system, he currently resides in New Jersey with his wife, Joanne, his first copy and language editor as well as creative associate.

SUNDOWN

Lou Manfredo

The water flowing in the stream was clear and cold and it sparkled in the sunlight, and though it held no color, it was colorful and it shimmered.

I watched the morning sun touch it, bright and hot and golden, and it seemed an ideal scene of late-spring splendor, and one of great peace and promise and appeal of the very best of nature. It was a wondrous day, the stream framed by a canopy of lush green and shadowed sunlight and warm breezes; it seemed a day of hope and great beauty and promise.

Except for the corpse at my feet. The body that sprawled stretched and broken and holding neither hope nor beauty nor promise.

It was ugly and real and far too familiar a sight to my jaded eyes and for my jaded mind and soul. And without need of the postmortem that would follow or the science and wonderous technical forensic methodology of our modern 1979 world, I already knew that which had transformed the body, taken it from person to object, from sacred to wretched, from living flesh to protoplasmic trash.

A bullet. As so often the case, a bullet. A mere wisp of lead, insignificant in a universe of vastness and awe, a lifeless lump of metal, benign in and of itself, deadly and murderous at the pleasured beck and call of man's intellectual conceit, pursuit, avarice, and cruelty.

Just another homicide to solve. Merely a new game for me to play, top of the first, kickoff time, set one, game one, match one. Just another blank Sunday crossword puzzle facing me and waiting to be challenged.

I know of no pursuit easier, more difficult, more purposeful or pointless, better or worse than catching a killer. Identical to the sunlight striking the clear stream water, or the twinkling emanating from the pebbled streambed, so intangible, so unpossessable, in a sense not really there, or anywhere.

But for me, Suffolk County PD Detective Joseph Oliver, it most surely *was* there. Often, it seemed, it was everywhere.

Murder. A pursuit not to be soon abandoned by mankind. For to hunter and prey, fox and hound, it remained just too damned empowering.

I tread carefully upon the soft stream bank. It was dew-covered grass, green and tender and yielding beneath my weight. I squatted and looked more closely at the body, sprawled in final disarray and indignity, lower half submerged in the clear, icy water, upper torso dry on higher ground, eyes fixed open, locked on my own, unseeing, glistening, dead. I turned to see my partner, Detective Mike Shay, as he squatted beside me.

"Female Caucasian, probably midtwenties, about five six, maybe one ten, one fifteen. Brown hair, blue eyes. No visible scars or markings," I said to him.

Mike nodded, picking up the narrative. "Small-caliber bullet wound, center forehead, no apparent exit wound. Fully clothed."

We went silent, forearms braced on upper thighs, hands dangling between our knees. I heard Mike let out a sigh.

"I never understood calling this stream a 'river,'" he said. "Hell—look at it. Maybe twenty feet wide and no more than a foot or two deep. Some river."

"Yeah," I said. "Connetquot River. Named by the Secatogue tribe centuries ago when they dominated this area. The stream widens and deepens south of here. Maybe that's the river."

We squatted there, nothing much else to say. The sun caressed the back of my neck, soothing and warm, and I wondered if any of its heat was touching the corpse, warming it gently, nurturing its departing soul. My intellect told me no, told me the girl was dead and gone, wasted and beyond the sun's reach, not traipsing through some magical afterlife; my heart told me the complete opposite. My intellect, so accustomed to victory, won out once more.

Still fixated on the dead girl's face, I spoke to my partner. "This cold water is going to complicate pinpointing time of death. Corpse cooled too quickly."

"The ME has a big bag of science," Mike said. "He'll figure it out."

He stood slowly and laid a hand on my shoulder. "Come on, Sherlock," he said, using his nickname for me. "Let's get started looking for the scumbag who did this."

The next morning, I sat opposite my grandfather, Gus Oliver, at a table in the local IHOP, breakfast before us. Granddad had served as constable for the Long Island hamlet of Central Islin, retiring in 1959 after thirty years of service. He and my Grandma Molly still lived on the family farm in the house built by Oliver ancestors in the 1800s. The farm is much smaller now, a glorified garden, really. My grandparents sold off most of the active acreage back in the late 1960s, suburban sprawl from New York City having arrived in Central Islin by then. The Oliver farm, like much of formerly pastoral Long Island, now sprouts four-bedroom, two-car-garage commuter homes in lieu of corn, potatoes, and cauliflower. Real-estate agents call it progress.

After he retired, Granddad had become a sort of unofficial private investigator, helping out local police and even an occasional lawyer who found himself in the unusual position of representing a client who was actually innocent. Over the years, Granddad had solved many a case, from the mundane to murder most foul. He was a natural investigator and something of a local legend.

So, as I often did when I caught a homicide, arson, rape—any A felony, I sought his counsel. See, despite my rather stellar reputation in the county detective division, and my partner's lofty nickname for me, I was, in fact, no Sherlock Holmes. I'm good, mind you, but not that good. Merely a competent and willing Watson to my granddad's folksy, flannel-clad Americanized Holmes.

I sipped some coffee, strong and black and touched by richness. My granddad's folded *Newsday* sat at the table's edge to my right, the paper's headline blaring the recent death in Hollywood of John Wayne. The Duke had pushed my tragic young murder victim to page two. Yet another reason to resent celebrities.

I watched Granddad butter a breakfast roll, then run his still Windex-clear blue eyes quickly around the IHOP interior, modern-splendid in its cookie-cutter Formica and faux wood, abuzz with conversation, cutlery clinking, fluorescents humming.

"A world away from Lang's, eh, Jo-Jo?" he said, referring to the long-gone rustic drugstore on Central Islin's Main Street where he and I had enjoyed ritualistic Saturday-morning breakfasts for many of my childhood years.

I smiled at the memory and his nickname for me. I was "Jo-Jo" to him long before I was ever "Sherlock" to battle-weary police detectives.

"Yes, it is," I said. "That CVS opening on Motor Parkway killed off Lang's Pharmacy and its meal counter. Progress, they call it."

After a moment during which I saw reflection and bittersweet memory dance across his face, he leaned slightly forward and locked onto my eyes.

"So—what do we have, Detective?"

I told him. Sara Wills, twenty-two, recent college grad. Lived with parents in Central Islin. Single gunshot, center forehead, probably from within a three-foot range. Twenty-two caliber handgun, hollow-point Remington round. Two kids fishing found her half-submerged in the stream Friday morning, nine fifteen. Prelim from ME says she was shot somewhere else and dropped at the stream.

"Where at the stream?"

"Behind the dead end of Ridge Boulevard, residential street off Connetquot Road."

He nodded. "I know the street. About fifty yards of woods from the dead-end tree line to the stream, and no access road or footpath."

"Yes."

His eyes narrowed. "How big a gal was she?"

I slipped my notepad from the inside pocket of my linen sport coat and flipped through it.

"Five five, hundred nine."

He nodded. "I guess a strong person or two could carry her through the woods easy enough." He paused, thinking. "Question is, why?"

"To hide the body."

"In the stream? Where every kid in town goes wading, fishing, playing cowboys and Indians? I can think of fifty better hiding places for a body within a mile of Ridge Boulevard."

"Okay. So, the killer is strong *and* stupid."

Granddad sipped at his coffee, then forked some hash browns into his mouth. He spoke only after chewing and swallowing.

"Boyfriend?" he asked.

Again, I checked my notes. "Yeah, Randolph Carter, twenty-three, from Bay Shore. Student at NYU Law School in the city. NYPD checked him out: body was found yesterday, Friday morning. ME puts time of death late Thursday afternoon, early evening. I had NYPD interview Carter. He told them he was taking a final exam until four thirty, went to his part-time job at five, worked there until eleven. The New York cops confirmed his alibi."

Granddad nodded, sipped coffee. "Well, sometimes it's easy, and he was the easy way out. No dice, I guess."

"No. No dice."

He tapped a finger against the tabletop. "Okay, then, so everyone is a suspect. Narrow it down, Jo-Jo. Narrow it down."

"Okay. I was planning to. Any suggestions?"

His eyes, kindly and soft most times, went hard. "Yes. The stream, that's the key. No way somebody shoots a woman and then carts her off through fifty yards of thick woodland just to lay her down in plain sight like that. The stream. It means something to the killer. He's making a statement. Find out what it is, and it'll point you right at him."

I nodded. "Well, all day yesterday, Mike and I ran down Sara's last known whereabouts. It dead-ended. She just dropped off the radar about four Thursday afternoon. Her parents called her in missing about six hours later. They were told about the twenty-four-hour missing-person requisite. Late last night her car was found in a strip-mall parking lot. The keys were in the ignition. Forensics team is doing a workup, nothing significant so far. The squad is checking the residents of Ridge Boulevard, looking for a likely. Wouldn't be too hard to get her to the dump spot if she was killed anywhere on Ridge."

"Sure. Check that. But you'll probably come up dry. You kill someone in your house, you don't dump the body a stone's throw away. Canvass for a strange vehicle seen at the deep end of Ridge, maybe parked at the wood line Thursday night. But—more importantly, find a link to that stream. That's the key here, Jo-Jo. I feel it in my bones."

"So," Mike Shay said. "What exactly are you saying?"

It was just after twelve noon, later that Saturday. Mike and I sat hunched over Pabst Blue Ribbon beers at the far corner of the battered old bar. The Green Lantern was one of the last of the old-time Main Street storefronts in Central Islin; Jill's Flower Shop had morphed into Ink Renegade Tattoo Palace about five years ago. Lang's Pharmacy was now a dollar store, Muller's Delicatessen a taco joint. And so on. But—against all odds, The Green Lantern survived. Of the dozen or so lunchtime patrons, I believe Mike and I were the only two not clad in flannel. And it was June.

There were no ferns in fancy pots scattered around the Green Lantern, no Tequila Sunrises in chilled shakers, but instead, old faded photos hung in frames on genuine pine–paneled walls: photos of Duke Snider and Johnny Podres in their Brooklyn Dodgers uniforms, of Say Hey Willie Mays rounding second in full gallop, his New York Giants cap flying from his head, of Mickey Mantle and his crooked boyish grin. It all blended well with the nicotine-stained tin ceiling and the flannel shirts and the well-used pickup trucks parked out front, perpendicular to the curb, mud-splattered fenders and dented dog-dish hubcaps glaring in the noonday sun. All so removed from the murder and mayhem, sin and spoil and commercial blight of the world it sat within and floundered above. It was a dream, a daydream of respite and warmth, taste and odor, sight and sound. The tavern was an oasis and one doomed to obsolescence. Soon, I imagined. As soon as the third-generation owner-operator decided that the obnoxious malls had consumed enough local farmland, the ubiquitous Hondas and Toyotas had replaced enough Fords and Chevys, and fancy coffees had displaced enough Maxwell House, she'd be gone, off to greener fields in the Carolinas or Florida, Arizona or Nevada. Soon.

"My grandfather says it's the stream. That's the key. The fact that the stream was the chosen dumping ground," I said to Mike, masochistically slamming myself back to 1979. The pain held some eerie satisfaction and I tried to ignore it.

Mike nodded, sipped at his Pabst. It was golden and afire in the glass, twinkling against the bar lights, frosty, cold even to the eye. I smiled at it.

"Okay," Mike said. "So, what is he saying? The killer is an environmentalist? *Silent Spring* guy? Is that it?"

I shook my head and raised my eyes from the beer to Mike's face, my smile gone.

"No. I don't know. But you really want to doubt him? You figure, 'Yeah, let's ignore the old man's hunch, 'cause we're, like, you know, two geniuses'?"

"Relax, Sherlock. Relax. So, it's the stream. Okay—where do we go from here?"

"Back to the vic's parents. We pry a little. Pick up the list of contacts we asked for. Get into the family history. You know—get annoying."

He nodded, drank more beer. It looked refreshing. I drank more of my own. It was.

"Well, hell, I'm good at that," Mike said. "Ask my wife. Or better still, my daughter. She's thirteen. I'm the most annoying thing in her life."

The house on Sportsman Street was old, maybe nineteen-thirty old. Depression-era workmen, craftsmen prideful in their work, had built it. It was furnished cozy, warm, a home, not merely a house. A structure is truly rooted to the earth, just as natural growth, but with man-made connectors—pipes, concrete, utility lines, sewers. An upward and downward flow of materials and fluids that gives the building a false life. But it is the people within that bring the house joy and warmth or sorrow and cruelty, bring it true life: the choice is there, and we all make our choice. Some better, some worse. Often—as now for the Wills family—the better becomes a worse. Shit happens.

I thought about this as I eyed Mary Wills, mother of Sara Wills, corpse. Wife to John Wills, devastated father. Mother to Karen Wills, shattered kid sister, eyes red, swollen, any remaining childhood glow now vanished from her eighteen-year-old face. A family ruined.

"Thanks for seeing us again so soon," I said to them, the three perched closely together on the living-room couch, huddling, it seemed to me; huddling against a chill that could never be abated, certainly could never leave them.

I needed to do my job. I leaned forward in the high-back chair I sat on, notepad in hand, heart in throat. I glanced quickly to Mike, seated to my left in an identical chair. He looked like a man waiting in a doctor's office to learn his biopsy results.

I spoke again to the Willses.

"We cleared Sara's boyfriend, Randolph. It was a formality, of course, but we needed to do it. Yesterday you told us you couldn't think of anyone who may have wanted to hurt Sara. Has that changed?"

They shook their heads slowly. "No," John Wills said. "We discussed it as a family last night. No one wanted to hurt her. She was a wonderful person."

Mother and sister sobbed silently at that. I dropped my eyes to my notepad, jotted down my dog's name just to appear to be doing something and to give them a moment. Mike took the opportunity.

"Have you put together that list?" he asked softly. "I know it's short notice, but the sooner we can get started . . ." He let his voice trail off.

And I understood why he did. The sooner we got started, what? We catch the killer? He goes to jail, has a trial, gets convicted, and goes off to the state prison? And what then? Does Sara come walking through the door, smiling, "I'm glad those two cops caught the guy. I'm alive again!" The thing about closure is, there is no closure.

"We have it," John Wills said. "Karen, it's on the hutch in the kitchen. Can you get it, please?"

The girl rose slowly, still sobbing. She shuffled toward the kitchen. If you are eighteen, you don't shuffle. You stride. If your sister is murdered, then you shuffle, and you aren't eighteen any longer.

Karen returned, a sheet of paper in her hand. She gave it to her father, then dropped heavily back onto the couch. He stood, crossed to me, handed me the paper. I glanced at the list. It looked detailed and thorough. They were intelligent people. Organized, detail-oriented, neat. Murder was not any of that.

I folded the paper and put it in my pocket, my hand brushing the Smith and Wesson revolver belted to my waist.

Every time I do this, every murder, rape, child-abuse case, every evil I deal with, I lose a little more of myself. I feel it floating away, like they say a soul does, and the lesser me remaining sees the cases become more and more merely a chase, a puzzle, a challenge, a game to win or lose. But for the victims and the survivors, their lives are altered, tainted for all time. To them, it's not a game.

Sitting there, I was ashamed of myself. I glanced again to Mike. He was too.

We asked the Willses all the usual questions and learned what we usually did about a murder victim: She was a wonderful young woman, not an enemy in the world, a bright future ahead with a wonderful young man, everything was going to be perfect. I wondered, as I listened to the sad, somber-proud parents tell us all this, where were all these wonderful people? Where were all these people without enemies, leading blissfully wonderful lives, moving happily through their bright futures? Where—among all the people who were not victims of murder—were all these wondrous creatures? Why wasn't I tripping over them on a daily basis?

After an hour of questions and half a notepad of scribbled names, dates, addresses, and phone numbers, we left. The Willses' disappointment followed us: Our visit had, as it usually did with victim's families, prompted some impossible hope within them. We were coming by to tell them a mistake had been made, it hadn't been Sara slaughtered and thrown into the stream, it had been the daughter of someone else, some unknown other people not in the lives of the Wills family. It was all going to be all right. Just a mistake. Sorry, folks. You have a nice day, Sara will be home any minute now.

Instead, they watched us, two strangers now their uninvited intimates, as we cop-walked to our black cop car and discussed our cop stuff.

And Sara, alas, was just as dead.

Later, we sat in the car and sipped tasteless coffee, the car backed against a white privacy fence in the cookie-cutter lot of the cookie-cutter Burger King on Lowell Avenue, the police radio occasionally crackling with reports of grief. With my left hand, I held the list of contacts John Wills had handed me in his warm, cozy living room.

"Jane Rossi," I read. "They notated 'best friend' next to her name."

"Good place to start," Mike said.

"Good as any."

"Yeah. Good as any."

I drained my coffee container and started the engine. I pulled the car forward to a telephone booth at the lot's edge. Rossi was at home in Bohemia. She would wait for us. Top of the first. The game was afoot.

Jane Rossi was twenty-two, tall and slim, jet-black hair and gorgeous blue eyes. She'd make a hell of a good-looking woman someday, after she lost some lingering youthful acne covered with too much pancake. Her eyes, like those of the Willses, were swollen and red. Reality has a way of swelling up eyes. Yet despite her grief, she had managed to get on makeup.

"I grew up on Sportsman Street, across the street from Sara. From when we were about five or six, we were inseparable, right up to when I was thirteen and my folks moved us to Babylon. Sara and I drifted apart for years, but once we got our driver's licenses, we reconnected. It was as though we had never been apart." Her eyes welled with tears, and she paused her narrative. I jotted my dog's name into my notes again. I looked like a TV cop. After a moment, I felt she was composed again. I looked up from my notes. The dog's name, by the way, is Molly. Like my grandmother.

"I know Sportsman Street pretty well," I said lightly, letting her composure deepen. "I grew up in Central Islin not far from that street. I remember where it dead-ends to the wood line, there was a footpath. It led down to the stream. I'd go there with my cousin to fish, sail our toy boats, catch frogs, play Swamp Fox."

"Swamp Fox?" she asked.

I allowed a casual laugh, lightening things further, like a real professional detective. I could feel Mike's awe at my skill set. "Yeah, old TV show with Leslie Nielsen. Like a Robin Hood, but during the American Revolution."

"Oh," she said. I guessed the old swamper couldn't compete with *Charlie's Angels*.

"Yeah, I spent a lot of hours in that stream," I went on. "Sometimes we'd wade south all the way down to the main pond, where it widens out and runs deep. How about you and Sara? Ever go exploring that stream?"

She smiled at me. "We'd usually wade upstream. There was a stretch where wild blueberries grew, and we'd pick them. We'd bring them back to Sara's mom, and she'd run water over them to chill them, then pour cream over them. It was a great treat."

I nodded, glancing at Mike. He poker-faced me, but his eyes said, "Yeah, follow this up."

Sara Wills's body had been found less than a mile upstream of Sportsman Street. I closed my eyes briefly, pulled up the scene:

yeah, blueberry bushes, just across from the body. Hanging over the water, flowering, budding.

"So, Jane," I said, my eyes open now, probing. I noticed with peripheral vision Mike stirring in his seat. Sometimes, we were both thinking, it's easy. Sometimes. "Who'd you pick the berries with? Just Sara? Just the two of you?"

"No, we were sort of a threesome then. Richie Field, he'd be with us a lot." She paused, smiling slightly. "Wow. Richie Field. I haven't thought of him in . . . well, not so long, actually."

"Why is that, Jane?" Mike asked. "You run into him lately?"

"No, not that. Sara mentioned him. Back when we first reconnected at seventeen. And—now that I think about it, a year or two ago."

"Tell us about that," Mike said.

"About Richie? Why? He's sort of a nonentity, you know. Nothing much to say, really. I haven't seen him in years."

I nodded at her. "Always something to say. For instance, when you were kids, what was Richie like? What sort of kid was he? I want to hear more about him and the stream."

Her eyes narrowed as she spoke. "You . . . you can't possibly think Richie had anything to . . . to do with Sara being . . . having died, can you?"

I let my face harden a bit. I didn't want a debate. I wanted information.

"One of two things happened here, Jane. One, Sara was the random victim of some maniac, or two, it was a motivated murder by someone who knew her. If it was random, forensics and luck may solve it, but most likely won't. If it was motivated, brains, forensics, instinct, and luck can solve it, and most likely will. Let's concentrate on situation two. What kind of a kid was Richie?"

After a moment of reflection and growing discomfort, she told us.

Richie was a weirdo. He had no male friends. He isolated himself as much as possible at school. He drew pictures on his face with grease pens. Everyone's parents were leery of him.

He had gravitated to Sara and Jane, and at the time he lived a short walk away on Connetquot Road. He seemed particularly taken with Sara. He would often wait for the girls to come out to play, "lurking," Jane said, in the woods along Sportsman Street.

"And he went to the stream with you?" I asked.

"Yes, all the time."

"Ever pick blueberries with you?"

"Sure. Lots. He always wanted to go upstream, always wanted to pick blueberries. I think he was happiest then, not so morose and withdrawn."

"Did the relationship continue into your teen years?" Mike asked.

She shook her head. "No. I moved away at thirteen, and I think he did too. Brentwood, I think his family moved to. I'm not sure when, sometime after I moved."

"You say Sara mentioned him when you reconnected years later and then more recently. In what context?" I asked.

And she told us. Richie Field had, for lack of a better term, been semi-stalking Sara in the not so distant past. Sending her letters when she first went off to college, telling her he loved her, they were meant to be together. At first it amused Sara, but then it annoyed her, and she had told him off. It seemed to end sometime around her junior year in college, almost two years ago.

The day after she graduated earlier this spring, Sara found a bag of blueberries on the hood of her car. There was no note. She told Jane she had a feeling Richie had left it.

"Did Sara tell her parents anything about him? Her sister or boyfriend? Anyone?" Mike asked.

"Not that I know of. She told me because, well, I knew how weird he was. We laughed about it."

I looked down to my notepad and wrote, "Field, Richie. Possibly Brentwood." I raised my gaze to Jane and watched as she read my eyes.

"Maybe," she said tentatively, her own eyes welling with tears once again, "maybe it . . . it wasn't something to laugh about, after all."

Late Saturday afternoon, we sat at our desks in the detective squad room at the Suffolk County PD 3rd Precinct. The desks were pushed together, front to front, Mike and I facing each other across their combined expanse.

I looked up from the printout the administrative aide had handed me moments earlier.

"Field, Richard, DOB May tenth, nineteen fifty-seven. Just turned twenty-two."

"And I wish him a happy friggin' birthday," Mike said. "Priors?"

"Textbook weirdo, partner, textbook. Two falls for cruelty to animals. Three for vandalism, one possession of a controlled substance, and, for his specialty, five separate harassment falls."

Mike shook his head. "And yet, he walks freely among us . . . great country, ain't it?"

My phone rang. Caller ID, a recent upgrade to PD phones, told me the call was from the forensic lab.

I picked it up, identified myself, hit the speaker feature so Mike could hear. The lab tech filled us in. It was good. Cross-contaminate transfer fibers were found on victim's upper garments, foreign hairs consistent with cat fur as well, additional testing pending. I thanked her and broke the call.

I stood up and slipped into my sports jacket. "Let's go, partner," I said. "We've got a miscreant to meet."

Mike stood. "Haven't done that in—what? Three days? Always a pleasant way to pass an evening."

If not for the car parked in the driveway and the red flag up on the mailbox, we'd have thought the house abandoned. Brentwood, I knew, was outpacing the surrounding Long Island communities in rate of deterioration. The Field house seemed a poster home for that sad fact.

The car was a sixty-eight Pontiac Tempest, battered and worn from ten or eleven years of Long Island salt air, dampness, and harsh winters. The windows were all rolled down; the green pine-tree air freshener hanging from the rearview mirror was faded and dried, looked brittle, and it stirred in the slight cross breeze passing through the car's interior.

Without verbal communication, something that seemed to grow less and less necessary as our time together as partners progressed, Mike and I walked to the Pontiac. We looked in. About what we expected to see: torn seats, ashtray brimming with twisted, darkened cigaret butts, fast-food wrappers strewn about.

But the odor. Mike and I faced each other. Again, wordlessly, we both knew we were where we needed to be.

Bleach. Faint, but distinct. It explained the open car windows. Silently, we moved as one to the trunk. Mike bent to the trunk deck seam and sniffed.

"Much stronger here, Joe. It's leaching into the passenger compartment, but it originates here."

I nodded. So Sara's body had been carted off to the blueberry patch in the trunk of this forlorn relic of an automobile. And then the trunk had been cleaned, bleach used by an amateur fool who mistakenly believed it would eliminate all traces of her blood.

It wouldn't.

"If Field is our guy, we can slam-dunk him. Blood, fibers, pet hair; his ass is toast."

I undid the button on my jacket, touched my Smith and Wesson lightly, illogically confirming its presence beyond any need to do so.

Our office investigation had told us there were two people living in this house: Field and his mother. No gun was registered to either. But an illegal, unregistered handgun on Long Island was about as rare as snow at an Eskimo wedding. My stomach knotted a bit.

"Let's see if he's here," I said.

The woman who answered our knock was hard to put an age to: as the mother of a twenty-two-year-old, it could range from thirties to above. She looked above. Way above. Her hair, stringy and dirty, hung in uneven strands around her face. She initially reeked of stale cigarette smoke, her skin and teeth yellowed and battered. She wore an AC/DC rock band T-shirt. Despite its deep black color, yellowish stains were visible at the armpits. The cigarette odor soon became the preferred stench of the woman.

She appeared neither surprised nor concerned at our appearance at her door. She merely glanced at my badge and ID card as I flashed them at her. She wasn't interested.

"You looking for Richie," she said. It wasn't a question.

"Yeah, we are. He here?"

She turned and walked deeper into the house, the door left open behind her.

"Yeah. He is. Upstairs."

"Get him down here," Mike said, and we entered the house.

She turned toward the stairs. "Hey, Richie," she shouted. "You got company."

After a moment, a low gravelly voice called, "Who?" from atop the stairs somewhere.

"You figure it out, asshole," she said. "Who is it always?"

Richie Field was tall and thin, but beneath his black shirt, sinewy muscles were apparent. He had dyed black hair in a tall, gelled Mohawk cut, his eyelids blackened with some sort of grease. Below each eye, centered on his upper cheeks, a black teardrop tattoo stood in contrast to his pasty-white complexion.

We got ourselves situated on the dank, moldy-smelling uphol- stered chairs in what passed for the living room.

Richie looked bored. Mike looked stone-faced. I felt my own face tightening. I hated this kid. Whether he had killed Sara Wills or not, I hated him.

It wasn't healthy. It wasn't logical. But there it was.

I decided to forego all preliminaries. The kid's mother had left the room, was out on the porch smoking, headphones on her ears, probably some dark rock blaring into her brain. I could say or do anything I wanted; the kid was the only witness. Mike and I could later write any script necessary. So—no preliminaries.

"Where were you Thursday afternoon, evening, and night, Richie?" I asked.

"I dunno," he said, voice and eyes flat, dead. He appeared indif- ferent. I hated him a bit more.

"Why? Why don't you know?"

He shrugged. "I dunno."

Mike stirred beside me. "Go get your ID and keys, kid," he said. "You're taking a ride with us. We have a lot of questions for you."

I stood and crossed the room to a black telephone on the windowsill. I needed to call the precinct, get a radio car out here to safeguard the Pontiac Tempest and its probable incriminating trunk. Later, we would get a warrant to search the house for the murder weapon, check fibers in the car's interior and trunk, grab the cat I had seen slink behind a chest in the room's corner and get a fur sample.

Field stood up, turned, and headed toward the staircase. Mike and I knew what needed to be done: One of us had to go upstairs with him. His gun could be up there somewhere, and he could come down ready to shoot. We looked at each other. Once again, without words, we communicated. Mike moved to his right, I to my left, separating the targets. We weren't going upstairs. We slipped our revolvers out, held them flat against our outer thighs. Our eyes locked on the upper stair landing.

In a moment, he reappeared, standing at the top of the stairs, smiling down at us benignly. Around his neck and dangling down on both sides of his chest, a huge, colorful, thick, shiny snake curled and squirmed, its black tongue flickering outward from its red mouth.

In his right hand, down at his side, Field held a long-barreled revolver. I made it for a twenty-two target pistol. As did the snake, the weapon conveyed evil; as did the snake, it dangled from Field's body.

"Drop it!" I yelled, going into a two-handed combat crouch, my revolver thrust forward, centered on his chest. Mike did exactly the same, our shouted words morphing into one voice.

Field smiled more broadly. I applied pressure to the trigger, felt it move, held my breath, steadied for a shot.

The barrel of the twenty-two came rapidly up to his temple, immediately exploding in flame and smoke and sound. The left side of Field's head burst open violently, gray-red mist spraying against the near wall.

Unlike with Sara, this time the weapon had produced an exit wound.

A dramatic one.

It all came together over the next ten days. Trace blood recovered from the Pontiac was a type match to Sara Wills's. Fibers from the worn trunk carpeting and cat hairs from an old blanket therein matched those found on her clothing. The ballistics came in confirming the gun Field killed himself with had also killed Sara. Mrs. Field, still with an air of distanced uninterest, told us that on the Thursday Sara was killed, her son had left home in his Pontiac at about three in the afternoon, not returning home until well after midnight. She hadn't asked him where he'd been, and he hadn't said.

Mike and I spent a rainy afternoon at our desks polishing the case file, then forwarded it to the Suffolk County District Attorney's office. Just two days later, they faxed us their findings. "Case closed, abated by death."

With a dead suspect unable to defend himself in court, there would never be an official proclamation of Field's guilt.

So, there is was. Case, indeed, closed. Sometimes, it was that easy.

Mabel Taylor, owner-operator of the Green Lantern, as her father and grandfather before her had been, served us personally, a show of her respect for my granddad. She placed the huge prime ribs and baked potatoes, garden fresh salads, and cold drafts of Pabst down onto the red-and-white checkered linen tablecloth. The blue-and-white patterned china plates and bowls were thick and heavy, the cutlery bone handled.

"Enjoy, fellas," she said, then winked at my grandfather, tucked her tray under an arm, and moved off to visit with diners, tend the bar, check on the kitchen.

I filled Granddad in on the final facts and minutiae of the Wills homicide. He listened attentively as he ate. His hands, weathered, liver-spotted, callused from farm work, had somehow remained graceful and deft in their handling of the heavy, antique cutlery. I envied him.

When my narrative ended, he put his utensils down, dabbed his lips with the cloth napkin, sipped some beer. Then he locked onto my eyes.

"I've got a question to ask you, Jo-Jo. One I'm guessing no one else has posed." Granddad paused, considering his word choice before continuing. "Maybe because no one wants to hear the answer."

"Go ahead, Granddad. Ask."

He nodded. "Okay. You had a murder suspect you were about to take in for questioning. You had a reason to suspect he had access to a loaded firearm. Yet—you both figured it was okay to let him go upstairs alone for his wallet and house keys." He paused again, concern creeping into his eyes. "I know you fellas aren't that careless."

I hesitated. Why had Mike and I really done that? We had certainly done it jointly, communicating something silently, moving away from each other to dissever the target, then pulling our guns and waiting.

"Maybe we are, Granddad. Maybe we are that careless," I lied.

He held my eyes for a very long five seconds before speaking.

"Okay, Jo-Jo. We'll go with that. But—maybe you and your partner need to discuss it sometime soon. Going forward, I mean. You need to discuss it."

We went back to our meals. The prime rib, just moments before warm and juicy and flavorful, red and comforting and fine, went tasteless in my mouth. I sipped beer. It was suddenly pale and lifeless in its pilsner glass, flat and bland on my taste buds. I put my cutlery down. The mournful whistle of a freight train running on tracks forty yards behind the Green Lantern touched my ears.

"How'd you do it, Granddad?" I asked softly.

He looked up from his meal, eyes warm with affection, brows raised.

"Do what?"

"Stay who you were. Who you are. Thirty years policing this town. How did you stay who you were?"

He thought a moment, then sighed. "Different times. Different world. Central Islin had only one murder in all those years, not a single rape. Biggest common crimes were deer and fowl poaching, fishing out of season. Some occasional bad things, sure—domestic violence, drunks beating in each other's brains—" He nodded around the room. "—some right here in this place. But it was all in all a good experience. I helped a lot more folks than I locked up." His expression went wistful. "Hell, I saw more evil in the three or four years working those private investigations after I retired than I did in thirty years' policing. It's why I quit it; maybe

I feared I might just lose myself. Maybe that was why I dropped it, concentrated on working the farm with Grandma."

After a few moments passed, I spoke. I found myself avoiding his eyes.

"I hated him," I said softly. "Richie Field. Hated him from the very second my eyes fell on him. Hated him."

"Did you," Granddad said.

"And now I feel guilty about it. The hatred. It was personal, outside my sphere as a lawman. It had no place in that sphere, so I made it personal. That . . . that was a failure."

He sighed, then leaned closer to me against his end of the table.

"Son, I'm no philosopher, just a simple country man, a farmer at heart. But—here's the thing. This new world of ours, it seems to function without a concrete 'good' or 'evil,' without a firm 'right' or 'wrong.' Changing circumstances seem to dictate those concepts, but what *governs* the circumstances? Do *we* govern them, or does our environment? And who or what governs our environment? Hell, what came first, the chicken or the egg? I guess I just don't know. But— here's what I do know. A man has to be true to himself, true to who he really is, good or bad. A man needs to step away from the world, especially a man who's a cop, and instead step into his own soul. Behave accordingly, and, for better or worse, there won't be any guilt. If you're true to who you are, whether good, bad, or indifferent, there'll be no guilt. Good men suffer no guilt. Nor do evil men. Only men who act contrary to their true nature suffer guilt."

He turned back to his meal, secure in who he was. I determined to emulate that. Or burn out trying to. A few minutes passed in silence; then I spoke.

"I pushed Jane Rossi to expand on that stream theme. Chased it down. Without your input on the significance it held, I'm pretty sure I'd have steered her away from reminiscence of childhood bright spots picking blueberries. I'd have missed it. Maybe never gotten Richie Field's name.

"You solved another one, Granddad. That's who *you* are."

Later, I sat alone on the streambed where Sara Wills's body had been found. I gazed across the water, glittering and tranquil in the dying sunlight. I saw the blueberry bushes along the opposite shore. I turned my eyes west, to the yellow-orange sun as it hung in descent just above the distant treetops.

I knew the setting sun would rise again with the new day. But to me, the setting seemed infinitely more final and dismal than the rising would ever seem promising and hopeful.

And as I watched, I wondered who I truly was.

A few years ago, I wrote a series of EQMM *stories set in the fictitious Long Island farming hamlet of Central Islin. The tales featured folksy and keenly intelligent retired town constable Gus Oliver and took place in the late 1950s, with the closing story a prequel set in the 1930s. In the 1950s tales, Gus has a young grandson he affectionately calls Jo-Jo. When the series concluded, I bade a fond farewell to Central Islin.*

Shortly thereafter, I found myself wondering: whatever became of Gus and Jo-Jo, and how had the idyllic community of Central Islin fared in more modern times? Thus, "Sundown" was born, with Jo-Jo now grown up and working crimes in the late 1970s.

Although nominally fictitious, Central Islin is based upon an actual Long Island town, with many locales, street names, even some characterizations based upon my own childhood experiences within that once-pastoral, countrified actual location. For a kid growing up in Brooklyn, summer weekends in my own Central Islin were magical; I miss them still, and that melancholy tug of nostalgia surely played a role in triggering this most recent visit to the past.

But—memory and experiences, strongly tempered by stark realities, have always driven my fiction, whether novel length or short form, and the dreamy vehicle of remembrance becomes less pristine with an awareness of the darker pursuits of the human character. Detective Oliver experiences Central Islin in a manner far more unsettling than any quixotic childhood memories of my own.

A shame, really. But, hey—that's what our beloved crime fiction is: a good stiff dose of reality to keep us all firmly and defensively grounded.

Annie Reed *is the award-winning author of more short stories than she can count. A great many of them are mysteries, although she writes in a wide variety of genres. Her stories appear regularly in* Pulphouse Fiction Magazine *and* Mystery, Crime, and Mayhem. *This is her second appearance in a row in* The Mysterious Bookshop Presents the Best Mystery Stories, *with her story "Little City Blues" appearing in the 2022 volume. A multiple Derringer finalist, her short fiction has also been selected for inclusion in study materials for Japanese college entrance exams. She also writes novels, and her mysteries* Pretty Little Horses *and* A Death in Cumberland *are two of her best. She lives in Northern Nevada.*

THE PROMISE

Annie Reed

Russell turned up the collar of his overcoat against a stiff November wind blowing from the north. The overcast sky was threatening rain. It might turn to snow if the temperatures dropped low enough overnight, or settle on that mix of rain and snow that made walking an exercise in squelching through half-frozen slush seasoned with car exhaust and grit.

The text he'd received that morning from Malachi said to meet him at three on the corner of Hightower and Seventh Avenue. Russell might have blown off the meeting if he'd been awake when the text came in, or if the request had come from anybody else.

Russell was still on nights, one of three detectives—not counting his soon-to-be-retired partner Vic Damonte—who rotated in and out of the night shift. When they were on night duty, he hit the sheets every morning about the same time most of the city was heading to work. Three in the afternoon was right in the middle of breakfast.

Russell had grown used to the late hours. The precinct was usually pretty quiet at night, and it wasn't like he had anyone at home waiting for him.

But this was Malachi Rosen. He hadn't heard from Malachi in years.

Fourteen years ago, Malachi's only child had been found beaten to death and stuffed behind a pile of black plastic trash bags full of donated clothes at the base of a donation bin in the alley behind the Catholic church on Seventh Avenue.

Malachi wanted to meet across the street from that church. That wasn't a coincidence. With Malachi, nothing was ever a coincidence.

In the years since Russell had earned his gold shield, a handful of homicide cases had gone unsolved. Each of those murders haunted him, but Malachi's daughter Rachel had been the worst.

Russell had been young and stupid and his detective's shield had still been shiny bright when he and the first detective he'd been partnered with had caught the Rosen case. Russell had made a stupid mistake. Said the wrong thing, something he'd never say now, no matter how devastated a homicide victim's family was. No matter how much they begged.

He'd promised Rachel's parents that he'd catch her killer.

He'd promised Malachi and his wife that their daughter would get justice, but the police hadn't kept that promise.

Russell hadn't kept his promise.

Not for a lack of trying. He'd worked the case night and day. Took the file home with him. Haunted the murder site. Pestered the lab techs. Canvassed and recanvassed the neighborhood.

All of it came to nothing. He'd never even come up with a viable suspect.

And now Malachi wanted to meet with him.

Russell had let dispatch know he had a meeting with a witness. It was only a little white lie—Malachi wasn't a witness—but it wasn't the first lie Russell had told in all the years he'd been a detective, and it wouldn't be the last.

Besides, Malachi might actually have something worthwhile to tell him. And if he didn't? If he just wanted to stand in the cold November afternoon and talk?

Russell would oblige.

He owed the old man that much.

Back when he'd been married, back when his wife had been healthy and cancer wasn't a part of their lives, Russell had worked the occasional night shift. He'd come home in the morning to the smell of pot roast or oven-roasted chicken, and they'd sit at their small kitchen table and eat dinner while the sun came up over the city.

Those were the days when most people could afford to put beef on the table a few days a week, even on a beat cop's salary. After dinner, Russell would stumble off to bed and his wife would go to work at a department store, and when he got up in the middle of the afternoon, he'd make himself breakfast. Scrambled eggs and toast. And bacon if he didn't oversleep and his wife had put in extra hours at the store.

His wife had been gone for years now. When he got home after work, dinner was something he could throw in the microwave while he was in the shower. But he'd kept up the habit of cooking himself breakfast, the same breakfast he'd eaten day after day.

Vic told him all those eggs would kill him someday. Screw with his cholesterol. Vic had suffered a minor heart attack a couple years back. He hadn't turned into a health food nut after that—he snuck in a donut or a bagel with cream cheese every now and then—but he enjoyed spreading the misery of a low fat, low carb lifestyle. Russell was a favorite target.

Vic might be right, but breakfast was part of Russell's routine. A piece of his married life he could hang on to like the framed snapshots of his wife he kept in his bedroom. If he knew how to cook pot roast like his wife had cooked it, he'd probably make that for himself every now and then too. Cooking eggs in the same frying pan his wife had used made the apartment smell, at least a little bit, like it used to when she was still alive.

Made the empty place smell like home.

This afternoon Russell broke his routine so he could get out the door in time for his meeting with Malachi. He'd stopped at a fast-food joint that served breakfast 24/7. He'd picked up a large coffee and a breakfast burrito that looked halfway decent on the menu board but proved to be disappointing in person. He'd thrown most of it in a trash bin he passed as he walked the few blocks up Seventh Avenue from the parking garage where he'd left his car.

At least the coffee was good. There was enough still left in the cardboard go cup to warm his hands. On a day like today, that was a plus.

Only a handful of people were out on the street. Not surprising. The parking garage was attached to a busy medical center. A pedestrian walkway connected the second floor of the garage to the medical center. Great for patients and the doctors and nurses and other staff who parked in the garage, especially on cold November days, but hell on local businesses who depended on foot traffic.

The closer Russell got to Hightower, the more the neighborhood changed from healthcare providers to a mix of small, independent businesses housed in buildings that had been built fifty years before the turn of the century. A CPA occupied the ground floor of a three-story walkup next to a beauty salon. Small apartments took up the second and third stories. A small discount clothing store, its storefront already decorated for the holiday season, shared the ground floor of another three-story building with a liquor store, an Asian grocer, and a Greek deli.

Stunted oaks, their bare branches rattling in the wind, lined Seventh Avenue on both sides, standing sentry in their caged planters every ten feet or so.

The trees had been planted a decade earlier, a low-cost concession by the city to entice the medical center's investors to build in the neighborhood. Electrical outlets had been installed near the base of each tree. In another week or so city workers would be decorating the trees with hundreds of twinkle lights.

The medical center was supposed to be a boon for the neighborhood. That's how the city had sold the idea to the existing businesses. And for some it had been a boon. The liquor store stayed open 24/7 now, and the Greek deli had extended its hours. Russell doubted the beauty salon or the discount clothing store had done as well. Some of the older homes in the area had been converted to doctors' offices, and while the former residents of those homes might take a walk to get their hair done or pick up a new outfit, the doctors and staffs in those refurbished homes rarely did.

After a few years, the local merchants had had enough. If the medical center could get concessions from the city, they figured they could too. They fought for any sort of improvements that would draw people into their stores.

The city planners took a look at the neighborhood and figured they were sitting on a gold mine. The older buildings brought in tax dollars, but newer buildings, taller buildings, modern commercial buildings, could bring in so much more.

So began the renovation of the neighborhood. Some of the oldest and most outdated buildings were torn down, to be replaced with shiny new multiuse, multistory complexes. The fact that those demolitions would displace residents and current businesses was just the cost of progress. The building that used to house a collectibles store and a new-and-used bookstore was gone now. In its place, a new high rise condominium was taking shape behind a boarded-up section of sidewalk.

Russell wondered how many more of the buildings housing current businesses and residences would be gone in the next couple years. If the current residents had wished they'd kept their mouths shut instead of pestering the politicians to improve their neighborhood. The new buildings would attract people, that was certain, but would any of the old merchants still be here?

As far as Russell was concerned, the whole mess was a prime example of "be careful what you wish for."

As he got closer to the intersection at Hightower, he realized why Malachi wanted to meet him in this particular place. Telltale orange cones and construction signs blocked part of the street in front of the church.

Or what was left of the church.

A bulldozer was busy tearing down the old brick-front Catholic church and the multipurpose hall attached to it. All that was left of the church was a portion of the front wall and the concrete steps leading up from the sidewalk to the entryway. A brick alcove facing Seventh Avenue was still standing, almost like it was protecting the statue of the Virgin Mary still standing inside. The multipurpose hall had been reduced to a pile of rubble.

Malachi was standing on the sidewalk on the other side of Seventh Avenue, almost directly across the street from that statue, his back toward Russell. The old man had on a brown fedora, a tan overcoat, and a black scarf wrapped around his neck.

Russell didn't call out a greeting. Between the sound of the ongoing demolition and city traffic, the old man would never hear him.

"I'd offer you some coffee," Russell said in lieu of hello when he reached Malachi, "but if I remember right, you don't drink the stuff."

Malachi grunted. "Never picked up the habit."

He didn't turn to look at Russell.

"Probably better off." Russell hunched his shoulders against the cold and nodded at the half-demolished building. "Didn't realize they were tearing this place down."

If the case had still been active, he would have known. Maybe he should have known anyway, should have paid attention to the renovations going on in the neighborhood in more than just the casual way someone does who reads the local news online over breakfast. But who would have thought the church would be among the buildings scheduled to be replaced?

"The developer offered the diocese a bucketload of money," Malachi said.

He turned his head to give Russell a sideways glance. Russell was shocked to see how old—how really *old*—Malachi looked. His chin and cheeks sported sparse white stubble, and the skin beneath looked sallow. The blue of his eyes behind wire-rim glasses had faded, the whites more ivory than white and shot through with tiny red veins.

He didn't just look old. He looked sick.

"They even kicked in some land for the diocese to build a new church complex," Malachi said. "Or so I heard."

That sideways glance held Russell's for a long moment before Malachi turned back to look at the destruction going on across the street.

The glance said *Why don't you know all this? Why did I have to tell you?*

The glance said, *You'd have known if you were still looking for the bastard who killed my Rachel.*

The glance said, *You broke your promise.*

Or maybe that was just Russell's guilt talking. You'd think after all this time, the guilt would have faded away.

But time, that old sonofabitch, had only made it worse.

A city bus swept past them, fouling the air with the diesel smoke left in its wake. Some of the buses in the city had been refitted to burn cleaner fuel, or at least the kind you couldn't see polluting the air. This wasn't one of them.

Russell took a sip of his coffee and grimaced. It was getting cold, and the cold made it taste bitter. He thought about throwing what was left in the trash receptacle halfway up the block, but he didn't want to walk away from Malachi and the old man didn't look like he intended to move from his spot anytime soon.

"Maryann used to keep in touch with some of the women in the church group," Malachi said. "Those old birds love gossip more than they love Jesus. I think that's one of the reasons she didn't . . ."

He shrugged but didn't finish the sentence. He didn't need to. Russell caught his meaning.

Maryann was Malachi's wife. She was also a devout Catholic who'd been a member of the congregation of the church currently being reduced to rubble. Her daughter's murder hadn't been enough to make her question her faith or her devotion to this particular parish.

"She doesn't talk to them anymore?"

"She passed away in April," Malachi said. "Cancer."

Seven months ago. Russell hadn't known that either. From the looks of her husband, Maryann might not have been the only one touched by cancer.

"I'm sorry to hear that," Russell said.

Malachi shrugged again. "It was quick. A mercy, the priest said. She didn't suffer, he said. As if he knew what suffering was."

The words were bitter, but the old man's voice was eerily neutral, like he was discussing the weather with a stranger on the bus. It was probably Malachi's way of working up to whatever he wanted to say.

Fourteen years ago, Malachi had been much more direct. He'd called the precinct every day, always asking for Russell, never Russell's partner. Malachi's questions were always the same. *Any news? Any leads?* So was Russell's answer. *We're working on it. We'll let you know when we get something.*

But they never had.

The department didn't have the money for all the high-tech stuff everyone saw on TV, even back then. Resources had to be budgeted. If it had been more than one little girl, Russell and his partner might have been able to convince the department to do the kind of analysis the general public assumed was done on every case. Samples had been collected, of course. Hair and fiber and other trace evidence. Photographs taken. All kept on file for comparison to whoever they hauled in for questioning.

There'd been no blood splatter at the scene. Malachi's daughter had been killed elsewhere and transported to church property. That meant something important to her killer. What, they'd never figured out.

Russell's partner at the time had had his theories. The little girl hadn't been sexually assaulted and there was no semen mixed in with the blood on her or her clothes, so the killer wasn't a garden variety pedophile. She'd been beaten with a blunt object, something like a baseball bat, but it had to be an aluminum bat since there'd been no wood fibers in the wounds. She hadn't been strangled. She was still wearing the clothes she'd left home with that morning before she went to school.

The first blow to the back of her head had caved her skull in and killed her outright. A blessing considering that her killer had kept hitting her until the bones in her arms and legs and most of her ribs had been broken. The autopsy had confirmed those blows had been postmortem.

Whoever had killed her had been angry. Furious. A beating like that came from rage.

There'd been no usable fingerprints found on her body or her backpack, which had been left next to the body. The alley behind the church was paved, and no useful tire tracks had been noted on the asphalt. No one in the neighborhood had seen anyone driving into or leaving the alley.

They'd investigated Malachi's family as a matter of course. He'd told the police he had no enemies, a sentiment shared by the people who knew him. Rachel had the normal amount of run-ins with the popular girls at school. Mean girls, they'd been known back in Russell's public school days, and some of them had been more than simply mean. But that avenue of the investigation led nowhere.

They'd widened the investigation to include anyone who'd threatened the church. The priest. The nuns or any of the catechism teachers. Russell's partner thought Rachel might have been a convenient substitute for whoever the killer really wanted to murder. A lot of people back then had been angry at priests, all Catholic priests, but the pastor at this church seemed universally well liked.

The more people they looked at, the more nothing they turned up.

All they had was Rachel's body and her backpack. With no leads, eventually the case had been back-burnered. Russell abhorred that part of police work, but all he could do about it was to continue working the case on his time off.

"She was only twelve," Malachi said now. "Twelve. She'd be twenty-six. Today." He sniffed but his cheeks were dry. "It's her birthday."

Russell didn't know what to say to that, so he kept his mouth shut. He hadn't realized that today was Rachel's birthday. He'd committed so many facts about her murder to memory, but her birthday hadn't been one of them.

Fair-haired Rachel had been the Rosens' late-in-life child. They had no other children and had given up trying years before. When they found they were going to have a baby, they'd called her a gift from God.

Malachi was Jewish, but his wife had insisted that their child be raised in her religion. It was a big thing for Catholics that any children be raised in the faith. Russell's own mother had done the same thing, raising him Catholic. Malachi loved his wife more than his own faith, and so Rachel had been baptized in the church that was now little more than rubble and memories.

A month into the investigation, when it must have become clear to the Rosens that the police might not ever find Rachel's killer, Maryann Rosen had brought an old-fashioned picture album full of photographs of Rachel to the precinct. Pictures of baby Rachel taking her first steps. Staring in wonder at her first Christmas tree. Chasing after the Rosens' dog in their backyard. Rachel in her frilly white first communion dress, her proud parents standing behind her.

Russell never asked if Malachi had witnessed his daughter's first communion. Malachi had told him once that he wasn't a practicing Jew, but he never mentioned if he went to Mass with his wife.

"I keep God in my own way," he'd said once. "For a Jew who fell in love with a Catholic woman, I always believed God would understand."

Russell hadn't given the remark much thought at the time. Russell kept God in his own way too. His own mother had been devout, and he'd kept going to Mass as an adult more out of habit than anything else. That stopped after his wife died and Russell found he no longer had the stomach for the religious rituals his mother had put so much faith in.

Now, though? As he stood next to the man who looked like age had finally caught up with him, Russell wondered if Malachi had ever lost his faith in God after his daughter's murder. Or if he'd lost his faith when the police hadn't been able to find her killer, much less bring him to justice.

The last and best theory Russell and his partner had was that whoever had killed Rachel must have spotted her leaving her catechism class the afternoon she'd been murdered. Classes were held in the church's multipurpose building, and witnesses—including the nun who'd taught the class—said Rachel had left on time for the walk home.

Somewhere in the mile between the church and the Rosens' home, Rachel's killer had snatched her off the street.

A crime of opportunity.

And a killer they'd never caught.

Rachel Rosen's murder had been the first homicide Russell had worked, long before he'd been partnered with Vic Damonte. His partner at the time had been a veteran detective who put up with exactly zero bullshit from a cop still learning the difference between being a beat cop and a detective.

Russell had been gungho and full of himself. He'd gone with his partner to do the notification to family. He'd watched Maryann Rosen collapse in the doorway of their home. Seen the blood drain from Malachi's face as the finality of what Russell's partner told them sank in.

Their daughter was dead.

Up until then, she'd simply been late getting home from catechism. The Rosens had called all her friends, all her friends' friends. All the catechism teachers and the women in Maryann's church group. Their friends had combed the neighborhood, gone to the stores where the kids sometimes hung out after school, went to stores where none of the kids hung out, all looking for Rachel while her parents waited anxiously at home.

Rachel's name was on the backpack found next to her body. On the school books inside her backpack. On her catechism books. The pastor at the church had given the police her address, and Russell and his partner had gone to the Rosens' home to notify her parents.

It had been Russell's first notification visit, and he'd made a serious mistake. He'd promised the Rosens that he'd catch their daughter's killer.

It was the first and last time he'd ever made a promise like that.

His partner had gone ballistic.

"You don't make a fucking promise you can't keep," he'd said. "You're not doing the family any favors. It'll eat you up inside, and they'll come to hate you for breaking your promise."

Russell had taken the rebuke as a personal insult. "How do you know we won't find the guy?"

He'd thought about saying that *he'd* find the guy. At least he'd been smart enough to keep that thought to himself.

"Because, smart guy," his partner had said, "unless the killer's as dumb as a doornail or makes a mistake somewhere down the line, or somebody has a beef with him and gives him up, it's fifty-fifty if we catch him or not."

His partner had gone on to cite manpower, caseload, the city's transient and homeless population, all the whack jobs on the street thanks to cutbacks in mental health services.

"We got too much on our plate as is," he'd said. "This case'll catch some media attention because it's a kid, so we might get a few extra days to work it, but then somebody's gonna shoot somebody else or a lot of somebody elses, and we'll have to back-burner this one."

Which was exactly what happened.

The case kept getting back-burnered again and again. Russell took the case file home, poured over the details while his wife was at work, followed up leads and reinterviewed witnesses as time allowed, but the case kept getting colder and colder.

When Malachi texted Russell that morning and asked for the meeting, Russell realized he hadn't looked at the file in years.

He felt guilty about that too.

"My liver's failing," Malachi said.

Across the street, the alcove holding the Virgin Mary's statue was reduced to a pile of bricks under a fresh assault from a bulldozer with a bucket bigger than Russell's car. The statue remained standing.

"I caught your expression when you looked at me," Malachi continued. "That look of shock you tried to cover up. I get that from people who haven't seen me in a while. 'You got old.' I hear that one a lot." He gave Russell a sideways glance again. "You shouldn't play poker with that face."

Russell shouldn't have been surprised. One look at Malachi's face had told him something was wrong, but Russell still felt a pang of sadness he hadn't expected.

He debated taking another sip of coffee, decided against it. "I'll keep that in mind," he said. "You getting treated for that?"

Malachi shrugged. "They tell me I need a new liver. I tell them give it to someone's got a life in front of them. Me? I think I've been around long enough."

Russell didn't know much about liver failure. He seemed to recall liver failure and alcoholism went hand in hand, but Malachi'd never struck him as someone who drank to excess. He certainly didn't look drunk now.

"That why you set up this meeting?" Russell asked. "You wanted to tell me you don't have much time left?"

Not much time for Russell to keep his promise before it was forever too late.

"Nope."

Across the street, the statue of the Virgin Mary joined the pile of brick rubble. Russell wondered why the church hadn't removed the statue, preserved it somehow. His mother would have been scandalized.

"I'm here to let you off the hook," Malachi said. "I took care of it for you."

He said that last part so quietly that Russell almost missed what he said thanks to the strident backup beeps from the bulldozer and a reverberating bass beat from a passing car on Seventh Avenue.

When the words sunk in, Russell turned to look Malachi full in the face. This time Russell didn't try to hide his shock.

"What do you mean, 'took care of it'?" he asked.

Another city bus went by, belching diesel smoke. The side of the bus was plastered with one of those wraparound ads for a chain store in the new mall south of town.

"A little over a year ago, I started getting these notes on my car," Malachi said. "Under the windshield wipers. Mostly bible verses. Didn't think much of it at the time." He shrugged. "Lots of crazies in the world today, but I don't have to tell you that."

A small ball of tension was settling in Russell's belly that had nothing to do with the few bites of the burrito he'd had for breakfast or the cold coffee he still held in one hand.

"Then Maryann got sick and the notes stopped for a while. To tell the truth, I didn't even notice."

Malachi shoved his hands into the pockets of his overcoat. His eyes had taken on a faraway look, like he was living in his memories, not standing on a city street across from where they'd found his daughter's body.

"They started again after she died," Malachi said. "Did I tell you she wanted a funeral Mass? I hadn't set foot in church since the day you came to tell me our Rachel was gone, but I honored her wishes. She got her funeral Mass." He nodded across the street. "In that church. It was a nice service. They got a new priest. He made an effort." Malachi's shoulders hunched as he took a deep breath. "I got the first threat the next day."

"You report this?" Russell asked. If Malachi had, no one had ever told him.

Malachi shot him a look. "So you could do what? Fill out another report that goes nowhere?"

There was a great deal of anger now in the old man's faded eyes. Russell had earned that anger, so he kept his mouth shut.

Traffic was getting heavier as the day wound down to rush hour. Russell stepped closer to Malachi so he wouldn't miss anything the old man said.

"I started writing back," Malachi said. "What else did I have to keep myself busy? I hear people do this on the internet, argue with the crazies. This was like that in real life. I left little notes under my own windshield wipers before I went to bed. They were always gone in the morning."

Russell couldn't keep quiet any more. "Do you have any idea how dangerous that is? This whack job knows where you live."

The world was full of fanatics who believed the world would be better off without whatever group was the current target of their hate. Jews had always been high on that list.

Malachi shrugged. "The world has always been a dangerous place. I shouldn't have to tell you that."

He pulled a piece of paper out of his pocket and held it out to Russell.

Russell reached out to take it, but Malachi held on for a moment too long, and Russell thought the old man had changed his mind.

"Don't forget us," he said, and he let go of the note.

Then he stepped off the curb and into traffic.

Russell grabbed for him but managed only to brush Malachi's overcoat with this fingers.

The first two cars swerved and missed the old man.

The city bus didn't.

They found a body right where Malachi's note said it would be.

Buried in a shallow grave in an empty lot east of town. Not the empty lot the developer had purchased as the site for the new church facility—even Malachi in his pain and his rage wouldn't have been that sacrilegious—but the site of a housing development that had gone bankrupt before the model homes were even built.

Malachi hadn't known the man's name, or if he had, he didn't include it in the note. The only thing in the shallow grave besides the body was a handgun, a little .22 pistol. Malachi's prints were on the gun as well as the bullets.

The coroner estimated that the man had been dead for at least four months. Cause of death was a single gunshot wound to the back of his head, almost in the same place where Rachel's killer had struck her with a baseball bat. The little .22 pistol had done its job.

The coroner also found marks on the body that indicated the man had been hit with a taser. The dead man was decades younger than Malachi. The taser charge explained how Malachi was able to subdue him.

The dead man's hair matched hair taken from Rachel's body. It tied him to Rachel, but would it have been enough to convict him in a court of law? Probably not, but it had been enough for Malachi. Maybe the man had even bragged about it. Russell wouldn't have put it past him. His prints were on file from when he'd been arrested at a protest outside a Jewish synagogue that had turned violent. He was forty-one years old, which meant he'd been twenty-seven when Rachel had been murdered.

Had he snatched Rachel deliberately because she'd been the child of a Jewish father? Or had the murder been a crime of opportunity, as Russell's partner at the time had believed?

They'd never know. If the man had told Malachi before he'd died, that information had died along with Malachi the day the old man stepped into the middle of rush-hour traffic.

Vic Damonte refused to have anything to do with wrapping up the case. "We got enough on our plate," he told Russell. "This is your albatross, you deal with it."

That was fine with Russell.

He filed reports as they came in, crossed all the *T*s and dotted the *I*s, and when he was done, he was finally able to cross Rachel's murder off the unsolved list.

Had justice finally been done?

He didn't know. Three more people were dead—Malachi and his wife, and a racist who'd believed Jewish people were less than human. A man who harbored hatred in his heart even as he hit his knees in church every Sunday and professed his love of God in the same church where Malachi had held the funeral for his wife.

The last piece of evidence that Russell put in Rachel's case file was the note that Malachi had given him. The note that explained what he did and where the police could find the body. It was part of the evidence of the case, not that anyone would ever open this file again. The case was over, at least officially.

Unofficially?

Russell's old partner had been right. This case would haunt him for the rest of his life. Not only because he'd made a promise he couldn't keep. A promise to a dead child and her grieving family that her killer would be brought to justice.

No, what would really haunt Russell was the look in Malachi's eyes right before he stepped off the curb. A look of such profound sadness that it made Russell's jaded heart break.

Especially when he read the last line Malachi had written on the piece of paper he'd handed to Russell.

I made a promise to her too.

---

*One of the inevitable side effects of living in the same area for most of my life is the loss of places that once held meaning as the old is torn down to make way

for the new. You'd think churches would be immune to that—but not so much. The old-fashioned church with its old-fashioned steeple where I went as a child with my father houses a bank these days.

One afternoon as I was driving home, I was surprised to see that another church, a place where I dressed as a ghoul one Halloween to scare a bunch of kids as part of a haunted house in the church's rec hall, had been reduced to a pile of rubble. It made me wonder how many memories—good like mine (the kids had a good time and so did I) or bad—might have been walled up inside. Memories that, thanks to a bulldozer, would see the light of day one last time. Thinking about that was the initial spark for "The Promise," the third story I've written so far featuring Detective Russell.

Anna Round *is a British/Irish writer based in Newcastle in the Northeast of England. Her fiction has appeared in* The Briar Cliff Review, *the* Fish Anthology, *the* Hammond House Anthology, *and elsewhere. She is a former winner of the Sid Chaplin Short Story Competition, and is working on a novel.*

GLASS

Anna Round

GLASS

The broken bottle is not Eddie's fault.

He thinks about saying so but Marissa isn't inclined to listen and anyway he would be addressing her bum as she bends forward to collect the glass. He regards the outline of her substantial pants under a clinging skirt that drops to her ankles, the hem gray where it skims the pavement. Shards and slivers have sprinkled all over the road. Marissa casts from side to side with her dustpan and brush after the rainbow spikes, muttering about danger to cyclists, children, dogs. She hates dogs.

"I'd've cleared it up," says Eddie, although he probably wouldn't.

"Hunh." She pivots and addresses the curb. "I leave it to you, we be findin' bits from now till Christmas. Move your boot!"

He retreats to the top step as Marissa whisks away the last pieces and straightens her spine, groaning. Her knees are bad and her bunions give her trouble, but her back is the worst. An old woman's ailments, but her face is unlined and her eyes are girlish sometimes, and in fact she is only thirty-nine while Eddie himself is knocking on sixty's door. He is tall and thin with a beaky nose and a graying ponytail that almost reaches his belt now. He can't be bothered to get it cut. Leaning against the front door, he lights a cigarette.

"Them things'll kill you," says Marissa.

"I know. Want one?"

She shakes her head. Often she says yes and they stand out here or go up to sit on the fire escape. She isn't allowed to smoke at home, although her neighbors mostly ignore the rule. Marissa lives in the ground-floor flat, which Ademoglu bought back in the nineties; he stripped out the fireplaces and plaster ceiling roses, flung up flimsy partitions, and let it out by the room. Tenants get a single bed and a skinny wardrobe and survival of the fittest in the kitchen and bathroom. Now he owns the whole first floor and half of the second. He's made a few offers for Eddie's attic, but he won't get his hands on that until Eddie leaves feetfirst.

Marissa wriggles her toes. Her feet are calloused in her wooden sandals, but she paints her toenails. Today they are bright plum purple and there's a tiny silver ring on her fourth toe. She hands Eddie the dustpan to take down to the bin, where the fragments land with a satisfying crash.

"Thanks for that," he says. "You working tonight?"

"Always working."

"Yeah, me too. I'm late."

"Always late. What today?"

"Bar in Stoke Newington. Journo I know's interviewing a hot young filmmaker. Or an actor, maybe? Hot young something, anyway."

"Hot, huh? Boy or girl?"

"Boy. I think."

"You think?"

"Ashley. Could be either or neither. What d'you reckon?"

Marissa shrugs and wipes her hands on her skirt. "I got no time for guessing games after pickin' up after God knows who. You get off now or you get fired."

"They won't fire me," says Eddie. He knows he's safe. He's not like Marissa, who gets fired fairly regularly although she's never late and picks up conscientiously after all and sundry.

He doesn't know if Marissa is legal. Some of the people downstairs aren't and he suspects she might not be, although one of her jobs is fairly legit. He doesn't ask. As far as he knows she has no family in England, nor anywhere else come to that. Once she talked about her brother, but when he hazarded an innocent question she clammed up and didn't accept a cigarette for a month. Her hours are too long for much of a social life. He isn't even sure that her name is Marissa. He didn't hear properly when she first told him, but if it's not, she's never put him right.

He came home drunk, four years ago, at midnight on a Saturday just after she moved in. Fumbling for his keys he dropped a bottle on the step and Marissa, returning from work, told him to pick up the pieces. They stood in the warm night, smelling spilled beer. Marissa watched him gather the smashed glass, then went back indoors.

A couple days later she was buying tomatoes and rice in the corner shop when he nipped in for cigarettes. Without knowing why he asked if she wanted to get a coffee and to his surprise she said yes. Afterward she said it was because he'd done as she asked him; she hadn't thought he would. They went to the smeary café and had espresso, and cheese sandwiches, and Marissa told him about her flat and about Ademoglu, whom she'd met twice (once to give him some of the deposit and get a key, once when he kicked out the guy in the next bedroom, with some helpers she didn't like the look of).

Since then they've been friends. She has never entered Eddie's flat nor invited him into her room. Instead they sit on the landing, the fire escape, the front steps, and talk. They talk about politics, music (she listens to the radio all the time but has no TV), London, the house, the neighbors, her work and his, and nothing very much. Sometimes a week passes, or longer, and they don't see each other. Eddie travels a lot and Marissa spends most of her time cleaning: offices, houses, a hospital cafeteria.

Eddie is the oldest inhabitant in the house, although he doesn't feel old. He's been there thirty years and he's seen them come and go. He remembers when the flat downstairs belonged to an ancient professor, who yellowed slowly behind his big beard and his thousands upon thousands of books. He died in the library, which must have been much like home, and his students came and packed up all the volumes and took them off to his college.

Then there was a hippy couple, with their friends and their babies. Smells of cannabis and shit wafted through their front door and up the stairwell. Then the flat was repossessed and Ademoglu bought it at an auction.

Eddie's always been on good terms with his neighbors, but Marissa is his first real friend in the house. One day, he knows, she will no longer be there.

Ashley, a boy, is better company than he expected and Eddie stays for a few drinks after he's taken the photographs. He still schleps around for jobs like this even though he makes more than enough from news gigs and commissions these days. He doesn't need the money. His flat's long since paid for, and since Heather remarried so is his divorce, but he likes to work. What else would he do?

Sauntering home around closing time, he breathes air heavy with spices and diesel. There's not much traffic, even around King's Cross. It's quiet all the way until he's nearly home and he realizes that he's walking toward a commotion; voices bubbling and agitated, engines running to stink up the summer night. Blue lights splinter over the asphalt, and when he turns the corner, an ambulance and two police cars are parked across the mouth of his street. Behind them, Ademoglu, rousted from somewhere, is dancing up and down on his fat little legs and shouting. His mouth moves like a cement mixer.

The street is full, everyone outside in pajamas and T-shirts and dressing gowns. Eddie recognizes the posh girls from two houses along and the Korean family from the basement. Marissa isn't there. He doesn't recognize anyone from her flat, but it's their front door that crackles with yellow police tape.

The camera is still around his neck. Before he knows what he's doing Eddie's looking through the viewfinder, taking pictures, catching people as they blink in the blue wash and the shock. His flash grabs wide eyes, pale brows, lips parted in question. The hallway gapes. He doesn't know what's happened, but he knows the fizz in the air that tells him something has. There's another photographer by the ambulance, a guy he sort of knows, and a woman with a notebook and a Dictaphone. *Bloody hell*, he thinks, *they got here quick.*

A cop runs over and plucks at his elbow. "No pictures. No pictures. I'm afraid I'm going to have to ask you to—"

"I live here." Eddie lets the camera go; it slaps against his leather jacket. "What's going on?"

"You live here, you say? What's your address, please?"

"Number seventeen. The attic flat."

"And were you at home this evening?"

"I've just finished work."

She arches an eyebrow, and Eddie shrugs. "What's happened, then?"

The cop demands identification. Eddie fishes out his driving licence and she checks her list, which he scans over her shoulder. The ground floor entry is sketchy and doesn't includes a Marissa, but "Edwin Green" is present and correct for upstairs. Reluctantly the cop scrawls a tick against his name and mutters that there has been an incident.

"What kind of incident?" Eddie asks, but her radio buzzes and she heads back to her car.

Eddie looks around for Mr. Youn, or his downstairs neighbor, but instead Ademoglu stomps over, waving his arms and scowling. "You see this?" he snorts. "They let this happen, then I can't get in my own property. What d'I pay my taxes for, man? Huh? For this shit, this crap? You and I, we own these places, we have rights! We'll tell 'em—"

"What happened?"

"One of them bum tenants of mine. He's dead. The fucker."

To Eddie's surprise the news shocks him. He has seen enough death, photographed it too, framed scenes of violence and destruction and chosen his favorites, peering at them in the chemical fug of his darkroom where the smell of blood fades in acrid developer, dark stains white and purified through the lens. He's used to turning horror into work. He thought he was hardened off, but now his hands shake and his head swims for a moment.

"Which one?" he asks, although he doesn't know any of the men by more than sight.

"Which one, which one, how do I know, I don't adopt them, I rent them a room. How do I know it's even his real name, how do I tell if they're lying to me when they rob me blind, they fuck off without paying me, they . . ."

Eddie suddenly wants to punch him in the face.

"Well, he isn't going to pay you now," he says shortly. Even in the dark he can see Ademoglu's face turn puce, but the cop returns before he can answer. They won't be allowed back in for a few more hours, perhaps until morning. Ademoglu lets out a squawk and launches into another tirade. Noone says how the man died.

He is looking for Marissa. He doesn't know this until he's halfway to Highbury, peering into convenience stores and cafés and down alleyways. She has mentioned a job near Islington Green, cleaning some building that closes up at eleven, but he can't remember where. A supermarket? A bar? No; one of those language schools over the shops, long banks of booths with computers and head-phones. She'd laughed about the students parroting their stilted sentences, the ones who stay late while she sweeps around their feet. He finds a couple places that might be the right one. At the first, he leans on the bell for five minutes but no one answers. The second is up a grimy stairway with two doors, neither locked. Eddie sticks his head around the door, where a woman is wiping at the headsets with a dirty cloth. She doesn't know a Marissa, she says. It's just her, nobody else.

On the way back down the Caledonian Road he keeps an eye on the all-night shops and burger bars. For a bit he follows the canal, remembering that she likes to walk there in good weather. A figure on a bench looks familiar from a distance, but it's not her; he doesn't know how he could have made the mistake. He remembers suddenly that she gave him a phone number, once; he saved it, and now he scrolls through his contacts and jabs at the screen. It rings and rings and rings.

The police car is still outside the house. Eddie doesn't bother trying to go home but checks into a cheap hotel for the night, takes a boiling shower, uses a tiny toothbrush from a plastic pack, drops asleep the second he lies down. He doesn't remember his dreams but they leave him shattered. Late the next morning he walks round to the house, shows his driving license again and rattles his keys at the two officers guarding the door. They let him in.

The entrance to the ground-floor flat is covered in plastic sheeting, and ghosts in white overalls drift on the other side. The house seems to be empty, apart from the police and Eddie himself. His steps echo, an unanswered question on the deserted landing. With relief, he slides his key into the attic door and falls inside where it's blissfully unchanged.

He puts on a CD, lies on the sofa, smokes, reads for a while.

The phone is ringing. Eddie's on his feet, grabbing the receiver, before he knows what he's doing and of course it's a wrong number. Marissa rarely makes calls—too expensive—but even she must count this an emergency. He showers and makes coffee, and thinks about working but he can't concentrate, disastrous in the darkroom. His phone is silent, dark, mocking, and he needs to get out.

On the doorstep, a cop asks where he is going.

"Does it matter?"

The man shrugs. "We'll have to take statements from all the residents, just as soon as forensics are done."

"Good luck with that."

"This is a serious situation, Mr. Green."

"Don't I know it," mutters Eddie.

He's wandering down Swinton Street when he spots a face through the misted window of a café. If he'd had to describe Marissa's neighbors he couldn't have done it but he knows the man behind the glass, a grubby copy of the *Mirror* in his hands and a black knit cap pulled low over his eyes.

When Eddie sits down opposite him, the man drops the paper and starts to stand up, but Eddie's hand is around his wrist. He pulls, but Eddie, to his own surprise, holds tight.

"What d'you want?" The words come out in a whispered shriek. "What d'you want from me? I done nothing wrong."

"I'm not here to make trouble. I just want to know if you've seen Marissa."

"Marissa . . . ?"

"From your flat. Have you seen her since . . . last night?" There were seven rooms, five of which had been occupied; Marissa and a silent, scarred girl who'd been there less than a month were the only women. "She had the room at the front. You know who I mean."

The man blinks a couple times, then smiles slyly. "Her?" he says. "Oh, yeah, her. You wanna know about her? I bet you do."

"Yeah, I do." Eddie keeps his voice flat but leaves his hand where it is.

"What's she to you, huh? Who's askin' about her? Who's . . ."

"Nobody. Just me."

"I seen her."

"When? Where?" Eddie notices that the man is shaking slightly. His nails are cracked and discolored, his thumb pads splayed. It would be good to photograph them.

"Last night." He wipes his mouth on his sleeve. "Last night, course. That's what you mean, innit? Oh yeah, she was home all right. She was home."

"What time?" says Eddie, but the man cackles and buries his face again in the mug.

"Late," he says when he emerges. "Late, late. Right before the police came. She was outa there, she was fast outa there."

"And you? Did you hang around to talk to the cops?"

"What—" The mug lands back on the table with a crack. "What you sayin'?"

"I'm saying it sounds like you both got the hell out of there. Don't blame you. So did I." The conversation annoys him; why did he even start it? Surely the only reason Marissa is out of sight is because she'd found the lowest place to lie, the one she needed because—unlike Eddie—she didn't have money, or a title deed to the flat she'd fled. She'd be back, stoic or sardonic, once the fuss had died down. And where did he get off himself, giving this poor bastard the third degree?

"Did you know him?" he asks more gently, letting go. "The guy who died?"

The man worries at the tabletop with his ravaged fingers. "No. Not—no."

"Hell of a shock."

The man shrugs. Eddie thinks about staying, buying him another coffee, but instead he gets up to leave. He's on his way to the door when the man adds, "But Marissa. Last week, man. She was yellin' at him, yellin' at him like she wanted to kill him."

He's yelled at enough people, been yelled at enough, to know it doesn't mean anything. Even so, he tries to visit all the places he's seen Marissa outside the house and every one of them is empty. A little before six he's outside a pub he sometimes visits off the Gray's Inn Road, and it feels like time to stop. He pushes the hefty wooden door but meets resistance. When he shoves harder he realizes that someone is on the other side, buffing the stained glass with a cloth. The person steps back to let him in; at first he thinks he's hallucinating when he sees it's Marissa.

"Christ almighty!"

Marissa shrinks. She backs into the shadows, the cloth twisted and hard in her hands and her eyes cast down to the floor.

"What are you doing here?" Eddie demands.

The cloth cracks. "Work," she mutters. "Work here, three days a week. I get off at six."

She's so matter-of-fact that he almost laughs, until the tear trickles down her cheek. "God, Marissa," he says. "You—you just came to work? Where were you last night?"

He has to lean close to hear her answer. "Laundrette. Twenty-four hour. And today, I . . . I got nowhere else to go. So I came to work."

It makes as much sense as anything else.

"But now . . ." She looks around. "Now, I go. I'm done here."

"You're going home?"

She shakes her head until her hair covers her eyes. "Can't . . . can't go home. You know."

He thinks of saying that the police won't care about her immigration status, not now, but it's probably not true. And he doubts she has a friend or a relative where she can stay. If she did, she'd be there already.

"I gotta go."

"Go where, Marissa?"

She avoids his eyes. "I can't go back."

She pushes past him toward the door but Eddie follows her. They hover in the vestibule, the glass half-cleaned.

"I know," he says. "I know that. But . . . let me help you. Work it out . . ."

"Work out?" There's an echo of her old sarcasm but it withers as fast as it came. "Work out? What can I work out? This is bad . . ."

He doesn't know what to say but he leads her to a booth and gets her a brandy, remembering that she's accepted it before as they sat on the fire escape at the end of a long week. The glass and the drink and the chintzy wall light make her face seem golden although he knows she's gray and pale.

Of course she is innocent. He knows because she hasn't even considered the possibility that the yelling might mean something else. She had bawled the dead man out after she caught him stealing food from the new girl in the flat. The first rule of having nothing is that you don't take from people who've less. Marissa tells Eddie this not to prove her innocence, but because it's what happened. She never even knew his name; she just called him a thieving swine. The girl was too scared to confront him but Marissa had standards. Eddie's had his own fridge for thirty years.

"So he was a prick," says Eddie. "Look, I'll vouch for you. I'll say—"

"But then I found him," she murmurs, twisting her hands in her skirt. She opens and closes her mouth and then words gush out so quickly that she might choke on them. "I come back and his door is open, the music loud, and I think, that asshole, people are trying to sleep, and I go to tell him, and—and he is there. On the bed. I know he—he is—he has gone. I seen enough people dead. And his neck . . ." She makes a clawing motion at her collar. "Torn. Like ribbons. Threads. Like if an animal . . . and, on the bed by him . . ." Her voice clots and dries.

"You can tell me," says Eddie. He's numb, like the first numbness of real cold, or drunkenness, or fever.

"The bottle," says Marissa. "*That* bottle. The one I clean up. The part left whole, the neck and the, the . . ." With her hands she describes the shoulders of a bottle. Eddie thinks how odd it is that there is no word for this. Marissa's clothes are clean, bloodless. "And I know, my—hands. My fingertips, on the glass . . ."

"Fingerprints," says Eddie. "Oh Christ."

"So—I ran. I ran."

"Ran. Right. And did anyone . . . ?"

"The other man, he come home. He see me. I pass him in the door."

Eddie pushes the brandy glass across the table and she drinks. "I don't know none of them," she says. "We all . . . come home, get up, we work. Too busy, also what we say, them and me? Nothing alike. Just we here, not somewhere else."

"Okay." He makes himself breathe deeply. "Okay. Look, I know a few decent lawyers. People who do criminal work. An immigration lawyer, come to that. I—"

"No."

"Fuck it, Marissa, this is a big deal." Eddie ran through the names of the lawyers in his head, people he'd met on news stories, a feature on refugees. What's a little murder charge between professional acquaintances? "Look, I get why you don't want to talk to the police. *All* the reasons, and I don't give a shit about those. But—"

"No. No, no."

Eddie knows he shouldn't believe her story, and he believes it all the more. He sighs deeply and watches her eyes swell in the globe of her glass. "Okay. Okay, then. No lawyer, not yet anyway. But, we'll figure this out, okay?"

Somehow he persuades her to come home with him, on the way buying a completely incongruous pizza, with anchovies and olives and extra cheese. Eddie scouts out the flat but the cop has gone. There's a cat's cradle of yellow tape across the locked door of the downstairs flat. He signals to Marissa who scuttles from the street corner to the front door and up the stairs, panting with the effort until she reaches his attic.

She hesitates on the threshold as he switches on the lights and the television and the kettle. Eddie thinks she might vanish, but at last she tiptoes inside and perches on the sofa while he makes coffee. She looks around, eyes sharp as knives. "Nice," she murmurs. "Not how I think your place is."

He laughs. "What were you expecting? Take-out boxes and dirty socks?" In fact the flat is clean and pleasantly cluttered with thirty years of living.

Marissa gestures, as if stroking a smooth surface. "I expect, not so many things. I think black, shiny, silver metal. Machines, loudspeakers."

"High tech minimalist. Not bloody likely." He sinks into his wheezing wicker chair. "How are you, Marissa? You okay? You must be knackered."

"Don't matter." She hunches her shoulders.

"You can hole up here for a bit, if you want."

"They will come back. To ask. They ask . . ." She breaks off, shivering.

"About you?"

"About him."

Eddie gives her a cigarette. Her lips tremble; it takes him a couple tries to light it. "Yeah, well. We'll deal with that. We can find another place for you, if you want. I'll call a few people, in the morning."

Does she know why she's here, he wonders? Because he doesn't. He looks around and his place is suddenly unrecognizable, a port in a storm, a life lived in a high attic. Marissa draws on her cigarette and gives him an unfamiliar smile.

"You don't—" she says awkwardly.

Eddie goes into the kitchen to fetch plates. When he comes back she is watching the smoke as it thins and vanishes.

"You don't have to help," says Marissa.

Eddie lights his own cigarette and cuts the pizza. They eat in silence, watching a black and white war film with chiseled men in uniforms and caps. "Heroes," Marissa says sadly. She takes the blanket that he's fetched for her and wraps it tightly around her shoulders.

I seen enough people dead, she'd told him. He's seen plenty of dead bodies himself, and photographed most of them, but he's never stumbled upon one unwarned.

At midnight he offers to sleep on the sofa so that she can have his bed. She refuses.

"I'll change the sheets."

"No. No need." She gets up and marches into the bathroom. Eddie thinks of her using his soap, the bathmat, the toothbrush he bought at the corner shop. He fetches pillows and another blanket and a quilt, knowing she will feel cold although the night is mild.

How will he sleep in a house where a man was murdered? Probably he has done it before without knowing, but not a few scant hours after a warm and pulsing throat was slashed, not with bloody footprints still downstairs on the carpet. In the next room Marissa turns, breathes, sighs. Outside there's shouting and a car spits and starts. Eddie's eyes won't close. He resigns himself to a long night, but when he jolts up and up through layers of dark he realizes he's been profoundly asleep.

Marissa stands by his bed, silhouetted like a vision in the light of the streetlamp. Naked she is taller and younger. Her body is all smooth curves and silky skin. He may be dreaming. Her breasts, which to his surprise he has never considered, swell like suns. Her legs are muscled, athletic; blinking and rubbing his eyes, he remembers that she walks everywhere. There is a long scar on her thigh.

She reaches out and folds back the bedclothes, and sits next to him. Cool fingers brush his chest and sadness pierces his heart. "Marissa," he murmurs. "There's no need . . ."

"I know."

"None—"

"It's not need."

"No—no. Sorry. I didn't mean that. You don't have to do this, I mean. You don't have to—I don't expect—"

Marissa smiles, sadly, sweetly. "I know."

"You don't owe me anything." He closes his eyes. "Go back to bed."

But she is still touching him.

"I don't expect anything from you," Eddie says again. "I mean, I don't . . ." He almost says "I don't want," but that would have been a lie, now. "You don't have to do this. That's not why I asked you here."

"I know," she says again, leaning close. She smells of almonds. "I know, but—this, I choose. This, I want."

Eddie struggles to sit up. "Marissa. Are you sure?"

"I'm sure."

"I don't want to hurt you . . ."

"You won't hurt me." Marissa grows small, cold, shading before his eyes into gray. If he pushes her away now she will dissolve into blood or dust. He doesn't understand—he likes to understand things—but he thinks she is hungry for human warmth, and that at least he has to give. "Oh, you are beautiful," he says, and takes her in his arms.

There is not love but they make a little in the silver beam of streetlamp and moon. He strokes her free, clean curls and she runs a hand through his long hair. They fall asleep in an easy embrace, her soft body curled against his bony one. When he wakes Eddie is warm and loose-limbed and the bed is half-empty. She has left as silently as if he had imagined her.

The police return to take his statement, and the ground floor flat is locked up. Ademoglu sells it a few months later. Eddie thinks often of Marissa. He wonders why he failed to photograph her and the thought hurts like chemicals in a cut. The man's killer is not found. Eddie works his crime desk contacts but he knows, he will always know, that Marissa is innocent. One night the crash of a bottle breaking outside wakes him. He jumps out of bed and stumbles to the window, hoping she will be there, smiling up at him and scolding over the mess. But she is not, and he lies alone in his clean bed and cannot forget.

---

* *"Glass" began with a chance glimpse of a man and a woman talking on a quiet side street. I was on the top deck of a bus, traveling south along the Gray's Inn Road, and if I hadn't turned my head at that moment, I would have missed them. I was thinking about the millions of small encounters that the city nurtures every day—some beautiful, some fatal, some so ordinary that we forget all about them until they fall into a bigger story—and the different ways people inhabit places, alone and together.*

Joseph S. Walker *is a college instructor living in Bloomington, Indiana. He has a PhD in American literature from Purdue University. He is a member of the Mystery Writers of America, the Short Mystery Fiction Society, Sisters in Crime, and the Private Eye Writers of America. His stories have appeared in* Alfred Hitchcock Mystery Magazine, Ellery Queen Mystery Magazine, Mystery Tribune, Guilty Crime Story Magazine, Tough, *and a number of other magazines and anthologies. He has been nominated for the Edgar Award and the Derringer Award and has won the Bill Crider Prize for Short Fiction. He also won the Al Blanchard Award in 2019 and 2021. Recent anthologies from small presses (which are helping to keep short crime fiction alive out of love and dedication, and are richly deserving of support) containing his stories include* Mickey Finn: 21st Century Noir Volume 3 *(Down & Out Books),* The Detective and the Clergyman: The Adventures of Sherlock Holmes and Father Brown *(Belanger Books), and* Weren't Another Other Way to Be: Outlaw Fiction Inspired by the Songs of Waylon Jennings *(Gutter Books). Find him online at jswalkerauthor.com.*

CRIME SCENE

Joseph S. Walker

When Adler got back to his private dock, Melanie Phelps was sitting at the end, legs kicking in the air over the water. Her Stevie Ray Vaughan T-shirt and khaki shorts made her look like the kid she'd been when they first met, thirty years ago. Adler hadn't seen her in more than a year. He cut the engine and let the little boat drift in, tossing her a line. As she tied it off, he climbed up onto the planks beside her, carrying his pole and a small cooler.

"Catch much?" she asked, nodding at the cooler.

"This is for beer," Adler said. "These days I let the ones I catch go. Too much trouble cleaning them." In truth, he hadn't wet a line in months. When he went out on the lake he mostly just drifted, staring out over the water. "How's your father?"

Melanie shook her head. "No change. Wish I could say different."

Lamar Phelps had spent decades as the country's top criminal talent scout, hooking crooks up with jobs from coast to coast for a slice of the proceeds. When a stroke cut him down five years ago, Melanie took over the family business. Adler went to Denver once to see his old friend, but found nothing of Lamar in the chair being wheeled from one sunny spot to another. Given the things Lamar knew that would be of interest to prosecutors, the fact that he was completely nonverbal was, Adler supposed, a blessing in disguise. It was one bitch of a disguise though.

"I was going to grill a steak," he said. "You want one?"

"You cook now?"

"Beats the hell out of driving an hour and a half for a Big Mac."

He grilled on the cabin's back deck. Melanie sat at the picnic table. He tried to remember how old she was while she chatted, mostly gossip about people Adler had long forgotten or never knew. She had to be in her forties, but she didn't show it. There was maybe a whisper of gray, barely detectable, in the blond hair at her temples.

By the time he served the food she was lapsing into a silence to match his own. He'd seen it before. The spell of this place. When a V of geese came overhead, close enough to hear not just their honking but the velvet sound of their wings cutting the air, she looked at them with an open delight that took her right back to childhood.

She finally pushed her plate away. "I can't remember the last time I had a steak and baked potato."

"I'm a simple man," Adler said. "Gonna talk about why you're here?"

"A job," Melanie said. "But you knew that."

He opened another beer and waited.

"One target," she said. "Your cut is a hundred K, twenty now and the rest after."

"Something with that kind of number attached has to be hairy."

"There are some complications. The target is locally prominent, and the customer wants him to get it in a very public place at a very specific time."

"Hold the pickles, hold the lettuce," Adler said. "Special orders don't upset us." He waved a hand at her confused look. "Before your time. Give me the details."

"Ever been to Dallas?"

"Passed through a few times. Never worked there."

"All the better if nobody local can make you." Melanie took an eight by ten from her bag and slid it across the table. It showed a silver-haired man in an expensive suit, his arms crossed. Some kind of publicity shot.

"Alex Lersch," she said. "Sixty-four years old, net worth a couple hundred million. Never married, no known children."

"Gay?"

"Don't know. Could be he's just allergic to sharing the pile. He got his start in real estate and software, but he's so diversified now that you couldn't really say what he does. Active in local politics and charities, mostly leans left, which isn't easy in Texas these days. Has a reputation as shrewd but basically honest."

"Who'd he piss off?"

"Don't know," she said again. At Adler's look she raised a hand. "Honestly. This one came through deep back channels. The money's real, but I don't know who the client is."

"I'm hearing warning bells, kiddo."

"I get you, but show me the cop who can put out this kind of cash just on the chance of netting somebody."

"What about the time and place?"

"You're gonna love this. Dealey Plaza on November twenty-second."

He gave her a flat stare. "You drove one hell of a long way for a joke."

"No joke. Lersch is an assassination buff, an obsessive. He's supposed to have the largest private collection of Kennedy materials in the world. Funds an annual conference that's a mix of legitimate historians and tinfoil nutjobs. One of the activities is a visit to Dealey Plaza that he leads himself on the anniversary. That's where you're supposed to tag him."

"Somebody's got a sick sense of humor."

"If you've got the money, I think it just counts as an eccentric sense of humor. Anyway, there it is. You in or out?"

He gave Melanie the extra bedroom to spare her the two-hour drive to the nearest hotel. After she went to bed, he sat on the dock, under the stars. It was too late in the year for fireflies, but the woods and the water were buzzing with the constant small sounds of living creatures.

Adler had done a lot of jobs in fields of work where nobody writes a résumé. He started in explosives, blowing safes for crews on the West Coast, then learned to hack alarm systems. He hired on for a handful of kidnappings, which always seemed to go screwy. There had been some hijacking, some smuggling. Eventually word got around that he didn't mind eliminating people under the right circumstances, and Lamar started steering hits his way. By his count, Adler had done thirty-four. If he thought hard, he could remember all their names.

Lately he'd been remembering them a lot, drifting around on the lake. It was always easiest to assume they all deserved what was coming. It was starting to bother him that for some of them, he didn't know. He didn't know why somebody in their lives wanted the hammer dropped.

The money from this Dallas job would be nice, but he didn't need it. He took it because maybe this time he could know why. Even thinking the question was breaking some rules, but he was too old and tired to care. November 22 was almost a month off. The way Adler figured it, how he spent that time was up to him.

He was going to spend it figuring out why somebody wanted Alex Lersch dead.

Two weeks later Adler set foot in Dealey Plaza for the first time. The Rangers ball cap pulled low on his forehead and the heavy black sunglasses covering half his face would complicate facial recognition programs that might be running on any one of the dozens of security cameras on an average American city block. The Cowboys jersey and the camera around his neck marked him as a tourist. He'd barely crossed the street into the plaza when a tall Black man with a canvas bag slung over his shoulder offered him a "personal tour" for a hundred dollars. Adler got away by giving the man twenty bucks for a reproduction of the November 23, 1963, edition of *The New York Times*. He held it loosely at his side as he wandered, letting it ward off the other hustlers.

On a pleasant Saturday afternoon, with the anniversary approaching, there were plenty of tourists for the hustlers to prey on. Some were rolling through on buses, the rehearsed patter of the guides echoing through tinny loudspeakers, but many were just walking around. Adler drifted among them, occasionally snapping a picture. In part of his brain, he held a sketchy biography of this version of himself. *Midwest. Retired schoolteacher. Middle-grade science. Widowed?* Mostly, though, he focused on getting a feel for the setting, finding the lines of sight, the obvious entry and exit points, the less obvious maintenance and structural features.

It was an odd place. The plaza itself was just a rough triangle of patchy grass, with the base along Houston Street to the east and the point at the west, where the streets defining the two sides swept under railroad tracks. All the energy and interest was along the north edge, where the former Book Depository squatted at the corner of Houston and Elm, Oswald's window clearly marked. Two big white *X*s in the middle of Elm showed the exact places where Kennedy had been hit.

In an hour and a half, Adler saw at least fifty people, most of them young men, stroll out into the road to take a selfie on an *X*, usually with the Oswald window in the frame behind them. They seemed oblivious to active traffic on the street, and he wondered how many got hit over the course of a year.

He heard at least twenty-five people, most of them slightly older men, looking back and forth from the window to an *X* and proclaiming it an easy shot. "He was right on top of him," they usually said.

He heard at least fifteen people, most of them middle-aged men, saying that their lawn back home was bigger than the grassy knoll.

They were inane, but they weren't wrong. The place had the aura of a back-lot re-creation, a three-quarter-scale model that didn't quite convince. It was the field of myth, the pressure point where the American century shattered. The most devastating rifle shot in history shouldn't be so short. The grassy knoll should at least be large enough for everyone mentioned in the conspiracy theories to stand on. If it wasn't for the sheer weight of the names, Dealey Plaza would look like what it was: a stunted, inconsequential green space tucked into an odd margin of a big city.

None of this mattered. He wasn't Lersch, trying to solve some riddle for the ages. He was a professional, here to do a job. He watched where the cops strolled and what they were looking at. He watched the traffic lights, timing them in his head. He walked five or six blocks in every direction, noting parking garages, bus stops, and buildings with multiple access points. He verified what he already knew: that from every corner of Dealey Plaza he had a clear, unimpeded view of the neon red shirt he'd hung in the window of his room on one of the upper floors of the big hotel a couple blocks to the southwest.

Before coming to Dallas, Adler spent a week in another hotel in San Antonio, buying the things he would need at several different stores using credit cards under several different names. One of the things he bought was a laptop. At night in his room he used it to read everything he could find about Alexander Malcolm Lersch—interviews, profiles, news stories, the last few years of the available records on his various businesses and charitable funds.

He found nothing that provided an obvious motive for the man's murder. Lersch had no living relatives. Upon his death, half his fortune would go into a trust for the "perpetual funding" of a Center for the Study of Assassination and Political Violence at the University of Texas at Arlington, which would also be the recipient of his personal Kennedy collection. The other half would be distributed to various local charities focusing on voting rights and hunger. In his business dealings Lersch was aggressive, but not ruthless, leaving no ruined rivals to dream of revenge. Even reading between the lines, Adler saw no evidence of scandal. No mysterious payoffs to former employees. No trace of money laundering or obvious bribes. From all appearances, Lersch was an upstanding citizen. The only unusual thing about him was his hang-up about the Kennedy hit.

Ideally Adler would have shifted from research to surveillance once he was in Dallas, but keeping eyes on a multimillionaire around the clock wasn't a realistic proposition. He could hardly hang out in the reception area of Lersch's offices, which occupied several floors in a downtown skyscraper. Sitting in a coffee shop across from the entrance to the attached parking garage, he did verify something mentioned in almost every profile: despite his wealth, Lersch still drove his own car, arriving at the office at nine every morning and making it a firm practice to leave at five. He spoke in many interviews about the importance of maintaining a balance between work and the rest of life, and of resisting overwork on one hand and unnecessary luxury or indulgence on the other.

Adler was grateful that Lersch's notion of "unnecessary luxury" did not extend to buying some anonymous sedan or SUV. He drove a silver Rolls Royce that was easy to follow. For several days in a row Adler trailed him from the office just after five, hoping to be led to something that would give him a thread to pull. A mistress. An underground sex club. A poker room. Every night, though, Lersch drove straight to his estate in Highland Park. Adler's research told him that the place was worth in the neigh-borhood of ten million dollars, and that Lersch lived there alone. Here, too, he couldn't just sit on the street and watch the place. In a neighborhood like that, the cops would have been on him in twenty minutes. He made several passes a night, though, and never saw any other cars go near the place or anything remotely suspicious.

Driving back to his hotel, Adler drummed his fingers on the wheel. He was starting to wonder if somebody had just pulled Lersch's name out of a hat, or if maybe this was some kind of elaborate sting. He was tempted to call Melanie to try to track the back channels she'd spoken of, but asking questions like that in the middle of a job would set off every alarm she had. Melanie was fond of him, but she would assume he was either going soft or had flipped on her. Either choice meant that she would be visiting another one of her subcontractors soon, and sliding a picture of him across the table. Adler was on his own.

He briefly considered registering for Lersch's assassination conference before rejecting the idea as too conspicuous. The schedule was online, though. There was nothing for him in the scheduled sessions on bullet trajectories and Cuban diplomatic archives. On the night of the twenty-first, though, there was a three-hour formal banquet, with a keynote address by Lersch himself. "Living in the Echo of Gunfire: The Continuing Legacy of Assassination Studies."

Poetic, Adler thought.

Lersch's estate backed onto a creek that, two miles away, ran through the grounds of a country club. An hour before the banquet was scheduled to start, with dusk gathering, Adler parked in the employee lot of the club. He walked to the creek and began following it, sticking as close to the edge of the water as he could. Most of the creek's path through the whole area was still heavily wooded, and along much of the way he was completely out of sight of any structures. He stopped occasionally to check his exact position on his phone's GPS. There was heavy undergrowth in many places, and the wet ground made for slow progress, but in forty minutes he was at the low wall marking the back entrance to Lersch's property. Ten minutes after that he was at the patio door at the back of the house.

The security system had been installed by one of the big national firms. Several years back, keeping his skills up to date, Adler used one of his dummy identities to go through the firm's hiring and training programs. There had been some updates since then, of course, but people in the security business are every bit as inefficient as people everywhere else. They couldn't always be bothered to, for example, check their systems for legacy back doors left by a previous generation of programmers.

He had the door open in twenty minutes. It took him another thirty to find the security system's central drive, disable the cameras, and wipe the last two hours they'd recorded.

The speech went well, Alex Lersch thought. Perhaps a little dry, but he hoped his sense of urgency came through. He had spoken at length of the coming establishment of the Center at UT-Arlington, urging his fellow enthusiasts to unite their scholarship and investigative powers around its banner. The time had come to set aside petty squabbles and ensure the security of future inquiries. Had he persuaded them? Time would tell.

Tomorrow would tell.

When he got home he went into the office, intending to make a few final notes before the tour in the morning. The sconce in the hallway cast a long canted column of light across the room as he crossed to the desk. He was reaching for the lamp, thinking that something seemed odd without being able to put his finger on what it was, when a calm voice came from behind him. "Don't turn around," it said. "And don't turn on the light. I have a gun."

The chair, Lersch thought. The chair that normally sat in the middle of the room had been missing. Pulled into some corner for this man's comfort, no doubt.

Lersch put his hands flat on the desk and waited.

Adler gave Lersch credit for not panicking. He seemed perfectly calm.

"There was a revolver in your upper right-hand desk drawer," Adler said. "There isn't now. Go behind the desk and turn the chair to face the wall and sit down."

Lersch did as he was told. "I don't suppose you'd believe me if I said there's not much here worth stealing," he said.

"No, but it doesn't matter. That's not what I'm here for."

"And what are you here for?"

Adler could just make out the curve of Lersch's head above the top of the chair. "You and I have an appointment tomorrow morning."

Lersch was slow to answer, the extra beat confirming what Adler already knew. "I have an appointment with a lot of people tomorrow morning," he said. "I'm leading a tour."

"Our appointment isn't about an old murder."

Rich people always have the quietest homes. Adler knew the air conditioning was running, but it didn't keep him from hearing Lersch's breath getting shallow as he answered. "I don't know what you mean."

"How long have you got, Lersch?"

The answer came with a touch of acid. "I guess that's up to the man holding a gun on me."

"I've seen your medicine cabinet. I'm no doctor, but I've had plenty of time to google the stuff you're taking. It's not for lowering your cholesterol."

For a time he thought Lersch wasn't going to answer.

"Two months," he finally said. "Probably a little less."

"You put the hit on yourself."

"I've spent my entire adult life studying assassination," Lersch said. "I knew the kind of people to get in touch with. The professionals."

"Very flattering," Adler said.

"But not very professional," Lersch said. "This is not what I paid for."

"I've been trying to figure out why anybody would want you dead," Adler said. "That's why I came here tonight. I wanted to know the reason."

Lersch made a noise in his throat. "I've bought many things and services in my life. I've never before had anyone demand to know why I wanted them." He made the noise again. "Not professional."

"I'll report myself to the union when this is over," Adler said.

"And now that you know? Does my motive meet your exacting standards? It's rather late for me to seek alternate arrangements."

"Now that I know? There's no reason you have to bleed out on dirty pavement, Lersch. I can do this right now. I can make it quick. Painless."

"*Not what I paid for.*" For a moment Adler thought Lersch was going to come out of the chair, but he brought himself under control. "Please. Follow the directions you were given. Tomorrow, at the plaza."

"Why?"

"Why, why, why. You're certainly consistent in your curiosity, Mr. Whoever You Are."

"You're not answering."

The outline of Lersch's head dipped, came back up.

"Because I want what they have," he said.

"They?"

"Kennedy. Oswald. Two paths crossed, and more than half a century later we don't fully understand why or how. You know what lasts, Mr. Killer? A mystery. A riddle. We'll talk about the two of them forever because there is no final piece to the puzzle. And me?" Lersch gave a low whistle. "One of the foremost experts on the assassination, cut down in exactly the same place by an unknown assailant for unknown reasons. There will be books about me. Podcasts. I'll be part of the story forever."

"Very pretty," Adler said. "Is it from your speech?"

"It's from my life."

It was Adler's turn to be quiet, for so long that Lersch finally stirred. "Did I put you to sleep?"

Adler stood up. "No, but you should go to bed yourself, Mr. Lersch. You've got a big day tomorrow. I'll leave the gun on your back patio."

A little over twelve hours later, a bus adorned with the logo of the conference made the tight turn onto Elm and parked at the curb directly in front of the former Book Depository. The plaza was already crowded with more people than Adler had seen there before. He was across the street watching, back in his tourist gear.

Lersch was the first person off the bus, followed by about two dozen men and women. He had a small megaphone with him, and he led the group along the sidewalk, gesturing at the street and occasionally the building. Adler couldn't hear the speech. What looked like a rather old-fashioned hearing aid in his right ear was playing the police radio band, at a volume high enough to drown out most of the noise around him.

Lersch led his group along Elm, taking them to the spot where Abraham Zapruder's 8 mm camera caught the only footage of the assassination, then on to the grassy knoll. He was using the megaphone less, and seemed to be getting drawn into conversations with one or two individuals at a time. Adler shifted from foot to foot, seeming to stare at his phone while actually keeping track of the group's progress. Finally, Lersch led the entire bunch across to Adler's side of Elm and started bringing them the right direction. He was focused on the building now, gesturing at Oswald's window. When he was ten feet away, Adler dialed the first of two preprogrammed numbers on his cell phone.

Four blocks east, the burner cell he'd dialed triggered a device in the base of a sidewalk garbage can. Adler always enjoyed a chance to go back to his earliest specialty. Demolition. The explosion blew out most of the windows in the nearest office building.

Which happened to house the Internal Revenue Service.

Within twenty seconds the voices in Adler's right ear exploded into pandemonium. The handful of uniformed cops standing near the corner in anticipation of the day's crowds clawed at their shoulder radios and began moving, slowly at first, in the direction of the explosion. The sound had been loud enough to be heard in the plaza, but as something distant and confusing. People looked around, slowly registering that something odd was happening, more from the actions of the cops than from what they had heard.

Lersch was five feet away now. He was standing near the curb, facing Oswald's window, still pointing at something. Adler slid through the crowd until he was standing immediately behind the man, and then keyed the second number.

This package was inside the big rolling suitcase standing against the floor-to-ceiling window in his hotel room. He'd built this one to be as loud as possible and to pour out a huge volume of smoke without actually starting a fire. In all of the plaza, his was the only head that didn't turn at the enormous *bang* to see black fumes billowing from a shattered window on an upper floor of the hotel.

The screams were immediate, from every direction. People began running, some toward the hotel, others away. Alex Lersch didn't scream or run, though. As he spun on his heel at the sound of the explosion, his chest met Adler's knife, coming in the opposite direction. Lersch's eyes widened. Adler put his left arm around the man's neck and pulled him close, the further movement of the knife masked by their two bodies, to all appearances just two men clinging to each other in the terror of the moment.

Many people nearby had fallen, either in shock or simply tripping out of panic. Lersch did not seem out of place as Adler eased him to the ground, on his stomach. There was no longer a cop in sight. He joined a knot of people moving north, away from what seemed to be the burning hotel, listening to the frantic voices in his ear coordinating the response to what looked very much like an organized attack.

His car was parked in the lot of an aquarium, half a mile away. On his way there he ducked into the YMCA, where he'd left another set of clothes in a locker. He was changing when the voice in his ear started talking about a body in Dealey Plaza.

Ten minutes later he was on the interstate, heading home.

"Not exactly stealthy," Melanie said when she brought the rest of his money a few weeks afterward.

Winter was slow in coming. There was beginning to be a bite in the air, but it was comfortable to sit out on the deck in light jackets.

Perfect bourbon weather, Adler thought. He poured another finger into his glass. "Stealthy was never an option," he said. "Not with what the client wanted."

"I guess not. But Christ, Adler, there's a damn federal task force on this now."

"Task forces aren't cops, kiddo." Adler sipped, feeling the warmth slip through him. "Task forces are politicians and press conferences and fourteen different three-letter organizations fighting over jurisdiction."

"You sound like Dad."

"There are worse ways to sound."

Adler was four years old when Kennedy got shot. Too young to really understand what was happening, but the memory was there, a dark time when every adult he knew suddenly seemed very angry and very, very scared. It must have been like that for Lersch too. In that moment when Lersch turned into the blade and his eyes widened, Adler saw the little boy who would spend a lifetime trying to understand.

"There are kids today," he said, not realizing he was going to speak out loud until he did. "Someday somebody will ask them what's the first big news story they really remember being aware of, and they'll say the explosions in Dallas."

"And this is a good thing?"

"Damned if I know," Adler said. "The mystery endures."

Melanie would stay in the extra room again. In the morning he would make pancakes for her and tell her he was retiring. She would protest but not much. After she drove away, he would untie his little boat, push off into the cold water, and try to decide if knowing why made any difference at all.

---

*In November 2019 I attended Bouchercon, the World Mystery Convention, in Dallas. It was my first time in Dallas, and my first Bouchercon—in fact, my first mystery convention of any kind. It was an overwhelming experience to find myself in the same room with people like Lawrence Block, and to be meeting and chatting with exciting new talents like S. A. Cosby. Throughout the weekend, I felt that I had found my people, and everyone I met made me feel that I was very much part of the mystery community.

The conference hotel was only a few blocks from Dealey Plaza, so it seemed fitting to stroll over for a look at the most famous crime scene in American history, the site of what Don DeLillo, in Libra, called "the seven seconds that broke the back of the American century." I'd seen pictures and film of the plaza hundreds of times, of course, but I found actually being there a powerful and disorienting experience, precisely because the pictures don't really convey what it's like. The whole area is more cramped than you imagine—or at least, than I had imagined. It's startling to see how little space you actually need to change history. Walking back to the conference, I was already thinking that I wanted to write a story set there, if only because I wanted to convey something of what I had felt (to what degree I succeeded, the reader can judge).

I left Dallas feeling exhilarated and determined to attend Bouchercon the following year, in Sacramento, and the year after that, in New Orleans. I didn't know that both those events would be forced online by a virus that wasn't yet so much as whispered of in the news, and that I wouldn't get to see my fellow mystery writers in person until three years later in Minneapolis. "Crime Scene" would end up being one of a number of stories I wrote while trapped at home, in the middle of a slow-motion catastrophe that seemed to be breaking the back of this new century (to what degree it succeeded, the reader of the future can judge). The story was a pleasure to write, because it was a doorway back to a time and place I was always happy to revisit. It's even better to know that the story has brought pleasure to some readers, as well.

My thanks to Otto Penzler and Amor Towles for the honor of being included here, and to the North Dallas chapter of Sisters in Crime for giving "Crime Scene" its first home in their Malice in Dallas anthology. I am especially grateful to Barb Goffman, the editor of that anthology, whose comments and suggestions made the story so much stronger.

BONUS STORY

BONUS STORY

More famous as a writer of mainstream literary fiction than of genre stories of crime or the supernatural, **Edith** *(Newbold)* **Wharton***, née Jones (1862–1937) won the Pulitzer Prize for her novel,* The Age of Innocence *(1920) and her novella* The Old Maid *(1935), adapted as a play, won the Pulitzer Prize for Zoe Atkins, yet her superb mystery and ghost stories spanned virtually her entire career.*

Born to enormous wealth in New York City, she rebelled against her privileged life among high society in New York, Paris, and Newport, Rhode Island, by writing fiction, which her family regarded as an eccentricity that was best ignored. Her earliest stories were written for Scribner's Magazine *and, when the editor requested a serial novel "in six months," she wrote her first big bestseller for him,* The House of Mirth *(1905). Six years later she published what many regard as her masterpiece,* Ethan Frome *(1911), ultimately writing more than fifty books.*

Although a popular figure in society, she sought privacy and bought a one hundred thirteen acre parcel of land and designed a house and gardens, declaring that she was a better landscape designer than novelist. She lived there with her husband for ten years before divorcing him and moving permanently to France, being awarded a Legion of Honour for her charitable work in the Great War.

Her crime story "A Cup of Cold Water," originally published in her collection Greater Inclination *(1899), was selected for inclusion in* The Best American Mystery Stories of the Nineteenth Century *(2014).*

Her ghost stories were collected in Tales of Men and Ghosts *(1910),* Xingu and Other Stories *(1916),* Here and Beyond *(1926) and* Ghosts *(1937).*

"A Bottle of Evian" was originally published in the March 27, 1926 issue of The Saturday Evening Post; *it was collected in her short-story collection* The Ghost-Feeler *(London, 1996, Peter Owen). It was later reissued as "A Bottle of Perrier."*

A BOTTLE OF PERRIER

Edith Wharton

A two day's struggle over the treacherous trails in a well-intentioned but short-winded "flivver," and a ride of two more on a hired mount of unamiable temper, had disposed young

Medford, of the American School of Archaeology at Athens, to wonder why his queer English friend, Henry Almodham, had chosen to live in the desert.

Now he understood.

He was leaning against the roof parapet of the old building, half Christian fortress, half Arab palace, which had been Almodham's pretext; or one of them. Below, in an inner court, a little wind, rising as the sun sank, sent through a knot of palms the rain-like rattle so cooling to the pilgrims of the desert. An ancient fig tree, enormous, exuberant, writhed over a white-washed well-head, sucking life from what appeared to be the only source of moisture within the walls. Beyond these, on every side, stretched away the mystery of the sands, all golden with promise, all livid with menace, as the sun alternately touched or abandoned them.

Young Medford, somewhat weary after his journey from the coast, and awed by his first intimate sense of the omnipresence of the desert, shivered and drew back. Undoubtedly, for a scholar and a misogynist, it was a wonderful refuge; but one would have to be, incurably, both.

"Let's take a look at the house," Medford said to himself, as if speedy contact with man's handiwork were necessary to his reassurance.

The house, he already knew, was empty save for the quick cosmopolitan man-servant, who spoke a sort of palimpsest Cockney lined with Mediterranean tongues and desert dialects—English, Italian, or Greek, which was he?—and two or three burnoused underlings who, having carried Medford's bags to his room, had relieved the palace of their gliding presences. Mr. Almodham, the servant told him, was away; suddenly summoned by a friendly chief to visit some unexplored ruins to the south, he had ridden off at dawn, too hurriedly to write, but leaving messages of excuse and regret. That evening late he might be back, or next morning. Meanwhile Mr. Medford was to make himself at home.

Almodham, as young Medford knew, was always making these archaeological explorations; they had been his ostensible reason for settling in that remote place, and his desultory search had already resulted in the discovery of several early Christian ruins of great interest.

Medford was glad that his host had not stood on ceremony, and rather relieved, on the whole, to have the next few hours to himself. He had had a malarial fever the previous summer, and in spite of his cork helmet he had probably caught a touch of the sun; he felt curiously, helplessly tired, yet deeply content.

And what a place it was to rest in! The silence, the remoteness, the illimitable air! And in the heart of the wilderness green leafage, water, comfort—he had already caught a glimpse of wide wicker chairs under the palms—a humane and welcoming habitation. Yes, he began to understand Almodham. To anyone sick of the Western fret and fever the very walls of this desert fortress exuded peace.

As his foot was on the ladder-like stair leading down from the roof, Medford saw the man-servant's head rising toward him. It rose slowly and Medford had time to remark that it was sallow, bald on the top, diagonally dented with a long white scar, and ringed with thick ash-blond hair. Hitherto Medford had noticed only the man's face—youngish, but sallow also—and been chiefly struck by its wearing an odd expression which could best be defined as surprise.

The servant, moving aside, looked up, and Medford perceived that his air of surprise was produced by the fact that his intensely blue eyes were rather wider open than most eyes, and fringed with thick ash-blond lashes; otherwise there was nothing noticeable about him."

Just to ask—what wine for dinner, sir? Champagne, or—"

"No wine, thanks."

The man's disciplined lips were played over by a faint flicker of deprecation or irony, or both.

"Not any at all, sir?"

Medford smiled back. "It's not out of respect for Prohibition." He was sure that the man, of whatever nationality, would understand that; and he did.

"Oh, I didn't suppose, sir—"

"Well, no; but I've been rather seedy, and wine's forbidden."

The servant remained incredulous. "Just a little light Moselle, though, to colour the water, sir?"

"No wine at all," said Medford, growing bored. He was still in the stage of convalescence when it is irritating to be argued with about one's dietary.

"Oh—what's your name, by the way?" he added, to soften the curtness of his refusal.

"Gosling," said the other unexpectedly, though Medford didn't in the least know what he had expected him to be called.

"You're English, then?"

"Oh, yes, sir."

"You've been in these parts a good many years, though?"

Yes, he had, Gosling said; rather too long for his own liking; and added that he had been born at Malta. "But I know England well too." His deprecating look returned. "I will confess, sir, I'd like to have 'ad a look at Wembley." (The famous exhibition at Wembley, near London, took place in 1924.) "Mr. Almodham 'ad promised me—but there—" As if to minimize the abandon of this confidence, he followed it up by a ceremonious request for Medford's keys, and an enquiry as to when he would like to dine. Having received a reply, he still lingered, looking more surprised than ever.

"Just a mineral water, then, sir?"

"Oh, yes—anything."

"Shall we say a bottle of Perrier?"

Perrier in the desert! Medford smiled assentingly, surrendered his keys, and strolled away.

The house turned out to be smaller than he had imagined, or at least the habitable part of it; for above this towered mighty dilapidated walls of yellow stone, and in their crevices clung plaster chambers, one above the other, cedar-beamed, crimson-shuttered but crumbling. Out of this jumble of masonry and stucco, Christian and Moslem, the latest tenant of the fortress had chosen a cluster of rooms tucked into an angle of the ancient keep. These apartments opened on the uppermost court, where the palms chattered and the fig tree coiled above the well. On the broken marble pavement, chairs and a low table were grouped, and a few geraniums and blue morning-glories had been coaxed to grow between the slabs.

A white-skirted boy with watchful eyes was watering the plants; but at Medford's approach he vanished like a wisp of vapour.

There was something vaporous and insubstantial about the whole scene; even the long arcaded room opening on the court, furnished with saddlebag cushions, divans with gazelle skins, and rough indigenous rugs; even the table piled with the old "Timeses" and ultra-modern French and English reviews—all seemed, in that clear mocking air, born of the delusion of some desert wayfarer.

A seat under the fig tree invited Medford to doze, and when he woke the hard blue dome above him was gemmed with stars and the night breeze gossiped with the palms.

Rest—beauty—peace. Wise Almodham!

Wise Almodham! Having carried out—with somewhat disappointing results—the excavation with which an archaeological society had charged him twenty-five years ago, he had lingered on, taken possession of the Crusader's stronghold, and turned his attention from ancient to mediaeval remains. But even these investigations, Medford suspected, he prosecuted only at intervals, when the enchantment of his leisure did not lie on him too heavily.

The young American had met Henry Almodham at Luxor the previous winter; had dined with him at old Colonel Swordsley's, on that perfumed starlit terrace above the Nile; and, having somehow awakened the archaeologist's interest, had been invited to look him up in the desert the following year.

They had spent only that one evening together, with old Swordsley blinking at them under memory-laden lids, and two or three charming women from the Winter Palace chattering and exclaiming; but the two men had ridden back to Luxor together in the moonlight, and during that ride Medford fancied he had puzzled out the essential lines of Henry Almodham's character.

A nature saturnine yet sentimental; chronic indolence alternating with spurts of highly intelligent activity; gnawing self-distrust soothed by intimate self-appreciation; a craving for complete solitude coupled with the inability to tolerate it for long.

There was more too, Medford suspected; a dash of Victorian romance, gratified by the setting, the remoteness, the inaccessibility of his retreat, and by being known as *the* Henry Almodham—" the one who lives in a Crusader's castle, you know"—the gradual imprisonment in a pose assumed in youth, and into which middle age had slowly stiffened; and something deeper, darker, too, perhaps, though the young man doubted that; probably just the fact that living in that particular way had brought healing to an old wound, an old mortification, something which years ago had touched a vital part and left him writhing. Above all, in Almodham's hesitating movements and the dreaming look of his long, well-featured brown face with its shock of gray hair, Medford detected an inertia, mental and moral, which life in this castle of romance must have fostered and excused.

"Once here, how easy not to leave!" he mused, sinking deeper into his deep chair.

"Dinner, sir," Gosling announced.

The table stood in an open arch of the living-room; shaded candles made a rosy pool in the dusk. Each time he emerged into their light the servant, white-jacketed, velvet-footed, looked more competent and more surprised than ever. Such dishes too—the cook also a Maltese? Ah, they were geniuses, these Maltese! Gosling bridled, smiled his acknowledgment, and started to fill the guest's glass with Chablis.

"No wine," said Medford patiently.

"Sorry, sir. But the fact is—"

"You said there was Perrier?"

"Yes, sir; but I find there's none left. It's been awfully hot, and Mr. Almodham has been and drank it all up. The new supply isn't due till next week. We 'ave to depend on the caravans going south."

"No matter. Water, then. I really prefer it."

Gosling's surprise widened to amazement. "Not water, sir? Water—in these parts?"

Medford's irritability stirred again. "Something wrong with your water? Boil it then, can't you? I won't—" He pushed away the half-filled wineglass.

"Oh—boiled? Certainly, sir." The man's voice dropped almost to a whisper. He placed on the table a succulent mess of rice and mutton, and vanished.

Medford leaned back, surrendering himself to the night, the coolness, the ripple of wind in the palms.

One agreeable dish succeeded another. As the last appeared, the diner began to feel the pangs of thirst, and at the same moment a beaker of water was placed at his elbow. "Boiled, sir, and I squeezed a lemon into it."

"Right. I suppose at the end of the summer your water gets a bit muddy?"

"That's it, sir. But you'll find this all right, sir."

Medford tasted. "Better than Perrier." He emptied the glass, leaned back, and groped in his pocket. A tray was instantly at his hand with cigars and cigarettes.

"You don't—smoke, sir?"

Medford, for answer, held up his cigar to the man's light. "What do you call this?"

"Oh, just so. I meant the other style." Gosling glanced discreetly at the opium pipes of jade and amber laid out on a low table.

Medford shrugged away the invitation—and wondered. Was that perhaps Almodham's other secret—or one of them? For he began to think there might be many; and all, he was sure, safely stored away behind Gosling's vigilant brow.

"No news yet of Mr. Almodham?"

Gosling was gathering up the dishes with dexterous gestures. For a moment he seemed not to hear. Then—from beyond the candle gleam—" News, sir? There couldn't 'ardly be, could there? There's no wireless in the desert, sir; not like London." His respectful tone tempered the slight irony. "But tomorrow evening ought to see him riding in." Gosling paused, drew nearer, swept one of his swift hands across the table in pursuit of the last crumbs, and added tentatively: "You'll surely be able, sir, to stay till then?"

Medford laughed. The night was too rich in healing; it sank on his spirit like wings. Time vanished, fret and trouble were no more. "Stay, I'll stay a year if I have to!"

"Oh—a year?" Gosling echoed it playfully, gathered up the dessert dishes, and was gone.

Medford had said that he would wait for Almodham a year; but the next morning he found that such arbitrary terms had lost their meaning. There were no time measures in a place like this. The silly face of his watch told its daily tale to emptiness. The wheeling of the constellations over those ruined walls marked only the revolutions of the earth; the spasmodic motions of man meant nothing.

The very fact of being hungry, that stroke of the inward clock, was minimized by the slightness of the sensation—just the ghost of a pang, that might have been quieted by dried fruit and honey. Life had the light monotonous smoothness of eternity.

Toward sunset Medford shook off this queer sense of otherwhereness and climbed to the roof. Across the desert he spied for Almodham. Southward the Mountains of Alabaster hung like a blue veil lined with light. In the west a great column of fire shot up, spraying into plumy cloudlets which turned the sky to a fountain of rose-leaves, the sands beneath to gold.

No riders specked them. Medford watched in vain for his absent host till night fell, and the punctual Gosling invited him once more to table.

In the evening Medford absently fingered the ultramodern reviews—three months old, and already so stale to the touch—then tossed them aside, flung himself on a divan and dreamed. Almodham must spend a lot of time dreaming; that was it. Then, just as he felt himself sinking down into torpor, he would be off on one of these dashes across the desert in quest of unknown ruins. Not such a bad life.

Gosling appeared with Turkish coffee in a cup cased in filigree.

"Are there any horses in the stable?" Medford suddenly asked.

"Horses? Only what you might call pack-horses, sir. Mr. Almodham has the two best saddle-horses with him."

"I was thinking I might ride out to meet him."

Gosling considered. "So you might, sir."

"Do you know which way he went?"

"Not rightly sir. The caid's man was to guide them."

"Them? Who went with him?"

"Just one of our men, sir. They've got the two thoroughbreds. There's a third, but he's lame."

Gosling paused. "Do you know the trails, sir? Excuse me, but I don't think I ever saw you here before."

"No," Medford acquiesced, "I've never been here before."

"Oh, then"—Gosling's gesture added: *In that case, even the best thoroughbred wouldn't help you.*

"I suppose he may still turn up tonight?"

"Oh, easily, sir. I expect to see you both breakfasting here tomorrow morning," said Gosling cheerfully.

Medford sipped his coffee. "You said you'd never seen me here before. How long have you been here yourself?"

Gosling answered instantly, as though the figures were never long out of his memory: "Eleven years and seven months altogether, sir."

"Nearly twelve years! That's a longish time."

"Yes, it is."

"And I don't suppose you often get away?"

Gosling was moving off with the tray. He halted, turned back, and said with sudden emphasis: "I've never once been away. Not since Mr. Almodham first brought me here."

"Good Lord! Not a single holiday?"

"Not one, sir."

"But Mr. Almodham goes off occasionally. I met him at Luxor last year."

"Just so, sir. But when he's here he needs me for himself; and when he's away he needs me to watch over the others. So you see—"

"Yes, I see. But it must seem to you devilish long."

"It seems long, sir."

"But the others? You mean they're not—wholly trustworthy?"

"Well, sir, they're just Arabs," said Gosling with careless contempt.

"I see. And not a single old reliable among them?"

"The term isn't in their language, sir."

Medford was busy lighting his cigar. When he looked up he found that Gosling still stood a few feet off.

"It wasn't as if it 'adn't been a promise, you know, sir," he said, almost passionately.

"A promise?"

"To let me 'ave my holiday, sir. A promise—agine and agine."

"And the time never came?"

"No, sir, the days just drifted by—"

"Ah. They would, here. Don't sit up for me," Medford added. "I think I shall wait up—wait for Mr. Almodham."

Gosling's stare widened. "Here, sir? Here in the court?"

The young man nodded, and the servant stood still regarding him, turned by the moonlight to a white spectral figure, the unquiet ghost of a patient butler who might have died without his holiday.

"Down here in the court all night, sir? It's a lonely spot. I couldn't 'ear you if you was to call. You're best in bed, sir. The air's bad. You might bring your fever on again."

Medford laughed and stretched himself in his long chair. "Decidedly," he thought, "the fellow needs a change." Aloud he remarked: "Oh, I'm all right. It's you who are nervous Gosling. When Mr. Almodham comes back I mean to put in a word for you. You shall have your holiday."

Gosling still stood motionless. For a minute he did not speak. "You would, sir, you would?" He gasped it out on a high cracked note, and the last word ran into a laugh—a brief shrill cackle, the laugh of one long unused to such indulgences.

"Thank you, sir. Good night, sir." He was gone.

"You do boil my drinking-water, always?" Medford questioned, his hand clasping the glass without lifting it.

The tone was amicable, almost confidential; Medford felt that since his rash promise to secure a holiday for Gosling he and Gosling were on terms of real friendship.

"Boil it? Always, sir. Naturally." Gosling spoke with a slight note of reproach, as though Medford's question implied a

slur—unconscious, he hoped—on their newly established relation. He scrutinized Medford with his astonished eyes, in which
a genuine concern showed itself through the glaze of professional
indifference.

"Because, you know, my bath this morning—"

Gosling was in the act of receiving from the hands of a gliding
Arab a fragrant dish of kuskus. Under his breath he hissed to the
native: "You damned aboriginy, you, can't even 'old a dish steady?
Ugh!" The Arab vanished before the imprecation, and Gosling,
with a calm, deliberate hand, set the dish before Medford. "All
alike, they are." Fastidiously he wiped a trail of grease from his
linen sleeve.

"Because, you know, my bath this morning simply stank," said
Medford, plunging fork and spoon into the dish.

"Your bath, sir?" Gosling stressed the word. Astonishment, to
the exclusion of all other emotion, again filled his eyes as he rested
them on Medford. "Now, I wouldn't 'ave 'ad that 'appen for the
world," he said self-reproachfully.

"There's only the one well here, eh? The one in the court?"

Gosling aroused himself from absorbed consideration of the
visitor's complaint. "Yes, sir; only the one."

"What sort of a well is it? Where does the water come from?"

"Oh, it's just a cistern, sir. Rain-water. There's never been
any other here. Not that I ever knew it to fail; but at this season
sometimes it does turn queer. Ask any o' them Arabs, sir; they'll
tell you. Liars as they are, they won't trouble to lie about that."

Medford was cautiously tasting the water in his glass. "This
seems all right," he pronounced.

Sincere satisfaction was depicted on Gosling's countenance. "I
seen to its being boiled myself, sir. I always do. I 'ope that Perrier'll
turn up tomorrow, sir."

"Oh, tomorrow"—Medford shrugged, taking a second helping.
"Tomorrow I may not be here to drink it."

"What—going away, sir?" cried Gosling.

Medford, wheeling round abruptly, caught a new and incom-
prehensible look in Gosling's eyes. The man had seemed to feel
a sort of dog-like affection for him; had wanted, Medford could

have sworn, to keep him on, persuade him to patience and delay;
yet now, Medford could equally have sworn, there was relief in
his look, satisfaction, almost, in his voice.

"So soon, sir?"

"Well, this is the fifth day since my arrival. And as there's no
news yet of Mr. Almodham, and you say he may very well have
forgotten all about my coming—"

"Oh, I don't say that, sir; not forgotten! Only, when one of
those old piles of stones takes 'old of him, he does forget about the
time, sir. That's what I meant. The days drift by—'e's in a dream.
Very likely he thinks you're just due now, sir." A small thin smile
sharpened the lustreless gravity of Gosling's features. It was the
first time that Medford had seen him smile.

"Oh, I understand. But still—" Medford paused. Through the
spell of inertia laid on him by the drowsy place and its easeful
comforts his instinct of alertness was struggling back. "It's odd—"

"What's odd?" Gosling echoed unexpectedly, setting the dried
dates and figs on the table.

"Everything," said Medford.

He leaned back in his chair and glanced up through the arch
at the lofty sky from which noon was pouring down in cataracts
of blue and gold. Almodham was out there somewhere under that
canopy of fire, perhaps, as the servant said, absorbed in his dream.
The land was full of spells.

"Coffee, sir?" Gosling reminded him. Medford took it.

"It's odd that you say you don't trust any of these fellows—these
Arabs—and yet that you don't seem to feel worried at Mr. Almodham's being off God knows where, all alone with them."

Gosling received this attentively, impartially; he saw the point.
"Well, sir, no—you wouldn't understand. It's the very thing that
can't be taught, when to trust 'em and when not. It's 'ow their
interests lie, of course, sir; and their religion, as they call it." His
contempt was unlimited. "But even to begin to understand why I'm
not worried about Mr. Almodham, you'd 'ave to 'ave lived among
them, sir, and you'd 'ave to speak their language."

"But I—" Medford began. He pulled himself up short and bent
above his coffee.

"Yes, sir."

"But I've travelled among them more or less."

"Oh, travelled!" Even Gosling's intonation could hardly con-
ciliate respect with derision in his reception of this boast.

"This makes the fifth day, though," Medford continued argu-
mentatively. The midday heat lay heavy even on the shaded side of
the court, and the sinews of his will were weakening.

"I can understand, sir, a gentleman like you 'aving other
engagements—being pressed for time, as it were," Gosling rea-
sonably conceded.

He cleared the table, committed its freight to a pair of Arab
arms that just showed and vanished, and finally took himself off
while Medford sank into the divan. A land of dreams . . .

The afternoon hung over the place like a great velarium of
cloth-of-gold stretched across the battlements and drooping down
in ever slacker folds upon the heavy-headed palms. When at length
the gold turned to violet, and the west to a bow of crystal clasping
the desert sands, Medford shook off his sleep and wandered out.
But this time, instead of mounting to the roof, he took another
direction.

He was surprised to find how little he knew of the place
after five days of loitering and waiting. Perhaps this was to
be his last evening alone in it. He passed out of the court by a
vaulted stone passage which led to another walled enclosure.
At his approach two or three Arabs who had been squatting
there rose and melted out of sight. It was as if the solid masonry
had received them.

Beyond, Medford heard a stamping of hoofs, the stir of a stable
at night-fall. He went under another archway and found himself
among horses and mules. In the fading light an Arab was rubbing down one of the horses, a powerful young chestnut. He, too,
seemed about to vanish; but Medford caught him by the sleeve.

"Go on with your work," he said in Arabic.

The man, who was young and muscular, with a lean Bedouin
face, stopped and looked at him.

"I didn't know your Excellency spoke our language."

"Oh, yes," said Medford.

The man was silent, one hand on the horse's restless neck, the other thrust into his woollen girdle. He and Medford examined each other in the faint light.

"Is that the horse that's lame?" Medford asked.

"Lame?" The Arab's eyes ran down the animal's legs. "Oh, yes; lame," he answered vaguely.

Medford stooped and felt the horses knees and fetlocks. "He seems pretty fit. Couldn't he carry me for a canter this evening if I felt like it?"

The Arab considered; he was evidently perplexed by the weight of responsibility which the question placed on him.

"Your Excellency would like to go for a ride this evening?"

"Oh, just a fancy. I might or I might not." Medford lit a cigarette and offered one to the groom, whose white teeth flashed his gratification. Over the shared match they drew nearer and the Arab's diffidence seemed to lessen.

"Is this one of Mr. Almodham's own mounts?" Medford asked.

"Yes, sir; it's his favourite," said the groom, his hand passing proudly down the horse's bright shoulder.

"His favourite? Yet he didn't take him on this long expedition?"

The Arab fell silent and stared at the ground.

"Weren't you surprised at that?" Medford queried.

The man's gesture declared that it was not his business to be surprised.

The two remained without speaking while the quick blue night descended.

At length Medford said carelessly: "Where do you suppose your master is at this moment?"

The moon, unperceived in the radiant fall of day, had now suddenly possessed the world, and a broad white beam lay full on the Arab's white smock, his brown face and the turban of camel's hair knotted above it. His agitated eyeballs glistened like jewels.

"If Allah would vouchsafe to let us know!"

"But you suppose he's safe enough, don't you? You don't think it's necessary yet for a party to go out in search of him?"

The Arab appeared to ponder this deeply. The question must have taken him by surprise. He flung a brown arm about the horse's neck and continued to scrutinize the stones of the court.

"When the master is away Mr. Gosling is our master."

"And he doesn't think it necessary?"

The Arab sighed: "Not yet."

"But if Mr. Almodham were away much longer—"

The man was again silent, and Medford continued: "You're the head groom, I suppose?"

"Yes, Excellency."

There was another pause. Medford half turned away; then over his shoulder: "I suppose you know the direction Mr. Almodham took? The place he's gone to?"

"Oh, assuredly, Excellency."

"Then you and I are going to ride after him. Be ready an hour before daylight. Say nothing to anyone—Mr. Gosling or anybody else. We two ought to be able to find him without other help."

The Arab's face was all a responsive flash of eyes and teeth. "Oh, sir, I undertake that you and my master shall meet before tomorrow night. And none shall know of it."

"He's as anxious about Almodham as I am," Medford thought; and a faint shiver ran down his back. "All right. Be ready," he repeated.

He strolled back and found the court empty of life, but fantastically peopled by palms of beaten silver and a white marble fig tree.

"After all," he thought irrelevantly, "I'm glad I didn't tell Gosling that I speak Arabic."

He sat down and waited till Gosling, approaching from the living-room, ceremoniously announced for the fifth time that dinner was served.

Medford sat up in bed with the jerk which resembles no other. Someone was in his room. The fact reached him not by sight or sound—for the moon had set, and the silence of the night was complete—but by a peculiar faint disturbance of the invisible currents that enclose us.

He was awake in an instant, caught up his electric hand-lamp and flashed it into two astonished eyes. Gosling stood above the bed.

"Mr. Almodham—he's back?" Medford exclaimed.

"No, sir; he's not back." Gosling spoke in low controlled tones. His extreme self-possession gave Medford a sense of danger—he couldn't say why, or of what nature. He sat upright, looking hard at the man.

"Then what's the matter?"

"Well, sir, you might have told me you talk Arabic"—Gosling's tone was now wistfully reproachful—"before you got 'obnobbing with that Selim. Making randy-voos with 'im by night in the desert."

Medford reached for his matches and lit the candle by the bed. He did not know whether to kick Gosling out of the room or to listen to what the man had to say; but a quick movement of curiosity made him determine on the latter course.

"Such folly! First I thought I'd lock you in. I might 'ave." Gosling drew a key from his pocket and held it up. "Or again I might 'ave let you go. Easier than not. But there was Wembley."

"Wembley?" Medford echoed. He began to think that the man was going mad. One might, so conceivably, in that place of post-ponements and enchantments! He wondered whether Almodham himself were not a little mad—if, indeed, Almodham were still in a world where such a fate is possible.

"Wembley. You promised to get Mr. Almodham to give me an 'oliday—to let me go back to England in time for a look at Wembley. Every man 'as 'is fancies, 'asn't he sir? And that's mine. I've told Mr. Almodham so, agine and agine. He'd never listen, or only make believe to; say: 'We'll see, now, Gosling, we'll see'; and no more 'eard of it. But you was different, sir. You said it, and I knew you meant it—about my 'oliday. So I'm going to lock you in." Gosling spoke composedly, but with an under-thrill of emotion in his queer Mediterranean-Cockney voice.

"Lock me in?"

"Prevent you somehow from going off with that murderer. You don't suppose you'd ever 'ave come back alive from that ride, do you?"

A shiver ran over Medford, as it had the evening before when he had said to himself that the Arab was as anxious as he was about Almodham. He gave a slight laugh.

"I don't know what you're talking about. But you're not going to lock me in."

The effect of this was unexpected. Gosling's face was drawn up into a convulsive grimace and two tears rose to his pale eyelashes and ran down his cheeks.

"You don't trust me, after all," he said plaintively.

Medford leaned on his pillow and considered. Nothing as queer had ever before happened to him. The fellow looked almost ridiculous enough to laugh at; yet his tears were certainly not simulated. Was he weeping for Almodham, already dead, or for Medford, about to be committed to the same grave?

"I should trust you at once," said Medford, "if you'd tell me where your master is."

Gosling's face resumed its usual guarded expression, though the trace of the tears still glittered on it.

"I can't do that, sir."

"Ah, I thought so!"

"Because—'ow do I know?"

Medford thrust a leg out of bed. One hand, under the blanket, lay on his revolver.

"Well, you may go now. Put that key down on the table first. And don't try to do anything to interfere with my plans. If you do I'll shoot you," he added concisely.

"Oh, no, you wouldn't shoot a British subject; it makes such a fuss. Not that I'd care—I've often thought of doing it myself. Sometimes in the sirocco season. That don't scare me. And you shan't go."

Medford was on his feet now, the revolver visible. Gosling eyed it with indifference.

"Then you do know where Mr. Almodham is? And you're determined that I shan't find out?" Medford challenged him.

"Selim's determined," said Gosling, "and all the others are. They all want you out of the way. That's why I've kept 'em to their quarters—done all the waiting on you myself. Now will you stay

here? For God's sake, sir! The return caravan is going through to
the coast the day after tomorrow. Join it, sir—it's the only safe
way! I darsn't let you go with one of our men, not even if you was
to swear you'd ride straight for the coast and let this business be."

"This business? What business?"

"This worrying about where Mr. Almodham is, sir. Not that
there's anything to worry about. The men all know that. But the
plain fact is they've stolen some money from his box, since he's
been gone, and if I hadn't winked at it they'd 'ave killed me; and
all they want is to get you to ride out after 'im, and put you safe
away under a 'eap of sand somewhere off the caravan trails. Easy
job. There; that's all, sir. My word it is."

There was a long silence. In the weak candle-light the two men
stood considering each other.

Medford's wits began to clear as the sense of peril closed in
on him. His mind reached out on all sides into the enfolding
mystery, but it was everywhere impenetrable. The odd thing was
that, though he did not believe half of what Gosling had told
him, the man yet inspired him with a queer sense of confidence
as far as their mutual relation was concerned. "He may be lying
about Almodham, to hide God knows what; but I don't believe
he's lying about Selim."

Medford laid his revolver on the table. "Very well," he said.
"I won't ride out to look for Mr. Almodham, since you advise
me not to. But I won't leave by the caravan; I'll wait here till he
comes back."

He saw Gosling whiten under his sallowness. "Oh, don't
do that, sir; I couldn't answer for them if you was to wait. The
caravan'll take you to the coast the day after tomorrow as easy as
if you was riding in Rotten Row."

"Ah, then you know that Mr. Almodham won't be back by the
day after tomorrow?" Medford caught him up.

"I don't know anything, sir."

"Not even where he is now?"

Gosling reflected. "He's been gone too long, sir, for me to know
that," he said from the threshold.

The door closed on him.

Medford found sleep unrecoverable. He leaned in his window and watched the stars fade and the dawn break in all its holiness. As the stir of life rose among the ancient walls he marvelled at the contrast between that fountain of purity welling up into the heavens and the evil secrets clinging bat-like to the nest of masonry below.

He no longer knew what to believe or whom. Had some enemy of Almodham's lured him into the desert and bought the conniv-ance of his people? Or had the servants had some reason of their own for spiriting him away, and was Gosling possibly telling the truth when he said that the same fate would befall Medford if he refused to leave?

Medford, as the light brightened, felt his energy return. The very impenetrableness of the mystery stimulated him. He would stay, and he would find out the truth.

It was always Gosling himself who brought up the water for Medford's bath; but this morning he failed to appear with it, and when he came it was to bring the breakfast tray. Medford noticed that his face was of a pasty pallor, and that his lids were reddened as if with weeping. The contrast was unpleasant, and a dislike for Gosling began to shape itself in the young man's breast.

"My bath?" he queried.

"Well, sir, you complained yesterday of the water—"

"Can't you boil it?"

"I 'ave, sir."

"Well, then—"

Gosling went out sullenly and presently returned with a brass jug. "It's the time of year—we're dying for rain," he grumbled, pouring a scant measure of water into the tub.

Yes, the well must be pretty low, Medford thought. Even boiled, the water had the disagreeable smell that he had noticed the day before, though of course, in a slighter degree. But a bath was a necessity in that climate. He splashed the few cupfuls over himself as best as he could.

He spent the day in rather fruitlessly considering his situation. He had hoped the morning would bring counsel, but it brought only courage and resolution, and these were of small use without

enlightenment. Suddenly he remembered that the caravan going
south from the coast would pass near the castle that afternoon.
Gosling had dwelt on the date often enough, for it was the caravan
which was to bring the box of Perrier water.

"Well, I'm not sorry for that," Medford reflected, with a slight
shrinking of the flesh. Something sick and viscous, half smell, half
substance, seemed to have clung to his skin since his morning bath,
and the idea of having to drink that water again was nauseating.

But his chief reason for welcoming the caravan was the hope
of finding in it some European, or at any rate some native official
from the coast, to whom he might confide his anxiety. He hung
about, listening and waiting, and then mounted to the roof to
gaze northward along the trail. But in the afternoon glow he saw
only three Bedouins guiding laden pack mules toward the castle.

As they mounted the steep path he recognized some of Almodham's men, and guessed at once that the southward caravan trail
did not actually pass under the walls and that the men had been
out to meet it, probably at a small oasis behind some fold of the
sand-hills. Vexed at his own thoughtlessness in not foreseeing such
a possibility, Medford dashed down to the court, hoping the men
might have brought back some news of Almodham, though, as
the latter had ridden south, he could at best only have crossed the
trail by which the caravan had come. Still, even so, some one might
know something, some report might have been heard—since
everything was always known in the desert.

As Medford reached the court, angry vociferations, and retorts
as vehement, rose from the stable-yard. He leaned over the wall
and listened. Hitherto nothing had surprised him more than
the silence of the place. Gosling must have had a strong arm to
subdue the shrill voices of his underlings. Now they had all broken
loose, and it was Gosling's own voice—usually so discreet and
measured—which dominated them.

Gosling, master of all the desert dialects, was cursing his subordinates in a half dozen.

"And you didn't bring it—and you tell me it wasn't there, and I
tell you it was, and that you know it, and that you either left it on a
sand-heap while you were jawing with some of those slimy fellows

from the coast, or else fastened it on to the horse so carelessly that it fell off on the way—and all of you too sleepy to notice. Oh, you sons of females I wouldn't soil my lips by naming! Well, back you go to hunt it up, that's all."

"By Allah and the tomb of his Prophet, you wrong us unpardonably. There was nothing left at the oasis, nor yet dropped off on the way back. It was not there, and that is the truth in its purity."

"Truth! Purity! You miserable lot of shirks and liars, you—and the gentleman here not touching a drop of anything but water—as you profess to do, you liquor-swilling humbugs!"

Medford drew back from the parapet with a smile of relief. It was nothing but a case of Perrier—the missing case—which had raised the passions of these grown men to the pitch of frenzy! The anti-climax lifted a load from his breast. If Gosling, the calm and self-controlled, could waste his wrath on so slight a hitch in the working of the commissariat, he at least must have a free mind. How absurd this homely incident made Medford's speculations seem!

He was at once touched by Gosling's solicitude, and annoyed that he should have been so duped by the hallucinating fancies of the East.

Almodham was off on his own business; very likely the men knew where and what the business was; and even if they had robbed him in his absence, and quarrelled over the spoils, Medford did not see what he could do. It might even be that his eccentric host—with whom, after all, he had had but one evening's acquaintance—repenting an invitation too rashly given, had ridden away to escape the boredom of entertaining him. As this alternative occurred to Medford it seemed so plausible that he began to wonder if Almodham had not simply withdrawn to some secret suite of that intricate dwelling, and were waiting there for his guest's departure.

So well would this explain Gosling's solicitude to see the visitor off—so completely account for the man's nervous and contradictory behaviour—that Medford, smiling at his own obtuseness, hastily resolved to leave on the morrow. Tranquillized by this decision, he lingered about the court till dusk fell, and then, as usual, went up to the roof. But today his eyes, instead of raking the horizon, fastened on the clustering edifice of which, after six days' residence, he knew so little. Aerial chambers, jutting out at capricious angles, baffled him with closely shuttered windows, or here and there with the enigma of painted panes. Behind which window was his host concealed, spying, it might be, at this very moment on the movements of his lingering guest?

The idea that that strange moody man, with his long brown face and shock of white hair, his half-guessed selfishness and tyranny, and his morbid self-absorption, might be actually within a stone's throw, gave Medford, for the first time, a sharp sense of isolation. He felt himself shut out, unwanted—the place, now that he imagined someone might be living in it unknown to him, became lonely, inhospitable, dangerous.

"Fool that I am—he probably expected me to pack up and go as soon as I found he was away!" the young man reflected. Yes; decidedly he would leave the next morning.

Gosling had not shown himself all the afternoon. When at length, belatedly, he came to set the table, he wore a look of sullen, almost surly, reserve which Medford had not yet seen on his face. He hardly returned the young man's friendly "Hallo—dinner?" and when Medford was seated handed him the first dish in silence. Medford's glass remained unfilled till he touched its brim.

"Oh, there's nothing to drink, sir. The men lost the case of Perrier—or dropped it and smashed the bottles. They say it never came. 'Ow do I know, when they never open their 'eathen lips but to lie?" Gosling burst out with sudden violence.

He set down the dish he was handing, and Medford saw that he had been obliged to do so because his whole body was shaking as if with fever.

"My dear man, what does it matter? You're going to be ill," Medford exclaimed, laying his hand on the servant's arm. But the latter, muttering: "Oh, God, if I'd only 'a' gone for it myself," jerked away and vanished from the room.

Medford sat pondering; it certainly looked as if poor Gosling were on the edge of a break-down. No wonder, when Medford himself was so oppressed by the uncanniness of the place. Gosling reappeared after an interval, correct, close-lipped, with the dessert and a bottle of white wine. "Sorry, sir."

To pacify him, Medford sipped the wine and then pushed his chair away and returned to the court. He was making for the fig tree by the well when Gosling, slipping ahead, transferred his chair and wicker table to the other end of the court.

"You'll be better here—there'll be a breeze presently," he said. "I'll fetch your coffee."

He disappeared again, and Medford sat gazing up at the pile of masonry and plaster, and wondering whether he had not been moved away from his favourite corner to get him out of—or into?—the angle of vision of the invisible watcher. Gosling, having brought the coffee, went away and Medford sat on.

At length he rose and began to pace up and down as he smoked. The moon was not up yet, and darkness fell solemnly on the ancient walls. Presently the breeze arose and began its secret commerce with the palms.

Medford went back to his seat; but as soon as he had resumed it he fancied that the gaze of his hidden watcher was jealously fixed on the red spark of his cigar. The sensation became increasingly distasteful; he could almost feel Almodham reaching out long ghostly arms from somewhere above him in the darkness. He moved back into the living-room, where a shaded light hung from the ceiling; but the room was airless, and finally he went out again and dragged his seat to its old place under the fig tree. From there the windows which he suspected could not command him, and he felt easier, though the corner was out of the breeze and the heavy air seemed tainted with the exhalation of the adjoining well.

"The water must be very low," Medford mused. The smell, though faint, was unpleasant; it smirched the purity of the night. But he felt safer there, somehow, farther from those unseen eyes which seemed mysteriously to have become his enemies.

"If one of the men had knifed me in the desert, I shouldn't wonder if it would have been at Almodham's orders," Medford thought. He drowsed.

When he woke the moon was pushing up its ponderous orange disk above the walls, and the darkness in the court was less dense. He must have slept for an hour or more. The night was delicious, or would have been anywhere but there. Medford felt a shiver of his old fever and remembered that Gosling had warned him that the court was unhealthy at night.

"On account of the well, I suppose. I've been sitting too close to it," he reflected. His head ached, and he fancied that the sweetish foulish smell clung to his face as it had after his bath. He stood up and approached the well to see how much water was left in it. But the moon was not yet high enough to light those depths, and he peered down into blackness.

Suddenly he felt both shoulders gripped from behind and forcibly pressed forward, as if by someone seeking to push him over the edge. An instant later, almost coinciding with his own swift resistance, the push became a strong tug backward, and he swung round to confront Gosling, whose hands immediately dropped from his shoulders.

"I thought you had the fever, sir—I seemed to see you pitching over," the man stammered.

Medford's wits returned. "We must both have it, for I fancied you were pitching me," he said with a laugh.

"Me, sir?" Gosling gasped. "I pulled you back as 'ard as ever—"

"Of course. I know."

"Whatever are you doing here, anyhow, sir? I warned you it was un'ealthy at night," Gosling continued irritably.

Medford leaned against the well-head and contemplated him. "I believe the whole place is unhealthy."

Gosling was silent. At length he asked: "Aren't you going up to bed, sir?"

"No," said Medford, "I prefer to stay here."

Gosling's face took on an expression of dogged anger. "Well, then, I prefer that you shouldn't."

Medford laughed again. "Why? Because it's the hour when Mr. Almodham comes out to take the air?"

The effect of this question was unexpected. Gosling dropped back a step or two and flung up his hands, pressing them to his lips as if to stifle a low outcry.

"What's the matter?" Medford queried. The man's antics were beginning to get on his nerves.

"Matter?" Gosling still stood away from him, out of the rising slant of moonlight.

"Come! Own up that he's here and have done with it!" cried Medford impatiently.

"Here? What do you mean by 'here'? You 'aven't seen 'im, 'ave you?" Before the words were out of the man's lips he flung up his arms again, stumbled forward, and fell in a heap at Medford's feet.

Medford, still leaning against the well-head, smiled down contemptuously at the stricken wretch. His conjecture had been the right one, then; he had not been Gosling's dupe after all.

"Get up, man. Don't be a fool! It's not your fault if I guessed that Mr. Almodham walks here at night—"

"Walks here!" wailed the other, still cowering.

"Well, doesn't he? He won't kill you for owning up will he?"

"Kill me? Kill me? I wish I'd killed *you*!" Gosling half got to his feet, his head thrown back in ashen terror. "And I might 'ave, too, so easy! You felt me pushing of you over, didn't you? Coming 'ere spying and sniffing—" His anguish seemed to choke him.

Medford had not changed his position. The very abjectness of the creature at his feet gave him an easy sense of power. But Gosling's last cry had suddenly deflected the course of his speculations. Almodham was here, then; that was certain; but just where was he, and in what shape? A new fear scuttled down Medford's spine.

"So you did want to push me over?" he said. "Why? As the quickest way of joining your master?"

The effect was more immediate than he had foreseen.

Gosling, getting to his feet, stood there bowed and shrunken in the accusing moonlight.

"Oh, God—and I 'ad you 'arf over! You know I did! And then—it was what you said about Wembley. So help me, sir, I felt you meant it, and it 'eld me back." The man's face was again wet with tears, but this time Medford recoiled from them as if they had been drops splashed up by a falling body from the foul waters below.

Medford was silent. He did not know if Gosling were armed or not, but he was no longer afraid; only aghast, and yet shudderingly lucid.

Gosling continued to ramble on half-deliriously: "And if only that Perrier 'ad of come. I don't believe it'd ever 'ave crossed your mind, if only you'd 'ave had your Perrier regular, now would it? But you say 'e walks—and I knew he would! Only—what was I to do with him, with you turning up like that the very day?"

Still Medford did not move.

"And 'im driving me to madness, sir, sheer madness, that same morning. Will you believe it? The very week before you come, I was to sail for England and 'ave my 'oliday, a 'ole month, sir—and I was entitled to six, if there was any justice—a 'ole month in 'Ammersmith, sir, in a cousin's 'ouse, and the chance to see Wembley thoroughly; and then 'e 'eard you was coming, sir, and 'e was bored and lonely 'ere, you understand—'e 'ad to have new excitements provided for 'im or 'e'd go off 'is bat—and when 'e 'eard you was coming, 'e come out of his black mood in a flash and was 'arf crazy with pleasure, and said 'I'll keep 'im 'ere all winter—a remarkable young man, Gosling—just my kind.' And when I says to him: 'And 'ow about my 'oliday?' he stares at me with those stony eyes of 'is and says: ''Oliday? Oh, to be sure; why next year—we'll see what can be done about it next year.' Next year, sir, as if 'e was doing me a favour! And that's the way it 'ad been for nigh on twelve years.

"But this time, if you 'adn't 'ave come I do believe I'd 'ave got away, for he was getting used to 'aving Selim about 'im and his 'ealth was never better—and, well, I told 'im as much, and 'ow a man 'ad his rights after all, and my youth was going, and me that 'ad served him so well chained up 'ere like 'is watchdog, and always next year and next year—and, well, sir, 'e just laughed, sneering-like, and lit 'is cigarette. 'Oh, Gosling, cut it out,' 'e says.

"He was standing on the very spot where you are now, sir; and he turned to walk into the 'ouse. And it was then I 'it 'im. He was a heavy man, and he fell against the well kerb. And just when you were expected any minute—oh, my God!"

Gosling's voice died out in a strangled murmur.

Medford, at his last words, had unvoluntarily shrunk back a few feet. The two men stood in the middle of the court and stared at each other without speaking. The moon, swinging high above the battlements, sent a searching spear of light down into the guilty darkness of the well.

THE BEST CRIME STORIES
2023
HONOUR ROLL

Additional outstanding stories published in 2022

Mike Adamson, The White Calf and the Wind
Black Cat Mystery Magazine, #11

Scott Adlerberg, The Killing at Joshua Lake
Witnesses for the Dead, ed. by Gary Phillips & Gar Anthony Haywood (Soho Crime)

Michael Bracken, Kissing Cousins
Starlite Pulp Review, Winter

Leah Cutter, The Missing
Mystery, Crime, and Mayhem: Cold Cases (Knotted Road)

Gregory Fallis, Red Flag
Alfred Hitchcock Mystery Magazine, March/April

G. Mikki Hayden, Forever Unconquered
Crime Hits Home (Hanover Square)

Natalie Haynes, The Unravelling
Marple: Twelve New Cases (William Morrow)

William Burton McCormick, House of Tigers
Black Cat Mystery Magazine, #52

Tim McLoughlin, The Amnesty Box
Alcohol, Tobacco, and Firearms (Akashic)

Andrew Miller, Samurai '81
Jacked, ed. by Vern Smith (Run Amok Publishing)

"Blind Baseball" by Doug Allyn. First published in *Ellery Queen Mystery Magazine*. Copyright © 2022 by Doug Allyn. Reprinted by permission of the author.

"The Adventure of the Misquoted Macbeth" by Derrick Belanger. First published in *A Detective's Life: Sherlock Holmes* (Titan), ed. by Martin Rosenstock. Copyright © 2022 by Derrick Belanger. Reprinted by permission of the author.

"Princess" by T. C. Boyle. First published in *The New Yorker*. Copyright © 2022 by T. C. Boyle. Reprinted by permission of Georges Borchardt, Inc., on behalf of the author.

"Cold Hands, Warm Heart" by Joslyn Chase. First published in *Mystery, Crime, and Mayhem: Cold Cases* (Knotted Road). Copyright © 2022 by Joslyn Chase. Reprinted by permission of the author.

"New Kid in Town" by Andrew Child. First published in *Hotel California* (Blackstone), ed. by Don Bruns. Copyright © 2022 by Andrew Child. Reprinted by permission of the author.

"Death at the Sundial Motel" by Aaron Philip Clark. First published in *Witnesses for the Dead* (Soho Press), ed. by Gary Phillips and Gar Anthony Haywood. Copyright © 2022 by Aaron Philip Clark. Reprinted by permission of the author.

"Dodge" by Jeffery Deaver. First published in *The Broken Doll* (Amazon). Copyright © 2022 by Gunner Publications, LLC. Reprinted by permission of the author.

"The Landscaper's Wife" by Brendan DuBois. First published in *Mystery Tribune*. Copyright © 2022 by Brendan DuBois. Reprinted by permission of the author.

"Strangers at a Table" by Kerry Hammond. First published in *Malice Domestic: Murder Most Diabolical* (Wildside). Copyright © 2022 by Kerry Hammond. Reprinted by permission of the author.

"Miller and Bell" by Victor Kreuiter. First published in *Mystery Magazine*. Copyright © 2022 by Victor Kreuiter. Reprinted by permission of the author.

"Two Sharks Walk into a Bar" by David Krugler. First published in *Mystery Magazine*. Copyright © 2022 by David Krugler. Reprinted by permission of the author.

"Pobre Maria" by Tom Larsen. First published in *Alfred Hitchcock Mystery Magazine*. Copyright © 2022 by Tom Larsen. Reprinted by permission of the author.

"Playing God" by Avram Lavinsky. First published in *Deadly Nightshade: Best New England Crime Stories* (Crime Spell Books), ed. by Susan Oleksiw, Christine Bagley, and Leslie Wheeler. Copyright © 2022 by Avram Lavinsky. Reprinted by permission of the author.

"Ears" by Jessi Lewis. First published in *Alaska Quarterly Review*. Copyright © 2022 by Jessi Lewis. Reprinted by permission of the author.

"The Smoking Gunners" by Ashley Lister. First published in *The Book of Extraordinary Femme Fatales* (Mango), ed. by Maxim Jakubowski. Copyright © 2022 by Ashley Lister. Reprinted by permission of the author.

"Monday, Tuesday, Thursday, Wednesday" by Sean McCluskey. First published in *Mickey Finn: 21st Century Noir, Vol. 3* (Down & Out Books), ed. by Michael Bracken. Copyright © 2022 by Sean McCluskey. Reprinted by permission of the author.

"What the Cat Dragged In" by Michael Mallory. First published in *The Strand Magazine*. Copyright © 2022 by Michael Mallory. Reprinted by permission of the author.

"Sundown" by Lou Manfredo. First published in *Ellery Queen Mystery Magazine*. Copyright © 2022 by Lou Manfredo. Reprinted by permission of the author.

"The Promise" by Annie Reed. First published in *Mystery, Crime, and Mayhem: Cold Cases* (Knotted Road) ed. Leah R. Cutter. Copyright © 2022 by Annie Reed. Reprinted by permission of the author.

"Glass" by Anna Round. First published in *The Briar Cliff Review*. Copyright © 2022 by Anna Round. Reprinted by permission of the author.

"Crime Scene" by Joseph S. Walker. First published in *Malice in Dallas* (Metroplex Mysteries) ed. Barb Goffman. Copyright © 2022 by Joseph S. Walker. Reprinted by permission of the author.

ABOUT THE EDITORS

AMOR TOWLES is the author of *New York Times* bestsellers *Rules of Civility*, *A Gentleman in Moscow*, and *The Lincoln Highway*. The three novels have collectively sold more than six million copies and have been translated into more than thirty languages. Towles lives in Manhattan with his wife and two children.

OTTO PENZLER is the founder of the Mysterious Press (1975), Mysterious Press.com (2011) and New York City's Mysterious Bookshop (1979). He has won a Raven, the Ellery Queen Award, two Edgars and lifetime achievement awards from Noircon and *The Strand Magazine*. He has edited more than 70 anthologies and written extensively about crime fiction.

Also Available

BEST CRIME STORIES OF THE YEAR
(edited by Lee Child and Otto Penzler)

BEST CRIME STORIES OF THE YEAR VOLUME 2
(edited by Sara Paretsky and Otto Penzler)